The Gailean Quartet, Book III

SYMPHONY OF CROWNS

Christine E. Schulze

WORDS MATTER
PUBLISHING
OUR WORDS CHANGE THE WORLD

© 2022 by Christine E. Schulze. All rights reserved.

Words Matter Publishing
P.O. Box 1190
Decatur, Il 62525
www.wordsmatterpublishing.com

Map Illustration Copyright © 2022 Stacey Hummel
Edited by Kira Lerner

ISBN 13: 978-1-953912-88-6

Library of Congress Catalog Card Number: 2022942269

Dedication

To Dr. Gail, who said,
"You all have a gift. It's free. It's the gift of song."

To Isaac,
my true Chamblin

To Kira, who sang this epic saga back to life
and helped make it everything it could be and more

And to God, for shining these and so many
Other lights into my dark world

Acknowledgements

Thank you so much to Kira, as always, for helping me resurrect yet another of my old tomes and breathe new life into it. Thanks to Isaac, my lovely boyfriend, for genuinely enjoying my ramblings and rants about plot and characters and all the challenges of publishing. And many thanks to the WMP team for taking yet another of my books and turning it into a visually beautiful masterpiece. God bless you and may you all be inspired!

Table of Contents

Map of the Four Realms

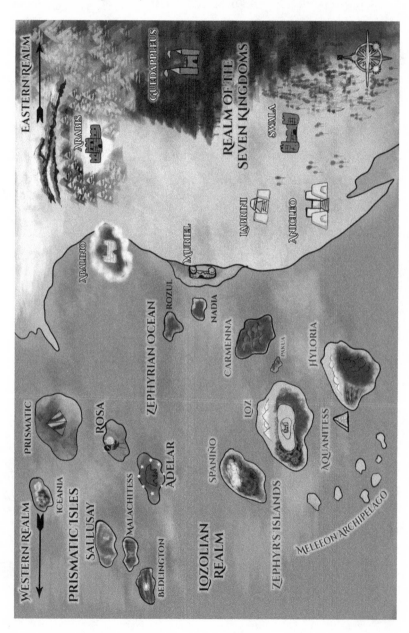

The Lozolian Realm encompasses all the islands in the Zephyrian Ocean, including Loz, the Prismatic Isles, and the Meleeón Archipelago.

The Realm of the Seven Kingdoms is located on the mainland, sometimes called "The Surpriser Mainland" from the time of the 100 Years' Curse.

The Western Realm lies far beyond Zephyrian waters and includes Asian, African, and European countries. Several explorers from the Lozolian and Seven Kingdoms Realms have adventured to this mysterious realm.

The Eastern Realm beyond the Seven Kingdoms is considered even more mysterious and little explored, though rumors tell of Giants living deep within the woods.

"At any given moment, we stand at a crossroads with an infinite number of possibilities. It may not seem so at the time, because this crossroads can be obscured by fears and other insecurities, but the choices we can make are truly limitless. If alternate universes existed, perhaps we could even sit back and watch many different versions of ourselves play out.

"But we only get one lifetime. Perhaps that is what can make our choices so intimidating. Because we only get one chance to be what we should and do as we dream.

"Whatever choices we make, one thing is certain: like it or not, they create the life we live. There is no reversing time or starting over. Spiritually, yes, but not physically. We have but one precious earthly life, and it is linear, moving ever forward; let us savor it and do our best to walk its path wisely."

~ Old Man Eldwin of the Mirtle Sprites

THE FIRST
MOVEMENT

CHAPTER 1

DUSK OF THE PAST

Thick clouds blanketed the sky. Their darkening hues blurred with the choppy ocean waters, painting the world into a singular canvas of gray.

A large island densely covered with trees cropped up on the near horizon. As the tide rushed away from its sandy shores, a small wooden boat fought against the currents, fueled only by the last lingering shreds of Gailea Fleming's magical strength.

She had traversed the high seas for months now in this fashion, stopping on the various Zephyr's Islands to rest and procure food for herself, her son Merritt, and her unborn child.

Merritt, a toddler hardly past his second year, now clung to the tattered fragments of her cloak. His wailing blended with the wind's cries, and he shuddered at the dawning cold. Gailea wrapped her cloak more securely around them both as a merciless chill ripped up her spine and through her entire body.

Her pains were deepening. Each jerk or flinch of the boat poked and prodded her like a skeleton's fingers grasping at her swollen belly. Their last stop had been nearly three days ago in Loz, and her strength was spent. Neither she nor Merritt, much less her unborn child, would survive a longer journey in these conditions. They had run out of both money and food a few days back. Gailea had managed to use one of her self-made song-spells to draw fish to their boat, charming them until she could snare them in one of the boat's small nets. However, the raw fish stirred her stomach, sometimes making her vomit what little she'd been able to take in. Worst of all, their supply of fresh water grew frighteningly shallow.

Reaching land was her most important goal. There, they could find shelter, warmth, food, and friends, if what Tytonn's father had promised was true. His uncle, Bromwell Jardis, was meant to help them, and right now, he was their greatest, perhaps only, hope of survival.

Gailea prayed to Amiel that it was so. She would not have sought refuge in the kingdom of Hyloria otherwise. Her husband's family ruled in the capital of Fyre and might have instilled his hatred against her within them.

At long last, the boat dragged against the shore. Gailea hefted her son from the battered craft. She ripped the torn sails from the makeshift mast to wrap around him for extra warmth. Then, mustering her flagging strength, she pushed toward the woods.

The worn, thin leather of her boots provided little protection from the rocky sand beneath her feet. As she cleared the beach and stepped beneath the cover of the close-knit trees, she sighed in relief. At least here they were partially sheltered from the battering wind.

The forest brought its own treacherous obstacles. Branches tore her dress, scratching her legs. Her feet throbbed. She could barely catch her breath and clutched her big belly as the pain burned. Deprived of much-needed sleep and food, she felt as though she'd been flung inside a torture chamber.

Meanwhile, Merritt squirmed and screamed, pulling at her hair, and the babe in her belly kicked furiously, as if it tried to run away from whatever dangers might yet pursue them. Her vision blurred and her mind whirled in dizziness. She struggled onward, promising both herself and her children to take another step forward, and then another. The Forest-footer village of Vian was meant to be only several hours' journey inland. If she could just make it there…

Pain seared through her abdomen as though someone had slashed through her flesh with a blazing sword. She ignored it as best she could, but after only a few more yards a warm wetness flooded from within her. Gailea could no longer deny what she recognized from Merritt's birth. Her water had broken. Her child was on its way.

For a brief moment, she wanted to cry as she realized what was happening, but instead she sank to the ground and leaned back against the nearest tree, bracing herself. It didn't matter how exhausted she was; she *couldn't* be. She must find the strength to do what needed to be done.

Gailea still held Merritt close to her breast, but as the pains came in more powerful waves, he began crying and squirming. She was crushing him. She released him, and he plopped down beside her, calling for her, pulling at her skirts. She opened her mouth to sing a calming spell, but the song erupted into screams.

Everything became a blur of misery and terror. She was too weak to move but feared staying in one place. She had no clue how close she might be to Vian and safety, or instead to enemies. She had not seen or heard any trace of her husband's soldiers, but that didn't mean they weren't searching.

Dizziness overtook her. Her head swam, throbbing, and she fell in and out of consciousness. Merritt's cries became a muffled whisper in her mind, but every now and then she would hear snatches of him calling for her and would fight to stay awake, to stay with him, to stay with the child inside her struggling to be born.

Dizziness soon turned to nightmares.

Her husband's best friend, Tytonn, whipped and burned to death because of the false crimes her husband had imagined against him. The other innocents her husband had murdered in his wrath, including his own sweet sister. Fire, war, the ravaging of Castle Adel. Lord Donyon claiming the Adelaran throne, sparing her kingdom from further harm. Her decision to flee. Holding her newborn in her arms for the first time, while Merritt peeked over her shoulder, staring down in frightened wonder....

But wait. That last thought was no memory. Only a dream. She could no longer feel the pain. She was numb. There were no cries. The baby had not come. She would die, and the baby would die as well. She tried to fight, but her eyes would not open. She prayed someone would find Merritt and give him the loving, safe home he deserved, the home she had never been able to give him.

~*~*~

Voices surrounded Gailea. Dim snatches of light faded in and out. Flashes of green ignited memories of the woods she'd found solace in. Distant cries drew her attention—Merritt—she must get to him. Who knew what beasts, thieves, or other dangers lurked in this unknown territory? She stirred, but her limbs felt weighted down against the soft surface stretching beneath her.

The pungent scent of bitter herbs bit her nostrils. Her eyes shot open, and she sat up a little, coughing, almost retching.

"Whoa. Whoa there. It's all right...."

Someone's hand pressed gently against her shoulder. With a single glance at the stranger, Gailea panicked and sang a charm that sent him slamming back with a loud thud.

Gailea glanced about wildly, now aware of two other figures, a green-skinned woman and man rushing about with linens and clay jars. A hand rested gently on hers. She flinched and glanced up to find another green face, a woman's, framed by dark green curls that had loosed from her intricate braid.

"You're all right. You're safe now. You're with the Mirtle Sprites, protectors of the Mirtle Woods. My name is Laisa."

Laisa sat in a wooden chair beside Gailea's bed and patted a cool, wet cloth against her forehead. This tender gesture began to soothe Gailea, as did the woman's serene presence. Growing up a ward of Moragon's had afforded her little chance to encounter a variety of races or cultures, but her late friend—Tytonn, the kind and ever-loyal horselord—had once told stories of the Sprites, an elemental people who used their ancient magic to tend the forests' plantlife. While the Sprites had known feuds between their various clans, they were valued for their extended peace and protection toward outsiders. Tytonn's father had promised that Bromwell himself was friends with the Sprites. Perhaps Amiel had used their arduous voyage to lead them into safe hands at last.

Scuffling sounds drew Gailea's attention to the end of the bed. The young man she had knocked down braced himself against the wall, rising to his feet. His sun-tanned skin and thick golden-brown hair stood out plainly against that of the Sprites' shades of green. In fact, his warm, honey-colored eyes reminded her of Tytonn, and her heart ached, wanting to trust him....

No. She could trust no one and nothing. Anyone she encountered might be some spy sent by her husband. She drew what little magic she could summon to the forefront of her mind. Her feverish body sweated a little more, as if on the verge of boiling, but she held her concentration steady.

Slowly, the young man raised his hands in the air and took a few steps forward. "Please don't be afraid. My name is Ashden, of the Jadiyah Fury Clan. My people and I, we found you and your children in the woods, brought you to the Sprites for healing."

"My children," Gailea gasped hoarsely. Clasping at her belly, she felt its stark emptiness. Terror poured inside her, and she narrowed her gaze at the stranger. "What have you done with them?"

Ashden kept his hands lifted where Gailea could see them while Laisa said, "Your children are both safe and well. The babe was delivered without any cause for concern. Willa, Clove."

Laisa motioned toward the Sprite woman and man who hurried through an arched wooden door.

Clove returned moments later, holding Merritt to his chest, and the toddler snuggled close, crying muffled sobs. As the Sprite whispered in his ear, Merritt looked up and cried louder, reaching his arms toward Gailea and squirming to reach her. Clove set Merritt on the bed, and he snuggled against Gailea's side.

"And the babe."

Gailea looked up anxiously as Willa returned, holding a tiny wiggling form bundled in thick green cloths. Gailea's heart seemed to stop inside her before racing wildly as the infant was lowered into her arms. Bright

7

violet eyes gazed up wondrously at her. Tiny fingers played with the edge of her blouse.

"A girl," Laisa announced. "A lovely, healthy baby girl."

Gailea cradled the child's head, with already-thick hair softer than flower petals and red as sunrise. Eyes filling with tears, Gailea smiled sadly. How much the infant looked like her father, the man Gailea had loved not long ago. Remembering this stabbed her heart with a pain almost as sharp as giving birth. She had spent so many days with but a single purpose, running from him as an enemy, that she had allowed herself to forget the deeper feelings she feared might never heal.

But that could not be her focus now. Her children must be, above all.

She glanced up at the tanned stranger, Ashden. He had lowered his hands but hadn't moved another inch forward. He stood smiling at her and her daughter, relief and admiration softening his otherwise stern features. It was a bittersweet relief to see any man study her children with such tenderness. Gradually, Gailea's nerves calmed a little. Though she must maintain a cautious spirit, this man did not seem an immediate threat.

"We should leave the lady and her children now to rest," Laisa said gently.

Clove nodded in agreement. "Indeed. Rest, get your strength. Our people will prepare some fresh clothes for you, food, and—"

"I need to get to Vian," Gailea said, quickly remembering her purpose. "A man named Bromwell Jardis. I'm a distant cousin."

"We know Bromwell," Laisa said. "A loyal friend of the Sprites. As soon as you're able, we will take you to see Eldwin. Then, we will make arrangements to get you to Bromwell as soon and safely as possible."

"Who is Eldwin, and why must I first see him?" Gailea demanded, her heart lurching at the need for urgency. As peaceful as this place seemed, she and her children could not be made to linger any longer than necessary. "Who is he?"

"He is our Chief Elder," Willa said. "He may be able to help you. After all, begging your pardon, but 'tis no ordinary piece of glass you carry on your person."

Gailea's hand flew to her pocket in a panic, only to realize she had no pockets. Her battered traveling clothes had been exchanged for a fresh, clean, linen gown.

Clove shot Willa a scolding look while Laisa said, "The crystal is safe." She nodded at Ashden who stepped forward slowly, unwrapped the Prism from a clean cloth, and ever so gently set it on the bed beside Gailea before stepping back again. Gailea's hand closed around the Prism in relief.

"Luckily, Ashden found it," Laisa said. "It fell from your pocket as we were transporting you here. We Sprites know much of Icean Crystal, and Eldwin is a man renowned in relics and prophecies. But there is no need to talk of these matters now. Rest, my dear. I will check on you in a little while."

Laisa rose and motioned for the others to follow. Clove, Willa, and Ashden all did so, but as they reached the doorway, Gailea called, "Wait."

They glanced back, and Laisa said, "Yes? Can we get you something?"

"No, not right now. I just...thank you."

"Of course. You are most welcome here, for as long as you need."

Gailea glanced at Ashden and held up the Prism for just a moment before letting her hand fall back on the bed. "Thank you for this as well. For returning it to me."

He smiled, and again his rough features softened. "It is always an honor to help those in need."

The Sprites and Ashden departed the room, pulling the door closed behind them.

Gailea released her breath in a great sigh. Her daughter began to whimper, nuzzling against her. Pulling open the laces of the loose gown's bodice, Gailea guided the child to her breast, and she fed readily. Gailea felt surprised that she herself was not just as ravenous. Perhaps the Sprites had used their magic to grant her some nourishment, or perhaps she was too far beyond the point of exhaustion to care.

As her daughter suckled, Gailea drew Merritt a little closer to her and studied her surroundings. Walls built from logs stacked on top of each other indicated that she was in some sort of cabin. Vines and branches laden with thick leaves grew right through the walls, entwining up toward the open ceiling. Stars gleamed above through the branches. Lamplight washed a quiet, orange warmth across everything.

Unbidden, tears trailed down her cheeks. This peaceful setting could not be more different from when she'd given birth to Merritt, and yet, even this serenity was marred by the same fear of her husband's vengeance. At least she was surrounded by allies this time, or so she hoped. She must continue to be wary, but if these folks knew Bromwell, she hoped her instincts to trust them were well founded.

Turning once more to the stars, Gailea let herself get lost in their eternally stretching light and beauty. If only for one night, she would allow herself rest and peace and the façade that this simple life belonged to her.

CHAPTER 2

THE PROMISE OF FYRE

Several days passed. The Sprites provided Gailea with all manner of fresh fruits, vegetables, and warm, sweet breads baked from a unique green grain much like maize, called "orna," that the Sprites were renowned for growing.

Laisa visited frequently to tend to her needs or to make pleasant conversation about the weather, summer plantings, and playful incidents her children had been up to that day. Laisa always kept her talk light and simple, and Gailea did more listening than responding, relishing those stories of normal, peaceful life and imaginging a future when, just maybe, she could live such stories of her own.

Willa and Clove came by as well, though this was more often to change her linens, bring food, or help care for her children. Willa especially had a soft spot for Merritt and the babe. Gailea felt the need to keep a close watch on her children at all times, but she would allow Willa to hold her baby girl or play with Merritt on the rug beside her bed. The young Sprite delighted in showing him different leaves from the forest or reading stories to him, and Gailea felt grateful for him to have this opportunity to make new friends. Her life thus far had been so insulated, and she wished the opposite for him.

Here and there, Ashden would stop by to inquire how Gailea was getting on. She could tell by his searching gaze that he wished to stay longer and talk more, but she never invited him to, and he was respectful enough to not linger.

The day after her delivery, Gailea had begged to get up and move about, hoping to regain her strength and be on her way as soon as possible, but her weary body had forbidden it even more than had the Sprite healers themselves.

At last, on the fourth day, she rallied enough to step outside, her baby girl in her arms and Merritt at her side.

The enchanting woods thrived with lush greenery. A myriad of other colors bloomed in the form of bright, unfamiliar flowers Gailea had never imagined inside the confines of the Adelaran castle. Several tents dotted the forest in between many log cabins and tree houses, and she was surprised to see many other people with fair or tanned skin and golden-brown hair. They dressed in deep turquoise or wine-red tunics with bejeweled belts, standing out against the Sprites' simple green or brown tunics and gowns, which she herself was wearing.

"Don't worry. You're not going mad," Ashden's familiar voice assured her. "This truly is the Sprites' home. The Mirtle Sprites are trusted friends of my clan. The roots of our friendship stretch as deeply as the roots of these trees. And so, in more recent times, we moved our camp here to take up residence with them."

Ashden walked up beside her. Beneath his gray cloak, he wore a tunic dyed a deep shade of turquoise, brown trousers, and leather boots; turquoise stones adorned his leather belt. Merritt rushed to him, laughing, and threw his arms around the man's legs. Ashden looked alarmed, not so much at the child, but at Gailea. With a smile, she nodded, and Ashden lifted Merritt gently. The toddler laughed again and ran his hands through Ashden's thick hair, making it stand up wildly on end.

"Thank you," Gailea said. "Again. For helping me and my children. For saving the crystal and returning it to us instead of taking it for your own."

"As I've said before, it was an honor." Ashden chuckled then, a seemingly strange sound for such a serious persona. "You know, not all of us are thieves."

Gailea frowned at him in confusion. "I beg your pardon."

"My people, the Furies?"

When Gailea continued to stare at him, embarrassment flashed in Ashden's eyes. "Forgive me. I had only assumed that was why you were so surprised I returned the crystal to you. Many Fury clans are infamous for thievery and kidnappings. My clan, the Jadiyah, have chosen to make our living more honestly. We craft weaponry, jewelry, and other goods to trade or sell. But I can see I was mistaken about you. Again, I ask you forgive me. It's only that I am used to being met with such eager judgments."

Gailea kept her cautious walls raised around her mind and heart but felt herself warm a little with compassion toward this honest new acquaintance. "I have seen the pain and danger that false judgments can bring. I ask you to excuse my ignorance. I am new to these parts, to the names 'Fury' or 'Jadiyah.' And if you would let me finish thanking you, the honor you afforded us was nobly brave, just like that of the Sprites. You didn't know what we might be running from or what dangers you yourself might be running toward in aiding us."

Ashden's gaze questioned, but he only said, "It is not my nature to pry. I would've helped you no matter the reasons. Although perhaps you might at least honor me with your name?"

Gailea studied him carefully. He seemed the opposite of her husband in every way. Even his outer beauty was rugged, wild, and free, a contrast to her husband's refined beauty. She wanted to trust him, to be able to place trust in someone new and call them 'friend,' but her heart had led her so far astray for so long that she dared not rely on its inclinations.

No. She would stick to her plan, taking on the surname of Tytonn's kin. "Lea Jardis," she said finally.

"A strong name. And his?" Ashden nodded at the toddler who'd fallen asleep against him.

"Darius," Gailea said. She had chosen a false name for him similar enough to her sister's, to make it easier to remember.

"A strong name, also. He's a beautiful child."

Gailea couldn't hide a proud smile. "Thank you. I wish his father had granted him such compliments."

"His father." Ashden's serious gaze hardened. "Is he still alive? Is it from him that you've fled?"

Gailea's smile faltered. "Amiel has led me here," she murmured, fingers twisting her infant's blanket. "That is all that matters now."

The hardness vanished from his eyes. "I can't say whether or not Amiel has anything to do with it, but forgive me for making you uncomfortable."

"What do you mean that you can't say whether Amiel...?"

"I do not claim faith in Amiel. Or in any god."

Gailea inhaled sharply. Could she trust a man who might be devoid of faith altogether? Of course, her husband's family had claimed faith in Amiel while distorting His teachings to suit their purposes. She didn't want to jump to hasty conclusions about Ashden. Hadn't his deeds proved his true nature?

He watched her closely, seeming to sense her discomfort. "I came to the decision to place my belief in no deities long ago. I've seen too much evil done in the name of faith."

Gailea nodded slowly. "As have I."

"It's my belief that we only have one life, here and now, that drives me to help others. Drove me to help *you*."

"Isn't that…sad?" Gailea asked, choosing her words carefully, hoping to avoid any insult. "Isn't it lonely, worrisome even? Having no eternity, no hope to look forward to? My faith alone kept me going some days, when…"

Her voice trailed. It wasn't time for that talk, nor especially the emotions accompanying it.

"Sometimes I do envy people like yourself," Ashden said gently. "People who constantly have some hope to hold to. But I like to think I can place my hope in my people, in the ones I love."

"The ones we love can't grant inner peace. And there is no guarantee they will always love us back. Or that they won't change. Become different people altogether. People are not constant. Amiel is."

She studied him, and he watched her gently in return. "I can tell you're a wise woman. Perhaps you have answers I do not. Just as some of mine elude you." His smile was almost teasing. "Maybe someday we'll get it all sorted out together."

"I would welcome such a talk."

"As would I. But for now, more important matters are at hand. I came to see you because, if you're feeling up to it, Master Eldwin is ready to speak with you regarding the Prism."

Gailea perked up. "And then we can leave?"

Ashden nodded. "We've been making arrangements—Laisa, Clove, Willa, and a few other of the Mirtle Sprites, and me. We'll be taking you to Master Bromwell ourselves. It'll be rough going, but Bromwell's home in Vian is only a couple days' journey from here, and the Sprites can take us on the safest, most secluded course. The Alder Sprites, a second clan, have also agreed to help. They'll meet us about halfway through to lead us the rest of the way."

"Thank you," Gailea said. "But you needn't come as well. Nor Laisa and the others. You've all done enough."

Ashden shook his head. "I cannot speak for them, though I doubt you could sway them otherwise. As for myself, when a Jadiyah takes someone under his or her refuge, a sacred vow of protection is made. Until I see you safely to your goal, you are my responsibility. Though I would do the same even if you were not."

His intent gaze made Gailea uncomfortable, and she instinctively sang a spell inside her mind to cast up a mental song-shield against him, just in case.

"Come," Ashden muttered, glancing away, and looking irritated with himself. "I will take you to Eldwin."

Still holding Merritt, who slept on his shoulder, Ashden led Gailea into the thick of the woods. Massive trees towered over them, some broader and taller than the towers of Castle Adel. Thick, dewy moss and vines cloaked the trees, glistening in the sun like emerald armor. Gailea felt free and yet protected in one breath. What a rare and refreshing feeling, one to savor.

Soon the trees thinned out enough to reveal more cabins like the one she'd been staying in. Sprites sat sewing or cooking around small fires, while others tended to large patches of high-waving green stalks. The orna plans, Gailea realized.

Laughter drew Gailea's attention upward, where children raced to and fro on high, precarious-looking tree branches. She almost cried out, but she soon saw that they slid along the slippery moss and jumped from branch to branch with ease.

Ashden led Gailea to one of the massive trees. It was the widest among its brothers and sisters, and thick roots stretched up all around, creating great archways. A long opening had been split vertically in one side, serving as a doorway. Ashden stepped inside, and Gailea followed.

Rich, overwhelming scents of cloves, thyme, ginger and other herbs and plants nearly made Gailea swoon. She tilted her head way back, gazing up in awe. Vines criss-crossed all the way to the top of the tree, with dried herbs, fruits, and vegetables strung all along them. Hazy sunlight filtered through the windows carved at intervals around the tree's perimeter. Moss-covered steps had been hewn inside the hollowed tree, winding from its base and around the perimeter toward the branches high above.

"Master Eldwin?" Ashden called, his words almost lost around the busy surroundings.

Merritt stirred in Ashden's arms then, lifted his head, and gasped. His bright blue eyes widened, and he reached a hand toward a set of hanging gourds. Ashden lifted him higher, and Merritt grabbed one of the gourds, tapping a pleasant rythm and smiling, clearly pleased with the sound. Gailea smiled and cuddled her baby girl, who'd finally fallen asleep, a little closer to her heart.

"Yes, I am here," a voice answered. "Welcome."

A man glided down the spiraling steps. Thick green robes waved behind him, the colors blending almost perfectly with his weathered skin. A thick, green beard and mustache sprayed with white and gray hugged his wrinkled face. He turned to Gailea with a grin, and the serenity filling the tree seemed to flow from him as well. Gailea hoped this was no trick on the elder's part, that her intuition to trust him was sincere, but just to be safe, she continued humming the mental song-shield melody in the back of her mind.

"Welcome," the elder repeated as he stopped before them. "I am Master Eldwin. It is an honor to meet you and your children." He smiled at Gailea. "Laisa informed me that you carry a sacred secret with you. Come, let us talk of these matters."

He motioned them toward a large stump in the midst of the room, likely left over from the tree's carving. They sat on soft pillows around the table-like stump.

The baby began to squirm and whimper, but Gailea hummed a gentle lullaby into her ear, the one Brynn had sung for her and her sister, Darice, when they were small children. Gailea had used that song to spark the war that had allowed their escape. As the babe settled back into a serene slumber, Gailea felt a bittersweet gratitude that the song could still fulfill such a pure purpose of granting rest to innocent souls.

Merritt had meanwhile crawled over to watch a small bird that lighted inside one of the lower windows. As the bird tweeted a merry tune, Merritt studied it closely and cooed, raising and lowering the pitch of his voice as if trying to mimic it.

"The child has an affinity for beasts, it seems," Master Eldwin said with a warm grin, "not to mention a talent for song."

Gailea's chest tightened. How bittersweet, if he happened to share the gift of taming animals, just like the dear friend who had been murdered for his existence.

18

She shuddered to think how her husband would have reacted to see such a similar affection. The mere sight would have solidified his insane accusations about her infidelity and might have driven him to the edge of bringing harm to their son.

"What is his name?" Eldwin asked.

"Darius," she said quietly.

"And the girl?"

Gailea glanced at Ashden. "I've decided to name her after both you and Laisa, for saving us. I'm calling her 'Ashlai.' Ashlai Brynn, after my mother as well."

Surprise flashed on Ashden's face. "That is an honor indeed."

"And the Prism, my dear," Eldwin said. "May I see it?"

Reaching into her pocket, Gailea removed the perfectly round piece of Icean crystal bound in its cloth. She unwrapped it, then cupped it inside the cloth in her hands, admiring the heptagonal shape etched in its center. Sunlight streaming through the tree's doorway and windows made the Prism's smooth surface glisten with many rainbow hues.

"The Prism forged from the Meirian Crystal," Eldwin breathed, gazing upon it with vivid admiration. Fearing this awe would turn to covetousness, Gailea prepared defensive song-spells in her mind and clutched it tighter.

However, the longer she watched him, the more she saw that his desirous stare was not born from lust, but from sheer awe and reverence. And, she thought, a glimmer of fear.

His focus dragged, reluctantly, it seemed, from the Prism to Gailea. "My dear, if I may ask, where did you acquire such a gift?"

Gailea studied him, defenses raised once more. The memories leading up to her obtaining the Prism assailed her mind: her husband's hate, his uncle's ruthless envy. Harmless as Eldwin's intentions behind such a question may be, a fully truthful answer could prove harmful for her and her children.

"No matter." Eldwin gently shook his head. "I can see such memories trouble you. Instead, what do you know of the Prism itself? Or of Hylorian history and lore?"

"Nothing really, I'm afraid."

"This Prism was forged from a greater crystal called 'the Meirian.' The Meirian, crafted from Icean Crystal, is an ancient relic housed in the lighthouse in Fyre, Hyloria's capitol. The Meirian, or Meirian Crystal as it came to be called, has the power to grant wishes to those who gain mastery over wielding the Prism itself. The Prism serves as the Meirian's heart, if you will, the source of its deepest magic. But it was stolen long ago by a sorcerer."

Eldwin paused, as if searching Gailea's face for any signs of recognition. *Chevalier*, she guessed. The court sorcerer who had gifted her with the knowledge needed to obtain the Prism from its hiding place in his chambers, right before he had fled her husband's kingdom, and thus his wrath. She wondered briefly if Chevalier was alive or dead and which fate she desired for him. At any rate, she did not say his name, still uncertain of the elder Sprite's motives.

"The Prism, also known as 'the Promise of Fyre,' can grant a person one wish, but only once reunited with the Meirian from whence it was forged. Until then, I fear it poses a great threat to you, my lady. Some evil chased you here. Not merely an abstract. A man, yes? He desires the Prism above all else, except for vengeance. You know of whom I speak. He will seek the Prism to your death, and to the deaths of your children. But your musical magic may be the key to—"

Gailea struggled to her feet, clutching Ashlai close.

"How much do you know? *How* do you know? My children, my magic?"

"Lea—"

Ashden grabbed her hand, but she wrenched away and glared at him in alarm. Merritt had inched toward him, but she took her son's hand, pulled him to her side, and snatched the Prism from Eldwin, burying it deep in her pocket. "Did you bring me here to trap me?"

"*No!*" Ashden started to stand, but as Gailea backed away, he lowered himself to the ground again. "I told you Master Eldwin has a ken for visions and prophecies. I should have elaborated more specifically. He can see many things besides the future. He *knows* things."

"It's not what you are thinking, dear lady."

Gailea snapped her attention back to the old man, who sat looking apologetic. "I understand what you've been through, but the Sight is not the same as mental intrusion. I cannot enter your mind or read your thoughts. The Sight is more of a strong intuition. Anything might trigger my visions. The sight of the Prism itself may have conjured the memories embedded deep into its history. Your humming to the babe allowed me to infer that you likely wield a gift for musical magic. I understand why trust is hard for you. But please believe me. I want to help you with this burden. You *need* help, for it *will* be a burden. But it need not be a hopeless one."

Gailea eyed the elder a few moments more, a trapped animal breathing swiftly. Her knees buckled beneath her, and she stumbled. Ashden half caught her, supporting her as she found a comfortable sitting position once more. She glanced at him in silent thanks, then turned back to the elder and said, "Forgive me for being so quick to accuse you of such a horrible deceit."

Master Eldwin shook his head. "There is nothing to forgive. I too have suffered the trauma of mental control. It is one of the most terrifying breeds of magic one can ever contend with. You have every right to react with such caution and anger."

Gailea shuddered as the face of Moragon, her husband's uncle, loomed before her, ever trying to prove her thoughts. Her husband had tried to rule her by controlling her heart, Moragon by trying to control her mind and magic. Both had proven equal horrors in their own rights.

She shoved the dark memories aside. "The Prism. How can I keep him from getting it? How can I keep my family safe?"

"The Prism is a strange creation," Master Eldwin said. "Its makers created it so that it could be split into seven pieces. This happened once, long, long ago, during the First Age of Dragons. Its pieces were scattered to the winds, with the intent to keep it from landing in the hands of one who sought to use it for evil. Those who eventually found the seven pieces were each granted a special sort of protection.

"I tell you this because it seems history may be bound to repeat itself. The wisest course of action would be to split the Prism. You have the power. Musical magic is the only thing that can sever Icean crystal, besides Icean crystal itself. If you make this decision, the pieces will scatter and hide themselves. One piece would be left with you, which you could leave with your children, to protect them."

"Protect them? How?" Gailea clutched at Ashlai's blanket, uncomfortable again at what he seemed to suggest. "And what do you mean leave it with my children? You're saying I should abandon them? That I might imperil them, even with a piece of the Prism to protect them?"

"I do not know for certain. The Prism's protective powers have always been somewhat mysterious, due to their mutable nature. Its protection works differently, depending on who controls it. During the Age of Dragons, the seven who found the individual shards were placed inside a protective sleep until the time came for them to awaken. These seven awoke at the proper time to utilize the shards' magic to defeat the dragons' evil. I've heard other tales from the more distant past where the wielders of the Prism shards were only protected as long as they followed certain rules, like refraining from touching the shards or using their individual powers. I suspect these arbitrary variations may have been infused into the Prism as a further protective measure. If the manifestation of its protective qualities changes over the course of time, it would make it more difficult for those qualities to be tampered with.

"All this is to say that because of the Prism's mysterious nature, I believe it would be wisest to stay away for as long as possible, until any danger against your children from those desiring to take it had passed. After all, music mages are relatively rare, compared to other magic users. Even if you sought to hide your magic, a simple mistake could give you and them away, and—"

"*No*," Gailea cried. An agonizing terror ripped through her, as if the old man had slashed a hole in her heart. She staggered to her feet, holding Ashlai tight against her bosom. "No, I will not abandon my children."

With a darting look toward Ashden, Gailea wrenched Merritt from his side once more, muttered her thanks for the old man's warning, and turned away toward the tree's split.

But Master Eldwin called to her, "My lady! There may come a time when it there is no other choice but for you to part with your children, for their safety."

Gailea lingered a moment more. Then, with a curt nod, she hurried from the tree.

She broke into a swift walk, clutching Ashlai close to her breast and holding Merritt's hand firmly. She wove through the trees, getting lost in the woods and wishing she could escape the miasma of troubled thoughts choking her. She had always known her husband would seek to come after her, to destroy her and her children. Why would the sorcerer Chevalier have granted her a relic that would make him pursue them with an even greater thirst for vengeance? Had the sorcerer's apparent sympathy for her been some twisted pretense after all?

"Lea."

Gailea stopped. She gazed up at the expanse of trees and green and dappled sunlight showering her. She didn't know how long she had been walking or where she was.

"I'm sorry." Ashden walked up beside her. "I didn't take you there to upset you. I thought you would want answers."

"And I thank you for that," Gailea said, more curtly than she would have liked. "But the idea of separating myself from my children is ludicrous. Not after all we've been through. Who better to care for any child than their own mother or father? Barring any parent given over to abuse or madness, which I am not. Rather, that's the sort of person I run from with them! Do you think I've chosen to flee on some flippant, exciting adventure?"

"I know you flee to protect them." Ashden's voice remained level, filled with its usual, serious calm. He didn't dare to step closer, respecting her space, but he did meet her eyes intently, in a way that unnerved her, not because his gaze was unsavory, but rather because it emanated such strong truth. "I would never tell you to part with your children. I would only caution you to consider Master Eldwin's words, to store them in your mind instead of disregarding them entirely. Unbeknownst to him, his intuition may have sensed that a time is coming when you may have to make such a difficult choice. I haven't known you well or long, but I believe that you would never put your own desires above their safety."

He glanced between Merritt, Ashlai, and finally back to her. The gentleness softening his serious demeanor calmed her, as did the truth of his words as they sunk deep inside her. Her remaining anger transformed into a renewed determination, one as rock-solid as the Prism in her pocket.

"You're right. Their protection matters above all. And right now, that means doing what I already knew, the one thing Master Eldwin said that I can agree with fully. That the sooner I can flee this place and find a haven for my family with Bromwell, the better."

"Your name…it's not Lea Jardis, is it?"

Gailea inhaled a deep breath. "No. No, it isn't."

"Perhaps you'll tell me your real name someday?"

"Perhaps."

"Once you're safe in Vian, with Bromwell."

"Long after. When my husband is dead, and with him my entire past, which has proven nothing but a threat to me and my children."

She could see the disappointment wash over his face, but his steady focus remained on her. "Whoever he is, he is a fool. The Prism may be the treasure he seeks now, but it's clear that he lost the true treasure long ago."

For a moment, Gailea wanted to draw near him, to hide inside his safe embrace like Merritt did. But she had no time for affection, no room in her heart, nor could she afford the blunders that came with such distractions.

Her children were her family. Ashden was not. Before her face could betray her, she turned away, staring once more into the trees.

"Best head back to camp," Ashden said at last. "Now that we've seen Eldwin and you're strong enough, we can make preparations for the journey to Vian ahead."

CHAPTER 3

THE PROMISE
SHATTERED

Gailea, her children, and Ashden departed the next day with a band of five Mirtle Sprites—Laisa, Clove, Willa, and two Sprite brothers named Star and Sage—just as dawn bathed the green woods in a brilliant red-gold sheen. Mists clung to the lower branches and bushes, shimmering and shivering like the liquid silver of a certain magical sword Gailea had once known.

The trek through the terrain soon proved just as arduous as Ashden had promised, their path tangled with thick reeds, thorns, and trees often knit so close together that the group could barely squeeze through. Laisa promised that, while unpleasant, these paths were the most secluded. Aside from Sprites and perhaps a few Forest-footers, none would know they even existed. Besides this, should the need for further protection arise, Sage and Star were two of the Mirtles' most agile fighters.

The air grew dense. Between struggling to draw breath and squeezing in and out of tight places, Gailea felt almost suffocated. At times, she longed to return to the open, airy comfort of the Sprite Woods, but her children fueled her forward. The more abandoned the paths they took, the higher a chance they had of safely reaching their destination.

Laisa had helped Gailea weave special baskets from orna reeds and pliable tree limbs for the children to ride in. Gailea carried Ashlai close to her heart while Merritt rode on Ashden's back.

Ashlai spent most of her time sleeping. When she wasn't napping or suckling, she had a tendency to fuss, but Gailea's singing would easily soothe her back to sleep.

Merritt, on the other hand, was gratifyingly quiet and content as ever. The thick air seemed to make him extra tired, and he slept much of the time. At other times, he would stare in wonder at the towering trees or try to mimic the birds, crickets, and other forest noises.

When Merritt grew bored of these things, he would resort to his favorite hobby of playing with Willa or Ashden's hair, depending on whom he'd chosen as his current favorite companion. Gailea found herself sharing a smile with them many a time, and then she would quietly thank Amiel. Though danger still chased her little family, they had found a small reprieve in these new friends. She could not have asked for better guides and protectors.

As evening fell, Laisa and Clove found a small clearing within a cluster of trees and thorn bushes. Gailea was determined to keep going, but Laisa promised that a short rest would do far more good than harm. Besides, they still waited to receive word from Bromwell, and from the neighboring Alder Sprites who had promised to lead them the rest of the way.

"Why do we need the Alders' aid?" Gailea asked. "You and the other Mirtles seem to be doing well enough leading us."

Laisa had just finished helping Clove start a small fire and stood with a smile. "The Alders are skilled warriors. In the latter half of our trek, further south where the Alders make their home, the woods aren't quite as thick. They leave potential for us to encounter more people. There are still secluded paths we can take, but they've agreed to accompany us as an extra precaution. Bromwell also has friends among the Alders."

"You mentioned some sort of sign or message from Bromwell. How will he know how to find us and without giving us away?"

"We Sprites have our own ways of doing things." Laisa's eyes danced playfully. "Remember that we are close with nature. We can communicate with the birds and beasts, sometimes even the trees. Our messengers are often the least conspicuous because they don't appear as messengers at all. But enough worrying for now." Gently taking Gailea's hand, Laisa led her to sit on a log near the fire. "Rest, my friend! Rest and wait for this delightful dinner planned for us."

While Ashden, Star, and Sage skinned a brace of rabbits they'd caught earlier, Laisa helped Gailea remove the strips of leather binding Ashlai's basket to her shoulders and waist. Gailea laid the basket on the hard ground and set the infant within. Despite the chill in the air, she sweated from their long hike and removed her cloak, padding the babe's makeshift bed. Ashden had released Merritt who now ran around the fire, chasing fireflies.

"Lea."

She looked up. Willa had walked up to lay more firewood beside them. The younger Sprite frowned at Merritt with concern and then back at Gailea.

"Ought you let him play so close to the fire?"

Gailea offered a playful smile. "He *does* have Fyre blood."

When Willa's worry lingered, Gailea nodded toward her son. The moth Merritt had been chasing flitted over the flames. He stopped before the fire, instinctively cautious. Then, slowly, he reached his chubby fingertips toward the dancing embers.

"Oh!"

Willa reached toward him, but Gailea cleared her throat, making her pause. Merritt's fingers glowed a brilliant white-gold, and ever so carefully, he waved his hand back and forth through the flames. Gailea sang a little melody she'd composed beneath her breath, making the fire morph into a bright purple, a dark blue, a vivid green, and then back to orange. As the pattern continued, Merritt plopped down right before the flames and clapped his hands. Willa looked relieved and hurried off to collect more firewood, while Laisa laughed in delight before joining her.

"That's amazing," Ashden breathed. He'd glanced up from his work, his dark eyes alight with admiration. "To have his powers under control at such an age."

Gailea shook her head. "It remains to be seen if the boy will have magic of his own, and if so, what kind. He's never yet displayed any. But at the least, all with Fyre blood are born with some inherent safeguard. Even those who never display any affinity for fire magic have some degree of protection. They're drawn to flames, and it's good for them to be exposed at a young age. He could still hurt himself if the fire was too big or its heat too intense, but his instincts keep him from harm."

Gailea shifted in her seat with a groan. Laisa had provided her with the herbs, water, and small bowl needed to make a salve which she used now to tend the scrapes and cuts on her arms, hands, and face. Every muscle seemed to rebel inside her body, and she felt almost as broken as on the day she'd delivered Ashlai.

She shifted again, and something nudged the side of her leg. Reaching into her pocket, she drew out the smooth Prism. Ashlai cooed, and Gailea lowered it toward the infant, turning it in the firelight so that the multifaceted figure within reflected the light with soft rainbow hues.

Ashden sat beside Gailea. "Have you thought any more on what Master Eldwin said?" he asked gently. "About breaking it?"

"Yes..." Gailea gazed admiringly at her daughter before narrowing her gaze at the Prism. "If my husband were to find it whole, intact, there's no telling the amount of damage he might be able to do with it."

"You think it's safer with you, where you can keep an eye on it? Even though he's looking for you?"

Gailea hesitated. "That's where I struggle. But I also don't favor the idea of scattering the pieces to the wind for just *anyone* to find, even if they're meant to hide themselves well."

"Or the idea of having to sacrifice being with your children if you break it and leave a piece with them."

Gailea glanced up at him. For a moment, she almost appreciated his understanding, but then she wondered if he accused her.

"I would do *anything* to protect my children. Even if it meant such a painful separation."

Ashden frowned. "I know you would. I meant no insult."

A shrill screech made Gailea jump and glance up at the sky. A great beast swooped through the trees and landed before them. It looked like a bat but large enough that Gailea could have ridden it like a horse. Thick green fur covered its body. Large, fox-like ears twitched. Its huge mouth curled into a grin, and between its lips rested a folded piece of parchment.

Gailea stared, mouth parted in shock. As Ashden rose and stepped toward the creature, Gailea cried out in alarm, but he merely gave her a calming pat on her shoulder, nodded to the creature, and took the parchment.

After unfolding and skimming it, he looked at her. "It's from Bromwell. Your late friend's father wrote to him of your kindness to Tytonn, and he promises to make his home a refuge for you and the children."

"I'm glad to hear it. But what is this creature, and how did it know to find us?"

The beast opened its mouth wide and released a loud groan. Taking a step back, Gailea prepared defensive songs in her mind, only to watch as the creature completed its apparent yawning with a friendly, albeit toothy, grin.

"This is the messenger I alluded to earlier." Laisa breezed up beside Gailea, extending a bit of cooked rabbit to the bat who slurped it up with its long, purple tongue. "As I said, we Sprites have our own ways of doing things. Woodland Bats, or Sprite Bats, as they're commonly known, are our close companions. They're very in tune with nature, and with us. Good job then, Verde. Best be on your way." Laisa patted the beast's side, and it winged toward the heavens once more.

Gailea watched the sky in a daze a few moments longer. She had certainly never seen anything like that in all her years living in Moragon's castle. What other wonders and oddities did the world hold? Many, she hoped, to share with her children.

"Here, would you like to see the letter?"

Ashden handed it to her, and upon scanning its contents for herself, she sighed relief.

A wail pierced the quiet. Merritt lay on the ground, crying and kicking. Thick sweat lined his brow. Gailea hurried over, crouched on the ground beside him, and placed a hand to his forehead.

"A fever?" Ashden asked.

Gailea shook her head. "No...he's just hot from playing so hard and very tired. Hush, my son." She stroked his messy red curls. "I know it's been a long day...." Softly, she sang her lullaby that had once set her free. Lately, it set Merritt free from the realm of nightmares, granting him a peaceful rest.

Gradually, his sobs calmed. Ashden knelt beside Gailea, placed a soothing hand on the child's head, and sang along. His voice was low and rich, and he sang in a tongue foreign to Gailea. The boy ceased fidgeting. Even Gailea felt a strange calm descend upon her. She'd almost fallen asleep by the time her child lay still, sleeping soundly. Ashlai slumbered too.

Gailea studied Ashden curiously. "You know musical magic?"

"A little." Touching two fingers to the earth, he sang beneath his breath until a small green shoot emerged from the soil. He smiled up at her. "Mostly songs that have to do with growing or tending plants."

"Musical magic is an inborn gift. One cannot acquire it by studying."

Ashden shrugged. "So my elders have said, and the wisest Sprites too. The trait has only shown itself in the past couple of years. I'd like to learn more, but it's such a rare gift to my people."

"I could teach you sometime," Gailea said. "If you get the chance to visit us once we're settled in our new home."

Ashden hesitated before letting his smile fill his face. "I would gladly accept that chance to see you."

Gailea smiled back, leery yet admittedly with a small sense of pride that she hadn't felt in some time.

She heard the snapping of twigs farther down the path, barely audible beyond the sound of rustling leaves in the wind, but Gailea was alert enough.

"They are coming," she whispered, her arms reflexively drawing Ashlai nearer. "The bat, the message was a ruse."

"No, please don't be alarmed." Again, Ashden reassured her as he stood. "Those must be our new escorts."

Gailea clambered up and anxiously followed Ashden's gaze as seven Sprites entered the clearing from its singular entrance. They stood a little taller than the Mirtles Gailea had traveled with thus far, and their hair was a brighter shade of green, shining with inflections of yellow; even their dark brown eyes were gold speckled. They wore fierce expressions, thick leather, and breastplates painted with a golden bear crowned with silver stars.

"Are those the Alder Sprites?" Gailea asked.

Ashden nodded, studying the newcomers sternly.

"They're wearing the crest of King Donyon of Adelar," Gailea whispered, feeling an extra sense of relief. Perhaps Donyon, once a displaced lord, now king, had heard of her plight and wanted to help her, as an unspoken thank you. After all, it was her lullaby, transformed into the potent song-spell that had taken out her husband's soldiers, that had allowed Donyon to take back the throne.

"Did you know he was the one sending the Alder Sprites?"

Ashden made no reply but continued watching them more intensely.

Clove approached the Alders, with Star, Sage, and Laisa on his heels. The Alders addressed Clove in a strange, harsh language.

"Do you know...?" Gailea whispered.

Ashden shook his head. "No. The Jadiyah clan is newer to these parts. The Sprites' language is yet foreign to me." His voice faded, but his hand hovered over his sword.

The Alder's voice rose in pitch and intensity. He seemed to grow irritated with Clove, who suddenly paled. The other Mirtles closed in, standing protectively around Gailea, while Willa took both sleeping children into her arms.

Gailea instinctively slipped her hand into her pocket and clutched the Prism. Perhaps she had no swords or daggers like the Sprites, nor the training to use such weapons were they to hand her one, but she would protect her children as she always had, with her music. Silently, she sang another familiar, old melody inside her mind, channeling its magic into the Prism and concentrating to magnify its might, just as she once did with her lullaby. Now, as then, she had only one chance to get this right.

As the Alder warrior reached toward his belt, the Mirtle Sprites drew their swords. The Alders did the same.

Gailea braced herself, focusing more intently on her song-spell, but the Alder Sprite who'd been speaking only drew a small scroll from his belt. Gailea began to release the large breath she'd held in, yet as he opened the scroll and showed it to all present, both her breath and heart seemed to stop once more. The warrior pointed to a sketch of Gailea. Then, he pointed at Gailea. Clove started talking very fast. The Alder warrior talked back, yelling, pointing at Gailea. Laisa stepped beside Clove, talking calmly but sternly, seemingly trying to reason with the Alder. He spat at her and drew his sword, eyes ablaze with disdain as he shouted. Laisa drew her sword.

The Alder Sprite cut her down before she could utter

another word in Gailea's defense.

Gailea wanted to scream, but the noise lodged in her throat. Instead, she could only watch as Laisa lay motionless, abruptly transformed from a dear caretaker and new friend into an empty shell, blood steadily spreading from beneath her. The horrific scene felt so unreal that Gailea was certain it must be a nightmare, or perhaps she simply needed to believe this, to momentarily numb herself to the pain of yet another loss—at the hands of yet another person she had placed false, naïve trust in—and focus once more on the song-spell she was now absolutely certain she needed.

With a cry that rivaled her own anguish, Clove drew his blade.

The Alders and Mirtles charged at each other.

Swords clashed. Ashden and Clove rushed to the forefront. Star and Sage circled the Alders, performing turns and flips like an artful dance that kept their enemy on their toes. Without hesitation, Willa and burst with Gailea's children toward the thick woods. Gailea would not stop her. Willa surely knew better than her how to get her children to safety. But she couldn't let them from her sight without the Prism to protect them. Why had she been so selfish as to not to sever it before now?

While the battle raged around her, Gailea removed the Prism from her pocket and clutched it tight in both hands, chanting her melody over and over in her mind. She had created the simple charm long ago, during her days as Moragon's servant, to aid the chore of stoking the castle's many fireplaces. Often weak from hunger and cold, Gailea had lacked the strength needed to chop the large lumps of coal into smaller pieces. Instead, she had created a secret song-spell to do the work for her. She sang that same song now. All she need do is push her singular need for her children's safety into that song-spell and pray that, just as she'd once transformed her lullaby into more than a lullaby, she could also use this simple charm to provide deliverance for her children once again.

Sage staggered beside Gailea. Star fell, and blood oozed from thick gashes on both his legs and side. While quick on their feet, their lack of armor had gained them a greater number of wounds. Clove and Ashden closed in before Gailea, shielding her as two of the Alders attacked.

A warmth pressed into Gailea's palms as her magic flowed into the Prism. She tried to intensify her song, but the dreadful truth battered her mind over and over again: *He's found you. your husband has found you. Donyon betrayed you and joined your husband's side, and now he will turn you over to him.*

The warriors closed in. In a matter of moments, all Gailea's protectors would lie slaughtered. The Alders would drag Gailea back to her husband to claim their reward. King Ragnar would murder her children or worse: imprison her and force her to witness the torture of their son whom he abhorred and the mind-control of their daughter whom he was bound to worship as his self-proclaimed sole heir.

Fear wavered her spell, so she closed her eyes and focused, blocking out the sight of the blood, the shouts, the clashing of swords, the screaming of her children who'd just woken.

The Prism burned so hotly against her flesh it could well sink right inside her palms. Ropes of fire sliced across her skin and spiraled up her arm. She buckled at the pain. Her eyes opened again, and she watched Sage fall. Ashden stumbled against her, releasing a cry. Her children shrieked. She sang the spell again, this time at the top of her lungs,

"*Vergeria assundra!*"

A brilliant light burst from her hands, flooding the entire clearing. Immense power and heat flowed from the Prism, as if Gailea's song had awakened some dormant consciousness within it. She cried out and almost dropped it, but she managed to clutch it and glance up, squinting into the bright light. The Prism burst apart, flinging her hands aside. For a brief moment, the Prism hovered midair, its glow magnifying into a blinding white. The next instant, the light divided into seven colors, and seven shards hovered instead—red, orange, yellow, green, blue, indigo, and violet. Gailea snatched at the sky, grasping the one nearest her with indigo hues. It burned into her flesh, and she barely managed to hold it. Tremors traveled up her entire body, making her sweat.

She reached for the second-nearest shard, the yellow one, hoping that if she obtained one for each of them, maybe they would be protected enough for her to stay safely with her children, without endangering them. But as her fingertips grazed the yellow shard, a fiery heat shot from her fingertips up the entire length of her arm so vehemently that she swooned, and the indigo shard nearly slipped from her grasp. Gailea abandoned the idea of obtaining a second shard. Perhaps the Prism thought she meant to take multiple shards for herself and fought to prevent this.

As one of the Alder Sprites leaped toward the shimmering objects, Gailea flung her hand out, singing her separation spell again as loud and intensely as possible. The remaining shards scattered in all directions. The one in her hand tried to lunge, but Gailea clutched it tight. She whirled about in the direction Willa had fled with her children.

To her shock, Willa and her children remained in

clear view. On the farthest edge of the clearing, Willa had knelt before one of the larger trees. Holding Ashlai with one arm while Merritt clung obediently to her side, wailing great tears, Willa used her free hand to etch what appeared to be the outline of a door on the tree's side. She drew slowly, face twisted with intense concentration. It seemed Gailea wasn't the only one who'd been focusing on a vital, life-saving spell.

Gailea darted across the clearing, ignoring Ashden's frantic protests. One of the Alder warriors slammed into her from the side, knocking her to the ground and the air from her lungs. Her mind spun, but she concentrated once more on her separation melody. Exhausted, what little magic remained came to her clumsily. She opened her eyes in time to see a long blade sweeping down at her. As she sang her song at full force, she and the warrior flew through the air in opposite directions. Gailea sang a charm to slow herself, sparing her from crashing into a thorny bush. She glanced up to find the warrior lying motionless at the base of a tree.

A cry alerted Gailea back to her children. Willa had just completed her spell, an arched door swung inward on the tree's thick trunk, and she swooped the children up, ducking inside.

"Willa, wait!" Gailea shrieked, stumbling as she ran for the tree.

Willa did not stop, and Gailea picked up speed, reaching her and grasping at the hem of her cloak. Willa paused and stared at Gailea in alarm.

"If you're coming too, we must hurry!"

"I can't," Gailea gasped as her tears abruptly came. She pushed them back. Not yet. The time to break down and mourn and release every righteous anger and pain was not yet. Not until her children were safe.

Gailea ripped a large strip of cloth from her tunic

and bound the shard up tight. Then, she shoved it into Willa's pocket, gasping desperately, *"Please.* Take them to safety, and keep this with them, always. It will protect them. And tell Bromwell to make sure that my son knows someday that his true name is 'Merritt.' Now go!"

Willa nodded, a look of promise in her gaze. She would not rest 'til she had fulfilled a mother's last wish. Ducking inside the tree and kneeling on the ground, Willa began tracing the dirt and chanting. Merritt screamed for Gailea over and over again. The remaining three Alder Sprites rushed in, and Gailea barely kept them at bay with spurts of protective songs that repelled them for a few moments.

Ashden leaped toward her, blocking one of the warriors with his sword and yelling, "Go, Lea, now!"

Gailea inhaled a shuddering breath. She glanced wildly at her children and crouched inside the tree. She watched as the pattern Willa had traced crumbled and fell away, revealing an opening into tunnels below. Willa glanced at her, demanding a final answer. Suppressing another sob, Gailea shook her head.

"Mama, Mama!" Merritt cried. *"Mama!"*

Each time her little boy called to her, another small part of her heart tore away. She tried to smile, but it was useless. The child was old enough to know she was abandoning him, just as he was not old enough to understand why. He shrieked her name over and over again, kicked, pulled Willa's hair. Gailea longed to touch her son, to embrace him one last time, comfort him, but Willa disappeared with Merritt and Ashlai inside the tunnels, and the opening sealed itself behind them. Gailea collapsed to her knees, whispering, "I love you, Merritt, I love you," needing him to know and believe it even though he couldn't anymore.

"Lea, come on! We have to go! *Now!*"

Ashden's words were a dim jumble in her mind, strange and distant. A part of her knew she should move, but she couldn't. She'd lost all desire and strength. Without her children, her heart, she was nothing. She knew she should rejoice over their safety, but in being separated from them, her husband had won the war between them after all.

"Lea, *please*." Ashden gripped her arms firmly, lowering his face to hers so that she was forced to look. "You *will* see them again someday. I promise you. But if they are to be safe, *we must leave now*."

Their safety. Yes, that was the only way she could keep her children, by knowing they were safe somewhere. Yes, that had been the plan.

Gailea glanced at the thick blood pouring from the long gash in Ashden's arm. She saw his labored breathing, and the injured Sprites scattered across the clearing. They were not all accounted for, including a couple of their enemies. Panic lit Gailea's heart. Scrambling to her feet, she helped Ashden stand. Then, together, they fled into the woods.

Within moments, dozens of arrows split the air toward them. Behind but gaining fast, more of Donyon's Alder Sprites snarled, shouted, and raced furiously toward them.

"*There she is!*"

One of the Sprites blew a loud note on a horn, and the warriors thundered in their direction. Sorrow fled from Gailea's heart, replaced by fear and an imminent need for focus and speed. She and Ashden pushed through the trees, leaping over gnarled roots and prickly bushes. Furious shouts, cries, and bodies crashed through the woods toward them. Arrows rained on all sides, and they barely managed to duck out of range.

Ashden collapsed, bringing Gailea down with him.

She screamed as they rolled down a long hill. When they slammed to a stop, Gailea sat up, stunned. Ashden sprawled on the ground, his arm bent grotesquely. An arrow stuck cruelly into his right side. Blood soaked his clothes and bloomed against the vivid green grass.

He pushed himself halfway up, groaning loudly. Gailea reached a trembling hand toward him, singing one of her healing charms beneath her breath, but the song's magic echoed pure emptiness. Both her strength and spirit had abandoned her. There was nothing she could do to help him. She had lost Laisa, her children, and now she would lose him too.

"I'm sorry. I can't help you. I have nothing left to help you."

"*Go,*" Ashden gasped. "You must keep going!"

"I can't just leave you this way, and I've nowhere to go besides. There's nowhere left for me to hide!"

"That's not true. Find your boat. Sail north for Loz."

"That boat was practically destroyed!"

"I had the Furies fix it. Just in case. It should be waiting where you left it. Loz is a large kingdom. You can lose yourself there, become someone new."

"I *can't.*" Gailea trembled more violently. "I can't leave you too, after all you've done for me."

"You can, and you must." Ashden forced the words. He gripped Gailea's arms, only to wince and recoil. "Lea, your children are safe now. Willa will know where to take them. They have the shard. You must place as much distance now between yourself and them as you can. You know you must. *You must keep on.*"

Gailea swallowed her tears. A part of her wanted to die beside Ashden, but she knew he was right. She still had her children. She must fight to stay alive for them and, Amiel willing, someday return to them.

She bent over and gently kissed his forehead. He smiled faintly, his golden-brown eyes reflecting both physical pain and yet a strange peace.

"I return now to my brothers and sisters of the earth," he whispered, before exhaling and drawing still.

Gailea wrenched away. Without a second glance back, she tore away through the woods toward the ocean.

CHAPTER 4

THE KING'S INSTRUMENT

F ar north of Hyloria, on another island kingdom,
Carmenna, Castle Alaula's thick walls well protected its few remaining inhabitants from the raging rain
and thunder outside. Carmenna was usually warm and
sunny or had seemed so to the young woman now standing against one of the stone walls that had always kept
her safe. Lady Lorelei had relied on their safety more
heavily in recent months, thanks to the increasingly sin-
ister acts developing within the walls of her once beloved
home.

She lifted her fingers, paler than their usual dark
red brown, thanks to the fear drawing blood away from
her feet and hands, and muttered the familiar spell over
and over again, all the while touching the amulet at her
heart, invisible and fused magically inside her. Just as its
protective presence was embedded within her body, so
she would soon fuse with the stone wall at her back, long
enough to pass through it to the secret passage on the

other side. If only she could concentrate properly.

As she pressed her body close to the stone wall, chanting the amulet's coalescence spell, *Amalgamation*, it burned so vehemently she thought her very heart must catch ablaze. Then, at last, the magic took root. She slipped inside the wall, so quickly that she felt like her entire body was collapsing in on itself, crushing her heart and lungs, her very bones. Tumbling into the secret passage beyond, she ached all over. She rested against the wall, muttering a healing charm. The amulet's burn faded. Within moments, her strength was fully regained, and she hurried down the corridor.

The secret passage was one of many that formed an interconnected maze of narrow corridors and stairways built inside the castle's very walls. Lorelei's old nurse, Lady Alma, had told stories of those passages, presumably crafted for the purpose of providing the Carmennan royal family with secret escapes from their enemies. This secret was passed down only to the royal family and their absolute closest, most trusted friends.

Unfortunately for the late King Noheah, the usurper Samil's attack to steal the Carmennan throne had come too swiftly and unexpectedly for him to make use of the passages. But fortunately for Lorelei, her father, Master Lorens, was close enough friends with the king to be aware of them. Lorelei's father had shared his knowledge with her with hesitation, knowing her to be a bold and curious creature, but King Samil's terrifying reign had driven him to it. Master Lorens said that he had seen enough dead or tortured needlessly at Samil's hands to want his daughter to have every opportunity of protection and escape available to her.

Lorelei hurried through the narrow passage. Her father would meet with King Samil soon—he might already be in the throne room—and she must watch to make sure he was safe. The king had grown increasingly violent. Lorelei's father said some secret challenged his patience, something he desired greatly but could not attain. Many feared that the king's unfilled greed would drive him mad.

In Lorelei's opinion, King Samil had come to them mad. He was no native Carmennan, to be sure. Though he shared their jet-black hair, it was stick-straight, and his skin was white as a corpse's, a stark contrast to her people's various shades of dark brown. He had swooped in from some other land and stolen theirs seemingly overnight, murdering the royal family and setting himself up as king.

That had been just two years ago. Lorelei had feared how the transition would affect her family. Thankfully, thus far, her father had won favor with Samil by crafting musical instruments for him. Samil seemed to possess no musical skill himself but obsessed over anyone who shared any magic connection to music. He had spent the past several weeks parading strangers through the throne room, making them play, sing, and dance, all the while seeming to search for something. All in vain, a fact that only served to enhance his unstable, ill temper.

Lorelei slowed her pace as she heard voices echoing beyond the other side of the wall. Their words were too muffled to distinguish, but those who spoke them were familiar enough. This was the spot.

She crept alongside the wall, carefully tapping the stones at intervals until a certain, hollow sound with a slightly higher pitch caught her attention. As she slid the small, loose stone from its place, she touched the skin above her bodice, where the amulet was embedded. Its warmth pulsed beneath her fingertips, just like her heartbeat, and its song echoed faintly to her. Calmed as ever by its presence, she crouched down to the opening revealed by the loose stone, allowing her to peer into the massive throne chamber below.

King Samil sat on the throne perched atop a dais at the end of a long, solid stone room. Thick pillars supported the lofty ceiling, each intricately carved with nymphs, fauns, and other creatures playing musical instruments. Between the pillars, musical instruments of all sorts hovered inside floating glass cases. Tapestries woven from rich purples, reds and golds lined the walls, and between them on one wall, tall arched windows permitted starlight. This blue-white glow, accompanied by the orange din of torchlight, sent strange shadows spiraling across the floor. The shadows seemed to dance to the music radiating from below. Lorelei squinted, trying to decipher the source of the music flowing toward her.

A shadow-cloaked figure stood on the red carpet leading up to the throne, facing away from Lorelei. At first, she couldn't tell if it was a man or woman, Carmennan or foreigner. Thin, shorter than her father, this might even have been an older child. But she recognized that the instrument so skillfully played was stringed and played with a bow like a vielle or lyra. But its sound was...unique.

Samil leaned toward the man beside him. Reynard, his right-hand man, a Carmennan and therefore, in Lorelei's mind, an ultimate traitor. Samil and Reynard were constantly connected, moreso than some romantic pairings Lorelei had known.

Samil motioned with his right hand, and someone else stepped from behind one of the pillars.

Lorelei's heart skipped a beat. Though difficult to make out details, she would recognize her father's tall frame and confident gait from any distance. Master Lorens was not a proud man, but neither did he display fear in Samil's presence, as did many others. "He's just a man," her father always said of the false king.

Lorelei suspected this fearlessness was part of what had earned him such respect in Samil's court and kept him alive and unharmed for this long. Sometimes she wished she could give her amulet to her father. Being under the king's constant watch, he was in more danger than she. But the protective gem had ever been embedded within her body, and she'd not yet deciphered how to undo its magic. That had been her mother's cleverness.

Her father handed something to the person playing music, likely one of his creations. When the figure turned, Lorelei could now see it was a young man, possibly not much older than her own thirteen years. Moments later, the boy switched to this new instrument. Like the one before, it was stringed and played with a bow, and Lorelei had never heard the likes of it before. It evoked emotion vividly, seeming sometimes to laugh and other times to cry. She found herself entranced by its sad yet striking melody. The amulet near her heart burned fiercely. The tune was clearly a musically woven spell, and the amulet worked hard to safeguard against whatever sway it sought to hold over her. The music pleaded, *ached* to get inside her mind, but she reacted, singing the word *Salmána* beneath her breath, a powerful song-shield that acted as a countercurse.

Most people in the room below had neither amulets nor musical charms to protect them. Lorelei watched, partly horrified, partly awed, as guards marched forward from all sides of the room and knelt before the young musician wielding the instrument and its song as a weapon.

King Samil rose from his throne, walked down the steps of the dais, and stopped behind the boy. He placed an almost paternal hand on his shoulder, leaned down, and whispered something. The music changed, became a series of dissonant chords. One of the guards drew his dagger, raised it, and drove it straight through his own heart.

The song abruptly ended with a squealing chord mingled with a choked scream. Lorelei barely stifled a shriek as the guard collapsed and blood ran in all directions. The other guards, their hypnosis broken with the music's abrupt ending, staggered back, yelling and pointing at their dead comrade. Lorelei's father stood perfectly still, not saying a word, but she could imagine the revulsion flooding him, the same horror that nearly made her retch.

A loud command from the king sent everyone scattering. They had been dismissed, except for Reynard and the young man, who had dropped to his knees, the instrument slumped in his lap.

When her father left the chamber, Lorelei darted back down the corridor. He would seek solace in their shared chambers, specifically his workshop.

Lorelei wove down the series of secret passages until a sharp chill told her she had reached the castle's lower level. She traveled a little further until she finally hit a dead end. Too impatient to bother tinkering with the secret switch, Lorelei pressed both palms against the wall, chanting her coalescence spell once more.

She pushed through the stones, spilled out the other side, and stood hugging herself for a few moments, breathless from the effort. Then, she smoothed the folds of her dark red dress. Her mother had died nearly a year ago during a fever epidemic, but it was custom in Carmenna for loved ones to wear red and midnight blue, the colors of mourning, for at least a year. Lorelei's father would wear red until he found another bride.

Lorelei hurried down the deserted hall. As it was

so close to the dungeons, hardly anyone ever came this way, and the cold made her quicken her pace.

A few winding passages, then up a flight of stairs, and she found herself in a warmer part of the castle. Cheerier too, with tapestries and paintings of Carmenna's past monarchs, knights, and musicians lining the walls between torches, a few heralds to the royal family's past glory. Samil had redecorated much of Castle Alaula to match his tastes, but this was one of few corridors he seemed to have overlooked, and Lorelei was glad of it. Seeing these familiar artifacts lent hope that someday things would be put right.

At last, she reached the corridor housing hers and her father's quarters. At thirteen, she was two short years away from being of age. She dreaded that day, when she would be removed from him to take up a new room in the section of the castle that lodged all the other noble ladies. The amulet protected her, but it couldn't give her the same reassurance and courage as being so near her father.

Within their chambers, she passed by her father's room, stepped into the large room beyond, and paused, observing. The Royal Fabricator's workshop was spacious, its ceiling high, the windows permitting much sunlight by day or, as now, starlight. Candlelit lanterns glowed softly upon the furniture, musical instruments, weapons, and various other items carved from wood and stone organized about the room. Started projects, finished ones. The sweet scent of wood shavings wafting through the room, the same scent that clung to her father's clothes and skin. Lorelei inhaled deeply, and her nerves calmed a little as she walked forward.

Master Lorens stood at the far end of the room at one of his worktables, carefully whittling some small object. Lorelei watched him before glancing at the collection of similar objects lined up on the table. Tiny horses, houses, people.

Lorelei frowned curiously. Her father was such a practical man, rarely crafting whimsical objects. And he had been given explicit orders to craft nothing except whatever the king himself ordered. What use could the king have for children's toys? Even if Samil had a child of his own, he would likely teach it about warfare and dark spells. Fanciful toys would serve no purpose.

Master Lorens hissed, dropping the knife and half-formed horse figurine. A thin stream of blood trickled from his thumb. He grabbed a cloth and held it to the wound. Then, with a frustrated sigh, he plopped down onto his bench.

"Papa?"

Her father glanced up, and a weary smile touched his lips. "Why Lori! Forgive me, Little Mouseling. I did not hear you enter."

"You were busy carving your thumb," Lorelei said playfully, then sighed. "The king works you too hard. All your woodworking, now all these sudden audiences. You're so tired."

Eyeing her, Master Lorens raised a speculative bushy eyebrow., "You were there again. You followed me."

"I have to make sure that you're safe."

"That's not your responsibility. It's *I* who must watch over *you*."

"*You* have no fancy amulet to protect you."

He smiled a little. "Point well made. Still, there are things you don't need to see. I tell you what goes on in the castle, as much as is necessary for your safety." His gaze darkened. "You don't need to witness such horrors. Please tell me you did not see—"

"I did." Lorelei swallowed at the memory of that poor guard's suicide. "That musician, the one who forced him...."

"Under orders. He is but a boy," Master Lorens muttered. "Near your age, with a keen gift for music, but not yet aware what its power can do. His Majesty lacks the skill but not the knowledge. *He* knew the spell-song would impel the soldier to do his bidding."

"Through his mental magic," Lorelei said softly. "He played the boy like an instrument."

Her father did not answer, a sign that she'd already gotten him to divulge more than he felt safe. "Put it from your mind. It is not suited for you to know such things. Much less see them." He returned to his work. His hands, usually so sure and strong, trembled.

Moving closer, Lorelei nearly asked if she could comfort him, but concern for his pride changed her request. "Would you mind if I sang? I think it would help calm me."

He nodded. "Yes. I would like that."

Lorelei thought for a moment, then chose a song she'd composed long ago, one that had been a favorite of her mother's. Though lacking magic, Mamma was talented and well versed in the musical arts and had helped Lorelei refine and perfect many of her tunes. In the year since her loss, Lorelei had added a refrain that wove within its notes a soothing charm. She sang it now:

"Calm your breath, ease your mind:
May this song's serenity help you unwind...."

Her father began to relax, his shoulders slouching a bit as his whole body eased.

Suddenly, his head jerked up. "Wait, Lori, no. Don't. No magic!"

Lorelei sang on. She needed the song just as much right now. Anything to wash away the vision of that poor solider sacrificing himself for his cruel king.

"Lori, I warn you—*Lorelei*!"

Cutting off when her name exploded from his lips, the girl froze and stared at her father. At no time could she recall his having used such a harsh tone with her. An uncommon fear filled his entire face, making him look abruptly old and eerily exhausted.

Sadness softened his gaze and he walked over, taking her by the shoulders. "Forgive me. But I cannot tell you again. *No magic.* You must not squander your safety by displaying even a hint of your skill. That goes for the both of us. We must give him no suspicion that musical magic runs through our veins, but especially yours. I won't see anything happen to you like what happened with that boy today."

Lorelei breathed deeply, regretful to cause her father such obvious distress. "I'll do what you ask, Pappa, but I don't understand. What could the King want from me? He has plenty of court musicians to entertain him with spell-songs."

Her father gave her shoulders a gentle squeeze. "I promise that you are better off not knowing the answer to such a question."

"But why?" Lorelei pressed. She didn't wish to exasperate her father further, and yet she couldn't contain her own frustrations. They had always talked with each other about everything.

"When Mamma was alive, she encouraged my spell-singing. You did too. I remember when we used to create new song-spells together. What's changed? Can't you help me understand?"

Pain reflected in her father's eyes at the mention of Mamma, and he drew a long breath. "Much has changed, Lori. Too much. I can see I'll have to tell you what little I know."

Lorelei waited eagerly, equally surprised and pleased that her father trusted her with whatever information he prepared to divulge.

"King Samil continues to seek something of value to him and grows more frustrated as he does not find it. It's some kind of weapon connected to musical magic. Many of the men, women, and children he has brought in to test their musical skills have vanished without a trace. Many others have been executed as spies, thieves, or whatever petty crimes Samil has imagined them to have committed. He's an unbalanced man, and that is the most dangerous sort. One never knows which way the scales will tip, or when. Thus far, they've tipped in our favor. But should he ask me to do anything against my conscience, those scales might tip in the blink of an eye. I fear such a day approaches. I can almost feel it.

"But *you*, sweet daughter..." Master Lorens cupped her face in his palms. Lorelei smiled, comforted by their familiar, leathery texture. "As long as you endure, there is nothing they can do to me. And as long as you keep your secret buried, there is nothing Samil will desire to do to you. The amulet protects you from much harm, including death. But there are some things even more terrifying that it cannot safeguard against. I have seen what Samil does to those he no longer has use for, and worse still, those he *would* use but cannot. Keeping your magic under close, secret watch is the only thing that can protect you from such a fate. Do you understand?"

Lorelei nodded. With a sigh, her father slipped his arms around her, and she gladly returned his embrace.

Then he gently drew back and again clasped her shoulders. He gave her his familiar smile that conveyed how precious she was to him, but now Lorelei could see a terror within him as well.

"I'll be fine," Lorelei said. "I have no reason to be careless, to reveal my magic."

"Promise me," Master Lorens said. "Even if I become

the king's enemy and fall under attack, you *must* promise me that—"

Approaching footseps froze his tongue, and they both glanced up as a knock sounded on the door.

"Open up in the name of the king," a man's voice announced.

Master Lorens cast his daughter a wary look before stepping over to open the door. One of the king's guards stood in the doorway, with Samil's crest, a phoenix spreading fiery wings over a golden harp, painted on his breastplate.

"The king requests your presence," the guard declared.

Lorelei watched, paralyzed. Had Samil overheard their conversation by some magic? Did he have spies where they couldn't see them? Perhaps he had discovered the secret passages in the walls after all? Her father had only just returned from the king's chambers. What could Samil possibly want with him now?

"Yes, of course," Master Lorens said quietly. "I will come at once. Daughter…" He turned to her, touched her cheek, and gazed seriously into her eyes. "Stay here. Stay here and remember."

Lorelei nodded, unable to speak.

Her father followed the guard and shut the door behind them. Lorelei waited until the din of their footsteps faded to deafening silence.

Then, she ran.

She raced from her father's chambers into the hallway beyond. Carefully, she scurried along the corridors, making certain to slow her pace in the presence of a stray guard or servant, until she reached the empty hallway with the familiar tapestries and paintings. Pressing her body close to the stone wall, she chanted the coalescence spell, *Amalgamation*, and felt her body contorting and compacting as it became part of the stones for a few, painful moments before tumbling into the secret passage beyond.

Once she had recovered her strength, she scurried down the passage, trying to calm herself. She was likely shaken because of the heavy secret her father had just shared with her. The king couldn't possibly know about such an exchange, and even if he did, he couldn't have sent a guard so quickly. No, that wasn't it. Perhaps instead, King Samil simply wanted to grant some new information on his plans. It seemed he trusted her father enough to include him on important matters, at least where musical magic was concerned.

At last, she reached her hiding place. She had forgotten to replace the stone earlier and crouched down, peering through into the throne room below. Her father was already there, standing before Samil's throne. Guards stood as they typically did, beside the pillars upholding the room and around the base of the throne's dais. Nothing seemed amiss.

Samil rose from his throne, paced, and began to talk. His tone sounded tense, displeased, but as usual, the sound barriers masking the room made it impossible for Lorelei to clearly decipher his words.

Samil's voice rose. He raised his arm, and Lorelei's heart jolted as she prepared for some spell to hit her father, but instead, he threw something at Master Lorens's feet. Many small somethings that rolled around on the black-and-white marble floor and then lay still. Master Lorens kept his head held high, hands folded, feet planted in a confident stance. He spoke calmly to the king.

Samil yelled. His voice thundered.

Master Lorens interrupted, only to be slammed back against one of the pillars. Lorelei heard the sickening crack, or perhaps imagined it. She clutched the side of her peep hole and pressed her face as close as she could, praying for her father to stand. He staggered to his feet, and as a distorted song reached her ears, she knew he was singing. Singing to defend himself.

Samil rushed forward. Master Lorens held out his hands and began weaving them through the air around his head. He likely crafted one of his invisible shields to place a barrier between him and Samil's mental attacks, formed not with audible words but inside the mad king's lethally powerful mind. Her father had always been keen on detecting such magic. *He'll be all right. He'll avoid the king's wrath until it passes—*

Her father slammed back against the floor, sliding until he hit another of the pillars. Samil held one arm outstretched, fingers curled, and with a spell dragged her helpless father as if clutching him by his heart. Even once her father lay beneath the king's feet, Samil did not stop twisting, squeezing sadistically. Master Lorens screamed, clutching at his chest, clawing the ground.

No, Lorelei whispered to herself. No, she could not bear it. Her father was all she had. This king was no one. He didn't frighten her. He couldn't harm her. She wouldn't let him harm her father.

Lorelei darted from the corridor. Guilt at her own disobedience flitted through her mind, but she would not be held back. She hadn't actually made the promise to her father and in truth didn't care even if she had. Her father's songs could not outmatch Samil's mental force. No one's could. But she would try. She *had* to. She wouldn't just let her father be slaughtered before her eyes.

Lorelei burst from the secret passages and rushed toward the throne room's towering double doors. Guards advanced at her. Some cast streamers of fire magic. Others snapped whips made of water or lightning tendrils. Each spell bounced off Lorelei's body as though an invisible shield encased her, the one formed by her amulet's protection. She felt the attacks as someone brushing or tapping her skin, but no harm befell her.

"*Abré*," she sang, and the doors opened.

She flew inside and burst down the gold-trimmed, blood-red carpet, her gaze locked fiercely upon Samil and her father. More guards pursued her, throwing a fresh barrage of elemental attacks that bounced off her. One of the guards snatched out and caught her around the middle. Lorelei flailed, screaming in mingled fear and frustration, but then Samil's voice commanded,

"Let her go."

Lorelei's feet touched the ground, and she bolted toward her father once more, singing a charm inside her mind to erect a shield around it. She should be alarmed that the king commanded the guard to release her, but anger boiled inside her, eradicating any sense of caution as she shouted, "Stop! Leave him alone!"

Samil glared at her, then grinned. "How precious, Master Lorens. Your daughter comes to beg for your pitiful life. Perhaps you'd like to tell her of your great betrayal against your king. Have you made her just as much a traitor—?"

"I said let him go!" Lorelei commanded, an unfamiliar power thrumming through her. As long as she kept her mental shields raised, the amulet would protect her mind. Hopefully, Samil wouldn't see any of her thoughts or intentions.

Lorelei stopped mere yards away from the foot of the dais where Samil held her father prisoner with his outstretched hand and whatever wicked spell he wove. Master Lorens still clawed at the floor, his chest, his throat. Blood trickled from gashes he'd sliced open in his own flesh. He gasped, sputtering for breath. All around him, tiny wooden figurines lay scattered across the black and white marble floor, their smooth golden edges gleaming in the torchlight.

"Let my father go this instant, or I'll rip this whole castle to pieces." Lorelei's words rang through, despite her own difficulty catching her breath. She could barely keep her magic in check. Music flowed through her veins, begging to be released in a tidal wave of force she'd never known.

Samil laughed and did not release his grasp on her father.

"Your daughter's spirit impresses me. I don't know whether she is bold, ignorant, or some blend of the two. But she will suit for a fine replacement. Of course, the absence of your particular skills will be of a great loss to me, but perhaps she can make up for them in other services."

"*Lorelei,*" her father choked, his gaze begging her.

Fear clutched at Lorelei's heart. Did he beg her to help him or help herself?

"Silence, traitor," Samil hissed. "You have betrayed me on the lowest level. You have bowed before me, called me 'lord,' and yet laughed behind my back the entire time. I have dealt before with such servants, those meant to be my closest allies. Those allowed the most freedoms, always corrupted. I won't deal with it a moment longer. You will bow to me now with your last breath."

Samil twisted his wrist, and Master Lorens' entire body contorted, bones breaking with sickening cracks. He moaned and began grappling at the floor again, struggling vainly to get away. Samil raised his hand, and Master Lorens shot up into the air. He hovered, digging at his neck, scratching it raw.

"What's this, Master Lorens?" Samil sneered. "Disobedient, even at the end. How dare you stand! I command you: *bow* to me—"

"*Magnighta!*"

As Lorelei sang the powerful notes at the top of her lungs, they split and magnified until, instead of a single melody, chords vibrated from her throat, merging into chilling harmonies. Lorelei staggered in shock at this unexpected power rushing from within her but then regained her footing, surging straight toward Samil. Her piercing soprano vibrato echoed throughout the throne chamber, rebounding off the pillars and walls, making the entire room quake. Small chunks of debris fell from the ceiling, causing the guards to leap out of harm's way. Bits of stones slammed against the throne, splitting the back of it, while others rained toward Samil who dodged to the side, his concentration severed.

Released abruptly from the king's spell, Lorelei's father collapsed to the ground. His eyes were tightly shut, and one hand grabbed at his heart, his breathing ragged.

Lorelei rushed over and fell beside him. "Pappa…"

She reached for him, but he pushed her hand away. He gasped, and she thought he was still choking, but then he looked up, weeping softly. The hopelessness filling his face stabbed Lorelei with dread. As a shadow stretched over her, the knife dug a little deeper inside her heart, twisting as Samil said in a tone too quiet, too tame for a man who'd been a wild beast moments before,

"Well done, Master Lorens. You hid her secret so cleverly that even I would have never suspected. It is with some regret now that I must praise and punish you in a single breath. *Guards!*"

Lorelei jumped as Samil's whisper rose instantly into the harsh command. Guards rushed forward, grabbed her father, and began dragging him away. Lorelei scrambled to her feet to follow, but Samil's hand snatched out, clutching her wrist so tightly she feared he meant to rip her arm off.

Grappling for control, she sang *Salmána* silently in an attempt to shield her mind, but Samil only pulled her close and snarled in her ear, "No, my pretty thing. You cannot fool me with that trick twice. This is *my* castle. I make a personal note of knowing every single person who is capable of besting me at my own tricks, and making certain I render them *in*capable of doing so."

Lorelei cried her father's name but could only watch as the guards pulled him farther from her reach. Her head spun. Fear overwhelmed her, whether moreso for her father or herself, she didn't know.

"Don't worry, Lorens!" Samil thundered. "Your daughter is in capable hands as my new ward, and quite possibly as my new instrument. I thank you for your services, and for hers, in advance."

Lorelei watched numbly as her father disappeared from view. The great doors to the throne room slammed shut. A hollow echo reverberated around the room.

As Samil's mental magic began to probe her mind, Lorelei struggled to free herself but couldn't. She searched her memories to find the counter-spells her father had taught her but couldn't. Samil was crawling inside her head, extracting her greatest fears and desires, and she could only stand, powerless in his arms.

The king held her closer still and whispered in her ear, "Don't worry, my pretty thing. Your father has shown me a great betrayal, and his use in my court has expired. But yours is only beginning. The things I do to him will be mere child's play to the plans I have in store for you and your magic."

Samil kept his arm around her, forcing her toward a door opposite the one her father had disappeared within.

She knew that beyond that door lay a new fate, a new life. But this fate would not be one where she would join this monster. Her father had fought hard to serve King Samil without crossing any moral boundaries, and yet served he had, to keep her safe. Lorelei would not waste that service by betraying her father's memory. Even if it meant her death, she would fight to keep her magic, her world, safe from this madman's desires.

CHAPTER 5
THE BARD'S POSITION

The scent of Lila's famous beef stew wafted through Bron's Inn, just as it had when Gailea had arrived in Loz four years past.

The night she'd left her children with Willa and left Ashden to die had been the last she'd seen any of them. The days-long journey to the great island kingdom of Loz had been fraught with several terrifying, close encounters along the way. Ultimately, she'd stumbled, exhausted, into the Forest-footer town of Willardton along Loz's southern borders. There she had found refuge at Bron's Inn, now both her home and place of work.

The inn had looked just as it did this evening. The welcome lamplight, a fire blazing in the hearth. People scattered at the various tables of the dining room, eating, and chatting. Two tradesmen, regular customers, bartered over the cost of linen. A jolly bunch enjoyed mugs of beer and ale at a larger table. The broad-shouldered innkeeper, Bronson, stood behind the bar talking to his closest mate, Kaia, a spindly Carmennan woman with graying hair. Two other young women scurried around the room, refilling mugs, or delivering bowls of stew with brown bread.

Bronson, along with most of the inn's guests, were Forest-footer Elves, a kind and generous lot with fair skin, curly hair, and a gift for growing all things green. Living in Loz had afforded Gailea a thorough education on many of the races outside Adelar and how their magic worked. Some races, like Adelarans, Carmennans, and Spaniños, did not boast any specific magical traits. Each person could be born with any type of magic, or none at all, much like anyone could be born with a natural inclination toward poetry, mathematics, or physical sport. Certain types of magic ran in some families, none in others, and even those born without magic could learn to cast some types of spells via studying elemental alchemy and other sciences.

But with other races, like the Forest-footer Elves, all individuals shared the same magical gifts. Born with literal green thumbs through which they channeled their magic, legends said they had grown the entire Southern Wood where they now made their towns and villages. Living among them had provided a healing balm for Gailea's weary soul.

Some wounds, however, took an eternity to scar and even longer to fade. Now, in just a few weeks, Ashlai's fourth birthday would dawn, followed by Merritt's sixth. An ache pulled inside Gailea, surprisingly stronger than it had last year at this time.

"It's gonna rain *again*. I can promise you that."

Distracted by Bronson's lazy drawl, Gailea glanced up from scrubbing the rough wooden table. Her hands continued to move in their familiar patterns, making the old wood shine and smell of fresh herbs, but her gaze strayed to the nearby window.

Clouds shielded the seaside town of Willardton, and

the tall sandy reeds swayed gently in the cool breeze. Twilight's gentle pink hues spread across the sky like the healthy flush of her children's cheeks, Merritt as he played in the woods, Ashlai as she slept soundly in her mother's arms. That was how Gailea tried to remember them. Not the nightmares of how they'd screamed and cried for her while she'd abandoned them.

Gailea refocused on her work, taking several deep breaths to clear her mind with the fresh air. Its usual sea-salt was now supplemented by the mossy scent of autumn's rain-kissed grass.

Finished with the table, Gailea lifted a tray of cleared dishes and hurried down the back corridor toward the kitchen. She deposited the load in the sink, exchanged a few polite words with Hilda the dishwasher, and headed back toward the dining room.

Only to pause at the mirror in the hallway. She adjusted her spectacles and tucked a strand of auburn hair behind her ear. After all this time, she should have no doubts. It wasn't likely her spell-charmed new appearance would simply vanish, and she was diligent to repeat the spell at the first hints of her hair fading back to blonde. But in her twenty-four years spent among powerful mages and even a sorcerer, she'd seen much stranger things happen and dared not become complacent.

She had just finished latching the windows—the air had turned muggy, and Bronson was likely right about the rain; he always was—and resumed cleaning the tables when the door slammed open. Wind blustered in, along with a light spray of rain. A man stood in the doorway, dressed in a wine-red wool doublet embroidered with gold threads over a white linen blouse, with black breeches and shiny black boots, a stark contrast to the simpler tunics and dresses worn by the rest of the inn's current inhabitants. A bulging leather bag was slung over one shoulder. A canteen, dagger, and several small round trinkets dangled from his belt. The warm lamp-light gave his rich brown skin a copper sheen, and he was as tall and lanky as an adolescent boy. His thinning silver hair stated that he was beyond such an age, but the mischief in his gaze begged to differ as he grinned wide at the faces suddenly staring at him.

He bowed low. "Forgive me such an entrance, good gentlemen, and ladies. I've just barely won my race with a squall."

"No trouble, Chamblin, no trouble." Bronson nodded toward him. "It's glad I am to see you. No matter how many months or years span between visits, you know you're always welcome here."

He walked from the bar toward a square table near the fireplace and motioned Chamblin to follow. "Come, have a seat. Kaia will bring us some drinks, and we can catch up on your latest adventures."

"Thank you, Bronson. That would suit me quite well."

Chamblin loped amiably over to sit across from Bronson. Gailea returned to her work but kept a curious eye on the newcomer. Bronson's friends dropped by regularly to share stories and reminisce about old times, but in the nearly four years she'd worked at the inn, Gailea had never seen this stranger's face before.

She settled back into her work, catching occasional snatches of conversation between the two men about the mysterious Western Realm and the Prismatic Isles and even the legendary underwater city of Larimar. She was used to Bronson's friends being filled with tall tales, but this man's beat all.

"...After all that, I decided it was time for a reprieve. I would've made straight for the academy, but I was running short on food and stopped on Hyloria's northern shores. Fyre's a beautiful city but brewing with turmoil."

Gailea froze, as ever when anyone mentioned the Hylorian capital, where her husband was last known to take refuge, and her mop bucket sloshed water as it nearly tumbled from her hands. Her gaze locked on the silver-haired man but darted away when he glanced in her direction. Setting the bucket down, she began mopping again, focusing on the floor but inching closer to listen:

"The city appeared as cordial and peaceful as it could, but unsettling rumors about recent goings-on were everywhere."

"Go on," Bronson said, leaning forward. "Some trader I met on market day let drop that a mad former king from Adelar still takes refuge in Hyloria. 'Which mad former king?' says I. Hard to know with that lot. And he didn't know. Barely spoke Lozolian anyway. Is it the young one, or the one wot burned all those sorcerers?"

"Young Ragnar, as he styles himself."

Even near the fireplace, Gailea shivered. She'd dwelled much upon her husband in the past few years but had not uttered his name aloud in all that time. This stranger's doing so now was like breathing him back into existence, reminding her just how real he was. Gailea could imagine him standing before her with his crown of fiery curls and fierce, loathing gaze.

Ragnar.

It was odd yet to think of him that way. To her, he'd always been Crispin. But, of course, the boy he'd been, the one she'd loved, had disappeared from her life long before the bitter man now known as Ragnar had. If the former had ever existed at all outside her childish, romantic fancies.

"At any rate, I made certain to flee that city as soon as possible. I'd had enough trouble with the Chinese emperor. No need to get myself involved with any trouble in Fyre."

"No, indeed." Bronson looked pensive. Then, with a grin, he said, "Tell me more of your adventures to the Western Realm across the seas. This here kingdom called 'China,' you talked some on it last you were here. Are the mountains there really as treacherous as the legends claim? Ruled by great white bears with black masks?"

With an irritated sigh, Gailea continued mopping, circling near their table, listening for any signs that they had returned to their discourse on Fyre. After what seemed an eternal discussion on China's local flora and fauna—Bronson's curiosity, normally endearing, for once proved a bane—the innkeeper finally remembered, "Aye, but what about Fyre? So caught up was I with the bears and tigers that I near forgot: what new gossip on that Ragnar fella?"

"Well, usually, all gossip in Fyre must be taken with a grain of salt. Several grains, where one can spare them. But the majority of folks I encountered seemed to share the same tale...."

Chamblin's voice dipped, and Gailea edged closer. Try as she might, she couldn't catch a single word more. In fact, the only noise at all was a muffled sort of low rumble, as though the two men's voices had been submerged beneath a pool of water. Some sort of shielding charm and, by the feel of it, musical in nature, she realized with surprise. Bronson wasn't known to be gifted in any magic outside his natural Forest-footer gifts. It must be some trick of Chamblin's. Like her, he must be a music mage.

Gailea mopped beneath one of the nearby tables, glancing at Chamblin, debating: she could sing a charm inside her mind that might magnify their voices, but that left the matter of making them clear and coherent.

Before she could formulate the rest of her plan, she caught Chamblin's gaze, briefly, before it darted about the room with a curious frown. Propping his elbow on the table, he waved his hand in a gesture that would be interpreted as dismissive to most eyes, but Gailea recognized it as an extra "lock" of sorts, to tighten his spell and prevent any prying.

Frustrated, Gailea resumed her tasks around the rest of the room. Despite his playful demeanor, this newcomer could also be cautious and clever when the need arose.

The night stretched on. Gailea completed her tasks, passing by Chamblin and Bronson every now and then, hoping for some other glimpse into the happenings of Fyre, but the subject didn't come up again.

After a time, Bronson resumed his post at the bar. Once alone, Chamblin lifted the well-worn bundle he'd been carrying, reached into its depths, and retrieved an impressive number of maps. He spread them across the table and ran his finger along various paths and landmarks, muttering indecipherably as if planning his next adventure.

As the night dragged on, customers drifted out of the inn, returning either to their homes or the lodgings upstairs. There was nothing left for Gailea to clean, and there were only a few men to serve, to keep their glasses full.

Retrieving her small sewing basket from the kitchen, Gailea settled into a corner at one of the tables. She earned extra coins by mending villagers' clothes and was glad to get off her feet now.

Some movement caught her attention from the corner of her eye. The dining room was almost empty, but Chamblin remained, drawing a curious-looking contraption from his bag. As he set it on the table before him and began to tinker with it, Gailea recognized it as a musical instrument, albeit one she was unfamiliar with. Shaped like a wooden box, with five strings across that he plucked with his fingers. But why couldn't she hear whatever song he played?

His protective charm must yet surround him, blocking out any sound in his near vicinity. Carefully, Gailea found herself stretching out some of the threads she'd been working with, trying to replicate his movements. She tried to imagine how the notes would play inside her head and closed her eyes in concentration.

"Close. But you'd want to strike the *gōng* and *jué* notes like so."

With a gasp, Gailea glanced up. Chamblin looked right at her, beaming a playful smile. He plucked the strings again, and this time, she heard their strange, whining sound. The tune he played was light, merry, and made Gailea relaxed. And even more curious. The melody line was like none she'd ever heard, and she peered more closely at the man's fingers to watch the patterns they made, but they too were unfamiliar. He struck a strange chord and grinned in expectation. Gailea's cheeks warmed, and she hoped the firelight's glow hid her flush. She was unused to being bested in music.

"It's a different scale," he explained. "The Chinese use what's called a 'pentatonic' scale. Similar to ours, but with its focus on five notes instead of octaves. If you like, come join me by the fire, and I'll show you."

Gailea hesitated. The man seemed friendly enough, and she liked to think that by now, she had learned a thing or two about trusting people. Leaving her sewing behind, she followed him and sat across from him at the table, grateful to be near the fire's warmth.

"See here. The notes are called *gōng, shāng, jué, zhǐ,* and *yu*." Chamblin plucked them each in turn. Gailea's heart sped, and her fingers itched to mimic the sounds. As if sensing this, Chamblin pushed the instrument toward her and said, "There. Give it a try."

Gailea considered his good-natured smile, the playfulness in his gaze. Taking the instrument into her hands, she plucked the five notes, running through the scale backward and forward, trying different combinations.

"Fascinating," she breathed. "What is it called?"

"It's called a 'zhu.' It's an ancient instrument. There aren't many left, and I was quite fortunate to get my hands on this one. The adventure behind acquiring it is no small tale, I can assure you of that."

"Do you travel often to the Western Realm?" Gailea asked, fingertips lightly brushing the strings and weaving her own melody. "I heard you talking about China earlier."

"No, this was my first trip, actually. I've spent a lot of time exploring the Spectrum Isles and the various uncharted Zephyr's Islands. But never to the Western Realm. When I received an offer from the king of Muriel to join an expedition to China, I couldn't refuse. I've been on my fair share of adventures to learn about new wildlife and cultures, and I'm always excited to find what unique musical instruments other cultures use. But China was a whole new world. It's absolutely astounding, China is. The sheer size, the number of people, and the strangest wildlife. Bears made of black and white markings, as if painted with tar and snow. Great cats striped with orange markings like fire and twice the size of the panthers I've seen on the Seven Kingdoms Mainland. The forests and mountains are extensive. The palaces hold all the splendor of the Aquanitess palace but are ten times the size at least!"

"It sounds wonderful," Gailea said, crafting another tune on the zhu. "I'd love to travel someday. Exploring, is that what you do for a living, I suppose?"

"That and map-making. My family has long been close friends with the royal Muriel family. Meaning, I've got a leg in, anytime there's a new expedition planned for Muriel to explore new lands, discover new wildlife, establish trade routes between the Lozolian Realm and other lands....

"Of course, I'm quite often just along for the ride. And for my expert mapmaking skills, of course. For me, such trips are the perfect opportunity. I get to travel and make maps, two of my greatest loves. Meanwhile, I get to see and learn all sorts of fascinating things, but without the pressure of being the one responsible for recording them. It's almost like a free holiday, if a bit fraught with danger now and then."

Gailea continued to play, but her gaze trailed to the maps sprawled beneath the zhu. Her glance lighted upon the name "Fyre" and froze there before hurrying onward.

But he was too observant. "You seem to have a great interest in Fyre. Before, when I was talking to Bronson about my travels there, you were intrigued."

Gailea glanced up warily, but he was studying her with friendly interest. "I...I have friends there. When you mentioned the former king of Adelar, I became concerned for their safety."

Chamblin nodded. "Understandably. May I ask how much you know? The recent rumors have caused quite a stir further north. Hence, my desire to place the protective charms around me and Bron. No need to cause undue alarm and panic, though I fear I may have unwittingly awakened such a reaction in yourself."

Tensing up, Gailea said, "As I said, I have friends there. If there have been...recent developments regarding Ragnar, once king of Adelar...." She forced herself to utter his name, suppressing a shiver. Speaking it out loud made him feel a hundred times more real and closer than when Chamblin had said his name earlier. "I know that he's a relative of the Hylorian king, by Moragon's marriage to the late Queen Marlis. After Ragnar was deposed some years back, I've heard that he sought refuge in Fyre, with the royal family there, Marlis' family, now being his closest relatives."

Chamblin nodded. "Though the royal family granted him protection, they were uneasy about it, and justly so. The more recent rumors say he went there not for refuge, but to conquer. To take their throne as he once did Adelar's. They'd like to exile him but fear what he'll do if they did, how he might retaliate. It seems possible there was some recent skirmish inside the castle walls, some attempt on Ragnar's part to rebel against the relatives who so kindly took him in. So, he's become a ward of theirs, like a prisoner, placed under careful guard. Thankfully, the royal family is an ancient and powerful one."

"You think they can keep Ragnar under control."

At her flat words, Chamblin looked thoughtful. Too thoughtful. This man seemed to see and guess too much about her.

But then he smiled again and said, "I think they can. For a time. For a good long while. A man that full of hatred and anger with nothing left to lose is most dangerous to allow near the royal family. And yet, as they say, it's sometimes necessary to keep your enemies close by."

Gailea nodded slowly. She knew this truth, as well as the danger of it. She prayed Marlis' family would be more stalwart in keeping Ragnar under close watch than his uncle Moragon had been. Moragon had been the most magically powerful man Gailea had ever met, but with allies, Ragnar had been able to take his throne. Gailea, to her sorrow, had been one such ally and knew personally how convincing Ragnar could make himself.

The feel of something soft brushing Gailea's hand startled her. Chamblin was reaching toward the zhu. His sleeve must have touched her hand by accident.

"May I?" Chamblin asked.

Gailea glared sharply before realizing he meant the instrument.

"Of course. It's yours, after all."

Chamblin took the zhu into his hands. A thoughtful frown lowered his brow as he touched the strings delicately, as if trying to remember how they should be played. Gailea was about to ask him if he needed help when he finally began weaving a simple but cheery tune.

The song lit Gailea's heart with a strange sort of serenity. She found herself smiling, almost laughing, until Chamblin struck a dissonant chord that made her cringe.

She allowed the insult to ring in her ears twice more before grabbing the instrument and declaring, "Please, for the love of Amiel. Play *these* strings together, like *this*."

She strummed the correct chord several times and then integrated it into the snippet of song he'd been trying out. A small sense of pride tugged inside Gailea. She'd mastered the new chords and their progression from mere tinkering around. Soon, she was playing the entire song, top to bottom.

"Astounding!"

Chamblin's voice jarred her concentration. For a moment, she feared he might be upset with her for stealing his creation and transforming it, but his face shone with sheer fascination.

"Your ear is impeccable. Clearly you have a gift," he said, beaming at her.

"Thank you." Mastering the challenge had been more than fulfilling, but even moreso was the fact that Chamblin did not seem insulted in the least at her correcting him. How refreshing, if strange indeed, to find a man who seemingly wasn't ruled by jealousy or an inane desire to turn every small event into a competition or quest for power. Even more refreshing was the fact that he simply took pleasure in her music instead of finding her talents shameful.

"Say…" Chamblin struck the awful chord once more. Gailea winced, but he quickly resolved with the correct chord, a wiggle of his eyebrows, and a smile like a naughty child, and she laughed a little despite herself. "I also help teach a class here or there at the Lynn Lectim Academy. Right now, I'm merely passing through to gather some of my maps, but oftentimes between my travels, I lecture there about my discoveries, geography, mapmaking…" He waved a hand as if to dismiss this impressive list. "With your affinity for music, you oughtn't be stuck working as a scrubmaid. Have you given a thought to being a tutor?" Before she had a chance to respond, he hurried on. "Because if you like, I could inquire if there are any openings available for a talented musician like yourself. That is, if I might have a name to pass along."

Gailea hesitated. The offer was tempting. To be able to use her music once more, without fear and for a noble purpose, surrounded by children who *wanted* to learn her craft.…

"Lea Byrnes." She had since abandoned the name "Jardis" to place even more distance between her and her children.

She stood to curtsy. Chamblin met her with a graceful bow, then surprised her by gently taking her hand, which was red and chapped from her duties, for a light kiss. "A true honor, Miss Byrnes." He stood to his full height, which was considerable. "Tomilias Chamblin, though I am 'Chamblin' to most."

"Well then, Chamblin. I'm grateful to you for your offer. But there is a difficulty." Gailea paused. "Isn't Lynn Lectim a *magic* school? I could only teach students how to play or sing. I've no musical magic, I'm afraid."

Chamblin studied her carefully, as if he could pick apart her lie, and Gailea held her breath.

"Perhaps that wouldn't be necessary," he said at last. "Even musical magic students must begin with the fundamentals of the art before they start mastering song-spells. I think Miss Lectim would have use for you. She's always searching for new talent to expand the school's offerings. It would also be a safe place for you."

Gailea inhaled sharply. "Safe," she said hoarsely. "Why would you think I need—?"

"I don't mean to be presumptuous. You must be very capable, to work hard and provide for yourself as you do. But surely any young unwed lady needs a safe harbor. And Miss Lectim's academy would be so. You wouldn't have to worry about anything."

Gailea was calmed by his words and the kind warmth in his silver eyes, which held an uncanny wisdom as well. She trusted this man, more than most, anyway. He was too intuitive for her liking, and yet she was glad of his help.

"I would appreciate any inquiries you can make on my behalf."

Chamblin nodded. "It's decided then. Perhaps in the meantime, you can help me with another song I've started composing?"

Gailea glanced about the inn. Even fewer customers lingered in the dining room, and those who did looked content. Bronson still chatted with a group of friends, and the other maids had taken to gossiping at one of the tables. "Yes, I would like that."

"Perfect." Chamblin grinned. "Consider it practice for your first teaching position."

CHAPTER 6

GREAT EXPECTATIONS

After their first meeting, Gailea did not see Chamblin for a few days, which was expected. He had many things to do upon his return from abroad. But before the week was out, he returned to Bron's Inn with a letter voicing Headmistress Lynn Lectim's interest in Gailea's skills and requesting her presence at the academy as soon as possible. Gailea happily sent word ahead, promising to visit that next afternoon.

Now, at the appointed time, Gailea waited, standing inside the headmistress's small but cozy chamber. A mahogany desk with matching chairs spanned before Gailea, with neat piles of parchment stacked on its surface. Bright sunlight streamed through the window behind the desk. To her left, a matching table with chairs rested near a small fireplace. Plants hung in clay pots all along the ceiling. Some emitted a soft, sweet scent that Gailea tried to focus on, wishing they could set her at ease.

The door opened, and a woman breezed inside. At once Gailea bobbed in a curtsy, which was returned almost perfunctorily before the headmistress took her seat in a chair behind the desk and indicated that Gailea should sit in the chair before her. At last, they faced each other, Gailea anxious, Lynn Lectim wearing a wide smile.

Lynn's skin was fair as moonlight, and her strawberry blonde curls fell around her shoulders in wild spirals. Flamboyant pink and green robes flowed from her tall, curvy frame. Her golden-brown eyes were keen yet warm. "Chamblin has spoken most highly of you, Miss Byrnes. It is an honor to meet you."

The older woman's rich mezzo voice immediately imbued Gailea with a sense of calm. Lynn Lectim carried herself with commanding confidence but engaged warmth as well.

"And you, madam. Although I don't know how much Chamblin could have told you. We'd met only once before he came to you on my behalf."

Lynn laughed, eyes dancing. "Chamblin clearly learned enough to esteem you greatly. Enough to compel my interest in you as a music instructor for our students. Chamblin has done so much traveling, met so many people, that I trust his intuition. His judgment of character has ever been proven wise. I can already sense that I will like you. But tell me about yourself, about your music. Have you taught before?"

"Yes." Gailea had spent half the night lying awake in bed, pondering exactly how she should answer the questions most likely to arise. Some with truth, others with half-truths, others with cleverly made lies that she could easily unravel and rebuild if need be. "I've been a music tutor. Flutes, stringed instruments, voice. Nothing very in-depth, but there was little opportunity in my situation. If you wish to test my skills...."

Lynn shook her head. "One thing at a time. We'll do so later, though I've no doubt Chamblin knows a good musician when he sees one. For now, tell me, why did you make the decision to come here now? Have you not considered teaching before?"

"I'm still fairly new to these parts," Gailea said. "I know little of the school, to be honest."

"Do you know anything of the Mass War?"

Gailea breathed relief. Despite her youth being spent within the insulated confines of Castle Adel, the history of the Mass War was infamous enough that even Gailea had some knowledge of that time. The Mass had been a cult of fairies and elves who'd turned their interests to the darker arts, particularly shadow magic known as "Obscura." They'd tried to use this magic to overcome the Lozolian Council, the group of elite magicians and knights who collectively made decisions for the good of the realm and advised the Lozolian king and queen. Lynn Lectim herself was renowed for spearheading the Council's initial establishment. The Mass had wished to rule Loz for themselves and indoctrinate others with their beliefs that those born with magical blood were superior.

Gailea shared this knowledge, adding, "I know that you had some important role in ending the war and overthrowing the Mass, though the details of that role are a mystery to me."

Lynn smiled gently. "As they are to many. You know your history, as well as music, yet another skill to admire in a teacher. Or in any woman. The reason I inquired about your knowledge of the Mass is because this academy was founded during the Mass War. I wanted a place where magical people of all kinds could hone their skills to the best of their abilities and learn how to protect themselves from dark magic and other evils. This building, Willard's Mansion, was once the headquarters for Willard, leader of the Mass himself. When he turned to our side to fight *against* the Mass, the mansion became his hiding place, his fortress, if you will. He died destroying the evil entity that he had originally created. He died on these very grounds, where the last battle took place. The school has served as a symbol of hope, safety, and security ever since. A beacon shining in the fight against all evils. We prepare our students for the real world, teach them practical magic. We don't teach them to fear evil as if it might lurk around every corner, but to be wise enough to know how to guard against it. That is our philosophy."

"I would gladly uphold such a philosophy. I've had my fair share of fighting evil in my life."

"So many of us have at one time or another. You say you're not from Loz. Where, then?"

"Prismatic."

"Prismatic…" Lynn's face fell into a pensive frown. "That's far from here. But I've heard that many have relocated from Prismatic lately, seeing as they've had their share of troubles."

"They have," Gailea said firmly, bringing to mind the latest gossip she'd heard of Prismatic, the island kingdom far north of Loz. Prismatic was removed enough from Loz that even if someone suspected she lied about her origins, no one was likely to go scrounging for the truth. Not least of all because the latest rumors spoke of Prismatic's young, reckless king dabbling in shadow arts, making the kingdom just as unfriendly a place to visit as Adelar was during the time she'd lived there, if not moreso.

"I have no family left there," Gailea said. "My mother has since passed. I stayed for a few years, wishing to remain in the house we grew up in. Leaving it was the most difficult thing I'd ever done." She swallowed hard as sudden tears threatened to assail her. Instead of the imaginary house she narrated about, her children's faces flashed before her. At least tears would help solidify the believability of her tale. "I had worked as a seamstress and maid, as I've done here, so I could get by on my own. But talk of the king's unstable moods, his experimenting with shadow magic, people disappearing, it all made me unsettled. So, I saved up enough money to get on a ship. I wasn't sure of my final destination when I started. Just somewhere away. And the away led me here, to this peaceful town."

"And you've been happy here, in Willardton?"

Gailea thoughtfully tilted her head. "Perhaps 'content' is a more fitting term. I've not lacked any need. In that, Amiel has truly blessed. I've had sufficient work, food, a roof over my head. I suppose what I've lacked is companionship, as well as stimulation. I've always held a great love for music. Being able to teach others and share my passion. I think that could provide me the stimulation I've been missing."

"And companionship too." Lynn's smile warmed. "I think at Lynn Lectim, you will find not only an outlet to fulfill your passions and those of others', but new friends as well. We consider ourselves a large family. I hope you will come to feel quite at home here."

Gailea stared with mingled excitement and disbelief. "You...you'll really take me on then?"

"I'm rather inclined to do so, yes. I admire your grit, your enthusiasm for working hard to make a better life for yourself. All the same, while I'm obviously one for a woman making her own way in the world, it is easier, and often safer, in the company of friends, as opposed to entirely on one's own. Chamblin chose wisely in spotting a young woman of such ambition and intelligence as yourself in need of good friends. We've only yet to see if he was on target regarding your musical talent. I've no real cause for concern, but I'd not be much of a head-mistress if I didn't put your skills to the test. Come. Dre-wit and Valarie, our other two music teachers, are wait-ing for us in the sitting room just down the corridor."

Lynn rose to her feet and exited her study, and Gailea followed behind, astonished at what really seemed to be a turn of good fortune at last. As long as she didn't fail whatever musical test Lynn had prepared for her. There seemed a thin chance of this, unless she let her nerves get the best of her.

Gailea tried to shake this thought aside as she fol-lowed Lynn down a short hallway painted a soft golden hue, flanked by landscape paintings and flickering oil lamps. They stopped before one of the polished wood-en doors, too soon for Gailea to properly gather her thoughts. Lynn knocked on the door to announce their presence before opening it and slipping inside.

Forest green walls surrounded them, and a fire blazed in the hearth along one wall. Sunlight poured through windows on one wall, and bookshelves lined another. Flowers grew in pots hanging from the ceiling.

Gailea found herself soothed by the room's earthy appearance and scent and bright sunlight. She then found herself surprised as she gazed not into two faces, but three, the last of which was refreshingly familiar and put her at even greater ease.

"Chamblin!" She curtsied in his direction. "It's good to see you again. Thank you again for the recommenda-tion to bring me here."

With a light-hearted chuckle, Chamblin stood from the large armchair beside the fireplace. "'Tis not every day such a lovely lass grants me such a fine curtsy. Allow me to return the favor..." He bowed low, throwing his arms out in a dramatic flair, before straightening once more. "...and inform you that you are most heartily welcome." Glancing at Lynn, he added, "I trust she's lived up to your expectations, or she wouldn't be here now to meet Drew and Val?"

A snort drew Gailea's attention to the two other people in the room who had also stood to their feet. Valarie, a woman with dark brown skin and long, black hair plaited into dozens of tiny braids, shot Chamblin an annoyed glance before smiling warmly in Gailea's direction. Drewit, a shorter man with dishelved mess of sandy-colored, curly hair, rosy cheeks, and pointed ears, smiled as well, his gentle eyes radiating serenity.

"You did set rather high expectations," Lynn said to Chamblin with a playful smile, "but, yes, thus far she has met them. I thought it only proper for her to come meet the rest of the musical crew and allow them to assess her current musical skill for themselves."

"That seems a fair enough plan."

"Lea, I'd like you to meet Drewit Ferneus and Valarie Malhia."

Valarie nodded at Gailea. "An honor to meet you."

"I hope you'll be quite happy here." Drewit bowed as had Chamblin, though with far less flourish.

"Come," Lynn said, "let's all sit and have a chat." She breezed over to one of the two armchairs by the fire. Chamblin looked at Gailea and motioned at the one he had sat in.

"Are you sure?" she inquired.

Chamblin waved his hand in a dismissive gesture. "Quite. I've been sitting about, grading maps by amateur cartographers all afternoon. Charming work, to be sure, but tedious, to be even surer. At any rate, I could use the chance to stretch my legs."

Gailea took her seat in the armchair, while Valarie

and Drewit resumed their spots on the settle, a long bench with arms, a back, and inlaid with green velvet cushioning.

"Now we're all comfortable," Lynn said, "I thought the two of you could share about your own positions here at the academy. Then, we'll get an idea of Lea's personal skills and talents."

"Of course." Drewit nodded, still wearing his soothing smile. "To begin with, I'm a heartsong seer. Are you familiar with the term?"

Gailea hesitated. Showing too much understanding of such terminology might raise suspicions that she possessed some magical talent after all. "I've heard the name, but I'm afraid I don't know what it means."

"It's a rarer gift. It essesntially means that I can hear the songs playing in others' hearts. Every person's heart is constantly playing a song that reflects their current emotions and intent."

"That must be overwhelming." Gailea hoped this declaration would get him to reveal a bit more of how his gift worked, without showing her sudden fear that he could read her own heart right this very moment. What truths might he infer from her heart's song?

Drewit chuckled lightly. "It was indeed when I was a lad and first coming into my magical abilities. But that was many years past. Nowadays, I only hear another's heartsong by choice, and with their full permission, of course."

Gailea released a relieved sigh. "Of course."

"I don't explain all of this to blow my own horn, as they say, about having some fancy, rare gift. But rather because there have been times where folks overheard about my gift and assumed that I was listening in on their emotions unawares. I would never make such an intrusion. That being said, my gift is also rare enough that in my ten years teaching at the academy, I've only ever had the opportunity to teach one other student with the same gift. Otherwise, I spend my days teaching the basics of musical magic. How to control spells via different pitches, volumes, various musical charms, and so on. I also teach in-depth lessons to those who desire them."

"That sounds like a lovely job. Not even a job at all, really."

"Quite right. It is rather too fun to be considered work."

A wistful smile curled on Gailea's lips. Drewit's enthusiasm for his students and the nature of his lessons reminded her of Lady Aline, the mentor who had discovered Gailea's gifts and set her on the path to honing her own musical magic craft. If she could instill such enthusiasm and confidence in others, she might feel a sense of purpose again at last.

"I think one's work *should* be fun," Valarie said. While she yet smiled in a pleasant way, she sat straighter, and her demeanor reflected a more serious aura. Her eyes watched Gailea with a sharp observance. "May I ask what your musical skills are? Chamblin mentioned you being a fast learner who could set a solid example for the children."

"I've some experience in playing various musical instruments, singing. I had the opportunity to work with a music teacher when I was younger. It was for only a short time, but she once said I have perfect pitch. And I can both transcribe and transpose nearly any song."

Valarie raised her brows. "Speaking of tedious tasks. I consider myself the best between Drewit and me at reading music, but transcribing has always bored me, transposing eluded me."

Gailea smiled gently at the humble praise. "What do you teach?"

"Musical combat and defense. Song-spells that allow students to shield their minds, protect their bodies, and defend themselves from any foes who might befall them." Valarie made fluid motions in the air, as if crafting an invisible shield.

"That is impressive," Gailea said, "but surprising. I'm not sure I've heard of an academy that offers to teach such skills to all its students."

"As stated earlier," Lynn said, "the academy was founded during dark times. It's unwise to wait to train others to defend themselves until danger is upon them. By then, it's usually far too late. Even you need not play the role of just a teacher. We offer teachers and students alike the opportunity to advance their learning. Lessons on mastery of a sword and bow, elemental chemistry—these and more would be offered you."

"Thank you. But…" Gailea shifted in her seat, growing a bit restless. Lynn spoke as though she had secured her home and position here, and yet they still hadn't come to their original purpose for meeting with Valarie and Drewit. "…don't you still need to test me? To make sure I'm qualified to teach?"

Lynn's smile warmed once more. "I assure you that, even were your musical skills to prove unsatisfactory, as I'm sure they will not, I would still offer you a home and work. Cleaning, sewing, we can always use more hands on deck with so many souls to care for. But yes. Now we know each other a bit better, let's put your mettle to the test."

Valarie and Drewit led the way from the sitting room. Gailea and Chamblin stood in unison, and Chamblin motioned for her to follow ahead of him before dipping into another of his flamboyant bows. Secretly grateful at how his dramatics placed her at ease, she followed the two music teachers. Chamblin followed next, with Lynn behind him.

They traversed several corridors with walls painted goldenrod until they returned once more to the long, open hallway overlooking the entrance hall on the floor below. Wide stairs led down to main floor where children and teachers bustled about, chatting as they scurried to their next classes. A variety of races and skin tones met Gailea's eyes, along with a variety of tunics, dresses, robes, and other clothing. As when she had first entered the hall, she found herself astounded at the sight of so many different people gathered peacefully in one location. Never would such a glorious sight have existed in the Adelaran castle. King Moragon himself couldn't even stand his own wife being a Fyre.

They continued forward until the entrance hall was out of sight, passing more students as they went. The northern wings were reserved for classrooms and were thus livelier than the southern wings, which housed most of the teachers' and students' living quarters.

After winding through several more corridors, Gailea found herself entering a large room filled with such a wondrous sight that she took in her breath and held it some moments, nearly forgetting to breathe again.

Tall windows dazzled radiant sunlight across dozens of musical instruments—different-sized harps, lyres, lutes, and other stringed instruments, shelves filled with flutes, recorders, shawms, cornets, and trumpets. A harpsichord stood in one corner, its wood weathered but evidently cleaned and cared for. On a desk was piled several stacks of parchment. A few music stands were scattered in one corner, a collection of various-shaped drums and gourds in another. Never had Gailea seen such an array of instruments, outside of Moragon's crystal collection. This one was different, more hodge-podge and welcoming. Here, it felt as though the instruments were well-played and well-loved by many students.

Chamblin came up beside her. "It's like releasing a child into a room full of toys, isn't it?"

"Is my awe that obvious?"

Chamblin's lips pulled into a teasing grin. "You lit up just like a forest of fireflies in summer."

"Go on then," Drewit encouraged, walking over to one of the harps and strumming a few notes. "Explore, try anything you like. We collect instruments from all over. Quite a few are donated by our families who are more well-to-do, others hand-crafted by some of the students who are learning carpentry. They've been played and loved by many, so it won't do any harm for you to do the same."

Gailea stood frozen for a few moments more, hardly knowing where to focus her attention. Then, she wandered forward, running her fingertips along the harp strings, plucking a simple melody on a zither. Coming to the shelf filled with woodwinds, she selected a flute and played a cheerful melody, one of the happier ditties she had learned from Lady Aline. It didn't contain any magical quality, but how she and Aline and the other students had used to love dancing to it!

"Lea."

Gailea glanced up at Chamblin who motioned her toward a wooden table where several smaller stringed instruments sprawled.

"Have you ever played anything like this before?"

He sat in a wooden chair and rested an instrument across his lap, the likes of which she had never before seen. Its shape was similar to that of a lute, with several strings, but most curious of all was the small crank resting at its base. As Chamblin turned the crank and pressed a row of keys connected to the strings, unexpectedly rich and vibrant tones flowed from it.

"What is this odd contraption?" Gailea breathed, so mesmerized that she hardly paid heed as Valarie, Drewit, and Lynn gathered close around her and Chamblin.

"'Tis a hurdy-gurdy, my good madame."

"What a ridiculous name for such a fascinating instrument."

Chamblin ceased playing and jumped to his feet. "Would you like to give it a go?"

Gailea nodded eagerly. If she must be tested on her musical skills, what better way than to attempt to play such a magnificent instrument? Even if Lynn denied her the job, she would first relish such a unique experience.

After taking Chamblin's place in the wooden chair, she gently cradled the hurdy-gurdy as he lowered it into her arms. At first, Gailea admired the instrument: its weight, the sheen of its wood, the smoothness of the ivory row of keys connecting to its five strings.

Then, placing her fingers to the keys, she turned the crank and began to play. At once, her hands found familiar notes, but not as many as she might have on a harpsichord or harp. Like the zhu, this instrument utilized a different sort of scale than what she was used to. She experimented with different combinations of keys until the patterns began to make sense, and soon she whipped up a simple but lively tune.

"See, what did I tell you?" Chamblin did a little jig, locking arms with Drewit and Valarie and spinning them about. Drewit laughed out loud while Valarie rolled her eyes, though a hint of a smile tugged on her lips. "Just like with the zhu. The woman's a musical genius."

As Gailea brought her song to a snappy end and the dancing ceased, she glanced up at them and declared, "Thank you for such an amazing opportunity."

"You're most welcome," Lynn said. "And thank you for such a delightful performance. I've seen more than enough. If it pleases you, I would offer you a position teaching our students how to play various musical instruments, as well as teaching voice lessons. A choir, perhaps. What say you?"

Gailea stared at Lynn while Chamblin returned the hurdy-gurdy to its perch on the table beside the other stringed instruments.

"I hardly know what to say, other than to accept wholeheartedly and thank you again." She glanced from Lynn to Chamblin. After all, he deserved at least half the praise for taking notice of her skills in the first place and, instead of being overcome by jealousy or greed, helping her use those skills to seek out better opportunities than she had ever known before.

"It's settled then," Lynn declared. "You will help set a foundation in music basics for all students with an interest in music, whether they are magic mages or not, thus allowing all students who love music to pursue their passion. Now come..." She leaned forward and took Gailea's hand with a warm smile. "Let us show you to your new classroom and teacher's office. And around your new home."

CHAPTER 7

TESTING METTLES

O ne whole year had passed since that day when Gailea first met Drewit, Valarie, and Lynn. One whole year since they had led her, along with an ever-supportive Chamblin, down the hall from the room filled with instruments to the large room panelled with golden wood and brightened with sunlight from its row of east-facing windows.

Gailea stood there now behind a lectern, sheet music spread before her, facing the thirty-three students who comprised the academy's first choir. The students stood on wooden risers in three rows, each elevated a little higher than the one before it, and sang "Zephyr's Elegy," the latest piece she'd challenged them to master. Each student wore a badge of one of four colors—indigo, orange, turquoise, and wine red, indicating what year they were in—and Gailea's heart swelled with pride. The choir had provided an excellent opportunity for children of all ages, cultures, and abilities to come together to enjoy a common passion. She had watched many friendships forged inside her class and had formed many herself.

Of course, she made it a rule not to get too close to any singular student. Sharing her music with the children partially filled the void of her own childrens' absence, but she knew it could never fill it completely. She did not wish to place such fanciful expectations on any student or to give herself false hope that it could be so.

Still, she had found peace and solace in their presence and enthusiasm for music. In a way, she felt as though she had taken on the role of Lady Aline, honoring her memory by granting joy through music in much the same way Aline had done for her.

Gailea grinned as her choir resolved the final chord of "Zephyr's Elegy."

"Brilliant, everyone. Absolutely fantastic!"

She clapped her hands, and the students smiled, some with relieved sighs.

"I think at last we've perfected it. When we conclude our concert with this piece, the lords and ladies of the Seven Kingdoms will be rendered speechless."

"They'll only be speechless 'til they start making demands for all their students to come to *our* school!" Zavier said.

The three rows of students laughed. Gailea gave Zavier an over-the-spectacles glare for talking out of turn, but then she smiled and said, "Well put. All right then. Class dismissed for the day. I must attend to my own studies."

Gailea ducked from the choir room into her adjoining office and plopped the sheet music onto her desk beside the stacks of other songs. After watering her hanging moon blossom plant, she hurried from the room, down the music hallway, and into the branching corridor beyond.

Swordplay was today's intended practice in the weaponry class Gailea had taken up. While she must keep her magic hidden, she had chosen to take advantage of every opportunity to learn to defend herself by other means. Her first three months had been spent getting to know her students, developing her lessons, and settling into new life at the school. After that, she had taken an archery class, which taught her that she would likely never be a master at the sport, but at least she understood the basics. It had been a fun and empowering experience, to realize she could learn new skills outside of music that could allow her a greater sense of independence.

She had higher hopes for this new class. She had always held an interest in swordplay and thus far, she was catching on faster than she had with bow and arrow. Gailea thought this was because she could equate swordplay with dancing. The footwork, stances, and variety of ways to position your body and arms all made it feel so.

Gailea hurried down several corridors and soon emerged into the Sparring Hall. The Sparring Hall's vast ceiling, lofty windows, and ornate wooden pillars had at first reminded her of Moragon's great hall. However, after her first class, she had soon learned that there was much more to the hall than first met the eye.

It was imbued with magic that allowed each teacher to transform it to suit their class' needs. Today, the wooden floors had been transformed into a soft lawn of grass, perfect for padding someone's fall during a swordfight. The white walls Gailea had known upon first sight instead reflected a soothing, sage green. The sunlight shimmering through the tall arched windows reflected on soft blue curtains, and young men and women talked gaily, ready to learn. It was a far more welcoming atmosphere than anything she had ever encountered in Castle Adel.

Gailea's gaze fell upon a tall, muscular young woman with brown skin. Valarie's long black hair was pulled into a thick braid, and as usual during sparring sessions, she wore a black leather tunic, leggings, sturdy boots, and dark red leather gauntlets. She stood at a table, laying out her knives and examining them before sheathing them and drawing her sword. Valarie was already skilled in all manner of weaponry and, in Gailea's opinion, didn't really need classes on the subject. However, when she'd voiced as much, Valarie said it was good to refresh herself on techniques and that she preferred to practice with friends as opposed to always doing so on her own.

"Good morning, Valarie!" Gailea greeted her.

Valarie glanced up, and a smile softened her serious expression. "Good morning indeed."

"You've brought the full arsenal, I see."

"Never know when Tress might decide to throw us a challenge. One class last year, we were meant to practice archery, and she gave us crossbows."

Gailea's eyes widened. "I suppose one has to be prepared for anything in battle."

"Agreed," a man's voice rang out, "though I thankfully don't anticipate any battles coming to this school."

Gailea and Valarie smiled up at Drewit as he approached, his crooked smile warm, his sandy-colored hair messy as ever.

"Tress has seen war up close," Valarie defended the other teacher, one of her closest friends. "We shouldn't speak too lightly."

"Where *is* Tress?" Drewit asked, sweeping a glance across the room. Gailea and Valarie did the same. Pairs of students had drawn their blades, creating mock battles, practicing techniques from last week's session. Usually throughout such sparring, Tress was a familiar figure darting about, correcting their form and posture. The experienced swordswoman was punctual as the finest timepiece. If anything, she was often early. Today, she was nowhere in sight.

"How's your good lady bride?" Gailea asked Drewit with a teasing smile, hoping to distract herself and her friends from worrying too much about this anomaly.

"Wonderful, as Aislin always is," Drewit muttered, his frown deepening. He again scanned the room.

"Any luck yet?" Valarie asked, picking up on Gailea's game of distractions.

"No, but we're nearly there. The house should be completed just in time for us to welcome the baby into a proper home, and—"

"Good morning, damsels, and sirs!"

The man's familiar voice stirred Gailea's attention, but it didn't jog her memory fully until a chord twanged on a stringed instrument. Her head snapped up to find Chamblin breezing into the room. Sunlight turned his prematurely silver hair into a halo while his smile reflected his constantly cheerful outlook on life. He toted a large leather bag on one shoulder while strumming a lute strapped around the other, and a sword hung in its hilt about his waist.

"He's back," Drewit said, sounding amused.

Valarie murmured something under her breath as the curious combination of plucky explorer and traveling minstrel stopped in the center of the room and motioned everyone over.

"Come on then, don't be shy. Surely you lot know by now that I don't bite. It's my singing you have to watch out for!"

Gailea and her companions trailed over, joining the crowd circling Chamblin. Since the day of her interview, she had only seen him once, and then he had only been in town for a few weeks.

"Ah, there we are. Well, I know you're all wondering why I'm here. I'll be resuming my old mapmaking classes, and for now, I'll also be filling in for Tress. Her sister has taken ill, and Tress is helping with her family in Birkton. She may be gone a few weeks. But no fears! I just returned from the Labrinian capital with the most wonderful gifts to share with all of you."

Chamblin knelt on the ground, and his giant bag hit the floor with a clunk, while his lute twanged a chaotic dissonance of chords in protest when he nearly sat on it. After rearranging his things, he opened the leather bag and pulled out an ornately carved box coated with a shimmering turquoise paint and studded with jewels. Opening the lid, he walked around, showing off a collection of sharp knives with ruby-encrusted hilts.

"Let's say we skip the boring ol' swordplay for today?" Chamblin quipped, flashing one of his cheery, mischievous grins. "Who's up for some good, old-fashioned knife throwing?"

"Mastery of the sword is not boring," Valarie said, crossing her arms, "and it requires consistent study."

Gailea couldn't resist a grin as Valarie's serious demeanor clashed with Chamblin's light-hearted spirit. She found them both equally endearing for these opposite qualities.

"Rightly put, Val," Chamblin said, making Valarie roll her eyes, as ever, at the nickname uniquely used by him. "And you may certainly keep up with it on your own time." He quickly added, "I mean no disrespect to Miss Tress's domain. But using these particular knives, holding them, even *looking* at them, is a once-in-a-lifetime opportunity! More important, knife-throwing is an art, and a quite useful one at that. You might think that anyone can throw a knife. Well, I suppose anyone *can*. But doing it properly, and aiming true, without lopping some luckless bystander's head off, is easier said than done.

"Now, let's split up into small groups." He turned toward the distant north wall of the hall. "I see we have… hmm…six archery targets. Those will do. Luna, if you wouldn't mind performing a charm to change the nature of the materials, make them more conducive to this type of activity? Something akin to a soft wood, like a nice pine or spruce, ought to suffice."

Luna, a young Woodland Sprite student well-known for her gift of shape-shifting objects and altering their textures, gave a firm nod.

"Of course, Master Chamblin."

"Perfect. Everyone assemble your groups, and let's begin!"

Luna rushed over to the targets and, one by one, touched them and uttered a spell to transform the straw into a woodier texture, while everyone else broke up into four teams. The class was a mix of teachers and students. Tress always said it was good for people of different ages and abilities to work together, as that allowed for more learning opportunities for everyone.

Gailea, Valarie, and Drewit remained as one group, along with Rosamund, a deceptively delicate-looking Prismatic girl clad in a red leather tunic, her dark indigo hair intricately plaited behind her back. At just fifteen years of age, she already displayed extraordinary fighting skills, and Valarie and Rosamund always enjoyed competing against one another.

Each team formed lines before a target. When they were all ready, Chamblin explained the correct way to hold the knives and throw them, demonstrating each step as he spoke:

"All right then, my good sirs and ladies! Feet shoulder-width apart like so and place one foot forward, whichever foot feels most comfortable. Grab the knife by the tip. Yes, that's right, the pointy end. Not what you were expecting, eh? Lift it over your head like so, then extend your arm forward. Make sure to release the knife just before your elbow straightens all the way...."

Chamblin's knife went sideways, seeming to bounce off thin air—one of the invisible barriers spaced between targets for students' safety. Chamblin tried two more knives, again explaining the process as he threw them. These found the wooden target, but neither stuck, instead landing on the ground with a thud.

"Well then..." He picked up the knives with a shrug. "That's the other part of the lesson: finding your correct distance away from the target can be tricky. It's important for the blade to make a good, half-rotation before flipping around to strike, but that distance may not be quite the same for all of you. Depends on your stance, the thrust behind your throws, and so on. Shall we all just give it a go?"

Rosamund was first up on Gailea's team. She set her stance, stepping one foot in front of the other just as Chamblin had. Grabbing one of the four knives they'd been granted by the tip, she extended her arm back then flung it forward with impressive strength. While she didn't hit the center each time, her shots did land on the target, sticking fast. Gailea watched her every move carefully, wanting to be ready when her turn came.

Once Rosamund had finished her first turn, she moved to the back of the line, flashing a challenging grin in passing. Next in line, Valarie shrugged casually, though Gailea could see the gleam in her sparkling brown gaze. She picked up her first knife and let it fly. A perfect bullseye. Gailea and Drewit cheered while Rosamund stood with crossed arms, one eyebrow arched, but clearly impressed.

Gailea's attention strayed to Chamblin, who assisted one of the other groups nearby. A burly man named Red tried to throw his knife, but it went far amiss, impacting against the invisible barriers spaced between the targets before clattering safely to the floor. Red's face flushed to match his name, but with a patient smile, Chamblin helped correct his body positioning.

The longer Gailea watched Chamblin, the more her thoughts wandered. During the past several months of travel, had he returned to Hyloria? Had he heard anything more of Ragnar's activity?

"Lea...Lea?"

A hand gently shaking Gailea's arm jarred her thoughts back to the present. She glanced up at Drewit whose face had pulled into a concerned frown.

"Are you all, right? You seem ill at ease."

"Is my heartsong that loud?" Gailea asked, attempting a smile.

"No..." Drewit shook his head. "But your eyes look troubled, and just now you seemed to be thousands of miles from here."

"I suppose I was, in a sense. This is a difficult time of year for me. Memories."

"Prismatic?"

Gailea nodded. Drewit and Valarie didn't know about her true past. None at the academy yet did. While she would have trusted either of them with her very life, the fewer people knew her secrets, the better for her children. Like Lynn, Drewit and Valarie supposed she had fled from Prismatic, losing her family and home. The latter wasn't entirely untrue, and it granted Gailea some comfort to feel a sense of empathy and solidarity from her new friends, even if they couldn't know the full cause behind her pain.

"Well, you're next anyway." Drewit handed her the first of the four knives their team had been granted. "You need a lot of force and control behind your throw, and that has partly to do with how you stand."

"Yes, I've been watching." Gailea stepped forward and tested the unfamiliar heft and balance of the knife. "Thank you, Drewit."

Gailea focused on the target, or tried to. She wished Chamblin's presence weren't such a distraction, but he was the greatest link she had known to the outside world, and in the months since she'd known him, he had been away more often traveling than here teaching. She chose to insulate herself inside the school for her family's protection, but that made it difficult to glean news of anyplace else.

Crispin's face flashed before her, and she turned back to the target. Perhaps if she imagined throwing the knife at his heart.

But even that was difficult. For a time, she *had* loved him, and much as she hated to admit it, some pain yet lingered from this attachment.

Trying to push everything from her mind, Gailea flung the knife. It flew a bit low, headed toward the second ring from the center, but fell at least a yard short.

"That's all right," Drewit said. "The first time I threw knives, all my shots went amiss entirely. At least your aim is true. Try stepping closer and use more strength if you can."

Gailea appreciated his praise but couldn't help feeling annoyed with herself.

Concentrate, Gailea. Concentrate.

Taking a few steps forward and refinding her stance, she let Moragon's face hover before her instead. She didn't know whether he yet lived, but unlike with Crispin, no emotional attachments hindered her desire to see the older man dead. She let the second knife fly—

Same results. True aim, but the blade's point merely grazed the target before clattering to the ground. Gailea exhaled in frustration. "Why are we doing this anyway? How often would we even use this type of skill in combat?"

"Not likely often, to be fair." She jumped at Chamblin's sudden words from behind her.

"Forgive me for startling you," he said. "But that's the, er, point, if you'll also forgive the knife pun. To throw you off-balance. Require more than you're used to. All of you," he added to the rest of her team. "A situation where you might need to aim a knife is rare, and the ideal circumstances—a well-marked target, familiar weapons—are even rarer. Today's class is all about testing your mettle."

He paused and then flashed his smile. "And I don't mean iron metal." When the group groaned and Gailea's scowl deepened, Chamblin lifted his hands in mock defense, then moved back toward Gailea. "Might I correct your stance a bit? It should give you more strength behind your thrust." When she nodded, he took a knife and demonstrated. "Here. Place your legs like so...."

Gailea mimicked his moves without a word, flustered and a bit embarrassed by his having seen her poor performance. This was fast becoming more frustrating than archery class had been, and not least of which because she couldn't stop her competitive spirit from flaring to life in this man's presence, just as when they'd first met. She held the knife but hesitated, glancing at Chamblin's encouraging grin. He was the instructor. She couldn't ask him to turn away. Biting her tongue, Gailea looked to the target and threw the third knife.

Again, too weak! Chamblin opened his mouth, no doubt to give her advice, but she snapped her hand out and grabbed the final knife, and he seemed to know to fall silent. She rubbed her temple with her free hand. A headache was coming on, likely from her spectacles.

From time to time, they made her head throb. Now they seemed an unnecessary distraction. Gailea removed and pocketed them. Then, she focused on the target once more and flung her arm back in preparation.

She couldn't help herself. Just before she let the knife fly, Gailea's mind sang a silent, fierce charm demanding more momentum, more power. Sure enough, the jeweled weapon thudded into the target, sticking perfectly in the target's center. Her team cheered. Gailea inhaled deeply and stepped back, feeling too triumphant to regret her impulse.

Chamblin joined in the applause, nodding wisely at her. Gailea belatedly realized what she'd done and stiffened in alarm. Had he guessed she'd used some magical charm? But his gaze was one of pride, not suspicion. "Well thrown," he said with a smile, and then moved on to help another of the teams.

Gailea heaved a sigh of relief and, despite her own vow, let new confidence guide her. So many months without a song-spell! With her inner voice free, her headache vanished as if a tight leash had been released. They practiced for several more rounds. Gailea continued to secretly use her music to aid her throws.

After two more rounds of knife throwing, Chamblin declared they had plenty of time yet before class' end to share the special tea he had brought with him from China. Lynal, a Fyre mage teacher, created a ball of flame that hovered midair. Chamblin pulled from his sack an iron teapot which he had also acquired from China. Then, slipping on a bracelet containing a bit of elemental powers, he muttered a spell, and the teapot hovered over the flames. Melina, a Water Nymph student, volunteered her help, waving her hand over the teapot to fill it with water, and Chamblin inserted the tea leaves, letting them steep for a few minutes.

Everyone sat on the grass floor, sipping tea and enjoying a few moments' reprieve and friendly conversation. The tea was light in color and even lighter and airier in taste and texture. It calmed some of Gailea's nerves despite herself.

Someone asked Chamblin to tell about his latest adventures, and he enthusiastically obliged. Gailea listened enraptured, hoping for any mention of Hyloria or its capital of Fyre. None came, but Chamblin's narration was full of such animation that she couldn't help but be comforted by his tales. Perhaps he lacked seriousness, but his enthusiasm toward his work, toward everything, made him an engaging personality to be around.

After finishing the tale of how he'd won the tea they drank from a bet with a Chinese tradesman, Chamblin announced that they could spend the last minutes of class practicing any of their skills that they wished.

Newly eager, Gailea grabbed one of the wooden practice swords and began going over the various steps and sword strikes they had learned in a more recent class. As she spun about, her sword collided with another, and she staggered back in surprise.

"Chamblin!" she gasped, her face burning.

He stood a few feet away, sword in hand, eyes dancing with amused anticipation.

"Care for a quick duel?"

Gailea replied by clutching her sword hilt a little tighter and squaring up, determined.

The pair circled one another slowly. Gailea flew at Chamblin, slicing toward his heart, but he easily blocked the attack. His light step danced away, then darted forward when he aimed a blow at her knees. Gailea thought he'd miscalculated, but throughout the battle, his sword swept and thrust low, even with his greater height. She parried successfully each time, but her agitation grew until at last she shouted, "What in all Amiel's worlds are you doing? What kind of strategy is that, aiming for my feet?"

"My good lady, I'll have you know that I've felled many a foe by bringing them to their knees, quite literally. While most aim for the heart or head, I like to catch a man off-guard with a good, strong, underhand stroke."

Gailea snorted. "Underhand stroke? I've never heard of such a thing."

"Of course, you haven't. It's an original turn of phrase coined by yours truly...."

He leaped forward, aiming at her knees again. She countered the strike, singing the same melody in her head as before with the knives. Chamblin's sword went flying, and he sprawled on his back.

"You were saying?" she asked, pointing her sword at his heart before moving it aside so he could jump to his feet.

"Well met, Miss Byrnes. Had your sword been real, you'd have played quite the pretty tune across my ribcage." She looked at him with concern, but he simply added, "How appropriate for a music instructor."

Fresh worry gripped Gailea. Did he allude to some suspicion that she possessed musical magic talent?

She quickly shook the idea aside. Unless he was a mental magician—she was certain he was not, and even if he had been, he was not the kind to intrude into another's mind unawares—he had no way to tell that she had just used a simple music charm. Her secret remained safe. Perhaps, just as when she'd lived under Moragon's rule, she could enjoy her gift in secret here and there, just a little. What a thrill, to be reminded of how fulfilled she felt in being her truest self.

The clock tolled then, announcing the class's end.

"Spared by the bell, truly!" Chamblin said with a playful grin. "You're a worthy match, Miss Byrnes. A worthy match, indeed."

Gailea rolled her eyes but thanked him in reply. After replacing the wooden sword, she found Valarie and Drewit and promised to meet them later for their evening meal. Everyone filed from the room, heading their separate ways to their next classes and other duties.

"Miss Byrnes?"

Gailea paused at the door and turned back. What could Chamblin possibly want now?

"I just want you to know, if you ever need to talk, if you need anything at all, you *can* trust me. I know I'm always flitting about from one mission to the next and we haven't had much opportunity to get to know each other well. But, if you're interested, I'd like the chance to prove my offered trust and friendship to you."

Gailea studied Chamblin carefully. His gaze was sincere. He had caught her attention and extended an offer of friendship but didn't force her to take it. He was almost like Ashden.

Only far less serious. A youth inside a man's body. A man with such a constant cheery and optimistic demeanor toward every aspect of life couldn't have seen evil and hard times like she had. He couldn't know heartaches and losses like she'd experienced. Even now, his smile promised great things and yet made her discredit those promises.

"Thank you. I'll keep that in mind."

Chamblin nodded. "I hope things are going well for you here?"

"Yes. Yes, quite well," Gailea said. "The students and teachers have proved wonderful, as has the work itself."

"Good. And I hear you've started a choir?"

"Indeed. We're hoping to perform in Labrini next year, to honor the fortieth anniversary of the peace treaty between the Seven Kingdoms."

"What a delight! Unfortunately, I think I may be on my way to China once more by then."

Gailea's brows rose. "Another great voyage?"

"Yes, indeed. I've spent the last few months exploring and creating more maps for Muriel's king. He paid me a fair sum, and now I'm using my earnings to fund another trip he's been trying to persuade me into for some time now. A second trip to China. Muriel is fascinated by their silks, spices, their language, every aspect of their culture. They want to learn more and establish peaceful alliances of whatever sort possible. I'm just a humble mapmaker and that's often how I prefer to keep things. But the king thinks I've a natural sense for diplomacy and wants me to accompany other of his diplomats for the cause. I finally gave in. Said I'd try anything in exchange for another free trip to China."

"That all sounds very exciting. But..." Gailea paused before taking a step forward and venturing, "have you heard anything else about Hyloria? About Fyre and the mad king?"

"No, I haven't, I'm afraid. But the vessels I've sailed on have passed close by without incident. With borders open and no news otherwise, let's hope things are stable."

Gailea nodded slowly. Silence could indeed be the best indicator that evil had lain dormant, but it could also mean that evildoers were scheming under that cloak of silence.

She sighed and stared up at him. "Chamblin...I'm sorry if I seem cold at times. I'm not so easily trusting of others. But I do have you to thank for all of this..." Her hand lifted, gesturing toward their surroundings. "I am truly grateful."

"You are most welcome, my good lady. It was truly my honor, as was teaching you today. You are an attentive and quick learner. I can't say whether I had more fun today or in watching your face light up over learning the zhu so quickly. But now I'd best get going. Time to drop all this off in my office and dive into the books once more. Or the maps, I should say."

"Is that the class you teach next? Geography?"

Chamblin smiled. "Close. Cartography. Enjoy the rest of your day, Miss Byrnes."

He turned on his heel, whistling gaily down the hallway and out of sight.

CHAPTER 8

MAPPING FATES

As Gailea started back toward her office, she reached into her pocket, fiddling with the bit of spare parchment there to distract herself, when her hand brushed something else. Cool to the touch and smooth as ice.

Gailea frowned and drew out the small item. Pausing in the hall, she held the gem carefully in her hand, turning it and letting the sunlight through the window illuminate its red facets. A ruby, or perhaps a carnelian. But how had it found its way into her pocket?

The knives. The ones they had just used to practice knife-throwing. Their hilts had been adorned with small red stones.

With a sigh, Gailea turned in the opposite direction. Such extraordinary treasures must be valuable. They seemed precious to Chamblin, and considering his keen attention to detail, he would likely notice the stone missing.

She swept upstairs and, upon searching the plaques posted in the hallways, soon found the corridor housing Chamblin's office. She stood before his door, knocked, and called to him. The door swung open, but no reply echoed from within. He must already be at his cartography class.

Gailea slipped inside, and immediately stopped short. The office was a terror to behold. Stacks of papers and books piled high, maps too numerous to count, compasses and many devices she couldn't recognize, strange little carvings and other odds and ends from his travels. Afraid of knocking anything over, Gailea waded carefully toward his desk, the top of which could barely be seen, and peered about for the box he'd carried into the sparring hall.

There was, she discerned, a sort of order in the chaos. Sections of the belongings, though not well distinguished from one another, were organized by location. She searched for the heaping mass of items related to China and, soon enough, recognized the chest. Once the lid was open, the dagger with one jewel missing gleamed up at her. Carefully, she set the gem in the box's corner and turned to leave.

A name hooked her attention, peeking from the corner of a map rolled up like a scroll: *Hyloria*. Gailea gasped and hurried over. Several such maps stood erect inside a large basket. She slowly removed one and spread it wide open on the nearest horizontal surface.

Hyloria loomed before her, its illustration large, detailed, almost tangible. She let her fingers trail along the high peaks of the mountains surrounding Fyre, along the tiny drawn towers and turrets of the capital's castle. Crispin—Ragnar, she reminded herself—lived there as an exiled refugee, practically a prisoner in his new home. How ironic, Gailea thought, as she had spent most of her life playing such a role herself.

Her fingers danced past more mountains and fields and forests, all the way down to the southern Forest-footer town of Vian. A few tears slipped down her cheeks. Her children felt so close, and yet so far away. She wished she could make up some song that would drop her inside the map to right where they were.

She couldn't do that. She didn't even know if any such magic existed. But there were less fanciful ways to accomplish such a goal. The autumn holiday drew nigh, during which the Academy would cease classes for a period of fourteen days. Hyloria was close enough for Gailea to make the short journey to Vian. The map showed a high hill overlooking the forests housing Vian. She might be able to catch a glimpse of them via a type of magic known as scrying. Scrying through a scry glass allowed one to view a certain place from a distance, like a strong telescope of sorts, but one uninhibited by barriers such as trees and walls.

Of course, Gailea had never attempted such magic before, and so she couldn't possibly scry all the way from Loz. But perhaps in Hyloria, atop that hill, she might get close enough. Her husband was no longer an imminent threat. She knew going all the way to her children, interacting with them, could still be too dangerous for them. But, oh, just to catch a glimpse of Merritt as a grown boy, or her sweet Ashlai so near her birthday.

Footsteps alarmed Gailea, followed by Chamblin's cheery whistle. Gailea flung a glance about the room. Her eyes locked on a side door. Two baskets stuffed with scrolls blocked it, but she could easily push those aside. The place was such a disheveled jumble that even Chamblin's keen eye wasn't sure to notice.

The matter was whether to take the map. She hadn't finished looking at it and certainly hadn't memorized where she would need to go. She could borrow the map long enough to copy what she needed from it onto a separate parchment and return it before he found it missing. After all, there might not be another such opportunity. She didn't know when he intended to leave town again, and even then, she might find his chambers locked. There were sure to be maps in the library, but she couldn't be certain they were as detailed as Chamblin's.

Rolling up the map and rearranging the others so that it wasn't immediately obvious one was missing, Gailea pushed the baskets aside and opened the side door, breathing a sigh of relief that it wasn't locked. Slipping inside, she shut it silently behind her just as she heard the front door to the office opening.

Gailea found herself at the top of a winding stair. Down she crept, moving as fast as she dared without making a noise. Gradually, the sounds of Chamblin shuffling about his office faded, and she found herself at the base of the stairs.

Carefully, she opened the door to find herself in a short hall. A cool breeze blasted at her, along with the scents of fresh bread. She must be near the kitchen. She had been in this area only once and didn't remember it well, but now that she was out of Chamblin's chambers, she could take her time.

Gailea wandered past the kitchen and down several halls, making a mental note of how many turns she took or any interesting paintings or statues she saw to help her recall the way. Finally, she found another staircase. This one wound back up, and at the top, she found herself in a corridors housing some of the classrooms. From there, she was able to navigate to the music hallway, to her own classroom, and finally to her adjoining office.

Stepping inside, Gailea collapsed back against the closed door with a huge sigh of relief. After singing a soothing melody to ease her nerves, she straightened herself, fully prepared to set to work. She didn't have a lot of time. She must focus.

But first, she must do her best to ensure no one would likely disturb her. After peeking out her door once more to make sure no one was afoot, she closed it and, as quietly as she could, sang a short melody, *Dumkana*, that had the power to either magnify or diminish sounds. She sang the version of the song that would work to muffle any sounds she made within her office. The fastest way to copy the map would be via her musical magic. She was aware of another song that could help her accomplish this, but it wasn't one she'd ever practiced enough that she could do so silently, inside her mind. Such magic required a deeper concentration and practice. She must sing it aloud.

Once Gailea had completed the song to diminish sound, spreading her arms and turning in all directions to make certain it sheathed the entire space, she unrolled the map and spread it on her desk. For the first time, she noticed the inscription of the map's artist: *T. Chamblin*. Gailea bit her lip as she realized how much painstaking work he must have put into this. Just as she did for her own music. A wave of guilt passed through her.

Pushing it aside—after all, she wasn't stealing the map, merely borrowing it—she quickly formulated her plan. She would copy the map and then, hopefully, she had memorized the way well enough to return through the side door to Chamblin's office and therefore draw less potential attention. Once she'd secured the map, she could use the remaining weeks until the holiday to learn all she could about scrying and work on obtaining a glass, elemental powders, and anything else that might be needed to make a scry glass from the school's magical sciences supply.

Grabbing an empty piece of parchment, Gailea rolled it out beside the map. It was a comparably small piece of parchment, but she didn't need to copy the entire map, only the southern regions. She spread her right hand out on the map and her left on the empty parchment. As loud as she dared, she began to sing, focusing intently on the map and the information she needed transferred to the parchment. At first, her mind wavered with doubt, and she couldn't help but fling an anxious glance at the door. Taking a deep breath, she sang her calming melody once more to refocus and then began the copying spell anew.

Gradually, the same images on the map appeared on the blank parchment. The same lines, shapes, letterings. The color was more faded but clear enough to be deciphered. Gailea had completed nearly half of the copy when a knock on the door startled her.

Abruptly, she ceased singing. Heart racing so hard she thought she might be sick, she turned the copy of the map over. Then, as the knock sounded again, she opened the door.

Chamblin stood in the doorway, smiling in his serene way, eyes twinkling. Gailea stared, trying not to look alarmed. As her gaze drifted, it rested on the item in Chamblin's hand. Her spectacles. Gailea touched her face where the spectacles should have been, and her cheeks flushed.

Chamblin released a light-heart chuckle. "I apologize for startling you. Only I returned to the Sparring Hall where I'd left the rest of my tea, and I found these and thought you may have need of them."

His eyes shone playfully, but panic gripped Gailea as she took the spectacles, donning them. Her throat felt abruptly dry, and she forced herself to swallow. "Thank you for returning these. Though you didn't have to rush. I'm sure your class is waiting for you."

Chamblin waved a dismissive hand. "Several students have taken ill. I've cancelled the class for today. Besides, truth be told, as I was nearing your office, I couldn't help but admire your lovely music."

Gailea reeled, as though someone had punched her in the gut, knocking all of the air from her. As she staggered, Chamblin reached toward her in alarm.

"May I help you, Miss Byrnes?"

Gailea grabbed the edge of her desk to resteady herself, but Chamblin had already stepped over the threshold into her office, and his glance caught the map sprawled on the desk.

"Is that one of my maps?" His voice wasn't accusatory, merely confused. He ran his fingers across it and then, in a movement too smooth for her to stop him, flipped over the smaller parchment.

Gailea was caught. The evidence glared so blatantly at them that she couldn't try to deny it. Her instinct was to sing some magical charm that would render Chamblin immobile or put him to sleep, but such was a reaction from her days living under Moragon's rule that would not serve her well here. She couldn't attack a teacher, not after Lynn had so generously taken her in. Above all, she could not attack the man who had selflessly sought out her current position, securing work and home and ultimately friendships for her.

"Chamblin, I'm sorry—"

Her trembling words were the last straw. Overwhelmed, she burst into tears and sank down into her chair.

"Ahh, dearest lady..." Chamblin's tone was tender as he knelt before her. Reaching into one of the pockets in his tunic, he drew out a handkerchief and handed it toward her. As she took the cloth and wiped her tears, a terrible guilt panged her. She had stolen from this man who'd done nothing but try to help her, and still he was giving to her, doing his best to care for her.

"Madame, I hope I do not speak too boldly in revealing that I know some darkness chases you, that you're running from something." When she glanced up in alarm through her tears, he quickly added, "No one has told me as such. It's pure intuition and life experience, if you will. I could tell you needed a safe refuge from the time we first met." He glanced over his shoulder at the door and then back at her. "May I close this, for sake of your privacy?"

Gailea nodded. "Yes, thank you. Though I suppose it won't do much good, if you were able to hear my music after all."

"Your muffling spell was clever." He stood long enough to shut the door and then sat on the floor before her, his demeanor relaxed and unassuming. "Its magic was one of the things that drew me in, made me linger. I truly intended to return the spectacles without a word, but as I approached, I could sense some sort of musical aura, though dampened, and the source of it was distorted, uncertain. Intrigued, I used one of my own musical charms to try to figure out the source. The charm clarified that the source of musical magic came from your office. I'm afraid the charm also allowed me to hear beyond your sound barriers. Forgive me. Twas no intentional instrusion."

Gailea laughed bitterly through her tears. "It's I that should ask your forgiveness. My taking your map was certainly intentional, though I did intend to return it."

"May I ask what you wanted with it? And why you simply couldn't ask? I would've gladly let you borrow a map without question. Now, begging my pardon, while I can't see you as having any ill intent, I feel compelled to ask. If not for the integrity of my maps, then for your own safety, and that of the school. If you plan to do anything reckless...."

"Up until minutes ago, I didn't plan a thing. I was in your office to return one of the red stones that had fallen from one of your knife handles...." A gentle smile filled his face, and she glanced away, uncomfortable by his continued kindness and grace and fearful she might burst into tears again. "I saw the map, and something inside me just...snapped. Suddenly, I had to have it."

"Is it about your friends in Hyloria?" Chamblin's tone remained calm, not pressing in the least.

Gailea breathed deeply, considering. She could say yes, yes it was her so-called friends in Hyloria. She could easily fabricate a believable tale. She'd done so plenty of times within the past year.

And yet she ached to release the truth, even if just to one soul. And what better soul than this man who, though a perfect stranger, had sought to care for her and be a friend to her from the start? True, she had formed closer friendships with others like Drewit and Valarie. But Chamblin had already unraveled that she was a music mage. More than that, he'd suspected for over a year now that she ran from some danger and had held the respect and dignity not to breathe a word to her, ask questions, or prowl for answers.

Gailea took another deep breath and then released it, along with the words, "It's not friends I have in Hyloria. It's my children."

With those two words, "my children," Gailea felt a massive weight falling from her shoulders and shattering into pieces. Overwhelmed anew, her tears came afresh even as Chamblin stared at her, wide-eyed. The room was silent except for her tears, until moments later when she heard Chamblin's soft words:

"Your children?"

Gailea nodded, dabbing at her eyes with the hand-kerchief and inhaling shuddering breaths to steady her voice. "Yes. A boy and a girl. They'd be close to seven and five years old now. It's been nearly five years since I've seen them, held them...."

"That's terrible, Lea. May I ask how you were separated from them?"

"Yes. The reason I came here was to protect them." She lowered her ice-cold hands, staring up at him. "My husband is mad. He would kill us all, or else turn them against me. I was forced to leave them with a family friend. And I just thought, if during the autumn holiday I could make a brief trip there, just to see them with my own eyes, just once...."

Chamblin had started to reach toward her but now was still. "You have a husband? Who is your husband?" Gailea pulled back, forcing herself away from his comfort.

"Why? What have you heard? What do you know?"

"Nothing, I swear to you. Upon my very life and the lives of every person I've ever known or loved. But truly, Lea, if your husband is as dangerous as you claim...does Lynn know? I ask only for the safety of the school, of the children. If this person is someone who would still wish you harm...."

"Lynn doesn't know," Gailea whispered. "When I first came here, I didn't know who, if anyone, I could trust. Now...you may be right. Even if it meant my exile, maybe Lynn deserves the truth. For everyone's safety, as you say."

Chamblin shook his head. "I don't think Lynn would turn you away if you were honest with her about what's happened and why. Remember that she once housed many refugees fleeing the Mass. I'd be surprised if she didn't do the same for you. I'd even help you speak with her if you like. But can you tell me any other details of your story? Something that could help me plead upon your behalf, if it came to that?"

Gailea stared at Chamblin, astonished once more by his selfless concern. Agonizing as it was to reveal more of her truth, his sincere compassion made the words come a little easier.

"You know of the mad king who hailed from Adelar but took refuge in Fyre some years ago?"

"Ragnar? Yes, we spoke of him during our first meeting, as I recall."

"Did you hear also how he came to be in Fyre? How in Adelar, he was cast down by his wife the queen, also a musical mage?"

Chamblin nodded again, face twisted into a pensive frown.

Gailea told him everything then in halting sentences. Her history of growing up in Moragon's courts, Moragon's twisted desire to puppeteer her through her music, her brief romance with Crispin before he took the throne from Moragon. Chamblin's eyes widened but he said nothing until she'd cut herself off, afraid to say more.

Then, he reasoned out loud, "The tale of the Adelaran throne, cruel King Ragnar—*Crispin* Ragnar. You are Queen Gailea?" With a deep sigh, he added, "Lea. Gailea. Of *course*."

Gailea clenched her fists. "You must tell no one."

"Of course not. But with all due respect, I believe you yet should."

"My children...." Gailea argued weakly, heart tearing in two complete opposite directions. She knew Chamblin was right. Lynn should know for the sake of protecting the children here, but she must protect her own.

"Dear Gailea, I do travel a lot. I hear many rumors, stories, legends...your story is not entirely silent. It may have lain dormant for several years now, but I believe I could promise you that seeking out your children would not be what's best for them at this time. You wouldn't want to risk leading that lunatic to them. They are far safer being left alone. As long as you trust whomever you've left them with."

Gailea nodded. "I would have trusted him or any of his kin. A relative of his was one of my few allies. A dear friend."

"Then let them be," Chamblin said gently. "It may not be easier that way, but it is best, for the safety of all."

"I just wish I could see them," Gailea whispered. "I know you're right. I just wanted to see them once more."

"You will." Now he did reach out, placing a hand atop hers which rested on her knee. "I promise that one day, when things are more settled and it's safer, I will help reunite you with your children myself. If I can, and if you need it, I will help find a safe place, a true home, for all of you."

Gailea smiled faintly through her fresh tears. "You may be an insufferable musician at times, but you're a true friend. I'm sorry, for taking one of your maps without asking."

Chamblin shook his head. "It's no trouble. If I loved someone and their safety weighed constantly on my mind, I might do rasher things than borrow an unsuspecting teacher's maps. Would you like me to help you later, to know what to say to Lynn, accompany you?"

"I think it's best if I speak to her alone. But I would welcome talking it through and any advice you might give."

"Under Lynn's guidance, I might also speak with Drewit and Valarie as well. Not to tell them everything, but at the least that you possess musical magic. With them being the two other musical magicians teaching at the school, I think it would be good for them to know. It would be difficult to hide your secret forever, and you don't want the wrong person to stumble upon your magic by accident as I did, to misjudge you or misconstrue your actions."

Chamblin's words rang true. Drewit and Valarie were her friends. She didn't think they would judge her too harshly. And yet, a year truly wasn't that long to know and trust someone. Those bonds were still somewhat fresh, and she had no desire to taint them.

"Very well," Gailea said, rising to her feet; Chamblin did the same. "I'll consider talking to them as well, if you can help me figure out what to say first to Lynn."

"Certainly."

Gailea's smile grew a little, and he seemed pleased.

"Come..." He turned her toward the door. "The day is beautiful. If I can't help you find your children just yet, at least allow me to escort you on a refreshing walk."

CHAPTER 9

TIDINGS OF CHAOS

The young woman flew through the corridors of Loz's Council Chambers.

Men and women alike flung spells at her. Lightning, water, fire, and wind bombarded her. She whipped her head back, clawing her thickly matted black hair from her face so she could counter the attacks rushing at her on all sides.

She may have broken into the Lozlian Council, but she'd had no choice. They had declared her deranged at the castle gates and wouldn't see her any other way. The matter she brought to them was well worth the risk of injury, even death. In truth, the Council could inflict nothing more painful on her than she had already suffered in the past five years.

A volley of electric sparks hurtled toward her. She lifted one hand and sang a charm inside her head to block it, nearly stumbling over her own feet. With the other hand, she clutched at her chest, feeling the amulet's warm protection radiating through her.

Flames surged toward her, and she screamed. Shielding her head with her arms, she dived and rolled out of harm's way. Fire was the amulet's one great weakness.

With nothing to burn, the fire extinguished itself, but she was already far away, scrambling up to resume her desperate sprint. She need only make it to the inner chamber. There, she would be recognized and welcomed, as her father once was long ago.

At last, the double doors painted with the emblem of a golden sword inside a silver cross loomed into view. As she neared them, guards rushed at her from the corridors extending on either side. They hurled various elemental spells of wind and water while others tried to freeze her in place, but she sang another charm to cast a momentary shield around her body. While the attacks couldn't cause her physical harm under the amulet's protection, their impact could slow her down long enough for them to capture her.

More guards braced themselves directly in front of the doors, swords drawn. "*Abré!*" she sang at the top of her lungs. Her voice cracked, but the doors slammed open, flinging the guards aside. She threw herself inside and collapsed before the massive triangular table.

The men and women seated around the table stared in shock. Several had risen to their feet. One was quicker to act than the rest, rushing to meet her at the entrance.

The girl collapsed to her knees, hands clutching at the council member's soft velvet gown. Her vision blurred, but the woman's face was familiar and gave her just enough hope to cling to consciousness a few moments more. This was the person she'd come to see, the one who could help her.

Lynn Lectim fell at her side, brushed a few locks of singed hair from her face, and gasped. She stared up at the council members who had piled into the room, all bewildered.

"Fetch the healers at once!" Lynn commanded. "She is the daughter of Master Lorens. Lorelei. She is the one we've been searching for."

~*~*~

Gailea hurried down the corridors of the academy toward Lynn Lectim's study chamber. Though late at night, a messenger had announced that Lynn required her presence at once.

Fear flitted through Gailea that perhaps it was some news of her husband, that he had found her at last. After revealing her story to Chamblin, she had kept her word and told Lynn all her tale. Lynn had expressed understanding and gratitude. Gailea apologized for potentially endangering the school in any way by not speaking up sooner. Lynn agreed that knowing her full circumstances would have been best, while also assuring the school had many safeguards in place at all times. She swore also to keep her secret sealed safely tight.

Afterward, Gailea had brainstormed with both Chamblin and Lynn to come up with a tale to share with Valarie and Drewit that could reveal her musical powers without giving her cause to share her entire history with more people. She'd felt uneasy enough revealing all to Lynn, despite believing how safe the headmistress would keep her story. When revealing her musical magic to Valarie and Drewit, Gailea told them she had learned to hide it it because such magic was sought after by Prismatic's king. Rumors said that he was seeking sorcerers and other rare types of magicians, so this was a believable enough tale.

Despite her faith in Chamblin's and Lynn's confidence, her story being released into the world at times gave her an irrational fear that it had traveled beyond and found her husband's ears. Thus, as Gailea entered the room to find Drewit and Valarie gathered as well, she couldn't help but wonder: Was Ragnar coming for her? Did Valarie and Drewit now know the truth because Lynn was forced to tell them? Had they summoned her to reveal what they knew and gently break to her that she must leave the school, once again losing home and family and all that she loved?

Gailea shook this notion aside as she saw the looks on Drewit's and Valarie's faces. They seemed equal parts troubled and confused. Drewit stood leaning with one elbow on the mantel, holding his forehead in his hand and rubbing a pattern of small circles on his temple. His lips moved, as if he attempted some charm to calm his nerves. Valarie sat in one of the chairs surrounding the mahogany table, arms crossed, face hardened into a frown.

Gailea sat beside Valarie. Running her hands across the fronds of the giant plant potted beside her, she tried to break the tense silence. "Good evening. Any clues as to why our headmistress has summoned us at so late an hour?"

Drewit shook his head, sitting on the edge of the chair next to Valarie who muttered, "No, none."

The door swung open, and Lynn rushed inside. Collapsing into the large mahogany chair at the head of the table, she released a huge sigh and held her head in her hands a few moments. Then, recovering her fortitude, she looked up at her colleagues.

"Forgive me for waking you at such an hour. But there's an important matter I must discuss. One that requires the knowledge of musical mages such as yourselves. A girl came to the Council tonight..." Lynn glanced at Valarie. "...from Carmenna."

"Carmenna!" Valarie gasped.

Carmenna, Gailea thought. *Usurped by that wicked king, Samil.* The kingdom had been so insulated by his rule for years now that the Lozolian Council had not been able to send spies inside without most meeting their deaths.

"What is she doing here?" Valarie asked, looking both suspicious of and concerned for her fellow countrywoman.

Lynn shook her head. "You needn't mistrust her. She appears to have escaped."

"But *no one* has escaped those walls." Valarie still seemed stunned. "Not since Samil set himself up as king."

"It's Lorelei. I've spoken to you of her before."

"She's the lost girl," Drewit said, looking at Lynn in shock, "the one the Council's looking for. Isn't that right? Her father was a longtime ally?"

Lynn nodded. "They'd disappeared in Carmenna, swallowed up by the tumult as many people were. I thought we would never see them again. Hearing of Master Lorens' death several months back was a striking blow, but when I heard nothing of his daughter, I prayed that silence meant hope. And I suppose it did... but she went through much hardship to find us." She breathed deeply, looking uncomfortable as she continued, "Regretfully, the Council as a whole did not grant Lorelei the most open welcome. Many thought she was a spy. She's still being closely watched. Samil's mind manipulation spells are among the most powerful." She paused, then turned back to Drewit. "I thought perhaps the gift of a heartsong seer might help to confirm or deny her sincerity."

Drewit sat back in his chair, looking astounded. "Me? But will the poor girl allow such a thing?"

"I don't wish to use any mental intrusion," Lynn said. "Apparently, she has suffered many such violations at Samil's hands. But she is willing. She wants to be trusted. And of course, you will be gentle. A heartsong seer need not intrude. Simply listen."

"Is that the only reason why you gathered us here? To help this girl?" Valarie's question was more of a demand.

Gailea watched Lynn's fingertips tapping fervently on the arm of her chair. Valarie's inclination was right. Lynn had more to say. Much more.

"No," Lynn said at last. "Helping Lorelei is only a small part of this. Whether friend or foe, she did choose to tell us much about the horrific goings-on in Carmenna. Some things we knew, others we did not. She could prove quite helpful in the war against the evil there."

"I thought the Council was too busy with its own affairs to get involved with the troubles of other lands," Valarie said, her tone sharp. Drewit placed a hand on her arm and hummed one of his calming melodies, while Gailea sent her a sympathetic look. The Lozolian Council had grown large enough since its initial founding to extend its reach of guidance and military aid to other kingdoms outside of Loz. Thus, it had become a sore point to Valarie that, in recent months, the Council had offered so little aid to Carmenna. Logically, this was because the Council's resources were already stretched thin, but Gailea could understand Valarie being upset enough to point irrational blame.

"You're not entirely wrong," Lynn conceded. "Which is why I would like to propose the creation of a new committee, protected by the Lozolian Council, connected, but separate, its own entity. A small council of musical magicians. It's something we have considered for some time. As Samil gains more power and knowledge in the musical arts, I think it becomes necessary to create a protective circle who can focus solely on musical magic." She hesitated, then sat straighter and folded her hands on the table. "This new council would guard the songs of the Lozolian Realm and use their knowledge to help overthrow Samil."

"A war. To save Carmenna," Gailea said softly. A grave matter, but one she thought served a noble purpose.

"Or perhaps," Valarie said, "they only care to contain the evil to Carmenna, so that they don't have to worry about it spreading to Loz."

Drewit looked pained. "Valarie, you mustn't—"

"The Council have become weak, lazy cowards! If they'd acted earlier, the entire royal family might not have been slaughtered!"

"It's not that simple!" Lynn thundered.

A deep silence cloaked the room. Even Valarie dared not speak.

"Already, we are overwhelmed," Lynn said, quiet but firm, "what with the unrest in Prismatic. Whenever the Council interferes in another kingdom's affairs, we risk opening Loz to danger. We must pick and choose our battles. That makes us prudent, not cowards. I'm not trying to ignore the issue in Carmenna. I am trying to help it. By proposing this new council of musical guardians."

Gailea eyed Valarie, who was very still, then returned her focus to Lynn. The headmistress continued, her words more measured, "These guardians are to protect our entire realm, of which Carmenna is but a small part. Samil is a threat to us all. According to Lorelei, her father believed he was creating some kind of weapon. Over the past few years, Lorelei has watched Samil use musicians in horrifying ways. Forcing them to play songs that can torture, even kill, songs that can enslave masses of people. He's using music to violate people's very will. Music is more powerful, more persuasive, than almost any other form of magic."

"Yes." Drewit's eyes flashed horror. "We all know this."

At last, Valarie stirred, tall and determined in her chair. "So where do we factor into all this?"

"To begin with," Lynn said, "I would like your opinion on the formation of a musical council."

Gailea's head spun with all she'd just learned of this brutal king. This was not just another cruel ruler; they were common, as she knew too well. Lynn's revelations frightened her to the core. Samil's obsession with music and his keen ability to control people like puppets struck terror inside her, and an old but too-familiar face flashed in her memory....

Impossible. She hadn't heard of Moragon in years, even longer than since she'd heard mention of Ragnar's name.

Her jaw tightened, but she made herself speak up. "I think it's a wise suggestion."

"Valarie, Drewit?" Lynn glanced at each of them in turn.

Drewit didn't hesitate. "I agree with Lea."

"And I," Valarie said. "Something must be done before things grow completely beyond our control."

Lynn nodded. "It is decided then. A council of musical guardians will be formed. And I'm requesting that the three of you become its first members."

"Us?" Drewit's brow furrowed. "I cannot speak for these ladies, but I myself don't have enough knowledge of the musical arts. My strength lies in being a heartsong seer. I have knowledge of other charms and spells, yes, but no great gift outside of being a seer."

"That makes you perfect for the job." Lynn's glance included the others. "Each of you has strengths. Lea, for your ability to compose new song-spells. Valarie, for your brilliant musical memory. You soak up new songs like a sponge. I've also used my connections throughout the Lozolian Realm to garner other willing souls. There are roughly a dozen applicants. Lorelei herself will be invited. There will be tests, trials. I would like the three of you to head those as well."

"How many guardians will be required?" Gailea cast a quick glance at her colleagues, who returned her look. None of them had missed the realization that the head-mistress had already decided on this council, long before asking them.

"Eight," Drewit sauggested firmly. "There is no more powerful sound or spell in the musical realm than the octave. In heartsongs, the octave reverberates the most powerful emotions. It can read minds, save lives or kill them." His questioning gaze drifted to Gailea and Valarie, who both nodded their agreement.

"Eight it is then," Lynn said. "The prospective members should arrive in Loz by week's end. We'll hold the trials. And then, whoever seems the best fit will form our new Council, the Octavial Guardians of the Lozolian Realm."

CHAPTER 10

OCTET

The entirety of the Lozolian Council gathered inside the Great Hall of Castle Iridescence, both the main council of seven and the hundreds of members comprising the lower-ranking First and Second Echelons. Various-colored flowing robes draped over the men and women comprising the main council, while the First and Second Echelon wore respective dark blue and wine-red tunics embroidered with golden swords inside silver crosses.

The hall itself was a massive chamber built from light gray stone, with arches and pillars supporting its lofty ceiling. Sunlight dazzled through the many tall windows formed from colorful stained glass, painting vibrant pictures across the polished, wooden floors. Between the windows, blue and wine-red banners hung, matching the Echelons' garb right down to the embroidered gold swords and silver crosses.

The Octavial Guardians stood atop a wide stone dais at the far end of the room, facing the several hundred

130

Lozolian Council members watching and waiting to welcome them into their fold.

Lorelei squinted in the sunlight pouring through one of the tall arched windows flanking the room. She took a step back, shielding herself from the sun's glare, and Lynn Lectim suddenly came into focus as she walked down the blue carpet flowing through the room's middle, looking proud and prepared.

The exact opposite of how Lorelei felt.

This act of being appointed a Guardian was too public. Too extravagant. The formalities were strange and unnecessary. A Guardian named Lea had also balked against such a display. Lynn had argued for tradition, promising that the entire premise was heavily sheathed inside protective charms and spells. All the same, Lorelei hoped Lynn would get on with it already.

Lorelei glanced at the other Guardians. Lea was only a few years her senior, and yet, judging by her guarded nature, she too had experienced deep pain. Valarie stood tall, wearing her proud and solemn demeanor, while Drewit smiled softly. Lorelei sensed a quiet song radiating from him, a soothing charm. She found it difficult to let that calm aura wrap around her but appreciated his effort.

The willowy, silver-haired woman with milk-white skin and a serene spirit, Marger, had fairy blood and had been close friends with Egan, the short, dark-haired man, for many years. Despite his diminutive size, Egan was no child; his face showed mature features. Egan could not speak, but Marger had shared that he could hum perfect pitches. Apparently, he had an ear for all types of music and could sing plenty of spells in his mind. He talked using a special hand language which Marger interpreted for him.

Lorelei recognized the purple-haired Meleeón woman, Elya, and the sturdy-built Forest-footer man named Bernhard but hadn't interacted much with them yet. The only thing she had yet gleaned of their personalities was that Elya seemed an enthusiastic soul, while Bernhard's demeanor seemed to teeter on the pessimistic side.

Lynn stepped onto the dais and smiled at each of the Guardians in turn. Then she faced the crowd. Spreading her arms wide, she declared, "My dear Council. This day we welcome the formation of the Octavial Guardians into our fold. They will now be officially appointed and become one entity."

She turned toward them again, and her glance fell on Drewit.

Drewit stepped forward, stood beside Lynn, and faced his fellow Guardians. He lifted his hands as if to conduct a great choir. He began chanting several notes and then, one by one, he pointed at his fellow Guardians. One by one, they opened their mouths and let their voices soar, all the way from Drewit's deep, vibrant bass to Lorelei's airy soprano. They sang the "Song of Appointment," which Lorelei and Gailea had composed together:

"Now let the eight become as one,
Seal our new fate now begun.
Servants all to one another
Joined as new sisters and brothers.
Lift us now one single voice,
To evil dispel and vict'ry rejoice...."

As they sang on, vocalizing overlapping harmonies, Lorelei felt a strange warmth flowing through her, similar to that created by her amulet's protection. It coursed through her entire body and purified her voice. Their voices blended to create a lovely harmony with what

Drewit had declared as "just the right amount of dissonance." With their permission, he had listened to the heartsong of each applicant, examining their harmonies to help determine how their personalities would twine together. They were each unique but fit together as a perfect puzzle.

The warmth radiated from Lorelei's heart to her shoulder, and down to a singular hot point on her forearm. As she sang, she turned her arm over and watched as the word "Ut" etched itself into her skin, as if an invisible hand burned the symbol with glowing, golden ink. They would each receive such a mark based upon Lozolian solfège, the syllables representing the musical scale they collectively understood best. As there were only seven distinctive notes in the scale, both Lorelei and Drewit would receive the symbol "Ut," representing the highest and lowest notes in the octave scale, whereas everyone else's would reflect the other six notes in the scale.

The song ended. Drewit returned to his place beside his fellow Guardians, and Lynn turned to the Council, declaring, "I present to you the Octavial Guardians of Loz. Welcome your new brothers and sisters!"

Cheers erupted from the crowd. The Guardians cheered and waved, but Lorelei had to force such pleasantries. She was exhausted by so many eyes watching her.

Lynn led the Guardians back through the crowd and into the council chamber beyond. The space boasted a large, triangular table carved from white and silver marble, surrounded by many wooden chairs painted white. Carved into the table's midst was Loz's crest of the sword within a cross. Sunlight gleamed from tall, thin windows, and the ceiling stretched up to a high, singular apex.

Lorelei repressed a shiver as both Lynn and the Octavial Guardians sat in their chairs, bathed in silence.

Such tense quiet always meant a calm before a storm, or so it always had in Samil's fortress.

"What a beautiful ceremony." Lynn broke the silence, beaming at them each in turn. "I congratulate you and thank you again for your service. I know that a difficult task lies before you and that some of you arrived only a few days ago." Her glance strayed to Elya and Bernhard before returning to all of them. "If you have any questions or regrets, please be sure to let me know."

"What if something happens to us?" Bernhard asked gruffly. "What if we get ill or our family is in trouble or some other circumstance outside our control calls us away from our duties, gives us cause to resign? Resigning *is* an option?"

Surprise flashed on Lynn's face before her calm smile returned. "This is not a position of entrapment. You are all here by choice. You've chosen to undertake a weighty responsibility. It would not serve the cause to keep members who despise their position."

Lorelei eased a bit as she was reminded of this point. While she had no intention of abandoning the Guardians or any chance to defeat Samil, it was refreshing to feel part of some purpose without being coerced or trapped inside it.

"But what would happen then?" Marger twirled a strand of her long, silver hair, a nervous habit betrayed by the worry in her eyes. "Without eight members, we aren't as strong. Even the Appointment Song works strongest with eight of us, grants us extra musical strength. And certain song-spells are strongest when we combine our harmonies...."

"Should such a thing happen," Drewit said, "we would then set about immediately holding trials once more to find a replacement."

"What about circumstances you can't forsee?" Elya

leaned forward, studying Drewit closely. "What if, Amiel-forbid, one of us were to die unexpectedly?"

"Amiel forbid that would happen indeed. But even then, we have prepared for this worst possibility. In the case of a Guardian's unexpected death, an emergency appointment would then occur. Lea, Valarie, Lorelei, and I worked out the details of this magic, though they can always be changed as needed. The spell of emergency appointment was designed so that, upon a Guardian's death, a new one is chosen as swiftly as possible. This choice is made not by a council, but rather through the magic of the Appointment Stone, which is protected within the Chamber of Music, right beneath this castle. The stone is imbued with spells that allow it to send out magical pulses if you will, searching for the next musical magician most suited to work in harmony with the remaining Guardians."

"And if *that* person refused?" Bernhard huffed, waving a dismissive hand before crossing his arms.

"Then they would likewise be free to resign. But in the meantime, the strength of having Eight Guardians would endure, hopefully allowing us the time needed to replace that person."

"Mind you, emergency appointment is not the same as the official appointment spell," Gailea added. "A new Guardian appointed by emergency will not have received their personal musical instrument or the full strength of their powers. But the emergency appointment at least allows us to work together and combine our magic when needed. The 'Song of Appointment' also binds us, as Guardians, to the magic of the Appointment Stone, which sends out a pulse to certain Lozolian Echelon who've agreed to serve as our messengers. Their purpose is to find any newly appointed Guardian and bring them safely to us."

"And how would the Echelon find this new member?" Elya tapped her fingers on the table, face pulled into a look of deep concentration. "That sounds the wildest of goose chases to me. Especially if the new Guardian could be anywhere in the Lozolian Realm. That's not exactly a small radius."

"The Echelon have been gifted with smaller stones," Lynn answered, "that pulse and glow the closer they draw to the new Guardian. The Appointment Song ties all of it together—you, the Appointment Stone, the smaller pulse stones."

A grunt turned their attention in Bernhard's direction. He cleared his throat again before speaking. "Another important question then: what are our first steps in fighting Samil? I've only arrived, Elya too, but surely the lot of you hasn't waited until this moment to discuss some sort of plan."

"We have met on a few occasions now," Drewit said. "Sometimes alone, as now, other times with the First Echelon, men and women trained in the arts of battle and politics. Shall we begin with what we discussed at our previous council?"

Drewit kept his tone light and cheery, which helped to calm Lorelei's nerves a bit more. Lorelei trusted him the most out of all the Guardians so far. He had read her heartsong some weeks ago but had made the process so gentle that, to her surprise, she had been glad to open her heart to him, without feeling invaded in the least.

"The Chamber of Music." Valarie, the other Carmennan woman, swept her sharp, midnight gaze across them. Lorelei didn't know if Valarie had ever lived in Carmenna, but she spoke much in defense of their people. "We had intended to start seeking out songs and collecting them for the Chamber."

Egan signed with his hands, and Marger verbalized for him, "Egan asks what this means, 'seeking out songs.'"

"Knowledge of any song-spells should be collected," Lea said, adjusting her spectacles as she swept her steady gaze across each of them. "Through research of various spell books, history books, and such, we can collect more songs, especially those of attack and defense, and store their knowledge inside our Chamber. Then, when the time comes to prepare for battle, we'll have an arsenal of songs at our fingertips. The more songs we collect the sooner, the better. And, of course, in the Chamber they'll be well-guarded, well-studied, and put to good use. We don't know exactly how much Samil knows about musical magic, but there's no sense in leaving any knowledge on the subject lying out in the open for him to find."

"What do we know of Samil and his own intentions?" Elya's eyes were bright with readiness, as if she was prepared to face Samil on the spot.

At every mention of Samil's name, a desire to bolt flashed through Lorelei, and she nervously adjusted the skirts of her silk gown. She should be used to such finery by now. Samil had similarly clothed her, his own personal doll. But she had been on the run for the past year, and now the delicate fabric made her self-conscious, like an animal attempting to act tame, trying its hardest not to rip off its collar and run for the hills. She focused on the warmth of her embedded pendant while silently singing a calming charm.

Strains of another soothing melody drifted toward her. Drewit's again. She accepted it readily and with a thankful glance in his direction before tuning back into the conversation. Valarie was finishing an explanation about Samil controlling musical mages via his mental manipulation spells.

"We think perhaps he's building an army of sorts," Valarie added. "An army of slaves controlled by music."

"If that's the case," Elya said, "then he already has whatever musical knowledge he needs to do so. We can't stop him."

"But we can help the Council prepare for war," Drewit said. "War is inevitable, and if music is involved, we'll be in the thick of it. There's an island near Carmenna, Pakua, where Carmennans who've fled Samil's clutches take refuge. The Council has discovered rumors that they may be creating their own army, a resistance to fight against Samil."

"I've heard rumors of Pakua as well," Lorelei found her voice at last, as her parents had spoken fondly of Pakua. "Pakua is still considered Carmennan territory and is home to many old fortresses we've used in past wars. If the rumors hold true, it would be an optimal hiding place. But there is another, more recent rumor. Talk of an heir to the throne. It's been thought for years that Samil slaughtered the entire royal family. But now… it seems possible that an heir may have survived."

"Hmm…" Bernhard nodded slowly, his gaze pensive. "Having an heir would not fix everything, but it *could* help morale. A new leader to rally around and some hope for their future."

"It wouldn't surprise me if it was true," Valarie said. "The late King Noheah, the true king, had many mistresses in his day. It's possible one was overlooked, and her child spared."

Lynn leaned forward. "If this is true, then perhaps that should also be the Guardians' task. Appointing someone to go to Carmenna, to search for the heir."

"I could go," the words spilled from Lorelei before she could stop them. The idea of setting foot on Carmennan soil again terrified her, but her will to do everything she could to help defeat Samil burned just as strong. "I could search for the heir."

"*No,*" Lea said firmly, setting her fierce gaze on Lorelei. "You're blessed to have escaped Samil's wrath once. If he found you on his soil again, he'd slaughter you."

Lorelei held a hand to her heart. "My mother's amulet will continue to protect me, as it has all these years."

"What amulet?" Bernhard huffed, though he couldn't hide the intrigue in his eyes.

"It's made from earth magic. My mother had a special knack for healing. Before her passing, she made it from special plants and herbs that fused with my skin. I've never learned how to remove it, which I suppose is just as well. I always feared that Samil would find a way to force it from me, but if he knew I had it, he never tried. It protects me from all physical harm. It also strengthens spells that protect against mental intrusion. In exchange for its protection, I cannot cause direct harm to another person, but even then, there are ways to defend myself. For example, if an enemy chased me and I were to loose a boulder from a hill, the boulder could collide with that enemy because it would not be me directly laying hands on them."

"You sound quite confident," Marger said, exchanging looks of admiration with Egan before turning back to Lorelei. "I'm humbled by the fact that you would choose to go back at all, considering your long history with such a terrible place."

"Trust me, I'm terrified at the idea of returning to Carmenna." She gripped her skirt again, suppressing another shiver at merely speaking the idea aloud. "But I've known from the moment I fled that returning would likely be necessary, to stop Samil. I'm the only one of the Council who spent several years listening, watching, inside Samil's halls. The only one who might have an idea of how to begin searching for the truth. I wouldn't have to go immediately. I could learn from you first, strengthen my magical skills. Then, knowing that I would have you and the Council as allies, I think I could be brave enough to return and focus on doing whatever must be done."

"Out of the question!" Lea stood up, her palms on the table.

Lorelei gave her an alarmed look. She appreciated Lea's will to protect others, but she was no damsel in distress.

"Sending a Carmennan does make sense," Drewit said, his gaze drifting over Lea with concern. "It would likely draw less attention than an outsider. Not that I'm necessarily advocating to send the girl," he added quickly, meeting Lea's fierce glance, "though I believe it wisest to consider all options."

"I myself would relish the chance." Valarie tapped a fist to her heart. "I've never set foot on my native soil, so I certainly wouldn't be recognized."

"Perhaps not," Lorelei voiced. "But with all due respect for your willingness to volunteer, I still think it might be best if I were to go. I know Carmenna like the back of my hand, its customs, its dangers. And if it came to it, I know Samil and how his mind works likely better than anyone in all Carmenna."

"It's certainly something to consider," Drewit said. "Lorelei, if you don't mind, we can talk together later on the matter?"

He smiled gently at Lorelei, who nodded in reply. She glanced at Lea who stared at her with obvious discomfort and then away. She appreciated the woman's concern but...it was insulting. They weren't that far apart in age, and Lorelei wasn't a child. She certainly hadn't felt like one for years. She was a capable young woman who knew exactly what madness she offered to throw herself into.

Drewit went on. "Very well then. We can meet later, discuss things further. Make decisions after a full night's rest, after we've had time to clear our minds and work through these issues."

The plan was agreed upon. Overwhelmed and grateful for Drewit's camaraderie, Lorelei fairly fled the chamber and stepped out onto the adjoining balcony.

With the great expanse of the Lake Crystal and Loz's northern woods stretched before her, she gratefully gulped the cool air. She could almost imagine she stood on the wall stretching between the towers of Carmenna's Castle Alaula as the sun rose over the eastern horizon. That balcony had served as her single source of solace and hope all those long, torturous years. Watching the sun's continuous rising, how it chased away the shadows each morning, had provided her constant hope that eventually, the evil shrouding Carmenna would be dispersed for good.

"Lorelei."

Lea. Lorelei's heart skipped, but she stayed in place when Lea came up beside her, her intense gaze softened with a weary smile.

"I apologize if I offended you," she said. "I don't mean to imply that you're incapable of handling this task. It's just, I've dealt with my share of corrupt rulers in the past. I grew up in the halls of a man very much skilled in mental magic who enjoyed abusing that power, like Samil."

Lorelei stared up at Lea in surprise. While she'd sensed the woman held a troubling past, she wouldn't have guessed that her outburst in the Council chamber might mean they shared such a similar history.

Lea took her hand. "I only wanted to assure you that

I *am* on your side. I only want you to be safe. If you enter Carmenna again, and Samil knows, I hate to imagine what he might try to do to you."

"He can do nothing." Lorelei rested her hand over her heart. "I have no children. I have no family. There's nothing he can take from me that he hasn't already...." She paused, closing her eyes, and breathed deep to block the sudden memories of Samil stripping everything from her so brutally—her freedom, her dignity, and ultimately her father.

Lea squeezed her hand tightly, bringing her back to the present. She couldn't let the past haunt her to the point of inaction. She must do her duty to her people, and she must prove to the Guardians, and to herself, that she was capable, that she could be more than some frightened, wounded victim that awful things happened to, that she could be the one to *make* things happen.

Opening her eyes, Lorelei added, "If I'm chosen for this mission, I will return to Carmenna with fear, but with confidence as well. I *can* do this."

"I know you can."

Longing seemed to ache beyond the sadness in Lea's gaze. After giving Lorelei's hand a final squeeze, she turned and slipped back indoors.

Lorelei lingered on the balcony. Lea was more a kindred soul than she could have imagined. Lorelei vowed to open up to her, and in kind, to earn her trust and that of all the Guardians. Then she would return to Carmenna, face her fears, and find the heir who could throw Samil from his throne and rebuild a just and righteous kingdom for her people.

CHAPTER 11:

FROM ASHES TO DUST

S torm clouds gathered over Castle Alaula. Their gray claws stretched in all directions as far as eyes could see, veiling the entirety of the island kingdom of Carmenna like the silver cloths used to shroud the dead as they were laid to rest.

Such a respectful gesture would never be granted toward the dead found within the castle courtyard.

King Samil had ordered two more dozen men and women executed. Murdered. Slaughtered. Long wooden spikes lined one of the courtyard's walls, across from the benches where throngs had sat just yesterday, pretending to hail and cheer their king in hopes that they would not meet with the same fate.

One by one, servants removed the mangled bodies from the spikes. Samil's newer servants revealed their naiveté to his ways by cringing at the pungent smell of burnt flesh. They retched at the texture of melted skin, and the sight of bones jutting grotesquely from what little remained of the bodies.

A single stake went unnoticed. The chains that had bound its captive hung limp. Black ashes pooled beneath the stake. The body that had hung there had been entirely consumed, bones and all. A particular brand of shadow flames, imbued with powerful charms that prevented the victim from casting any spells to spare themselves pain, had seen that the task was thoroughly completed.

The clouds parted and released their torrents. It had rained often lately, an occurance nearly as frequent as the king's executions. As if the clouds wept for the dead when no one else would.

The rain did not wash away the ashes. It did not drive them deeper into the dirt, to dissipate into and become one with the earth, a far different rest from that of the bodies cramped together like refuse in their mass graves.

Instead, the ashes stirred. Shivered. Coldness passed through them. A tangible coldness, as if each tiny particle of ash was a conscious, living soul, a seed awakened by the water.

Within the wind, a thin sound whispered into life, the faintest echo of a voice, barely audible. It settled into a melody that wound its way among the ashes, stirring them like a graceful, sinuous finger. Only seconds later, the song faded into nothingness. The ashes fell still once more.

Then they choked. Choked on themselves like lungs that suddenly needed fresh air.

And then the ashes knew what lungs *meant*, and that they had them. They inhaled staggering breaths, grasping for air as the soft tissue began to reform. Lungs, stomach, liver, muscles, a beating heart at its core. Bones appeared and new skin grew over them.

At last, a body lay in the dirt, among the ashes' remains, its breathing so shallow that, above the subtlest wind and rain, never mind the thunder, such a feeble sign of life would not be detected.

Not far away, gravediggers, overworked servants of the king, were near the end of their exhausting day, ready to lug their wheelbarrows back to the stables, when one young man caught sight of the lone body on its pyre.

"Look!" He straightened over his barrow to stare. "How'd we miss this one?" By the horror in his eyes, he had not been in Samil's service long.

An older man followed the direction of his gaze. "I dunno. Coulda sworn we grabbed 'em all already."

"Well, you didn't," his wife beside him said with heavy disinterest, "so help me grab it now and let's be done with it."

She clambered over the soggy ground. The young man hesitated, but once the woman took hold of the body by its feet in preparation for dragging it along, he nodded in a delayed sort of reaction and pushed the barrow forward in readiness. Then, he carefully lifted the body by its shoulders.

"It won't bite," the woman muttered with shake of her head.

"Just trying to show respect."

"Nor can it acknowledge such gestures." The woman's tone was sharp, but the boy could see the sadness in her eyes.

They pulled the body onto the barrow and rolled it toward the giant pit. There, the boy gazed with remorse at the still figure. Skin badly patched with burns, a mess of wild curls obscuring its face. This had been human, once. Alive. Should have been *allowed* to live.

He blinked the thought away. Silent, he and the woman tossed the body into the pit.

It landed with a thud. What little breath it had collected was knocked clean out of it, losing what consciousness it had regained.

But as the magic that had begun by the ashes and the rain completed itself, it remembered. It *knew*. It knew *everything*. Though not all at once.

Gradually, *it* became a person. Then, a young woman. And then a name:

Iolana. Iolana Noelani.

Her eyelids slowly fluttered open, only to close a moment later, unwilling to greet even the dim light again too soon. Her stomach ached with the sharp pain of many days' hunger and thirst gone unmet. She tried to remember the days before this one, how she had arrived at this state of near-death. The memories soon returned like an ocean tide bringing an ill-favored storm.

For days leading up to her death, she had been starved. She had tried to sleep, but sleep had provided no rest. Samil had plagued her with continuous nightmares of her beloved Mika being tortured and killed in the most brutal ways.

In the dreams, she was always right beside Mika. His blood soaked her dress, too warm and real on her skin. His labored breathing pounded in her ears, as did his cries for her. She would try to comfort him, but he could neither see nor hear her. Then he died in her arms, his vacant, lonely stare eternally accusing her. Why had she not rescued him?

And every night Iolana awoke, sickened, guilty. The dreams were so real, and as time wore on and she grew weaker, she'd wake more and more confused, believing that she truly had harmed or even killed him. Sometimes it would take hours for Samil's hypnotism to wear off.

She remembered being sentenced to die. The day had come both too swiftly and with agonizing slowness. Here in this cold, clammy pit she could still feel the fire slicing every inch of her. Through a hoarse, choking throat, she'd chanted the song over and over, losing hope with every second it did not end her pain. Her lungs had burned, struggled, and then shriveled inside her.

Beyond that, everything else was a void. Until this moment.

That desperate song-spell had worked. She had returned.

Iolana stirred again as a breeze brushed her face. Its chill echoed her pain at being separated from Mika, but she couldn't think about him now. She had so little strength left, maybe not even enough to escape wherever she was. She could waste no time on any weakness, not even her sorrow.

Her senses were waking. She lifted a trembling hand ever so slightly. The effort made her whole arm ache, and it flopped back down onto something soft and moist.

She breathed in the air, stale, thick, wet. With her next breath, she almost vomited, overpowered by the sour smell. Opening her eyes at last, she blinked at the light—the sun, piercing through the dying rain—and then sat up.

She was lying in a pit filled with dozens of corpses. For once, she was surrounded by people but their heart-songs were extinguished. What a dreadful and grim relief. A void of silence beyond anything she had ever known.

She tried to crawl away, but the effort was too great,

and she gave up, falling back with a sob. Was there any-one above, nearby? For some time, she pretended to be dead, wondering how she would get out of the pit. She pushed back her continuous urge to retch. She couldn't risk the sound, nor could she weaken herself by empty-ing her groaning stomach even further.

At last, mercifully, Amiel sent another heavy rain. Anyone remaining above would surely head inside. She thought, maybe just imagined, she could hear receding voices and begrudging heartsongs.

Iolana struggled to stand, her trembling legs wobbly and uncertain how to balance. Her head pounded with the swift movement, and her vision faded in and out. She braced herself against the earthen wall of the pit until she was finally able to look up.

The earth wall of the pit was soft enough, and roots stuck out at intervals. Grabbing hold of the roots, she began to climb. It was a long, hard journey, but by some miracle she pulled herself out and stumbled onto solid ground.

On her knees, she glanced wildly in all directions, surveying her options. She wanted Mika desperately but was too exhausted to consider sneaking into the castle to rescue him. The time for that would come—she would not abandon him—but only when she could regain strength and bring help with her. Right now, she was too weak, frail, and past starving, her mouth parched with intense thirst. The song had brought her back to life, but it had granted her little more than a corpse's body.

Not that she would complain, for there had been no way to know whether the song would work at all. Her talents were still raw, and she was wise enough to know that a single slip of the tongue could have been enough to bring her life to an even more gruesome end than she'd faced at Samil's flames. Lingering patches of her damaged flesh still burned with a dull but constant pain, reminding her to be grateful that she'd used the song-spell as successfully as she had.

She must remain calm and think as Mika would think. She must observe, plan, and take action in what seemed the most logical way.

Iolana continued to survey her surroundings and realized that she stood outside the walls of the castle.

More than that, she stood on the other side of the great ravine that ran the entire length in front of the castle, a now-dry moat filled with hopeless shadows instead of water. The drawbridge had been lowered, bridging the gap. A single wagon lumbered over it toward the castle gates, but no other signs of life were in sight. The woods were only yards away. Her best hope was to hide there, seek nourishment, and then make for the coast. She would find a way to cross the ocean, seek aid and shelter. Then she'd decide what to do about Mika and Samil. Someone had to be *told*. Someone had to *know*. Samil was plotting something, and she had never known him to plot anything that was for anyone's good but his own.

Her body groaned as she began to walk, and her breaths came in short, raspy gasps. She forced herself onward, focused on a single purpose: survival. Survival had been her only true goal the past few weeks. Now, she survived in hopes of finding a way to live as a free woman, with Mika a free man beside her.

Determined, she dragged herself across the field and fled at last into the woods.

CHAPTER 12
RISING TIDES

The sun shone high, bright, and warm on the white beach stretching along Loz's southwestern coast. A party of Forest-footer Elves gathered near the ocean, playing flutes, recorders, strings, and drums. Dancing and twirling, they laughed out loud, merging their merry voices with the cheery strains of their instruments.

Further inland, grassy hills rolled up toward the town of Willardton. Atop one of the wider hills, another musical party took place, though of a more serious, studious nature. Gailea gathered with four of the other Octavial Guardians and several of her students. Elya had sailed to the Meleeón Isles to attend her brother's funeral, while Lorelei had departed for Carmenna two months ago to begin her search for any knowledge of Samil's plans or signs of a true heir.

The Guardians played their new instruments, including Gailea on her double flute. These had been gifts from the Lozolian Council, granted them shortly after their official appointment just over a year ago. Each was exquisitely crafted from Icean crystal and magically bound, responding only to its owner, and each came with a magic leather case shaped just like it. The small cases were exceptionally lightweight, and their instruments could either shrink to fit inside them or else be summoned from them by the Guardians touching them and singing their note of the solfége that matched their Guardian's mark.

Gailea picked up the pace on her flute, fingers moving lithely across its two rows of keys, challenging her students and fellow Guardians.

Bernhard followed suit at first, but then his curious gaze wandered toward the dancers on the beach, and his fingers skipped several notes on his lute. Valarie cast him a stern look as she beat the small drums secured with thick cords to her shoulders, but he paid her no heed.

Meanwhile, Egan played the strings of his small vielle so fast that his fingers were a blur. Marger played her horn beside him. When the spirit moved her, she flew up to dance circles around him. Gailea had been astonished the first time Marger had floated into the sky, moving about effortlessly and without wings, but Marger had since taught her that many with fairy blood were born with the inherent gift of flight, whether winged or wingless.

Drewit had laid aside his small harp to join some of the Forest-footers now dancing around in a ring on the beach. As Drewit did a silly jig, Gailea burst into laughter. The children surrounding Drewit laughed too, skipping in and out of the circle with him and urging him to keep dancing. As his gaze met Gailea's, they shared a knowing smile. Aislin's belly seemed to grow rounded every day, and he could hardly wait to welcome his new son or daughter.

Nerine, a tall Water Nymph who was one of Gailea's best students, played with the utmost vigor. Her big, brown eyes shone with delight, and her silvery-blue skin shimmered in the sun, as did the various blue and brunette hues of her long hair. She was a sweet girl, very intelligent, and a fast learner. Gailea yet clung to her vow to not get too close to her students, for the sake of protecting both them and her own heart. However, she admitted a special fondness for Nerine. As an only child, Nerine had spent much of her life traveling with her parents and, since coming to the academy, had found a difficult time connecting with those her own age.

A shrill, dissonant note burst from Nerine's fife, making Gailea jump. The girl's fingers never stumbled.

"Nerine?" she asked. "Are you all, right?"

Gailea followed Nerine's horrified stare toward the ocean. Many of the Forest-footers on the beach had paused in their dancing to stare too, backing away from the water.

Gailea hurried down the hill to the shore to get a better look. What seemed to be a mess of dirty rags and black feathers pushed through the waves and heaved itself onto the shore, like a small sea monster. But then the creature glanced up to reveal a thin brown face and dark eyes dazed with first fear, then relief. The feathers were a tangled web of matted curly hair. It was no monster, but a girl about sixteen or seventeen years of age.

The girl crawled onto the sand, panting hard. Her skin stretched thinly, and the sharp outline of her bones gave the appearance of a walking skeleton. Her dress was tattered to mere shreds and tangled with seaweed. At last, she crumpled to the ground, letting the shallow tide wash over her.

Several Forest-footers started for the girl, but Gailea burst forward and pushed past them.

Sloshing into the shallows, she scooped the girl up. A sour stench met Gailea's nose, nearly making her gag.

Recognizing the smell of sickness from her days living in the castle's less savory quarters, Gailea sang a simple healing charm, *Sealya*, beneath her breath, hoping to soothe the girl's suffering.

"We'll take her to my house," Drewit said, suddenly beside her. "Aislin will know what to do."

Gailea nodded and passed the girl into Drewit's arms. Drewit led the way up the hill toward his cottage, Gailea and the other teachers following, with Nerine trailing behind.

Valarie flanked Gailea and stared with dread at the girl. "Carmenna?"

Gailea made no reply. The girl's dark complexion and delicate features did appear Carmennan.

Over the past year, the Guardians had succeeded in acquiring knowledge of many of Loz's magical songs and storing that knowledge safely inside the Chamber of Music. But they had not been able to gain any new insight on Samil, and Gailea didn't want to imagine what terrors the girl might have fled.

After struggling uphill, Drewit panted, clearly out of breath. While the girl's frame was slight, Gailea could judge that she wouldn't have had strength to carry such dead weight over the hills herself. Valarie took over, holding the girl in the cradle of her arms. When they reached Drewit's small cottage, he rushed to open the door for Valarie, calling out his wife's name. A pale, round-faced brunette with a figure equally round appeared through a door, skirts sweeping the floor as she rushed into the entryway to meet the group.

"Poor thing!" Aislin cried. "What happened to her?"

Drewit shook his head as he carefully guided Valarie through a small sitting room with a small fire in its hearth. "Where's your brother?"

"Out for the day. Collecting herbs for me."

Gailea followed behind, watching the girl every second. They walked down a short hall and turned a corner into one of the cottage's two bedchambers.

Carefully, Drewit helped Valarie place the stranger onto a bed with a warm, soft quilt.

Gailea, Valarie, Drewit, and Aislin were the only ones who could fit into the tiny space. The other Guardians, along with Nerine, crowded in the hallway.

On the bed, the girl groaned, and her brows lowered as if she tried to focus on something. Gailea heard a few soft, indecipherable noises escaping from her lips.

What is she doing? Egan signed from the doorway, leaning up on his tiptoes to get a better look.

Gailea leaned her face a little closer to the girl's and gently touched her hand. "She's trying to tell us something."

The girl took in several shuddering breaths and muttered a few incoherent syllables. Then, slowly, her eyes opened, just enough for Gailea to see their dark shine. She turned her head toward Gailea and whispered, "Fi... re. Fire...Samil...." Just those words seemed to exhaust her, and her head fell limp on the pillow again.

Immediately, as though the girl's declaration had been some trigger for a spell, her skin burned beneath Gailea's fingers. Sweat covered her body. Gailea looked helplessly toward Valarie but was quickly distracted when her friend's eyes widened with alarm. Behind them, Drewit placed a steadying arm around his wife. Gailea's attention returned to the girl. Beneath the ragged sleeve, the girl's skin was red and raised where fire had distorted it. The stench of burning, infected flesh lingered, potent enough to turn Gailea's stomach.

Drewit murmured something to Aislin, who shook her head. "This is beyond my abilities to heal, or that of any other Forest-footer. She needs Headmistress Lectim's magic."

Gailea nodded in agreement and prayed silently. The girl needed immediate and more intensive help than any of them could give.

Drewit faced his wife, holding her by the shoulders and asking, "Will you be all right? If I go and help them?"

Aislin nodded. "My sister was to stop in soon. If I need anything, she'll be here. Go and help the girl."

Drewit kissed her forehead. Then, he turned toward Gailea, took the girl into his arms, and led the way from the cottage.

Drewit soon found a man who agreed to drive them to the school. Gailea was about to jump inside when a small voice stopped her:

"Miss Byrnes? Miss Byrnes, can I ride with you?"

Gailea whirled about. She'd forgotten Nerine. The Water Nymph gazed up hopefully at Gailea, eyes shining with deep worry.

"Nerine, this need not concern you," Gailea said gently. "Go back to the beach. Enjoy the day."

"No." Nerine's reply was unusually firm, and her lifted chin showed the same determination that Gailea felt. "I want to make sure she's safe."

"Very well." Gailea admired Nerine's compassion, and she was too eager to tend the injured girl to argue.

Everyone piled in the carriage. It was a tight squeeze with eight of them, but Egan volunteered to sit on the floor, and Nerine joined him.

Within minutes, they had reached the mansion and were rushing inside. Upon reaching the healer's wing, they met Healer Cassias who led them swiftly to one of the empty beds, where Drewit lay her on fresh white linens. Cassias inspected her burns, his touch light and delicate as always, but the more he searched, the more his face seemed to fall. He ran a hand through his thick, black curls, a gesture that signaled he was nervous, a gesture Gailea did not much favor. The girl still lay motionless, the white sheets drowning her small frame.

"I will fetch the Headmistress," Cassias said at last, "and will have an herbal soup prepared immediately. She will need some nourishment."

"If she can take it," Valarie muttered, her stare haunted, and Gailea could guess why. This was the second time in the span of a year that one of Valarie's countrymen had fled to Loz, clearly having been sorely mistreated, tormented.

Nerine wandered over and watched the girl, a pensive frown stretched across her face. "She doesn't look that much older than me."

Swift footsteps made Gailea look up as Lynn glided into the room, followed by Healer Cassias. Lynn gently placed her hands on Nerine's shoulders and guided her away from the bed. Then, sitting on the wooden chair near the bed, she pushed up one of the girl's sleeves and stared at the grotesque burns before closing her hand tightly around her arm. The girl emitted a soft groan and fidgeted. Lynn closed her eyes and bent her brows in deep concentration, murmuring incantations.

Her eyes opened abruptly, and she swept a sharp glare across each of them. "All of you, out of here. Lea, Valarie, Drewit, Bernhard, wait for me in the Octavial study. Marger and Egan, escort Nerine back to her room before joining us. I want no one disturbing this girl until I say she's ready for company."

Everyone slipped into the hallway. While Drewit, Valarie, and Bernhard made their way to the study, Nerine asked Gailea, "Will the Headmistress be able to heal her? Will she be all right?"

Despite her frazzled nerves, Gailea managed a smile. "It may take time, but I think so. But you must go now.

As Lynn said, it's best that she rests and regains her strength before seeing too many visitors."

Nerine's face fell a little, but she turned toward Marger who smiled sweetly and led her away, Egan following alongside them. Gailea breathed a prayer of thanks for Marger's tenderness, a trait she simply didn't have the capacity to show right now.

Gailea hurried from the western wing into the northern one, winding through corridors and past classrooms until she at last entered the study with its soothing green walls and hanging plants. Almost identical to Lynn's personal study, this room had been granted to the Octavial Guardians for their personal use. The Guardians who didn't live at the school had taken up residence nearby and often visited to discuss Octavial matters. The Lozolian Council's headquarters was several hours away, making the academy the more logical choice for a regular meeting place. Hence, Lynn had granted the Guardians their own space which they had collectively shrouded in shielding charms, preventing outside ears from hearing any activity or conversation happening within.

Drewit paced before the small fireplace. Valarie sat on the settle, staring sternly into the fire. Bernhard sat in one of the four armchairs, elbows propped on his knees, his somber face resting on folded hands.

Gailea almost shut the door behind her, but a loud cry made her glance back and realize that she had nearly shut the door right in someone's face. Opening it again, she found herself staring at Chamblin.

"Tomilias Chamblin! What a pleasant surprise."

"Likewise, my good woman."

"I'm afraid this reunion will have to be cut rather short. Lynn called us here for a special meeting requiring utmost privacy."

"Then it would appear I am in the right place."

Chamblin stepped inside and swept into one of his low bows, nodding at each of them in turn. "Good afternoon, ladies, sirs."

Gailea's heart skipped with mingled calm and joy as his eyes, joined by his constant smile, met hers.

His smile sobered then. "Lynn stopped by my office and mentioned that you'd found a girl washed up on the beach. How is she?"

"Lucky to be living. And luckier still if she's just escaped what she *appears* to have just escaped."

Moments later, a woman with a mane of fiery red hair and thick muscles, Tress, their weaponry teacher, entered as well, followed by three other instructors: Cameron, a Spaniño with tanned skin and jet-black hair who taught mathematics, Gwen, a blonde Scintillate woman who taught elemental magic, and Laina, a brunette Forest-footer who served as the head reading and writing instructor while also leading one of the history classes.

These four teachers comprised their own small council dedicated to the protection of the school. They had met altogether only once before, right after the Octavial Guardians were first established, to share current knowledge of Samil and discuss how to add extra enchantments of protection to the school that would alert the teachers if any intruders or suspicious magic showed itself on the grounds. After that meeting, Lynn had taken it upon herself to pass along any information either group needed to know. The fact that they all met together now signified that the girl's arrival was of utmost concern to both the Guardians' plans and the school's security.

Lynn was last to enter, hurrying over to her favorite mahogany and leather-cushioned chair near the fire and motioning for everyone else to join her.

Gailea sat in another of the large armchairs, and

Chamblin pulled a rocking chair close to her, while Valarie, Tress, and Gwen shared the settle, Drewit and Laina drew over chairs from the small wooden table, Cameron eased onto the large footstool, and Bernhard drew his armchair closer. As Chamblin rocked back and forth, the chair's creaking placed Gailea's brittle nerves on edge, making her shift restlessly.

Valarie seemed just as impatient. "How is the girl?"

"She will live and should heal," Lynn said. "Beyond that, she's a mystery. The burns were severe but patchy. It seems impossible that fire could have caused such incredible wounds only on certain parts of her body, unless she was tortured by very specific fire magic. Even then, it's a greater wonder that she's alive, or that she managed to make it to our shores. The question at present is what remains to be done with her. We don't know yet if she has any family, or where she came from, though my guess is Carmenna."

"If she is from Carmenna," Gailea said, "she may have some further insight into Samil and his plans. She spoke his name. She may have fled him just as Lorelei did."

Lynn nodded. "That is a possibility. I'm willing to send Drewit in later to read her heart. She may have traveled here because she has family or friends living in Loz. Or it may be she has no one, and this seemed the closest, safest refuge. If the latter is true and she has nowhere else to go, I'm not opposed to her living here until better arrangements can be made. If she has magical blood, she may even study here, though that wouldn't be required. What say all of you?"

"Certainly," Drewit said. "I see no reason not to take her in. We've plenty of room and resources here."

"I agree." Cameron gave a firm nod. "I remember when I first came here from Spaniño. No home, no work. Just the clothes on my back and my knowledge of numbers. Anyone else might have turned me away based on my clothes alone, in absolute shambles, but not this place. This place has always stood as a home to the homeless."

"It certainly has," Gwen confirmed, sharing a meaningful glance with Laina, Cameron, and Drewit in turn.

"How can I disagree, after Cameron gives such a beautiful speech?" Tress threw a playful smile at him, and he nodded in turn.

"I'm for it," Laina piped.

"And I," Chamblin said firmly.

Gailea shared a slight smile with him. "As do I—"

A scoff sounded from Bernhard. "Just because we've stood as a beacon of hope for the homeless doesn't mean we should readily accept every stray that passes our doors. Some degree of caution seems warranted, seeing how little we know of this girl. And by little, I mean absolutely nothing."

"I'm inclined to agree with Bernhard." Everyone turned to Valarie, her face pulled into a solemn frown. I fear you all too quick to trust. We've been trying to discover the secrets of Samil's powers for the past year, without success. Who knows what evil this girl just fled from? Would you risk bringing that evil upon our school?"

Valarie's gaze rested on Gailea, who stared at her in disbelief.

"I understand your fears. We all understand the risk. But we accepted Lorelei as one of our own. And what about me? Lynn took a risk taking me in as well, for which I'm eternally grateful. Why then should we turn this girl away?"

"Lorelei wasn't as complete a stranger as this girl," Bernhard reminded them. "Lynn knew her father, knew who she was. That's more to go off than we have with this one."

"I'm not saying we shouldn't show caution," Drewit said, all the while rubbing his temple. "But Lorelei came to us for help and has been a great aid to us. This girl could be the same."

"Or she could be some spy sent from Samil."

"Or she could simply be an escapee in need of refuge." Cameron directed his defensive gaze at Valarie. "Just as I was."

"And I," Gailea agreed firmly.

"And as Lorelei was too," Gwen said, stroking her blonde braid over her shoulder.

"We did consider at the start that Lorelei may be a spy." Lynn's expression was both guarded and concerned. "Valarie, why do you seem to fear this new girl even more?"

Valarie's hands clutched the chair arms. "Because Samil has had even more time."

"Aye." Tress leaned forward, her gaze intent. "Time to plot, time to perfect. His spies may have become cleverer."

"If I may offer my opinion," Chamblin said with a calm smile. "Can we not help the girl while also exercising caution? We can help a lost sheep *and* make sure there's no wolf hidden beneath."

"He makes a fair point, Valarie." Drewit's glance at her was prompting. "Show some sympathy."

Lynn's gaze hadn't left Valarie's, but now she switched to the whole group. "There *is* some truth in what Valarie says. There is some truth in what *all* of you say. I believe we shall keep a close watch on the girl, but not to lock her up. We don't want to make her feel like she's a prisoner, especially if she's just come from a similar situation. That will not gain us her trust."

"What about placing protective charms on her?" Laina's brow had bent with deep thought. She glanced at Gwen, uncertain, but when her friend nodded, she continued, "We could use charms similar to those we've placed around and within the school. Charms that will alert us if she tries to escape or send any outside messages."

"Yes..." Tress nodded slowly, and Gailea could almost imagine the ideas turning over in her mind like spokes on a wheel. "That might allow her freedom to move about the school grounds freely, without tethering her, but while giving us peace of mind."

"Would she feel them?" Drewit asked. "These protective charms? She's been through some horrible ordeal. We don't wish to alarm her further, cause undo anxiety."

Gailea gave him an empathetic smile, grateful that he was able to consider the girl delicately, just as she would have wanted to be treated after suffering torment with Moragon and her husband.

Gwen shook her head. "Unless she is particularly skilled in mental magic or has had much experience being around such magic, then no. Most people would not detect such subtle spells."

Cameron sighed deeply, face bent in an internal debate. "I suppose even if she did detect such charms, better that route than locking her up, caging her like some prisoner."

"Perhaps, or perhaps not," Gailea voiced. "The girl may indeed have been subjected to mental magic." She shuddered as memories of Moragon fighting to claw his way into her mind so he could puppeteer her music waved through her. She added quickly, "She may have indeed been tortured by it, if she has any connection to Samil."

"Is that a risk we are willing to take?" Lynn asked. "I think it's a small price to pay, placing security charms on a complete stranger who most likely won't detect them.

We must consider the school's security first and foremost. And I think it's a better option than the alternative of keeping her locked up or having someone follow her at all times."

Nods and words of agreement echoed around the room. Even Gailea found herself nodding. While wary and concerned for what the poor girl might have gone through, the safety of their hundreds of students was of equal importance, nor did she wish to see the poor girl caged, if she was innocent of evil as Lorelei had been.

"We will give her what freedoms we can but place charms upon her that will alert us if she tries to escape or send outside messages. Is this a fair bargain?"

Lynn swept a sharp gaze across all of them, suggesting that her words were more of a final statement than a question.

Everyone conceded, even Valarie, who still looked irritated, but Tress had soon swept her up into a quiet conversation that seemed to set her at ease. Soon everyone got up to leave, Gailea lagging behind in thought.

She looked at the others, could see the unique emotions written on everyone's face, the moods evident in their gait. Her gaze drifted to Chamblin with an uneasy frown. When she recognized what she was doing, she exhaled, now irritated with herself. The truth was, like it or not, his words at the fencing lesson long ago now seemed prophetic.

Everyone's mettle was being tested.

CHAPTER 13

AWAKENINGS

Iolana slowly stirred back into the realm of consciousness.

Soft blankets wrapped her with velvety warmth. The sweet smell of freshly washed bedlinens was foreign to her and though pleasant, she shrank from it. Where was she?

In the next breath, she wondered *how* she was here, lying in this veritable heaven. The fog hazing her mind lifted a little, allowing familiar aches to throb dully throughout her body. She shifted a little, and as her skin rubbed against the fabrics, its burned patches stung, making her wince.

Someone gasped.

Iolana lay still, listening. In the stillness, the din of a troubled melody reached her mind. Someone's heart echoed a frantic song. Voices stirred ever so quietly in the back of her mind, whispering to her that she was trapped. She tried to push them away with protective charms, but they lingered, weighing her down.

A hand touched hers.

Iolana blurted out a repelling song-spell as forcefully as her hoarse voice would utter. A cry rang out, followed by a loud thud.

Iolana struggled to sit up. The panicked heartsong lingered nearby, beating just as wildly and now with confusion. Iolana's limbs were too weak to support her, stiff and sore. She shielded her mind while preparing another wave of offensive spells, then turned toward the stranger staggering to her feet and staring at Iolana with round, brown eyes.

It was a girl with blue skin such as Iolana had never seen. Merely a girl, but Iolana had learned that evil could come hidden in many disguises. Pushing her mind beyond the intruder's trembling figure and innocent face, Iolana dug deep for her heartsong. There it was. She maintained her mental grasp, listening once more.

Alarm plagued the girl's heart. No ill intents, only curiosity and kindness. Iolana had encountered many hearts difficult to decipher, but this one was so pure that Iolana sensed its owner would not know how to deceive her even if she tried. Iolana sighed and released her hold on the girl's heartsong, relief letting her breathe again.

Until she heard the voices, whispering in the back of her mind. Holding her down, forbidding her to be fully in control of herself.

Then she knew: they were binding spells, tracking spells. Her rescuers, or perhaps captors, thought her a spy or some other threat. Iolana couldn't be certain what the charms meant, but she hated their restraint. They suffocated her. Just like in the grave. Countless decaying corpses, crushing her on all sides....

Iolana shook the memory aside. She could never forget the past, but she would not allow its pain to claw its way into the present. For now, she must focus on unraveling this new place, these new people, this new girl.

"I'm sorry," Iolana said at last. The rasp in her voice surprised her, and she paused, inhaling to let the cool air soothe her throat, still sore from the fire. "I didn't mean to scare you. I wasn't fully awake and didn't know who or what you were."

"No, no, it's all right," the girl said quietly. She hurried over and sat on the chair beside the bed, smoothing out her dark brown skirts. "Are you...are you feeling better?"

Iolana nodded. "I'm still tired, but I think so." She eyed the girl carefully. "Who are you?"

"I'm Nerine. I'm one of the people who found you when you washed up on shore. May I ask your name?"

"I'm Iolana." She almost smiled. How strangely refreshing to share that small piece of her with another soul.

Nerine's face brightened, and she leaned forward eagerly. "That's a lovely name."

"Thank you. Can you tell me where we are?"

"Oh! Of course. We're in Loz, at the Lynn Lectim Academy. I'm a student here. Miss Byrnes, one of our teachers, rescued you from the water, and she and the others brought you here. Headmistress Lynn and the other healers helped you as best they could. You were hurt so badly."

Nerine's voice trailed off, and Iolana followed her gaze as it wandered to the exposed skin of Iolana's arms and legs.

The skin was still stretched so thinly that Iolana could clearly distinguish the shape of her own bones. She'd been bathed and changed from her filthy rags into a white tunic stretching all the way down to her ankles. It was short-sleeved, exposing her arms where the nasty burns had been. Now, the burn marks had faded. A few black scabs remained, but her skin already looked far healthier. Iolana admired the thorough healing work.

Then, as all Nerine had shared so far sunk in, she glanced up and said, "Do you mean *the* Lynn Lectim?"

Nerine nodded.

Iolana felt awed and relieved at once. She had set her sights for Loz, deeming the vast kingdom as the perfect place to regroup and make plans to rescue Mika. She had heard of the Lozolian Council and hoped she might find some way to reach them and plead to them to help rid Carmenna of Samil's terrorized reign. But she could never have predicted such good fortune as finding Lynn Lectim herself, the woman famous for fighting against the Mass. Lynn would never support a ruler like Samil. That didn't make Iolana feel entirely secure. Spies could abound, and pure hearts could be swayed. But it meant she was in no immediate danger and could trust her new captors a little more readily. Amiel truly had blessed her. Perhaps He wanted her to rescue Mika as much as she did.

Her gaze found Nerine's again. "I'm grateful for your help. I don't trust many people. But I do trust you."

"Why?" Nerine's head tilted in curiosity. "How do you know you can trust me?"

"Because I can sense it. I can hear it inside you, inside your heartsong. At least, I did at first. The song's faded now. The ability comes and goes, sometimes by its own will. It can get tiring after a while."

"You're a seer?" Nerine's eyes widened again. "So is Drewit, my musical charms teacher. Maybe he can help you learn more. How old are you?"

"Eighteen or so. I think. It was hard to keep track of time inside the prison."

Nerine's widened eyes filled with tears. Iolana grew tense, uncomfortable at the haunted way the girl stared at her. She didn't want to be pitied as some victim, nor did she wish to be hailed as some hero. She only wanted to leave this place as soon as possible to save Mika.

"I'm fifteen," Nerine said at last, "and a half."

Approaching footsteps caused Iolana to jerk her head up. Nerine glanced about with a frown, apparently not hearing the same, but when Iolana motioned her to leave, she slipped through the curtain surrounding the bed and hurried noiselessly in the opposite direction of the footsteps. Iolana supposed the girl must know another door for entering and exiting the healing wing. At any rate, she didn't worry about Nerine getting into any sort of trouble. Despite her timid nature, she obviously had a knack for sneaking about and possessed enough daring to do so.

Iolana sank back against the pillows and closed her eyes, praying she looked asleep and wouldn't have to deal with anyone else. None would likely be as easy to contend with as Nerine.

The footsteps and whoosh of robes faded into the distance, but someone else stepped inside the room, through the curtain, and stood by Iolana's bed.

Iolana tried to remain still as stone, kept her breathing shallow, and listened, but deciphering this newcomer's heartsong was much more difficult. This heart was laced with layers of defense. This person's mental abilities were strong, well-seasoned, and had thrown up thick guards before entering the room.

However, the longer Iolana listened, the faintest strains of a heartsong began to seep through the sturdy mental walls. Fear sang in this new heart, a fear that intrigued Iolana greatly. She had never heard her own heartsong but felt this fear was akin to hers.

The longer Iolana listened, the more relaxed she became, and the more intensely she felt a sense of a kindred heartsong. She thirsted to understand why. She hesitated a moment more, then opened her eyes.

A woman stood over her, wearing a simple but well-made blue gown that accentuated watchful blue eyes ringed by oval spectacles, and thick, auburn wavy hair that was woven into a braided coronet.

"How are you feeling?" the woman asked, her voice pleasant but every bit as cautious as the guarded strains of her heartsong. She sank onto the chair, her posture noticeably rigid.

Iolana swallowed. "Better. A little stronger."

"Good. My name is Lea Byrnes. We found you on the shores of Willardton, near the Lynn Lectim Magic Academy. I'm a teacher here. Can you tell me your name?"

"Iolana. And thank you for helping me. Miss Byrnes—"

"Please, call me Lea."

"How long have I been here?"

"Just overnight, so far. You need more time to heal. Headmistress Lectim and other staff have been discussing your situation. For now, you may stay here. As you heal, if you like, you may attend classes. In the meantime, is there anyone we can notify? Any family or perhaps a friend?"

"There's no one," Iolana said quietly. "My parents died when I was young. I know no other family, and the only friend I have, I was forced to leave behind."

Lea studied Iolana intently before replying, "I see. As I said, you may stay here, though you may not leave the premises, not yet."

A fist of dread tightened around Iolana's heart. "So, you're imprisoning me?"

"No...not exactly. It's a precaution. Some of us are concerned where you may have come from, and for what purpose. You will be under close watch until we get to know you better. Your past, your reasons for being here..."

Iolana cringed away, her heart palpitating. *Get to know you better.* She knew what that meant. Prying, observation. Was she never to have private thoughts?

Lea seemed to sense Iolana's concerns. "Please, don't be afraid. Your mind will not be examined. That much I can promise you."

Gratitude washed over Iolana. As suffocating as the protective charms were, this woman's assurance seemed credible. Iolana's mind, her *soul,* would not be violated, as it had been countless times under Samil's rule.

As if they were linked at the mind, the mere thought of Samil allowed Iolana to hear Lea's heartsong a little clearer. Iolana dug deeper inside the heartsong and focused on the familiar fear until at last, snatches of a terrified melody broke through. Visions of Mika dying flashed before Iolana, and suddenly, she understood.

"You know," she whispered, struck breathless. "You understand. You too have known grief at the hands of Samil."

Lea drew a long breath. Her body tensed as though Iolana's perceptions made her uncomfortable, and yet Iolana couldn't miss the intrigue in Lea's watchful eyes. Lea swallowed, and then she managed to murmur, "Not Samil, but another cruel king. Two such kings, if I'm truthful. But how could you know that?"

"I hear songs sometimes," Iolana whispered back. Samil had always tried to use her for her gift, but she wasn't afraid to show it to this woman who had known similar pain. If she was to take advantage of this place and its educational opportunities, she must take the risk of showing her capabilities to the right people. Learning more about her talents, expanding and perfecting them, may be the only way for her to get back to Mika. "I hear songs within certain people. I heard your song, and its pain was kin to mine."

Lea inhaled, seeming to hold her breath. "That is one of the rarest and, if trained correctly, strongest kinds of musical magic. The gift of heartsong."

Iolana nodded slowly. "So Samil always said."

"Samil..." Lea's face dipped into a frown, but not one of distrust. Rather, she looked curious and concerned, lost deep in thought as she debated her next question. "Where exactly are you from? What is your connection to Samil? If you aren't quite ready to share, if the pain is too fresh, I will understand. But we will need to know eventually, the other teachers and I, for the protection of the school, and to know how best to help you."

Iolana took a deep breath and closed her eyes for a few moments, instinctively trying to block out the memory of being burned alive. Of course, closing her eyes only made the memories crisper, closer, feel realer in the blackness.

Opening her eyes again, she said, "I lived in Samil's castle for years. I was supposed to be one of his servants. He wanted to use my heartsong powers for himself. For what ultimate purpose, I was never really sure. He tried to control me with his mental magic, torment me with nightmares. But I rebelled against him. It's what landed me in his prison, and ultimately, at the mercy of his shadow flames."

Lea winced, visibly wounded by Iolana's pain. "I am sorry you've suffered such horrors. No one should ever be subjected to mental torture. But here, we can help you, teach you to use your magic for good, teach you to control it and defend yourself. Would you like that?"

Iolana pondered. Maybe whatever these people could teach her could even help her eliminate the charms they'd placed on her, and thus escape. If not, they likely had a library and other resources that might prove useful.

"Yes," she said. "I'd be glad to learn here. I learned much under Samil's tutelage, but only what he wanted me to, so that he could use me. I want to know how to *really* use my magic."

"Samil taught you?" Lea raised a curious brow. "How so? From what we know, he possesses no musical magic abilities of his own."

"Yes, but he has studied the art extensively. And he knows how to play various musical instruments, how to sing. He would teach us these things, as well as song-spells he had read about. He would bring in music mages and instruct them to teach us exactly what he wanted us to learn. Songs that allowed us to seduce or persuade or do harm, mostly. We think he was trying to build an army of musical mages."

"You keep saying 'we.' How many of there were you? Did you know a girl named 'Lorelei,' by chance? She came to us as well, having fled Samil."

Iolana's brows raised as she felt genuinely impressed that someone else had managed to escape, and without Samil thinking them dead. "I'm not sure how many of us there were altogether. He tutored us individually and kept us in separate quarters. But a few of us, including my friend, Mika, we would sneak out. We had formed this secret alliance, hoping to form a plan that could help us all escape. I know the name 'Lorelei.' She was one of his favorites. But he kept her so close to him that I hardly ever saw her. But I know he hurt her, in even worse ways than he hurt me or my friends. There were enough rumors around the castle for us to know they were more than rumors. And that's why I want to see him, Samil, ended. So that he can no longer harm anyone else. If he finds out I'm alive and comes for me, I want to know how to fight him. Can you help me with that? What do *you* teach here?"

Lea sat, seemingly abashed some moments before replying. "I admire your courage. Thank you for sharing your story with me. For my part, I teach basic music classes, which might not be a bad place to start. Even if you already have strong skills, a good foundation in the basics is necessary to truly master and control any technique."

Iolana smiled, grateful for this woman's help. Perhaps she could prove just as useful an ally as the girl, Nerine.

A strong tiredness rolled over her then like a wave. She yawned wide, and her eyes struggled to stay open.

Taking this unspoken cue, Lea rose from the chair and gave Iolana's hand a squeeze. Iolana yanked her hand away, alarmed. The only physical touch she knew was Mika's tenderness and Samil's torture, and because of the latter, did not often welcome it.

Lea withdrew at once, contrition written on her face. "I'm sorry. I shouldn't have—"

"It's all right. I just wasn't expecting it. I don't usually like to be touched."

"I understand," Lea said softly. "And I do apologize. Rest now. I'll come visit you again tomorrow." She parted the curtain and slipped out.

Iolana sank back onto the pillows, mind whirring with all that had just happened. Exhausted, she let her eyelids close so that sleep could come. She would need as much rest and recovery as possible to learn as much as she could from this place.

~*~*~

As soon as Gailea left the healing wing, she broke into a sprint down the hall. Her heart raced with fear at Iolana's solemn declarations, but even moreso, soared with excitement.

This enthusiasm practically spilled from her as she flung herself inside the Octavial study and shut the door behind her.

"Drewit! She's like you. She's a heartsong seer."

Egan and Marger remained lost in their chess game on the rug near the fireplace, but Drewit and Valarie stared up at her from the settle. From their flustered appearance, Gailea wondered what sort of heated argument she had likely interrupted. "She truly is, Drewit. You must come and see."

Bewildered, Drewit continued to stare until a playful grin spread across his face. "Just couldn't resist checking on her, could you?"

Gailea gave a wry smirk. "I suppose not."

"Well, I for *my* part do not wish to get into any sort of trouble with Lynn. More than that, I think the girl does need her rest. But I'll check on her later. You really think she has the gift?"

"I do."

"Even if she is a seer," Valarie crossed her arms and touched her chin pensively, "we must ask ourselves what Samil would've been doing with such a gift."

"I don't think this girl is a threat to us," Gailea said. "She spoke with fervent hatred against Samil and her desire to see him overthrown, to rescue the friend she left behind. Her own rebellious acts are the reason he tortured her with fire magic. Samil has no musical magic by nature, and while it seems he had other music mages there to assist, I doubt he would've allowed a full, proper training."

"But she has been trained by someone?" Drewit asked.

"She told me that I had known pain at the hands of a dark lord just like her. Without me breathing a single word on the matter, she was able to sense it."

Drewit and Valarie both leaned forward, interest and concern mingling in their expressions.

"That is a more advanced skill," Drewit said.

"I wonder if Lorelei knows anything," Valarie said.

"Not likely." Gailea shook her head. "Iolana said that she was aware of Lorelei, but that Samil kept her under especially close watch. It doesn't seem the two interacted."

"Has anyone received word from Lorelei lately?" Marger asked, as she and Egan had sat up on the rug, listening intently.

"Nothing," Drewit said. "Not since she left Pakua to continue her research on the Carmennan mainland."

Valarie's frown deepened. "We need to reach out to her again. Tell her about Iolana. Even if they never met, Lorelei may have overheard something. And even if Iolana turned out to be a spy, she could prove useful. You *know* it's true," she added with a cautious glance at Gailea.

"Yes, I know," Gailea muttered, remembering the sorcerer Chevalier who, at heart, had not agreed with Moragon's evil schemes but had succumbed to them to protect his family. "When Moragon was king, he tried to manipulate me, and others, by using the people we loved. Samil may have done the same with Iolana, using the friend she left behind to manipulate her. Samil's restlessness may be tied to Lorelei's reason for leaving the safety of Pakua to seek answers in Carmenna."

Valarie's gaze narrowed with all seriousness at Gailea.

Egan and Marger glanced at each other, their eyes reflecting the same idea.

Drewit spoke for them all. "The lost heir of Carmenna. Perhaps Lorelei has found some clue at last."

"I'll write her," Gailea said. "About the girl. Perhaps she may be a link to something Lorelei has learned about Samil or the heir."

"Very good," Drewit said. "Elya should be back within the week, and we can fill her and Bernhard in then. I will assess Iolana's powers in a few days, when she's had sufficient time to heal and regain her strength."

"Thank you, Drewit," Gailea said, before jumping up and hurrying from the room toward her personal office.

CHAPTER 14
WANDERINGS

Iolana kept her eyes shut as the healer cleaned her burns and applied herbal ointments that refreshed the patches of tender skin. She had been awake for some time but pretended to sleep, not wishing to risk a confrontation filled with questions. The healer's heartsong pulsed with a steady compassion and desire to help, but it also wavered with fear, and Iolana had no way of knowing whether this fear was bred from concern or distrust. Last night, her sleep had been interrupted by the heartsongs of people standing outside the healing wing. She had fought to block them out, but her body was still weary enough that finding strength to do so had proved impossible. All through the night, the heartsongs had faded in and out, along with snatches of conversation from curious students trying to decipher where she had come from.

As the healer finished and left, Iolana opened her eyes and basked in the blessed silence engulfing her. Faint gray light filtered from the window through the slightly parted bedcurtain to her left. It must still be early morning. Perhaps she could sneak out for a half hour or so, explore the school a bit, find her bearings. Even if these people proved to be entirely friends, she hated being trapped, lacking the option to flee when necessary. Now and then, the voices still whispered in the back of her mind, a subtle reminder of the tracking charms placed upon her. She must find a way to work around them.

One of the other patient's heartsongs began to beat with a swift melody. At first, Iolana thought the person must have an animated dream, but as the song intensified, she realized they must be awake.

Within moments, the person hovered near her bed. Iolana shut her eyes and held still, listening. In the next breath, she recognized the sweet, pure song. It overlapped with a nervous, more frantic melody, but that too quickly became familiar. With a sigh of relief, Iolana gazed up at Nerine.

Nerine's face lit up with a smile. "Good morning, Iolana."

"Good morning."

"Sorry, did I wake you? I didn't mean to. I can leave. I just wanted to check on you."

Iolana reached out and grabbed Nerine's hand. "No, it's okay. Stay, please. I would appreciate company for a bit."

Nerine glanced down at Iolana's hand wrapped around hers, looking bewildered. Iolana let go and expected the girl to leave, understanding too well what it meant to hate being touched by strangers, but then she seemed to relax and sank onto the edge of the nearby chair, as tentative as she had been yesterday. Questions stirred in her gaze, but she seemed either too shy or too polite to ask them. Iolana appreciated anyone who knew when to stay quiet. Perhaps this girl could prove even more useful than she had originally thought.

Cupping her hands, Iolana sang a quiet song-spell, *Luma*. Her hands glowed, and a ball of light formed inside them. Nerine's eyes widened at the expanding light, which Iolana set on her lap.

"How did you do that?" Nerine breathed.

Iolana smiled and shrugged. "It's a simple spell. I've always had a talent with music. *Emonie*," she sang. The light blossomed into a bright blaze and then vanished like a dying star.

Nerine stared, captivated, and Iolana laughed a little at such sincere awe.

"It's really not that impressive. Don't you see magic here every day? Magic that's far grander, I'm sure."

"Yes, of course I do. But *my* magic has only just started to show itself. Both my parents are Water Nymphs, so of course I have those abilities, but my father was also a music mage, and I seem to have inherited a small part of his musical gift. Sorry, I'm rambling."

"It's all right," Iolana assured her. "I like talking with you. Please, continue."

Nerine smiled and relaxed a little more at this encouragement. "I've just started learning about my waterpowers and how to control them. Here, I'll show you: *Undina*."

She held very still. Ripples darted across her skin. As her brows furrowed in deep concentration, both her hair and body transformed into flowing currents of water, and Iolana found herself gasping then grinning in delight. Nerine had changed from solid to a liquid that somehow held her human shape. She stayed that way a few moments before solidifying herself.

"It's just for show. Not very useful. Not yet, at least.

Although, I *can* turn into a complete puddle of water and sneak around. Only for a few moments though."

"Useful or not, it's lovely," Iolana insisted. "And it made me smile, which I've really needed. I get so restless. I've been on the move for so long now. I know you probably see this place as a safeguard, and I'm trying to see it that way too. But I don't like feeling trapped or contained. Small places, I've had too much of them."

Nerine only nodded, listening closely. Iolana carefully searched her face for any change, any sign of worry or judgment, but she looked just as curious and concerned for Iolana's welfare. Nerine didn't seem like the type to break rules, but perhaps Iolana had lured her in enough to convince her. The curtains surrounding her bed seemed to shrink and press in closer, caging her in. She needed to explore her surroundings, get a feel for the layout of the school.

"Nerine...do you think you'd be willing to take me on a walk, show me around? It would ease my nerves."

Nerine's brows rose in surprise and then dipped into a concerned frown. "Do you think you're strong enough? I really don't want to get us in trouble."

"There will be no trouble. I can hear heartsongs, remember? That will help us. And my burns are feeling much better. Just think. It'll be like our own secret adventure. We could come back before anyone found me missing."

Nerine lifted her chin. Her gaze wavered with concern, but she seemed to make up her mind. "I'd love to show you the school. And I never get in trouble, so even if we get caught, I don't think they'll go too hard on us."

"I never had much of a chance for school," Iolana said, "but my curiosity probably would've gotten the best of me. I'd have been in trouble all the time."

With a laugh, Nerine leaped to her feet and reached toward Iolana. "I'll help you up."

Iolana hesitated a moment before she clasped Nerine's hand with a smile.

While most of Iolana's burns had been healed, the fabric of her tunic brushed uncomfortably against those that lingered, making her wince. Fresh scabs had formed on the bottom of her left foot, causing an unusual limp. Adjusting to place more pressure on her right foot, she followed Nerine past the other currently empty beds and whispered, "The healer gave me some wonderful soup last night. But I *am* hungry again. If we're to be true explorers, is there any chance of stocking provisions for our quest?"

Nerine seemed to ponder as she peered out the door, looking both ways.

"It's clear," Iolana whispered. "No heartsongs in close range."

Nerine looked at Iolana, who now noticed a shift in the girl's gaze, a hint of uneasiness. "You know, I think your gift is wonderful. But my teacher Drewit always says that heartsongs should only be listened to with the greatest discretion."

Iolana tensed at this criticism. "I don't listen with the intent of intruding into others' emotions and using those against them. It's only for my own protection. Besides, I can't always help it, overhearing others' songs. I was never really taught how to properly control it."

Nerine looked skeptical a moment before nodding, seeming to accept her answer. "The dining hall will be serving breakfast soon. I think I have a place I can hide you, and then I'll grab us some food."

"Sounds like a plan."

Nerine slipped from the healing wing and motioned

at Iolana. Iolana followed noiselessly, moving as fast as she could while limping on her better foot. Stealth had been another skill necessary for surviving Samil's domain. Nerine noted her limping and paused with a concerned stare, but Iolana nodded for her to continue. Nerine turned and fled quietly down the hall, Iolana on her heels.

Nerine checked around corners and gestured when to pause. Iolana helped by stopping them when she heard a heartsong, giving them plenty of time to hide from passersby by pressing against the gray stone walls or ducking behind statues or passage doorways.

After a time, they came to a large hallway. Great double doors spanned to Iolana's left, and she barely suppressed the urge to bolt through them. This place had food and healers and magic she could learn. She could start preparing her escape but must not let fear push her into making stupid choices or risk getting placed on an even closer watch. She'd have only one chance to go back to rescue Mika and couldn't afford to ruin it.

The light shining through the large, leaded glass windows was dawn's soft yellow-orange, and Iolana guessed that everyone would be up soon. Heartsongs began to drift toward her, followed by chatter, and she sang a shielding charm in her mind, trying to muffle the heartsongs before they became too overwhelming. Nerine motioned for her to hide, but Iolana was already diving under a table cloaked in a green cloth with vases of flowers resting atop. Nerine crouched by the table and whispered, "I'll get some food and be right back."

Nerine's heartsong faded with her footsteps, and Iolana's heart lurched with a strange anxiety in the calming girl's absence.

A large group approached. Still on her knees, Iolana pressed herself up against the wall, praying her silhouette couldn't be seen through the tablecloth. Heartsongs waxed and waned, blending together in a dissonant mixture of chords as more people passed through the hallway. Iolana's head ached and began to spin. Sometimes she could block out heartsongs, but when her anxiousness soared like it did now, focusing became nearly impossible.

Iolana crouched down, flinging a wild glance beneath the tablecloth, barely resisting the urge to dart from her hiding place to flee the barrage of heartsongs. So many melodies and harmonies clashing together in a rising discordance. As she held her head, her glance fell upon something several feet away, beneath another table on the other side of the doors, also overlaid with a green cloth. The something appeared to be a hook, jutting up from the floor.

Iolana braced herself, listening as the din of heartsongs ebbed and flowed, watching the shifting shadows of passersby. After a couple painful minutes, both heartsongs and footsteps had diminished. A few still approached from either direction, but with a deep breath, she took her chance, scurrying like a mouse from one table beneath the next.

She collapsed beneath the table, breathing heavily, trembling. When no hands snatched at her to drag her out, she softly hummed a favorite melody to regain her composure. Few enough heartsongs lingered now that she was able to silence them with her mind-shielding charm.

Then, finding the small, iron hook, she grabbed it and pulled, gasping as one of the floor's tiles slid aside with a squeak. She froze, equal parts mortified and thrilled. Perhaps this might lead to some secret part of the mansion that could hold the key to a way out. If not, it at least alluded to the fact that the mansion may have other such secrets to explore.

Ever so carefully, she slid the tile open a little at a time, tensing every time it scraped sharply and listening for the next small wave of people to pass by. At last, she had opened a space large enough for her slight frame to slip down inside. The dim light beneath the table illuminated a stone staircase hewn against one wall, spiraling down into darkness. She lowered herself through until her feet touched one of the steps and then dropped down. Cupping her hands, she sang her *Luma* spell softly, and a ball of light glowed from her palms. Stepping carefully, she descended the stairs, using the light to guide her path.

After descending deeply, her feet at last found level ground, the end of the stairs. Darkness engulfed her, and she almost bolted back up the steps. Darkness held enemies jumping out and snatching at her in the nightmares Samil had once assailed her with. As fast as she could, she sang several more balls of light into existence and flung out her hands, singing another series of notes that sent the balls of light bouncing about the room. Keeping one of the lights cupped in her hands, she wandered her new surroundings.

She stood in a wide circular room ringed by cells formed from thick iron bars. The cells' doors were thrust wide open. She wondered if the Mass had perhaps kept prisoners here.

Iolana wandered over to one of the cells and stood in the doorway. Her stomach churned as more memories flashed before her, as if the cell were a living, breathing entity with its own heartsong that could evoke such visions. She saw herself being tortured, burned, and thrown into a cell half this size with nothing but stale air for food and cold stones for a bed.

She turned to head back upstairs, but a noise made

her linger, the subtle whistling of a breeze. Its coolness brushed ever so softly against her skin. Wind could mean a way outside.

Slowly, Iolana crept inside the cell. She flung a glance over her shoulder, half expecting its door to slam shut and seal her inside. When it didn't, she walked forward, exploring. No heartsongs reached her here, no traces of human presence.

However, a different sound flowed subtly to her. It sounded almost like water. She felt the walls and knocked on the stones. Her knock turned hollow and echoing in one spot, and as her hand pressed one of the stones, the back wall shifted to reveal a smaller room beyond. Empty shelves lined the room, and on the far side, an opening formed close to the floor. Perhaps a sort of tunnel or conduit to a sewer.

A heartsong approached Iolana. Stepping back from the secret room, she pressed the same stone as before, and the wall covered the room once more. She would return here later to explore the tunnel beyond.

Moments later, Nerine stood behind her, whispering, "Wow. You found it. It took me *ages* to find this place."

"It's strange," Iolana muttered, "finding a place like this in a school. Maybe that's just my fate, to be surrounded by iron bars no matter where I go."

"You were kept in a place like this?" Nerine's wide eyes gleamed with shock and compassion.

"I did stay in a cell like this. It was so quiet. This quiet is different. Peaceful. This would make a suitable hiding place for us. It could be our secret."

With a smile, Nerine said, "I would like that." She held up a small bundle wrapped in cloth, unfolding it to reveal two large pieces of bread with poached eggs.

"Here. It's not as much as I'd hoped, but I didn't want to look too suspicious."

"It's perfect." Iolana snatched a piece of bread with the egg, eagerly devouring what proved to be one of her best meals since she could recall. Not only was she starving, but she shivered as the room's draftiness began to cut into her, and her feet numbed on the cold stone floor. Nerine ate quickly too, seeming to understand.

With a curious glance at Nerine, Iolana asked, "Don't you have classes to attend? Or friends who will be missing you?"

Nerine shrugged. "Classes don't begin for another hour or so. And…I haven't really made any close friends yet. It's difficult for me. I traveled with my parents all my life. I'm not used to people my age."

"But you're talking to me just fine."

"You are a few years older than me, at least. And you feel different than most people our age." Nerine studied her pointedly while adding, "Besides, if I've been lonely and in need of a friend, I figure so have you."

"Yes, that's true."

As they ate, Iolana watched Nerine with interest. They were only three years apart, and yet the Nymph's sweetness and naivety made her feel younger. Iolana would have to keep her guard up. Manipulating the girl would be easy to do, and she didn't want to take advantage of her or place her in any real danger.

After the meal, Iolana led the way from their secret place. For a while, they crouched beneath the table in the hall, listening as waves of students passed by. Heartsongs assailed Iolana, making her head reel again. She needed to get away from the noise as soon as possible.

"Let's just step out," she whispered close to Nerine's ear. "If we act normal enough, no one will even notice."

Nerine looked concerned but nodded, following Iolana as she listened for a small gap in the sea of heartsongs and emerged from beneath the table.

Students walked away from the table on either side in small groups. Each involved in their own conversations, none seemed to notice Nerine and Iolana. Their chatter wasn't as loud as Iolana had thought. But the sound of their voices seemed to expand as so many heartsongs churned like waves seeking to choke her.

She started down the hall, Nerine trailing behind.

"Hey, what're you doing?"

Iolana whirled. A boy had just stepped from the stairs that wound up to the second floor. A host of other students descended the stairs after him, watching Iolana and Nerine with curious stares. Iolana inwardly scolded her foolishness at stepping out so quickly. Curses on the heartsongs clouding her judgment, as ever.

"Good morning, Sion," Nerine chirped in her cheery voice, clearly trying to smooth things over for them.

"What were you doing under the table?" Sion advanced closer, and Iolana threw up a mental shield. This boy looked as young as Nerine, but that didn't make him trustworthy. Most of the boys she'd encountered living with Samil had only ever been after their own gain. Besides, deciphering his heartsong to test it in a sea of so many was impossible. Her anxiety mounted, and she wished Nerine would pull away and stop ogling the boy like a drunken idiot.

"Oh, I had dropped my quill on the way to class, and we were just trying to retrace our steps and find it. You know how clumsy I can be," Nerine added quickly with a roll of her eyes. Iolana cringed, hoping she wasn't overacting.

Sion gave a friendly nod and smile at Nerine, seeming to accept her story, before turning a skeptical glance to Iolana. "You're that new girl from the healing wing. Should you be out of bed?"

"I really don't think that's your business," Iolana

snapped, taking a defensive step forward.

Sion threw his hands in the air. "I didn't mean to pry. I was only wondering if you're all right. If you need any help getting back upstairs."

"Why would I want your help? I don't know you. Better yet, you don't know me. Why offer to help a complete stranger? What do you know about me?"

Sion looked stunned, as did Nerine who reached out a hand toward Iolana. "We should really head back…"

Iolana wrenched away and marched forward.

"I asked you a question, *boy*."

"I—I'm sorry. I don't know anything about you. I only meant to help—"

Iolana's emotions spilled over, and she let the dissonant melody slip from her lips. A wild wind swirled around her and then surged forth.

The boy slammed back onto the floor and slid several feet, sending students screaming and darting out of the way.

Iolana approached the boy who half-scrambled to his feet before tripping and falling back down. He scuffled backward across the floor, eyes wild with fear. Several students cast gusts of wind or water in Iolana's direction, and someone threw a small bolt of electricity, but Iolana sang a repelling charm to dissipate their pathetic attempts at defense.

Iolana stood over the boy. He sat pinned against the bottom step of the staircase, breathing hard, staring up with hands raised, silently begging mercy. Satisfaction swelled inside Iolana. This boy, this ignorant little fool, thought he could trap her or pry whatever information from her. He thought he was superior, but he was nothing. He wouldn't hurt her. *No one* would hurt her again. She raised her hand back, prepared another spell—

"Iolana, *stop*!"

Nerine grabbed Iolana's wrist and held it with surprising strength. Iolana fought her at first, determined not to let her enemy escape with his life. But then heartsongs assailed her once more, some angry, others frantic and pleading.

Iolana stumbled dizzily as she broke from her reverie. The hall was just a hallway. Not one of Samil's torture chambers. And this boy was no spy. He was as innocent and terrified as Nerine.

Trembling at what she had prepared to do, Iolana let her arm fall and motioned for the boy to leave. "Just go. Now."

Sion staggered to his feet and fled around the corner out of sight.

Iolana turned to face Nerine, who stood staring at her uncertainly. A new fear shone in her eyes, and Iolana hated that she was its creator.

More frantic heartsongs floated toward them, and then Lea stood in the hallway alongside a Forest-footer man with brown curly hair. Both stared at Iolana wide-eyed. After a moment, the man nodded. "Yes. She is definitely a heartsong seer. And perhaps much more. Call her over."

"Iolana," Lea said, "please come here."

Iolana studied the man a long while. Her mind was too flustered to examine his heartsong properly, and she turned a desperate gaze to Lea, who made a beckoning motion with her hand. Iolana started forward, her gaze locked on Lea's, needing her reassurance, but her stomach dropped when she found anger brewing in the teacher's eyes. As they all wandered into a nearby, empty classroom, Iolana found her mind scrambling for any defensive and offensive charms she had ever learned, needing to be prepared, just in case.

"Iolana." Lea spoke her name not unkindly, but with

a sternness that made her shiver. Surely, after their previous conversation, Lea would not treat her harshly as her captors had done in the past. "I know you have been through an ordeal. I know you must be frightened and overwhelmed. But you cannot attack other students, especially considering that some, like Sion, are Lateborns who do not yet possess the magic needed to defend themselves."

With Lea's every word, Iolana could feel the symbolic noose tightening around her neck. She couldn't afford to lose Lea's trust faster than she had started to gain it. She couldn't afford to lose this opportunity of safety and education. "I didn't mean to harm him. He was asking questions he had no right to ask, and I got scared."

"He only asked if you were okay. He was concerned about you."

Iolana flung a glance at Nerine, shocked but admittedly impressed as the timid girl defended Sion. Nerine looked away, seemingly ashamed for shedding any negative light on Iolana.

"I am disappointed to find you out of your bed at all." Lea's voice was solemn, like Iolana imagined any teacher's might be when protecting her students from harm, but Iolana couldn't help hearing harshness more than mere firmness. "You are still healing, and what's more, we don't know much about you yet, about what your magic is capable of, if it's safe to keep you around. It's not just us who must gain your trust, but you who must gain ours. If anything like this happens again, we may be forced to remove you from the school, or at the least place you under closer guard."

The idea of being abandoned or imprisoned again snapped the feeble threads holding Iolana's emotions in check. Her tears flowed, and she collapsed into a heap of sobs.

"I'm so sorry. It won't happen again, I swear. Please don't send me away. Help me. I need help controlling my magic. The heartsongs are too much and I can't always handle them, block them out. Please, please don't send me away...."

Arms closed around Iolana, and she glanced up, recognizing the auburn hair of the woman who'd crouched down, drawing her into a close embrace.

"It's all right," Lea said, her voice softened. "There's no need for such upset. We'll help you as much as we can. We're not sending you away, dear girl."

Lea's voice broke then, and Iolana felt her entire being calm as she realized the woman's empathy and compassion. Her sobs quieted, and she embraced Lea even harder. It had been so long since anyone had held her. Being held like this freed her in a way only one other person had ever been able to.

"All right," Lea said, gently drawing back. "Drewit here is a dear friend of mine. I promise you can trust him. Let's go talk together. Nerine, I'll speak with you in my office after your last class of the day."

As Lea led Iolana after Drewit, Iolana glanced back over her shoulder at Nerine. Nerine still looked bewildered but, despite the fear Iolana had struck inside her, the affectionate, admiring way Nerine watched after her did not lessen. She was a true ally indeed.

CHAPTER 15

TAKING NOTES

Gailea, Drewit, and Iolana gathered in Gailea's office. The subtle fragrance of moon blossoms hung in the air, helping to subdue Gailea's nervous energy as she examined the girl sitting in the chair across from her and her fellow teacher. Drewit had studied Iolana for some time, humming gentle tunes and returning her curious yet cautious stare with his own deep watchfulness.

At last, he spoke. "Hearing heartsongs is not unique to being a musical mage. It's one of the rarest magic gifts, to be sure. But various types of magic wielders have been known to possess it. Do you know if you have any other musical magic, or just the heartsongs?"

"I know several song-spells," Iolana said, keeping her sharp gaze fixated on Drewit. She clutched the sides of the chair, looking emotionally overwhelmed. "Charms of offense or defense. I used a song to throw back that boy in the hall. I'm not very good at the shielding spells. The heartsongs are usually too overwhelming for me to block out. But Samil did what he could, to research songs to teach me. Songs he wanted me to use against his enemies. Though, I often refused any time he wanted me to torture someone."

Gailea and Drewit exchanged an uncomfortable glance. Iolana spoke with such ease about such terrible things. Gailea supposed that wasn't out of place, considering such horrors had been part of the girl's natural, everyday life. Still, it set her nerves on edge, reminded her of her estranged husband's mind—brilliant, but always straddling the line of taking his powers too far. Eventually, the horrific had become mundane and commonplace for him as well. She supposed the difference was that while Ragnar had embraced and created such atrocities, this girl showed strength in continuously resisting them. She yet had a chance to grow into something beyond the circumstances she had been thrust into.

"...I said your flute, Lea. May she?"

Drewit's words jolted Gailea from her deep memories. She drew the double crystal flute from her desk drawer and held it out to Iolana. The girl turned it over in the sunlight streaming through the single window. As it shimmered with rainbow hues, she stared and cradled it with all the carefulness of someone holding a newborn baby.

"It's breathtaking...."

"It is a rare and special gift," Gailea said. "All of the Guardians have their own instruments hewn from Icean crystal."

"The Guardians?" Iolana continued to study the flute wih a curious frown.

"The Octavial Guardians are a council comprised of eight musical magicians, including myself and Drewit. As for you, have you ever played a flute before?"

"No. But Samil let me play other instruments, though only a few."

"Well, see if you can play this one now."

Iolana studied the woodwind closely, as if it possessed a heartsong that she tried to decipher. Lifting the flute to her lips, she blew a long, clear note. She crafted a short melody which soon transformed into a longer, more passionate tune.

The more she played, the more deftly her fingers danced along the instrument. She squeezed her eyes shut, and her brows dipped in concentration as she conveyed the emotion of the song. Sad to hopeful, longing to triumphant.

Gailea's heart beat wildly, overcome by the robust emotions thrust upon her. She glanced over at Drewit, whose face reflected the same shifting exhilaration, mourning, anticipation, victory. They both sat spellbound, trapped by the emotions Iolana wove with her music.

At last, her song ended, and she lowered the flute. Drewit's face reflected awe as he said, "You indeed are gifted. Who knows what other talents may be revealed through proper training and practice? You say Samil taught you other song-spells, mostly for attacking or defending?"

Iolana faced him again. "Some, yes. Other song-spells, I learned myself."

"You'll learn much more here. How to use and control all sorts of musical spells. And how to foster that heartsong talent of yours."

Iolana shifted in her seat. "My heartsong skills are strong enough."

"But not *controlled* enough. Not if you're finding them so overwhelming. A trained seer doesn't find themselves bombarded constantly. They're able to tune out heartsongs and choose only to listen to them at will. And with a person's permission, of course." He added the last bit with surprisring sternness, but Gailea felt grateful. It was obvious that Iolana held little regard for boundaries when it came to protecting herself. Gailea couldn't blame her, but nor could she justify such actions, having experienced the damage that prying into another's mind and emotions could do.

"Your magic lacks focus," Gailea added. "You would agree that your behavior against the boy in the hallway was hardly controlled?"

"No," Iolana muttered, downcast. "It wasn't. I couldn't distinguish his heartsong among the others."

"That's perhaps the most trying aspect of being a heartsong seer," Drewit said. "I'm still learning myself. Forgive me, Iolana, but I couldn't help but read some of your own heart, its song was playing so vehemently. You're a strong young woman, fueled by much passion. And what you learn here can make you even stronger."

Iolana inhaled deeply. "I'd like nothing more. And thank you for the compliment. But any strength I have comes from Amiel. If not for my faith in Him, I think I would've lost purpose and given up long ago. I know there must be a reason why everything that happened with Samil brought me here."

Her gaze locked fervently with Gailea's.

"I *do* hate Samil," she continued. "I hate him with every fiber of my being. But it's for the love of those I saw sacrificed, as well as those I left behind, that I want to fight for." She hesitated before adding, "Do you think... do you think I *can* help them someday? Avenge them? Do you think I can use my music to help others, just as Samil used it to hurt them?"

"Musical magic is tied strongly to a person's blood, heart, and soul," Gailea said. "You must be born with it. You cannot learn it through other means. Yours is a true gift. And I think that with the proper tools, you can certainly use it to overcome the evil you've fled. A war is coming. Samil has started gathering allies to himself, while creating others through his mind manipulation. Loz is making preparations for war. When it comes, I believe you'll be more than capable and ready to join the fight."

"And we'll help you," Drewit said. "I can start teaching you how to better hone your heartsong skills, how to control them, to reach out and hear individual, specific hearts, and also to block them and choose not to invade another's privacy. If your faith is important to you, then remember that it's only Amiel who should know what's inside everyone's heart."

Iolana nodded slowly and watched Drewit with intent, seeming to carefully absorb and process his words.

"I'll set you up in some of our other classes at once," Gailea said, smiling at the girl whose face shone with a determined readiness. "I'll talk to the Headmistress, but I think she'll forgive how late in the year you're starting. I can give you any private tutoring needed."

"I'd be glad for that," Iolana said. "Very glad indeed."

~*~*~

Iolana followed Nerine down the music hallway, a stack of papers in tow.

A couple of months had passed, and Iolana continued to heal, both outside and within. She took several music classes, including all Lea had to offer, and Lea's classes provided a refuge that she highly treasured.

She'd happily joined a weaponry class with Tress and had also taken on a Lozolian history class and private tutoring lessons on mathematics and writing with teachers Cameron and Laina respectively. Iolana could do simple addition but had never been granted the opportunity to receive much education on mathematics. She could read fairly well, as Samil had insisted that was an important skill, but her writing skills hadn't been given much attention either.

Iolana found the work challenging and, at times, frustrating, but she perservered, knowing it would all serve her in the end. Not to mention having next week's excitement to keep her motivated. Lea would set sail to Labrini with the other Guardians for the celebration honoring the fortieth anniversary of the Seven Kingdoms' peace treaty. Nerine and the rest of Lea's choir would attend, to sing their own special music.

At first, Iolana had worried at the idea of the Guardians gathering all in one place and for such a public spectacle. What better opportunity for Samil to plot some deviousness?

But Gailea had assured her that the Guardians had carefully thought through the plan and that they, along with the Lozolian Council, would be shrouding the Labrinian theatre with all manner of protective charms, preventing anyone entering or exiting without the Echelon guard knowing. What was more, the Guardians traveled under the guise of being simple music teachers from the Lynn Lectim Academy. Samil might have spies anywhere, but thus far the Echelon's spies had not found any indications that Samil knew of the Guardians' existence.

Once these fears were satiated, Iolana had implored Lea to let her come along. After getting approval from Lynn, Lea had agreed to take Iolana, provided she kept up with her studies.

In the meantime, Lea had assigned Nerine with the task of transcribing a few last songs for the celebration. The Guardians had no need for the sheet music, but some of the less seasoned students did.

Nerine led Iolana into their favorite practice room,

which housed an old harpsichord. They sat on the bench together, Nerine set one of the songs on top of the harpsichord, along with spare parchment, ink, and a quill, and they set to work scribbling staffs, notes, and other musical marks across the page.

After vigorously working a few minutes, Nerine paused to rotate her arm, groaning softly, face twisting with discomfort.

"Still sore from practice with Tress?" Iolana asked.

"Yes, but I'm finally improving at swordplay. I think she pushed me harder than ever today, but it was worth it."

"Always is with Tress." Aside from Lea and Drewit, Tress was one other teacher whom Iolana not only respected but had come to really like. It was clear that Tress knew what she was doing, and Iolana admired her passion for teaching anyone and everyone, regardless of age or sex, how to defend themselves.

After stretching her arm, a bit more, Nerine resumed her transcribing work, and Iolana marveled at the grace with which Nerine's quill dashed across the paper. She hadn't known much about notation, but Nerine had been eager to show her. The two of them had been working hard over the past couple of weeks and were nearly done, all thanks to Nerine's efforts.

Iolana pulled her own stack of parchment into her lap, dipped her quill into ink, and began carefully transcribing another of the songs. For her, the work was painfully tedious. At times, she was forced to cross out several lines and start over.

Finally, with a growl, she slammed the parchment down. Nerine's quill still flew, and she focused so closely that her nose nearly touched the parchment. Transcribing songs was like a second language to Nerine, as detecting heartsongs was for Iolana. Iolana might have found the work equally simple if Lea had allowed them to use her charmed quills, but Iolana hadn't been able to persuade Lea in this instance. Lea had rather insisted that it was important for them to learn by hand, to truly understand the techniques before using magic to complete the task.

"I wish *my* mind could work that way!"

Nerine glanced up, and Iolana grumbled, "I keep fumbling over the notes, all the little sharps and flats. It's one thing to hear the music. It's another to apply it to paper."

Nerine smiled gently. "Just give it more time. You'll catch on."

"Maybe, with you as my teacher. If Lea had left the task up to me alone, I'd have the whole school singing a disaster. You're so talented when it comes to music theory."

"Just as you're talented with your song-spells." Nerine looked quizzical, and Iolana mentally prepared herself. Nerine rarely asked questions, but sometimes her curiosity got the best of her. She could clearly read the desire on Nerine's face, the urge to connect with her in whatever way possible.

"May I ask...may I ask *how*? How you do it? Sing that way? Command such attention with your voice?"

"Mika taught me," Iolana replied softly, her heart shuddering with longing.

"The one you were in love with."

"*Am* in love with." Iolana's gaze sharply met Nerine's. "I know he's still alive. That's why I have to learn as much as I can. I have to be ready. When I go back, I'll only have one chance...."

Nerine's face clouded with concern. "You talk a lot about going back. When you do, would you do so alone?"

"You wouldn't want to come," Iolana said flatly. "I

wouldn't let you. It's no place for you. It's not safe."

The worry in Nerine's gaze intensified. Iolana hated to see her that way. She relied on the girl for comfort and strength, to be her ray of joy when she needed it most. She wondered if she might place too much pressure on the poor girl, but it was difficult not to. Nerine was always so eager and willing to be there for her.

"I'm sorry if I'm so cynical at times. Bitter." Iolana sighed and put down her quill. "I try to help it, but it's hard. I've seen many friends die, others imprisoned. When Mika came along, I clung to him fiercely. I needed him like a drunkard needs strong drink. If I get too wrapped up in thoughts of Mika or talk about going back, I'm not trying to worry you. It's just what I need to do."

"It doesn't worry me," Nerine said, even as the tremor in her heartsong revealed the falseness of her words. "Well, we'd best get back to finishing these." She turned and resumed furiously scribbling across the parchment.

After two more painstaking hours, Iolana had finished one song, and Nerine the final three.

Once they gathered their parchments, Iolana followed Nerine from the music hallway into the adjoining choir room. Nerine rapped lightly on the door to Lea's office, and Lea beckoned them in.

The teacher greeted them, adjusting her spectacles, and Iolana held out her stack of the music. "We finished the songs you asked us to transcribe."

"Here they are," Nerine said with a beaming smile.

Lea took one of the songs from Nerine. Her gaze darted swiftly across the page and then widened in obvious pleasure. Iolana felt a small sense of pride for her friend, especially as Lea said, "Exquisitely and flawlessly done, Nerine. Exceptional work as ever." She flipped to the next page, continuing to scrutinize the notes.

"Nerine did most of the work, as you can see," Iolana said. "I was lost without her."

"Yes, well, that's why we each have our own talents. Speaking of which,Iolana, this piece. I've been meaning to show it to you. Since you'll be attending the celebration, I thought perhaps you'd be interested in singing something? I've already cleared it with Lynn and your healers. Come, look. It has the loveliest harmony at the end."

Iolana wandered forward to read the music over Lea's shoulder. Lea began to sing in her soothing alto, and Iolana soon chimed in with her high, clear soprano, shivering with delight at the beautiful harmonies formed by both their voices and heartsongs.

As they sang, some slight movement made Iolana glance up to see Nerine lay the remaining stack of papers on Lea's desk. She glanced at Iolana and Lea with a sort of longing before exiting the room.

Guilt gnawed at Iolana, but she shoved it aside and kept singing. She had as much right to Lea's attention as Nerine did, perhaps more. Lea alone understood Iolana's pain, and Iolana needed her too much right now to share whatever care and attention the older woman was willing to offer.

CHAPTER 16

THE LAST MUSICIAN

On the sultry night of the celebration, the Octavial Guardians gathered backstage inside the grand Labrinian Theatre, housed inside the Labrinian Palace, minus Lorelei, of course. At least she had finally been able to send a message through one of the Echelon spies. She continued to search Carmenna for the heir and returned often to Pakua, Carmenna's last free stronghold, for reprieve and replanning.

Gailea peeked out from the curtain. She had just finished leading the Lynn Lectim Academy choir in their finale. As they filed behind the curtain on the opposite side of the stage, a Labrinian nobleman stood to make some announcement.

"Are you all ready?" Gailea asked over her shoulder. "It's nearly our turn."

Bernhard grumbled, pulling at the collar of his doublet. Labrini had graced the male Guardians with blue satin doublets stitched with silver thread, and the ladies with blue satin, silver-trimmed gowns. "I'm surely ready to leave behind this ridiculous kingdom with its hellish heat."

"Hush," Valarie scolded. "You're only so hot because we're behind this stuffy curtain. The Labrinian palace has been decently cool."

"Cool for a desert. Not for someone accustomed to living by the ocean."

Elya snorted as she patted her purple hair, pinned up off her neck. "The Meleeón Isles are as hot as any desert and thoroughly surrounded by beaches."

"A beach and a desert are rather alike, aren't they?" Marger remarked, her silver eyes sparkling with whimsy. "A desert is like a huge beach, just without the water." She shared a grin with Egan, all the while helping him tune the strings on his vielle.

"There's no point to a beach without water," Bernhard muttered.

"Perhaps not, but the young lady makes a solid point with her parallels. Many deserts once were seas or lakes or other giant bodies of water."

As this last voice registered with Gailea, she looked up with a wide grin, pleased to see Chamblin striding toward her, eyes twinkling as he sashayed in the most ridiculous way. The bow he took before her was long, sweeping, and equally ludicrous.

"Do stop all that nonsense, you silly fool," Gailea huffed, though she couldn't help smiling. "I'm so glad you could make it after all."

"Likewise..." Drewit walked up, strummed a final chord on his harp, and gave a satisfied nod at its tuning. "But aren't you meant to be in China again?"

"He is," Gailea confirmed. "But his trip was cancelled, allowing him to grace us with his jovial presence instead."

Chamblin shrugged. "Glad as I am to be here, the cancellation was a bit of a nuisance. We were quite a way out into the ocean when we received word from China. On a dull stretch of ocean at that. No mermaids, no Larimar, no sea monsters. It was entirely the most boring expedition, probably too boring to even be called 'boring.' Anyway, I decided that the next best plan was to come here and support you in your festivities."

"They're no mere festivities," Gailea corrected. "We're honoring a most sacred peace treaty, if you recall."

"How could I forget? The peace here may be only a few decades old, but what precious years those have been. My great-uncle was a Surpriser, you know, back before the curse was broken and everyone was still walking around half-man, half-beast. Uncle Mark was a fox-man, to be exact, which terribly disappointed him. He said he'd have preferred to be a bear. Family says I caught the travel bug after him, and—"

"Lea!" Drewit whispered from right outside the curtain. "Come on then. They've just announced us!"

Gailea hurried to follow the rest of the Guardians onto the sprawling stage, and the audience spanning the rows upon rows of theatre seats applauded with enthusiasm. People from each of the Seven Mainland Kingdoms had gathered for this special occasion honoring their peaceful union. The dark-skinned Labrinians, Anicleans, and Swalians dominated the audience, all hailing from the desert kingdoms and swathed in colorful linens, silks, and satins. A few sun-kissed representatives from the seaside kingdom of Muriel attended, along with several Guedappleaus diplomats sporting wild brunette curls and artfully embroidered leather tunics, and a handful of fur-clad Arabisians from the northern mountains. Even a few men and women from the airborne island kingdom of Abalino were present, with their snowy skin and hair and their elegant, white-feathered wings folded behind their backs.

Everyone wore an array of colors, made more fanciful in the glow of torches circling the theatre and the candlelight from the immense chandelier branching overhead. Velvet-draped seats rose all along the perimeter of the room. Gold and jewels adorned every inch of the walls. Layers of silk curtains hung on either side of the stage. Never had Gailea performed in such an elegant setting. The theatre's opulence reflected Labrini's status as the wealthiest of the Seven Kingdoms.

As Gailea and the other Guardians arranged themselves in a semi-circle facing the crowds, the sounds of scuffling and voices drew her attention to the left side of the stage. Iolana and Nerine shoved against each other, trying to get a clear view. Amused, Gailea nodded at the two girls, who waved before giving each other a challenging glare. At last, Nerine crouched down while Iolana peered over her shoulder and several other students gathered round.

Gailea glanced at the opposite side of the stage toward Chamblin, who nodded with an encouraging grin. He clutched the side of the curtain, bouncing on his feet like a small child about to watch a favorite play, and Gailea quickly turned her attention to her fellow musicians. He would have her laughing like a buffoon and making a mess of them all if she kept her sights on him.

Gailea raised her flute to her lips. Drewit, who stood to her left, gave a subtle nod, and the Guardians began to play.

The music soared, the "Butterfly Fantasia," a triumphant piece renowned on the Isle of Malachitess. Gailea played with enthusiasm, immersed in the beauty she heard from her colleagues' instruments, along with her own. She barely remembered that there was an audience. Before the music had begun, the crowd had murmured, coughed, and shuffled restlessly, but now everything was still. Everyone was transfixed.

A sharp pain jolted through Gailea's temple. Her breath faltered, and her fingers nearly slipped from the crystal flute. She retained control, but the pain persisted and again she fumbled, skipping a few notes. Valarie's gaze snapped in her direction. Gailea blinked, trying to indicate that she was all right. She'd been prone to headaches of late, what with all her classes, caring for Iolana, worrying over Lorelei....

Valarie missed a beat on her drums, frowning at the instrument as though it had conspired against her. She picked up where she'd left off with the song, only to miss several more beats. Egan and Marger glanced up at Valarie, clearly perplexed. But then Egan cried out and twanged a few unpleasant notes on his vielle, while Marger's horn seemed to wail rather than soar above the clouds as it usually did. The piece shifted from joyful melodies to a stormy rage of minor chords edged with doom.

Mortified, Gailea ceased playing and glanced about at her fellow Guardians. Drewit had stopped strumming his harp and looked just as baffled. The others continued playing, and the audience leaned forward, seemingly entranced. Some frowned, possibly insulted by this new rendition of a piece considered sacred among their allies. Some looked intrigued, others confused.

Again, pain sliced at Gailea's head, as sharp and destructive as an arrow piercing straight through her skull. Voices seemed to pour inside the invisible wound, subtle whispers, incoherent at first, but then they commanded her fingers and lips, trying to force them to play an utterly unfamiliar melody. Her fingers trembled, aching to reach for the notes, and her mind swam as she fought against whoever tried to enter it. After chanting a defensive song over and over, she had slammed up a mental shield, blocking the intruder. She scanned the room, and her gaze locked on a man who stood behind the curtain where Iolana and Nerine had been only moments before.

Gailea's soul screamed inside her. The sharp angular features of his face, his moon-white skin, his dark hair and darker eyes, all these features painted the image of a man she would recognize anywhere, in sleeping or waking nightmares.

Moragon stared at her. A bewildered recognition flooded his face before he flung another mental spell in her direction. She sang several spells beneath her breath, raising shield after shield. She would not let him enter. She needed to keep her mind free so she could protect her fellow Guardians, and the students, wherever they'd gone—and Chamblin! Where was he? Had Moragon taken all of them?

Valarie cried out and collapsed to her knees. Tears and sweat rolled down her face. Her fingers bled as she played jumbled rhythms on her drums, struggling against whatever command Moragon forced upon her and the others. Drewit raced toward her.

Egan's entire body shook and turned bright red, seeming ready to explode any moment. The others had grown pale and trembled. Marger staggered forward and fell, toppling right off the stage with a sickening crack, but she clutched her horn and played on.

The crowd gasped, shrieked, stared. Guards filed down the aisles toward the stage while some of audience members leaped over the stands and hurried over to help.

Moragon slammed a mental attack at Gailea so viciously that her entire body throbbed from the head down. Her fingers strained along her double flute, toward the octave notes he commanded them all to play, but with a mustering of all her will, she instead sang a counter-curse, *Gyféria Bin*, at the top of her lungs.

Moragon's spell rebounded, striking Drewit. Gailea's friend stumbled forward as if driven through with an actual sword. He staggered, wide-eyed for a moment, and then strummed the single, minor chord on his harp. One by one, the other Guardians followed suit. The chord built and swelled until the entire theatre rumbled with its might.

People shrieked, racing from the theatre. Bits of gilded rock tumbled from the ceiling. Guards shouted commands, ushering everyone from the theatre at once. The concertgoers trampled each other, flowing in choppy, uneven waves toward the doors. The Abalinos grabbed whomever they could carry and winged them from the room.

The Guardians played several more octave chords, perfectly in tune and just as eerie as before. All Gailea's concentration went to preventing herself from lifting the flute to her lips. She flung up another mental wall of defense.

The new chords emanated more violently throughout the theatre than the first, swelling to a deafening roar.

"Lea!"

Gailea barely had time to comprehend Chamblin's yell as he bolted across the stage, shoving her, and sending her flying, just as the roar of music morphed into an explosion of fire and blood.

Smoke and ash veiled the room like an eclipse. Screams deafened as the crowd continued to push against each other, desperate to evacuate.

Gailea coughed and sputtered, stumbling across the stage, shivering at the onslaught of shrieking and wailing. Blind within the cloud of debris, she dropped to her knees, feeling the floor for the other Guardians. Panic turned to denial. This could not be happening. This wasn't real. It was just some horrific dream.

As some of the smoke began to lift, Gailea froze. She stared out across the stage.

Her friends all lay dead.

Dead. Their bodies scattered at grotesque angles, their blood splattered on walls and the burning fragments of shredded curtains.

Chamblin was nowhere in sight. Had Moragon taken him hostage after all? Had he seen the man's passion in protecting Gailea, and now would use him as some bait or bargaining tool?

Bargain for what? Gailea thought as she squinted into the smoke and crawled across the stage, ignoring the pain of fallen rubble splintering into her knees and charred bits of wood burning her palms. *What else is left?*

Dazed, she dragged herself to each of the Guardians, listening for their heartbeats, checking their necks for a pulse. Bernhard and Elya had reached for each other at the last moment. Marger and Egan lay side by side, their heads almost touching. Egan's large eyes were frozen wide open, empty of everything but fear, and with a shuddering breath, Gailea closed them. Valarie lay with her arms spread wide, her brows knit in a last, fierce attempt to resist Moragon's spell.

Gailea glanced up, breathing hard, watching as the audience finished fleeing the theatre. She listened as their cries diminished. One small sob escaped her before her heart seemed to go entirely numb, uncertain what to feel or if she could trust the nightmare unfolding so quickly before her. She couldn't believe it, didn't want to believe it. All her friends, dead in the blink of an eye.

A shriek snapped her head up, and her tears released after all, blinding her as she scrambled toward the body at the front of the stage. Drewit lay on his back, eyes closed, as if he might have been sleeping. Gailea froze when a figure staggered onto the stage, wailing before collapsing at his side. Aislin, Drewit's wife. She sobbed loudly and crawled toward him, one hand clutching her round belly, the other trembling violently as it grasped Drewit's. She fell on his chest and wept bitterly.

Gailea wrapped a trembling arm around Aislin. She glanced at Drewit's face, as empty now of life and joy as it had been full just moments ago, and then wrenched her gaze away. She needed to be here for Aislin. She needed to comfort the poor woman through Drewit's death, but she couldn't do that without being able to deny that his death was devastating for her too.

"Aislin, we have to go." Gailea's voice tremored with her body. "Look, you're hurt." She nodded at the burn showing between the fragments of Aislin's torn sleeve. "We need to find you help."

"Look out!"

Arms grabbed Gailea and pulled her from the stage. Instinctively, she sang a defensive charm that sent her captor flying back. She whirled to see it was not Moragon, just a man wearing purple Labrinian robes. Two women had likewise grabbed Aislin and guided her from the stage, and none too soon. A smoldering beam of wood crashed down right where she and Gailea had been.

"Please, I can't leave him! Please, I need to be with my husband. Don't make me leave him!"

Aislin's screams chilled Gailea down to her soul. As several soldiers ushered her into the hall outside the theatre, she struggled to push against them to reach Aislin, but the crowd packing the hall had soon swallowed all sight and sound of her.

Instead, Gailea allowed the crowd to take her as

far from the theatre as they could. At last, the corridor branched off, and she slipped into an adjoining hall, so breathless that she feared she might pass out. She stopped, falling against the wall. After taking several deep breaths, her spinning mind settled on Iolana and Nerine. Had Moragon taken them, along with Chamblin? Was Iolana what he had come for? And what of the other students? Had they made it out safely, or had the explosion harmed them too? Still shaking head to toe, she forced herself onward, prepared to find another way back to the theatre to look for them.

"*Don't!*"

Gailea whirled as Lynn rushed up the hall toward her, several First Echelon soldiers dressed in dark blue on her heels. Gailea stared at her desperately, gasping, "The students..."

"Most of the students are fine," Lynn said. "We're trying to track down Iolana and Nerine right now, but I'm sure we'll find them."

Gailea practically felt her heart crumpling inside her. "And Chamblin?"

"We'll find him as well. But you cannot go back there. The Labrinians and Swalians are up in arms with each other. The latter think the Labrinians conspired to kill everyone as a sign of breaking the treaty. This chaos is exactly what Samil wants, and he'll use it as a perfect opportunity to target you, the one musician who—"

"Not Samil." Gailea's voice felt abruptly tight, and she choked out the next word: "Moragon."

Lynn stood stunned into silence. For once, her ever-placid demeanor looked shaken, and fear gleamed clearly in her eyes.

"Lea, what are you talking about? I understand if tonight made you relive past horrors from your time with Moragon, and I empathize with that. But before I found you, I and the Echelon were fighting off a rebellion of disloyal soldiers who clearly wore Labrini's emerald."

"His crest may be Labrinian, but his person is not!" Gailea grasped Lynn by the shoulders. "I saw his face, clear as you see mine before you. And he saw me. He was equally shocked to see me as I was him, but he recognized me. It was him. Samil is Moragon—"

Breathing life into this realization made Gailea's knees collapse beneath her. Lynn caught her, trying to steady her, but all Gailea could do was tremble and cry, "This is my fault. He looked surprised to see me, and yet what if that was just some act. What if he knew I was here? Maybe he was just shocked that I survived his attack. Oh, Lynn, what if I did this? Their blood—my friends' blood—is on me!"

"No, Gailea."

Gailea froze, her attention snared as Lynn called her by her true name for the first time. Lynn held her firmly by the shoulders, staring her in the eye. "Whether or not Moragon knew you were here, their deaths are not your doing. Neither will allowing yourself to be killed or captured justify those deaths. If Moragon and Samil truly are one, then that is all the more reason for you to flee. I may know your true connection to Moragon, but there are many more who know the stories he and Ragnar spun to work against your favor. In this panic, they could believe you conspired with him and kill you before the night was through. I will find the children. I will take them back to the academy. You must head to Pakua at once."

"Lorelei!" Gailea felt even sicker. Lorelei had shown such incredible bravery in returning to Moragon's realm, but at what cost? Now that Gailea acknowledged the truth of Samil's identity, she feared tenfold for the girl.

"Yes, Lorelei." Lynn kept her voice as level as she could, though Gailea could hear its strain. "Amiel willing, you will meet her there. At any rate, the Carmennans there will grant you safety if they know you are her companion and a Guardian. Idalin, Cenwin, escort Gailea to the stables." Two Echelon women stepped forward, and Lynn handed one of them a small, leather purse. "Take these coins and tell them Lynn Lectim has need of their fastest horses and carriage. Then, head due west, until you reach the ocean. Find a ship setting sail for Pakua, and if there are none, rent a boat, and don't stop until you reach Pakua." She turned then to Gailea, placing a hand on her shoulder. "Go, and be safe, my friend."

"The girls," Gailea pleaded. "And Chamblin—"

"We will find them, but you'll be no help or comfort to them if you're dead or...."

Time and space seemed to freeze around Gailea as a figure darted past in the adjoining hallway where the crowds had since thinned. Gailea took a few steps forward, brushing past Lynn. The figure backed up, and then Moragon and Gailea stood in full view of each other once again. Both Moragon and the soldiers following him wore Labrini's crest on their dark silver breastplates, a purple amethyst centered inside a golden sun.

Moragon flung his hands wide, and Gailea could feel his mental curse trying to claw its way inside her mind. Gailea sang a protective shield, pushing back against him, even as Lynn lifted her hands high, and light beams poured forth to create a protective shield.

The light sheathed Lynn but didn't reach Gailea. Gailea sang with as much intent and intensity as possible, but the pain and exhaustion from the night's ordeal started to ensnare her body as much as Moragon fought to ensnare her mind. Slowly, the poison of another curse dripped inside her mind as if through a sieve, *visions of her friends' dead and mangled bodies, visions of Chamblin wailing in pain that she hoped weren't true....*

The visions vanished so abruptly that she staggered back, mentally whiplashed. Shaking her head, she looked up to see that two of the Echelon now flanked Lynn, arms raised, extending the light shield so that it stretched between the corridor's walls, blocking Moragon and any attacks he might send toward them.

"Go, Gailea," Lynn groaned over her shoulder. Her face twisted in intense concentration, and sweat trickled down her face. Other of the Echelon braced themselves just beyond the light barrier, swords drawn, fire and electricity and other spells poised at the ready. Several of Moragon's soldiers rallied likewise around him. Lynn and the Echelon could only hold the barrier for so long. It would shatter, and then the two small armies would clash. Gailea must be long gone by then.

With a grateful nod at Lynn, Gailea tore herself away, flying down the hall. Idalin led the way while Cenwin followed behind Gailea. Gailea pushed herself forward numbly. She pictured the Myrtle Sprites who so bravely defended her and her children, sacrificing their lives. She hoped Lynn and the Echelon would not meet the same fate. She couldn't bear the idea of another soul dying on her behalf.

Idalin and Cenwin wound with her through a maze of corridors and stairs. Here and there, they had to fight through a skirmish between Labrinians and Swalians.

At last, they burst outside into the desert night. The sultry air had cooled, but Gailea still felt stifled. The two women led her across the courtyard to the stables, and the next few moments happened in a whirlwind. Gailea entered a carriage along with the Echelon soldiers. Their carriage burst forward, hitched not to a team of horses but to two, shaggy, whale-like creatures with long, spiraling horns that dove in and out of the sand in rapid arcs, pulling the carriage at twice the speed of any horse team. Gailea thought the creatures were called "sandwhals." Chamblin had prattled on about them once when relaying one of his many stories of the Seven Kingdoms mainland.

Gailea tried to focus on all these mundane details, the sway of the carriage, a glimpse through the window of the sandwhals' fur shimmering in the moonlight, the pattern of the stars gleaming bright in the clear sky, but nothing could erase the nightmare of her friends' murders from replaying over and over again, as freshly as though she was still in the theatre, reliving them anew.

As their carriage fled across the sand toward the ocean, the harsh truth struck Gailea that she was not returning home. The academy was no longer safe. Or rather, she was no longer safe for it. Her presence would only bring danger there, just as it had ever followed her and those she loved. It was likely she would never see any of the teachers or students ever again. This was good-bye, but without really getting to say it, just as with Ashlai and Merritt.

Grief crashed through her numb reserve, and she buried her head in her hands, sobbing bitterly. A hand brushed her arm, one of the Echelon, likely reaching out in concern, but she slapped it away. She couldn't stand to be touched right now. She was overwhelmed, forcibly confined to this small space with two strangers and her swelling guilt. Years ago, her affection for Tytonn, however innocent, had led him to be killed by the madness of his best friend. Her very existence had endangered her sister, Darice, and Brynn, her adoptive mother. In fleeing Ragnar, she had fled them too. She had abandoned her children, saving them but killing Ashden in the process.

Now, almost everyone she loved had been killed once again, and she was the cause of it. The truth seemed so plain now, Samil and Moragon being one, that she wondered if she truly had never suspected it, or if her mind had simply buried such a horrific possibility from surfacing, for her own safety and sanity. How she wished now that she had been aware enough to figure it out. Perhaps Moragon showing up and forcing the Guardians to play the Chords of Death could have been prevented. In the initial confusion, she hadn't recognized this ancient, powerful curse for what it was, but now, she knew. It was one of many songs she and the Guardians had researched, just as Moragon must have, before they had sealed away the tome containing it. Clever of him, to leave the tome behind, so that none would suspect that he had already gleaned from it.

She would not allow him another such chance to get the best of her. As soon as she reached Pakua, she would begin her plot for vengeance and justice.

CHAPTER 17

RESOLUTIONS

Iolana and Nerine raced down the Labrinian Palace's corridors, clutching each other's hands.

The moment Iolana had recognized the man falsely wearing Labrini's crest as King Samil, she had fled the theatre, dragging Nerine with her.

"Iolana, what's going on?" Nerine cried. "What did you see?"

An explosion rumbled from the direction of the theatre, and the entire corridor trembled.

The two girls picked up their pace.

They wove between the crowd shouting and pressing too close together. Guards rushed forth, trying to usher people out safely. The scent of smoke and ash fouled the air, making Iolana cough and want to retch. Too familiar. Too evocative of a deep pit glutted by corpses and the stench of her own burned flesh, newly remade.

"What about Lea?" Nerine choked, tugging on Iolana's hand.

Iolana whipped her head behind her, straining to catch a glimpse of what was happening inside the theatre beyond the waves of frantically escaping crowds. She saw only a sea of smoke.

"*Lea*," Nerine repeated. She squeezed Iolana's hand as if to bring her to a halt, but the crowd would not allow this. Panicked courtiers shifted constantly and pushed the two girls forward in their desperate attempt to escape, forcing them to follow their flow.

"They'll trample us!" Iolana shouted above the din. "I'm just as worried for Lea. But we have to get out of here first!"

"Why did you take me out of there?" Nerine demanded again. "How did you know something was about to happen?"

"I can't tell you now," Iolana said. "I will, but not now!"

"Labrinian scum!" someone shouted. The sound of metal against metal rang out, followed by culminating cries, shouts, and cursing. Insults flung back and forth in languages Iolana could not comprehend, but their tones were vicious, accusatory. A single voice let out a scream that ended in a pain-stricken groan. *Someone's been killed*, Iolana thought grimly.

The mobs went mad. Swords, fists, daggers, magic, people used whatever they could to fight one another.

Men and women rushed with children away from the disorganized battle. Others grabbed torches from the walls and spears from the decorative armor lining the hall. Blood and screams flew. Bodies fell, barricading their path.

Iolana weakened. Her legs shook and threatened to give out. She had seen this kind of horror. By now she should have gotten used to it, but never had, despite her years of service to Samil. She ducked low, weaving between the crowd, and tightened her grasp on Nerine's hand.

The bitter aroma of smoke overpowered. Nerine began to cry, tripping as they ran. This was no place for such a sheltered creature, for any living creature, good or bad. Iolana must get her away from here.

Iolana flung them around a corner. At the end of the corridor stood a man with a silver breastplate over his black tunic and a purple cloak. He and a half-dozen soldiers stared at something in the adjoining hall. The cloaked man raised his hands as if preparing a spell.

"*Samil*." Iolana clenched Nerine's hand so tightly that the girl cried out.

Samil flung a spell down the hall. A loud explosion sounded, making the entire hallway shudder. Iolana braced herself against the wall and held Nerine, who fell against her. Her head spun with a sudden, sharp pain. Though not meant for her, the mental attack had been strong enough that some of its energy had reached her, leaving her momentarily stunned.

When she regained her senses, she saw Samil fleeing down the hallway where he'd cast the spell. She noted the armor of the soldiers running with him, Labrinian silver and purple. But these were no Labrinians. Her glance caught a familiar face, and everything fell into place. These were disguised Carmennans.

The man she recognized, Reynard, was valued by Samil for one main reason, his skill in mass transport. Samil likely meant to transport back to Carmenna, but he must make it outside the castle for this magic to work.

Iolana wrenched away from Nerine and bolted down the hallway after them. Samil was heading back to Carmenna. Back to Mika. This was her one opportunity to return. She would get just close enough for the mass transport spell to encase her.

But she was distracted by sound of following footsteps. Whirling in alarm, she glared at Nerine. "Stay put! Find a way out, or somewhere to hide 'til the fighting is done!"

Iolana turned back just in time to see Samil and his men disappearing around the corner at the far end of the hall. Cursing beneath her breath, she broke into a sprint, pushing herself so hard that her lungs burned, begging air.

Samil and his men slipped around another corner. Iolana followed, careening down a wide set of stairs toward a pair of ornately carved, golden doors. As the doors shut with a hollow *boom*, a whiff of fresh, cool air met her. Beyond those doors lay Samil's path to freedom, and her path to Mika if she could make it in time.

Iolana stepped over several cruelly mangled bodies on the stairs. She paused just long enough to reach down and grab a dagger that its owner would never need again. Then she dashed outside, into the night.

At the bottom of the palace stairs, Samil and his men huddled close, faced away from her.

Iolana ducked behind a pillar and peered out. She could hear someone chanting. Reynard raised a stone that glowed a bright blue. They were preparing to complete the instant transport spell. All she need do was get close enough at the last moment.

The silvery blue aura radiating from the stone expanded, encompassing the entire group. Any moment now, the spell would be complete. Iolana hurtled herself from her hiding spot behind the pillar and fled down the stairs, dagger in hand.

Something knocked into her from behind, sending her sprawling into the soft desert sand. The dagger flew from her hand. Reynard's blue light intensified to a blinding brilliance, and Iolana struggled to stand. When she couldn't, she tried crawling toward its glow, grappling handfuls of sand in desperation, until the weight pressing against her nearly crushed her. She felt heavy as lead and unable to move no matter how much she scrabbled against the sand.

Only after the light faded was her body freed. She jumped to her feet, staring at the empty space where Samil and his men had stood only moments ago. Her heart sank. *Mika...*

"Iolana."

Iolana whirled in fury, expecting Nerine. Instead, she found herself glaring at Lynn Lectim, who stood gazing back at her, too calm and collected.

"Why didn't you let me go?" Iolana cried, her voice and body shaking. "I have to get back to Carmenna. My friend there needs me! I could've handled Samil. I could've stopped him, could've saved—"

"The time for that will come," Lynn interrupted. "But it is not now. You cannot stop him on your own. You know this."

Iolana clenched her fists. "I could. I hate him. I hate him with every fiber of my being. I would have rescued my Mika, had you not intervened."

Lynn said nothing. It was impossible to read anything beyond her stern expression, and Iolana realized that she could not detect the woman's heartsong. Lynn guarded herself well. This only deepened Iolana's frustrations.

"I think," Lynn said slowly, "that Lea would agree that putting yourself in such blatant danger would not have been the best course of action."

"We'll see what she thinks about that herself," Iolana snapped, marching forward. "Let me see her. Let me talk to her!"

"She's gone."

Iolana froze, fear crashing through her anger. "What do you mean she's gone?"

"King Samil knows she's here now. She's no longer safe. Not that she would have been anyway, as it's clear he wants all the Guardians dead. She's heading to Carmenna to find Lorelei, the only other Guardian now living."

The words struck Iolana like a fist in her gut. "The Guardians. They're all dead?"

Faces flashed before her, sweet Marger and Egan, compassionate Drewit, adventurous Elya, the stern but well-meaning Valarie and strong Bernhard.

"I thought you knew. That you saw." Lynn looked furious with herself.

"No. I ran with Nerine the moment I saw him. But... if this is true, you're letting Lea walk right into the realm of that madman?" Iolana practically spat her last words, trembling with mounting anger and anxiety.

"This is out of my hands," Lynn said. "For now, my job is to protect the school and all those within it, including you. Come. We sail back to the Academy at once."

Like a sentinel, Lynn waited for Iolana to follow. Iolana stared at her a long time, debating. It would do little good to try to run from the Headmistress again, not right under her nose. She sighed in exasperation and kicked at the sand. Then, she trudged forward, with Lynn leading the way around the perimeter of the empty courtyard.

Nerine stood right outside the double doors to the palace and soon fell in line beside Iolana. Iolana could feel Nerine staring at her and wished she wouldn't. She focused on the back of Lynn's head, almost wanting to rip it off for keeping her from doing the same to Samil.

"Iolana?"

Iolana inhaled sharply. She knew Nerine had never experienced anything like what had happened tonight and must be terrified. She knew that she should comfort the girl. But her mind was too intent on how she had missed her chance and what she could do to get another.

"Iolana, it'll be all right," Nerine said. "Lea will be fine. She's very smart and brave."

"I know," Iolana muttered.

"Do you think the fighting's stopped?"

When Iolana shrugged, Nerine went on. "It was horrible. Did you hear all those people, what they were saying? Everyone blaming each other. Blaming the Labrinians for betrayal, just like in old times."

"It wasn't them," Iolana snapped. "It was Samil. His men disguised themselves as Labrinians. Probably to make it look like they broke the treaty. It was just a diversion for him to escape. It was him. *All* of it."

Iolana took a deep breath and released it slowly. The mere mention of Samil's name made her shake with the rage radiating from her very core.

As they rounded the castle's outer wall and headed down a sloping, sandy hill toward a carriage, Iolana knew exactly what she must do.

It was time. No more waiting. Mika could not spend another moment in that monster's hell. She didn't care what Lynn Lectim thought she knew about Samil. Iolana knew much more, and on a much more personal level. She'd lost too many people she loved to Samil. She would not lose Mika, or Lea, for that matter. She would save them both.

CHAPTER 18

INTO THE WEST

The corridors of the Lynn Lectim Academy were silent tonight. Iolana made not a sound, creeping her way through.

Sunrise was only a couple short hours away. Over the past several nights, Iolana had observed the patterns of the new guards inside the school and had decided that early morning would be easiest for her to slip past them.

The closer Iolana drew to her goal, the more heavily the weight of her mission pressed against her. In Labrini, on that dreadful night, she'd wasted no time. She'd instinctively leaped after Samil to protect the ones she loved. Without thinking, without question.

Since then, she'd had too much time to question herself.

A wave of fear made her wish she'd asked one of her teachers, perhaps Tress, for some sort of counsel. But she knew what they'd say: It was too dangerous. She was being too reckless.

No. Asking for aid would only slow her quest, perhaps even halt it entirely. Both Mika and Lea were plunged into deeper danger with each passing moment. She must keep moving.

Iolana rushed down corridors, dancing around the guards' patterns. At last, she reached the sweeping stairs and crept down to the entrance hall. The closest guards weren't due to enter the hall again for a few moments. She'd have just enough time to reach the table, dive beneath it, and drop into the secret passageway.

"Wait!" a familiar voice whispered behind her.

Iolana froze on the bottom step but did not turn to face her friend.

"Iolana," Nerine said, now just above her on the stairs. "You're leaving, aren't you? You're going to look for Lea."

It wasn't really a question. Nor were Nerine's next words:

"I'm coming with you. I want to help too."

Surprise flitted through Iolana at what seemed a bold declaration from the girl, though one born of ignorance. Nerine didn't know what she'd be getting herself into. Iolana knew she should forbid her. Samil was no villain out of some children's tale. His savagery was warped, twisted, and very real.

But Iolana couldn't linger on the stairs, doing nothing. The guards would enter the hall any moment. She had no time for pointless debate or arguments. And Nerine wouldn't back down. The urgency in the girl's voice echoed Iolana's own. Nerine wouldn't take "no" for an answer that easily.

Without looking at Nerine, she nodded and continued forward.

They knelt and crawled beneath the table together. Iolana found the unobtrusive hook and slid the tile open. She disappeared down the hatch, Nerine following.

Iolana led Nerine downstairs and into one of the

open cells, illuminating the space with her light orbs. She felt along the cell's back wall until she touched the stone that was smoother than the others. She pressed it in, and the wall shifted to reveal the secret room beyond.

Iolana led Nerine inside and pushed another stone to close the wall behind them. Beside her, Nerine exhaled, staring at Iolana's treasure store in wonder.

The small room was stocked with ropes, maps, extra clothes and strips of fabric, wooden staffs, leather satchels, flasks of water—Iolana had made sure to refill them regularly to keep the water fresh—and all sorts of dried fruits and meats, separated into small pouches.

She began stuffing several of the preserves into two leather satchels. Nerine watched for a moment before asking, "Is there anything I can do to help?"

"Grab one of the larger linen sheets, a coil of rope, and one of those staffs."

Nerine rushed to obey. "Did you put all this stuff down here?"

"Yes." Iolana stuffed two water flasks each in the satchels, adjusting the food pouches to make them fit. She tightly folded a cloth and squeezed it inside. Then she secured the satchels shut, tossed one to Nerine, and set about helping her to choose a staff.

"What's it all here for?" Nerine asked.

"Just in case."

"In case of...?"

Nerine's voice trailed, and Iolana was glad. She was too distracted with assessing what they needed to answer unnecessary questions.

Iolana's gaze fell upon a wooden staff, which she snatched up. She had collected several to use as possible weapons, unable to procure any knives from the kitchen where it seemed someone was always working. Hefting a coil of rope around her shoulder as Nerine had done, she motioned her friend over to the room's far wall. Crouching, she pointed at the small, square opening near the floor. As they peered inside, it seemed to lead into black nothingness, but Iolana had explored the tunnel last week.

"If we follow this," she explained, "it'll lead us to a river beneath the school. There are two paths, both leading to the ocean. One path leads to the docks for merchant ships. We'd never be able to slip away there. People will be working already. Our best bet is with the other path. That'll take us to a bunch of small rowboats. They're usually unattended until later in the day. That's our path."

Iolana lowered herself all the way onto her stomach, prepared to crawl into the tunnel, when Nerine blurted, "*What* will be our path?"

Iolana hesitated at the apprehension in the girl's voice. Glancing back at her, she asked, "What? Don't you trust me?"

"I do," Nerine said, "but I think I deserve to know what I'm getting into before jumping in completely."

Again, Iolana paused. Every time she'd mentioned Samil in Nerine's presence, Nerine had seemed deeply uncomfortable, moreso since the Guardians' murders.

"Lea needs to find Lorelei. They're the last of the Guardians. She's heading to Carmenna already. And so are we."

"*Carmenna?*" Nerine's eyes widened with such frantic uncertainty that Iolana was sure she'd turn back.

Then she lifted her chin a little, probably in an effort to make herself as brave as she wanted to be. "All right. Let's go find Lea."

Iolana studied the girl a moment longer, worried but admittedly impressed by her determination. If this was Nerine's choice, then Iolana was glad for the company.

And Nerine's water magic might prove useful at sea.

She nodded and peered into the black crawlspace. "The way will be slow going with all these supplies. It'll be rough going, especially once we reach the water. Things will only get worse. Harder. More dangerous."

She gave Nerine a final questioning look, but her friend had already lain on her stomach, mimicking her. Iolana gave her a faint but genuine smile. She'd known few friends in her past, and most had been stolen from her, either through death or their own treachery. Nerine was the most loyal ally she'd had in a long while.

Iolana pulled herself into the narrow tunnel and began dragging herself along. "There are grooves in the stones that you can grab onto, help pull yourself through."

The stones beneath Iolana pressed icily against her skin, especially as her tunic kept pulling up. The rough stones scraped her stomach, arms, and legs, but the pain seemed negligible. She'd had to fight through far worse. The hardest part was trying to drag the wooden staff with her. She managed to keep the rope coiled around her back, and the satchel and cloth were easy enough to manage, but the staff kept catching on the stones, bumping her in the head, or poking her ribs. Gasps and grunts from behind indicated that Nerine faced similar challenges.

Finally, they came to a bend in the path, and a dim gray light appeared. Iolana's staff proved too long to fit around the corner. Thankfully, Nerine's was a little shorter, and they managed to wrestle it through.

Once around the bend, the faint gray light leading them strengthened a little. The path dipped steadily downward, and then, at last, Iolana felt the damp shock of cold water beneath her.

This meant they were almost free of the crawlspace

and could stand at last. Encouraged, Iolana pulled herself along with greater vigor, and minutes later, the small tunnel heightened into a sort of narrow corridor. Iolana got to her feet and helped Nerine, who already looked weary, but proud that she had been able to complete the first leg of their journey.

They sloshed through the shallows of the underground river. With a murmured spell, Nerine transformed her legs from her knees down into her water form to merge with the shallows. This seemed to rejuvenate her.

They had traveled several yards when they came to a fork in their path. The rightmost path led southwest to the docks where the giant ships were harbored. Workers flowed constantly between the port and the town. The left path would take them south to the quiet fishing port, where borrowing a boat would prove vastly less challenging. Iolana headed in that direction.

The gray light gradually brightened until, when they rounded a bend in the tunnel, the light of sunrise nearly blinded them. They'd reached the end of the river. Iolana motioned for Nerine and crept along the edge of the tunnel's mouth. The path ended at a cliff, fortunately not tall, where the river poured down in a little waterfall right into the ocean below.

Peering carefully out from the tunnel, Iolana observed several fishermen rowing back to shore in small sailboats, nets wriggling with fish. They had been out all night and would surely soon go inland to rest for a little while.

The sun had climbed above the horizon by the time the fishermen headed up the small hill and out of sight. Iolana couldn't hear anything over the rush of the waterfall, so she waited a few minutes more, just to be certain.

Then, after motioning again for Nerine to follow her, Iolana jumped over the cliff's edge and plummeted the short distance into the ocean. She sensed the strong pulse of Nerine's heartsong and turned back to see that the Nymph had shifted her entire body, as well as her clothes, into its liquid form. Her skin and hair flowed in nearly transparent rivulets that blended with the ocean's gentle waves. Only the shape of her face and eyes gave her away.

The two girls swam over to the rowboats. Iolana treaded low in the water, her head just above the surface, and peered around, scanning the shore as far as she could see. Spotting no one, Iolana clambered into one of the boats. She spied several nets resting on the floor and gave a satisfied nod. Her two requirements for the right boat had been a sail and nets to catch fish in. Iolana reached down, grasping Nerine's hand with a gasp. What a strange sensation, to grip water firmly, as though it was solid. Stranger still was how the water from Nerine's arm flowed around Iolana's hand and through her fingers like a cool stream.

Iolana pulled Nerine inside the boat. Then, she took the oars and rowed as quickly out to sea as possible. Nerine, who'd changed back to her solid form, placed her hands in the water and whispered a spell. Small waves pushed out from Nerine's cupped palms, and they picked up speed. Only when Loz was a faint line on the horizon did Iolana dare to let go of the oars to rest her weary arms and smile at Nerine.

"We did it."

Nerine released a long sigh as if she'd held her breath the whole time. Sitting back with a grin of her own, she said, "That was incredible. Now what?"

"Now, we sail, if we can figure out which direction we need to go."

"That's easy. Carmenna is northeast from here. The sun will tell us which direction we need to go."

Iolana's brows rose. Nerine may prove useful in more ways than she had originally thought. "When did you become such a master of navigation?"

Nerine shrugged. "I used to travel with my parents a lot, before coming to the academy. We would sail sometimes too. Here, I'll show you how to loose the sails, and I can control the rudder. We'll use the oars when needed, but hopefully we can get by without them."

Once more, Iolana felt both grateful and impressed as Nerine helped her loose and trim the sails, tying the lines in their proper positions, and then explained how she would turn the tiller to control the rudder below the boat and thus the direction in which they needed to go. After this brief lesson, Nerine set them on course and they sailed east, into the rising sun.

~*~*~

Four days had passed by uneventfully as they drove toward Carmenna.

Nerine dove out of the boat from time to time to catch fish for them to eat. She would turn into her water form, camoflauging to snatch the fish in the small nets. Toward the end of the sixth day, their fresh water rations began to run low, a problem exacerbareted by the sun's beating. Despite Iolana's best attempts to shield herself with the linen cloth she'd packed, the skin on her face and bare arms had begun to burn and peel. Nerine was thankfully able to replenish her strength and cool her skin by dipping her arms or legs into the water and absorbing the sea's currents. She had tried turning some of the salt water into fresh water to drink, but this magic had proven too advanced for her.

They would simply have to hope that Nerine was as capable in her directional skills as she had seemed thus far, and that land would show itself soon. Iolana wanted to keep trusting Nerine to lead them in the right direction, but her own voyage from Carmenna to Loz had lasted a mere three days, and that was in a more battered craft and without her being entirely sure of the way.

Iolana lay down in the boat, trying to rest, but the fears and doubts pressing on her mind often robbed her of proper sleep. They tugged at her mind now, steadily wakening her...as did something sharp and cold pelting her face over and over again.

A startled cry from Nerine made Iolana bolt up, wide awake. Her friend sat looking as dazed as she felt.

"Are you all right?" Iolana asked.

"Yes. Are *you* all right?"

Iolana nodded. Then, she noticed how dark it was and frowned. Had she actually slept that many hours? It had been mid-afternoon when she'd settled down for a nap, but she was as weary as if she'd taken only a two-minute reprieve.

Tiny flecks of icy spray bombarded her, seering her already-tender skin, and her frown deepened at the thick, black rain clouds. The wind picked up, and their small vessel began to rock. It wouldn't be long before the gusts of chilled air grew powerful enough to capsize the boat.

Iolana surveyed their surroundings. There was an island far in the distance. Their best bet was to turn the sails and fight for it.

A loud splash alerted Iolana. Nerine had leaped overboard, transforming into her liquid form. She clung to the side of the boat and swam hard, but as the wind picked up, it wrested the boat from her grasp. She began floating away, and Iolana panicked, but Nerine was strong enough to swim back and climb into the boat.

"I'm sorry," she said, panting, and returned to her usual appearance. "But the currents are too strong. I can't maneuver properly."

"It's all right," Iolana said. "We'll just have to ride it out, hope we can reach that island."

"I'll handle the rudder. Row as hard as you can. The wind's against us, but we'll have to sail into it anyway, with everything we've got!"

Nerine angled the rudder, driving the boat toward land. Iolana rowed vigorously, fighting the uneven waves as they grew choppier. The wind howled, and the next instant, a torrent of rain blasted from the sky. Iolana held firm to the oars and kept rowing, ignoring the intense cold and the weight of the rain pushing her back. The waves rose, pushing them higher and higher, but she fought on.

Suddenly, their boat spun, and Iolana whipped her head back to see that Nerine had abandoned the rudder and instead stood to her feet, gripping the mast to steady herself. Looking uncertain at first, she then aimed her fierce concentration at the water ahead. Iolana was about to shout and ask what she was doing, but then, amidst the madness, a song found Iolana's ears. A song flecked with fear but radiating courage and even hope.

Nerine focused on the waves. Her hair now flowed in waves of water that extended in long arcs down into the ocean. Her skin morphed into its liquid form, and she spread her arms wide, a great queen commanding the sea to be still.

They jerked forward, and Iolana fell against the side of the boat, staring up in amazement. The brutal waves now stretched away from one another, parting before her eyes to create high walls of water on either side of them. The boat rocked uneasily, and Iolana's awe turned to panic. Nerine's magic was impressive but still new to her, and the storm was picking up speed.

"Nerine, get down! I don't want you getting hurt!"

"I'm fine!"

The boat swayed. Iolana took up the oars, guiding it along the path Nerine had created. The island seemed so small and far away, but in clear view. Perhaps they would make it after all.

The song vanished, and Iolana's heart lurched.

Nerine tumbled inside the boat, landing with a hard thud against the wood. She didn't get back up, and a small trickle of blood ran down her forehead.

The waves sprayed mist into Iolana's face, blinding her. She could no longer see the island or anything else except a solid sheet of gray, cold water. The shadow of a giant wave loomed over them for a few terrifying seconds before it crashed down.

Black and steely blue surrounded Iolana as she twisted and turned, hurled in every direction as the ocean tried to rip her limb from limb.

Then it all ceased. The sea calmed itself, its waves no longer attacking everything in their path. Iolana broke the surface, sputtering and struggling to catch her breath. She spotted the boat yards away, upside-down. Nearby, Nerine bobbed in the water, clearly unconscious.

Iolana swam over and grabbed her friend. Holding her as tightly as she could with one arm, she fought to stay aloft with the other.

After what seemed a long time, the rain lessened just enough for Iolana to make out what she thought was the shore of the island not far in the distance. Perhaps it was just her imagination playing tricks on her, or perhaps Amiel had granted them some mercy in allowing the wild wind and waves to carry them in with the tide.

Perhaps Amiel had even sent the storm to push them closer toward their goal.

Relief flooded Iolana as they were borne up to the shore and slid onto the wet sand. Iolana dragged Nerine farther up the beach, where the tide couldn't reach her.

Then, exhausted, Iolana collapsed beside Nerine and closed her eyes, waiting for the storm to pass.

CHAPTER 19

MARK OF THE GUARDIANS

Nerine stirred from sleep. The chilly air was first to wake her with its shocking sharpness. Then the wet, hard ground beneath her amplified the cold.

Shivering, she opened her eyes and tried to sit up, but her limbs shook and ached all over. As her senses returned, she heard a soft crackling near by. Warmth now radiated toward her, not enough to erase the coldness gripping her body, but enough to tempt her into seeking it out.

Nerine sat up. She was on a sandy beach, still drenched from head to toe. The boat rested on the sand and appeared to be miraculously unscathed. When she turned away from the shore, she saw a thick forest rising in the distance. Just a few feet across the sand, a blazing fire roared on, its heat beckoning her.

Crouched by the fire, Iolana turned several fish on a sharp stick. Between her tunic's ragged appearance, her intense gaze, and her wild mane of hair that curled up like spiraling smoke, she looked like one of the heroes stranded on an island in the stories Nerine's father told. Nerine was impressed watching this brave, capable side of Iolana, but now that their sea journey was over, part of her felt small, out of place. Iolana had been through so much more than Nerine could ever fathom. She'd known this all along, but it was an entirely different thing to watch how natural it was for Iolana's survival skills to care for them both.

Carefully rising to her feet, Nerine walked over and knelt by the flames. The iciness slowly melted from her body.

Iolana's brows furrowed deeper, and Nerine worried that speaking might interrupt some important thought or plan.

But then Iolana blinked and glanced up. Her face softened with a tired smile.

"Glad to see you're awake. Are you hurt at all?" When Nerine shook her head, Iolana's smile widened. "That's good. Supper is done, actually, so you're just in time."

Iolana drew the stick-pierced codfish away from the flames. She set two fish on a large leaf and then wrapped the remaining fish in several other leaves, binding the package with what looked like seaweed.

She unfolded another leaf package, and Nerine's mouth watered when bright red berries gleamed up at her. They were huge, and she imagined how sweet they would be, but she'd never seen anything quite like them.

"How can you be sure they aren't poisonous?" she asked. The heroes in Father's stories always had to be careful about that sort of thing.

Iolana smiled again. "When I escaped Samil, I came across these berries in the woods. I was starving and I didn't much care if they were safe or not. If they were, great. And if not, then it was Amiel's time to call me to his spiritual Haven, and I wouldn't have to suffer or worry about starving anymore."

Awe stole Nerine's words away, and then she flushed, irritated by her own question. Of course, resourceful Iolana would have sense enough not to feed her anything she didn't know was perfectly safe.

Iolana portioned the berries between their two makeshift leaf platters and handed one platter to Nerine, along with one of their flasks of water.

"It's the only flask that survived," Iolana explained. "But there's a small stream not far inland where I was able to refill it. We can do so again before setting sail. Probably good to drink as much as we can before then."

Nerine thanked her and savored the food. The fish was especially flaky and delicious. And, as she'd predicted, the berries proved delectably sweet.

"You know," Iolana said as she tore into her meal, "what you did out there, your magic, that was amazing."

Nerine glanced toward the ocean, its waves still white-capped but far less tumultuous than during the storm.

"I'm sorry it didn't work. I just...I wasn't strong enough to hold my form against the storm."

Iolana took Nerine's hand. "Someday, you will be."

Surprised by Iolana's touch, Nerine looked down. "Thank you. That means a lot to me. I think I knew that the magic was beyond my capabilities, but I wanted to try." She glanced up again. "I'm sorry if I haven't contributed enough yet to this quest."

Surprise flashed in Iolana's eyes. "You've contributed more than your share. I'm sorry I'm not good at saying thank you. But I'm grateful you came with me, Nerine. You've not only been a great help and companion. You may have actually saved our lives, more than once. Your knowledge of sailing, for one. When I took a boat from Carmenna to Loz, I had no clue what I was doing. And then, with your magic. You may see it as a failure, but really, you did push us closer to the island."

Nerine smiled at last, allowing Iolana's sincere praise to sink in. "You were equally amazing. All of this, planning the escape, getting us to the island, finding and cooking the food...How do you know so much about surviving out in the wild like this? You've told me so little of your past. There's so much about you that I still don't know."

She studied her friend, hoping she hadn't asked too much while yearning for Iolana to open up and trust her, to let her in just a little more.

Iolana smiled at her, but the smile seemed strained.

"I'm sorry," Nerine said. "I really don't mean to pry."

"I know. And I appreciate that you don't often pry. And even though it was your choice to come along, maybe I do owe you some explanation, as my friend, for sharing this danger with me. Just...not now. I can't bring myself to tell you everything now. Not yet."

Perhaps not ever, Nerine thought, disappointed, but she understood. If whatever Iolana had been through was that horrible, Nerine wouldn't push her to relive it.

"You know," Iolana added, "I envy you too."

Nerine sat taken aback.

"You're still a girl," Iolana explained, "while I was forced to grow up, in many ways, far too quickly. I can no longer be given over to fancies and fairy tales. My faith in Amiel is very real to me, but it's the only truth I've been able to cling to. Life has shown me that men are cruel, and dreams are crueler. I've seen enough to believe that ignorance is true bliss. That's why I was hesitant for you to come with me. Your innocence, your sweet spirit...I admire you for these things, and I don't want you to lose them. I don't want you to change."

Nerine stared in astonishment. Iolana, strong and

stalwart, was envious of the exact traits Nerine had begun to wish she could exchange for some measure of
Iolana's toughness.

"Then I won't change," Nerine said, "unless it's for
the better." She shared an encouraging smile before adding, "So, the storm. Did it throw us too far off course?"

"No." Iolana's face brightened at the change of subject. "Actually, it might have helped us get closer faster.
See that island over there?"

Iolana nodded toward the thick, hazy outline of an
island on the dark sky's distant horizon.

"I *think* that's Carmenna...."

Nerine scanned the skies for some glimpse of the sun.
It shifted subtly between the lingering clouds. Judging
by its current position, Iolana might just be right.

"The way I see it," Iolana added with a grin, "we can
be there tomorrow."

~*~*~

As predicted, by the end of the next day, the island of
Carmenna loomed close against the backdrop of a star-
strewn sky. Jagged cliffs towered high like dozens of sentinels, and thick forests ruled the lower lands.

What Iolana couldn't have predicted was the thick
fog that descended as they rowed closer and closer toward shore.

The air was heavy with moisture, and Iolana felt dizzy. Nerine coughed and looked pale. At times, she'd dip
her hands in the ocean, trying to refresh herself, but this
seemed to do little good. Iolana began to panic. Was the
fog laced with poison?

Nerine seemed to guess her thoughts. "It's safe, but
there's some sort of spell or charm placed on it. Since fog
is moisture, I should be able to draw strength from it,

same as the ocean, but something is blocking me...." She was interrupted by a coughing fit again before catching her breath. "It's not natural. Maybe we should leave."

Iolana studied her friend with concern, sharing her suspicions. The fog had appeared out of nowhere. The day had been otherwise sunny. Maybe it was some cruel trick of Samil's. Maybe he'd discovered that they were trying to help Lea, and this was meant to halt them.

"I think you're right," Iolana said at last. "If I can figure out how to row us out of this mess, we could observe from farther out, perhaps find a place where the fog's thinner and approach from there, and—"

An abruptly blinding light silenced her. Shielding her eyes as best she could, she squinted across the ocean. The giant, shadowy outline of a ship approached, silhouetted ghostlike against the thick fog. The fog shimmered an eerie silver in the glow of a huge flame blazing atop the watchtower on deck. Someone shouted a word Iolana did not recognize, some sort of spell, and the flame's glow expanded, whitening like a lighthouse beacon and dispersing the immediately surrounding fog.

"Halt!" a voice shouted. "Go no further toward Carmenna! Row your boat to our ship, and we will bring you aboard."

Iolana glanced at Nerine, who sat very stiff, unable to conceal her fear. Iolana was uneasy at the newcomers, and yet they had little choice. This might be their only chance to be rescued from the fog. Iolana took the oars in hand, turned the small boat around, and rowed toward the ship.

Once their rowboat was alongside the ship, two ropes with loops at the end were cast down. Iolana helped Nerine slide her legs inside one of the loops and watched as her friend was lifted up, her frightened face soon swallowed by the fog. Iolana secured herself to the other rope and allowed herself to be pulled up.

No sooner did Iolana's feet touch the deck than she was surrounded by a crowd of men and women. By their tightly curled black hair and deep brown skin, she could tell they must be fellow Carmennans.

Someone clutched her arm, startling her, but it was only Nerine, huddling close and shivering. Iolana couldn't blame her. The mass of strangers watched them, their expressions demanding or accusing.

The crowd parted to let one man pass through. He was taller than most, thick muscles lined his arms, and his many tiny braids were plaited into a single, thick braid down his back. Like the others, he wore dark shades of gray, brown, and blue that blended with the fog, his skin, his hair, the night. His fierce eyes seemed to burn through the darkness, and Iolana shuddered.

"My crew tell me they saw two spies rowing toward Carmenna. They tell me you are these two spies. Is this true?" His voice was deep yet smooth, almost melodic. In other circumstances, Iolana might have thought it pleasant.

"We are no spies," she assured. "We come from the Lynn Lectim Academy on the island of Loz, in search of a missing friend of ours."

"Your names? And what is this friend's name?"

"I...I would rather not say. We believe she may have embarked on a task of special importance and secrecy."

The captain drew a long sword from beneath his cloak and pointed it straight at Iolana's heart. She drew back swiftly, and Nerine threw a hand over her mouth to stifle a scream.

"Our shores have been too plagued by spies as of late to waste our time on your half-truths. Identify your-selves, and name the friend you seek, or I will be forced to take you and your companion captive to await judgment, young though you appear."

Iolana opened her mouth to speak, but the answer caught in her throat. Telling these people about Lea could cause more trouble for her than she was already in.

However, saying nothing at all would seal their fates, and that would help no one. Iolana took a deep breath. "I am Iolana. She is Nerine. And the friend we seek is Lea Byrnes."

A wave of murmurs swelled across the crowd. The Carmennans closed in, locking the girls inside an even more tightly knit human cage.

"Traitors!" someone shouted. "Murderers and thieves!"

"How did you find her?"

"Don't let them get a step closer to our shores!"

Their shouts turned into an indecipherable chorus of accusations and calls for justice and blood. Iolana was overwhelmed by a maddening clash of heartsongs roaring with anger, fear, and a hunger for vengeance. Struggling to shut out the noise, she glanced frantically at each face, searching for some friend among their foes—

Someone snatched Nerine. Iolana cried out and reached for her friend, but the mob had already thrown her at their captain's feet. Nerine cowered in his shadow, shaking, and sobbing violently.

"Enough!" the captain barked. "We do not know yet if they be friend or foe. We will take them down to the hold, question them further—"

"No!" This second voice was rough, wild. "Don't give them the chance. *Kill them!*"

A man jumped through the crowd, his gaze lit with a mad fury. He pushed past the captain and lifted his sword high.

"*No!*"

Iolana dove for Nerine, shoving her out of the way and rolling to the side just as the sword sliced down. Its blade ended with a chilling *thwack* against the ship's deck, inches near Iolana's head.

With a grunt, the accuser hefted his sword and lifted it high once more. Iolana tried to scramble backward, but the man brought the blade swiftly toward her neck and she turned away, closing her eyes tight.

A slash of fire burned across her neck, yet she was still alive. How? Why had the crowds ceased their jeers and calls for her blood?

Opening her eyes, she saw the captain standing over her again, a sword clutched in one hand. He breathed hard, and his expression had dissolved from skeptical doubt into sheer wonder and fear.

The man who'd attacked Iolana lay sprawled on the deck, seemingly unconscious. His sword was still in his hand, not a drop of blood staining it. But if his blade hadn't seared Iolana's flesh with a burning fire, what had?

She realized then that the captain's stare wasn't aimed at her face, but her shoulder. No, just above it. She reached up to her neck, and immediately gasped in pain, withdrawing her hand. Then, carefully, her fingers crept back to the small spot burning with an incredible heat.

As the pain intensified, Iolana hissed sharply, and then she heard music. A single, shrill note screamed inside her mind like a flute or fife gone wild. She held her head, trying to push the noise right out of her skull.

"Iolana!" Nerine gasped, falling at Iolana's side, and gently sweeping her hair to examine her neck. "Are you all right? There's a strange mark here. A word. *Ut*, one of the notes of the Lozolian solfiége. How strange...."

The tone faded to a dim hum, but a dull pain lingered. Iolana felt the mark and, sure enough, Nerine spoke truth. She could just trace its outline, etched into her skin. What could it mean? Where did it come from?

An instant later, she shoved away her curiosity. She didn't care. Whether this new omen was good or bad was irrelevant. Its mysterious magic or meaning had blazed to life and saved them, and that was good enough for her.

The pain and musical tone having diminished, Iolana looked up at the captain. Slowly, as if it took him a long time to accept what he was seeing, he stepped back and sheathed his sword.

"Forgive me, and forgive Kamahele for attacking. For some of us, the lines between loyalty, fear, and zeal for our cause have been blurred as of late. Our shores have been home to far too few friends. I offer my full apologies. I am Pono, captain of this ship and, once upon a time, of the royal Carmennan guard. I offer you my full service and protection and will safely escort you to Pakua where Lea Byrnes takes refuge."

Pono extended his hand toward Iolana, but she hesitated. She could detect his heartsong, but faintly. Her powers were worn from being bombarded by the entire crew's mad heartsongs. But though faint, its sound was pure, and his offered friendship shone as sincerely in his eyes as his suspicion had done only moments before.

Iolana reached out her hand, which he clasped to help her to her feet. Pono's gaze swept across his crew, who stood in awed obedience.

"These two here are our friends. Provide them now with food and rest. By remaining on this ship, you swear total allegiance to protecting and guiding them. May anyone who brings them harm be cursed, both in this life and the next."

Turning back to her, he added, "You are most welcome here, Iolana of the Guardians, as is Nerine."

Iolana's fear mingled with excitement, and she whispered a silent prayer of thanks. Amiel had brought them this far, and now they were closer than she could have imagined to finding Lea.

~*~*~

Iolana and Nerine stood on deck, staring across the misty gray sea. Hardly a few hours had passed before a new island had cropped up on the horizon and Pono announced it as their destination, Pakua.

The nearer the ship drifted toward the mountainous isle, the more Iolana's anxiousness to reach it intensified. What truths might be revealed in her reunion with Lea? What was the meaning of the mark on her neck and the crew's claim that she was "of the Guardians"? Certainly, it couldn't mean she was now an Octavial Guardian like Lea. The idea was hardly fathomable. Her magic was not yet tempered enough. She could never fulfill such a massive role. But the mark had saved them once already. She could only hope it would prove to be a boon when she unraveled its true significance.

Once they had drawn a little nearer to the shore, Iolana, Nerine, Pono, and several other Carmennans boarded the rowboats that were lowered from the ship.

"Why are we still so far from shore?" Iolana asked.

"Because," a woman said, "we've been so overrun by enemies lately that we've been forced to become spies in our own land."

A crewmate nodded. "It's for this same reason that our ships move like ghosts in the fog." He gestured to the thick air surrounding them. "Captain Pono himself created this, both as deterrence to outsiders and as a shield for us, to maintain secrecy."

Iolana studied the cliffs stretching up a few miles inland. She found an arched hollow set high up in their midst, like the mouth of a cave, and hoped that was not the way into Pakua. Heights were not her favorite challenge, and the thought of having to climb all that way made her dizzy. But she would do it, if she must. She'd come too far to turn back now, and the crew, by whatever grace the mark gave her, thought her too valuable to let any harm come to her.

The small boats rounded the island to the side opposite the cliffs and brushed against the shore, and everyone climbed out in disciplined silence. Pono had given both girls thick, warm tunics and gray woolen cloaks to wear, as well as special boots made of a soft but heavy leather that protected their feet while also muffling their footfalls.

As they traveled further inland, the fog cleared at last, revealing a black sky studded with stars that illuminated their way. The shore was strewn with uneven rocks, and Iolana and Nerine both tripped along. The Carmennans knew the way well, and Iolana watched them, trying to weave across the stones in their exact path while helping Nerine.

Past the shore, they entered the thick wood and traveled up a gentle incline for a long while. They still had roots and wild shrubs to navigate, but the way was much easier than the rocky beach.

Unexpectedly, Pono grabbed Iolana's arm, bringing her to a rough halt, and Nerine stopped behind her.

"Forgive me," he whispered. "But we are here, and I didn't want you to topple over the edge."

"We're where?"

"Pakua."

Pono pulled the tree branches aside and led them beyond. Iolana stared in wonder, and Nerine inhaled sharply.

Right before them, a cliff dropped nearly straight down. The precipice overlooked a deep, lush valley ringed on all sides by vertical cliffs. The far cliffs were the tallest and shaped exactly the same as those Iolana had viewed from the boat. She wondered if, on the other side, one of them bore the cave-like opening.

In the valley below, she could just make out houses with smoke curling from the chimneys and firelight in the windows. A waterfall spilled over the left-most cliff, forming a moat around the city below.

"Come," Pono said. "We must make our way up."

They proceeded in a straight line, heading up around the perimeter of the valley. When they came at last to the tallest cliffs on the far side, Pono put his ear to one of them. He made his voice trill like a bird's, and the outline of a door appeared in the stone. He slid it open, and Iolana walked inside, Nerine and the other Carmennans following.

They traversed a narrow corridor that rose steadily upward, dimly lit by orange torch-glow. When Iolana glanced behind her, all traces of the door had vanished.

The path continued to rise steadily, and it soon became apparent that they were not heading into the valley part of the city. As they stepped out onto a balcony, the rest of the city stretched before them, several stories tall, massive buildings elegantly carved right into the stone. All lay swathed in peaceful silence. Firelight glowed within a few of the windows. The walls closed in toward the very top of the vast cave but did not shut completely. Instead, a long strip of open, star-scattered sky peeked through, allowing a fresh breeze.

Pono swept an arm out. "This is Chahuru. The central nerve of the city. Here is where all business is conducted. As you can see, there are many homes built into the caves. But our business lies inside Castle Kanoah."

Iolana followed his arm's leftward motion and immediately wondered how she could have missed the fantastic sight. Castle Kanoah was built right into the cave's far wall, stretching up nearly all the way to the chasm permitting the starlight. In front, two great pillars flanked two massive stone doors that could be reached by wide steps. Intricately carved vines wrapped around the pillars, with flowers arranged as though the vines served as music staffs and the blossoms were the notes. Huge torches blazed brightly all along the front of the castle. It was so massive that it could have been built for one of the legendary Giants who lived beyond the Seven Kingdoms.

"It's breathtaking," Nerine whispered.

Iolana nodded, stunned into silence by the castle's magnificence. Pono led them down a spiraling ramp to their left. Once they'd reached the ground level of the city, he led them toward the castle.

If Iolana thought she had been intimidated by the mere sight of the cliffs, that reaction was dwarfed by how she felt in the castle's presence. Not only did its colossal size and strength daunt, but the way it had been so precisely carved gave it a reverential importance, like a living entity deserving of respect.

"Lea is being housed in the Outcrop Wing," Pono said quietly. "The rooms there are our most secure."

He led them up the stone stairs, and the double doors swung silently inward, as if their company had been expected.

They all stepped inside. Castle Kanoah looked even grander within, winding staircases, arched hallways, ornate pillars, every bit of stone carved so elegantly and flawlessly.

Iolana and Nerine followed Pono toward one of the staircases, while the other Carmennans separated down the halls left or right.

Pono led the girls down corridors and up stairs lined with torches. Despite Iolana's talents for memorization, they wound around so much that she knew she could get truly lost in this place. This made her feel trapped again, but then she supposed that was the point. Lea was meant to be trapped, in a way, protected in a place that would make reaching her difficult.

Finally, Pono stopped before a door and rapped on it gently. "Lady Fleming, are you still awake?"

Iolana frowned. Lady Fleming? Why the strange title? Perhaps she had taken on a new identity to protect herself.

"Yes. What is it?"

Iolana's heart raced at hearing Lea's voice, first with relief, but then with a small panic. What would she say to the woman who'd taken her in as her own, sought to protect her? Now Iolana had thrown herself into the midst of so much danger. What would Lea say to her placing Nerine in the same danger?

"You have visitors, madam."

"May I ask who they are, at this late hour?"

"Iolana and Nerine from Loz."

There was a long, dead-silent pause.

At last, Lea said, "Send them in, please."

Pono opened the door.

CHAPTER 20

A GATHERING OF GUARDIANS

Gailea stared in sheer disbelief at the sight of the two girls entering her chamber.

Pono bowed and shut the door, leaving them in privacy, but still no words came to her. Two of her students were, inexplicably, here. One had once been a prisoner of the man who'd murdered all of Gailea's friends. The other knew nothing of evil, except perhaps what her parents had read to her in adventure tales where the heroes always triumphed.

What was to be done with them? They couldn't possibly stay.

"Miss Lea," Iolana said. "We're so glad to see you're all right."

Gailea's heart ached. With a weary sigh, she rose up from her seat before the large, open-air window and hurried toward the girls. They raced forward, and she drew them into a tight embrace.

"As I am you," she whispered, squeezing them closer.

Then, something caught her eye.

She drew back, staring at the mark glowing faintly on Iolana's neck. With trembling hand, she touched it, only to recoil at its fire-hot temperature.

"You came here because you're one of the new Guardians."

A curious frown lowered Iolana's brow, and Nerine stared blankly.

Gailea's voice wavered as she tried to hold back a flare of anger. "You *did* come here because you're a Guardian? You were sent here? Summoned?"

"The Carmennans who found us said that I bore a mark of the Guardians," Iolana said. "But it appeared so suddenly, and I didn't know what they meant."

"What do you mean they *found* you?" Gailea demanded, her patience waning. Her nerves had been so depleted over the past week that she found it difficult to contain her emotions.

Iolana took a deep breath. "We didn't come here because of the mark. We came here because of you, to make sure you were safe."

Gailea's anger threatened to boil to the surface, but as she studied the girls' faces, filled with such love and concern, she felt abruptly too tired for anger, too tired for anything except a desperate wish that their standing before her were nothing more than a dream.

"Do you know how I've been worrying about you, wondering if *you* were safe, ever since the attack? Do you have any idea how foolish, *reckless* it was for you to come here on your own?"

"Begging your pardon, Miss Lea," Nerine interrupted. "But we've been just as worried about you. After all we've been through, I don't think it's fair for you to be *too* upset, especially not at Iolana. She's been so brave. I wouldn't have survived without her."

"Neither would I, without you." Iolana shared a smile with Nerine. Then she turned back to Gailea, eyes soft with tender pleading. "After everything you've done for me, how could I not do this for you? You're one of the last people I have. I couldn't abandon you. Especially if any of this has to do with—with—"

"*Him*," Gailea finished for her. She sighed heavily and stood, defeated. "Forgive me," she breathed, as a few tears slipped down her cheeks. "I do understand. And I thank you both. Though I wish our reunion came by a safer path, your love and concern are an encouragement to me. The two weeks I've spent here have been filled with dark memories. It worries me greatly that you should become one of the Guardians. But then, perhaps your righteous anger against Moragon's injustices will make you one of the strongest allies against him."

Iolana frowned, shaking her head. "Moragon? I don't...who is he?"

Gailea's throat went dry. Of course. Of course, they didn't know. The horrific truth had plagued her mind, becoming such a harsh reality that she forgot others wouldn't yet know.

"Come, have a seat. There's much you need to hear, especially you, Iolana, if you are indeed meant to be a Guardian."

Gailea led them over to the velvet-covered bench placed snugly in the alcove before the open, airy, window that looked out across Pakua's shores. Moonlight glimmered on the distant ocean, painting a peaceful scene. How often Gailea wished to drown all thought and memory in its endless black expanse.

They all sat on the bench, and Gailea leaned back against the stone wall, looking at the two girls. "To begin with, my name is not Lea Byrnes. It is Gailea Fleming. I took a different name to go into hiding, both from Moragon, the one-time king of my home country, Adelar, and from…from another who would seek to harm my children." Nerine gasped at this revelation, while Iolana stared as though Gailea had turned into a ghost. "They too have been forced into hiding, and I've not seen them now for many years.

"It would seem Moragon also took on a new name. That he has been subjugating Carmenna as 'King Samil' for the past seven years. I didn't realize, but all the clues were there. I should've known. I simply did not wish to see them.…" She glanced away, flooded by guilt.

"This isn't your fault," Iolana said, placing a hand on Gailea's knee. "What Samil did at the concert, that was about the Guardians, wasn't it? If you were hiding, he didn't even know you were one of them, did he?"

"No, I don't think he did. Sweet girls…I'm so sorry. So, so sorry for everything you had to see at the concert. No one should see such hateful violence and death. And that I invited you too, placed you in such danger.…"

"It isn't your fault," Iolana repeated more fervently, her gaze surprisingly stern, as though she was the adult comforting the child. "Besides, we didn't see anything. At least, not the Guardians dying. We left before that. As soon as I recognized Samil, I took Nerine from the theatre."

"We're the ones who should be sorry," Nerine added. Tears slipped from her eyes which narrowed with such sincere compassion that Gailea almost dissolved into tears herself, overwhelmed by her grace, a gift that, in the moment, she found it difficult to deserve or receive. "You're the one who had to see all your friends killed in front of you. I'm sorry you had to go through that. And I'm sorry for all of them, for their families. They were good souls, all of them. And Drewit was one of the best teachers…his poor wife.…" Nerine's words faded into a shuddering breath as she wiped away more tears.

"I wish I had known," Gailea whispered. "I wish I had made the connection. I hadn't heard of Moragon in so many years—no one has—that I didn't dream it might be him."

"It would've made no difference," Iolana said, her voice bitter. "Samil—Moragon—would've found a way to kill them anyway. He always finds a way. I suppose this means we truly do share a common experience, moreso than we thought. We've both been his prisoners."

"Yes." Gailea brushed away a few tears as Iolana watched her so tenderly. "What a strange kindredship we share. We have both suffered at his hands, both seen what he is capable of."

"And you both escaped to tell the tale," Nerine said, her voice filled with admiration.

"To tell the tale and to fight back," Iolana said. "And for me, it seems that means becoming a Guardian."

Gailea cringed at this declaration but tried to conceal her fear. What was done was done. Besides, at least Gailea could keep a closer watch on Iolana. Moragon would likely come for them both, for escaping his clutches and making a mockery of him.

"Iolana," Gailea said. "Let me get a better look at your mark." She moved to the girl, who tilted her head. Gailea smiled faintly. "*Ut*. Mine shifted from *So* to *La*, I suppose once the new Guardians were chosen." She drew up her left sleeve, and both Iolana and Nerine stared at the mark on her shoulder. It was more faded than Iolana's and no longer glowed, but its scrawl was similar.

"*Ut* and *La*,'" Nerine mused. "The solfège scale. Is that how the Guardians identify themselves?"

"Yes, my dear," Gailea said, smiling with pride at Nerine. "As observant as ever."

Nerine grinned. "It's just like in the tales of Lord Juu that Chamblin used to tell. There's a similar story in Chinese legend, only those Guardians each sang a specific song to identify themselves."

Gailea's spirit fell. Chamblin had been one of many names she hadn't dared to breathe and couldn't erase from the constant pains bombarding her mind. It was evident by Nerine's lack of concern that she hadn't seen him the night of the concert. How could she tell this girl, who loved him so, that he might be dead, or worse, captured and tormented at Moragon's hands?

She turned back to Iolana, gently rubbing the girl's mark. "Does it still hurt?"

"No," Iolana said. "It did for a little while, but now it just itches."

"Good. That too will fade soon enough."

"But why did your mark change, now I'm a Guardian?"

Gailea smiled, warmed at both girls' curiosity even under such dire circumstances. "The marks are dependent on a Guardian's range. There are two who are granted the note *Ut*, being at the beginning and end of our chosen scale, completing the octave. You're no bass or baritone, so you must now be the highest singer in our new group."

"What happens now, Miss Gailea?" Nerine asked, leaning forward with a gleam of eagerness in her eyes. "What happens with the new Guardians? Have others already received their marks like Iolana has?"

"Likely, yes," Gailea said. "The spell of emergency appointment was designed so that, upon a Guardian's death, a new one is chosen as quickly as possible. It's not the same as the official appointment spell. None of the new Guardians will have received their instruments or the full strength of their powers yet. But the emergency appointment at least allows us to work together and combine our magic when needed."

"How does it work?" Iolana asked.

"There is a special stone imbued with various magical properties, housed inside the Guardians' headquarters. This stone sends out pulses of musical power across the Realm, searching for the next best candidate to be a Guardian. The Guardians have no leader. They are eight equal members. Their powers and voices must have a natural balance of both harmony and dissonance. The stone's spell searches for those who will best fit together."

"And the other new Guardians?" Nerine asked. "Where will they go once they're chosen? How will we meet them?"

"Once appointed, a messenger from our headquarters is dispatched to track down the new Guardian and tell them where to go."

"That didn't happen with me," Iolana said.

"Likely because you've been moving about all this time. Tracking spells are difficult enough to follow under the best of circumstances. The new Guardians will be sent here, to Pakua. It is well fortified, and the Carmennans here have been planning to fight Moragon for some time. For now, we must simply wait. And pray for the others, that they will reach us safely. In the meanwhile, tell me of your adventures."

Iolana and Nerine took turns narrating. Nerine awed over Iolana's bravery, and Iolana looked slightly uncomfortable at her praise. When it was her turn, she told of Nerine's remarkable commanding of the ocean waves.

Gailea smiled proudly at Nerine. "Your gifts truly are starting to show signs of their true strengths. Why, give it a few years, and you'll be able to command the *entire* ocean—"

Another knock sounded on the door. Gailea and the girls looked up curiously, and Gailea called, "Yes?"

"Lady Gailea," said a woman's voice. "There are two more visitors for you, sent by Lozolian escorts. They are two new Guardians."

"Please, send them in."

The door opened to reveal a fuller-figured woman with sun-kissed skin and dark brown hair plaited into a long braid. A gentle happiness danced in her warm, brown eyes.

Gailea stood to her feet but could then only stare, trembling in shock. Her sister? How could this be? "*Darice!*" She could see something glinting on her sister's cheek, another Guardian's mark. Filled with dread, Gailea couldn't move, but Darice raced forward and caught her in a tight embrace.

"My dear, sweet Gailea," Darice whispered in her ear. "How I missed you!"

"And I you. I've worried all this time. Sister…" Gailea squeezed her tight. "I thought I'd never see you again. I prayed you were safe after escaping Adelar, but—"

"I know." Darice stroked Gailea's hair, and the tears they shared blended on Gailea's skin. "Oh, dearest… I tried to find you, tell you I was alive. Eventually, I stopped looking, thinking perhaps it was safer for you if I stayed away. But I've prayed and loved you each and every day."

"I've done the same."

Something moved in the doorway.

Gailea glanced up over Darice's shoulder and inhaled sharply. Again, shock hit her like a blow. "No—no, it's impossible!"

A tanned, rugged man leaned against the doorframe, arms crossed, eyes gleaming with admiration and great joy.

Gailea withdrew from her sister's hold and walked slowly over like a woman entranced. She reached up one hand to touch the man's scruffy face, the strong outline of his jaw, his soft, golden-brown hair at the base of his neck.

"How can this be?" She placed her other hand to her heart, hardly catching her breath. "I saw—I saw you die before me!"

"And now you see me live before you once more. Gailea...."

Ashden took her hand and kissed it. She pulled him forward into a tight embrace, which he readily returned. For the longest time, she stood in his arms, surrounded by him, his protection and warmth, and a nervous energy skittered through her.

"My dear friend," she whispered against his strong chest.

After a few moments, she remembered the girls and took a step back, just enough to gaze up at him in bewilderment. "Iolana and Nerine, over there is my sister, Darice. And this—this is Ashden. A dear old friend who once saved my children and me...at the cost of his own life, or so I'd thought." She returned his tender smile, and he drew her a little closer.

She patted his back fondly and led him toward the fireplace, Darice and the girls following along. "You must tell us everything. How you survived, how you're here. Are you also a Guardian? Your mark...?"

"My back, close to my left shoulder," Ashden said. "Believe me, I was as bewildered as you looked just now. I tried to figure out why my entire back seemed to be on fire. Not as conveniently placed as Darice's...." Darice tilted her cheek toward the firelight and smiled playfully. "I was relieved when the messenger arrived to explain things and bring me and the First Echelon here."

"The First Echelon?"

Gailea, Darice, and Ashden sat on the tapestry-cush-ioned settee close to the fire, while Iolana and Nerine sat on the black rug embroidered with silver swords crossed over a purple lyre to represent Carmenna's true royal family. For once, even Iolana looked whimsical, like a child expecting to be told some grand bedtime story.

"Yes, the First Echelon," Ashden said. "The Lozo-lian Council is sending some of them to escort the new Guardians, for their added protection."

Gailea nodded slowly. A wise call on Lynn's part to send the Lozolian Council's elite soldiers, and most ap-preciated.

Thoughts of Lynn faded when she couldn't take her eyes off the man miraculously sitting beside her. "What happened to you, Ashden? I saw you filled with arrows. Saw your blood stain the forests, your last breath as it left your body. I've thought you long dead, and I the cause of it."

Ashden placed an arm around her and held her tight, while Darice squeezed her hand.

"No, dearest," Darice said. "It would never have been your fault. Moragon's and Ragnar's evil—*they* drove Ash-den to his near death, not you."

"May I not tell my own story?" Ashden leaned for-ward to give Darice a mock stern look, and she laughed in reply.

Ashden then straightened, returning to Gailea. "She's right though. It was never your fault. *None* of it was."

"None of it," Darice reassured her. "Even the most recent losses."

Gailea's heart dropped like a heavy stone, but her sister's kindness was a balm. "You've no idea how I've needed those words. I only wish I could believe them."

Ashden brushed her tears away. "You must try. I am

so sorry for all you've been through." After a moment, he brightened. "Let me tell my tale, before Darice too eagerly steals my glory."

"I'd be glad for the distraction, and for you to satiate my curiosity. What happened that day, when I left you?"

"After I'd fallen and you escaped, I drifted in and out of consciousness. Pain seared my body, and for a while, I truly wished for death, that Ragnar's men would come and finish me off."

"Not Ragnar's men," Gailea said flatly. "Donyon's."

"Donyon's?" Darice said, looking stunned.

Ashden took this in. "During our journey here, Darice shared some of your history with me. Is he not the lord you helped take back the Adelaran throne?"

"Yes, the very same," Gailea couldn't conceal the bite from her voice. "But as with all kings, it seems to have taken little time for his loyalties to shift to accommodate his ambition. The Alder Sprites who attacked us, I recognized their crest. It was most definitely Donyon's."

"Well, then it was his men whom I wished would end my agony," Ashden said. "They captured me, dragging me back to a camp they had made in the Southern Wood. I was barely coherent to what was going on around me. I remember being forced to stand before someone, accused of treachery. I remember speaking what few words of defense I could muster. And then I remember hearing that I was to join the slain Sprites who had fought beside me. Soon the men threw me into a mass grave...."

A soft sob made Ashden pause his tale. Iolana sat wiping away a few tears. Her face looked strangely soft, younger, vulnerable. Nerine rubbed her shoulder, whispering words of comfort in her ear.

"Are you all right, child?" Ashden asked. "Should I stop?"

Iolana shook her head. "No. Your story stirs up difficult memories for me. But it's all right. Go ahead, please finish."

Ashden studied her with concern before continuing, "I was lying in the grave. I'd accepted death. But then, a pure light washed over me, accompanied by the purest song. The song itself was like light, easing my pain and erasing fear from my heart. I heard shouts and cries from the guards above the pit. A woman's face flashed before me, but my consciousness was fading again. It was like going to sleep, and I thought perhaps these were a final few moments of peace before death found me. I hadn't believed in any sort of god up until that point, but for a moment, I believed some spirit of light had come to take me to rest with the spirits of my ancestors.

"Then darkness swallowed me, until I awoke safe and clean, and in a clean bed, and the woman from my vision was real and taking care of me. It was Darice."

"She rescued you." Gailea stared at her sister in amazement. "But how? By Amiel's grace, how did you find him?"

Darice held her hand firmly. "When I heard news of things unraveling in Adelar, of Donyon retaking the throne, Ragnar fleeing, your disappearance, I set out to find you myself. Of course, where to begin such a search? If you didn't come to me and Mother for aid, I knew danger must chase you that you didn't wish to lead to us. So then, in trying to think where else you might hide, I remembered Tytonn having family in Hyloria and hoped that I might be able to find you, to help you and the children. Of course, I didn't find you. But while traveling the Southern Wood, I was able to expand my music skills to focus more on healing. There were many rebellions and fights then, between various Sprite clans. I was out accompanying the Mirtles, healing their wounded from a recent fight, when we found Ashden."

Gailea tightly squeezed her hand. "Just like he once saved me, you saved him. I can never repay you."

Darice's smile warmed. "Seeing you alive is enough."

"It is indeed." Ashden said softly.

"Have you two been companions since?" Gailea asked.

"Yes," Ashden said. "For a while, we traveled together, searching for some sign of you or your children. When none came, we hoped no news was good news. I returned to my people, while Darice gained work in Kadenza. Both light magic and especially music are valued there, and so the Elves welcomed her warmly."

"Light magic?" Gailea eyed her sister. "You've grown much since last I saw you."

"I started studying light songs," Darice said, "learning how to infuse my music with light."

"We visited each other frequently, wrote to one another," Ashden added. "Our correspondence waned over the years. We each grew busier in our own work. Until just a week ago, when each of us received the mark of the Guardians and then were summoned. We were given an appointed meeting place in Hyloria, where we were astonished to find one another again, to realize we had both become Guardians." He nodded proudly at Darice, then concluded, "With the Echelon escorting us, we traveled here together."

"Isn't it curious really that we all know one another in some way?" Darice asked, glancing across them all. "The girls here seem like close friends, and they're your students. Ashden and I being connected to each other, and again to you, sister."

Gailea tensed once more. Part of her felt relieved at their familiar presence, while another part dreaded dragging them into greater danger. "It does seem curious, but I think there may be a logical explanation. Musical mages are not abundant in the world compared to other magical types, and thus are even more limited within the Lozolian Realm. And the Octavial Eight works together most strongly when there is just the right amount of harmony and dissonance."

"I suppose our knowing each other would speak to harmony then. I can't agree with there being dissonance between us, as far as I've seen."

"Don't speak too quickly," Ashden said. "We've yet to meet the remaining Guardians." He turned a playful smile to Gailea. "Have you nothing to say though, for our story, now it's concluded?"

Gailea shook her head in wonder. "It's an amazing tale. Truly one worth celebrating."

"Then let us do just that," Ashden said. "We've still a few moments' calm left before the great storm approaching us hits. There's perhaps a day or more before the rest of the Guardians show themselves. Unless we are compelled to do otherwise, let us rejoice."

They talked late into the night, sharing stories of the past and their more recent adventures in coming to Carmenna.

Nerine was the first to fall asleep, and then Iolana, huddled close to her side. Ashden was next, his head on Gailea's shoulder. She stroked his thick hair, reveling in the feel of its softness slipping between her fingers.

"Gailea," Darice said quietly, "may I talk with you for a moment?"

Darice's gaze begged a little privacy. Gailea nodded and stood up, slipping a pillow beneath Ashden's head. Then she led Darice to sit before the large window.

The two women sat across from each other, staring out at the stars.

"Isn't it dangerous?" Darice asked. "Having this great, gaping hole where anyone could enter?"

"Most would be hard-pressed to try, and it's protected by many charms besides."

"That's a relief. It *is* lovely, sitting here and watching the stars, being almost close enough to touch them...."

Gailea studied her a few moments before venturing, "I think your mind is on more than the stars."

Darice stared at her, wide-eyed, like a child caught sneaking sweets.

"What do you mean?"

Gailea smiled fondly. Though the idea hurt a little, she'd accepted it from the moment she'd realized what was before her eyes. "Several years and many changes now stand between me and Ashden. You've been more to him than I was, and I'm happy for you. Does he feel the same?"

Darice flushed scarlet. "I didn't know if I should tell you, with you just finding out he's alive. I know he still cares for you, and that you must care something for him."

"I do care for him, yes. But we didn't know each other well or long enough for those feelings to blossom into love. Not for me. Our time is past. I think he would be a brilliant match for you, if you think he truly cares for you in the same way."

"I'm not certain." Darice glanced back at Ashden's sleeping form. "That is, I know he cares. He's often been the one to set up times for us to visit one another. When we were corresponding, he was most faithful in writing to me. But sometimes I fear part of his affection for me stems from his affection toward *you*. I'm sorry. I don't mean to make you feel badly."

Gailea clasped her sister's hands. "I know you don't. There really is no need to hang onto this guilt. I would caution you to be careful, to guard your heart, as I would caution any woman. My experiences with love have been mostly disastrous. But I do know Ashden to be an honest soul. I don't think he would show you such attention if he wasn't sincere. At any rate, whatever happens, you have my full blessing."

Darice grinned. "Thank you."

They embraced, and Gailea asked, "Did you wish to tell me something else? Or to simply trade childish gossip about our mutual lover?"

Darice laughed softly. Then, reaching into the large pocket of her tunic, she presented a weathered envelope sealed with a circle of red wax.

Gailea accepted it and turned it over, looking in vain for any indication of what was inside. "What's this?"

"Inside are diary accounts. Our mother gave them to me last I saw her."

Brynn! Gailea gasped in delight. "How is she doing?"

"She's thriving. Sewing away, as usual. Happy. She misses you terribly. But she understands the needed separation, for everyone's safety. She's proud of you."

Gailea inhaled deeply and swallowed her tears. "I'll be with her again," she vowed to Darice and herself. "I'll reunite with her, and my children, and we'll all be together, a family at last."

"I've no doubt of it."

"What of this envelope? A diary, you say?"

"Mother says she's wanted to give it to you for a while, but it wouldn't have been safe while you lived with Moragon. I'll admit I did read them myself. You won't like everything you find within, and yet I think she's right. You should know as much as you can."

Darice's solemn, sad tone frightened Gailea, as did her lack of a straight answer.

Again, Gailea looked at the envelope. The thick

parchment was turned brown, its sides jagged, corners bent. Nothing extraordinary about its appearance.

Yet as she opened it, unfolded the pages within, and let her gaze rest upon the first few words, time seemed to stand still. She held her breath for what seemed a long while before releasing it and staring at her sister.

"These are accounts from Gillian, my *birth* mother. How did our mother come by these?"

"The accounts explain all," Darice said. "They were close friends, our mother and yours...."

Darice's voice seemed to fade as Gailea read, and her mother's words seemed to leap off the page. She tried to imagine how her mother's voice would have sounded. She reread several passages, awed by some things, horrified by others.

The fire had dwindled in the hearth when, finally, Gailea laid the accounts to rest. A singular thought stuck out in her mind, making a new anger boil steadily inside her.

"So, my mother and father died trying to purge their respective countries of their ignorant prejudices, long before I helped Donyon take the throne. Adelar and Rosa stopped their warring with one another. And Donyon...."

"Yes," Darice whispered. "It seems he was obsessed over Gillian."

"And I helped him," Gailea muttered. "I helped that envious madman take the throne. He abused my mother, would've taken my children from me—killed them, killed us all—who knows what? I can't fathom."

"Some rulers are corrupt no matter what."

"*All* rulers are corrupt," Gailea said bitterly. "As far as I've seen."

Her gaze wandered over to Ashden, Iolana, and Nerine. They looked so peaceful in sleep, permitted a few sweet hours with their minds devoid of the dangers approaching.

"I hate it," she whispered. "I hate how connected I am to all of you. Even more than I was the other Guardians. Even Iolana. I've become so close to her, in the absence of my own children. She too was Moragon's prisoner for a while. And Nerine. Sweet Nerine. She isn't a Guardian. She *must* be sent back."

"Do you think she'll go?" Darice asked. "She and Iolana seem very close."

"She must go," Gailea repeated. "There's no purpose to her staying here, caught up in this madness." She turned back to Darice. "Go ahead then, take the bed, get some sleep. I'll join you shortly."

"Are you sure you'll be all right?"

Gailea nodded. "I just need time to pray and think."

Darice gave her sister a wary look. Then she slipped beneath the covers of the massive bed and, within moments, had fallen fast asleep.

For a moment, Gailea envied her sister. Envied the simplicity of being able to sleep so easily and soundly. She even envied her sister's connection to Ashden. Not that she would wish to tear their newfound love apart, but what a comfort to have a constant partner at her side. Was such a blessing even possible for her at this point? She doubted it. Men like Ashden seemed a rare exception. Gillian's last accounts more than proved this.

Gailea returned her attention to the parchment and began re-reading, committing as much to memory as she could. As war unfolded, and possibly expanded, she might come into contact with Donyon again. When she did, she wanted her hatred for him to be deeply brewed and ready for retaliation.

THE
SECOND
MOVEMENT

CHAPTER 21

THE KING OF CARMENNA

The iron carriage rattled along the dirt path through bleak and barren woods. As it emerged from the trees and approached the massive stone castle, a sure, feminine hand parted its ebony curtains.

The young woman glanced out, her dark eyes filled with dread. At long last, Lorelei had passed through the forests bordering the northern fringes of the capital, Alaula, named after Carmenna's first queen. Beyond the forest, the castle sharing the same namesake stretched before her. Nestled against the cliffs rising behind and on either side of it, the sturdy fortress had once housed Carmenna's royal family. Now, it stood as the stolen stronghold of the false king, Samil.

Lorelei gazed up at the stone gargoyles leering along the walls and towers and shuddered. Her heart sped as the familiar nightmare drew closer and closer, especially as they crossed the drawbridge spanning over what seemed an endless abyss. Many years had passed since she'd been dragged to the edge, Samil holding her by her hair and threatening to fling her into the chasm if she refused to obey him. Such memories descended on her now like a deafening chord, their sting surprisingly fresh.

She let the curtain fall back into place and pressed her hand to her heart. The pendant still hung about her neck, embedded within her skin. Her mother had crafted it from anemone blossoms, or windflowers as they were sometimes called, a special plant native to Carmenna and renowned for its rich healing properties.

Its warm pulse was her solitary light in this land of shadow. She touched it, drawing courage from it and all it stood for. Even had she not been summoned, she would have readily volunteered for the task she now raced toward. She'd been free of Samil for over a year, and now, she returned as a more educated and powerful rival, a worthy enough match for the man who'd won the throne by murdering the royal family...

Except for one.

One yet remained. One true heir. It was he—or she, the rumors never specified—that Lorelei must find. It was for this heir that she now allowed herself to reenter the darkness of the castle quietly, seemingly tamed, and ready to submit.

The carriage passed through iron gates and stopped before the wide steps leading up to the massive double doors of the castle. Someone opened the carriage door and bade her to get out.

She stepped from the carriage. Two guards clad in dark red armor led her toward the castle. She gazed up at its immensity and, with a shiver, passed from the free world back into its shadow.

The doors closed behind her with an eerie groan, ending in a thunderous clang. The noise echoed as if mocking her, before fading into a stark silence that reflected the finality of their closing. Except by some strong spell or miracle, they would not reopen again for Lorelei, nor for anyone. Not unless Samil himself bid it, and that would be a strange miracle indeed.

Torches and candles from chandeliers cast an orange glow inside the castle, but the light couldn't make Lorelei feel welcome. Each guard grabbed a torch and led her along. They wound through several corridors, passing many Carmennan servants and courtiers. Most wore dull, defeated expressions. Others' eyes looked entirely vacant, like walking corpses, those for whom Samil's mental manipulation schemes had not ended particularly well. As chilling as it was to be immersed again in such an atmosphere, Lorelei forced herself to look upon each face, wondering with aching heart: what is his story, or hers? How had they come to grief at Samil's hands? And was *this* the One? Was this the heir she risked ultimate danger to find?

The guards' winding path stopped Lorelei before a set of red doors adorned with a golden phoenix spreading its wings over a golden harp and said that she prepared to enter the chambers of the magnificent King Samil. An unnecessary announcement. She had faced these doors countless times, whether walking through them or being forced through them with spells or chains.

Bracing herself and donning her calmest, bravest face, she stepped inside.

The doors shut behind her, and once more she stood shrouded in silence, waiting. The floor sprawled in a pattern of black-and-white marble swirls. Gold, purple, and red tapestries displaying Samil's phoenix-and-harp standard lined the walls. Intricately carved columns supported the lofty ceiling. Between them, Samil's collection of various musical instruments encased in Icean crystal hovered just out of reach. Beyond the instruments, at the end of a deep red carpet, a stone dais beckoned. Upon the dais sat a throne, and upon the throne, a man.

Mental magic crept around the fringes of Lorelei's mind, touching, seeking entry, but it would not be satisfied. She'd sung a protective song before arriving, enacting the pendant's guard against mental attacks.

"Powerful and mysterious as ever. Don't stand there like some common slave. You're a guest here. An honored servant. Come forth, Lorelei."

His voice flowed deep, alluring. Pleasant, to untrained ears. But years as one of his favorite slaves had taught her every nuanced note of falseness and deceit in his words.

Slowly, Lorelei glided forward. She kept her gaze ever forward, upon the throne, not wanting to show any fear. Her heart thrummed mercilessly, but she matched its wild rhythm by singing the melody for mental shielding over and over in her mind, reinforcing its will.

As she drew closer still, Samil's familiar features were made clear. Handsome but stern, with sharp angles. Milk-white face with dark, glittering eyes. A gaze that reflected his heart, strong in everything but compassion, kindness, and peace.

Finally, she had passed the vast collection of musical instruments and stood at the foot of the dais. The man who called himself "king" spoke again:

"How glad I am to welcome my once dearest servant back into my fold. Surprised, to be certain, that you survived. But then again, that merely adds to the intrigue that always drew me to you. Since learning of your rise from the dead, I have hoped to welcome you back. And now, here you are, the finest of them all."

"If you brought me here to become your slave again, you've wasted your time."

"Not a slave, but a servant," Samil corrected patiently. "I would be a fool to bring harm against you. After all, you stand before me now as a *lady*, with powerful friends and allies…though perhaps fewer than before."

Samil paused, letting the hurt of his words sink in. Lorelei's reserve wavered, but then she gave in to her hatred toward the monster of a man and felt stronger again.

"If you do choose to serve me," Samil continued, "you will have an easy time here. If you succeed in becoming a faithful servant, you will be forgiven your past slights and granted great riches and privileges. If you do not obey me, however, you will suffer the consequences. Of course, you know this full well."

"I do." Lorelei's anger mounted inside her. "I know well enough. You murdered six of my friends for simply standing in your way."

"Six, yes," Samil muttered, "though I'd aimed for seven."

"Only seven? So, you had no thought to murder me, had I attended the concert?"

A smirk crossed Samil's lips. "No, my sweet girl. And, once I saw things for what they were, I set my sights on sparing yet another. In fact, perhaps you might guess for yourself once proper introductions are made. I see you haven't bothered to address me properly. But when you do refer to me, be sure it is no longer as 'His Majesty, Samil' but rather, 'His Majesty, Moragon'."

Lorelei stared, caught off guard. Her mental shields faltered for a moment, but as Samil—no, Moragon—clawed inside, she quickly slammed him back out.

"Moragon," she said. "The disgraced king from Adelar? The one whose throne was usurped by a nephew barely out of boyhood. And Lea, she was once one of your slaves. You meant to keep her alive. To torment her even more than you already have."

Moragon tilted his head, and an amused smirk pulled at the corners of his lips. "I had no idea the treasonous witch was still breathing until that night. Alas, she slipped through my fingers once again."

"Again?" Lorelei echoed.

"Indeed, again. Lea isn't Lea, you know. She's Gailea, the Lady of Adelar, or Gailea Fleming, as she is better known for debasing herself with some commoner's surname."

"The lost princess Gailea," Lorelei whispered, awed and humbled at this revelation about the woman who'd become a solid ally and friend, especially as the details fell into place. She met his gaze and spoke resolutely. "The true blood heir to the Adelaran throne. The one who cast you from your stolen throne with a single song."

"Yes," Moragon growled. "But not this time. Once this war begins full force, no doubt she'll stick her nose in it, especially as a Guardian."

Annoyed by his familiar arrogance, Lorelei lifted her chin and declaimed, "Gailea once found courage and power to overthrow your Adelaran reign. She did the same to Ragnar as well. She's grown stronger yet, enough to destroy you a second time around."

"Gailea is a powerful music mage," Moragon admitted, hatred burning in his gaze. "But the musical knowledge I obtained before the Guardians' formation, combined with my mental gifts, will soon be impossible for her, or anyone, to contend with. Truth be told, you will provide a fine substitute in her absence, to test the strength of my newfound magic."

"Your power holds no sway over me, Moragon." Lorelei's confidence grew a little, especially as she felt the pendant pulsing beneath her skin. "There is nothing you can do now to harm me."

"Need I remind you that my men *were* able to capture you?" Moragon sneered, his false patience visibly waning. "Obviously, my power is still greater than yours."

His eyes narrowed, and Lorelei could tell he was searching for something. How she longed to tell him, just for spite, that she was here of her own free will, that she had led herself into being captured. But hard as it was, she must keep silent and not spoil her plans. They were too vital. She *must* carry through with them.

With a sigh, Moragon eased back into his throne. "I believe this has been more than a sufficient welcome back into my service. Surely, you're weary from your travels. Mikanah, my trusted servant, will lead you to your room. In fact, he will be your escort in all matters."

Mikanah. The name rang a vaguely familiar bell, but not clearly enough for Lorelei to attach any significance to it. Moragon had trained many a young servant, including herself, but hadn't often allowed them to intermingle, perhaps for fear of rebellion. Lorelei had heard rumors of secret gatherings planning some sort of uprising but was never sure if such rumors were founded. When she had first become Moragon's prisoner, she had used her coalescence spell to wander the castle, searching for allies or escape. Over time, those excursions had dwindled as he placed her under closer watch. She never dared to utilize her coalescence spell in front of his guards and servants, for fear of being chained or otherwise robbed of what little freedom she had yet possessed.

Moragon whistled a shrill note. Moments later, a young man stepped into view, near one of the columns. How had she not seen him?

His dark skin and tight, dark curls revealed that he must be a full-blooded Carmennan, and his onyx eyes watched Lorelei intensely.

Lorelei held her mental strongholds firm. She

couldn't imagine what purpose Moragon had for pairing her with this young man with his icy stare, but she knew he had one. She could play this game. She had once accompanied Moragon when he questioned spies and suspects. Sometimes he would make a game of it, and she had to admit that she'd enjoyed trying to guess the subject's true agenda before he did, at least until Moragon started torturing them and forced her to watch. She had grown rather skilled at guessing correctly. Her strength now would lie in working to decipher this boy's agenda before he could decipher hers.

"Mikanah, this is Lorelei, our new guest, the one I told you about. You are to be her escort."

"Yes, Your Majesty," Mikanah replied. His voice was even more devoid of emotion than his cold gaze, and yet he did not strike Lorelei as one of Moragon's insensible puppets. Perhaps he was merely a great actor, capable of hiding away all feelings, except for his obvious annoyance.

"You will take her to the chamber I spoke of earlier, and ensure she stays there until tonight's concert. Then, you shall collect her and bring her to the theatre."

"Yes, Your Majesty."

Lorelei broke her silence. "What concert?"

"A performance by Carmenna's finest artist, an absolute genius, the likes of which you've never before heard. I actually think you'll find the experience quite enlightening."

Moragon dismissed them, and Lorelei followed Mikanah from the throne room. Mikanah led her on another winding path of corridors and stairways, pointing out certain tapestries, statues, or other visual cues to help her remember her way around. Even though she knew much of the layout, she remained quiet and let him lead on, all the while trying to catch some hint of emotion beyond his irritation.

Finally, they stopped before a door.

"Inside is your room," he said. "As King Moragon said, you are to stay here until I fetch you for the concert. Someone will bring you a meal."

"Thank you."

He didn't reply but continued to stare at her. Perhaps he was trying to read her as eagerly as she tried to read him.

"You're displeased with your new task," Lorelei guessed. "This is different from most work you do."

Mikanah narrowed his gaze. "Yes, that is correct. My usual work is less personal and of much higher prestige than playing nanny for spoiled, high-bred maidens. Of course, at least I have been granted the task of watching over a lady of such beauty."

He placed a hand on the wall and leaned forward, looming close to her, almost trapping her. Up close like this, she noted a dark blemish near his left eye, shaped vaguely like three music notes clustered together, likely some sort of scar or birthmark. His eyes bored into hers, but none of their ice had melted. It was a poor mimic of Moragon's seductive arts; this boy hadn't quite mastered them. Amusement curled Lorelei's lips. She tried to remain sober, but he'd seen her mockery, judging by the way he pouted at her.

"Thank you, my lord," she said, resisting another smirk as she feined new deference. "If you please, sir, I'm quite weary and could use some rest before tonight's event."

At first, he looked taken aback by her demure composure. Then his lips narrowed to a thin line, and anger flared in his eyes. Lorelei worried he might attack her and held her ground.

He took several deep breaths, and his rage faded

into an irritated scowl. He certainly was no benumbed captive. A great deal of life and will still lingered within his young soul, however deeply buried.

"Then rest," he snarled, "but do not call me 'lord'. Moragon affords that honor only to a select few."

"Of course. Then what am I to call you?"

Mikanah glanced away, looking more furious that he had revealed any hints of jealousy or displeasure against his master.

"'Sir' will do," he muttered before turning on his heel, promising sharply to pick her up at half-past six, and striding out.

Lorelei watched until he disappeared from view. She hesitated outside her room a few moments, contemplating whether or not to enter. Strangely, they had encountered a sparse amount of guards or servants. Stranger still, none stood posted outside her door. Whether or not this was some trick of Moragon's, she couldn't know. Perhaps he had grown arrogant enough to believe that fear of his vengeance would keep people from fleeing his walls. At any rate, she must take the risk and chance while she could, for who knew when another might arrive. Both her body and mind were exhausted, but she didn't dare succumb, as she would surely do if she saw a bed. She must keep on the move.

She walked down the marble hall, weighing her options. One of the castle's several libraries might be a fair place to spend her time. She doubted Moragon would have kept any important artifacts accessible, but it couldn't hurt to check the older tomes for any possible clues pointing to the heir's maternal lineage. During her months-long mission, she had searched Carmenna's various cities and scoured their archives. The more she had researched, the less mere legend the heir had become. History had soon breathed life into this unknown figure, spurring Lorelei to search more and more. While she still didn't know the heir's identity, she had learned enough to believe the heir was real.

One of the late King Noheah's mistresses had proved elusive many years, before Moragon caught up to her and slaughtered her like the rest. While there were vague records of her having children, there was no record of their names, their sexes, or their deaths. As orphans, they would have likely been sold into slavery, and that meant Castle Alaula was a likely place for them to end up. Where better to further her search?

Thus, here she was, having allowed herself to get captured by Moragon, and thus she must keep up the illusion that she was here entirely against her will. He had taken the bait more readily than she'd thought he might, all the more reason for her to keep her wits about her. If he wanted her to be seduced by Mikanah, as seemed rather clear, she must pretend to be seduced. If he wanted her to be drained of her senses like the rest of his servants, she must pretend to be insensible.

Lorelei snaked through the corridors of the castle, up and down flights of stairs, reacclimating herself with the castle she'd lived in nearly all her life. The longer she walked, the deeper a silence seemed to descend upon the entire castle. Servants, guards, and other courtiers all appeared fewer and farther between. With the approaching concert, a strange expectancy hung over the castle, like a curtain waiting to be raised. The anticipation was so omnipresent Lorelei could almost sense its weight.

At last, Lorelei stopped before the doors leading into the library. She grabbed the handle, turned, and pushed—

Without any effect at all. She tried the handle again, with the same results.

"Sweet girl, you won't get in."

Lorelei whirled. A Carmennan woman with a wrinkled face stood before her, streaks of gray in her jet-black hair. The shape of her face showed she might be younger than she appeared, perhaps aged by the cruelties of the castle. Her shoulders hunched slightly, and her gray gown, so dark it was nearly black, trailed the floor behind her; she might have risen from the very shadows. As frail as her body appeared, her eyes shone with a stark alertness. If Mikanah's eyes had been ice, this woman's were fire.

"No, you won't get in at all," she continued, her voice soft but unsettling. "In fact, I would get back to your room as quickly as possible. Then again, it may be too late. They may have locked that too. You don't want to get caught out here, my dear. But I suppose you must be new and wouldn't know that."

She took a few steps forward and tilted her head.

Lorelei shuddered. She hated to judge based on appearances, but the woman's wild eyes made her look almost possessed.

"You..." the woman said. "You have seen hardships. But your face has a softness about it. You haven't been here long enough. You haven't *seen*. You wouldn't *know*."

"I have seen enough at Moragon's hands," Lorelei said, finding her voice. "But why do they lock the doors?"

"You have not seen *enough*," the woman insisted, "if you do not know why they lock the doors."

"Is it just the library doors?"

"No, naïve child. 'Tis all the doors they lock every night, exactly one hour before the concert. As I said, you'd best head back before your room is sealed tight. No one will open their door to you once closed."

Lorelei wondered what happened to those who got locked outside their rooms, but she did not wish to see with her own eyes. And yet she felt compelled to linger a moment more. This woman understood how the castle worked. She might know other things.

"My room is far away. If yours is close by, might I come and seek refuge with you?"

The woman narrowed her gaze. She scrutinized Lorelei for a while. "If the king thinks this was my idea, it'll be a nasty consequence for certain."

"He'll know it was my idea."

"You seem to think he knows you well. Intimately, even, I'd say." An almost wicked grin pulled at the corners of her lips.

Lorelei suppressed a shudder. "Are we going or not? Or shall we stand here until we're both locked out and he has both our heads?"

The woman's grin vanished. With a vicious glare, she motioned for Lorelei to follow and turned down the hallway. Within moments, they had entered the woman's chambers.

Lorelei heaved a sigh of relief and looked about curiously. Four-poster bed, elegantly carved furniture, roaring fireplace with a small study area, and adjoining garderobe. What favor had this strange woman won to be granted such lavish quarters?

"Come, sit," the woman said, taking a seat in one of the massive armchairs by the flames and motioning for Lorelei to do the same.

Lorelei sank onto the edge of the other chair. "Thank you, Lady...?"

The woman chuckled, a low, raspy sound. "I no longer bear such an extravagant title. My birth name, 'Pua,' will suit well enough."

"Thank you, Pua. My name is Lorelei."

"Lorelei." The woman's smile dipped ever so slightly, and her gaze seemed to scrutinize once more. "Named after the ancient river enchantress...." Lorelei sat tall, forcing herself not to shift and reveal her discomfort. "Anyway, what were you intending to search for inside the library? Few of Moragon's wards are literate, and fewer still have the time or interest to pursue the art of reading."

"I am not one of his mistresses, if that's what you mean."

"Oh?" The woman tilted her head, and Lorelei couldn't decipher whether she was more curious or disbelieving of Lorelei's declaration.

Lorelei considered her next words carefully. If Pua was one of Moragon's spies, she'd been taught to easily detect a lie. Lorelei must make her lies simple and believable. "I'm not native to the mainland. I was raised in Pakua. I'm interested in learning about the royal family's history."

Pua chuckled. "The royal family's history? Ahh, but the books won't speak those truths, dear girl. Dates and names, important wars and marriages. All lies, in a sense, veiling the unseen secrets in between." She clapped her hands in delight. "Take the late queen for instance. Addicted to anemone root. It's how they say she became unable to bear children and ultimately went mad. Drove King Noheah to seek mistresses, especially in hopes for an heir, a *sane* heir at that."

Lorelei's heart lurched. What if some of Moragon's whispers had infiltrated her mind after all and extracted just enough of her thoughts? What if he had planted this woman in her path?

Then again, if this woman knew even an inkling of some fact that might get her closer to the heir, she must take that risk and press on. Just in case, she sang her shielding charms in her mind, making certain they locked securely around her thoughts.

"Did he succeed?" Lorelei asked, doing her best to sound only mildly interested. "In producing an heir? I'd thought all the royal family was dead."

"I just said the queen was infertile, didn't I?" Pua snapped. "Of course, it's possible that at least one of his little bastard 'heirs', of which I assure you there were many such claims, was genuine. But before that could come to fruition, our great King Moragon had the whole lot of them slaughtered—except for the one. Ah, yes, they always miss one in these stories, don't they?"

Lorelei leaned forward a little. "Did one survive?"

Pua nodded and shifted closer too, wildfire shining plainly in her eyes. "I saw the young child once, many years ago. Still can't be certain whether it was male or female. They say it possessed a great rare talent that His Majesty, Moragon, could not resist. But then something happened. Maybe the child was an intolerable brat as these whores' sons often are. The child disappeared."

"Any chance the child survived?"

Pua narrowed her gaze again, and Lorelei wondered if she'd pushed too far. "Unlikely. If His Majesty had taken interest in the child, we'd know. Otherwise, it would've been killed or turned a slave. But my..." She leaned back in her chair, straightening as much as her hunched back would allow. "You've developed a sudden fascination for the tale."

"It's one I've never heard," Lorelei said. "I'm interested in knowing more about where I come from."

"No...no, it's more than that." Pua gripped the arms of her chair. "You're one of those Defiance swine."

Lorelei's heart seemed to melt under the woman's fiery stare. She had encountered few members of the Defiance in Carmenna. Most stayed in Pakua, building resources and allies in the safety of the cliffs. Any member of the Defiance known on Carmennan soil would be slaughtered at once.

"I'm not," Lorelei said, her voice less certain than she wished. "I'm merely curious about—"

"No. You would plot against His sweet Majesty. You would help those rats steal his throne and murder him in his sleep. Traitor, *traitor!*"

Pua screamed the accusation at the top of her lungs and lunged forward. Before Lorelei knew it, the woman's hands were around her neck, squeezing and clawing so hard that both breath and thought were knocked from her. She grappled for a spell that would fling the woman aside.

"Hands off her, you stupid crone!"

Lorelei was yanked roughly away from the woman's grasp and into another's. She gasped for air as Mikanah held her. He stared past her, looking furious. A loud shriek summoned his attention, and he shoved Lorelei to the side.

Lorelei caught herself on the chair, wheeling just in time to watch as two guards dragged the woman from the room while she kicked and screamed vulgar accusations at them.

"Come on," Mikanah muttered, grabbing Lorelei by the arm, and pulling her down the hall.

Mikanah had soon unlocked her door and lurched them both inside the room. Slamming the door behind them, he glowered at her. "Just what in all the realms were you thinking? Did I not leave you here with express instructions?"

"So, the whipped dog has some bite after all," Lorelei snapped, still shaken and trembling.

Mikanah stared at her, taken aback, before saying, "You could've gotten yourself killed. That woman may look like just an old hag, but she's dangerous. She'll twist your words in an instant. Many have died for treason by her lips."

"If not just an old hag, then who is she?"

"To be honest, a quite young one. She was once beautiful but also rebellious. Moragon punished her many times for her disobedience, creating her madness. She worships him as much as she hates him. She spends her days lurking about the castle, tormenting whoever she supposes are his new mistresses."

"And Moragon trusts *her* judgment?"

Mikanah snorted in derision. "He doesn't. He trusts her judgment for those he wishes to condemn and condemns her for accusing those he wishes to see innocent. He...."

His voice trailed. For a brief moment, he looked worried.

Lorelei raised an eyebrow. At last, a bit of fire broke through the ice as he admitted his master's manipulative ways.

"That room we were in, it was well appointed. I take it that wasn't hers then?"

"Used to be," Mikanah said with a shrug. "When she was his favorite. She still fancies it hers. He punishes her, every time she sets foot inside. Makes no difference. She keeps going back."

"I'm shocked he hasn't just had her killed. That's his usual method for dealing with anyone who displeases him."

"He keeps her around because she hears things, sees things..." He stopped himself again. "Much like *you*, actually. Poking your nose into business where it doesn't belong. You'll end up like her if you're not careful."

"What difference would that make to you?"

Mikanah looked surprised again. Then his expression hardened. "It makes no difference to me at all. It's *your* life. I only thought that might make a difference to *you*."

Silence passed between them. When it seemed evident that he would reveal no more, Lorelei ventured, "What she said, was it a lie? There *is* no danger in being outside my room before the concert?"

"In that she spoke the truth." Mikanah took a few steps forward and reached out toward her.

Lorelei flinched and instinctively took a few steps back.

"What are you doing?"

"I had only wanted to check that you're all right after that witch grabbed you. At least move your hair aside so I can see."

Mikanah made no move to touch her again, but a chill rippled through her, and she flung up an extra mental shield, just in case. Then, sweeping her hair up, she held it as he examined her neck with a curious frown. "The way she grabbed you, there should be marks of some sort. Bruises, scratches. But I don't see any…"

Lorelei's pendant seemed to respond by blooming its heat beneath her skin.

She crossed her arms. "*Now* who's asking too many questions?"

Mikanah's jaws worked, his mouth a thin line. Reining in his obvious impatience, he waved a dismissive arm. "Never mind. Just stay here. I'll fetch you for the concert in a half hour's time. *Stay. Here.*"

Lorelei said nothing but simply waited until he seemed satisfied enough to turn and leave the room.

Then she let herself fall back on the bed. She breathed deeply and hummed a soothing melody to calm her quivering nerves. The mere act of Mikanah almost touching her, whatever his intent, had flooded her with fresh panic that only this place and its memories could invoke. She closed her eyes, begging a short rest before the concert and whatever horrors this mysterious gathering brought with it. In returning to Castle Alaula, she had truly, *willingly,* reentered a living nightmare.

CHAPTER 22

THE KING'S MUSIC

The knock on her door jerked Lorelei from her haze of dreams.

She opened her eyes just in time for the person to knock more intently. Without waiting for a response, the door opened and Mikanah stood in the doorway.

"What time is it?" Lorelei muttered, lifting a hand to her aching shoulder. Today's tension had wreaked havoc on her muscles. "Did I miss the concert?"

"No," Mikanah said with a scoff. "Had you missed the concert, we would've both woken in far less savory quarters, if at all. Come. It's time to go."

Lorelei didn't move at first, still foggy from being so abruptly woken from such a deep sleep. She looked beyond Mikanah to the corridor outside, bright with torchlight and candlelit chandeliers, then glanced about the room, looking for a window or any other way to judge the hour. Finding none, she rose and followed Mikanah. She remembered the large, gilded astronomical clock hung on the wall opposite the throne room entrance. They would pass it on the way to the concert, if it was in the Great Hall, as most entertainments had been when she lived here.

At any rate, her interest in the time was mere curiosity more than a real need to know the hour. Day, night... they would all blend into one humiliating experience after another.

They walked in complete silence down the corridors and winding stairs. Mikanah didn't look at her once, focused on the path ahead.

As they passed a dark corridor lined on either side with several long, narrow windows, Lorelei saw stars shining in the jet-black sky.

"Mikanah, how long is the concert?"

Still, he said nothing.

After traveling several more corridors and down a long, oak-paneled stairway, the vacant halls came to life again. Guards led groups of servants and courtiers toward a singular direction. Everyone stared vacantly, unblinking, like mere statues or puppets animated by some magic.

Finally, their destination rose into view, a pair of red doors, swung open wide. Under any other circumstance, Lorelei might have admired their intricate carvings—wild beasts playing musical instruments and dragons with breath aflame, entwined by a ribbon of a musical staff, complete with tiny notes. She had the impulse to learn the tune engraved there, but she wasn't near enough to examine it closely. As they drew closer, she realized that she didn't recognize the doors at all. And this wasn't the Great Hall, either. Had Moragon managed to build an entire theatre inside the castle?

They entered a short hall surrounded by ebony wood walls, their panels inlaid with gold, and crimson velvet curtains. The crowds streamed inside the hall in perfect rows, at a perfect pace, as if pulled along by invisible ropes. Lorelei, unnerved, slowed her own pace until Mikanah grabbed her arm and jerked her forward.

Within moments, the hall branched open wide. Lorelei gasped but kept walking. The theatre sprawled like a giant cave hewn from gold, ebony, and velvet. The seats ringing the massive theatre sloped down what must have been at least a hundred rows to the stage below, and they were packed. It seemed every single courtier, soldier, and servant had been gathered. Lorelei wondered that Moragon would allow even the lowliest to attend.

Above, the ceiling domed high, supported by pillars carved intricately with seductive nymphs, fauns, and small winged fae playing flutes and stringed instruments. Tapestries and iron sconces with thick white candles, alternating with torches, encircled the wall. The whole place was both beautiful and terrible. The beauty was for the eyes; everything else was drowned by an atmosphere of utter hopelessness. A weight hung over them all, stifling every feeling of freedom, making good thoughts and even breathing difficult. Even the glow of the flames, large and small, seemed dim, tainted by their surroundings, and lacking enough air to feed them. Strong, oppressive magic filled this room, blasting over Lorelei in wave after stormy wave.

Everyone filed to their seats. As Mikanah led Lorelei down the long stair set between the rows, her gaze fell upon Moragon. He sat on a gilded throne atop a dais near the stage, wearing a deep red doublet and a black, gold-embroidered cloak. A Carmennan man in a richly embroidered red tunic—Reynard, she recognized—sat in an ornate chair to his right. A similar chair sat unoccupied to his left. The instant Lorelei saw it, a new swell of unease rippled down her spine.

Sure enough, Mikanah guided her down to that very chair. Lorelei sat, her body stiff and awkward. She knew the seat to the king's left was traditionally a queen's place in Carmenna. Fortunately, Moragon seemed to pay Lorelei no heed.

She turned to thank Mikanah, but he had already slipped from her sight. Her gaze roamed to the stage, built from a dark ebony wood, with royal blue velvet curtains hanging in the backdrop, deceptively elegant and alluring like everything else about the theatre and the man who controlled it. Her interest focused on the single instrument hovering over the stage midair, illuminated by the flames hovering around the stage's perimeter.

A violin.

Her gut wrenched as she recognized the unmistakable instrument with its beautifully unique curves, polished golden-red wood, and long, delicate bow. This was the same instrument she had seen the young boy use to murder the guard, on the day Moragon had nearly murdered her father and had first learned the secret of her musical magic. Since then, she had seen him use other of his servants to play the instrument. Its strains, overflowing with emotion, could seduce, enslave, conquer. What deceitfully lovely nightmare would the violin craft tonight?

"Exquisite, isn't it?" Moragon said.

"Indeed," Lorelei returned curtly. She wanted nothing more than to jump on stage and use the violin to play a song that would torture Moragon for all the grief he had caused the Guardians, their families, and all Carmenna. Of course, even if she could make it to the stage without Moragon's guard seizing her, the pendant would forbid her. The protection it granted her came at a price. While she wore it, she could not directly harm anyone, nor had she yet learned any way to remove it. She could play a song that could quake the entire theatre, perhaps crushing Moragon, but of course she would never risk the lives of the hundreds gathered. She must enact her vengeance the same as she ever had her plans: with calculated control and patience.

"If you think the instrument is beautiful, just wait for the music itself. Mikanah plays with a command that very nearly equals my skills of the mind."

She inhaled sharply. "*Mikanah?*" The young man with the icy stare. Moragon had chosen him to play at this eve's concert? Even if his knowledge of music was great, Lorelei couldn't imagine that he possessed the passion necessary to enchant an entire crowd, not even one seemingly as dazed and ready to blindly receive as this.

"Yes, did he not tell you?" Moragon asked. "Mikanah is my chief musician."

Mikanah walked onto stage then, clad in fine clothes that echoed its grandeur, a doublet made from shimmering royal blue velvet and a gold-trimmed whisk framing his neck, black breeches, and black boots over blue hose. All lights extinguished, except for the hovering flames enlightening the violin with their haunting aura.

"Good evening and welcome." Mikanah bowed at the audience. "I stand here honored to play for you tonight. Listen well as I share with you *La Sirena*, a gift from the Spaniño kingdom."

Gifted or stolen? While the Guardians had quested to locate, learn, and protect as many musical spells as they could, Moragon had likewise set about a similar mission. Lorelei doubted he had been as diplomatic as the Guardians in obtaining such knowledge.

The Chief Musician took the violin, rested it beneath his chin, and set the bow to the strings. Out of the corner of her eye, Lorelei could see Moragon smirking. An almost maddened ecstasy leaped inside his gaze, and his smirk spread into a grin.

As Mikanah began to play the first rich, sinuous notes, Lorelei locked her gaze on him, instantly mesmerized. How, with a single instrument, could this young man, who'd seemed capable of communicating only coldness and anger, induce so many different emotions?

Her captivation quickly spread beyond that of the violin and toward the musician himself. Potent melodies and harmonies flowed from his inner core into his fingertips, through the strings, and straight inside her mind and heart. She could somehow feel the music emanating from every fiber of his being, calling to her, fighting to get inside her. As if the violin were a lover or slave, he leaned, swayed, and turned, both dancing with it and commanding it, seducing it along with his audience. His fingers lightly caressed its neck and brushed against its curves. He made the bow skip silkily across the strings, which sang and laughed and sobbed at the bow's lightest touch. Mikanah closed his eyes and parted his lips. He surely knew his music had conquered his captive listeners, and now he made love to them.

Lorelei shuddered, almost feeling his hands creeping along her body. She breathed, swallowed hard, and clutched the edge of her seat, wanting to tear away, but his spell ensnared her mind, compelling her to watch and listen on. She sang protective charms inside her mind to keep his infiltrating spells at bay, but she could not stop his emotions from becoming one with hers, could not shake their created desire to submit everything to him. His body and the violin became one, and they became one with her. Their seductive dance and song swelled stronger passions within her than she'd have ever thought possible, passions she could neither define nor comprehend.

At last, Lorelei found strength enough to sever her

gaze.

The disconnect knocked her breath away. She bowed her head and placed her palm over her pounding heart. *La Sirena*—indeed, *The Siren*—had entranced her nearly senseless, even with her pendant's protection. Fear now broke through all enchantment, and she wanted nothing more than to flee the theatre.

Instead, she glanced about at the audience, only to find herself staring in complete shock. No one else seemed moved by the music. . Instead, they all stared at Mikanah with the same blank, trancelike stupor.

Lorelei looked up at Moragon. He was staring at her, a twisted ecstasy filling his entire face. Suddenly she understood why Moragon had chosen Mikanah as his chief musician. Moragon kept his subjects under his perfect control by using Mikanah's music to enslave them. His hypnotic music was surely why Moragon had wanted her to see the concert. Thankfully, her pendant and mental shields protected her, but she must pretend as though her spirit began to break.

When the piece ended, everyone clapped mechanically. Their dismal expressions held firm, and Mikanah lowered his instrument to take a bow. As he scanned the audience, his eyes met Lorelei's for the briefest moment. He bowed again in her direction before turning and exiting the stage.

After the clapping ceased, the crowds filed from their seats into the corridors beyond. They glided fluidly, like rivers flowing toward the ocean, needing neither reason nor heart to guide them. They were simply flowing where they were meant to.

"I hope you enjoyed the performance tonight," Moragon said. "You will surely hunger for many more."

With these words and a cryptic final look at Lorelei, Moragon rose, as did Reynard, and joined a band of four guards. The crowds parted like waves, deferring to them as they walked through.

Lorelei followed the throngs of drone-like servants, uncertain what else to do. She tried to slow down, to match their drawling pace, but as their stiff bodies bumped against her and their empty, uncanny stares made her skin crawl, she wanted nothing more than to dart as fast as she could from their fold. She almost ran, but then she stopped herself. How deeply had they been manipulated this evening? If she dared do anything outside their routine, might they turn against her?

Someone grabbed her arm and whispered harshly in her ear, "Come. We must leave this place."

Mikanah pulled Lorelei back through the crowd, flowing against their current. The strangers bumped along like mere buoys bobbing in the water, easily falling right back into place while Lorelei and Mikanah pushed through. Lorelei averted her gaze, unable to bear so many lifeless stares.

Mikanah pulled her up onto the stage, around the back, and down another short set of steps. He opened a door, and they disappeared beneath the stage.

They flew down another flight of steps, a long corridor, and at last up a long, winding staircase that led into a vacant, drafty room. Lorelei shivered at the sharp breeze, but even this coldness seemed warmer than the chill of so many eyes watching her emptily.

At last, they emerged through a door into the night, onto a wall spanning between two of the castle's towers, known as an "allure" or "wall walk." Lorelei gratefully breathed the cool air and gazed with relief at the stars that twinkled and danced untamed, as if they possessed wills of their own; in some worlds, they did. Even these stars contained more will than the lost souls now trapped inside, forced to serve a man who would slaughter them all if it meant advancing his reign.

Mikanah left her side and walked across the allure. He picked up speed, and for a moment, Lorelei had the wild thought that he would fling himself off the edge. She nearly cried out, but he only leaned over and inhaled deeply, as though music instead of oxygen had fueled his body inside the theatre.

Slowly, Lorelei walked over, leaned against the short, crenelated wall, and watched him. The iciness had melted from his eyes, replaced by the fierce flames she'd glimpsed before. He looked alive with a sudden ferocity, with the same urge to flee that she'd felt inside the theatre.

"You played magnificently," Lorelei said. "A shame your gift is used for the service of Moragon."

Mikanah laughed shakily. "Don't compliment me. I hear no beauty in my music anymore. Not that it matters." He gave her a skeptical glance. "I'm not even certain why I brought you here."

"But now you have, you may as well give me some answers."

His gaze narrowed, but he said nothing.

"The theatre," Lorelei prompted. "It wasn't here when I served here before. I swear it wasn't. But it's right in the middle of the castle. It has to be near the throne room, from what I recall. How could he have had it built so quickly?"

"He didn't," Mikanah said. "At least, not directly. He reconstructed the castle's inner chambers, the same as he does most things, through his slaves. Manipulating workers to drive themselves too hard, past exhaustion, even to the point of death. Some, he promises unimaginable rewards. Others, he threatens with harm to them or their families. What promises he desires to uphold, he does. Others work for him for nothing. It's all the same to him, as long as the job is completed. Working people to the bone, using both threats and promises to persuade them to submit. It's all just more mental preparation for them to receive his enslavement spells."

"*Your* enslavement spells."

"Yes," Mikanah muttered. "The compositions are collaborative efforts. His Majesty has much knowledge of the mental arts, which can be quite useful in musical magic."

The direction of his gaze strayed, and Lorelei let hers follow.

Here on the castle wall, she could see all Carmenna spanned out below them, beyond the abysmal moat. The realm's thick, deep green woods stretched toward more cliffs towering in the farthest distance.

"Despite everything," Lorelei breathed, "it's still beautiful. It's still home...or might be again someday." She glanced at him, trying to gauge his reaction. Everything that had occurred so far—her being permitted to wander the castle, Pua taking her under her wing only to attack her, Mikanah's coming to the rescue then as now, his abrupt willingness to speak treason against his master—Lorelei couldn't help but wonder if it was all part of Moragon's ploy to make her think of Mikanah as a protector, to make her trust and be ultimately beguiled by him. Sensing no change in his demeanor, she asked casually, "Why did you bring me up here anyway?"

"Watch."

Lorelei gazed out. All lay swathed in night and shadow. But gradually, along the farthest border of Carmenna, something orange, red, and yellow peeped over the horizon. The sun cast brilliant rays as far as it could across the land, persevering toward the castle as if hoping to overcome Moragon's darkness by its sheer will.

"It's wonderful," Lorelei said. "But if it's morning,

that would mean an entire night has passed, which seems impossible."

Some of Mikanah's awe at the sunrise melted from his face. "That, too, is part of the spell. Everyone is required to be in their rooms before the concert because a certain mist is released, a sort of hypnotic training that makes their minds relaxed and open, ready for the real thing. The mist is imbued with strains from a magic lullaby, also played by me. This extra step isn't necessary. People obey Moragon, whether from love or fear, without any need for the mist, but he started releasing it as an experiment, to see how musical and elemental magics could be combined."

"For which reason do *you* serve Moragon, love or fear?"

Lorelei asked the question with a tilt of her head, making herself seem innocently curious.

Mikanah did not react, except to narrow his gaze ever so slightly, a gesture that might have indicated simple annoyance at her interrupting his explanation. "The mist makes people lose track of time. You've surely noticed by now that Moragon's removed all of the clocks in the castle." He looked at her closely. "The mist didn't work for you at all, save to put you to sleep. Nor did my music affect you in the slightest." Anger burned in his eyes, and beyond that, a hint of fear.

"Don't worry," Lorelei said, guessing his thoughts. "I've known Moragon long enough to understand how to twist his own games against him. I can make him believe your music has swayed me."

A wry smile crossed Mikanah's lips, and he returned his gaze to the lightening heavens. For a moment, a wistfulness touched his face, making him look less hardened.

"Why did you bring me here?" Lorelei asked again, gently. "This place seems to haunt you."

"I come here every day because it makes me think of a friend of mine. She was all I had left, but then His Majesty took a great interest in her. Of course, he punished her for disloyalty, as he does to all those who displease or tire him."

Lorelei guessed she was dead, but he seemed unable to breathe this truth aloud and she would not do it for him. Instead, she focused her eyes at the sun as it peeked just above the horizon. "Where there is still light, there is still hope, right?"

Mikanah scoffed. "The proper phrase is, where there is life, there's hope.' Which is something she might have said...."

He scowled at her again and took a step back. "Where *do* you get your powers from?"

"I'm no mental magician," Lorelei assured him. "I don't read or influence minds."

His disbelief was obvious. "All the same, it seems impossible that you could resist *all* my attempts this evening. Is that by some magic of the Guardians? I can't understand how you're so powerful and clever, but the rest of your lot got annihilated so easily."

Lorelei's entire body tensed. "Do *not* speak of my friends in that manner. Their deaths are still near to me."

"*Friends*," he sneered. "Saying the Guardians are friends is as foolish as saying anyone could be 'friends' with His Majesty. Though Reynard would like to tell himself so. He's the man who sat with His Majesty this evening. At any rate, the Guardians are a ruling faction in their own right. And such factions always have leaders, hierarchies, but no true friends."

"We rule nothing, you ignorant brat."

Mikanah's eyes widened. He opened his mouth to retort, but Lorelei stepped forward and said, "We *protect*. That is our sole purpose. How dare you insult the memory of my companions. Surely you have seen people you care about suffer at Moragon's hands. To insult me thus is to insult yourself, and the memories of those you love."

"You've some nerve, especially referring to His Majesty without the proper terms of respect. And I know exactly what it is to lose the only people I ever cared about to him."

"Then there is the difference between us," Lorelei said, clenching her fists at her sides to contain the anger emerging from her pain. "I have lost people I love but keep fighting for the right side, against him. You, on the other hand, have succumbed to his will, making you even worse than his poor benumbed slaves or—"

"Get out of here!" Mikanah snarled. Rage filled his face, and he raised his hand, whether to slap her or cast a spell, Lorelei was uncertain, and she mentally prepared herself for either.

"Leave," he repeated. "Now."

She stood her ground. "You are my escort. Moragon will punish you if he knows you've left me running about the castle on my own."

"He will punish me more if I lose control and lay a hand against you. Just go, *now!*"

Lorelei studied him coolly a few moments. He breathed heavily, his fury rising like a wild beast's. She wasn't scared of him, nor did she pity him. He wasn't like Moragon, devoid of human feelings. He felt far more than he was willing to let on, especially to himself. But he was just as volatile, trapped inside the mind that he had allowed Moragon to mold for him.

Without another word, Lorelei turned, hurried across the allure, and slipped inside the tower.

CHAPTER 23

THE KING'S SECRETS

Lorelei rushed down the long, winding tower stairs. Out on the wall walk, filled with righteous anger at Mikanah's insults, she had felt fearless. Now, her thoughts clarified, and she realized what a fool she'd been to defy him. He was not only Moragon's chief musician, but he dared to speak with detest against Reynard, Moragon's right-hand man. He was clearly fighting for the king's favor, whether for survival or some higher ambitions.

Lorelei emerged into a main wing of the castle and froze in place when she discovered the guards marching down an adjoining hall several yards away. Reynard himself trailed on their heels, his face hardened with determination.

Lorelei waited until he and the guards had disappeared from sight. Then, noiseless as the gray daylight slipping through the tall windows, she sped down the hall and peered around the corner, watching as the small entourage turned another bend.

She knew where she was and where they were going. After the briefest contemplation, she made her decision.

Without Mikanah looming nearby, this might be her only chance to gain new information.

Conjuring her old coelescence spell from her memory, Lorelei chanted the word *Amalgamation* in her mind, pushing against the wall until she began to fall through. She focused adamantly, nearly blacking out as the stones seemed to crush her, as if they passed through her body instead of her passing through them. Just when she thought she might lose consciousness, she tumbled through the wall completely to the secret passageway beyond, breathless.

Reeling dizzily, she braced herself, filling her lungs with air. Regaining a full breath took some effort. The passage was narrower than she remembered, the air heavier, staler. When at last her mind cleared, she scurried down the passageway, taking the many twists and turns until she had reached her goal.

It was still there, her secret peephole. Removing the stone that covered it, she crouched down and peered through. Moragon sat on the throne. His guards surrounded the room.

Lorelei recoiled, trembling. It was the same tableau as when he'd accused her father of treason and, in essence, sentenced him to die. That scene still haunted with her final memory of him, not strong and whole and happy, but terrified and bereft of all hope.

For the first time since she'd learned of the Guardians' slaughter, Lorelei buried her face in her hands and wept, incapable of restraining the silent tears for as long as they would come.

Someone brushed her shoulder, and she sang a musical charm, *Fonia*, to create a gust of wind that slammed the person back with a loud thud. Lorelei whirled to discover the intruder, rubbing his head with a groan.

"Mikanah!" she gasped. "Why are you here?"

"I tried to follow you," he whispered back. "Just as I found you, you were disappearing inside the wall. I didn't think anyone else knew about these old passages."

"Neither did I," Lorelei said curtly. She tried to conceal her fear, but her body tensed as she uttered her next thought aloud. "Does anyone else know...?"

"If you mean Moragon, then no. I highly doubt it. I know of them because my friend showed them to me. She was a master at discovering and keeping secrets. It seems the knowledge of these passages was only passed down to the royal family and their closest friends. My friend...she was always eager to plot some escape or rebellion. She managed to sway one of those friends, before they were found to have connections to the late King Noheah and met their untimely demise."

Lorelei scrutinized Mikanah, once again trying to decipher how much truth lay behind his words. If his sole purpose was to seduce and win her trust, he might run to Moragon with the knowledge that she was sneaking about the castle to spy on him. Except, it appeared that Mikanah's own sneaking about was unbeknownst to Moragon. Perhaps he was not as loyal to the king as he wanted to convince her, and his own self, that he was. Perhaps she might have a chance of turning the game on its head by luring him to her side. Meanwhile, continuing to take a defensive stance might be best, especially until she was certain of his intentions.

"If you've come to take me from here, you'll have to fight me and draw attention to us both. I've waited too long for this opportunity, to learn what he is up to."

"Don't worry," Mikanah said. "So have I." Whether he lied or spoke truth, he did so fiercely. "There are things he doesn't tell me. Things he tells only to Reynard. I came here once before, just recently. Moragon was telling him of some new relic or weapon, but I couldn't catch most of what was said."

"Then let's see if we can find out."

Lorelei motioned toward the peephole, and they hunched down. Reynard had entered the room and knelt before Moragon's throne. Moragon spoke, but as usual, the words flowed together in a garbled jumble, distorted by the sound barriers encompassing the room.

All of a sudden, their speech became clearer. A melody wafted to her, and she glanced at Mikanah in amusement. No sound came from him, but she knew he must utter some song-spell in his mind. He broke through the room's barriers just enough to make the conversation understandable. Lorelei leaned forward, listening intently:

"...and the Cynwrig traitors?" Moragon asked. "They've been dealt with as commanded?"

"Yes, Your Majesty," Reynard said. "Drawn and quartered, along with the rest...."

Moragan continued to dole out commands for dealing with prisoners. Many punishments were vile, a few petty. Lorelei cringed at how casually he rattled off people's names and fates, as though he recited a simple list of ingredients for Reynard to collect from the marketplace.

"What further progress can you report on our new Vessel?" Moragon asked.

Mikanah nudged Lorelei who turned to him and said, "This is what they were talking about before?"

"I think it might be."

"Some sort of boat or ship?"

Mikanah shrugged. "Perhaps. He's been making overseas allies. One of them might have gifted him a new ship."

They listened closely again as Moragon said, "Have you tested it properly as I commanded?"

"No, Your Majesty," Reynard said. "It is not time."

"War approaches us. The Lozolian Council grows ever more suspicious. Already, they amass their own allies. You understand how war works, Reynard. I will have my army, but the Vessel is necessary to see this war's full triumph. It must be tested sooner rather than later. *Much* sooner."

"I understand, Your Majesty. But to try and fill it with so much power right now would break it. It is not strong enough."

"Then *make* it strong enough. The Guardians will also be replenished soon enough and will make their move, and we cannot trust them to be so careless again—"

Moragon's last words increased significantly in volume, and he sent a fierce, searching gaze about the room.

Mikanah fell back and severed his spell. Silence engulfed them once again.

Lorelei glared at him before returning to the peephole. Below, Moragon seemed to be scanning the entire room, likely seeking the source of the magic he had sensed infiltrating his protective walls. At last, he returned his focus to Reynard, and their conversation resumed.

Mikanah grabbed Lorelei, dragging her back through the passageway. Several rooms and corridors later, they climbed a stair and entered the annex and corridor housing Lorelei's chambers. Mikanah led her inside, slammed the door behind them, and whirled on her with a lethal glare.

"What were you thinking?" he snapped. "Skulking around like that, do you hunger for death? That's what we'd be facing, had he caught us, as you well know!"

"Then perhaps you should be more careful with your spells! If you can't control yourself while playing spy, then you shouldn't do it at all!"

Mikanah's lips drew into a thin line. His fists clenched and he shook all over. Lorelei prepared for him to fly into a rage.

He managed to calm himself just enough to breathe deeply. "My spell wouldn't have failed if I hadn't seen Reynard. I can hardly bear him, his smug and pious ways. Moragon claims to prize me as his most useful servant. And yet this one, obviously important matter of the Vessel he keeps secret from me." He stopped short, looking furious with himself. "I don't even know why I'm telling you all this." He turned and stormed toward the door.

"Because you need someone to talk to," Lorelei said. "Besides Moragon and his minions. Someone you know you can trust."

Mikanah glared back at her. "I trust no one."

"Except yourself. You trust that what you're doing for Moragon is the right path. You make yourself believe your own lies."

"I don't desire to harm you, but you will not insult me." He pointed his finger at her, before jerking his thumb at himself. "I *am* fighting for the right side, the side that won't get me killed. Any thought of saving others died long ago. I couldn't save them and nearly destroyed myself. Now I fight to live, and to obtain what power I can. To surpass Reynard, and to regain some control over my life."

"You really believe Moragon will let you have that control?"

"No. I will take it for myself. But we will talk no more on this subject. You will not denigrate my decisions for my life. In return, I will not belittle the deaths of your companions. And you will never speak to me again as you have. Is this understood?"

Lorelei studied him skeptically. He really was a stubborn young fool, a boy grasping at any slim straws of power in hopes of feeling like a man.

But as they were to be companions of sorts during her stay here, and as gaining his trust might work to her advantage, she did not wish to be on ill terms.

"I understand," she said at last. "Now, if you would excuse me, I'm very tired."

"Of course," Mikanah muttered. "If you need something, or wish to go out again, pull that cord by the door. I or a servant will come." He slipped from the room, shutting the door behind him.

Lorelei released a heavy sigh and fell back gratefully on the giant bed. The warmth of the blazing fireplace engulfed her, and she begged sleep to come, but many thoughts played at the edges of her mind, taunting her, reminding her that as long as she was here, she could not fully rest.

She recalled what Pua had said yesterday about a child with a rare talent. The woman had clearly been insane, but Lorelei suspected there was some truth in her words. Perhaps an heir had survived right under Moragon's nose.

More than that, what of the Vessel? Was it truly a boat as she suspected, perhaps a great warship? Equally mysterious to the Vessel itself were the tests Moragon had hounded Reynard about performing, to ensure the Vessel's readiness. What exactly was this Vessel made of, and how did he aim to use it?

CHAPTER 24

THE KING'S FURY

Lorelei's head pounded as the deep, low sound boomed over and over, calling to her like war drums. Her sleep was disturbed with images of Carmennans being led by a masterful musician, sacrificing themselves to his music's will.

These same nightmares had filled her mind every night for the past week. She spent every day locked in her room, except when Mikanah might fetch her to eavesdrop on Moragon and Reynard. They hadn't spoken of the Vessel again since, nor anything else of significance, making such excursions feel like a waste. She would spend the rest of the day sealed away in her room, with only her whirring mind for companionship.

She and Mikanah had slipped into a routine of acting cordial to one another, but she hadn't seen him enough to build the rapport she felt was needed to gain his full trust. Aside from their brief ventures into the secret passage, she only saw him for his nightly performances. While his music couldn't fully infiltrate her mind, the energy it took to resist him began to drain her, and the emotions his playing invoked overwhelmed her, drowning her dreams in twisted memories. Blood filled her visions, blood that consumed her father over and over, along with hands coursing over her skin, fear running rampant across every inch of her body.

The drums intensified, and someone shook her roughly. She flew awake to see Mikanah grabbing her by the arm and demanding, "Come on! His Majesty has requested an audience with both of us. Best not to keep him waiting."

Lorelei pulled her arm from his grasp and rose from bed. She ran a hand through her wild curls and straightened her dress, all the while staring at him, trying to detect some emotion beyond his icy mien.

As soon as they stepped into the hallway, Lorelei stumbled to a halt. Reynard stood outside her door. With a curt smile and nod, he led them silently down the hall. Lorelei walked abreast with Mikanah, matching his brisk pace. He wouldn't look at her, only stared with loathing at the back of Reynard's head.

Lorelei's heart tumbled inside her. The three of them in a room, together with Moragon?

He knows, she thought with a shudder. *He knows it was us sneaking about. Or perhaps Mikanah's betrayed me.* Beyond his blatant loathing for Reynard, it was impossible to tell what Mikanah felt, whether he was afraid or indifferent to whatever plight they rushed toward.

Trumpets cried out in the distance. Their call intensified until something bright flashed down the hallway and Reynard stopped dead, motioning for Mikanah and Lorelei to do the same. The bright flash hovered before Reynard, fading to reveal a folded, shimmering piece of parchment. He snatched it, unfolding it and scanning its contents.

Lorelei raised her chin ever so subtly, hoping to catch

a glimpse of the message, but in the next breath, Reynard had muttered something into the parchment, and the words vanished. Lorelei froze, fearing that he had caught her trying to spy, but as he continued to speak into the parchment, fully concentrating, she took a couple steps forward and caught some of his words:

"...the intruder...the King's Wood...His Majesty... an interrogation...keep searching...."

After finishing his speech, Reynard folded the letter, muttered a few more words, and the note blinked down the hall in a bright flash before vanishing just as quickly as it had arrived.

Reynard turned to Mikanah. "Some urgent business has arisen that requires my immediate tending. Finish escorting her to His Majesty." His distracted gaze fell briefly on Mikanah before he turned on his heel and hurried down the corridor.

"What do you think that was all about?" Lorelei asked. "It seems like some sort of spy or assassin has infiltrated the castle grounds."

"It also sounds like he's soon to get himself caught," Mikanah muttered. "As would anyone who's foolish or brazen enough to attempt such feats."

"Do you think we should follow him? See what the commotion is about, see if we can learn something useful? Especially while everyone is so distracted."

She started in the direction Reynard had gone, but Mikanah ran forward and grabbed her shoulders, rooting her in place.

"What is the *matter* with you? His Majesty will have both our heads if we disobey his summons. Let's go— *damn it!*"

Mikanah hissed sharply, and his hand flew to his mouth. Wincing, he sucked on the skin between his thumb and pointer finger. Then he stared at his hand, turning it over and over as if trying to puzzle out some riddle.

"What *is* this?"

"What happened? Are you injured? Let me see!" Lorelei grabbed his wrist, jerked his hand toward her, and froze stiff, staring in mingled shock and horror.

"Ouch! You're pinching," Mikanah snapped, drawing away. "What is it? Have you seen it before?"

Lorelei nodded slowly. Gathering up the folds of her sleeve, she showed him her shoulder. He glanced at her faded mark and then at his, the word *Mi*, still glistening like gold and fire on his hand, then back again. He turned ashen, and for once, true fear shone on his face. "No. Impossible. I can't be one of them. I *can't*."

"But you *are*," Lorelei said, now the one to lead as she pulled him down the hall. "Trust me, I'm no happier about this than you are. But we have only one priority now—getting you as far away from here as fast as possible while everyone is distracted with the intruder."

A horrific theory struck her. A sudden intruder. Mikanah's Guardian mark appearing. Was the timing pure coincidence, or was this intruder possibly one of the Guardians' messengers, those who were dispatched whenever a new Guardian was chosen? Lorelei's stomach twisted into knots. If her suspicions were correct, the messneger was doomed to torture for whatever information Moragon could obtain from him, followed by whatever grisly death. She didn't want to imagine how much worse Moragon would do to Mikanah, one of his most loyal and powerful servants, once he discovered Mikanah had become one of the very Guardians he so despised.

She picked up their pace. "We have to get you out of here at once."

"No!" Mikanah twisted from her grasp and stepped

back. "I'm not going anywhere with you. I've worked too hard to gain His Majesty's favor to throw it all away, to make myself his enemy!"

"You *are* his enemy now! Do you not recognize that? Do you think he will spare the life of any new Guardian just because you've served him all this time? That mark changes everything. It changes *you*, who you are to him. You are no longer his favorite servant. You're his worst enemy."

Mikanah stared as if she'd knocked him over the head and stunned him. Lorelei exhaled loudly, exasperated. She didn't have time for this. *He* didn't have time.

Amiel, forgive me, she prayed, *but this? How can this self-centered fool be the musical dissonance You desire in our fellowship?*

Mikanah took another step back, finding his voice again. "I don't care what you say. I'll tell His Majesty you forced me against my will. I'll tell him how my music doesn't work on you. Better yet, you'll remove the mark."

"I have no such power. No one does, save the Lozolian Council, and they're miles upon miles from here. You're leaving unless you want to be killed. You're leaving with *me* at once."

"No! I will not sacrifice everything I've worked so hard to achieve just to be tethered to another master!"

"The only way you'll be tethered is if you stay here, likely to a wooden stake, burned as a heretic or traitor or whatever other tale Moragon manages to conjure about you. Now come. I won't say it again."

She reached for his hand to pull him along, but he yanked away and slapped her cheek. The impact had hardly registered when a strong melody threw her against the wall. Her head throbbed, but the amulet's warmth pressed against her heart and radiated upward, soothing the pain from both the slap and the knock on her head. Her mind cleared just in time to hear another musical attack surging toward her. This time she was ready. She sang a tune inside her head, the amulet burned, and a shield rose between her and Mikanah.

Lorelei stood tall and defiant. "You do not wish to fight me."

Across from her, Mikanah snarled and studied her with wild eyes, like a freed beast that feared its newfound freedom and would rather be flung back inside the only torturous existence it had known rather than take any risks by leaving.

"How?" he blurted. "How do you do it? Why do none of my attacks work against you?"

He almost screamed the next spell rather than singing it, but Lorelei held her mental shield steady. The curse rebounded, slamming him against the wall.

"You're not the only musical mage here," Lorelei said. "There is more to this gift than using sheer force and manipulation—"

The sound of clanking armor cut through her words.

"Guards!" Mikanah shouted, running toward their sound. "Guards, help! This madwoman has bewitched me!"

Lorelei stretched her arm out, pointing to him. She sang the song-spell *Fraziolda* straight toward Mikanah, who stopped dead in his tracks as if he'd run into a brick wall. His shoulders slouched, and Lorelei worried that she had overdone it, that he would collapse and fall asleep on the spot. Thankfully, he remained like a statue on his feet.

Lorelei hurried over, took him by the hand, and turned him around. His expression was blank, vacant. With her gentle nudge, he walked forward. She hated to manipulate him, but he gave her no time to choose otherwise.

The footsteps thundered closer. Within moments, Moragon's guards would turn the bend, and Lorelei and Mikanah would be surrounded. Lorelei might survive an act of rebellion, especially with the amulet intact, but Mikanah's mark, so easily visible, doomed him.

Lorelei began feeling along the walls. She pressed her fingertips close and chanted, searching for some hollow beyond, but the walls here were all at least five feet of solid stone.

She would have to try anyway.

Holding Mikanah's hand, she pressed her body against the wall, chanting *Amalgamation* over and over. She began slipping inside the wall, but much more slowly than usual. At this rate, she would never get them both through in time. Positioning Mikanah in a casual stance, she said a fervent prayer and fused inside the wall.

There was no secret passage beyond this wall. Instead, she remained stuck fast inside the stones, gasping for breath. Her whole body felt like it was being crushed from the inside out. She forced herself to listen as the guards swept past. One of them spoke, and then the footsteps receded. She waited as long as she could before spilling from the wall. She took several great breaths, recovering as quickly as possible. Then, taking Mikanah by the hand, she led him along, racing down the hall.

More guards approached. Quickly, Lorelei positioned Mikanah so that one of his arms wrapped around her shoulder while the other clutched her arm, making it look like she was the puppet and he the master. They rushed past the guards without so much as a suspicious glance.

They reached the servants' quarters. If only Lorelei could remember the exact room. She checked one where a woman sat sewing and glanced up, bewildered. Lorelei apologized, praying she wouldn't report them for wandering about. The next door over perhaps....

Yes. An empty room with a simple washtub. Lorelei moved aside the faded tapestry on the wall to reveal a door. She stepped inside, pulled Mikanah in with her, and then shut the door behind them.

They rushed down several narrow corridors, twisting and turning into the depths of the castle. The longer they traversed, the more Lorelei's mind raced to recall the exact path. She had only trekked the paths leading into the woods beyond the castle once, and now she began to doubt.

Two doors rose before them. Uncertain, she chose the rightmost door. She and Mikanah tumbled outside into an open courtyard.

Several guards stood only yards away. "Where did *they* come from?"

"It's Mikanah with that new wench of Moragon's."

"Get them at once!"

The half-dozen guards surged toward Lorelei. She threw herself in front of Mikanah and sang *Ochiá*, a stunning charm. Two of the guards came to a halt. Lorelei's next song forced them to drop their weapons. She swept up both swords and raised them in a protective cross. The remaining four guards rushed forward, drawing their own blades. Lorelei braced herself.

Swords clashed. Lorelei spun around, dodging blow after blow. She had taken a weaponry class with Tress but was no great swordswoman. Surely, it was the amulet's grace and protection that allowed her to avoid so many attacks. Other attacks, she blocked with the crossed swords, though their heavy weight soon encumbered her so that she dropped one of them, clutching the remaining blade with two hands. One of the guards darted toward Mikanah, but Lorelei sang *Fonia* to summon a wind that blasted him back against the wall where he fell still.

Another guard hefted a giant sword. At his muttered spell, flames sprang to life along its broad edges. Lorelei staggered at the sight of the fire, and a blade sliced into her side. She cried out, fell back, and turned just in time to block blows from two of the guards. The amulet burned, and her pain soon vanished, along with the wound that had caused it.

Lorelei danced between the five guards—the sixth still lay unconscious—conspiring how she would take them down. Since she couldn't deal direct harm, she would have to be clever about it. Her stunning spell worked for only one or two people at a time and exerted quite a bit of energy. Already, her body began to move clumsily.

The guard with the flaming sword flew at her. Lorelei ducked, jumped back, and stumbled from blocking the weight of his massive sword. She began composing a melody inside her head. Making up songs was better done when she wasn't weaving between arcs of flame and several swords. If it was to work, she would have to push past her fear and focus on the melody's serenity.

Once she had the song in her head, she held onto it tight and sang beneath her breath, pushing the song from her mind and through her body, down to her core. Her racing heart slowed. Her mind began to ease. She continued to dodge blows, keeping as much distance as possible and defending herself with the sword while praying her song-spell would take root.

The flames on the sword extinguished. Not exactly what she had meant to put asleep, but she'd take it. The guard stood aghast, long enough for her to disarm him. He dove for his sword, only to topple clumsily, knocking his head against the wall.

The other guards rushed at her, but as she continued to chant her new lullaby, their movements grew sluggish, and they fell against one another into a heap.

Lorelei gasped for breath, taking stock of her work with a measure of pride, before recovering enough to take Mikanah by the hand, dragging him back through the door they had come through, and choosing the other path.

They raced down halls and flights of stairs. After a while, the torches ceased leading their way as stony halls turned into the caves hidden beneath the castle. Lorelei sang *Luma* to summon a ball of light to hover beside them.

They descended deep, deep into the caves. Then, after a while, their path turned upward again. Mikanah moaned behind Lorelei, but she squeezed his hand and continued to pull him after her. He tugged against her, but she only quickened their pace. As they delved further, iron doors built into the cave passages appeared on either side of them. Good. That was a sign they were on the right trail.

As they passed through one of the doors, two guards attacked them with halbards, but Lorelei sang *Segmunda*, a repelling charm that sent them flying back.

Lorelei pulled Mikanah down a narrow cave passage and through an invisible doorway. To the naked eye, this magic-made opening was just another part of the wall. It led deeper inside the caves, to passages that were charmed so that no light or fire magic could be used to guide the way. Their balls of light entinguished, and Lorelei had to rely solely on instincts and memory.

Finally, they emerged from the secret caves and stood surrounded by woods. Lorelei stared, breathless at the sight of Castle Alaula rising behind them, between the trees. They had made it to the forest. They were free.

"What—what's going on?" Mikanah muttered. He grabbed his head and made a sour face. Staggering, he leaned against a tree for support and rubbed his temple. He gazed up at the castle and around the woods in bewilderment.

Then, as reality dawned, he turned on Lorelei, face red with rage.

"*You* did this! You messed with my mind! I don't even remember leaving the damn castle!"

"I told you it was come with me or die."

"No!" Mikanah marched toward her, fists clenched, but his feet twisted clumsily. He grabbed a nearby birch tree to keep from falling. "You don't get to make those decisions for me. No one does. I'll decide if and how I want to die."

"Your decisions no longer affect just you." Lorelei held her ground, sword clutched. She was exhausted, but she mentally prepared herself for an attack just in case. "Besides, it's too late. We've already left the castle. We need to find our way through the King's Wood and leave here as soon as possible—"

"No!" Mikanah yelled, his voice cracking. "No one is leaving here until *I* say so. This is *my* territory!" He drew his sword and swung at Lorelei.

Lorelei blocked the sloppy attack. "I didn't exactly want to leave yet either!"

They circled one another. Mikanah stumbled forward as he delivered several more blows, all of which Lorelei easily side-stepped.

"I still had a task I was meant to complete here," she went on. "I certainly had no desire to take *you* with me. You having anything to do with the Guardians, let alone *being* one, is a nightmare to me. But I have to accept it. It is now my job to free you of this land that has poisoned your mind."

"Poisoned?" he spat. "It's *you* whose mind is warped. Have you any idea how hard I've worked to achieve favor with His Majesty? And then, in one breath, you think you have the right to come and steal everything I have, leaving me with nothing!"

"I thought you already had nothing. I thought Moragon took everyone you loved. And now you think him a saint who's bestowed all this wonderful prestige upon you. What will presitige grant you? I don't see you living a gloriously happy life as Chief Musician. And yet you cling to that title, hide behind it instead of doing what you know to be right."

With a growl, Mikanah swung with his sword and flung a musical spell at her. The melody warbled, and Lorelei sang back at him, countering the spell and making him freeze in place.

A moment later, she released him. He sang another curse at her, but she returned with a high-pitched defense spell that made him cover his ears and cringe.

Once the noise ceased, he glared up at her but lowered his blade. "How do you know so many spells?"

"I'm a song-weaver," Lorelei said, lowering her blade as well. "My strength lies not just in learning others' song-spells, but in creating my own. You too would have access to learning powerful magic, if you would only come to your senses and accept your new fate. For whatever reason, Amiel sees fit to use you as one of his instruments, and I think you could learn quite a bit, if you were more grateful and took the opportunity."

"*Instrument*," Mikanah sneered. "Keen choice of words. Though if that is what I am, then I am an instrument bound to the service of His Majesty, not some made-up figment in the sky."

He swung and stumbled forward again. Lorelei disarmed him, caught his sword, and let him fall flat on his face. He scrambled to get up, but she kicked him to the ground and rested his blade at his throat.

"You belong now to the Guardians. Which means you will serve them, and the Council. And you will be glad to do so. Because you will serve freely, whether you understand this or not."

"Freely?" Mikanah chuckled darkly. "With your blade ready to slice my throat open? I don't believe a damn thing you say, any more than I believe in your made-up god."

Lorelei threw his sword to the ground beside him. "Then believe this. You are a Guardian. That mark proves it. Only death can spare you that fate." Guilt pricked her as this lie spilled so easily from her lips, but she didn't know what else to do. If Mikanah wouldn't listen to reason, then perhaps she must trap him into obedience, for his own good. After all, Moragon's men could show up at any moment. Quickly, she added, "And only Moragon's death can spare you from now being his enemy." That much was true. "By now, he will know we've escaped. We have to get as far away from here as possible."

Mikanah sat staring up at her, wide-eyed, like a child who has just woken to the worst nightmare and begs for it not to be as real as it seems. He glared at his Guardian's mark in disgust. Refusing to meet Lorelei's gaze, he clutched his blade and rose to his feet. "How do you even know which way to go?"

"I don't." She glanced up at the sky. "There're too many clouds and trees right now for me to see the sun. But you can just see the castle through there—" She pointed through trees. "—so, as long as we head in the opposite direction. Once there's less cover and we can see where we're heading, we need to make for the southwest shores. From there, we can take a boat to Pakua."

A nearby coughing sound alerted Lorelei. She and Mikanah froze still, listening keenly for another noise, watching each other warily. The cough began again, this time persisting.

"What do you suppose?" Mikanah whispered. "The intruder?"

"Maybe. Let's go see." Lorelei crept forward, stepping carefully over branches and bramble to avoid making too much noise.

"Are you insane?" Mikanah hissed, though he trailed after her. "You just said how urgent time is. Moragon's soldiers could find us any moment! And what if it's a trap?"

"If the intruder is who I think it may be, then it's no trap. Rather, we may owe him our allegiance, to do all we can to help him."

"Who could possibly...?"

Mikanah stood silenced as he stumbled after Lorelei upon a gruesome sight. A man lay on the grass, his pale face painted sky blue, his limbs bent, tunic smeared with blood. The tunic itself was curious, as were his tights and boots. All had been made from a shimmering fabric that seemed to shift colors as he moved, allowing him to blend almost perfectly with his surroundings. Red stained the grass from multiple arrow wounds, and he panted hard, fighting to pull himself up. As he angled his body toward them, Lorelei noted the shape of the silver symbol pinned to his chest, a treble clef wrapped around a sword. That symbol, known secretly to the Guardians and those sworn to help them, solidified her suspicions.

Ignoring Mikanah's protests, she rushed over and fell beside the messenger. He flinched at first, drawing back, but Lorelei sang a soothing melody that made him draw still and then said, "Shh. Peace. It's all right. I'm Lorelei, one of the Guardians. As is Mikanah." She glanced up at him, reaching for him, but he stood stiffly beside her.

"We need to go," he muttered. "We don't have time

for this mercy, nor does it serve any purpose. We need to go."

Lorelei narrowed her gaze at Mikanah, seething at his insolent callousness, but the messenger said, "He's right. You must hurry. They're looking for me. I am sorry, sir, and to you, Lorelei...that I have failed you, that I cannot take you back to safety."

"Don't worry about that," Lorelei said, forcing back tears. She took his hand and smiled down at him. "You have served faithfully."

Feeling the amulet at her heart with one hand, she placed her other hand upon his chest. Singing another healing charm, she pushed the amulet's warmth and from her body into his. Some of the pain receded from his face, but his wounds remained, and he continued to bleed. A sob escaped her. "Rest now in peace..." She hummed her new lullaby and added a few notes, while pressing her hand firmly over his heart. His eyes closed, and his breathing grew shallow. Then, after a few more feeble breaths, it stopped.

"See that?" she snapped, glaring at Mikanah. "Would you really have *that* be your fate?"

An arrow sang past and landed a hair away from Lorelei.

No sooner had she leaped to her feet than four guards rushed in, two on horseback, all with swords raised. With several short, high-pitched notes, Lorelei flung the two riders off their horses. They jumped up and ran at her. She glanced around wildly for Mikanah. He had hidden in the bushes, and his lips moved as if he muttered some spell.

The guards collapsed to their knees, gasping, panting, clawing at their throats. Their faces turned red. Their eyes bulged. One man drew his own blood, while pulling himself across the ground toward Lorelei. He reached toward her, but she backed away, mortified. Glaring at Mikanah, she commanded, "That's enough! We're not killing them. Quick, we can take their horses and flee."

Mikanah seemed to hesitate, but then he released the guards from his spell, and they collapsed, wheezing and sputtering, fighting to regain their breath. Lorelei grabbed at the reins of the chestnut-red horse, but the creature reared up with an alarmed whinny before bolting off through the trees.

The second horse, pure black, pawed uneasily, and Lorelei panicked, especially as one of the soldiers had dragged himself to a tree and braced against it, slowly staggering to his feet. She couldn't afford to get recaptured or for Mikanah to get killed, but the wearier she became, so did her magic. They needed the horse's speed. Ever so slowly, she stepped toward the beast, but it rocked its head back and forth with an uneasy whinny, eyes widening in terror at this woman whom he likely associated with his master's current suffering.

Lorelei caught snatches of a song then, drifting in the horse's direction. As the beast calmed, she glanced over to see Mikanah steadily approaching, all while singing a serene melody. He reached out his hand, and the horse stepped back, snorting. Mikanah froze again, singing on until the beast seemed wholy subdued, watching Mikanah with a careful but accepting gaze.

"I can tell that horse training isn't one of the Guardians' specialities." He smirked and lifted his chin, a sneering sort of gesture, before hefting himself onto the horse's back. "Horses don't trust just anyone. They must be persuaded."

"Or seduced by music," Lorelei said flatly.

"Are you coming or not?" Mikanah extended his arm

toward her.

Lorelei hurried over, and Mikanah helped pull her onto the horse's back behind him. The guard who'd managed to stand lunged toward them, swinging his sword clumsily. Mikanah pulled the reins, and the horse side-stepped the attack—even as an arrow whizzed right past Mikanah's ear, sticking fast in the tree beside him.

More arrows shot past. Lorelei and Mikanah dodged. The horse snorted and whinnied, pawing at the ground once more. Lorelei clung to Mikanah, terrified of being thrown from the beast's back into the snare of the approaching enemies.

"I need you to listen," Mikanah said sharply. "I need you keep the horse calm so I can get us out of here. I can't concentrate on singing and riding all at once. Can you do that?"

"Yes."

"Then hang on tight, and let's go!"

Mikanah urged the horse into a forward trot. The horse shook its head and danced back and forth, clearly uncomfortable, but Lorelei sang, doing her best to mimic Mikanah's earlier charm. Another volley of arrows found them. Soon, the horse picked up speed, and moments later, its frantic twisting and turning smoothed into a straight line.

Mikanah urged the horse from the clearing. The din of horses' hooves and the commands of men swelled not far behind them. Lorelei could glimpse the riders through the trees. She placed her hand at Mikanah's waist again, holding on tight while switching song-spells. The horse seemed subdued for now, and she instead concentrated on her lullaby. She hadn't had time to perfect it, especially targeting so many people at once, but it would have to do.

Mikanah glanced back at Moragon's men before

spurring their horse to go even faster.

Lorelei returned her full focus to her spell. The riders wove in and out so that it was impossible to concentrate on all of them at once. She would have to take them out one at a time.

Lorelei pushed her song as hard as she could. Its melody pulsed from deep inside her heart, which sped to match the song's intensity. It flowed through her veins with the same fluidity that began to make her targeted rider sway and lose balance. Moments later, he toppled from his horse, which came to a rearing halt.

Arrows continued to blur past. Lorelei deflected them with protective charms. She managed to put a couple more riders to sleep, but more joined their ranks, drawing ever nearer. She would never subdue them all in time.

Mikanah whipped his head over his shoulder, glaring fiercely at Moragon's soldiers as a new song poured from his lips. Their horse began to zig-zag, and he looked forward once more, steadying it before looking back to the soldiers. Lorelei prayed he wasn't about to do something stupid, as every ounce of pain, hatred, and betrayal he possessed seemed to burn inside his dark eyes, emanating with whatever spell he had aimed at their pursuers. One by one, Lorelei heard the horses cry out. Her heart lurched, and she looked back, hoping he didn't harm the beasts—

And found herself staring in astonishment. One by one, the horses turned and fled back through the woods, ignoring their masters' commands to continue forward. All trace of them had vanished, save for the subtlest sounds of receding hooves.

Mikanah took the reins again while Lorelei wrapped her arms around him once more.

"That was astonishing," she said. "Where did you learn that?"

"From His Majesty, of course. One of his servants in Adelar used to be a tamer of beasts. Where to now?"

"Southwest, toward the ocean. Ride as far as our steed will take us before resting."

Drained from all the magic she'd exerted, Lorelei let her head fall on Mikanah's back. Her eyes closed, and she absorbed the rhythm of his body moving in graceful arcs with the horse's every gallop, up and down, up and down. She exhaled deeply, at last allowing herself to relax as the horse's dance and Mikanah's warmth swept her into a deep contentment.

THE THIRD MOVEMENT

"For whatsoever from one place doth fall,
Is with the tide unto another brought:
For there is nothing lost,
That may be found if sought."

~ Edmund Spenser, *The Fairie Queen*

CHAPTER 25

FLYING FREE

S unlight stretched its dim warmth across Mikanah's face, along with autumn's chill breeze.

Warm and cold, darkness and light. Contradictions. His dreams had been full of them last night. When he wakened more fully and realized that he slept on the ground beside the woman who served as his new captor, he remembered that his life was now full of contradictions as well.

Opening his eyes, he stared at the lightening sky. A gentle rain fell from intermittent clouds. It hardly pierced the canopy of trees shielding them, but the droplets that reached him struck his skin like ice.

Sitting up, he took in his surroundings. The forest spanned in all directions, as far as his eyes could see.

A soft groan made him look at the woman sleeping at his side. Lorelei. A mysteriously powerful and annoyingly persistent force. She wanted him to trust her, now they were both Guardians, but why should he? She had already used him like a puppet to spirit him away from everything he'd ever known.

On the other hand, she had helped him escape.

But for her own agenda, he was sure. He suspected she might turn on him at a whim, just like His Majesty, the king. Moragon. Now enemies, he may as well get used to using his king's name plainly, and his new one, at that. Not Samil. Moragon would now afford him no respect. Neither must Mikanah show him any.

A vivid pain burned on his hand then and he jerked it to his lips, hissing and sucking on the tender flesh.

"Damn it...."

He stared with disdain at the Guardians' mark. It glared up at him, taunting him. The word *Mi* was nothing more than an insipid blemish. If not for its otherworldly shimmer, it could almost be a birthmark, like the one near his temple. How had something so small destroyed everything he'd spent a miserable lifetime to achieve in a single night? Unfathomable. Moragon would never stop searching for them now. Mikanah knew too much, was too great a liability.

He rose to his feet. Perhaps it wasn't too late. He could return to the castle, beg forgiveness, plead for his life....

And yet, at his core, he knew Lorelei was right. He couldn't prove that he hadn't aided her somehow or revealed His Majesty's secrets to her. The only way he might prove his loyalty to Moragon was to kill Lorelei before she woke, but even that was risky. If Moragon was dissatisfied with such a gesture, Mikanah would still be punished.

No. He could not go back. He was bound to a new master. He must use his new position with the Guardians to gain as much power and knowledge as possible. At least, he might finally be able to throw down Reynard.

"Going somewhere?"

Mikanah whirled. Lorelei sat up, pinning him with

her calm, ever-watchful stare. Her gaze probed much like Moragon's, if in a less forceful way.

"If you go back, you've signed your death sentence. Moragon won't let me near you again. I won't be able to help you a second time."

"Why would you think to 'help' me at all?" Mikanah muttered, sitting across from her. He shifted uncomfortably on the cold, rock-hard ground, wishing for his soft, sprawling bed. He'd had one of the finest rooms in the castle, yet another thing she'd taken from him. A petty loss, but a loss, nonetheless.

"Because you are a fellow Guardian," Lorelei said. "We are sworn to protect one another."

A wry grin played at the corners of his lips. Good thing he'd decided not to kill her, then.

"What now?" he asked. "You know Moragon will chase us."

"We leave Carmenna as soon as possible and head straight for Pakua. From there, we meet up with the other Guardians and plan what to do next."

Mikanah scoffed. "If the new Guardians, including myself, even make it to Pakua in one piece. You've said they have no leader. Perhaps it's time we reconsidered. Perhaps it's a lack of leadership that got the last batch of you killed."

Storms brewed in Lorelei's eyes. "You lack humility for a man who's been Moragon's plaything—"

"*Don't* call me that."

"Then don't speak disrespectfully of my friends' deaths. We had agreed."

Mikanah inhaled deeply but said nothing, defeated. He was a man who strove to keep his word. His word and his will, for what little they were worth against Moragon's, had been two of the only things that had always been his, that he'd always been allowed to keep, thanks to his faithful service.

"There is strength in our numbers," Lorelei added, staring at him evenly, "in combining our powers and ideas instead of relying on a single person to make choices for us. Working as a unit is stronger than standing on your own."

Working together also creates the risk of dying together, Mikanah thought, but said only, "What can I learn? In becoming a Guardian?"

"Your potential is limitless. You have a sharp mind. I could easily teach you any of my spells, and others besides. You would have access to the Chamber of Music, where we house and protect knowledge of all the musical spells we have found."

Mikanah studied her carefully. "Why trust me so readily? I could easily take all that you've said and use it against the Guardians."

"I *don't* trust you. Not yet. You've become one of us and I am therefore bound to treat you equally. But I'll tell you nothing you could not learn readily on your own. Our secrets, our most powerful spells, *they* must be earned." She paused, examining him. "Though, to be honest, I'm still not convinced that you're as loyal to Moragon as you want me to believe. I think you want revenge against him the same as I do."

"His Majesty. *Moragon...*" Mikanah shivered. It was strange to speak his name so freely as she did, though it also filled him with an odd sense of superiority. "Moragon taught me everything I know. I worked hard to rise to power in his service. But if being a Guardian can give me the power to rise above him, then I might embrace that chance."

"You speak much of power," Lorelei said, not accusing but looking curious.

"Power is a man's gateway to freedom. Power and

freedom are intimately linked. One cannot exist without the other."

"Power stole my father from me. And it stole those you love as well, didn't it? The girl you spoke of?"

"Yes, and..." Mikanah paused. Could he reveal this pain to her? Lorelei had saved his life, hard as it was to admit, and now she gave him a chance. Most who'd seen the persuasion of his music would barricade him from their presence at all costs.

"And my brother," he said at last.

Lorelei's mouth parted in surprise. "You have a brother?"

"Yes. I did. Jerah. He was in Reynard's care, and the bastard had tortured him. Jerah went mad—he was just a small boy—and he jumped out the window, maybe hoping to fly away from all his pain." Mikanah's anger flared. The sight of his brother's frail, mangled body being carried away would forever haunt his memory. "That's what fuels me to fight, to grow in magical knowledge and strength. Yes, Moragon tormented the girl I loved, for defying him at every turn. But Reynard, the way he treated my brother, an innocent child, just to win the king's favor...."

Overwhelmed, he fell silent, and Lorelei's sighed softly. She twisted a leaf in her hands, her face knit with obvious pain. "Why? Why would he do such a thing?"

"Jerah had strong magic. Musical magic, like me. But he was too young. He couldn't do what Reynard asked, what the king demanded. He couldn't even use it to defend himself." Mikanah swallowed the bile choking his throat. "So yes, Lorelei of the Guardians. I would see revenge enacted against Moragon. But even more so upon Reynard. Power may have taken my family, but power can also win their vengeance."

"Blood with blood, power with power," Lorelei said

quietly. "And yet such a fight cannot and will not return our loved ones to us. Our solace comes from looking forward to the day the silver stags reunite our bodies with the earth and our spirits with Amiel in the Forever Havens."

Mikanah snorted and turned his stare to the ground. "My only solace will come from someday lying buried beneath the earth, unable to think, feel, or understand. If my vengeance is never reached, then at least in death, I will no longer know it."

"You really don't believe in Amiel?"

Her tone didn't accuse, nor did her eyes. Rather, a haunting sort of sadness seemed to linger within them.

Mikanah hesitated. "I did once, as did the girl I spoke of. She believed up until the end. But I abandoned such foolish myths. No higher being would allow the evil I have seen in the world to exist."

"Evil does endure, but it does not prosper forever. In this world or in the next, good ultimately triumphs. That is what I believe." At Mikanah's cynical glance, she lifted a palm to forestall him. "And besides, Amiel did not create evil. Man did that well enough on his own. Amiel only grants free will, the ability to choose good or evil. If we were each His puppets, we'd be no better off than Moragon's servants, mindless slaves forced to do his bidding."

"Moragon does fancy himself a god," Mikanah muttered. "At any rate, even if some sort of afterlife exists, I doubt I would see her there. She was a pure soul. She fought him 'til the end. I did what I had to, to survive. I make no excuses for that. But I *have* manipulated people, used them."

Lorelei studied him. She seemed to think Mikanah a puzzle to be deciphered. "All are capable of receiving Amiel's redemption. There is no evil that, once repented of, cannot be forgiven. There is nothing inside a person that they cannot change if they want to. But come. We had best be on the move. We've been fortunate no one's followed us, but tarrying would be folly."

She clambered to her feet and stretched her back with a groan. Mikanah stood as well, scanning the woods. "Are you sure we haven't been followed?"

Lorelei grasped his arm and gave him a stern look. Placing her other hand to her heart, she said, "I can't promise we haven't been followed. But I can promise to keep you safe. I wear this amulet for protection. It keeps me from all physical harm and makes it easier for me to guard against mental magic as well. Should we be attacked, as a fellow Guardian, I will do my best to defend you."

He gazed curiously at the bare bit of skin right beneath her clavicle. No physical traces of any amulet could be seen. Perhaps she was just tricking him. He wondered, were he not a Guardian, if she would protect him just the same or leave him to Moragon's whims.

They mounted their horse and started through the woods at a steady gait. They rode mostly in silence, though now and then Lorelei would share a fond memory of her father or some other tale to pass the time. After several hours, they paused to search for food. Lorelei had spent enough time surviving on her own to recognize safe berries and mushrooms. She hunted both for them to eat while Mikanah found a small stream. An empty flask hung from the horse's saddle which they filled, uncertain when they might next find a fresh source of water.

After eight days, they at last reached the town of Kailani, along Carmenna's western shores. The sun was just setting as they crested a grassy hill, which gave them a view of the ocean, their destination. Blood reds, burnt oranges, and kingly golds all dazzled the ocean that spanned endlessly into the horizon. Sky and water became one majestic, infinite entity. Mikanah vowed to be that, someday—infinite in power and prestige, ruled by nothing except his own unstoppable will.

"Kailani," Lorelei announced with seeming relief as they passed by the first stone cottages. Mikanah knew her body ached, stiff and sore from riding bareback behind him all this time, and her stomach surely churned with hunger just like his. Berries, mushrooms, and a few fish caught in a stream were meager rations stretched over a week-long period.

Despite these pangs, Lorelei perked up at the signs of life surrounding them. A few children played in the dirt streets. Men chopped wood or tended horses while women hung laundry in the breeze. Clouds of smoke billowed from chimneys, turned a deep blue gray against the sunset sky.

"My father brought me here once," she said, her gaze looking ahead but, Mikanah suspected, viewing the past. "To buy me my first musical instrument. A lyre, just right for my size. The carving was rough, but the strings were well tuned. I've always preferred using my voice above anything, but I did love that lyre. I was happy to discover that my Guardians' instrument was a lyre as well." Traces of a whimsical smile played at the corners of her lips.

"Are we resting here for the night?"

Lorelei shook her head. "I hadn't planned to. We could still make it to Pakua before night settles in too deeply. However..." She stopped them before a shop. The scents of herbs and plants wafted from within, confirming the small sign in the window: *Apothecary*. "...if we wish to reach Pakua in a timely manner, we must see if we can secure a bit of flying powder."

"Flying powder?" Mikanah said as they slid from the horse and tied the reins to a nearby fence. "Moragon mentioned it once. That's a rare substance, isn't it?"

"Yes and no. Its invention is still fairly new. The combination of elements is complex and thus costly. But if one knows the recipe, any able spellcrafter can create it. I've learned the basic knowledge. It's the cost that concerns me. I've a small pouch of coins tucked away that might fetch us a decent meal, but certainly not such a sophisticated spell."

"Don't worry. I'm a master at bargaining." Mikanah led the way. "Come. We'll be in Pakua within the hour."

The moment they entered the apothecary, a whirlwind of scents blasted Mikanah. Bitter, sweet, savory, garlic, onion, cinnamon, ginger, all manner of flowers, weeds, herbs. He wrinkled his nose as he struggled to take in the heavy aromas.

They wandered past shelves laden with herbs, spices, and plants, as well as potions, powders, and a variety of elements—silver, copper, and various metals, different-colored gases contained in glass jars. At the far end of the small shop, a short, bespectacled Carmennan man with a thick mess of tightly coiled hair stood behind a counter. He took several powders, green, blue, and bright lavender, and measured them in a glass bowl by the remaining light streaming through the window.

"Excuse me," Mikanah said.

The man glanced up, only to frown at them before returning his focus to his work. "Yes? How can I help you?"

"We're looking to purchase a small amount of flying powder."

The man glanced up again and raised his brows. Mikanah couldn't tell whether he was amused or thought them mad. "Flying powder? Those ingredients will cost you a fair penny, especially with the restrictions His Majesty has placed on various dusts and powders. Some are limited, others are outlawed completely. I'll warrant that'll soon include the elements for flying powder."

"Then perhaps it's best we take them off your hands, save you the trouble of having to rid yourself of them later." Mikanah leaned against the counter, smiling politely. "Name your price, my good sir."

The man finished mixing the colorful powders before returning his gaze to Mikanah. Eyes shining with skepticism, he said, "Flying powders these days don't sell for less than five gold coins an ounce."

Mikanah couldn't help feeling shocked at such a price and felt his brows raise. "Five gold coins, you say? Seems lofty, for such a small amount as we need."

"Uh-huh. And how small an amount are we talking?"

"Enough to reach Olina," Lorelei spoke up, and Mikanah glanced at her in confusion. Weren't they bound for Pakua? Had she deceived him even in that?

"Well then, you'll be needing ten gold coins for two ounces."

Doubt and annoyance crept inside Mikanah, especially as the man stared at him like he was some foolish little boy and as Lorelei watched him expectantly, but he wouldn't let this show. Maintaining a calm smile, he said, "Perhaps a trade then, instead?"

The man arched a brow. At last, Mikanah struck a chord of intrigue with him. "Perhaps indeed. A solid trade can be worth more than gold. Name your offer."

"We've some valuable goods that you might find well worth the trade. Lorelei, our journey's nearly at an end. Perhaps now it would be safe to part with the amulet?"

Lorelei had studied him curiously, but now her face turned ashen, and horror glinted in her eyes as she subtly shook her head. Mikanah breathed slowly, trying to hide his embarrassment. Either Lorelei had lied to him and wore no secret amulet after all, or else, as her face seemed to give away, she truly did, and he had nearly given away the one thing protecting them. Feeling a fool, he turned once more to the man and declared, "Never mind. I forgot the gem had such sentimental value to my friend here."

"Pity," the man said, glancing with mild interest at her. "Jewels are rare enough these days to fetch a pretty price, especially if imbued with any magic."

"But may also soon be outlawed," Mikanah said. "As you say, they've become rarer, thanks to His Majesty's mining policies. He may desire or demand to keep all such treasures for himself. In that case, I offer you a better trade. We've a fine horse outside. Horses will never be outlawed. We could trade the beast, along with saddle and bridle, all of excellent craftmanship, in exchange for taking the powders off your hands. She should bring quite a decent price if you don't keep her."

The man glanced out the window. "She *is* handsome."

Mikanah nodded. "We've ridden her for days now, and she has proven a tireless, faithful beast. What say you? Do we have a deal?"

The man hesitated a moment more. His gaze narrowed desirously at the horse outside his window. Keeping his calm composure, Mikanah sang a silent charm in his mind to nudge man's decision in the right direction.

Then, with a firm nod, the man grinned up at them. Shaking Mikanah's hand and then Lorelei's, he declared, "We have ourselves a bargain."

"Thank you, good sir."

"Truly we're grateful," Lorelei said. "Like I said, we need just enough to reach Olina. I've got the formula if you need it."

The man shook his head. "I've a sharp mind for

spells and potions. I've had two other folks pass through in need of the same. Go to the inn next door if you've a need for some refreshment. Take the horse to the stables there for me while you're at it. Tell them property of Sigmis. Return in a half hour's time. The powders will be ready, you have my word."

As soon as they had exited the apothecary, Mikanah stepped in front of Lorelei, blocking her path, and demanding, "What game do you play with me? I thought we were going to Pakua. Another lie to manipulate me into doing your bidding?"

Lorelei stared at him, looking alarmed. Her surprise soon melted into annoyance, and she heaved a great sigh. "You speak of games, and yet you lack the apparent skills needed to play the game that will keep us alive. I did use deception, but not toward you. Olina is near enough Pakua that the flying powders should be enough to get us there all the same. Or do you want that man to be able to tell His Majesty's guard about two strangers heading to Pakua? You saw how eager he was to strike a bargain. Do you think he wouldn't bargain for our lives?"

Mikanah stood struck silent, lips drawn into a thin line as embarrassment burned through him once more. "Sorry," he muttered. "I am not prone to trust, especially toward someone who is, for all intents and purposes, my captor."

"Not your captor. Your fellow Guardian. We are both equally bound to this fate. And I don't expect to win your full trust right away, as you've not won mine. But you must trust me inasmuch that I've no desire to get us killed. Now, come. I should have enough coins to land us a decent meal and ale, if you're thusly inclined."

After tending to the horse and enjoying a much-needed hot meal at the inn, Mikanah and Lorelei returned to the apothecary. As promised, a small glass vial filled with a glittering indigo powder awaited them.

Mikanah followed Lorelei from the village, down a sprawling hill sprayed with sand and tall waving grasses, and to the ocean shores below. The sun had nearly completed its majestic departure. Lines of orange and gold still hovered on the horizon, while darkness bathed the rest of the sky in a rich royal blue speckled with stars.

"You were a decent bargainer," Lorelei said. "You've a gift of persuasion, even without use of magic."

Mikanah shrugged. "Never said I didn't use magic."

Lorelei stared at him flatly. "You charmed the man."

"Just a little."

"Such acts won't be tolerated now you're a Guardian. We use our magic to protect, help, heal, not to manipulate minds. I know that's what you're used to, but it's a horrific habit you'll have to break."

Mikanah snorted and shook his head. "Self-righteous words for a woman who wears a relic that protects her from all harm. Bolder still for a woman who used magic to turn me into her puppet and steal me away from His Majesty's castle."

Lorelei scowled, looking irritated, whether with herself or with him, he couldn't tell. "I did what I had to, to save your life, to get us both out of there alive."

"And I did the same. I assured our survival by securing the flying powders for us. I hardly did a thing, really. Only nudged him into making the decision he was already considering. Now, show me how to use these powders."

Lorelei studied him in silence for a moment, and he felt satisfied that he'd been able to strike her into submission. Maybe she would see that right and wrong weren't always so straightforward and that he had merely leveled the playing field she had set out for them.

Then, Mikanah watched as she took a pinch of powder, sprinkled it beneath her tongue, and said, "It's not an exact science. We may need to take it at intervals while we're flying, to ascertain we don't fall."

Mikanah took a similar amount to what Lorelei had used. Its taste sliced into his tongue, bitter and unexpectedly salty. He let it dissolve and then looked to Lorelei for further instruction.

"The spell for flying is '*Anemoius*.' You needn't sing it, nor does it require a great deal of concentration. Once airborne, your body will remain suspended until you choose to land. I've only done this a couple of times, and it does take a little while to learn how to maneuver oneself midair. On that note, are you ready?"

"*On that note?*" Mikanah arched a brow and grinned. "Was that a musical pun?"

Her face lit up with a slight smile. "Not on purpose. Though I think this is the first sign you've shown that you might just have a sense of humor buried beneath all your rigidness."

"It's something about the idea of flying, I think. It makes me feel excited. 'Playful' maybe is the right word. I haven't felt playful in...well, I can't recall. But I recognize the feeling, however distant its memory."

"It's more than playfulness. It's freedom."

Mikanah said nothing. He was still bound to her, to the Guardians, and in a way, he was still bound to Moragon. He would never be rid of one—Guardians or Moragon—without the other. Thus, despite Lorelei's insistence otherwise, he would not yet be free for a long time.

As Lorelei recited the spell and floated slowly off the ground, Mikanah allowed himself the rare luxury of pushing all his worries to the back of his mind. Repeating the spell after her, he closed his eyes, focused, and imagined himself soaring over the ocean like a mighty god.

A nothingness replaced the solidity beneath his feet. Cool breezes wrapped around him, slinking over and around his body. Their chill intensified, and he shivered. Then, he opened his eyes.

Mikanah gasped. Little surprised him anymore. But as he and Lorelei rose high above the village to meet the darkening sky, he was bewildered at his weightlessness. Wind buffeted him, and he fought it until he realized he was part of the wind. He could move anywhere. He felt possibility. He felt power. He *was* possibility and power. He embodied them, became them.

"We'll have to start pushing forward," Lorelei said. "It's said there comes a point where the air chokes and freezes a man to death, so we can't just keep letting ourselves rise upward. Directing yourself can be tricky, but you merely have to push your body in the direction you wish to go. For some, it helps to move their feet like they're running, though this isn't necessary. Here, I'll help you."

Lorelei reached toward him then hesitated. Mikanah watched as her hand hovered in the air between them. Before, his touch had seemed to alarm her. Taking charge in this case might induce the same reaction, and then they would get nowhere. He must let her make the choice herself.

At last, she firmly slipped her hand in his. Then, she bent downward and forward and started pushing herself through the air. Mikanah copied her, and soon they were gliding across the midnight sky together.

CHAPTER 26

GIFTS AND MEMORIES

Lorelei picked up speed, and Mikanah pushed harder, matching her pace. Soon they sped over the ocean. The peaceful waves shining with the moon's reflection blurred beneath them, while the stars blurred above. Mikanah felt like a king diving through a secret treasure trove filled with diamonds.

"You're quite a natural!" Lorelei called above the wind whistling past. "I think it's *you* leading *me!*"

A black outline appeared on the horizon and gradually thickened. Mikanah's heart sped a little faster. He had never set foot on shores outside of Carmenna, and the night was rapidly revealing more and more wonders to him. He felt almost happy for once, but such a feeling frightened him, made him anxious. Perhaps he was only dreaming it.

At times, Lorelei would halt them midair and make them take a bit more of the powder, just in case. The last thing they needed was to plummet unexpectedly into the ocean. The nearest shores were too far to swim to, and they would surely drown.

Minutes later, the island rose more visibly in sight—rocky shores with woods beyond, and walls upon walls of high cliffs beyond that. They soon reached the island but did not land. Instead, they pressed on toward the cliffs, and Mikanah's excitement waned. Pakua was Carmenna's last stronghold against Moragon. He had found welcome with Lorelei, but he couldn't expect to find welcome here, or for her to be able to protect him, even with her pendant. After all, she couldn't hold his hand forever.

Lorelei raised her free hand, waved it in the air, and sang several spells beneath her breath. A stark iciness shocked Mikanah, who immediately plummeted from the sky as if an intense weight pulled his entire body, making every inch of him feel a thousand times heavier, limbs, face, torso, down to his very skin and bones. Even his lungs crushed, and he gasped for breath.

But then he shot up into the air again, and he and Lorelei soared toward the cliffs once more.

"What was that?" he demanded.

"A protective barrier, enacted by the Council," Lorelei said. "I apologize. I should have warned you."

"Where are we going now?"

Lorelei said nothing but veered downward. They landed on a small ledge jutting out from one of the towering rocky walls. Two armored guards stood on the ledge, bearing Carmenna's crest of two crossed swords beneath a purple lyre on their breastplates. They braced spears in their direction, but then they relaxed as recognition sparked on their faces.

"Lady Lorelei," one of the guards greeted her with a bow of his head. "Long has it been since you graced Pakua. I am grateful to see you safe and well. Gailea is here.

She will be glad to see you, as, I'm sure, will the new Guardians who've arrived. Who is your companion?"

"This is Mikanah, another of the Guardians." She raised Mikanah's hand so that his mark gleamed. "Thank you, Simoni, for your kind words. But if you'll excuse us now, it's been a long journey."

"Of course." Simoni and the other guard knocked the ends of their spears on the ground in a synchronized rhythm. A stone panel slid aside, revealing a doorway. After a final grateful nod to the guards, Lorelei ducked inside, and Mikanah followed. As the door closed behind them, Lorelei took a few steps forward and inhaled deeply. She closed her eyes, and relief seemed to douse her like a fresh spring rain.

"Welcome to Pakua," she said. "Most people are likely sleeping, so we'll make our way quietly. I've one thing to show you, and then I'll find you a room where you can sleep."

"What about the other Guardians?"

"Likely sleeping as well. We'll wait until morning to meet them."

Mikanah couldn't complain. He wasn't eager to meet them. Surely not all of them would accept him as Lorelei had done.

After winding through several halls, Lorelei led him inside a room that was small but handsomely furnished. The sprawling bed, desk, and chest of drawers were all crafted from a warm, light-colored wood. A small stone hearth nestled in one wall. A black tapestry showing Carmenna's crest of two swords with a purple lyre hung on another wall, along with a painting of several birds perched among a tree's spring blossoms. Emerald silks hung from the bed's four posters.

"My father's favorite color," Lorelei said, running the silk through her fingers. "And mine."

347

She knelt before the chest at the foot of the bed and opened it, rummaging through parchment and fabric.

A small object spilled over the edge and clattered to the floor. With a curious frown, Mikanah stooped and picked it up. It was an intricately carved wooden faun playing a flute.

"This craftsmanship," Mikanah breathed, setting it on the desk. "It's flawless. My brother used to play with figures just like this."

"My father's handiwork," Lorelei said. "I think, at one time, he might have been making toys in secret for prisoners and their children, to bring them comfort. At least, until Moragon caught him and put an end to it." She drew out a long package wrapped in cloth and bound by leather straps before standing to her feet. "This too is my father's. Not his creation, but his design."

She handed it to Mikanah. He stared down at it numbly. He could tell what it was by its shape and weight but didn't believe she was giving it to him.

"Open it, please," she prompted.

Mikanah glanced at her, his eyes questioning. She nodded. Ever so carefully, he untied the leather and peeled back the cloth to reveal a long sword. Both hilt and blade glistened silver. Emeralds adorned the hilt. Mikanah turned it in the firelight, admiring its sharp edges before gazing at Lorelei with bafflement.

"Why do you give this to me?"

"Because," Lorelei said, "I know what it's like to have been a captive for so long, and then to come to a new place. You don't feel safe. You don't trust anyone. I had my amulet to help me feel safe. I cannot give you anything nearly as precious, but I thought a sword might be appropriate."

"It's perfect." Mikanah carefully ran his hand along the impeccably smooth surface of the blade. "I am forever indebted to you, both for this and for saving my life. But *this*. This makes me trust you a little."

Lorelei turned her head, a touch of mischief sparking in her tired eyes. "I would have thought carrying you safely over the ocean might've already accomplished such a feat."

Mikanah nodded, affording a small smile in turn. "It did. But this moreso. Holding it gives me extra hope that I will see Moragon and Reynard both brought to justice. I will name it 'Jerah's Justice,' after my brother."

"My father would be honored, to know it was granted such a name and purpose. I'm glad you enjoy it. But come. Let me show you to a room so we can both rest for the night."

Mikanah followed Lorelei down several more corridors and stopped before another door. "Inside here. Guards are posted throughout Pakua. I hope that, along with your sword, makes you feel safe."

"That, and the presence of such a powerful woman as yourself. Perhaps someday I'll be glad that we have become allies after all."

Hints of a smile tugged at the corners of Lorelei's lips. "You no longer resent my taking you from your 'home'?"

"I resented you taking me from my glory, my power, my life's work. My bitterness lingers in that regard. But Carmenna is no true home, for me or any man. I've never known a home, except as a prison, a place to serve. Or perhaps they are one and the same...."

"Lady Lorelei?"

Mikanah and Lorelei looked up. A guard approached them.

"I have announced your arrival to Lady Gailea. She is still awake and wishes to meet with you if you're not too tired."

Lorelei inhaled, and her tired eyes shone wide awake, lively, and perhaps a bit anxious. "Thank you. I'll be glad to."

"I will take you to her."

Lorelei nodded before turning back to Mikanah. "I haven't seen her since long before the attack on the Guardians. I'm sorry to leave you so hastily, but we'll be able to talk more tomorrow. Until then, get some rest."

~*~*~

Iolana woke to a gentle singing. Sitting up, she saw that Nerine had moved from her place on the rug beside her to Gailea's sprawling bed, while Darice still sat beside Ashden on the settee, still quietly reading aloud. It was a familiar scene, as they'd spent nearly every night the past week visiting in Gailea's chambers, sharing stories and songs until they could no longer keep their eyes open. The singing drifted from Gailea who sat inside the carved-out window, gazing out at the stars.

For a while, Iolana listened to her wistful melody, afraid to interrupt and break the moment. She listened a long time before deciding to stand and approach Gailea.

"That's very pretty."

Gailea turned toward Iolana in surprise. "Did I wake you? I apologize."

"No, not at all," Iolana said, sitting before her on the bench. "Can I ask what it is?"

Gailea's smile was melancholy. "It's about my mother. Not Brynn, the mother who raised me, but my birth mother, Gillian. Princess of Adelar."

Iolana's curiosity swelled, and she found herself suddenly wide awake.

"Darice gave me some old diary accounts from her." Gailea glanced across the room, sharing a wistful glance with her sister who peered up from the book. "That song.... Brynn used to sing it to me. Even though I couldn't have known then who it was about, I've hidden it in my heart for many years. The diary accounts have brought it back to life."

Gailea looked out the window once more and began to sing, while Iolana listened, captivated:

"Adelar's realm sits proud and strong,
Beside the river Shila long,
Through the heart of the Chamroq Dell
Where the Adelaran people dwell.

Behold! The fairest of the fair
With sunlight gleaming in her hair,
Of her people she sits and sings
Each song a prayer for peaceful tidings.

Gillian, the Lady of Adelar.
Within each eye reflects a star,
Lured and caught by her warmest gaze,
Her gentle hand, her loving ways.

Weaving music with skillful hand
Singing sweet words to calm the land
Her music drives life's woes away
And causes all to pause and say:

"There she is, our princess fair,
Harsh words are spoken by her ne'er;
The truest heart, the kindest face,
A maid blessed by Amiel's grace.

And ever shall the people sing
Of she whose light to all doth bring
A joy to people near and far,
Gillian, the Lady of Adelar."

"It's beautiful," Iolana said. "It sounds as though her people truly loved her. Did you—?"

A quick rap on the door interrupted them. A bit anxious at what such could mean at this late hour, Iolana stared after Ashden who opened the door to reveal a Carmennan soldier.

"Lady Lorelei," he announced. "She has returned at last with another of the Guardians. I know the hour grows late, Lady Gailea, but I thought you may wish to see her."

Gailea looked apprehensive at first, and Iolana could guess why: this was the first Gailea would see Lorelei since the other Guardians' deaths. Iolana reached for Gailea's hand to comfort her, but Gailea stood to her feet and hurried to the door. "Thank you. I will meet with her at once. Please, lead on."

She slipped from the room. Darice beckoned Iolana over. Iolana joined her and Ashden on the settee but despite Darice's best efforts, Iolana could not immerse herself in the story she read.

Rather, a thrill rippled through her. Everything up to this point had been a mere overture. They stood on the brink of beginning their true quest. After the past week's revelations, who might this other new Guardian be? What connections might he or she share with them?

~*~*~

Lorelei sped down the hallway. She took deep breaths, trying to calm herself before realizing she had no reason to do so. Gailea would understand both her delight and her panic.

Seeing Mikanah standing with a sword in his hand, looking so ready to deal death and judgment, had shaken her, but she had forced herself to hide her nervousness. They were both Guardians now. She must show him that she was capable of trusting him, just as he must learn to trust her.

Besides, the larger feat would be winning Gailea over.

Lorelei tried to formulate what she would say to her. She toyed with various arguments, but the moment the door to the small study opened and she saw her dear friend, all reason fled her as emotion took control.

Lorelei rushed forward as Gailea rose from her chair by the fire and caught her in a tight embrace.

"My sweet girl." Gailea held her a little closer and tenderly stroked her head. "What a blessed relief to see you alive, whole, and well. At least, I trust you're well, my dear?"

"Yes, I'm well," Lorelei exhaled in a sigh of relief, savoring the woman's warm hug. While her protectiveness could seem overbearing at times, Lorelei appreciated when it shone through as gentleness and compassion, making her feel like Gailea was an older sister welcoming her home. "I'm even better now that I'm here. It's truly good to see a friendly face again, Lea."

"Gailea," the other woman corrected gently. "Now that the truth is known by Moragon, there is no need to hide it. My true name—"

"You don't need to explain." Lorelei stroked the back of her hair. "I learned the truth in Carmenna, from Moragon himself."

Gailea stiffened in her arms. "You encountered him?"

"I went to the castle, seeking answers about the heir."

"Lorelei!" Gailea gave her a tighter squeeze. "Oh, you insanely brave young woman. I am extra glad then, to see you safe and well. But I'm also sorry.....". Her voice trembled with tears. "I'm so sorry about the others."

"No!" Lorelei held Gailea closer. "It's not your fault. No one could have known Moragon would be there, or what he might do."

"But the similarities, their love for music...." Gailea pulled back from their embrace, torment shining visibly in her gaze. "I should've put two and two together, Samil and Moragon. Too many coincidences."

Lorelei took her hands. "Sometimes our mind shields us from truths it doesn't think us strong enough to handle. I wasn't certain I'd dare go back to Carmenna. But I did. I faced my fears, just like you're doing now. I found truth just like you. And I brought back one of the new Guardians. It's why I returned. I meant to continue my search for the heir, but then I found one of our new Guardians instead."

Gailea led Lorelei toward the fire, and they sat on the settee together. "Yes, I heard. But tell me, did you find any news of the heir? Did you make any progress at all before you were forced to flee?"

"A little," Lorelei said. "There was talk of a child with unique powers. I didn't gain this information from the most reliable source. But I think there may be something to the story."

Gailea looked thoughtful. "Iolana, the young girl I wrote you about. She was a slave of Moragon's, one he tried to have killed. She's a heartsong seer, and somehow managed to escape, just like you."

Lorelei felt the blood drain from her face.

"Lorelei?" Gailea leaned forward and took her hand.

"Sorry, it's just...memories." Lorelei forced the words and took a deep, shuddering breath, as visions of her first, grisly escape flashed through her mind. "Everything being so recent, my going back there and escaping a second time, maybe it all affected me more than I'd thought. Are you suggesting that this girl might be the heir to the throne?"

"I think Iolana must be something special," Gailea said wistfully, before her face pulled into a brooding frown. "If there's one thing I know about Moragon, it's that he collects rare and valuable treasures. I would've thought he would keep a heartsong seer alive, unless he had a greater reason for seeing her dead."

"Perhaps…" The wheels turned in Lorelei's head, illuminating her memory. "Mikanah and I also overheard Moragon talking with Reynard, his closest servant, about a 'Vessel.' They talked about how it wasn't ready yet. Moragon seemed eager to try it, but Reynard warned against overexerting its power."

"A Vessel," Gailea said. "That term is familiar to me. Before, in Adelar, I think Moragon was working on a similar device, something linked to Obscura, shadow magic."

"Shadow magic? From the way they were speaking, it seemed like the Vessel might be a great warship of sorts. Do you think a ship could be utilized along with this Obscura magic?"

Gailea's brows dipped in deep thought. "It's possible. He had used Obscura magic to create this sort of cursed substance called 'the Dusk' that was strangely both liquid and mist. It moves fluidly and has the ability to spread rapidly, like a rampant disease or wildfire. Maybe he's building a ship that could tolerate carrying a large amount of such magic, to bring it to his enemies. Or, if it's a sea war he's after, maybe he would even hope to release it into the water so that it spreads all the more quickly, though I imagine he would need a great deal of it in that case. It's something to keep in mind, certainly." Her face softened then with a smile. "You've done so well. We must contact the Council as soon as possible, let them know everything you've discovered."

"Perhaps you might inform them also of the death of their messenger. I don't know his name. There wasn't time to find out. But as Mikanah and I were fleeing through the woods, we found him, a messenger sent to locate Mikanah as the new Guardian to bring him here. A needless, brave death, one that should be honored...." She shivered to remember her music flowing into him, even as his life had flowed out. A needed mercy on her part, she reminded herself, though that made it no less difficult to think about it.

"I'm sorry to hear it," Gailea said gravely. "Of course, we will tell the Council. They will know who the messenger was, give the news of his passing to any family he may have had."

Lorelei nodded. Needing to distract herself with talking about anything else, she said, "The new Guardians then, when will I get to meet with them?" Nervousness flitted through her. These new Guardians existed only because the previous ones, her friends, had all been slaughtered. She was reluctant to get close to an entire new group of people, for fear of losing them just the same. And yet, she felt ready to forge new connections and see who now joined with them in the fight against Moragon.

"We can meet them at once, if you wish," Gailea said. "We'd been joined in my quarters before you showed up. I'd wanted a few moments with you to myself, but I'm sure they're all eager to meet you, and Mikanah too."

A bittersweet warmth lit Lorelei's heart at Gailea's declaration. She, too, had been grateful for that private time between just the two of them, the last two survivors from their original Guardian family.

The warmth in Lorelei's heart faded as thoughts turned to Mikanah and how Gailea might react. "I've left Mikanah to get settled for the night. It's been a long journey for both of us. I'm likewise exhausted, but eager enough to meet the new Guardians. That said, I think it's best if everyone waits until tomorrow to meet Mikanaha, after I've had a chance to tell everyone about him. There are some things that may initially come across as...alarming...that I think would be useful for us all to discuss."

Uncertainty shadowed Gailea's face, but she said, "Very well. Come, I will take you to meet them, and then you can tell us all about our new Guardian."

Gailea led Lorelei from the room. Traversing down the corridor and around the bend, they soon entered a spacious room. Two people sat on the thick, furred rug laid out before an ornate settee, beside a hearth carved into the cave's wall, where a steady fire blazed. A four-poster bed sprawled on the opposite side of the room, and at the room's furthest end, a great arched window revealed a clear, starry night.

As Lorelei and Gailea entered, the two people looked up, a muscular man with sandy-colored hair and kind gaze and a curvier woman with dark, braided hair and a motherly warmth in her twinkling eyes. They rose to their feet as Gailea made introductions:

"Lorelei, please meet two of our new Guardians, Ashden, an old friend of mine, and Darice, my sister."

Lorelei's brows rose. "Your sister? You already know both of them?"

Gailea's smile drew into a thin, strained line. "Curious, indeed, how the Appointment Stone's magic works. Harmony is required for the Octavial Eight to be at their best. I suppose our connections would enhance that opportunity for harmoniousness."

"Indeed..." Breaking away from her intrigue, Lorelei smiled warmly at Darice and Ashden and walked up to them, curtsying at each in turn. "Pardon my rudeness. It's an honor to meet each of you, truly."

"Likewise." Ashden gave a small bow.

"Indeed!" Darice beamed at her, her smile pure enthusiasm.

"Where are Iolana and Nerine?" Gailea turned a concerned gaze to Darice. "Did they head out for another walk?"

"No, they're right over there." Darice nodded toward the great bed, where Lorelei caught a glimpse of two figures cuddled against each other, fast asleep. The shadows made it harder to see, but in the firelight's glow, they looked young. "I thought Iolana went to wake Nerine, but it seems she fell asleep herself instead."

"You know of Iolana," Gailea said to Lorelei. "Nerine is her friend. Stole away with her here if you will. We still need to send her back to the academy."

Gailea shared what seemed an uncertain gaze with both Darice and Ashden, and Lorelei sensed there had been some disagreement on this subject.

Quickly, Darice brightened and said to Lorelei, "Gailea has spoken so highly of you, and with good cause. You've been in Carmenna these past months? How truly brave, to return to a land that I'm sure must have caused great pain for you."

"Thank you. Actually, that's why I've come to talk to you at such a late hour, aside from being eager to meet you, of course."

"Yes, you must be quite exhausted." Darice gently took her hand and led her over to the settee. Lorelei sat alongside Gailea and her sister. Ashden offered her a saucer of warm milk, which she readily accepted, before settling on the thick rug, facing them, arms slouched over his knees.

"I'm almost as keen for a warm bed as I was to meet you," Lorelei admitted with a small, playful smile. "But before I retire, as I was telling Gailea, I think it's important we discuss a few things together, as Guardians."

"Of course." Ashden nodded and motioned toward the bed. "Should I wake Iolana then?"

Gailea shook her head, keeping her voice hushed. "Let her sleep. Whatever she needs to know, I can share with her later. For now, let the girl have her rest from such heavy subjects—the both of them."

Lorelei summarized what she and Mikanah had overheard about the Vessel, and Gailea shared their thoughts on it being a possible warship to transport or utilize Obscura magic.

"I'll try to talk to Mikanah," Lorelei added, "see if he knows anything more. He's been reluctant to share anything, but he might be more willing now that he begins to trust me a little."

"This Mikanah," Gailea said. "What can you tell us about him?"

"He's a very skilled musician. His skills are rough around the edges, but powerful."

"Similar to Iolana's then. She has much natural talent, but she lacked knowledge in even the most basic music theory."

"Not so with Mikanah. Though I think much of his knowledge is self-taught. He's a very ambitious young man. He was Moragon's chief musician." Lorelei paused, and she felt her entire body tense as she watched them, bracing herself for their reactions as this grave declaration sank in.

"Really?" Darice shared a shocked look with Gailea.

Gailea's face darkened with a frown, and anger seemed to flare in her eyes to overshadow her fear. "Chief musician? So, he was close to Moragon's side. And you trust him? How do we know he's not spying for Moragon as we speak?"

Lorelei did her best to carefully choose each word while maintaining honesty. "I can't say I trust him yet. I remain wary. Cautious. He was quite loyal to Moragon. I was hard-pressed to convince him to come along. Actually, I had to use a bit of magic to convince him." She tried to keep her voice as even-toned as possible. Gailea was looking more and more uncomfortable, and between her long journey and now sipping the warm milk, Lorelei was too tired for a fight, even one that was well meant.

"Is he still loyal to Moragon?" Ashden asked with a calm curiosity, his tone devoid of judgment.

Gailea's tone portrayed the opposite. "If he's still loyal to our greatest enemy, how is he meant to join us in our fight *against* that enemy?"

"Moragon was his teacher, his mentor. All Mikanah knows, he owes to him. But he also wants to see Moragon pay for the pain he's caused to people he loves. Moragon and his right-hand man, Reynard, are responsible for his brother's death, and he wishes to see that death avenged. I think he's capable of changing loyalties. I think he believes being a Guardian will grant him power, and he wants that, to avenge his brother."

"Such a thirst for power concerns me most," Darice said, seeming to echo Gailea's thoughts as they shared a meaningful glance. "If we give him our secrets, he could run back to Moragon and use them against us. I don't trust him, and I won't pretend to. Trust must be earned."

"But he can't earn our trust if we never give him the chance," Ashden said, gently placing his hand on Darice's.

Darice nodded, still looking wary but less tense, as though Ashden's touch grounded her back in the present. "Agreed. There are eight Guardians altogether. Surely as a whole we can keep an eye on him."

"Unless he truly is Moragon's spy!" Gailea whispered sharply, looking more upset. "If Mikanah is truly bound to Moragon, it will be nearly impossible to undo those bonds."

"But he's *not*." Lorelei grew impatient. As she finished the last of her milk and set the saucer on the small wooden table, all she wanted was her bed and her fire's warmth. "He is not like many of Moragon's servants. He still has his own mind, can still make his own choices."

"All the more reason to exercise nothing but the most fervent caution. I've watched corrupted rulers make corrupted choices of their own volition for many years. I know you want to trust him. But doing so freely is a naïve risk the Guardians cannot afford."

"I am not naïve," Lorelei said, her patience snapping altogether. "Please do not insult me. We were both prisoners of Moragon. We both know what he's capable of. You know what it's like to be under Moragon's thumb. Give Mikanah a chance."

"I don't wish to insult you," Gailea said, her voice a little gentler. "But I lived with Moragon all my life, many more years than you. Please, I beg you to show the utmost caution."

Lorelei took a deep breath. There were times that Gailea didn't realize her own tactlessness. It wasn't her fault, for there was much Lorelei had never told her, had never told anyone. But Lorelei knew exactly what Moragon was capable of and hadn't needed an entire lifetime in his courts to discover it.

"I'll remain watchful," she said at last. "But Gailea, all of you, please, give him a chance. He needs to feel welcomed like any other Guardian."

"I'll do my best."

"As will I," Darice agreed, with Ashden nodding beside her.

"Good. I should get some sleep now." Lorelei rose to her feet. As Gailea stood with her, Lorelei drew her close in another tight embrace. "I'm very glad to see you safe and well again."

"And I you," Gailea said tenderly.

Lorelei bid everyone goodnight before gratefully stealing away to the familiar comfort of her chambers.

As Gailea allowed her weary body to recline on the large canopy bed beside the two girls, her mind raced with a myriad of emotions. Tonight, her worlds had collided. Lorelei, Darice, Ashden, and Iolana were now part of one world. Gailea felt that Iolana and Lorelei would love each other just as fervently. Once more, there were Guardians, and they would instinctively become a family.

But this hope seemed overshadowed by the fact that another, also meant to be a Guardian, could not possibly ever harmonize with their family. Moragon's vengeance, lust, and wrath had destroyed the Guardians once already. In Gailea's mind, this Mikanah *was* Moragon's vengeance, lust, and wrath. Even if he desired retribution against his king, he could not stop Moragon from using him if he so chose.

If Gailea knew anything about Moragon, it was that he did not willingly relinquish ownership of his favorite playthings. Moragon likely still had a plan for Mikanah. With or without Lorelei's help, Gailea must watch him as closely as she could. She would not let him, or anyone, destroy her new family.

CHAPTER 27

UNMASKED VISAGE

Mikanah's sleep that first night in Pakua was plagued with nightmares—men and women seduced by his music, executed by fire, familiar faces pleading at him through the flames. Watching himself succumb to his own songs, only to be captured and dragged toward one of the wooden stakes, screaming and pleading. His gaze had met Lorelei's, but hers had only accused, reflecting the same coldness of Samil's—no, Moragon's, he reminded himself, just as her face had *become* Moragon's.

Now, as Mikanah followed Lorelei through Castle Kanoah's twisting stone corridors early the next morning, his body trembled with an aching tiredness. His nightmares had kept his mind alert so that he may as well have been wide awake all through the night. Thus, as hard as he struggled to shove the eerie visions aside, doing so was impossible. His weary mind forbade him rest, whether sleeping or awake.

The truth was, Lorelei had become his new master. She had fled with him here against his will. True, she had also proven an ally; the sword at his side was proof of this. But Moragon had also granted him gifts to use for his own purposes.

Thus, Mikanah couldn't help feeling confused about Lorelei. Strangely, he wanted to trust her, a feeling he rarely had toward any human, but he couldn't decide just how different she was from Moragon, aside from her apparent kindness. Powerful factions hardly ever allowed freedom without consequence. In leaving Moragon, that consequence was his life, if the king ever caught up to him. Lorelei had said that only death could spare his being a Guardian, but he now suspected this was a lie to manipulate him into coming with her. After all, she'd also suggested that the Council could remove his Guardians' mark. Even so, he couldn't know what punishment the Guardians might invoke if he tried to abandon them or did anything else to make himself appear as a danger or threat.

Not that they would likely want him to stay either. He, a servant of Moragon's, now meant to become one of their so-called "equal" allies? He scoffed the notion that they would allow this. But if they were indeed fools enough to take him into their fold, he must do his best to make a good impression. He must learn to make himself accepted, likeable, through pure charm alone. This thought drove his already-exhausted mind into an anxious sort of panic. Outside his persuasive magic, he'd never held any skill for making allies. And Lorelei had made clear that such magic would not be tolerated here.

At last, they stepped through a door flanked by guards. Beyond, a spacious room boasted a roaring fire, a sturdy, long oaken table surrounded by several chairs, and shelves filled with books. Along one wall, sunlight glistened through many tall, narrow windows dwarfed by the stones surrounding them. Several guards stood about the room, silver swords within golden crosses stitched across their wine-red leather tunics, the crest of Loz, Mikanah recalled. Two women, one with wavy auburn hair and another with a long, dark braid, and a strong-built man with tanned skin, stood up from one of the cushioned benches near a window.

"Good morning, fellow Guardians." Lorelei greeted them with a warm smile. "This is Mikanah. Gailea, if you would introduce yourself and the others?"

"I am Gailea Fleming," said the woman with auburn hair, her blue-green eyes gazing sharply over her oval spectacles. "This is Darice, my sister, and Ashden, a dear friend of ours." She motioned to them each in turn, and then to the guards stationed about the room. "These here are the First Echelon of the Lozolian Council, sworn to protect us from any who would wish us harm." Her gaze locked pointedly on Mikanah, who had to fight against curling his fists at the clearly accusing remark.

"It's an honor to see all of you again," Lorelei quickly broke the tension, curtsying at them before granting Gailea a warm embrace.

Mikanah shifted uncomfortably. This was not the way servants addressed their superiors. This was not even the way servants addressed servants. This was not the way anyone of any important rank addressed one another in Moragon's courts. He wasn't sure he knew how to talk to these people without offending, but he would have to try his best. He needed to make at least as good an impression as he had managed with Lorelei.

She motioned toward him now. "Our escape from Moragon's domain was overwhelming, to say the least. We arrived only last night, so Mikanah may yet be tired."

Mikanah walked over, appreciating Lorelei's cover, and yet loathing it. He didn't want to look like some impotent victim in front of these Guardians. He wanted to appear capable and gain their trust so that they would grant him as much knowledge and power as quickly as possible.

Ashden grasped Mikanah's arm in a strong embrace, and Darice curtsied with a warm smile.

Then he came to Gailea.

"Lorelei has spoken highly of you," Mikanah said, the words well meant, but they were cold and clipped, especially as she kept staring at him with a stony resistance.

"An honor to meet you," she replied. Her tone was perfunctory at best, her gaze almost toxic.

"Where are the girls?" Lorelei asked.

"They rose just as I had finished getting ready," Gailea said. "I expect they'll be in—"

The door opened behind Mikanah, and his body tensed. He was not eager for more company, for more potentially judging eyes and ears.

"*There* they are!" Darice said. "Over here, girls."

"*Mika?*"

The entire room stilled, shrouded by an abrupt, heavy silence.

Mikanah wasn't certain if the silence was real. Perhaps the sound of her voice held the power to make every other noise melt away in his mind. He whirled, faced the doorway—

Faced *her*.

Iolana.

His Iolana. Standing there. Alive. Or else a ghost. Though if the latter, a ghost who looked healthier than he'd ever seen her look while living. A ghost everyone else could clearly see, by the way they stared between her and him. No, she must be alive. But she couldn't. For her to be alive was...

"Impossible."

"Mika."

Iolana raced forward and threw her arms around him. Mikanah started to embrace her but then staggered back, grabbed her arms, and pushed her away. Holding her at arm's length, he stared. Her raven curls, as untamed as the desperation gleaming in her wide eyes. Her lips' familiar fullness. Her subtle curves beneath her tunic. Her delicate hand reaching for him, fighting against the invisible wall of space he'd thrown between them. He inhaled her scent, recalled the softness of her skin.

Every detail that was her made him ache inside, made him want to hold her close and love her as he had so many times in Moragon's domain—or Samil's, as they had known it together. But things were not the same. *He* was not the same. He was not the man she imagined herself running to now. All he could see were the flames consuming her, eating her alive. He had since sent others to similar deaths. He had done many things she didn't know about, *couldn't* know about.

"Mikanah?"

Lorelei's voice broke through his whirling thoughts.

"I take it that you two know one another?"

"Yes," Mikanah said, his voice too flat for the depth of emotions building inside him. They twisted like a hurricane, overpowering but incomprehensible. Old emotions he hadn't felt in so long that he couldn't define them. New emotions that flooded him with both relief and anxiety in one breath.

"Yes," he cleared his throat. "She's the girl I mentioned before. The...the friend I mentioned." He choked out the word "friend" and glanced away as Iolana's face dipped into an uncertain frown.

"Indeed," Lorelei said quietly. "Perhaps we could grant you some privacy?"

Mikanah stood still as stone, again uncertain what to

feel or respond. This was all he had wanted, to stand in her presence again. But now it came to it, what could he possibly say to her? What *should* he say? What should he do?

Iolana answered for the both of them. "I need some air. Come. I'll lead you to the gardens."

She grabbed his hand and dragged him after her.

They wound down several corridors and two stairways. At the bottom of the second stair, Iolana led him through a door and an intricately wrought iron gate, and they were suddenly outside in the cool morning air. Fresh sunlight danced between the many branches of lofty trees embracing high above. Despite winter's dawn, a few flowers still grew, bright blue blossoms with layers of pointed, star-like petals surrounding several taller petals that met at a single apex. Rosals, they were called. Tall, perfectly vertical cliffs surrounded the garden, serving as impassable sentinels.

Iolana released his hand and paced to the middle of the small clearing, breathing deeply as if panicked. At first, he worried she had regretted her decision to speak with him. Perhaps she might dart away like a frightened deer. Perhaps she truly was a dream that would just vanish in a puff of smoke, and he would wake to find he was still locked in a cruel nightmare. Much as he didn't know what to do or say, he couldn't stand the idea of her leaving his presence so quickly after reentering it.

Then she turned and faced him, her gaze pleading. Pleading to be invited to run into his arms, to hold him again and for him to let her this time. Pleading for him to reassure her that everything could be as it once was. It couldn't be. It already wasn't. But the longer she looked at him, his heart melted. He longed to comfort her, even as he longed to tell her the truth and knew he couldn't.

Finally, unable to resist, he bridged the gap between

them.

"Iolana Noelani." He reached out. "My Lani." When his fingers brushed her face, the velvet touch of her cheek made the surreal dream solidify, especially as she pressed his hand to her face.

"Lani, how...?" He shook his head. "When I last saw you...You were tied to the stake. And the fire, and the ash—I *saw* you die. I saw your body ruined!"

"You did." Iolana kept her eyes locked fervently on his. "You did see all of that. It was no illusion. It's what you *didn't* see that spared me. Moragon was enraged after the night I last saw you, the night we last kissed, and insisted I must be trying to plot with you against him. I think even then he sensed your potential. And he was right. You are now a Guardian, after all."

She smiled, filled with pride, but Mikanah only nodded, focused solely on her as she continued, "I knew it was only a matter of time. I'd seen hundreds go to their deaths for treason or disobedience. I was locked away in one of the most carefully guarded cells, with no way to escape or look for answers, before...before being sentenced to death." She choked out the last words, and Mikanah wrapped his arms around her, needing her to know that she was safe. He doubted she could be safe with him in the long run, but he needed her to feel safe now, for a few, precious minutes. He knew she had likely not shared her pain with anyone else. She needed to know that she could release it to him, just as she always had.

She remained silent, gazing up into his face, admiring. Her unwarranted admiration made him nearly tear away again, but he forced himself to hold his gaze steady, to make her know he was ready and listening. Her silence persisted, and then she tore her glance from his, but not before he had glimpsed the deeper pain within.

She had buried that pain, and it shackled her heart and mind. He must help her to free herself of it.

"What else?" he said, firm but tender. "I see it in your eyes. What else did he do to you?"

"No," she released a great sigh before sucking in her breath, clearly trying to hold back tears. "You don't need to be troubled with all of that. I'm here now, alive. That's what matters."

"Your pain matters too. Talk to me, as you once did. Let me bear your burdens with you. I want to take that pain away from you, as much as I can." He didn't add what a fitting punishment it would be for him, to bear all that pain after what she had suffered for him, after he had made others suffer.

Iolana drew close to him, leaning her forehead against his chest. As he held her, it seemed his touch gently eased the words from her, and she whispered, "Before my execution, he tortured me. Many days. I don't know how many. Most terrible of all were the dreams he forced upon me. Nightmares in which he tortured *you* relentlessly, and I—I was powerless to help you." She swallowed hard, again as if fighting tears, but he stroked her hair, silently telling her she could let them come. "I often woke to believe the dreams had been real. I felt so much guilt over them." She pressed herself as close to him as she could, weeping freely at last.

He held her as tightly as he dared. "I hate that he made you feel that way. All you ever did was help others, help me. Make our lives better, brighter. You never did anything to feel guilt for. Please know that. For whatever it's worth coming from me, I hope you can believe it."

After a few moments, her sobs quieted, and she looked up at him, gaze mingling torment and tenderness. "It means everything coming from you. You should know that."

Again, her loyal admiration, blind to the man he truly was, made him want to draw away, but he made himself stay put, for her sake. "Can you tell me how you survived? How you escaped?"

Iolana's eyes narrowed with fresh pain, and he added, "If that's too much, you don't have to tell me right now."

"No, I want to. Just…thinking about the execution itself.…" She shuddered head to toe, and he kept his arms locked firmly about her waist, to make her steady and secure. "I'd been feeling along the stones inside my cell for any means of escape. I'd gone over those stones so many times, I was certain there was nothing that could help me. But then one of the servants who had been kind to me, as kind as anyone was allowed in that place, granting me a bit of extra food here and there, one day she brought me an extra flask of water."

"That was gracious indeed. Do you recall her name?"

"I'm not sure. She was an older woman. I think I would know her face if I ever saw it again."

Mikanah couldn't think of any circumstances under which he would want her to be able to reconnect with that woman. All the same, he vowed to thank her if ever they met.

He nodded at Iolana to continue.

"The woman threw the water in my cell, and at first that seemed an uncommon act of callousness. But when I went to retrieve the water, I realized that one of the stones in that corner had shifted. I wedged my fingers between the stones, trying to move them, hoping in my delusion for some secret source of escape. They budged just a bit more, but then I pulled something out from between them, a thin piece of parchment. On it was scribbled a spell called 'The Phoenix Rising.' The writing said it was a song empowered by fire and meant to triumph over death. I knew it was my one chance of saving myself.

"That day, tied to the stake, I sang the song over and over again. The fires consumed my body, and I panicked, wondering if I had sung it right, and then I lost consciousness to the smoke. A day later, I woke in a grave. Risen from the dead. I crawled out and fled into the woods, toward the ocean."

"My sweet Lani." Mikanah's thumb swept a few tears from her cheeks. Beyond his amazement at her bravery, fresh anger stoked the fires blazing in his heart toward Moragon.

Iolana swallowed hard. Inhaling a long, trembling breath, she continued, "The next couple of weeks were running and surviving, often just barely. For a while, I did all right, but gradually, my body began to succumb to weakness and illness. '*The Phoenix Rising*' had saved my life, but it didn't entirely heal my burns. And I imagine it didn't entire cure me of whatever ailments I suffered from inhaling so much smoke.

"Once I reached Carmenna's borders, I found a small boat and set sail. I didn't care where the waters led me, as long as it was far from Carmenna. I rowed to the first island I saw, Loz. That's where Gailea rescued me. My strength was almost gone when I met her. Without her, without the other Guardians and teachers, I would've died."

Mikanah shook his head. Her story explained much, including the loathing with which Gailea had studied him. If Gailea had once been a prisoner of Moragon's and had also rescued Iolana, she had more than enough reason to distrust him, especially with whatever information Lorelei had divulged to her. Lorelei may have only spent a week with Mikanah in Moragon's castle, but he felt that was more than enough time for her to become entrenched in the depths of his music's beguilment. If she had shared a single shred of how he used his skills to snare others' minds, Gailea would not only distrust but likely despise him. He would have to fight to earn her favor.

He stroked Iolana's cheek. "Why are you here now? Why would you come so close to Carmenna, of all places?"

"Because I thought Gailea was in danger. And also, there's this."

She stretched her neck toward the sun. Something shimmered on her neck, just above her shoulder. He leaned closer to examine it and then immediately recoiled as the word *Ut* glared up at him.

"No," he snarled. "This can't be."

"Mika, why are you upset?" Iolana stared, looking surprised at his sudden display of anger. A part of him wanted to wrap his arms around her again, forget about the mark and return to soothing her. But the fury that the mark ignited in him wouldn't allow him such grace.

"Why am I upset? Why aren't you? Why should you be appointed as a Guardian, chosen to fight him, after all you've been through? Isn't it enough that you escaped death from him once?"

"Mikanah, this is no one's fault. The way I understand it, the Guardians are just...*chosen*. You too are a Guardian, after all." She stepped toward him, gently taking his hands in hers.

"Chosen?" Mikanah echoed skeptically. "If not by Lorelei or Gailea or whoever is in charge of all this, then by who?"

"I don't know exactly how it works. It sounds like, in cases of emergency, like when the other Guardians died, that new ones are chosen by some magic. Or perhaps it's just as well to say I've been chosen by Amiel."

"*Amiel.*" Mikanah sneered and pulled away. Iolana's face fell at the separation abruptly forged between them. Guilt tugged at his heart, but he couldn't give in. There was so much she didn't understand.

"Lani. Do you thank Amiel for the fate He dealt you? Dealt us?"

Her eyes narrowed, reflecting a new pain as she reasoned out the truth. "You no longer believe in Amiel. You've abandoned our faith."

Our faith. The accusation stung. "Yes. Does that change things?"

"I don't know. I honestly don't understand how you can shun Him."

"Forgive me for speaking a truth you don't want to hear. But Amiel is dead to me, Iolana. Know that. And if He *is* real, then He did nothing to save us."

She flinched at his harsh words but then reached for him again. He almost pulled away, but he allowed her to take his hands and hold them once more.

"But He did save us, Mika. Amiel led us back to each other."

"No..." His voice grew tender again, and he offered a small, solemn smile. "*You* led us back together. Your intelligence, your determination to conquer death."

Mikanah shifted closer. Hesitantly, Iolana placed her hands around his neck. He took a deep breath, trying to resist, but her constant gaze, still so eager, drew him in. He placed his hands on her waist and held her close, savoring the warmth pulsing between their bodies.

"You always were so delicate," he said quietly. "Delicate but with a hidden strength."

Iolana's attention drifted curiously to something at his side. "When did you become a swordsman?"

"It's gift from Lorelei. A sign of trust between her and me. She wanted me to feel safe here."

Iolana smiled, twining her fingers around the hair curling at the base of his neck. "You never needed a sword. Your magic is powerful enough to protect you from anything."

"That's beside the point," Mikanah muttered. He almost pushed her away again, but she clung to him. "Lani…In Samil's—that is, Moragon's—fortress, there was never any hope of our being free. I truly believed we would die there together. Now that we *are* free, I need to tell you…. There are so many things you don't know. Things that happened, terrible things you can't imagine. Things I have done."

"Tell me. You know you can tell me anything."

Mikanah searched her face intently. He yearned to tell her, but something stopped him. Lorelei knew first-hand what he was capable of, and yet she continued to place some hope and trust in him. Perhaps releasing his secrets to her and having one person see that side of him was enough. Perhaps it was best he divulged that side of himself with someone who was more a practical stranger, than his Lani, who could be hurt severely by his truth.

"We should probably get back. The others will worry." He saw the disappointment cloud her eyes and hurried on, "But I can share at least one secret with you first."

He reached inside his pocket and revealed a tiny glass vial. A bit of glistening indigo powder still rested at the bottom. He held it out toward Iolana, who took it in her hands, admiring it.

"What is it?"

"Flying powder."

Eagerness shone in her gaze.

"It's how Lorelei and I made it so quickly to Pakua."

Iolana tilted her head, and thoughtfulness filled her eyes. "She truly did save you. I owe her my life."

"She can teach us many things." Mikanah turned to the windows high above, as if able to see within. "They all can, these Guardians. We can become powerful enough to storm Castle Alaula and destroy him. Destroy Reynard."

Iolana nodded. "Destroy everyone who has ever served freely in his name."

Mikanah flinched at this declaration. It wasn't her fault. She couldn't understand the accusation she made against him.

Nor must she ever.

"Here," he said. "Hold out your hand."

She did so, and he tapped a bit of the powder into her palm. He took a pinch for himself, and she mimicked him as he sprinkled it beneath his tongue. She wrinkled her face as the bitterness struck him, making him smile at how silly she looked, like a child trying their first dose of healing tonic. He shared the magic word, *Anemoius*, and together, they rose steadily from the ground. With a gasp, Iolana held out her arms, struggling to balance as she wobbled in the air. Mikanah took her hands in his. He positioned one of her hands on his shoulder and then lifted her chin so that her eyes met his. Instantly, her gaze calmed.

They rose higher and higher, twirling slowly in a simple dance, creating an endless circle of them and only them, with no one and nothing else in the world. For those few moments, Mikanah let himself believe it was so, that there could be just them. No horrors of the past, no uncertainties of the future. Just her, his Iolana, in his arms.

"You didn't do *this* with Lorelei, did you?" Iolana whispered.

"No, of course not," Mikanah whispered back. "You've always had my heart. You and no one else. My heart died when you died. But it beats now stronger than ever. And it's ready to fight for you."

At last, he allowed himself to kiss her. As she kissed him back, her passion flooded over him, filling him from the inside out. Her passion felt like an ancient gift or dream from a distant lifetime, and yet familiar enough that he gladly let it devour him. In a single breath, it wrapped around his heart like a balm and surged through every fiber of his body like a flame blazed back to life.

His hands wandered her delicate neck, her shoulders, her waist. When he reached her thighs, her moan broke him at last from his trance. The castle was heavily guarded enough that someone had likely seen them already. Now was not the time for intimacy...if ever again with her, he thought soberly, gently severing their kiss.

She looked at him, breathless, awestruck, eyes hungering for more. More than desire reflected in her eyes. She still loved him. And he loved her...or did he really? It was hard to tell whether he had kissed her out of love or out of the same kind of selfish lust he had allowed to consume him after her death—and before her death, if he could be honest with himself. Guilt and doubts weighted him once more, and he began dancing them back down. They hovered for a few moments just above the ground. Then the spell ceased, and they landed on solid earth.

"That was beautiful." Iolana rested her head on his chest.

"It was," Mikanah said. "But we really must get back now. They'll be expecting us."

She took his hand and led the way back inside.

CHAPTER 28

EMBERS UNQUENCHABLE

Mikanah and Iolana approached the makeshift council chamber, where the others awaited them.

The nearer they drew, the more tightly Mikanah braced himself, preparing to enter combat. He imagined the Guardians split into two armies, meant to be allies but secretly enemies. Iolana was on his side, and Lorelei. But Gailea would hate him. If she was as influential as Iolana had described on their way here, perhaps the others would, too.

As they entered the large room, everyone glanced up from their seats at the long oak table and ceased their conversations until the room drew so quiet Mikanah could hear the flames crackling in the fire. Gailea's glance landed on him, heavy with accusation. An awkward silence fell, but Iolana broke it,

"Mikanah and I knew each other in Moragon's fortress. We were both prisoners there, both valued for our musical magic. He had thought me dead for a long time, and I had almost given him up to the same fate. But we are reunited now."

Mikanah resisted, but Iolana pulled him over and sat with him at the table beside Ashden and Darice, facing Lorelei, Gailea, and a blue-skinned girl. The guards wearing Loz's crest had gathered near the table. Iolana leaned into him, holding his hand. Trying to ignore Gailea's disdainful look, he allowed himself to embrace Iolana's comfort.

"In your absence," Lorelei motioned at Mikanah and Iolana, "a messenger arrived. The last two Guardians have been found. One sails not far from Rosa on a merchant's ship. The ship has agreed to meet us at specific coordinates on our voyage to the second Guardian, who dwells in Adelar."

"Our messengers were not permitted entrance to the Guardian in Adelar," said one of the First Echelon men standing near the table. "It's the Adelaran king himself, His Majesty Donyon."

"Of all the ironies," Gailea muttered, looking even stormier, before clearing her voice and speaking up. "The Lozolian Council says we will need to persuade Donyon in person, and I agree. Reluctantly, as I've no great desire to visit Adelar, but we don't have time to hope he'll have an unlikely change of heart or mind. We must take action. However, we won't be able to sail directly to Adelar. The Adelarans are an insulated people. They have great prejudice and paranoia against outsiders. Due to this fear, the Adelarans have sealed themselves inside their island. Donyon has researched the ancient, elemental magic barriers that once surrounded both Adelar and Rosa and, until recently, had still surrounded Rosa. He has had these barriers rebuilt around Adelar, two of fire magic and two of water."

"You have messengers who can fly," Mikanah said.

"Can't they fly over the barriers?"

"*We* have them," Iolana corrected gently, squeezing his hand.

Mikanah shrugged as Lorelei answered him. "No. They've tried, but the barriers stretch so high up that anyone who tries flying above them finds themselves suddenly unable to breathe. Adelar is now impenetrable, except with the aid of a very specific magic song. The keys to obtaining this song may reside in Rosa, Adelar's neighbor."

"*The Eagle's Ayre*," Gailea said. "The song is said to summon a great Eagle when sung by a Rosan or Adelaran in great danger, as long as the intents of their hearts are pure. It's especially sacred to the Rosans, as it was first composed by the ancient queen their island is named for. The Adelarans and Rosans have despised each other for generations now, so if one of them have tried summoning the Eagle, it's likely fallen on deaf ears. I have part of the song, granted me by my mother. Unfortunately, by the time I received it, the parchment was weathered, the song smudged."

Darice patted her hand from across the table with what seemed an apologetic smile. Gailea returned with a gentle smile that softened her hardened expression, allowing Mikanah to glimpse the caring spirit that had so infatuated Iolana.

"Obtaining our eighth Guardian will be no small task," Lorelei continued. "We must go to Rosa first, if we hope to have a chance of finding the song and reaching Donyon. This may also be an opportunity to convince both Rosa and Adelar to step outside their hatred for one another, to see the real danger approaching their shores and join with us in the war against Moragon."

Gailea scoffed, her softness vanishing. "If I were asked to wager on who is easier to convince, I doubt I'd bet on either. But does everyone agree with departing tomorrow morning, as soon as possible?"

Nods and murmurs echoed across the room.

"What about me?"

All eyes turned toward the girl with blue skin and flowing waves of blue hair streaked with brunette. Mikanah had hardly noticed her presence, and she seemed to shrink now against Gailea.

"Nerine and I have been talking," Iolana said, meeting her gaze. "She wants to come."

"This journey is not for you." Gailea looked Nerine sternly in the eye. "It will be too dangerous. The Guardians cannot be responsible for your protection."

"She is an ally and a friend. Do the Guardians only afford such protections to entire kingdoms with powerful armies?"

Iolana sat straight in her chair, meeting Gailea's challenging gaze head-on, and Mikanah smirked at her boldness.

"I do also have musical magic." Nerine spoke quietly, but with a slight lift of her chin. "I've also been practicing my water magic. The library here had an entire book on elemental magic that Captain Pono has since gifted to me. I may not be a Guardian, but I assume I could be quite useful, nonetheless. I could learn song-spells from all of you and add my strength to yours."

"Musical mages *are* always strongest when singing or playing together." Darice shared an uncertain look with Gailea, and Mikanah respected her for speaking this truth, whether or not Gailea wanted to hear it, and even if he didn't view Nerine's apparent timid nature as much of an asset to bring along. "Such a trait is not unique to the Guardians themselves."

"We cannot make her stay or go," Gailea said, sweeping an anxious glance across them all. "But surely, you see the foolishness of allowing her to come along?"

"I think the choice is hers." Ashden nodded at Gailea with an apologetic look. "I think she has the right to choose the same as any of us. What do you want to do, Nerine?"

Nerine's glance darted around the room, at last reaching Iolana, where it lingered a long while, seeming to plead for some answer. As Iolana granted her a subtle nod, Mikanah wondered why she couldn't just make up her own mind.

"I'll stay. Iolana is my best friend. I'll help her fight, keep her safe."

Gailea leaned toward the girl, peering at her. "Nerine, are you certain?"

"I am."

"Thank you." Iolana shared a smile with Nerine.

Mikanah almost felt good about the exchange. Iolana had never had a chance to make friends besides him. But Nerine seemed like a frail, unstable creature. He hoped Iolana wouldn't be distracted with looking after her.

A servant brought breakfast then, fresh brown bread, eggs, fruit, and clay glasses of milk served on wooden trays, and conversations turned to lighter subjects. After breakfast, everyone agreed that the best way to spend their last day in Pakua was to determine everyone's current musical skills and practice together. The new Guardians wouldn't obtain their crystal instruments until official appointments could be completed in the Chamber of Music, and Gailea declared that such appointments should wait until they could be completed all at once, when the Guardians were all together. Time was of the essence, and it would be too great a hassle to voyage back and forth to Loz multiple times.

Meanwhile, they sang a few simple songs and scales,

determining each other's pitches, ranges, how best to harmonize together, and what individual gifts they each possessed. Mikanah felt most drawn to Ashden's affinity for growing various plants in his hands simply by uttering the proper chants. Darice and Gailea both had healing knowledge and could use Ashden's steady supply of herbs to heal any minor injuries they might acquire.

Gailea and Lorelei promised to start teaching them songs of both offense and defense, songs they had woven themselves and those they recalled from their time researching and housing such knowledge within the Chamber of Music. Many song-spells used just a single word, while others required no words, just the correct notes. All required the spell-caster to sing with perfect pitch to guarantee their accuracy, while their strength could be enhanced by changing the volume, key, or by pouring their own emotion into each song's intent. Eventually, when all the Guardians had been collected and everyone made their way to the Chamber, they would gather other songs of use to learn together as well.

After a hearty lunch, more time was given to musical practice, as well as sparring with wooden swords. Gailea and Lorelei teamed up, along with Darice and Ashden, while Mikanah showed Iolana how to hold a sword, how to stand and move her feet, and how to block blows. Nerine alone refrained, instead sitting on a bench before one of the windows, either practicing the scales they had sung or else weaving different patterns and shapes of water with her hands, the book she'd mentioned sprawled before her. While pretty, Mikanah couldn't see much use for the Nymph's magic.

Throughout the afternoon, they switched partners. Mikanah made certain to spar with everyone, Gailea included, to gauge their skills. Not only did he want to know just how competent were the allies he'd gained, but it wouldn't hurt to know who might pose a possible threat to him. Gailea and Darice were both decently skilled, but he could manage their fierce fight. Ashden, on the other hand, proved a masterful duelist, but he seemed even-tempered enough that Mikanah didn't need to worry about him.

After dinner, they chatted late into the night. Mostly Gailea, Ashden, and Darice caught up on old times, which Lorelei, Nerine, and Iolana listened to keenly. Mikanah tried to pay attention, if only to seem friendlier and learn anything useful, but he was exhausted from the day and his mind easily wandered from their inane drabble. Only when Iolana began to fall asleep on Mikanah's shoulder did Lorelei announce that they should head to their rooms and get what rest they could before tomorrow morning's early departure.

Mikanah walked Iolana and Nerine to their room. As Nerine slipped inside, Mikanah kissed Iolana's forehead.

"I'll see you in the morning then?"

Iolana smiled up at him. "Of course. I'll be in the garden, to watch the sun rise. If you like, you should join me, and we can watch it together as we used to." She stretched up and whispered in his ear, "Perhaps even *be together*, as we used to."

His heart and body ached at her words, but he said nothing.

Iolana slipped inside her room with a final glance over her shoulder, a glance that made him wish he had pulled her a little closer, kissed her a little more deeply when they were in the garden.

But he couldn't think that way.

Not anymore.

For him, acts of love had not been connected to real love for a long time.

There was too much she didn't understand and never could.

~*~*~

Iolana stretched out on the bed beside Nerine, enveloped in the warmth of the covers, the flames from the fireplace, and Nerine snuggled up against her. They had cuddled this way last night, like sisters. Iolana appreciated the closeness again tonight, even while she ached for Mikanah's newly restored affection.

"So, who is he really?" Nerine asked. "Were you lovers a long time?"

Iolana hesitated. The memories of their separation still struck a painful chord inside her heart. She knew Nerine meant well and wouldn't pry any further if she forbade her. But maybe she needed this. Maybe she needed to talk about everything, to reason through her jumbled feelings.

"Mikanah is all I've ever known. He was my only friend in Moragon's fortress. He meant everything to me. He was strong, protective. I saw those things today, but...I saw something else. Something I can't place. He wasn't as warm as he once was. He didn't act like himself. Something was holding him back. Even his heartsong was almost entirely veiled from me. What little I could hear, I sensed passion, but also an unusual anger and fear."

The bed shifted as Nerine pushed herself up on one elbow. "He thought you were dead. Maybe he's still in shock. Maybe he's afraid to get close again too soon. But I think his affections are certainly sincere. The way he watches you is so intense, as if he's ready to pounce on anyone who tries to hurt you."

Iolana heard the doubt in her voice. "Do you think

that's a good or bad thing?"

"I don't know. I don't think there's any issue with his being so protective, after what you've been through. But...you mentioned anger, and I agree. I think he tries to hide it. But it's there, in the way he carries himself."

"He has much to be angry about," Iolana said. "He hasn't told me everything he's been through since my death...or even everything before, I don't think. But he was with Moragon a long time and is just now free. He hasn't had time to heal."

Iolana let her words fade as her thoughts sped. She could not deny Nerine's concerns on the matter. In fact, she shared the same reservations. She had tried to deny them when Mikanah had kissed her. After all, such a display of unbridled passion was what she had been craving. Their bodies had become a dance and song. They'd entwined together perfectly, as if truly created for one another. But something had dampened her experience. More than passionate, it seemed he had poured out his frustrations into his kiss.

Something had changed in him, something uncertain that she both feared and desired to know better.

"Iolana..." Nerine gently stroked the back of her hand along Iolana's shoulder. "I'm not trying to upset you. I don't judge Mikanah because I don't even know him. But I do know about *you*. You're a very all-or-nothing personality. And I love that about you. I just hope that you won't rush into things with Mikanah. I don't want to see you make a mistake that could hurt both of you."

Iolana nodded slowly, absorbing her friend's counsel. "I appreciate you looking out for me. I want everything to work out between us. I would fight to make that happen."

"Just give it some time," Nerine's yawn nearly cut

her words short. "If it's meant to be, it's meant to be. If not…"

Her heavier breathing signaled she had fallen asleep, leaving Iolana's mind to churn with heavy thoughts.

There was no "if not." There could not be. Iolana had never loved anyone as she loved Mikanah. He had been her singular source of comfort and strength. In Moragon's prison, they each had been the greatest gift that Amiel had ever granted one another. She could not lose him again.

~*~*~

Dawn crept through Mikanah's curtains, tingeing his bed with shreds of red and orange. He already sat upright. He had slept hardly an hour before nightmares had jerked him awake.

Slipping from the bed, he exited his room, declaring to the Carmennan guard outside his door that he was going to visit Iolana. The guard nodded in acknowledgment, and he hurried toward Iolana's room. He cracked her door open and peered inside. She still slept soundly, curled up close with her friend. Good. His heart ached to be near her, his body moreso. But he couldn't. Memory darkened such desires.

He sped through the corridors, passing several armor-clad Carmennan guards, as well as a few of the First Echelon. He didn't know his way around the caverns like Iolana did, but he could guess. He wound up and up until at last he emerged atop a high cliff overshadowed by a shorter ledge. Between two cliffs stretching before him, the sun rose. Its brilliant colors illuminated the space between the cliffs, blinding his view to all else.

Except for his vision of the fire, the flames. The flames in his mind that had tormented his nightmares and continued to torment him now, along with the shadows of every other memory building up to those flames....

His little brother, Jerah, chained down while Reynard performed magic experiments on him. Haunting, screaming melodies wrested from the small boy who trembled all over, jerking and convulsing as if the intensity of the magic forced on him might make him shatter at any moment....

The news that his brother had tried to fly away and, in doing so, had killed himself....

Mikanah rejoicing that his brother no longer had to suffer at Reynard's hands while mourning the loss of the one good thing in his life....

Mikanah throwing himself into the endless studies Moragon laid out for him, vowing to rise to power in Moragon's court, rise so far above Reynard that the man wouldn't even see it coming when he poured all his wrath and vengeance upon him....

Four years passed this way. Moragon was searching, always searching for some hidden gift among musical mages. Some said he sought a bride, to combine her powers with his. Other rumors spoke of a secret magic weapon he was working on. Mikanah overheard much of this weapon, though it was Reynard alone who was afforded the honor of learning about it personally.

As Mikanah grew into a man, his musical education was combined with Moragon's keen knowledge of mental magic. Mikanah's behavior began to mirror that of his master. All he learned, he learned from his king who served as a sort of twisted father. No other man had taken such an interest in him, such a pride in his talent. No other man had given him the opportunities his king did.

Moragon brought in young women, those he'd captured from Carmenna and other kingdoms, and invited Mikanah to join in what passed as simple revelry. Moragon gave him permission to exploit their attraction toward him, and he would. His good looks, his charms, they were all just bait for Mikanah to lure his prey. To take their bodies, overwhelm them with passion. In their moments of weakness, he would sing to them, using seductive song-spells to manipulate their emotions, lower their guards, make them eager to talk. Once entirely vulnerable to him, they would share any secret, including what powers they possessed. Many of these women he saw only once. If they were of no use to Moragon, they disappeared, never to be seen again. Mikanah didn't let himself get too attached. They were simply another part of his education.

Until Iolana arrived at the castle.

Moragon said Mikanah would not be testing her powers. The king already knew she was strong, that she was a heartsong seer. This was exactly the kind of power Moragon had been seeking, and she possessed it in its rarest and purest form. He could still mold her to his will. She was young enough yet for that.

Except that her will burned as equally strong as his.

"Break her," Moragon commanded. "Make her trust you. Make her love you. Do whatever you must do to convince her to use her powers for me."

Mikanah easily wooed her. But he could not control her. Nor could he tame her.

He fell in love.

What started as another of Moragon's assigned conquests rapidly evolved into something Mikanah had never experienced before. Touching her was different from touching the others. Kissing her was different. She made him alive, restored his sense of purpose. He craved her like the sweetest wine, and she needed him just as much.

The more deeply Mikanah loved her, the more desperately he warned her, and the wilder she became, determined to break free, to defy Moragon as so many had done before.

"Don't be afraid for me," she told Mikanah over and over.

She would be all right, she always assured him. She would be the one to make it.

Secret meetings, rebellions held in forgotten towers or dungeon rooms. Iolana was the queen of all of it. The escape plans. The plan against Moragon's life. Mikanah attended the meetings, never speaking a word but always watching her with pride. And fear.

A fear that began to dissolve over time. Iolana was so clever. She eluded Moragon for months. Maybe she would really do it. Maybe she could be the one.

But then Moragon caught up to her.

"Traitor," he labeled her. "Worse than that, instead of you bewitching her, Mikanah, she has bewitched you. She is a danger to our quest for power and glory. We are too close now. We cannot risk her ruining everything we have both worked so hard for."

But none of that was important to Mikanah anymore. The power, the glory. *She* was the goal that he had worked so hard for.

He pleaded with Moragon. Begged, screamed, threatened to kill himself. The king confined him to a single cell alone for months, stifled his magic, surrounded him with restrictive enchantments. Almost deluded him into believing that Iolana truly was some dark temptress.

Then Moragon made him watch her torture, and he knew Moragon was a liar. He had tried to deny it all these years, telling himself what a merciful soul Moragon had been for taking him in, teaching him, making him his favorite—next to Reynard.

Yes, next to Reynard. No matter what he did, he would always be second best.

He should have stopped it all. He should have helped Iolana with her rebellion. Maybe then Moragon would already be dead. Instead...

He watches as she is strapped to the wooden stake alongside many others labeled as traitors, heretics, lunatics, whatever name Moragon can give them to justify their demise. The flames are lit. Iolana's lips move as if she hopes to stop death with one of her musical charms. But the fire takes her, and soon her spell is drowned by her screams. She jerks violently against her bonds. Her beautiful wild curls catch ablaze. Her thin garments burn away, revealing her body, shaming her before it too is consumed by the flames. Skin melts, boils, strips away, filling the air with a sickening stench that makes Mikanah lean over and retch.

Then, at last, she is gone. She is silence. She is emptiness. She's not even a blackened corpse like the others surrounding her. She's a mere pile of ash, as if she never existed. As if she was never a soul or a voice or a spirit. She is nothing.

And he is nothing. He has nothing. Nothing except to return to his lustful quest for power and glory. Exactly what Moragon wants.

But he won't let Moragon have what he wants. He will learn all he can and use it to someday destroy those who destroyed the last thing he ever loved—

With a cry, Mikanah escaped his memories and blocked the sunlight with his arm, realizing that it was the sun and not the same fire that took her.

Trembling, Mikanah sank to his knees and held his head in his hands. He wished he could cry, feel something more human than the emptiness swallowing him whole, but such senses eluded him. When she died, he had become a mere shell, a hollow. He had wanted to kill himself but had never found the strength. Nor had he been able to cry. Those who are already dead have neither strength nor tears.

She was alive now. Which meant that *he* was alive, or

could be.

But things weren't that simple. Things weren't the same. She was changed. He was changed. The concept of *them* was changed.

She had been his Lani, and he had worshipped her. She had been the best thing in his world. She was his true savior, not Amiel. There *was* no Amiel, no gods of mercy and justice, no afterlife. The moment she had been stolen from him, Amiel as the Creator of all things good had become a vicious lie, one Mikanah could never believe ever again.

He could still believe in *her*, though. He must. When she was alive before, she was the one thing worth fighting for. Now that she was alive again, she must still be that one thing worth fighting for. She must be that one thing he loved, that fueled him forward.

And yet...

Did he love her? Or had he simply used her as a means of comfort, like he had all the others? Had their intimacy been of her own choosing, or had he seduced her with his music?

Did he even know what love meant?

Could he?

CHAPTER 29
ALL THAT IS GOLD

The Guardians, First Echelon Guard, and Nerine departed early in the morning. They packed sparsely, taking only what food, drink, and supplies they would absolutely need. The Carmennans had granted them each sturdy traveling clothes, linen dresses and tunics with belts, all in shades of green, gray, or blue, along with thick hose, leather boots, and leather satchels large enough to carry food, a map, or other small items.

As everyone boarded the small ship granted to them by Pono, Iolana and Mikanah held hands, whispering to each other, lost in their own world. Darice and Ashden's affections were less childish but certainly detectable. Nerine chatted with Darice excitedly. Lorelei alone looked solemn with her lips drawn into a thin line, brows knit, a clear unease in her eyes. However, as Nerine took Lorelei's hand and pulled her into hers and Darice's conversation, a smile lit Lorelei's face, dispersing some of its worry.

Gailea wished she could share their joy, however briefly. But she felt as solemn as the Echelon escorts marching onto the ship with them. The Lozolian Council had spared sixteen such soldiers to accompany them, including Idalin and Cenwin, the two women who'd helped Gailea escape Labrini after the concert. The Guardians were advised to go nowhere without their added protection.

Gailea supposed she should feel as secure as the others appeared to feel, but the past gnawed at her, along with its pains. The kingdom of Rosa was only the middleman, a necessary step toward rebuilding the bridge to Adelar, the prison of a home where she had grown up.

~*~*~

Over the next couple of weeks, their voyage passed uneventfully. They spent their time practicing simple charms of offense and defense, in between learning new songs, and practicing their sword skills. Nerine gleaned an elemental charm from her book to strengthen her concentration of water spells, much to her delight.

"*Ship ahoy!*"

A small vessel breached the horizon, speeding toward them on the still waters.

As the ship drew near, a familiar face beamed in their direction, and Gailea shouted, "Chamblin!" Mingled joy and disbelief overwhelmed her at the familiar sight of him, whole and well, even as Nerine and Iolana shouted his name, jumping and waving.

Two deckhands started readying a small boat for Chamblin, but he waved his hands in a nonchalant gesture and started running toward the side of the ship. Before Gailea could cry out for him to stop, he was playing a chord on the pear-shaped stringed instrument he held and leaping high through the air.

Halfway through his jump, he began to wobble. His

cocky grin faded, and he began tumbling from the sky. Darice leaped forward and sang a trilling series of notes along with the word *Élen-élen*, arms outstretched. Light beams shone from her her hands, weaving together to build a bridge of light that caught and lowered him safely to the deck of their ship.

"Well then," Chamblin huffed, brushing off his breeches, strumming a chord, and grinning up at them. "Thank you, my good woman, for a most charming rescue. Ever since I knew I was a Guardian, I've been practicing, but clearly, my musical skills aren't yet as fine-tuned as my skill with a sword or knife."

"They never were." Gailea grinned playfully, hurrying over, and taking his hands in hers. "Chamblin, I can't express how thankful I am to see you alive. At the theatre, during the attack, you saved me, and I...I left you there. I didn't mean to...." A rush of emotions flooded her heart. She cried, unable to stop the tears as a tenderness reflected in his gaze.

"My dear friend," Chamblin squeezed her hands warmly, "you did what you had to and exactly what I intended—you lived. You escaped. Escaped an old enemy of yours, I now understand, which makes me twice as glad that I defended you as I did."

Gailea quieted her tears, brushed them away, and smiled up at him. He smiled back, but she noted that he did not meet her gaze, even as he kissed her hand and declared, "What an honor to be reunited with so lovely a lady, Miss Gailea."

"Chamblin," she breathed. A flush crept into her cheeks, and she felt annoyed at her stark display of emotions. "You always did know how to make an unforgettable entrance. And departure, for that matter."

"I'm sorry to have scared you. I did take quite a blow, being so close to the explosion. But since I wasn't one of those singing, it wasn't automatically fatal for me. I had hoped to save them all. But when I saw what was happening, I knew I wasn't that powerful. But the mere idea of losing you, I had to do something. I don't even have words for such a nightmare. I'm so glad you're safe."

He smiled again in her direction, but when he still didn't meet her gaze, she noted the glazed look in his silver eyes and asked, "What *did* the explosion do to you? Are you…have you lost your sight?"

"Not yet." Chamblin's smile dimmed into a sober line. "Sometimes, I still see clearly, but that comes and goes by its own will. In this moment, I can only see lights, shadows, shapes, colors. None of it is well defined. The healers say it's only a matter of time before I lose my sight altogether, especially with the intensity of the explosion and the magic it was infused with."

"How long?" Gailea fought back another rush of tears. Losing her friends was a great enough horror, but now for Chamblin to lose his sight as well, and because of her.

"Could be weeks, could be months. Could be years or days. Who knows but Amiel Himself?"

"Chamblin, I'm so sorry."

"Don't be." He looked tenderly in her direction before drawing himself up in a dramatically proud stance. "Really. Don't be getting all soft and sappy on me now! Not when we've established the perfect friendship of sarcasm and mutual mockery. Above all, please don't blame yourself. I'd make the same choice a thousand times over. Now, while I may not be able to see well, I can see enough movement and colors to judge that you aren't commanding this ship yourself. I imagine I've other folks to meet? Fellow Guardians, perhaps?"

Gailea led him across the deck where everyone had gathered, waiting respectfully but with curious gazes.

"Hello!" Chamblin strummed a few silly notes on his instrument. "I am Tomilias Chamblin, though you may simply call me 'Chamblin.' A pleasure to be with you again, Nerine. You as well, Iolana."

Nerine's eyes shone wide with admiration. "I'm so glad to see you again, Mr. Chamblin."

"As am I." Iolana grinned up at him.

"Iolana is one of our Guardians," Gailea explained, "while Nerine is not but has chosen to accompany us for the time being. Allow me to introduce the other Guardians."

Gailea did so one by one. Chamblin gave a respectful nod and smile toward each of them.

Once introductions were made, everyone settled down to eat and rest for the remainder of the evening. Nerine suggested that it would be more refreshing to share dinner in the ocean breeze than to stay below deck, and as the sun set, they gathered on deck around a sturdy wooden table. Gailea, Darice, Mikanah, and Ashden had combined their voices to sing the song-spell *Hováría* that Gailea had taught them earlier, allowing them to levitate the table and accompanying benches long enough to float it above deck. Everyone sat on chairs or crates and stuffed themselves with bread and meat and dried fruits. Their supply was starting to run short, but they were meant to reach Rosa by tomorrow afternoon. They should have the opportunity there to replenish their supplies, but Gailea cautioned everyone to ration.

"After all," she said, "the Rosans can be just as prejudiced as the Adelarans. My birth mother, Gillian, fell in love with a Rosan, and their love fanned the flames of a war that nearly destroyed both kingdoms. Eighteen years later, when I served in Adelar as Queen, the Rosans often presented petty complaints in regard to trading, negotiating. It was established that trade between Rosa

and Adelar would occur peacefully, but fights and loot-
ing still broke out. Pirating on both sides was not uncommon. And instead of coming together, both sides
remained unwilling to trust each other, each believing
themselves superior to their self-proclaimed enemy."

Nerine released a wistful sigh as she rested her chin
in her hands, elbows propped on the table. "I still can't
believe you were a queen. I know it was a serious responsibility, having an entire kingdom of people to care
for. But it also does have a romantic ring to it, 'Queen
Gailea of Adelar'."

Gailea cringed, her lips drawn into a thin line. She
sang a shielding melody inside her head to contain the
dark memories flashing through her mind, along with
their accompanying flickers of pain, doubts, fear. "I'm
afraid I must disrupt your daydream by assuring you
that its seriousness far outweighed any romantic nuanc-
es or notions. Sometimes, all that appears gold does not
truly glitter."

As the night wore on, Chamblin happily received his
new audience by weaving songs and stories alike. The
gentle sway of the ship, along with the star-sprinkled sky,
created the perfect backdrop for his storytelling. Iolana
and Darice sang *Luma* to craft several balls of floating
light, better illimunating everyone while providing a
whimsical ambiance. Chamblin related many of his adventures to the more mysterious of Zephyr's Islands. He
also spoke of his most recent voyage with King Jorah
from Muriel and said that he intended to make a return trip to the Realm of the Seven Kingdoms once "this
Guardian business was over with."

"This Guardian business?" Gailea repeated, staring
at him. "I understand you're trying to put us all in good
spirits, and I appreciate that. But this is no game we
play. This isn't one of your flippant quests to barter with

Chinese merchants and bring back new spices from the Orient. The only reason you're here is because—"

Because the other Guardians died before him. And he almost died with them.

A lump formed in her throat. "Forgive me," she muttered, jumping up and hurrying toward the front end of the ship.

Blinking away her tears, she stared out over the bow where sky and ocean seemed to merge, creating a singular expanse of black speckled with stars.

"Gailea?"

Chamblin stood beside her. She folded her arms against her chest. She didn't need his comfort, and she certainly didn't deserve it.

"I'm sorry if I offended you," he said. "That is never my intent."

"I know," she whispered. Here, away from the others, hearing the sincerity in his voice, it was difficult to continue building the wall between them. Even still, she found it impossible to look at him, to look into his eyes that couldn't properly meet hers. "We're forced to go to Adelar. So many memories there."

"Because of Moragon."

"Not just him." Gailea roughly wiped away the few tears that had managed to escape. "Fear fills me when I think of Moragon. But bitterness takes hold when I think of Donyon. Because he pretended to be my ally. And I was his. I helped him take the throne back from Ragnar, and how does he repay me? By trying to slaughter me and my children!"

"I'm so sorry. What a miserable and utter fool he must be, to commit such a disgusting betrayal."

Gailea felt surprised at the bite in Chamblin's voice and glanced at him briefly, finding the same fierceness on his face. While she appreciated his defending her, she had never considered him capable of such a harsh tone.

"Do you have any idea why he would have acted thusly?"

Gailea shook her head. "My sister gave me some old accounts, letters, diary entries from my birth mother. Donyon tormented her constantly. He hated her for falling in love with a Rosan and breaking their engagement, an arrangement she never wanted and felt trapped in. Perhaps he wanted some vengeance on me, the child she had by the man she loved, the man that wasn't him."

Anger flared in Chamblin's voice. "If that's true, then what an arrogant and petty man indeed! To hold onto such hate for so many years."

Gailea sighed wearily. "Indeed. Maybe, by some miracle of Amiel's, he's become more reasonable since then. I doubt it, but...what can I do, seeing as we are forced to invite him into our fold? I've no choice but to attempt to trust him."

"*No.*" Chamblin spoke the word fervently, commanding her full attention so that she turned to him at last. "You're no more required to trust him than I'm required to enjoy my fading eyesight. We may have to each deal with these fates, but we don't have to pretend to like them. And, no, I don't say this to make you feel guilty over my blindness," he added with a dramatic wag of his finger that made her chuckle a little, despite herself. "I'm merely trying to make the point that you don't owe Donyon your trust, and he definitely hasn't earned it. If he is to be a Guardian, you'll have to learn how to work with him, yes. But you don't have to trust him. Or like him. I think it's terrible that you have to endure him at all, and terribly brave that you're willing to try. Amiel willing, he'll agree that the threat of Moragon overshadows any grievances he may have against you or your mother. But..." He took her hand. "...whatever happens, know that I will be right there to protect you. You know I would always protect you, as a Guardian or not."

Gailea smiled up at him. "I know. Thank you."

Chamblin wiped the last of her tears from her cheek. "Now, shall we get back and do our best to enjoy ourselves? We've one more day's journey, one more day before we need remember that worries even exist. Besides, it's a sorry looking lot over there since I stopped entertaining them."

Gailea glanced at the others. Iolana, Darice, and Nerine all stared across the deck at them, looking concerned, while Ashden and Lorelei seemed involved in some solemn conversation.

"Let's go, then."

As she and Chamblin took their seats, Chamblin glanced about at each wary face, lifted the stringed instrument over his head, and placed it in his hands, ready to play.

"This is truly the sulkiest gathering I've ever known. Anyone up for some pipa?"

"What's 'pipa'?" Nerine asked, her gaze alive with interest.

"This here…" Chamblin twanged a few loud, off-tune chords. Nerine and Iolana both laughed, while Gailea frowned, shaking her head in pretended disapproval. "This is a pipa. An instrument crafted in China, one of the largest countries in the Western Realm."

"China!" Nerine clasped her hands together, eyes shining with delight. "Isn't that quite a dangerous country?"

Chamblin shrugged. "No more dangerous than the kingdoms of the Lozolian Realm with their history of insane or sometimes downright ludicrous kings. I'd rather define China as extraordinary, brimming with adventure, fine art—and music."

He strummed a few mismatched chords, and their dissonant twanging made Gailea sincerely cringe. "Of all the choices in the Western Realm, you really brought home a pipa?"

Chamblin pouted, trying to look insulted. "Do you challenge my craft with the pipa?"

"No. I challenge your entire choice of instrument. The pipa is an entirely annoying contraption, at least in my past experiences. But by all means, go ahead, torture us. It'll be good preparation for the torture I'll feel setting foot on Adelaran soil."

Undaunted, Chamblin jumped to his feet, bowed low, and said, "As you wish, m'lady. I will now seek to overturn any negative dealings you've had with this glorious instrument."

Chamblin played several quirky melodies on his pipa and sang along. His rhymes and nonsense lyrics made Gailea roll her eyes, but even she couldn't resist clapping along, grateful for his distractions.

Ashden offered Gailea a dance. Gailea glanced uncertainly at her sister, but Darice nodded with a sweet smile, her eyes dancing brightly. Ashden took Gailea's hand and pulled her up. Within moments, Gailea found herself laughing as Ashden whirled her around the deck. His movements were somewhat clumsy, but then he allowed Gailea to take the lead. While not the most graceful team, at least he stopped landing on her toes.

As they leaped past Darice, Gailea extended her hand, Darice grabbed it, and Gailea pulled her into the fold. The three of them created a circle, dancing, skipping, and laughing like school children. Iolana and Mikanah skipped gaily to the music, and Ashden suggested seeing which team could go on the longest. Nerine and Lorelei joined in as a third contending team. In the end, none of them could hold out. Instead, they collapsed on the benches, declaring Chamblin as the winner.

When the hour grew late, they retired to the sleeping quarters below deck where they all shared a large room with several hammocks and a pair of bunk beds. Two Echelon guards remained posted outside the door at all times, while others patrolled the deck or slept in their own quarters.

Chamblin played soft tunes from his hammock in the corner. Gailea eased onto one of the lower bunks and tried to harmonize on her flute, but her heart wasn't in the music. Her gaze and thoughts strayed to Iolana and Mikanah, who had lain together on one of the bunks, Nerine sleeping beside them. Lorelei slept in the bunk above them.

As Darice and Ashden sat on either side of Gailea, Darice said, "Is something troubling you again, sister? You've looked worried about those two this entire trip." She nodded toward Iolana and Mikanah.

The orange glow of the hanging lanterns seemed to enhance the quiet understanding and kindness in Darice's face. Gailea's sister had always been well attuned to her feelings. The calm way in which Darice watched her, along with Chamblin's soothing song, seemed to draw the words out of Gailea, like removing a thorn from an old wound.

"I don't want to discourage their relationship...but the way he watches her, so intensely, reminds me of both Ragnar and Moragon. I don't want Iolana to make the wrong choice. I don't want her to suffer the same fate that I did."

"Nor would I," Darice said gently. "But Ragnar and Mikanah, they are not the same. And Mikanah and Iolana are both cut from the cloth of Moragon's imprisonment. Don't be so swift to dismiss that fact. I wouldn't worry about Iolana just yet, unless we see actual reason to. Nerine on the other hand…." She shared a concerned gaze with Ashden. "What about her? I know we advocated for her making her own choice to come along or not, but she seems a little lost now that Iolana is so absorbed with Mikanah."

Nerine still lay beside Iolana and Mikanah but had woken up and watched the couple with longing as they huddled together, speaking in hushed tones.

"She is determined to protect her," Gailea said. "Her parents traveled a lot. I think Iolana is one of the first real friends she's had. Staying is how she shows her love for that friendship."

"Are you sure it's not something deeper than that?" Darice asked.

Gailea frowned at her sister. "What do you mean?"

Darice's gaze lingered on Nerine before she said, "Nothing. Just an exhausted woman's ramblings. I think I should get some sleep. Good night, sister."

"Good night."

She climbed to the bunk atop Gailea's. Ashden bid Gailea a good night as well and soon tucked himself into one of the hammocks, pulling a blanket over himself.

All soon slept soundly, except for Chamblin, who continued to play a gentle melody, and Gailea, mind and heart racing anxiously. She took up her flute again, hoping music might comfort her. A foolish notion. Ever since the night of the Guardians' deaths, she had found it more difficult than usual to soothe her soul with song. Her music hadn't saved her friends, and now she couldn't seem to use it to save herself from dark emotions and dreams. It was almost as though her grief had numbed her to the usual joys of her music, making it become as intimate a part of her as blood and bones were to anyone else. Like breathing. Breathing couldn't comfort. Breathing was simply what one did to keep existing.

But then the music *did* begin to work its magic. Not hers, but Chamblin's. She laid back, prepared to let it pull her into the peaceful numbness of sleep when quiet footsteps alerted her, along with a cheerful humming that harmonized with Chamblin's song. She opened her eyes and then sat up, calling out to Iolana as she reached the door, "Are you all right?"

Iolana jumped in surprise before smiling warmly. "Yes. I'll be right back." Resuming her humming, she slipped from the room.

Gailea fell back on her bed with a sigh and tried again to sleep, but Iolana's interruption had severed the balm of Chamblin's music. Moments later, his music ended entirely, and quiet snores erupted from his hammock instead.

Iolana returned a few minutes later, still humming softly. Gailea debated with herself before sitting up and calling, "Iolana, can we talk for a moment?"

Iolana had just reached her bed and turned to face Gailea. She tilted her head curiously. Her eyes shone with a girlish sort of whimsy, and Gailea again hesitated. Everything in her screamed at her to talk to the girl, that now might be their only chance for some semblance of privacy. And yet, the idea of shattering such rare elation, however possibly misplaced, pained her heart.

As Gailea patted the bed, Iolana wandered over, perching beside her, and drawing her knees up to her chin. "What is it?"

Gailea savored seeing her so relaxed before diving in, doing her best to keep her expression and voice soft. "We haven't had a private talk in some time, just us two women. I couldn't help but notice that you seem quite distracted. Dreamy, if I may say so."

Iolana's smile grew a little. "I like to think I'm good at hiding my emotions when I need to. But it's hard with him."

"With Mikanah?" Gailea swallowed the lump in her throat.

Iolana nodded eagerly.

"And you've known him a long time?"

"Yes. It's hard to say how long exactly. Keeping time was difficult there. But I'd say a couple years or so."

"You seem quite close. If it's not too bold of me to ask, do you love him?"

"Of course, I do!" A fervent passion replaced the whimsy in Iolana's eyes. "With every fiber of my being. When I escaped, I would have gone back for him at once, if I thought I was strong enough to save him without getting caught again."

Gailea could feel her smile tightening, even as Iolana's expression sobered.

"Why are you asking? That is, I'm happy to tell you about him, but...why do you look so worried?"

"Not worried," Gailea lied gently, both to Iolana and to herself. "Only concerned. You both spent a large amount of time in Castle Alaula, I understand. But Mikanah was practically raised there, as a close servant of Moragon. I just want you to be careful, to know what you're getting yourself into."

A slight smile played on Iolana's lips, and she sat up tall, defensively. "I appreciate you saving me, guiding me. I love you and value your advice. But this is a choice I know I can make alone. That I've made for so long now and have never been wrong in doing so."

"I don't want to insult you," Gailea said, striving to choose her words carefully and not let her own emotions overrule her. "I know you're a capable young woman. But so was I, at your age. And yet, I chose wrong. I chose a man who grew up in the company of Moragon and other corrupt leaders. I told myself he was different, able to choose another path. Somewhere deep down, my heart tried to warn me, but I didn't listen. I never lost myself entirely to that young man, but I lost much to him. I couldn't bear to watch you make the same mistakes and live a similar fate."

Iolana's smile was tight, and she twisted her skirt in her hands. "Thank you for your concern. But Mikanah isn't a mistake. He never has been, never could be."

Gailea hated to see her happiness vanish, leaving anxiety in its wake, but she had to obey her heart's pleading. "I know it may seem that way now. Amiel willing, it will always be that way. Only promise me that if your heart would give you any warnings, you will heed what it's trying to—"

"I've never felt any such warnings."

A fierceness edged Iolana's eyes, cautioning Gailea against pressing the matter too far.

"But if you do, promise that you will listen. That you will ask counsel of myself or Lorelei or whomever you feel comfortable with."

Iolana nodded curtly and rose to her feet then. "I will promise. If you will promise to give Mika a chance. In this one thing, our stories are not the same. I understand why others might view him as a monster, but he's the tenderest soul I've ever known. Promise you'll give him a chance."

"I promise to try my best."

With a final, satisfied nod, Iolana slipped back to bed.

Gailea sighed deeply and laid back. As she closed her eyes, she prayed that her "best" would be good enough. She had no desire to sever the trusting bond she'd forged with Iolana, but while Iolana might not feel any warnings, Gailea wasn't convinced she could, or should, quiet those stirring inside her own heart.

~*~*~

Mikanah had lain with Iolana in his arms for a long time, absorbing the peacefulness of Chamblin's lullaby. He had hoped the soothing song could stave off the darkness that had crept into his mind. And for a while, there had been gratefully nothing. Nothing but the serene emptiness of sleep.

Then, the visions had come.

Iolana, consumed by fire, screaming his name, begging...why? Why did he not save her?

Mikanah sat up, wide awake, panting. He jumped back, startled, and pressed up against the headboard as he stared at Iolana's corpse resting in his arms, skin burned and blackened, face destroyed beyond recognition. He shook her frantically, praying that she still breathed—

Mikanah sat up, wide awake, panting. Iolana's corpse had vanished, along with what he realized was yet another horrifically lifelike nightmare. She wasn't dead. Wasn't burned or harmed in any way. She slept securely beside him.

Only, she didn't. Frantic, he threw back the blanket. Nothing. Stumbling from the bed, he let his gaze dart around the room. She was no where to be seen. Where was she? Had Moragon found them somehow? Did he send nightmares to torment them both?

Mikanah threw himself from the room. He staggered up the stairs, knocking against the walls in the ship's sway, hoping Iolana wasn't snared by some equally lifelike dream that had lured her overboard or into some other danger.

Spilling onto deck, he dashed toward the nearby stern, preparing to cry her name, cry to the crew for some help, when laughter alerted him. Coming to a halt, he whipped his head in the laughter's direction. There, some yards away, Iolana stood on the port side of the ship. Several Echelon patrolled the deck nearby, while Nerine stood beside Iolana, pointing at the ocean below. Iolana leaned over, eyes illuminated with a childlike wonder. Mikanah almost rushed over, afraid she might topple into the sea, when several small waves arched up. Nerine moved her hands through the air, fingers rippling in elegant patterns as she shaped the waves into dolphins leaping across the starry night.

As Iolana laughed in delight, Mikanah hardly recognized the sound. It was her voice, to be sure. But when had he ever heard or seen her looking so carefree? Never in Moragon's castle, not even in their secret moments together. Mikanah wanted to feel glad to see her so happy, but this desire was overcast by the fact that he'd never incited such a reaction of pure joy in her and most likely never could.

A bumping noise, followed by muttering, made Mikanah's hand fly to his sword hilt. He whirled, only to face the silly old minstrel, Chamblin.

"I apologize if I've startled you."

"It's all right," Mikanah muttered. "I've only just woken from a terrible dream. My mind isn't fully its own yet."

"Mmm. I was having trouble sleeping too and thought a few moments of fresh, salty air might do to cleanse my thoughts. Of course, I forgot that the darkness doesn't get much relieved by the moon's glow. Blindness takes more than a couple months to get used to, I suppose." He added the last bit with a wry grin.

Mikanah hesitated, glancing between the girls and Chamblin. "Do you want me to help you?"

Chamblin nodded. "I would welcome such an offer. Thank you."

Mikanah hooked his arm in Chamblin's and guided him across the deck, warning him when to step over a fallen coil of rope. Soon, the two of them stood at the starboard, leaning against the railing, facing the ocean. Mikanah relished the cool spray of mist as it splashed up on his face, all the while wondering if Chamblin could see the stars at all as he faced them.

"Thank you again," Chamblin said as he turned toward Mikanah. "You know, sometimes a stranger's lending an ear can seem less intimidating. Care to share what troubles you?"

Mikanah stared at him, stunned that any man would take the time and consideration to speak with him so intimately. The only other man who had ever cared to listen to his troubles had twisted them to suit his own will. Search as he might, Mikanah could detect no falseness in Chamblin's face nor, more amazingly still, any judgment.

Taking a deep breath, Mikanah tried to unravel his thoughts aloud, "I don't know how you do it. You seem so carefree. Despite what you've been through, Moragon's attack, your blindness—forgive me if it's rude of me to mention it."

"No, no," Chamblin said, waving the matter aside. "It's still an adjustment, to be sure, and will be for many months, no doubt, especially once the blindness completes itself. A man doesn't relearn all he's learned from birth in a new way overnight. But like it or not, it's my new reality. No good will come of pretending otherwise, with myself or with others."

Mikanah sighed. "Your spirit. I admire it. But I don't understand it. I don't know what that means, to live with such acceptance, without worry. With Iolana...I don't really know what I'm doing with her...."

Chamblin chuckled. "Don't fuss over that. I never

did meet a man so smitten who knew what to do about it."

Mikanah smiled a little despite himself. "I don't mean it that way. I wish I did, that I had just the simple, silly worries of most men in love. But I'm not the man she thinks I am. And I guess before, in Moragon's castle, when there was no other choice, that was all right. But out here, where she's free, I don't know if she can, or should, choose the man I've become."

The man you've always been, his mind taunted him, but he argued against it, fighting to silence such doubts. True, he had seduced countless women before Iolana, but most of them had desired him in turn. What was more, he had done so largely for pleasure and for extracting information for his king. It wasn't until after Iolana's death that his pursuits took a truly dark turn. He had first grown numb in his seduction of other women. Then, he had pursued them with a before-unknown ferocity, in his own twisted form of grieving. He had oftimes enjoyed winning the chase, only to crush their hearts.

"The only love I learned under Moragon's counsel was possessive, controlling. I don't even know if it was really love, or if what I feel for Iolana is love."

"What are you most afraid of?"

"*Most* afraid of? Hurting her. I know what I am, what I've become. She doesn't. She can't."

"Why not?"

Chamblin looked at him steadily, his demeanor collected but otherwise difficult to decipher. Whether or not Chamblin judged him now, at least he continued to listen. Maybe he was a fool for being open-minded, but Mikanah would appreciate it while it lasted.

"She believes in Amiel. I no longer do. She wants to be intimate. We both do, but I'm not sure if we should."

"There's always marriage," Chamblin suggested with a light chuckle. "Solves everything, you know."

"I don't think either of us would be ready for that kind of commitment. Iolana is a free soul. I don't want to cage her with me. Especially when I'm not sure I can be what she needs anymore—"

"Mikanah! Mikanah!"

Mikanah's head snapped up as Iolana rushed across the deck toward him, a half dozen Echelon on her heels.

"Heartsongs," she gasped. "Fast approaching...surrounding us...meaning us harm...They're everywhere!"

She fell into his arms. He held her close and swallowed hard, his throat dry. Her heartsong skills may yet be underdeveloped, but he'd never known her inclinations to be wrong.

A high scream split the air.

"Gailea!" Chamblin grabbed Mikanah's arm. "Let's hurry!"

Mikanah and Iolana helped Chamblin across deck. The Echelon followed.

No sooner had they tumbled into their room below deck than a brilliant white light blinded them. Mikanah shielded Iolana. A loud thud sounded, followed by a twang like the strings of an instrument snapping.

When the light faded, Mikanah saw that Chamblin had fallen, sprawled on his back onto his pipa. Mikanah helped him to his feet. Then, as something whooshed past with a growl, he ogled the sight surrounding them.

Dozens of hideous creatures swirled around the bunks. They were each hardly a foot tall. Their skin was a sickly green or moldy blue, weathered as leather, and shaggy black manes trailed down their backs. They stood upright and wore outfits stitched from leather, but beyond that, they were far from human. As they darted about, their chatter rose and fell like a dissonant symphony.

Gailea, Darice, Lorelei, and Ashden stood back-to-back, forming a protective ring. Darice sang short, high-pitched trills, emitting bursts of white light that sent the beasts shrinking back, though others quickly took their place with full force, clawing and gnashing their jagged teeth. Ashden sliced at them with his sword in one hand, while clutching a whip formed from vines in his other. Gailea played trills on her flute that sent waves of the small beasts crashing into the walls, while those nearest her flew in dizzy patterns, as if she had confused them. Lorelei's lips moved fast, and every now and then, a swirl of wind would twist from her hands, knocking the creatures back. The Echelon blasted the imps with lightning, wind, water, or flame, while others patched the burns blasted in the side of the ship.

Iolana rushed in to join the other Guardians, singing *Fraziolda*, one of the charms Gailea had taught them. The creatures immediately swarming her froze in place, and she sang another charm that made them drop to the ground, heavy as stones. Mikanah followed behind her, slashing his sword at the immobilized foes who burst with an apparent spray of blood before transforming into a smoky mist that dissipated. He situated himself beside Chamblin, swinging his sword in wide arcs. Chamblin yelled and made all sorts of a racket with his broken pipa, swinging the instrument about, whacking the beasts, and sending them flying with pitiful wails.

Iolana and Lorelei each wielded one of the creatures' short swords. Gailea played a new song on her flute that made many of the creatures whirl around dizzily before falling to the floor. The rest of the Echelon guards rushed in, swinging their blades or hurling magic spells.

"Close your eyes!" Darice shouted.

Mikanah did so just as another brilliant burst of light radiated from her. The monsters wailed and shrieked, and Mikanah fell to his knees, throwing his hands over his ears.

When the din had ceased, he lowered his hands and listened. A steady buzzing filled his ears instead. He wondered if his hearing was damaged by the creatures' noise.

Then, he opened his eyes and found that they were surrounded by a new problem. Instead of goblin-like imps, giant insects circled them. Stingers poked from the ends of long, curved tails, and their armored bodies were shaped like winged scorpions. They buzzed and darted about everyone's heads, diving down, repelled only by magical charms.

Mikanah instinctively swung his sword, but then a sharp pain seared his hand and he dropped it. He clutched at his hand, cursing beneath his breath as a fresh wound rose red and swollen around the thick stinger lodged in his flesh. He pulled it out, wincing. Then he swayed, his vision blurred, and he tumbled to the floor.

"*Mikanah!*" Iolana shrieked as he fell at her feet. He tried to stand, but his body felt like thick, heavy lead.

A thunderous noise and its vibrations sent Iolana spiraling back against the wall. Water and wind gushed in through the giant hole blasted in the deck above. Mikanah glanced up, dazed to see the sky starless and veiled by thick clouds. A thick rain fell. The buzzing culminated into a panic before the insects frantically dispersed.

The rain lightened just as abruptly as it had begun, and Mikanah watched in amazement at Nerine who stood up on deck, gazing down through the hole into the hull with arms outstretched, commanding the water flowing inside the ship with a song that ebbed and flowed like powerful ocean waves. Her skin and hair rippled blue and translucent. She turned her intense focus to the sky, and her song transformed into a gentler, more fluid melody. She sang until the rain ceased and the clouds vanished. Then she raised her arms, and the water filling the ship turned to mist until every last drop had vanished and dry floor stretched beneath them once more. Two of the sailors, alongside two Echelon, rushed over to patch the hole while Nerine changed from liquid to solid once again.

Ashden and Chamblin lifted Mikanah and carried him to one of the bunks. He sluggishly tried to sit up, with no success. Lorelei knelt beside him and pushed him down, making him lie still. Pressing the herbs that Ashden handed her to his wound, she sang a low tune beneath her breath.

"Will he be all right?" Iolana asked, kneeling beside him.

Lorelei nodded. As she finished her song, the heavy feeling lifted from Mikanah's body, and he sat up with a groan. Everyone had gathered around him, including Nerine who now stood beside Iolana.

"Ugh. What *were* those little menaces?"

"Kapua," Lorelei spat. "They're nuisances commonly found in the waters surrounding Pakua. The kapua would rob you blind but are otherwise harmless. When I stayed in Pakua, I would hear stories of them plundering our ships. I'm surprised to see them farther north."

"They may be another trick of the Rosans," Gailea said. "Or the Adelarans. Weak attempts to defend their land from outsiders and scare us away. You did well, Nerine, responding so quickly and using the rain to fend them off."

"Indeed," Chamblin concurred, clapping her on the shoulder. "That was an impressive show if ever I saw one—or heard it. You truly were the master of wind and rain with your songs."

"Thank you," Nerine said with a timid smile.

"Come," Gailea said. "Let's get what rest we can before morning. I've a feeling that the kapua will not be the only, nor the greatest, of the trials we shall face."

CHAPTER 30

A TALE OF TWO KINGDOMS

The sun had risen only a couple of hours into the clear azure sky, when Gailea had just finished helping Chamblin repair his pipa.

"Thank you." Chamblin looked astonished as he took the instrument in hand and strummed a few chords. "I had truly feared it might be lost for good."

"A few broken strings and a snapped neck? Nothing some twine and a couple healing charms can't handle." Gailea shrugged at him in a blasé fashion before sharing a smile with him. "I did wonder, as I was repairing it, at the strange markings carved on the handle?"

"Hmm? Ahh!" Enthusiasm lit his eyes as he turned the handle toward her. "Those are Chinese characters. They're how the Chinese portray the written word. Translated in our Lozolian tongue, it says 'Friend and Master of Music,' a most humbling title granted me by a dear friend I made in my travels. It was he who gifted me with the pipa, and 'twas he who also made me anxious at such a precious gift being destroyed forever, and so clumsily, needlessly." His expression of whimsical remembrance faded into an irritated frown.

"All is well now," Gailea said, resting a hand on his. "There's no need to dwell on what's past. We're all whole and well, including the pipa."

Chamblin's face lightened again with a soft smile.

Just then, someone cried, "land ho!" from above deck.

Anxious at once, Gailea jumped up and pulled Chamblin to his feet. They joined the others near the bow of the ship, gazing at the island they fast approached.

A solemn reverence filled Gailea as they neared the homeland of her birth father, Callum. All she knew of him was what her mother had written in the diaries Darice had given her. She had reread those accounts many times since, and they were enough to make her feel a kinship to the man who had so boldly loved her mother and dared to fight to free both of their kingdoms from the bitterness of hatred.

The island kingdom of Rosa drew into clearer focus, a seemingly endless dense forest of sturdy cedar trees, their thick red-brown trunks and wide branches adorned with thousands of blue-green needles. On the rocky beach, a giant statue hailed them. Its gray stone had been hewn into the shape of a woman with long flowing hair, queenly robes, and a crown woven from rosal blossoms, a flower much loved in many kingdoms but native only to Rosa. Two rubies comprised the statue's eyes, their many facets shimmering like fire in the sun's glow.

"Who is that?" Nerine gazed upon the statue with sheer awe. "She looks very important."

Chamblin delved into one of his narratives.

"That is a Rosa queen of old. The first, actually. The

Rosan and Adelaran kingdoms were once united under a pair of sibling monarchs named Rosa and Adel. What shame and heartache they would feel now if they could see how things have unraveled between their people since that time."

"Why are they so intent on keeping outsiders away?" Iolana asked, looking solemnly past the statue at the dense forests beyond.

"Much of their paranoia is due to pride, vanity, and hatred, especially toward one another, created over long years of abused trust. Instead of standing up together to their enemies, both kingdoms have sought to insulate themselves. Adelar, with ancient walls of flame and water that can only be breached by a song called *The Eagle's Ayre*. Long ago, these barriers surrounded both islands, to protect against outside enemies, and the Rosans and Adelarans traveled freely between their kingdoms on many Eagles who alone held the power to breach those barriers. But as their hatred grew and their fighting intensified, their magic, and that of the Eagles, began to fade. In particular, the Rosans' magic fades if concealed by isolation and disuse. In recent years, many Rosans have been born with lesser magic traits, and hence they lost their ability to hold the fire and water barriers around their island."

Gailea scoffed, her smile sardonic. "I'd be as surprised to learn that any of the Eagles survived as I am that the Adelarans retained enough knowledge to reconstruct such powerful barriers without the Rosans' aid. The Eagles' mysterious extistence is somehow bound to peace and unity existing between Rosa and Adelar. The two kingdoms' unraveling friendship, the fading of the Rosans' magic, the decline of the Eagles' race—it all truly is a tragedy."

"But just think about the possibilities," Chamblin

added, gripping the ships's rail in obvious excitement. "If this war could actually reunite Rosa and Adelar, get them to work for a common cause, and restore them to their original glory!"

A half hour or so later, the ship dropped anchor. The Guardians, Nerine, and all but two of the Echelon guards lowered themselves into smaller crafts and rowed to shore. The ship would dock for three days. If the Guardians and their escorts hadn't returned or sent word by then, the two soldiers remaining on the ship would contact the Council for further instruction. One of the Echelon women, Faina, was a light mage who could concentrate on a specific location or person in her mind to make objects carry over longer distances, almost as fast as light. In this way, they should be able to send a small message in an envelope.

Gailea shivered as they passed beneath the statue's cool shadow into the forest. One of the ancient queen's arms stretched toward her brother, Adel, whose statue stood across the seas on Adelar's shores. Though Gailea knew Rosa reached for her brother, she couldn't help but imagine that she held out her hand as a warning for them to stop and turn back.

Once inside the woods, they trekked along a rocky path for about an hour or so. Rich green ferns and thick roots covered the forest floor, with sprigs of spiky purple flowers popping up between them. At last, the trees and brush cleared to reveal an immense golden-brown stone wall, with square towers set at intervals. Its thick expanse stretched for many miles in either direction and loomed over the tops of the old trees.

As they approached two great doors set in the wall, Gailea's heart leaped and nearly fled her altogether. In Adelar, walls had always trapped her inside with evil, instead of shielding her and keeping evil at bay. Once they stepped beyond that wall, they weren't coming back out unless the Rosans permitted them.

Two guards flanked the doors, each with the Rosans' unique black banded mail armor and royal standard of a blue rosal illuminated by eternal flames that could never consume it. The same crest was painted across the giant red cedar doors.

"Halt, strangers! And state what business you have in Rosa!"

Their party came to a standstill before the guards, whose hands hovered by their sword hilts.

"We are the Octavial Guardians," Gailea announced. "Created by the Lozolian Council to protect the musical magic of the Lozolian Realm. The usurper, Moragon, has obtained much knowledge of musical magic and would use it to conquer your kingdom and as many others as he can."

The leftmost guard scoffed, fist clenching around his sword hilt. "I'd certainly like to see him try. Rosa would defend itself, as it has for countless ages."

Chamblin stepped up beside Gailea. "I would remind Rosa of the powerful influence musical magic can hold. Moragon manipulated music to murder many of the first Guardians. Most you see standing before you are newly appointed."

"He speaks truth." The other guard's voice was more even-tempered than his comrade's. "Let us hear them out, for the sake of our kingdom's safety."

The first guard nodded, and Chamblin added, "To obtain the last Guardian, we must go to Adelar, but to do that, we will need access to *The Eagle's Ayre*. Hence, our coming here to seek an audience with your gracious monarch."

The leftmost guard's austere face seemed to dip into a deeper frown. "*The Eagle's Ayre*? Of what do you speak?"

Gailea knew the man likely played bluff. After all, the song was a secret meant to be passed only to those of royal blood and their most trusted companions. With a lift of her chin, she declared, "My name is Gailea. My mother was Gillian of Adelar, my father Callum of Rosa. I learned of *The Eagle's Ayre* in Gillian's diaries. If you need further proof, there was also this song:

"Adelar's realm sits proud and strong,
Beside the river Shila long,
Through the heart of the Chamroq Dell
Where the Adelaran people dwell.

Behold! The fairest of the fair
With sunlight gleaming in her hair,
Of her people she sits and sings
Each song a prayer for peaceful tidings...

Gillian, the Lady of Adelar."

Astonishment filled the faces of both guards, and the one standing on the left spoke again. "You may enter the great wall. If found trustworthy, you might then seek an audience with our queen."

"Thank you," Gailea said.

The guard bowed his head in respect. "If you are who you claim, then we have waited a long time to learn of your survival, Lady Gailea. You are most welcome here."

He knocked a rhythmic pattern on the doors. As they slid aside, receding into the wall, anticipation pounded through Gailea alongside her fear. Perhaps they would be accepted here after all. Perhaps these walls would not be the kind that imprisoned.

The guard who had done the most speaking introduced himself as Niall and led them inside the wall where a plethora of guards patrolled, many glancing with intrigue as the entourage of Guardians and Echelon passed through their midst. Gailea's emotions teeter-tottered between hope and fear. If she could prove herself and they were accepted, the presence of so many guards would make her feel secure. If instead they were rejected as enemies, they would be hopelessly trapped.

A dozen more armed guards met them, some glowering in suspicion, others with gentler curiosity. After listening to their colleague's explanation, they accompanied the visiting party. Guided by the light of hovering white flames that glowed along the ceiling at intervals, they traveled inside the wall until they came to a wooden door.

They entered a large square room beyond, and Gailea guessed they were inside one of the towers. The room was furnished with a table and a few chairs. In the room's midst, more white flames crackled midair, waving, and shimmering an otherworldly glow across the golden-brown stone walls and tiled floors. They granted a soft warmth, making Gailea feel as though they had stepped inside a giant, magical fireplace.

Niall said they could make themselves comfortable before disappearing through an opposite door. The rest of the Rosan guards remained, positioning themselves around the perimeter of the room.

Iolana, Mikanah, and Nerine sat at the table together, talking quietly amongst themselves. The other Guardians remained standing, along with the Echelon who formed a protective ring around the group.

Time passed. Too much time, in Gailea's opinion. Her newfound hope began to fade, and she started pacing.

"You're worried, sister," Darice observed, head cocked in her direction.

Gailea paused to glance at her sharply. "Rightly so. Those guards might've considered me sacred for knowing that song. But others might think I'm some sort of spy. We can't afford to be too careful, or—"

The door opened, making Gailea jump. Niall had returned, along with four other guards.

"Her majesty will see you now. Come. We will escort you to her chambers."

Gailea shared a wary look with her sister who took her hand, squeezing it firmly. The rest of the Guardians, along with the Echelon and Nerine, followed Niall and the four other Rosan guards from the tower, while a half dozen of the Rosan guard who had stood watch inside the tower joined them, taking up the rear.

As the Rosans led them down the long corridor, the wind whistled through the stones, and Gailea glanced up. High above, she could glimpse murder holes in the ceiling, used to pour hot water, stones, or other traps onto enemies. Despite their apparent welcome, Gailea knew they couldn't be too sure and sang protective charms inside her mind. Judging by the deep concentration on Darice's face, she crafted her own shielding spells.

At the end of the corridor, they entered another of the vast towers, and from there another stone hall, this one plainer, with tall, thin windows higher above. Sunlight mingled with the floating white flames that continued to illuminate their path. A winding stair led them to another series of corridors.

Gradually, their path widened and brightened into a large hall, with red, gold, and deep brown tiles decorating the floor and elegant tapestries woven from the same colors adorning the walls.

Passing through an arched door carved from red pine, their surroundings expanded even more as they walked inside a vast hall. A great red stone structure rose before them, and it seemed they had entered from the back of the room, through a more secluded passage.

Gailea began to worry they had walked into a trap until, rounding the great stone structure, she saw it was an elevated dais, with a woman sitting at a long table, flanked on either side by two men and two women; they seemed to have entered a council chamber. The room didn't boast any windows, but the white flames floating along the walls, along with the light of oil lamps, filled the room like sunlight. Gold, red, and brown square tiles swept across the floor, accented by bright blue tiles shaped into rosals, and more bright tapestries lined the walls. On the far right and left of the room, giant white flames blazed, and Rosan guards stood at intervals all around the perimeter.

"Presenting Delia, Queen of Rosa!"

They stopped in front of the dais, the guards stepped back on either side, and Gailea looked up at the queen. Disregarding the fact that her hair flowed in thick waves of red and gold instead of gray, she reflected the image of the statue they had seen along the shore. Dark blue robes hung from her body, displaying the same pattern of tiny silver waves and stars. Green eyes watched them closely. Sapphires shaped into a rosal and embedded in gold hung around her neck, and smaller red and blue stones adorned the circlet of gold rosals on her head. Briefly, Gailea wondered if Rosa's ghost had wandered into their midst.

The two men and women flanking her dressed in gold velvet doublets and gowns with the standard of the blazing rosal stitched across their chest. Six more guards stood just behind the council table.

"Greetings, Gailea and companions. I am Delia, Queen of Rosa."

Ashden was the first to fall to his knees. The others followed suit, but Gailea had just reached the floor when the queen said, "Please, rise. Now is not the time for such formalities. Both Guardians and Echelon are welcome in these troubled times, if, indeed, you turn out to be who you claim. I know why you've come. I know of the evil brewing in Carmenna. But before I allow you inside the city, I must ask for further proof. As elated as I am to welcome you, Gailea, daughter of Gillian and Callum, both my counselors and my conscience could not excuse such careless behavior." She watched Gailea intently as she continued, "Normally, I would have sent someone else to do my questioning for me. But when my guards told me that you recited a part of the *Ode to Gillian* perfectly, I knew I had to summon you, meet you for myself."

"I can sing the rest, if you like."

Delia shook her head. "We've had many imposters over the years. Some who genuinely thought they might be descended from the royal line. Others simply trying to gain favor in Rosa for personal gain or malicious means. You look as strikingly similar to the old portraits of Gillian as everyone says I resemble Rosa, the great founder of our beloved kingdom. I don't believe you're an imposter, though of course that remains to be proved."

"Portraits?" Gailea asked, unable to hide her surprise from her voice. "There were portraits kept of my mother? I thought the Rosans despised her for marrying one of their own."

"My father, the late King Owen, did, I'm ashamed to admit. Unfortunately, he did away with said portraits. I never shared his prejudices, and neither do many of my people. There are those of us who admire both Callum and Gillian's courage, their willingness to risk all in the name of peace." Delia's advisors nodded beside her, their faces reverential. *"The Eagle's Ayre*. It was a gift to Gillian. A secret and sacred gift that has been preserved by a select few over the years. Might I ask how you came by knowledge of its existence?"

Gailea reached inside her satchel and drew out the faded parchment. Carefully unfolding the pages, she lifted them toward Delia. "These were Gillian's. They contain part of the song, as well as accounts of her final days."

Delia's gaze narrowed, glancing over Gailea with scrutiny. Gailea hoped that she hadn't taken things too far. Her knowing of *The Eagle's Ayre*, coupled with her claims, could easily be seen as a form of treachery, proof that she conspired with some spy or traitor of the Rosan court. Delia motioned to the man beside her, and he leaned in. They conversed in hushed tones, before Delia nodded, and then man stood and headed down the stairs toward Gailea.

"This is Rhys, my most trusted advisor. Hand the pages to him, so that we may get a closer look."

Gailea's stomach churned as she passed her mother's precious words into the man's hands. He took them delicately, and she prayed that, whether or not the queen believed their validity, Delia would likewise handle them with care.

Delia carefully took the pages. As she scanned their contents, her eyes widened. Upon reading further, she began to pass the pages to Rhys who examined them with a thoughtful frown. Together, they conversed again. Delia and Rhys spoke quietly with the other counselors, and Gailea held her breath. A hand squeezed Gailea's, and she glanced up gratefully at her sister who stood beside her.

At last, Delia nodded at Rhys who returned the pages to Gailea. She pocketed them with an inward sigh of relief while the queen locked eyes on her and spoke. "You are either the greatest imposter we've yet seen, or else the true daughter of Callum and Gillian. To decipher the truth once and for all, for the absolute safety of me and my people, I command a test be completed, a lineage test. One of our healers knows magic that can test a person's blood to see if it matches that of one's ancestors. We can perform the ritual today, though it may be early morning before the spell is completed and we see the results. Until then, I can grant you living quarters at Castle Rosa, somewhere discreet where you won't be troubled with questions, and well-guarded, for both our safety. If the test confirms you as being from Gillian and Callum's line, we'll have cause for celebration."

"And then you'll help us?" Gailea focused on keeping her voice steady, not wanting to reveal her desperation. They seemed so near to obtaining the queen's aid, but the situation was delicate until the blood test could be performed and prove her words as truth.

Delia tilted her head. "Perhaps. It depends on the nature of your request. Even for someone as beloved as Callum's daughter, I cannot take any risks that might place my people in danger. Please do tell: what exactly brings you to Rosa?"

"My companions and I, we are the Octavial Guardians. We are seeking our final member. Our messengers have confirmed this Guardian to be in Adelar, but Adelar will not grant them or the Council access. The only other way is to obtain *The Eagle's Ayre* and pass through the barriers."

A frown masked Delia's face, and the firelight seemed to leap to life inside her eyes. "Adelar would keep one of its own hostage, instead of exposing themselves to the outside world in any way, even to save it. Do you know who this Guardian is?"

Gailea hesitated, muscles stiff. She kept her voice even.

"No. Not yet, we don't."

"And how do you intend to convince the Adelarans? You'll be breaching their greatest strongholds. I doubt they will be eager to trust you after that, even if you can prove yourself to them. We in Rosa do not believe the tales they've told, tales of you aiding Ragnar while knowing fully of his madness. But many of them do."

Darice took a step forward, hands folded humbly before her. "I am Gailea's sister. Not by blood. I am a pure-blooded Adelaran. I grew up with her. I can vouch for her character. I am one of them. They may listen to me if no one else will."

Delia studied Darice before turning back to Gailea, looking pensive. "Come then. I will have my guards lead you to your chambers. Your guards may have their own rooms as well, or you may wish them to stand guard over your chambers, only understand that my own guards will also stand watch. I will give you time to rest. Then, in a little while, supper will be sent up. Gailea, someone will fetch you for the lineage test. We'll meet again in the morning, and if you are who you say, you will be more than entitled to receive *The Eagle's Ayre*. But you must promise to keep it to yourself. It's not for all ears to hear and master."

"I can promise not to impart the song directly," Gailea said. "But as a Guardian, I do have an obligation to add a record of the song in our Chamber, to safeguard its magic. There the Guardians will have access to learning it as well, if they so have need."

Delia looked thoughtful for a few moments more. Then she said, "Very well. I suppose the time has come for even Rosa to abandon some of its traditions for the sake of protection. Fionn and Conor, if you and your comrades could please escort our guests to their quarters. Go by the passage through the walls, right into the castle."

Two guards stepped forward and nodded. "Yes, Your Majesty."

The Guardians, Nerine, and Echelon followed after Fionn and Conor and a dozen other guards who led the way back through the corridor behind the dais.

As they left the hall's brightness to twist through several narrower corridors lit by oil lamps, Gailea couldn't contain a shudder. The more weathered stones signified this was likely an older part of Castle Rosa. She knew they likely traveled this way for sake of secrecy, but she couldn't shake the anxiety of impending confinement. Ahead of Gailea, Lorelei walked stiffly beside Nerine who cast her a concerned glance. Iolana and Mikanah tightly grasped each other's hands, and Chamblin and Ashden marched solemnly together. Darice smiled at Gailea, clearly trying to encourage her, but the dim gesture faltered, not quite reaching her eyes. Gailea took her sister's hand this time. Darice had grown up a prisoner just as Gailea had and needed the same assurance that everything was all right, at least for this moment.

At last, they emerged into a brighter corridor once more, floor patterned with the same colorful tiles, floating orbs of white flame enhancing the lighting with a warmer appeal. Thin, arched windows ran the length of the hall. Glimpsing the blue skies eased Gailea's nerves a bit, making her feel a bit less confined. They traversed one of the inner walls surrounding a green courtyard below. Towers each boasted several smaller turrets, and flags bearing the Rosan crest of the blazing blue rosal waved in the sunlight.

Finally, after what seemed an eternity, they reached their destination. They were granted three bedrooms to share between them, as well as an adjoining withdrawing room. After thanking the guards, they gathered in the withdrawing room, sitting around the long, cedar table situated on the right side of the room. Oil lamps and floating flames lit the room, and a bookcase with a settee were situated against the leftmost wall. Some of the Echelon stayed inside the withdrawing room, while others lingered in the hall.

"Well, that was exciting, eh?" Chamblin quipped with a smile, clearly trying to lighten the mood.

"I don't trust it," Mikanah muttered. "I don't like them keeping us locked away like this. With no one else knowing we're here."

"The Council knows," Lorelei said, her confident tone wavering. She had folded her hands on the table, and they tensed enough for Gailea to see her knuckles whiten.

"That's not what he means," Iolana said, both her voice and face riddled with tension. Mikanah wrapped his arms around her, but she only grew more rigid. "None of the other Rosans are being told we're here. If the queen decides we're enemies or they want to dispose of us for any reason, there's no one to defend us. No need for a trial. They could just get rid of us at a whim."

"I don't think that will be the case." Ashden's voice was calm as he manipulated the small vines sprouting from his fingertips, curling them around his hands. Perhaps keeping his hands busy prevented him being consumed by everyone else's blatant anxiety. "I believe Queen Delia and her Council simply do not wish to create an unnecessary stir or excitement. Once the blood test is completed, I'm sure we'll be known and will be granted more freedoms around the castle."

Lorelei frowned at Gailea. "Speaking of trust, you told them we didn't know who the last Guardian is. Why?"

"The tensions between the two kingdoms are obvious," Gailea said. "Did you see the way the queen looked at Darice, once she knew she was Adealaran?"

"I think your caution is wise," Chamblin said. "But I also don't think we should fuss too much. Let's wait for the Rosans to prove or disprove their trustworthiness. In the meantime, let's relax while we can."

He drew forth his pipa and strummed a few soft chords. Their notes mixed together with enough unpleasant dissonance to make Gailea roll her eyes. "*Must we?*"

Chamblin gave her an exaggerated frown. "It's either this or my story of the time I was assailed by man-eating mermaids. An event that lasted an entire week, so believe me when I say that its narration might take just as long."

"Your suggestions for 'relaxing' activities continue to astound me. Go ahead then. Play that poor, abused instrument. But know I'll be doing my best to drown you out."

Gailea revealed her double flute from its leather case. As she played along with Chamblin, her nerves began to melt. While Chamblin strummed the same repetitive refrains, Gailea played a melody that harmonized with it. Ashden joined in the refrain with his voice, chanting words in an unfamiliar language while the small vines continued to wrap around his hands, sprouting tiny flowers. As Gailea's nerves eased even more, she realized the two men performed some musical charm she was unfamiliar with. Judging by the unknown tongue, she surmised that it was most likely a charm common to the Fury people. Whatever it was, she felt grateful for the rare chance to unwind.

Iolana and Mikanah hummed along, Nerine vocalized with her soprano, and Darice's rich alto blended in. She sang some of the foreign words, confirming Gailea's guess that the song was from Ashden's Fury clan. Lorelei strummed on her lyre, smiling at Gailea with a bittersweet gaze that pierced the core of Gailea's heart. While Gailea and Lorelei had practiced several times now with the new Guardians, they had done so as teachers and pupils. Now, joined together with the sole purpose of soothing each other, their song gave her a glimpse of her old joy of performing. But, in the next breath, guilt crashed through her, for the last time she had played with the old Guardians so harmoniously was the night of their murders. Perhaps she didn't deserve the joy of such a union now.

They played through several songs when a rap on the door alerted them. To the delight of many, particularly the Echelon soldiers, two maidservants delivered trays heaped with a hot meal. They indulged in the rich beef and vegetable stew flavored with sesame, tangy ginger, and basil, with bread so fresh that small whiffs of steam rose from its surface, and berries with honey.

Everyone ate their fill, rested a little while, and then Gailea and Chamblin played once more as everyone else joined in pairs to dance: Mikanah with Iolana, Darice with Ashden, and Nerine with Lorelei. The Echelon paired up as well. Each person in the pairing would touch hands, spinning about one way before switching hands to spin in the opposite direction, all the while clapping a rhythm to accompany the music. As the night wore on, Chamblin played more vigorously, shouting a challenge for everyone to form a carola circle. Gailea matched his frantic pace while the others joined hands, dancing in a circle and laughing gaily.

When everyone was exhausted from merriment and Iolana had fallen asleep with her head in Mikanah's lap, they dispersed, choosing which bed chambers they would share. Each boasted two beds except for one which held a single larger bed. Each also held a writing desk, a chest filled with clothes, oil lamps on the walls, and one of the larger white flames hovering in the corner for extra warmth.

Mikanah carried Iolana to her bed before rooming with Chamblin and Ashden. Nerine joined Iolana. As Darice started toward Gailea, Nerine beckoned her. Gailea nodded at her sister, silently assuring her that she would be fine, and Darice followed after the younger girl. Gailea and Lorelei were left with the remaining room with the single bed. Some of the Echelon retired to their own rooms while others stayed in the hall, guarding alongside the Rosans.

Gailea changed into the sleeping dress and robe provided in the wooden chest at the foot of her bed. Then, she sprawled back on the giant bed swathed in fresh linen sheets and a silk blanket patterned with blue and gold rosal blossoms. The same fabric adorned the head sheet covering her pillow and the short canopy hanging above her head. She sank into the fluffy mattress, surely stuffed with feathers instead of strips of fabric as she was used to. While part of her felt grateful for such comfort, a part of her couldn't shake the memory of once sharing a bed like this with Crispin.

Lorelei crawled in beside her and asked, "How're you feeling?"

"Being stuck inside these walls makes me on edge."

"This place makes me feel unsettled too. Thank Amiel for Chamblin's music. My nerves would've never allowed me to sleep otherwise." She offered Gailea a sleepy smile. "Thank you, too, for playing with him, bringing us a bit of comfort and happiness. For a moment, I was almost a small girl again, dancing as my mom sang."

"You're welcome." Gailea granted her a small smile in return, the best she could muster. "And try not to worry. Amiel will protect us. He has brought us this far."

With a nod and wide yawn, Lorelei turned over. Her breathing became slow and steady.

Gailea tried to focus on sleep and the truth of her own declaration, thanking Amiel that He had allowed them a ray of hope in the Rosans' blessed welcome.

She was just drifting to sleep when a knock on the door roused her. She opened the door to a maidservant, whose dark eyes seemed huge in her face. The girl begged her pardon and whispered that she had come to take Gailea for the blood-testing.

Gratefully, the testing itself proved to be a simple matter. A tiny prick, a drop of blood collected into a vial. The healers would work overnight until the spells were completed to prove whether she was a match to Callum's bloodline. Gailea inquired how the magic worked, and the healer taking her blood informed her that it was custom in Rosa, when someone passed, to collect a small amount of their blood and hair, along with a tooth. A curious ritual, Gailea remarked, but the healer explained that in Rosa, it was believed one could pray and speak with one's ancestors, ask them for guidance and blessings. Only if these bits had been collected could this connection be made. One of Callum's cousins yet lived and had been summoned. Not only had they brought Callum's blood, but the cousin would also be tested in the ritual. If Gailea's blood matched both Callum's and his cousin, that was even more proof of her lineage.

Afterward, Gailea could do nothing except lay in bed, staring up at the canopy. Her stomach churned, whether with illness or unease, she couldn't be certain.

The soothing lull of the night's festivities had long since passed, and now her mind whirled. What if something went amiss in the lineage test?

A man's voice sounded from the hall beyond her and Lorelei's room.

Gailea froze still, listening.

Again, it came, more clearly this time: "*Halt!*" Multiple pairs of footsteps rushed down the hall.

Her heart seized in alarm, and she pushed herself to her feet. Intruders? Had Moragon somehow discovered their location?

Gailea hurried to the door. She cracked it open, peered out, and then gasped and swung it open wide, staring as a half dozen guards pursued her sister. She tried to rush forward, but her legs seemed to be made of stone, magically petrified, she realized, by one of the guards.

Darice shuffled down the hall, eyes closed, and dragging her feet with a painful slowness, as if laden with a heavy iron chain. Her limp arms hung at her side. She was drenched head to toe. Some type of liquid dripped and created a trail, shimmering red in the glow of lamplight. Gailea's stomach twisted. In rising panic, she wondered if it was Darice's blood.

Rosan guards followed Darice, surrounding her with drawn swords. Echelon guards trailed close behind, weapons drawn, except for those who had been stunned by the immobilizing spell.

Another door slammed open. "What's the meaning of this?"

Ashden emerged from his room and rushed toward Darice, but he too was stopped dead in his tracks. Chamblin hovered in the doorway. His unfocused gaze searched the corridor, but Mikanah stepped out beside him, whispering a quick explanation of what was happening. A presence behind Gailea startled her, but she sighed with relief to see Lorelei.

"One of the gardeners found her wandering around outside," one of the Rosan guards said; Gailea recognized him as Fionn from earlier. "She was soaking wet, just standing by the stream. The servant tried to wake her."

"Sleepwalking?" Ashden demanded. "She walked all the way up here on her own?"

"Yes."

"How did she get to the gardens to begin with, without anyone noticing? Surely, she shouldn't have been allowed anywhere without escorts?" His gaze roamed to the Echelon.

"When she first exited her room, we didn't realize she was asleep," Idalin nodded at the fellow male Echelon beside her. "We asked if we could help her, and she said she wanted some fresh air in the gardens. Two of the Rosan guards escorted us outside. For a while, Darice seemed to just wander the gardens, but nothing seemed out of place. Then, of a sudden, she vanished."

"I alerted other of my guard to search," Fionn added. "Then the gardener found her standing by the stream."

The Rosan guard whom Gailea remembered as Conor nodded, sharing a solemn glance with Fionn. "It was only then that we got a better look at her face. Her eyes were closed. She responded to nothing we said. We knew she must be sleep-walking. We did our best to guide her back here, but at times she would break into a run. We stayed close, afraid she might harm herself."

Gailea could not bear to see Darice so lost and distant. Fionn's explanation made her look closer, so that she could see Darice wasn't covered in blood. It was just the torchlight's reflection and her anxious imagination tricking her. Still, her sister remained trapped by whatever dream had taken control of her.

"Let us help," Gailea pleaded. "Please. I know we can draw her from it."

Fionn studied Gailea and Ashden with suspicion before nodding at another of the guards. When the weight of the immobilizing spell vanished, Gailea staggered forward. She and Ashden hurried to Darice. Mikanah followed after, leading Chamblin.

Gailea softly began singing her familiar lullaby.

"Close your eyes, my precious little treasure,

When you wake, the dawn will shine anew…"

Chamblin and Ashden joined in. Waking someone who sleep-walked too suddenly could overexcite them. The lullaby was an attempt on Gailea's part to rather soothe Darice's mind into a quieter sleep.

Gailea focused harder, fueling all her thoughts toward her sister, when Darice collapsed. Ashden caught and lifted her into his arms. He looked anxiously down at her, cradling her head. After a few seconds of examination, he heaved a great sigh of relief and said, "She sleeps calmly now."

"She's soaked through." Gailea's voice was barely a shaken whisper. "Take her to her room for me, please. I'll do what I can to dry her and help her back to bed."

"I'll help you," Lorelei said.

Ashden carried Darice into her room. Gailea followed, but as she reached the door, Fionn called, "My lady, she is your sister, yes?"

Gailea paused and nodded tightly, and he went on. "We will have to tell our queen of this strange behavior. Has she ever done this before?"

"No, she hasn't."

"I pray she is all right. Come on then, men." He led most of the guards from the hall.

Gailea slipped inside Darice's room. Movement alerted her to Iolana and Nerine, who'd sat up in one of the two beds, yawning and rubbing their eyes, squinting at the firelight. As Nerine's gaze fell on Darice, her eyes opened wide and she shook Iolana's arm, drawing her attention to the same.

"Is she all right?" Nerine asked.

Gailea nodded stiffly. "She will be. She's been sleep-walking, wandered down to the gardens. We just need to get her dry. Did either of you see or hear anything strange?"

"No," Iolana said, as Nerine shook her head. "We just woke up when we heard all of the commotion in the hall."

"Get back to sleep then. We'll care for Darice."

From the corner of her eye, Gailea could see the girls still watching as she hurried over to where Ashden had spread several blankets beside the glowing white flame in the corner. He laid Darice on the blankets and rested her head on a pillow. Carefully, Gailea and Lorlei worked to remove Darice's dress, hose, and boots. The fire's warmth would soon dry her soaked underdress.

Ashden sat beside Darice. Concern shone noticeably in his eyes as he stared down at her, fiddling with a wisp of her hair.

"What do you think?" Gailea asked quietly. "I've never known her to sleepwalk."

"I don't know. Maybe she's just especially tired. It's been a long journey for all of us."

"What of her eluding the Echelon and Rosan guards?" Lorelei asked. "Such a feat seems strange at best, suspicious at worst. What if the Rosans are trying to set us up in some sort of trap?"

"I've been trying to sort through that myself," Gailea said. "Ashden, you've spent more time with her than I in recent years. In her study of song-spells that utilize light magic, were there any that could possibly account for such behavior?"

Ashden clasped his hands beneath his chin, brows knit in deep thought. "Perhaps. She once showed me a song-spell that allowed her to sort of blend in with her surroundings."

Gailea had once disguised herself in a similar fashion. Darice might have used a comparable spell, or even the same one. The question begged...why? And especially while in her sleep? Did she run from some enemy in a nightmare, or did she feel just as trapped as Gailea, and her subconscious had begged her to flee and find freedom?

"I think we should stay up with her."

"Yes," Ashden agreed, stroking Darice's hair while gazing down at her tenderly. "Yes, we should. I'll take first watch."

"I'll take second," Lorelei said.

"Thank you." Gailea smiled at her and then at Ashden, but he kept his gaze fixated on Darice. A small yearning tugged at Gailea's heart. She remembered the safe haven Ashden's presence had granted her back in those days with the Sprites. For a moment, she wondered what she might have squandered in giving him up.

This thought fleeted away, like a stone skipping across a pond and then vanishing beneath the ripples. She'd had her chance for love. Darice deserved Ashden's shielding nature. Besides, as Gailea studied her sister more closely, she realized that her dark brown hair had begun to lighten to a more golden color, similar to Ashden's.

In reading her mother's diary, Gailea had learned that when an Adelaran fell in love, some of their magic abilities were transferred to their chosen partner, so that they both shared the same powers. It was likewise common for an Adelaran's appearance to shift to closer resemble that of their partner. This wasn't voluntary, but rather an inherent trait, an outer reflection of their heart's true desire. Darice's shifting hair color meant she had already given her heart to him.

Gailea cherished such a fate for her sister and could never begrudge her for it. Rather, she felt grateful that her sister had found love with such a loyal, loving man. Even now, as he watched Darice, he remained fully absorbed in her. He had never looked upon Gailea like that. Almost, but not quite.

And that was all right, Gailea confirmed with a smile. Ashden had rescued her once, and she once had feelings for him. But they were feelings born of desperation that had never had a chance to blossom into true love. What he shared with Darice was much realer, and Gailea was glad to stand back and watch it grow.

CHAPTER 31

DARK FLAME

Warmth brushed Gailea's cheeks. Even with her eyes closed, she could sense the pale golden light. She stirred, stretched, and blinked at the brightness of the rising sun. The velvety softness of a thick fur coverlet enrobed her like a cocoon. Heat radiated from the blazing white flames. She turned over to go back to sleep, slipping down deeper into her blissful, pillowy featherbed.

Covers. A bed. Morning.

Darice.

She sat up, dazed, and shielded her face from the sun streaming through the leaded glass windows. Hadn't she fallen asleep at her sister's side? Perhaps the entire event had been a dream. Perhaps Gailea had been the one having a restless night instead of her sister.

A sleepy groan jolted her mind to full wakefulness, and she glanced over to see Lorelei helping Darice with the back buttons of a clean blue dress. Darice looked perfectly alert as always, while Lorelei yawned widely. Ashden still sat by the fire, looking exhausted.

"Good morning," Gailea greeted.

Darice smiled at her warmly. "Morning, sister."

Sliding from the bed, Gailea donned one of the long, blue robes and walked over to her sister. "How're you feeling?"

"Well. Refreshed. Though I'm sorry it hasn't been the same for the rest of you." Her smile dimmed as she cast a sympathetic glance at Gailea, Lorelei, and then Ashden. "I don't know what could have come over me. I don't remember any of it. I don't even know if I had any strange dreams that would have led me."

Gailea took her hands. "It's all right. We've traveled far, exhausted, our mental and emotional limits pressed from all directions."

"Yes," Lorelei said, "and you're fine now, so that's what matters." Finished with the buttons, she gently touched Darice's shoulders. Then, she walked over to Darice's bed to finish donning a pair of stockings beneath her thick green dress. "Best hurry. The queen has summoned us to discuss the results of your lineage test."

Ashden left to change in his own chambers, while Gailea procured a green linen gown from the trunk. She wondered aloud where Iolana and Nerine were, but Lorelei promised they were just across the hall, sharing breakfast with Mikanah and Chamblin. Noting the fresh bread, honey, and slices of a yellow, star-shaped fruit, Gailea dressed as fast as she could and ate a small bit of each. Her stomach jumped in her throat as she thought about the lineage test. After last night's mishap, she dreaded that something else was bound to go wrong and prayed fervently this was just her nerves talking.

Shortly after they had dressed and eaten, both Echelon and Rosan guards arrived at their door. Once everyone was ready, they followed the guards through the castle. This time, instead of weaving through lesser-used, secluded passages, their surroundings grew more and more lavish. Carpets wove various crimsons, oranges, and golds in swirling flower patterns, accentuated by bright blue rosals. Tapestries and paintings sported many of the same sunrise hues, some showing rosal gardens, others depicting Rosa's past monarchs or the sun rising over various islands. Red cedar pillars gilded with golden flowers and vines supported vast halls. Even the tiles beneath their feet were painted gold. The walls were likewise painted a soft gold with subtle pink swirls and accented with rich, red brown wood panels. Golden chandeliers branched overhead, washing everything in a gentle, warm glow.

Despite the increasing opulence, the presence of life diminished. A few guards and finely clad courtiers traversed the halls, but not nearly as many as Gailea would have anticipated. Even Moragon, who considered everyone inferior, had filled his court to satiate his own arrogance. She expected an even fuller court from a queen as seemingly amiable as Delia, and this lack of normalcy only served to place her at greater unease.

They approached two immense doors painted with the Rosans' standard, the giant blue rosal, its petals blazing with eternal flames. The doors swung open inward, and they all walked through together.

More beauty surrounded them in the throne room, which was twice as large as the throne room in Adelar. Likewise, its extravagance and brilliant colors contrasted sharply against the cold black and white of Moragon's tastes. Arches and pillars painted gold supported a lofty ceiling. Arched windows with leaded panes and laced with golden orange silks dazzled in the sunlight. The floor was a mosaic pattern of blue, orange, gold, and red flowers and vines. An orange rug fringed with gold ran the length of the room all the way to the dais and its massive throne, and to Queen Delia, sitting in full royal opulence, wearing a gown of gold brocade draped atop an ivory satin underskirt. A brilliant blue rosal was stitched on her bodice. Her sleeves, bodice and hem were stitched with hundreds of tiny blue pearls. Despite her short stature, she did not look dwarfed by the throne's immensity. Rather, she stood out, shining like a bright sun, even amid such splendor.

"Welcome again, dear guests." Delia beamed a warm smile toward Gailea and her companions. "I bring you here to discuss news, both good and potentially ill. First and most happily, your test proves your word, Gailea. You *are* Callum's blood and thus his and Gillian's heir. However, the rest is most sobering." Her smile faded. The very light in the room seemed to dim as her demeanor grew stern. "There is just as much evidence to suggest that this woman—" She nodded gravely at Darice. "—poisoned our waters to create the affliction now making so many sick since early this morning."

Darice gasped, looking mortified, and took an instinctive step back, bumping up against Ashden who planted his hands on her shoulders as if to grant her some sense of groundedness. Even as Gailea watched her sister pale, she could feel the blood draining from her own face. Nerine and Iolana looked stunned, Mikanah stiffened, and Lorelei narrowed her gaze at the queen in an expression of betrayal.

"Perhaps we were too hasty to open our doors to strangers after all," Delia continued. "But as she is your sister, Gailea, I thought I should give her, give all of you, the opportunity to explain yourselves before I see fit to pass judgment."

Gailea's mind reeled. She stared into the queen's face, so friendly moments ago and now taut with apprehension, accusation, even. Delia believed her sister capable of this horrific crime.

All protested in outrage, with Ashden's words ringing the loudest. "What affliction? What are you talking about?"

"Many Rosans were stricken severely ill this morning. High fevers, vomiting, sweating, boils on their skin. I fear we've seen this before. It is all too familiar. The Dakazar, my people call it."

Gailea stood further stunned. The Dakazar! She hadn't heard that name in many years, but she clearly remembered the gruesome plague that had swept through Castle Adel, when she was a girl of fourteen. It was one of few times Darice had permitted her to use her musical magic, to spare them from catching the illness and to heal those for whom the illness had not yet hopelessly advanced. Gailea's skills then hadn't been nearly as refined at they were now, making the secret use of her magic even trickier. Her efforts had saved a grateful few, but dozens more had perished before her eyes.

"And what has this to do with my sister?" she demanded, finding her voice at last. "You readily accepted us into your fold last night. How can you be so quick to accuse her?"

Delia's somber gaze shifted to Gailea. "I don't want to look the hypocrite. But the Dakazar—you may know it as the 'Dark Flame'—is so very rare. A great bout of it happened years ago, in both Rosa and Adelar."

"I know. And Adelar provided you with the cure. So why now these horrid accusations?"

"Because Adelar 'provided' us with the sickness to begin with. Just one of many venomous attacks Adelar used against Rosa. Thanks to your king suffering a sorcerer in his walls, that vile Chevalier."

"I know." Gailea's words were heavy with the memories of that dreadful time. "He created the disease."

Delia seemed to flinch, her eyes narrowing. "Then

you likely know he released it into our drinking water. But somehow, it was also released into Adelar. Perhaps by a Rosan spy, perhaps by a traitor in Adelaran courts. Amiel knows there were many traitors on both sides. At any rate, only because the Adelarans suffered as well and only after much pleading did the sorcerer create the antidote. Chevalier kept the nature of the Dark Flame to himself. Only someone who grew up in Adelar might have learned of its secrets."

"Then why do you not accuse me?" Gailea said, stepping forward. "I too grew up in Moragon's courts. I too—"

"I will thank you to remember your place here," Delia said, stopping Gailea in her tracks. "You may possess royal blood, but you are no queen. My guards tell me that Darice was found in the garden late at night, beside a stream soaking wet. The pieces seem to align. Strangers enter my kingdom, one of them from the race of our sworn enemies. The very next morning, dozens and counting of *my* people are fallen deathly ill."

"I swear I did not do this thing, Your Majesty," Darice said, trembling.

"She was sleepwalking," Ashden said, still bracing her shoulders from behind. "She couldn't have known what she was doing."

"Was she?" The queen arched a brow. "Or was she merely pretending?"

"Impossible!"

"Worse things have been known to happen," Mikanah said, glaring at Delia, "especially if someone else was controlling her."

The queen's sharp gaze turned upon him. "The fate of the Guardians here stands on the edge of an unstable precipice, young man. You are asking a great favor to continue your quest. Do not challenge me. Do not seek to suggest that I or my people would dare to manipulate one of your own."

"Then what would you do?" Chamblin asked, frustration edging his usual calm tone. "You have no solid proof. You can't just punish her on a whim. The Lozolian Council would have all your heads."

"No. We won't punish her just yet. Not until we have more solid proof, as you say. But we will keep her under close watch. We will keep *all* of you under close watch. You will return to your chambers. You may visit one another's rooms, get fresh air on the balcony. But no one is to leave that corridor while my healers and alchemists investigate the water to get to the root of this mystery."

"What of *The Eagle's Ayre*?" Gailea nearly choked on the words as they tumbled from her. Exasperation gripped her, threatening to take control. Her body shuddered, and it took every ounce of will for her to maintain her composure. "It's difficult enough that my sister is accused of this wretched crime. But what also of our mission to obtain the last Guardian?"

"If any of you are saboteurs in the name of Adelar, then the last thing I will do is to send you to them so that you can plot further atrocities together. Your mission will have to wait."

"Wait too long," Lorelei stepped forward, "and you'll see that Adelar is the enemy you need worry about least. Moragon's power grows daily. There is no time for petty squabbles between two kingdoms who, by all rights and ancient history, ought rather to stand united." She watched the queen fiercely, with the same controlled outrage that Gailea fought to contain.

"There is no time for my people at all," the queen said, her voice wavering. "The the disease will work its way through them, and deaths will occur in just a few days."

"I'm guessing there must be those in the castle who are ill." Darice's voice cracked, but she bravely stepped forward and curtsied. "Your majesty, if we must be bound to this castle until my innocence is proven, perhaps we might at least do what we can to lend our aid."

Gailea's heart softened at her sister's compassion. "Yes, we have songs that can heal, soothe aches and pains. Not strong enough to overcome such a monumental plague, but songs that might ease some of its symptoms until help arrives."

Delia's lips drew into a thin smile, a feeble attempt at gratitude. She nodded in Gailea's direction, but it was clear her patience waned. "I thank you ladies for such a kind and generous offer. But I would not feel comfortable allowing any of you to interfere, considering the circumstances. If any of you possess ill intent, I would not place my people in further danger by sending their attackers to 'help' them. No, our healers will do what they can to slow the disease until the Adelarans respond to my messages."

"The Adelarans?" Chamblin looked aghast. "Why would you contact them? You seem so bent on pointing to them as the ones behind this mess."

"Because they also possess one half of the cure. The cure can be made only from a specific herb that grows in our woods and a specific berry from theirs. We have tried to grow the berry ourselves, but it simply refuses to thrive in our soil." Delia inhaled deeply, looking overwhelmed and exhausted. "I grow weary of this conversation. I have much work to do if there is to be any hope of restoring my people to safety. My guards will escort you to your chambers. Do not come to me until I send for you again."

~*~*~

449

The Guardians and Nerine sat around the table in their withdrawing room. The Echelon stood around them, with several Rosan guards lingering nearby.

"So, what do we think?" Lorelei kept her voice calm, despite the righteous anger burning in her gaze.

"I didn't do this," Darice insisted. "I swear to it."

"We know." Gailea took her hand before glancing up at the Echelon. "Do any of you know anything that may be useful?"

A Spaniño man whom Gailea recognized as Carlos shook his head. "Many of us questioned the Rosan guards last night, but they seemed just as confused at how Darice eluded us long enough to find the stream."

"I don't understand it either." Darice turned to Gailea. "I know that one spell of yours, sister, the one that allows a person to blend with their surroundings. But even if I used such a charm while sleeping, why and how?"

"Perhaps," Nerine spoke up, "you simply took another way to the garden. Like a secret passage."

"But how would I know of it? I'm entirely new to this castle—to this entire kingdom!" Darice swept her hands across the room before letting them fall defeatedly in her lap. "Even if there *was* a secret passage of sorts in the garden that led to the stream, surely the Rosan guards might have mentioned it when questioned?"

"I hate to say it," Chamblin said, "as I am neither a suspicious nor superstitious fellow. But I do believe some sort of mischief is afoot. I don't say we should blame the Rosans just yet, despite their clear lack of diplomatic skills. But someone is plotting something to make us appear an enemy."

"The Echelon will stay with Darice," Cenwin, one of the Echelon women, declared. "We'll take watches. If our banishment to these chambers extends into the night, we'll keep an especially close watch. Whoever is doing this, they seem to *want* Darice to be caught, to take a fall."

Darice heaved a heavy sigh. "I'm so sorry. I should be helping the Guardians, not hindering us."

Gailea squeezed her hand. Early in the day as it was, she was exhausted from their encounter with the queen but didn't want to display anything but the utmost support for her sister. "Don't worry. It's not your doing. No one will harm you here. I won't abandon my family to such a fate." She shared a meaningful glance with Ashden. "Not this time. The oceans will turn to fire before I allow that to happen ever again."

~*~*~

Outside the arched windows, the sky stretched like a black canvas, with a few sprays of white stars.

It was night, but Iolana was already crawling out of her skin, alert and alive and wishing for dawn, as restless as if she were caged inside Moragon's quarters all over again. There was no torture here, not yet at least. But a prison was a prison. The finery of the clothes, extraordinary tapestries, soft featherbeds, and succulent fruits and spices were all things of beauty and delight. But a trap was still a trap, however prettily disguised. Nothing good could come of it.

Darice had slept for the past hour. Peacefully, it seemed, in one of the two curtained beds. Nerine sat on the bed beside her, a few books piled carefully on either side of her. She had read to Darice until she'd fallen asleep. Now, she busied herself with weaving her hands through the air in various patterns, every now and then turning her arms to their liquid form or making shapes with water droplets midair.

Iolana couldn't stand it any longer.

"I'm going for a walk. Can you stay awake? Keep an eye on her for a little while longer?"

"Of course." Nerine glanced up. "Everything all right?"

"Yes. I just need some air."

Nerine nodded before returning her attention to her water magic.

Iolana stole from the room, nodded a greeting to the Echelon guards flanking the door, and headed down the hall toward the balcony at the far end.

"Care for an extra companion?"

Iolana smiled as Mikanah exited his room.

"How do you always know where I am? Like a mental magician of sorts."

"Don't call me that." Mikanah's frown was stern. "Not even in jest."

"I'm sorry." Iolana wasn't certain whether she felt worse at her mistake or at the way her heart twisted when he gazed at her with such disapproval. "It's been a long day. I want to see the sky, feel the breeze on my skin. I'd love for you to join me."

Iolana slipped her hand into his. He held it briefly before tensing and drawing away.

She paused, staring up at him. "What is it, Mika?"

"Nothing," he muttered. "Only...this place has a way of darkening my thoughts, even moreso than usual. Being trapped here, memories assail me in both waking and sleeping hours. Headaches, nightmares...."

"Nightmares of what?" Iolana took his hand again. She glanced back at the guards and whispered, "I know there are things you still won't tell me. Things that happened to you. We used to confide *everything* in one another."

"That was before. When we had no other choice."

She looked up at him fiercely. "And now that we have a choice, you *choose* to push me away?"

"You don't understand. And I haven't been pushing you away. I hold you. I stroke your hair to put you to sleep."

Iolana tensed with exasperation at the monotonous tone of his voice, the vacancy in his eyes. "You treat me like a father lulling his child. It's insulting, the lack of credit you give me. I notice the space between us. I feel it vividly."

She reached up to push a stray curl from his face. He closed his eyes, inhaled deeply, and let his exhale come with a shudder.

"I could make you forget those nightmares," she whispered close to his ear. "If you'd only let me."

Her hand crept down his chest, toward the leather belt around his breeches.

Mikanah staggered back, eyes flying open. "What do you think you're doing?"

"Trying to be close to you again, as we once were. But you have no intention of that. You're never going to touch me, are you?"

He looked guilty, but she didn't care. He needed to know how much he tormented her, needlessly. She could imagine the feel of his skin and hair. He had always felt surprisingly soft, but then again, she had supposed that, as one of Moragon's most valued servants, keeping Mikanah beautiful and clean would be just as important to Moragon as keeping him close. She longed for the strength of his chest against hers, his *lips* against hers. She stood so close, and yet the chasm he created between them seemed to expand by the second.

"Why?" She clung to him. "Why won't you touch me?"

He wrenched away. "Why are you so desperate? This

is neither the time nor the place!"

"These walls are closing in on me too. I feel—I feel like before. If they can accuse Darice, they can accuse any of us. We're not in charge here. *She* is—Delia—and this—" She grabbed his arms and pulled herself close. "—*this* could be snatched away at any moment. Just like before. So just hold me, kiss me, *please*—" She stretched up on her toes and caressed his cheek before drawing his face toward hers. He leaned into the kiss. Their lips brushed. His warm breath smelled of spices and wine.

He shoved her away and she stumbled back, her heart searing as if slashed in two.

"No, Iolana. I can't. You don't understand."

"I would if you'd tell me," Iolana snapped, fighting back angry tears. "I know you want me, too. You'll remember in time. I will *make* you remember. Come..." She grasped his hand. "You can at least indulge me with by walking with me."

With a reluctant scowl, he let her drag him down the hall.

~*~*~

Gailea sat up on the bed with a great sigh. Much as she needed rest, plaguing anxiety had permitted her none.

"Gailea—*Gailea*!"

Nerine flung herself into the room, two Rosan guards and several Echelon on her heels. Nerine caught her breath long enough to gasp, "Darice. They've just taken her. Arrested her!"

"What is the meaning of this?" Gailea cried, flinging a demanding glance at Carlos.

"Our deepest apologies, Lady Gailea." Carlos's eyes filled with deep remorse. "We didn't see her leave her room this time. She wasn't caught until she'd reached the garden again."

Gailea flew toward the door. She fled the room just in time to see her sister being escorted around the corner and out of sight, surrounded by a fleet of guards as if she were the deadliest murderer. A few Echelon drew swords or wielded elemental spells in their hands, assailing the Rosan guards who drew their own blades, blocking them and trying to shout words of reason.

"*Enough!*" Gailea cried.

The Echelon paused but remained poised to fight, faces flushed.

"Fighting will not solve anything," she added, before wheeling on the nearest Rosan guard. "But Amiel willing, talk will. I demand an audience with Her Majesty. Tell her we will wait no longer for answers."

CHAPTER 32

THROUGH FIRE AND
WATER

The doors to the throne room were thrust open wide. Guards led Gailea inside, along with the other Guardians, Echelon, and Nerine.

The queen sat on her throne, staring proudly. She was encompassed not only by guards but by four men and women clad in long black robes bearing the Rosan royal crest, her advisors from before. In the torchlight and moonlight, their red hair shimmered like fire.

Gailea thought of Adelar. Thought of Ragnar with his wild crimson curls and his eyes like violent purple storms. Fear shot through her, but anger crushed that fear as she saw her sister, hands chained behind her back, led by several guards, and made to kneel at the foot of the dais.

Gailea stood before the dais, ready to defend her sister, accuse the queen, or perhaps both, when she saw the water trailing behind Darice. That would be proof enough in the Rosans' already-suspicious minds, that she was the one tainting their water supply. What would Gailea say to defend her?

Ashden rushed forward, but two guards held him back while two others crossed their swords, blocking his path. He strained and gazed desperately at Darice before flinging a wild look at the queen. "What is the meaning of all this? Darice is innocent of any crime. The fact that she's soaking wet, that doesn't prove anything."

"Whether intended or no," Delia said, "my council and I believe she had something to do with the poisoning of our people. Perhaps she is a willing servant. Or perhaps she is a pawn manipulated by King Donyon himself. Whatever the case, she is clearly a danger. I could no longer keep the news of your presence secret. The people wanted answers regarding the plague. Now, they are calling for her blood."

"You cannot harm her!" Gailea's words were a shouted command. "Not without undeniable proof."

"We have enough proof to satisfy the Rosans' cries for vengeance. And though I would be disappointed to quell blood with more blood, I would also not risk any further harm to my people. My council and I have come up with a bargain. You would be wise to listen to it if you wish to spare your sister's life.

"We will grant you access to *The Eagle's Ayre*, as you wished. You will take with you some of our guard, who will ensure you do not betray us. You will travel to Adelar and secure the berries needed for the cure. What's more, you will convince Donyon himself to bring them. Only then will we be convinced of your innocence in these matters and spare your sister's life. Otherwise, her life is forfeit, and we will declare war on Adelar."

"That's absurd," Chamblin said, looking absolutely floored. "To ask a monarch to leave his kingdom and travel to that of his enemy, especially when that enemy is threatening war."

"Not so absurd, I think. If he is innocent, he will surely comply. If he refuses, then you may tell him we are willing to brave his walls of flame and water to finish the war he has begun with us. We will risk the flames, risk *anything*, to save our own. Adelar has deceived us into harm one too many times. My council has already begun making preparations for war, if needed." She narrowed her glare pointedly at Chamblin. "You may tell Donyon *that* as well."

"What will become of my sister in the meantime?" Gailea demanded, drawing the queen's intense stare to meet hers once more.

"She will be imprisoned and kept under the closest watch. I will order my most skilled magicians to place charms on her that restrict her magic. Whether by her will or another's, only the most skilled magic could've permitted her to slip from right under our noses unawares. My guard will now take you into a private chamber. Talk amongst yourselves, choose wisely. When you have decided whether you will accept this proposal, send one of my guards to me, and I will summon you when I am ready."

Delia nodded at the men holding Darice. They yanked her up and began dragging her from the room. Ashden darted toward her again, but the guards held him firm. Anger flared inside Gailea once more as she watched her sister treated like a wild beast.

"Don't worry, sister," Gailea called. "We'll get to the bottom of this. We *will* prove your innocence. We *will* free you."

Darice stared desperately at Ashden and then at Gailea. Her gaze remained locked on Gailea's until she was forced from their sight.

Like beasts themselves that might snap at any moment, they were quickly corraled by Delia's guard into an adjoining room. Once they had all clustered around the table set in its midst, the Rosan guards left them in privacy.

"I'm surprised," Lorelei muttered. "I expected to have them breathing down our necks the remainder of our stay here."

"Don't fool yourself," Mikanah said with a scoff. "They're likely right outside the door, listening to every word we say."

"There's one way to find out." Gailea swept a glance across her fellow Guardians before creeping over to the door and singing a songspell, *Dumkana*, ever so quietly. If there was even the smallest noise outside their room, the song would magnify it. Lorelei followed her to the door, joining in. For a few moments, silence prevailed, but just as Gailea felt satisfied enough to break away, a muffled cough met her ears, followed by the subtle shuffling of feet. A glance at Lorelei's irritated expression told her she had heard the same.

Gailea then focused her song-spell's purpose on concealing their voices, making them difficult for the Rosans to decipher. Lorelei sang too, along with Chamblin as familiarity sparked in his eyes. *Dumkana* was the same song-spell Gailea had used to douse her office with silence when she stole his map back at the academy.

Once satisfied their words were entirely muffled, Gailea said, "You're right, Mikanah. They're right outside, likely listening. If so, at least now they've nothing of importance to listen to."

The Echelon soldier named Idalin drew her sword, and lightning crackled along its edges. "If they wish to continue spying outside our doors, then I say we return the favor by stepping out that door with a little threat."

Several other Echelon drew their blades or summoned fire, ice, and other magic spells to their hands.

"If it's a war they want," Carlos declared, "then perhaps it's war they need, to knock them back to their senses."

"A battle here and now would be folly," said Seumas, a man with a gray stubble of a beard; scars across his cheek showed he was no stranger to battle. "Even with our magic, their warriors far outnumber ours. Guardians, we will gladly follow whatever orders you give. We will fight for the honorable Darice if you so command. But I must caution against it."

"As do I." Chamblin grasped the top edge of one of the chairs, for emphasis or balance, Gailea wasn't sure. "We would be outnumbered at once. We can't afford to shed more precious blood, nor waste time, either."

Lorelei nodded and moved to stand by him. "Rosa and Adelar are doing that well enough, instead of banding together to fight Moragon. We don't need to follow in their footsteps."

"That's what he wants," Gailea said, her tone grim. "Chaos. Where there is chaos there can be no unity, and he can easily sweep in while we're distracted to destroy us all. As much as I want to rush out there myself, that's not the wisest course of action." She exhaled in frustration. If the Octavial Eight, not to mention an entire castle filled with guards, couldn't defend her sister from whatever unseen force kept controlling her, then how would they ever overcome a king as powerful and twisted as Moragon?

Ashden took gentle hold of her shoulder. "What matters most is to make sure Darice is returned to us safely. We must do whatever is best for her."

Gailea met his gaze in an unspoken vow, then looked at the others in the room. "Which leaves us one choice. We do as they say. We talk to Donyon. He is a treacher-

ous, self-glorifying coward. I doubt he'll be easily persuaded to help us, let alone come here. But we must do
all we can to convince him."

"It's decided then?" Lorelei met Gailea's gaze head
on. "We agree to go to Adelar? Summon the Eagle, obtain the cure?"

Gailea nodded curtly, as murmurs of agreement
echoed across the room.

"Darice needs someone to support her," Ashden said
thoughtfully. "Someone who can be her voice, ensure
she is not ill treated. I will stay at her side, while the rest
of you go on."

Gailea offered him a grim smile, the best she could
muster. "Thank you. And that solves another problem.
Nerine, you'll stay here with Ashden."

Nerine's eyes widened, her gaze darting from Gailea
to the other Guardians, then back again. "But—but why?
I've been studying. I could be of help. Especially since
everyone keeps talking about walls of water."

"The Eagle is sufficient for that. Honestly, I ought to
insist you be sent home at once. This is just the sort of
reason I didn't want you along in the first place, to prevent you being flung into needless danger."

"I'm not leaving," Nerine insisted, so fervently that
Gailea could imagine her literally digging her heels into
the ground.

"I'm not trying to make you," Gailea said. "I know
you would fight the matter, and we've neither time nor
energy to argue among ourselves. But I at least can forbid you coming to Adelar, of all cursed places. I appreciate your desire to help, but Adelar is neither the time
nor place."

Nerine glanced at Iolana and Mikanah, who were involved in their own hushed conversation. She tugged
at Chamblin's arm, but he shook his head. "I'm sorry,

young lady. But while I know you'd be an asset, I must agree on this one. We've placed you in far too much unnecessary danger as it is."

Nerine frowned at the floor, clearly disappointed.

"Only one more thing I ask," Gailea said to them all. "Do not reveal the identity of the last Guardian. If I am loath to consider the fact, the Rosans will be even moreso, especially since they already consider us spies."

~*~*~

The Guardians gathered within Castle Rosa's inner courtyard. The sun had risen an hour or so ago. Gailea had risen with it, having been permitted to visit with her sister and offer encouragement, if only briefly.

A hazy light rested on the castle gardens. The Echelon stood nearby. Most would accompany the Guardians on their journey, though a few would stay back to watch over Ashden, Nerine, and Darice.

The queen emerged into the garden then, surrounded on both sides by many men clad in handsome, black leather tunics painted with blue rosals wreathed in flame across their chests.

"I am sending six of my trusted knights," she announced. "I think they will make sufficient representatives. Now, Gailea, if you will sing what you know of *The Eagle's Ayre*, then I will reveal the last few notes. Though, I must caution you not to be alarmed if the Eagle does not come. We have tried summoning him in recent years to no avail."

Gailea's stomach dropped a little. She hadn't considered the possibility that the Eagle might ignore or refuse her summons. She prayed to Amiel that her intentions for calling upon him—to save her sister, spare the lives of the ill, and obtain their last Guardian—were pure enough for the Eagle to deem them worthy of his help.

Then, she began to sing. From the moment she had first read her mother's accounts, she had stored the song in her memory.

Delia chimed in, adding in a few new bars at the end to complete the melody. Gailea quickly picked up on them and sang the song in full.

A great rush of wind engulfed the women's voices. Gailea looked up, just in time to turn and shield herself from the whirlwind caused by the Eagle's descent. The giant bird landed as effortlessly as an owl gliding at midnight in search of prey. Delia stared wide-eyed at the bird, as did the Rosan guards, all seemingly struck mute with wonderment.

Gailea crept over, gazing up in awe at the eagle who stood patiently observing her. Its eyes, one ruby red, the other sapphire blue, glistened with many facets as though inlaid with real gems.

"Would it be all right if I touch your feathers?"

The Eagle tilted its head, seeming to consider, before bowing its head in a nod. Gently, Gailea swept her fingers across the beast's soft, golden-brown feathers.

"Truly magnificent," Chamblin breathed. He ran his hands along its side, reaching up as if to gauge its height. "I can honestly say I have not encountered anything so magnificent in all my travels."

"Nor I," the queen breathed.

"Welcome, Eagle," Gailea said. "My sister, an Adelaran, is in danger, as are the people of Rosa. The Rosans are struck with a deadly plague, and my sister stands falsely accused. Adelar holds one of the keys to the cure, and we must reach them with all haste."

The Eagle flapped its wings wide and tilted its head back in a loud screech. Gailea staggered back, and several guards rushed forward to shield the queen.

"The Eagle is displeased," Delia said quietly, looking more somber. "He is said to hate any quarrel between Adelar and Rosa."

"We need you to take us to Adelar." Gailea again stroked the bird's feathers, all while singing a soothing charm inside her head; strains of a similar tune floated from Chamblin's direction. "We need to speak with King Donyon, convince him to help us."

As the Eagle released another valiant screech, Mikanah walked alongside it, examing its girth with sheer disbelief. "There's no way. Even considering its immensity, with the Echelon and Rosan knights, there's too many of us. There's just no way he can bear all our weight."

"Presuming he lends his aid," Gailea said, "legends do say that in times of great need, the Eagle can carry as many as it needs to. I've seen magic do stranger things, haven't you?"

"Pardon me, Gailea," Nerine stepped up beside her, "but his hame is Aneirin Dei, though he says we may simply call him 'Dei'."

Nerine's eyes reflected their usual curiosity, along with a gentle admiration as she gazed into the bird's eyes.

"How are you able to understand him?"

Nerine shrugged. "I'm not sure. Sometimes, on travels with my parents, they would study animals, and I could understand what they were thinking or feeling. Like an extra sense of sorts."

Gailea admired Nerine in turn, surprised, and yet supposing it was appropriate the girl could understand the Eagle above any of them, being innately connected to nature as she was. Fleetingly, she thought of Merrit and how, in his own way, he had likewise seemed close to beasts and birds.

"Please, Dei," Gailea addressed the Eagle, "may we ride you to Rosa? There are many of us, but our mission is dire. Both Rosa and Adelar's survival depends on this quest."

Dei screeched and bowed low before tucking his feet beneath him and sitting as low to the ground as possible. Gailea was first to mount him, climbing the creature's side by taking its feathers, bracing her feet, pulling herself up.

"Forgive me; I'm being as gentle as I can. Is this hurting you?"

Dei turned his head, watching her steadily.

"He says it's all right," Nerine declared. "Try to grab the feathers by their base so that it pulls less."

One by one, they climbed onto the Eagle's back. Those on top reached down to pull their companions up, while those below gave others a leg up, preventing as much pulling on Dei's feathers as possible. Mikanah guided Chamblin up, and he perched atop Dei's back with a grin. "It's softer than the finest king's velvet up here."

They continued to help one another along, stepping carefully. Gailea didn't know what it was like to have feathers or how delicate they were, but the bird held perfectly still, making no complaints, nor did Nerine voice any on his behalf.

Just when they thought they would run out of room, again they found room for one more. Some sat cross-legged, while others sat on their knees, grasping at the base of Dei's feathers for support. The bird seemed to grow larger the more people mounted him, and by this phenomenon, everyone fit. Everyone had a place, with wiggle room to spare, Guardians, Echelon, and Rosan knights.

"Is everyone ready?" Gailea called over her shoulder. She had crawled up front where the bird's head sloped down into the graceful arch of its neck. Declarations of readiness—or not, for some—met her ears.

"Wow, that's amazing." Nerine's eyes shone with wonder up at Gailea. "He says it's been nearly ten thousand sunrises since he last helped the Rosans and Adelarans."

"No doubt," Delia said, walking beside Nerine, her eyes lit wth hope as she turned them to Gailea, "seeing as Gailea's mother and father are the last in living memory to summon and ride the Eagle. Fly safe. And may Amiel grant you success in talking to the Adelaran king."

Gailea nodded at the queen. "Thank you, Your Majesty. We won't disappoint you. We will return with the cure."

Delia nodded back. "Seeing you ride the Eagle can almost make me believe it."

Leaning forward toward the Eagle's ear, Gailea whispered, "To Adelar."

With a mighty screech, Dei raised his head and wings high. Within seconds, he had swept them off the ground in a mighty rush of wind. Everyone held on tight to each other, closing their arms around the waist of the person in front. They rose higher until those on the ground shrank to the size of tiny bugs. Dei shot forward, and in a few breaths, Rosa rapidly shrank behind them before vanishing on the horizon altogether.

Gailea wondered that the rush of wind didn't catapult them all from Dei's back, but as she sensed an invisible barrier wrapping around them, she knew the Eagle must use some magic to keep its riders from falling. By all rights, the trip to Adelar should have lasted several hours.

However, thanks to the Eagle's speed, they found themselves wheeling toward the other island kingdom within the hour. A wall of dancing flames surrounded it, stretching hundreds of feet high.

As Mikanah and Iolana described the scene to Chamblin, he hugged his arms around Gailea's waist and said, "I can already feel the fire's heat radiating toward us. How exactly does this work?"

"I don't know," Gailea said. "My mother's diaries spoke of four barriers she passed through—two of fire and two of water—but she never clearly explained how to access all four barriers or pass through them or—"

Dei burst forward at an even faster speed and dove down toward the ocean, wings spread wide to embrace the fresh, salty air. Gailea realized just in time that he wasn't going to stop, even as one of the Echelon yelled for everyone to brace themselves and catch a breath. Gailea inhaled deep and hugged herself close to the eagle's body, clutching the feathers even tighter, bracing herself.

The cold impact of the water shocked Gailea, and she almost took a sharp breath but stopped herself. The force of the currents rushing against them should have knocked her off the Eagle's back, but whatever protective shield Dei had created held firm. Chamblin squeezed Gailea tightly, and she couldn't blame him as she clutched Dei's feathers for dear life. Their underwater journey was an altogether frightening sensation, let alone for someone who couldn't fully see.

Her initial shock from the water subsided just enough for her to feel that they had been doused in new magic as well. Another spell wrapped around them almost tangibly. While still terrified that the currents might rip her from Dei's back any moment, the spell provided a soothing that made her instinctively trust herself to take a breath. She could breathe underwater. The water zipped past, glittering as the Eagle's sapphire eye radiated with a magnificent blue glow. Perhaps Dei's magic not only penetrated the magic barriers of water and flame but also granted its riders the means necessary to do so as well, without risking harm to their bodies.

Gailea focused her gaze forward, and suddenly, she could make out a bright orange red through the blue.

The next moment, they had catapulted from the water into a vast cave, flying at top speed toward a wall of fire. Gailea glanced behind her and saw that, by some magic, the water did not penetrate the cave, as though an invisible barrier shielded the cave's entrance.

She focused on the wall of flame. Just before reaching it, the eagle's ruby eye shimmered. Bright rays of red light shone from its glistening facets, just as the sapphire eye had done, and they flew through the fire unscathed. It was amazing to be surrounded by fire, to be so close to something so dangerous yet know they had nothing to fear.

As soon as they emerged from the fire, they were surging beneath the ocean once more. Gailea marveled at such powerful elemental magic. How was it possible that the entire cave and wall of fire were housed beneath the very ocean? Only the strongest sealing charms could have kept the water from rushing inside the cave.

Dei surged up through the water. The bright morning sky shone through the clear ocean, tumbling nearer and nearer.

As the Eagle cut above the waves and winged once more into the air, the second water barrier appeared before them, this time rising in a high wall, just like the fire. They plunged through the wall of water, and Gailea braced herself for the impact, but she felt none. Another magic shield seemed to encompass them and the Eagle. The oddest thing was to stretch out her hand and be able to feel the water, but beyond that, to remain perfectly dry.

The Eagle passed through the second water wall, and the final wall of flame loomed into view, blazing bright blue only yards away. Its immense heat washed over Gailea, making her sweat. Her heart lurched, though not in fear of the flames, but because as soon as they passed through the fire, nothing would stand between her and Adelar.

Adelar. The home that had served first and foremost as a prison. She had cast out Moragon to help Crispin Ragnar, the young man who became her husband. The husband who had turned mad, turned against her, turned every good thing he had ever known in his life to poison. He had murdered his best friend. He would have killed his own son and manipulated his daughter against Gailea, had she not fled. Before escaping, she had seen to it that the Adelaran throne was stolen from Crispin and given to Donyon, a man she had then believed was righteous enough to rule.

But there were no righteous rulers in Adelar.

The world beyond the fire wall sped closer and closer. This was it. She couldn't run from her past any longer. She must face it head on.

They burst through the flames into Adelar.

CHAPTER 33

THE KING OF ADELAR

Flashes of silver glinted past, soaring so close they whistled shrilly in Gailea's ears. Realizing they were arrows, she sang a charm to deflect them. As more arched up from below, Gailea saw that beyond the fire barrier, a thick stone wall had been built around Adelar's perimeter. Anger brewed inside her, and her stomach turned. Yet another device to make Adelar more of a fortress than a place to call home.

"Sing everyone!"

Gailea sang *Dumkana* to magnify her voice's volume before resuming the song-spell that formed a temporary shield over her and the people nearest her, deflecting any attacks that would assail them. The other Guardians joined in, creating protection from the whirlwind of magic attacks and arrows that bombarded them.

They swept over a green valley layered with tall, wide-branching trees, with a gleaming river snaking around it, and Gailea wondered if these were the Chamroq Dell and River Shila named in her mother's song. A bittersweet whimsy flitted through her. She had spent most of her life cooped up in Adelar's castle. She had never been able to experience the beauty mentioned in *Gillian's Ode*, had never been able to see Adelar through that lens, and now she doubted she ever could.

Dei's flight soon reached the City of Delosia. Arrows assailed them from the walls and towers below, until they started vanishing mid-air. A different song floated to Gailea, and she glanced back at Lorelei and Mikanah, their faces fierce with concentration as they uttered the protective chant.

Castle Adel loomed mere miles in the distance, tall and proud against the bright blue sky, a splendid structure of gray stone and stained-glass windows. Flags bearing Adelar's crest—a golden bear crowned with silver stars—waved in the wind atop the towers near the castle and those situated at the four corners of the wall encompassing it. Bright sun gleamed on the colorful windows, fully restored as if they'd never been shattered by overwhelming chords of destruction, as if Moragon and all the torment he'd caused had never existed. Small hills surrounded the castle, giving it a whimsical look, almost like something one might find in a children's story.

Gailea would not let appearances deceive her. She had done so in her youth, but she was older now, too old for tricks.

They sped toward the castle. More arrows and elemental spells assailed them from the wall enclosing the outer courtyard. Lookouts blew horns of warning, announcing an intrusion. Adelarans yelled and ran into their homes, save a few here and there who stopped, pointed, and stared. Some called to their neighbors, watching the Eagle in awe before ducking into their nearby homes, shops, and inns.

They sailed past the castle's gatehouse and over the outer walls. Some of the guards continued shooting arrows, but most had drawn their blades or summoned magic spells into their hands and stood looking poised, ready, and yet terrified. Such a beast had not swept inside Adelar for many long years.

The Eagle wheeled down toward the inner courtyard. As it neared the ground, a man with brown hair and beard rushed out, his purple, fur-lined robe flowing behind him. A dark purple surcoat embroidered with gold fit snugly over his broad-shouldered form, and a golden livery collar hung around his neck, with a shining red gemstone ringed by smaller blue stones in its center. Golden rings with similar blue and red gems adorned his fingers.

Through all the finery, Gailea recognized him at once. Time and battle scars had aged his face, but this was the same man Gailea had seen marching toward Adelar as she'd fled with her children. The same man who'd sent the Alder Sprite warriors to assassinate her and her children.

King Donyon stared up at them, frozen a few long seconds until the Eagle landed with a screech.

"The Eagle?" he said hoarsely. "The Eagle of Spectrum?"

Recovering himself, he took a few steps forward, looking alarmed, as though he had strayed into a familiar nightmare. He stopped abruptly, still as a statue, and Gailea wondered if one of her companions had immobilized him.

A stern fierceness erased his bewilderment, and with a lift of his chin, he declared, "I am Donyon, King of Adelar. We have not seen the Eagle in these parts in long years. Who are you that ride upon him, and what tidings do you bring?" His attention landed on the Rosan knights, and at once he reached for the silver sword at his side. "Ill ones, methinks, if you bring the enemy's fighters."

"You ought to know that the Eagle would not have brought us here if we had ill intent," Gailea declared firmly, commanding the king's attention. "We are the Octavial Guardians of Loz. I think that much you know as well. We've all been through it, so do not aim to lie and deny the mark that was surely granted to you."

Donyon's lips pulled into a thin line, but once his gaze fell upon Gailea, his mouth parted in shock. He shoved the left sleeve of his robe up, revealing the Guardian's mark, the solfége word *Ut*, shimmering high up on his forearm.

"I did receive the mark a few days ago. Your messengers were forbidden access. These are troubling times. No one can be trusted. But I knew what it was…" He covered the mark with a scowl. "I have heard tales of the late Guardians' deaths, the new Guardians' appointments."

Lorelei released a short, irritated breath. "Then why did you not heed the mark's call? You really think Moragon would stop in Carmenna? You really think you would be safe behind your walls of water and flame? Against someone of his mental prowess, and with a musical weapon or army at his back?"

Donyon studied Lorelei a long moment. His troubled glance strayed across all of them and then back to Gailea, haunted once more.

"We will discuss this further. In my Council chamber, with my own advisors. Your soldiers may wait outside the chamber, under close watch of my sentinels. As for the Rosan knights…" Contempt hardened his baleful stare. "…I'll not let them take a single step further in my grounds. They stay out here, in the courtyard, or our conversation ends here."

"Coward as ever," Gailea muttered beneath her breath.

Donyon glanced sharply at her but said nothing. Turning on his heel, he said, "I will ready my advisors. Men, escort them when they are ready."

Donyon disappeared inside his castle, his velvet surcoat rippling behind him. The Eagle lowered its body so everyone could climb down.

The Rosan knights were immediately surrounded by Adelarans, whose raised swords and shields created a cage around them. Before the Rosans could react with violence, Gailea held up her hand and declared, "Peace. Remember your queen. I know you would spill your blood in her honor, but she doesn't wish that fate for you."

"Remember that we are here to *save* precious blood," Chamblin added, "not set more of it running in the streets."

Gailea leaned close to the Eagle's head and whispered, "Please, wait for us. We will do what we can to convince the king. We will get the cure. And then we will need your help to take it back to Rosa."

The Eagle lowered its head, folded its wings, and stood still as a statue.

Adelaran guards encircled both Guardians and Echelon, leading them not through the gates Donyon had passed through, but instead to a small wooden door.

Once they stepped inside, Gailea's anger once more battled with her fear. They were so very near the kitchen where she had spent endless days scrubbing and cleaning, breaking back and skin for a few scraps of food, being pursued by wolves like Moragon and Lord Alistor, who had sought to use her magic for their own pursuits.

They wound down several corridors and up stairs until they emerged from the servants' quarters altogether. Within no time, Gailea passed by a whole new string of memories. The immense Great Hall, where

Moragon's birthday celebration had revealed her magic to the world, and Crispin's as well, initiating a spiral of events that had led to her husband's ultimate downfall. The throne room, where so many had hailed Moragon as lord, not out of love, but from fear of what he might do to them if they did not display their utmost loyalty. Later, she had sat in that throne room alongside her husband, ruling as equals for a precious year or so. Once Alistor had begun to poison Crispin's mind against her, Gailea no longer stepped foot in that room, let alone ruled there with her husband.

They approached two doors, ornately carved but not as grand as those leading to the throne room or Great Hall. Gailea had passed these doors many times but had not been permitted entrance, either by Moragon or her husband.

The Guardians entered the Council chamber. As the door closed, locking them inside, Gailea watched Donyon, who sat at the middle of a long table. Five members of the Privy Council, no doubt the most trusted noblemen in the realm, sat on either side of him, clad in long blue robes that matched the blue tapestries lining the walls, all embroidered with golden bears crowned with silver stars. The Council faced the Guardians with stern distrust, while Donyon's gaze kept falling to Gailea, curiously haunted. The Guardians paused before the table, and the Echelon and Adelaran guards dispersed about the room.

"Will you not kneel before the king?" one of the advisors demanded.

"We are not here for the king." Gailea glared at Donyon. "We are here to speak to our fellow Octavial Guardian. We have no ruler. You are not our king, and the Echelon," she motioned behind her, "are honorable protectors of the Lozolian Realm, of which your kingdom is a but a miniscule part."

Donyon stared back at Gailea. "I should punish you for such boldness," he began, his tone unexpectedly quiet. "Except you remind me of another, unnervingly similar soul."

My mother, Gailea thought, wishing she could keep her face from burning. *You did not value her boldness. You thought to crush it right out of her.*

He shook his head as if clearing it and went on. "Excuse any affront you may have felt from Celegrave, here. His intent was regard for me, not insult to you. But you will forgive me. The entire event of your visit, especially the manner in which you arrived, was quite shocking. I will do my best to treat all of you with respect from now on, if you can do the same. Please, state your business. I trust it has to do with more than my status as a Guardian, considering the Rosan guards you brought along."

This apparent ploy by Donyon to maintain false composure—he had certainly displayed none toward her mother—took Gailea aback. She paused long enough for Chamblin to step forward and say, "Your Majesty, Adelaran representatives. A foul plague has struck the people of Rosa. The 'Dark Flame' it's called."

The Council members reacted with shocked grunts, gasps, and expressions of alarm.

Lord Celegrave eyed Donyon, then Chamblin. "Impossible. It's a farce!"

Donyon held up a hand to silence him. "Stranger things have happened as of late. I am sorry for the Rosans' fate, but what has this to do with me and my people?"

"The Rosans claim you hold one half of the cure," Chamblin said. "We were sent here to obtain it."

A derisive chuckle fell from Donyon's lips. "The Rosans have been infuriating to deal with the past few years. Even with our great fire and water barriers, they find ways to tease at war. Their pirates attack our ships, steal our goods. All manner of childish goading. And now they would expect a cure from us? I say they don't deserve it."

"Innocents are the ones being attacked!" Lorelei cried, throwing her hands up. "Not pirates and bandits and other menaces. Women and children who will die if you don't help them."

"Better yet. Fewer women means fewer chances to continue their miserable race—"

"How *dare* you." Gailea stormed forward, shaking with rage. "It's bad enough you're too much a coward to face your duties and join with the Guardians. It's bad enough you would cower behind your enchanted walls while the world crumbles around you. But to resist the call of innocent people in need is unforgivable. No wonder the Rosans are willing to risk war against you. And if they did, and if I were able, I would gladly fight in their ranks."

One of the counselors leaped forward in his seat. "Insolent witch!"

Donyon held up a hand to silence him. The man looked outraged, but Gailea kept her fierce gaze locked on Donyon.

"I received word yesterday about the plague," Donyon said quietly. "I suspected we might somehow get blamed for it. But for Rosa to threaten war, as my spies inform me, is absurd."

"They're willing to do whatever is necessary to protect their kingdom," Chamblin said. "Even risk your walls of fire. Granted, the Eagle is back, so that proved the easier part of our quest."

"Yes, and how did you convince the Rosans to give you *The Eagle's Ayre*? Or are you simply very clever thieves? You stole the song, and those few Rosan guards outside are your captives?"

Lorelei sighed obvious frustration. "This is a matter of the Octavial Guardians. One that you are now an integral part of, whether you wish it or not."

Gailea nodded grimly. "And if you don't care that the Rosans are dying and willing to wage war for the cure, perhaps it may interest you to know they are accusing an innocent Adelaran, one of your own, of creating the plague."

Donyon studied her a while longer. The haunted look passed across his face once more.

"It's still no concern of mine," he said. "And I cannot be a Guardian. My place is here, defending my kingdom, especially if I am to be laid siege by the Rosans."

"Why must it be that way?" Chamblin's voice pleaded, humble but exasperrated. "The Guardianship is a larger matter and certainly one we may discuss further. But the cure—why not just hand over the berries and be done with it?"

"Because he is still just as selfish," Gailea snapped. She saw the sharp side-glare from Lorelei and heard Chamblin's muttered warning but ignored them both. "He has known the horrors of the Dark Flame. He was one of few to survive it. Yet still, he would not help others overcome this wretched disease. Just as he would shirk duty as a Guardian and let Moragon consume the world."

"Peculiar, isn't it, Your Majesty?" one of the advisors said. "That Rosa would know such intimate parts of your history?"

"I'd call 'suspicious' a more fitting word." Celegrave cast a warning look at his king. "Perhaps they truly are Rosan spies."

Gailea slammed both hands on the table, her gaze fixated on Donyon. "Rosa knows nothing. Just as *you* know nothing. Only I know—thanks to my late mother's narratives."

The counselors muttered among themselves again but this time, Donyon didn't bother to silence them. He focused solely on Gailea. He leaned forward across the table, peering as if trying to decipher some puzzle.

"And who, pray tell...?"

He hesitated. Gailea knew his question, but he seemed too terrified to ask it—or to hear its answer.

"Princess Gillian," she said boldly. "Daughter of the late King Weston. I am her daughter, Gailea, true heir by blood to the Adelaran throne."

The counselors' voices rose with loud curses and insults.

"An outrageous affront!" one of them cried. "She's an imposter!"

"No." The king cut through their protests, gazing now with full recognition at Gailea. "She is who she claims. I can see it."

"It took you long enough," Gailea said, her eyes boring right into his as she directed her every bitter word directly at his heart and soul. "Then again, I'm not surprised. You were always too focused on yourself to see what was happening right in front of you. That's why my mother was able to escape, hardly before you even knew she loved another. And that's why you don't care one whit for dying Rosan children. After all, you sent your soldiers to murder my own children for whatever twisted profit you had in mind. So, believe me when I say I care nothing for you, or for Adelar's fate. Let the Rosans attack. Let them raze it to the ground. Except that I would not see more innocents die, at your hands or anyone else's."

Donyon continued to stare at Gailea, his face drained of all color.

Gailea watched him, her anger joined by pride and self-assurance. At last, she stood in Adelar's courts with power. At last, she had a voice. Donyon was breaking visibly right before her eyes.

"I do not know why you accuse me of wishing harm upon your children. I deny this, absolutely. I owe you everything, Gailea, daughter of Gillian. You gave me this, your kingdom, rightfully yours by blood. Your mother… I owe her much as well. Your mother only ever wanted peace between our kingdom and Rosa—a wish I have sorely ignored." His words were now the mere whispers of a ghost. "I will grant your request. I will grant the cure."

Gailea stood silenced, not so much by Donyon's sudden submission and willingness to grant the cure, but by his outrageous insistence that he had nothing to do with the attack on her and her children, where she had been forced to leave them crying and traumatized, without chance of a real goodbye, and where so many Sprites needlessly gave their lives.

"Wait, Your Majesty," Chamblin said, and Gailea glared at him, hoping he wasn't about to unravel all her hard work. "There is one matter more. As the Rosans blame you for the poisoning, one stipulation they gave was that, in order to believe you're in earnest and avoid war, that you bring the cure yourself. In person."

"Madness!" Lord Celegrave shouted. "Would you have us send our king straight to the slaughter?"

"Why must the king go?" another counselor asked. "Even if Rosa blames His Majesty, if we simply send along the berries, what does Rosa stand to lose? If they wage war on us then, it would be pointless!"

Chamblin swept his glance across the table, in each

advisor's direction. "My good lords, if I may, having traveled much and knowing a thing or two of diplomacy, I understand that it's an absurd notion to make a king travel to an enemy kingdom threatening war. But I've seen such ridiculous proposals followed and carried out peacefully. The Rosans are frightened. They need to see with their own eyes that Adelar is sincere."

Donyon sat a little straighter but stiffer in his chair, his frown filled with uncertainty. "I would be willing to go. But as Lord Brewer points out, the Rosans only need the berries. That alone should prove my word. Placing my life in such reckless danger, in times like these...."

Gailea lost her little remaining patience. "Yours is not the only life in danger. Remember that we did not just come for a cure. Moragon grows in power with every moment we waste."

"If this is about the Guardians yet again...." Donyon sighed and waved the matter aside. "I know the dangers. Battles are breaking out everywhere. I can better protect my kingdom by staying here, where I belong, and—"

"Don't play the fool with me, Donyon."

The Council gasped; even Donyon sat looking stunned that Gailea would address him with such contempt. She continued mercilessly, "You can't hide here forever, and I think you know this. Cowardice disguised as duty shouldn't stop you from hearing the truth. Moragon has been enslaving the minds of countless innocents by combining his mental magic with the songs of music mages. He's building an army of mindless slaves. Moragon *will* come for you."

Stark silence doused the room. Neither the king nor his noblemen seemed able to form a response. Gailea's disgust roiled. It shouldn't require such arguing to make them consider the danger they were in.

At last, Donyon found his voice, but any emotion he

felt was well hidden. "The day grows late. I am weary, and I would not make a final decision too hastily. You may dine here, stay for the evening. Even the Rosans will be given rooms, though they will certainly be watched carefully—"

The doors burst open behind them, and a guard stumbled in.

"Your Majesty," he blurted, "another intruder."

CHAPTER 34

DISSONANCE

Donyon shoved back his chair and jumped to his feet, glaring at the solider in alarm. His advisors rose from their seats beside him.

"Who? And how did he possibly surpass the barriers?"

"She washed up on our shores, sire. A young girl. We can't fathom how she might have gotten past the barriers."

Bewildered, Donyon motioned to a band of guards who entered, circling the accused intruder. Between their tight-knit ranks, Gailea could catch glimpses of blue and hardly knew who to be more enraged at—the Adelarans for treating the girl as if she were some dangerous sorcerer, Ashden for not keeping a close enough watch on her, or the girl herself who ought to have known better.

Iolana cried out, "*Nerine!*"

"She is one of your own?" Donyon demanded.

Chamblin looked astonished. "Not a Guardian, Your Majesty, but a close companion traveling with us. We left her back in Rosa."

Lord Celegrave lifted his chin proudly. "If she came directly from Rosa, she too may be a spy. This may serve to prove that this entire event has been a trap after all."

"Your Majesty."

Everyone turned to Iolana. Her eyes shone with terror, and Mikanah muttered something tensely in her direction, but she lifted her chin and continued, "May I say something in defense of my friend? She is a Nymph, very skilled in water magic, but no danger or threat. She is the purest, most honest soul I have ever known."

Donyon studied Iolana carefully. His gaze drifted to Nerine, who stood completely still, eyes wide with alarm, and motioned at the guards. They parted without delay, and Nerine stumbled forward, flying into Gailea's arms.

Gailea held her briefly, but her nerves were too on edge for her to grant much comfort. She grabbed Nerine by the arms, pushed her away, and shook her. "What made you do such a thing? Had you any idea of the danger? That the Adelarans might have killed you on sight?"

"I'm sorry." Nerine shivered as tears spilled onto her cheeks. "But I didn't want to be left behind again. There was nothing for me to do in Rosa. I thought I could be of more help here."

Gailea breathed deeply, fighting against her irritation. Chamblin placed a hand on her arm, and she released her grip on Nerine.

Iolana drew her friend next to her. "I don't know how you did it. But I think it was fiercely brave."

"I have to agree with your protégé," Chamblin said to Gailea. "We underestimated Nerine. She's become used to it and took advantage of it, clever girl."

Gailea glared up at him. "You're as mad as she is. This might have placed us all in danger again."

"Indeed, it might have," Donyon said, and they turned their attention back to him. "But I do believe this young woman." He gestured to Iolana briefly. "The water Nymph has an unguarded manner ill suited for a spy. Still, no one has ever passed through the barriers before, Nerine—as the Guardians have not introduced themselves, I know none of your names but hers," he added dryly before sighing with heavy tiredness. "And I must now ask how she was capable of accomplishing such a feat."

Iolana held Nerine's hand, but Nerine pulled gently away and stepped forward, steadily meeting the king's gaze. She spoke in a calm, clear tone, "Your Majesty. I've been practicing my coalesce skills. I turned into my liquid form." She held out her arms, transforming them to pure water, watching the amusement passing over the king's face before solidifying them once more. "I became one with the waves and dove down beneath the water until I reached the bottom of the barriers' magic. I swam so far that at first, I feared there was no end to the barriers at all. But at last, I could feel where their magic stopped, and the rest of the ocean continued. Then I merely swam beneath the barriers and emerged on the other side. I'm sorry for causing any trouble."

"You've caused no greater trouble than your friends here." Donyon's lips drew thinly into a sardonic smile. "You certainly caused quite a stir, but I believe there to be no true danger from your actions."

"No, I should think not," Mikanah said. Irritation seemed to fuel him, making him find his voice at last. "If anything, the girl here has done you a favor by showing you the vulnerability of your kingdom after all. If *she* can get inside, others can too."

Donyon's body tensed at this declaration. "In all the countless years that Adelar and Rosa alike have utilized such barriers, there is no record of them having ever been breached. I will have my fire and water mages re-examine their security, ascertain that we have not missed any steps in their recent reconstruction. The one solace I can grant myself is that at least water Nymphs themselves are not a great threat. They are peaceful beings. Nerine here is a perfect example of their nature. They have never once, as a people, sought aggression against any other race or kingdom."

Gailea fumed with frustration. "The desire or nature of water Nymphs is of little concern to Moragon! You truly don't understand, do you? Moragon can control entire armies of people with his mind. Lorelei, Iolana, Mikanah—" She motioned to them. "—we've all seen it. He can bewitch people and make them do things they'd never dream of doing. If Moragon suddenly discovered that he could use water Nymphs to swim beneath the barriers, they would become instantly worthless."

Donyon remained silent for a while, studying Gailea intently.

At last, he said, "There will be more talk later of the dangers of Moragon and what is to be done with him. But I refuse further talk until I have had proper time to rest and think. You would all do best to do the same. My guards will escort you to your chambers. We will meet again come tomorrow."

Their chambers boasted a spacious solar room with two fireplaces on either end, both ablaze. One wall was taken up almost entirely by three large rectangular windows, their glass covered in a diamond lattice pattern and separated by separated by vertical oak mullions. Sky blue curtains flanked the windows. A settee with two armchairs and a small oak table with wooden chairs nestled near one of the fireplaces, while a larger oak table with chairs rested near the opposite fireplace. A soft rug depicting horses galloping across a flowery field ran the length of the room, woven from soft blues, purples, whites, and greens. Tapestries with similar calming colors and scenes hung along the inside wall. Even the oak panels framing the fireplaces and the large oak overmantels above them depicted elegantly carved horses, flowers, and fields. Aside from the sunlight gleaming through the large windows, candles gleamed from three small, iron chandeliers overhead, brightening the place even further.

Despite Donyon's decorative tastes being lighter than Moragon's harsh black, red, and white décor, Gailea couldn't stop her spirit from feeling like it wanted to crawl right from her body and flee as far and fast from the castle as it could. Even the windows that made the room so open and airy felt restrictive, reminding her of the ones she'd shattered the first time she defeated Moragon. That memory, while victorious, could hardly be deemed happy, especially considering that just moments before, Moragon had tried to rape her with intent of gaining complete mastery over her musical gifts.

Everyone gravitated toward the larger fireplace with the settee and comfortable chairs. On the table rested several books, a quill and ink with a few pieces of parchment, and a basket of dried fruits and nuts for refreshment. Chamblin played a soothing tune he'd learned from the friend who'd gifted him the pipa, while Iolana suggested that they practice some of their song-spells, both to distract their minds from the day's tension and to not forget what they had already learned. Mikanah, Lorelei, and Nerine readily agreed, while Lorelei promised to teach them a couple new tunes as well.

Gailea wandered over to the table. She took a seat and pretended to involve herself in one of the books.

She was glad everyone could enjoy a moment's peace, but too many anxious thoughts whirled in her mind for her to relax with them.

Chamblin came to sit beside her, still strumming his calming melodies. "Care to share what's a matter of such displeasure at present?"

Gailea propped her elbow on the table, resting her chin in her palm with a deep sigh as she glanced across the others. "I'm still upset about Nerine. Mostly over what could've happened to her."

"Begging your pardon, Gailea, but just because I'm going blind doesn't mean I'm growing equally dim-witted."

She frowned up at him, but before she could retort, he spoke again with a playful grin, "I can still feel it, you know. Any time you glare at me, that is. I might not be able to see it properly, but I can still tell."

Gailea hoped he couldn't see her hastily changed expression, the blush assailing her cheeks.

"This is about more than Nerine," Chamblin continued gently. "I know you're impressed with her, same as I. But...well, it's this place. You're terrified because she chose to come *here*. You're terrified because *you're* here, and—"

A knock sounded on the door. A guard entered and announced, "His Majesty, King Donyon."

Gailea and Chamblin rose to their feet, and the others started to stand too, but Donyon waved his hand and said, "Do not rise for me. I wish only to speak with the Lady Gailea. If I could have a word with you in private?"

Gailea clenched her fists, too overwhelmed to handle any further confrontation. "Anything you have to say to me may be done so in the presence of the other Guardians. We stand together as one harmony."

Donyon narrowed his gaze, seeming to understand her jab at his reluctance to join them as a Guardian.

Nodding toward an unused corner of the room beside the smaller fireplace, he said, "Might we talk over there then? Might you afford me some small semblance of privacy? This is not a Guardian matter."

Gailea stared hard at him. "I owe you nothing. No respect, no honor. But I will grant you this wish for privacy. I imagine we both have difficult things to say to one another, after all these years."

She joined him at the other fireplace. They each drew one of the oak chairs from the larger table and sat facing one another. Silence drowned them, save for Gailea's thoughts which seemed to scream in a mindless jumble. Briefly, her gaze wandered to the horses galloping across the oak overmantel and surrounding tapestries. She wished she could embody such a free spirit and fly from Castle Adel, never to return.

Then her thoughts turned to Tytonn, faithful horsemaster and friend, and sadness made her tear away, resting her gaze once more on Donyon. Sadness merged with the fury still burning inside her toward him. And yet, the hard-to-define, almost tender way in which he watched her baffled her, made her question that fury.

"Gailea," Donyon said quietly. "I hardly know where to begin. When I first saw you in the courtyard, it was like seeing a ghost, or like perhaps I had become a ghost. Gillian might have been standing before me, through a glass or some other veil. She was there again, but unattainable, untouchable."

"I was surprised you didn't use your mental powers to extract the truth from me. My mother wrote of your 'gifts'."

His gaze shifted to the fire, mirrored in his dark

brown eyes. "I once used my mental gifts to force my way into the minds of others, but that was long ago. I'd never infiltrate your thoughts—or anyone's—without their express permission. I ceased using such pervasive magic many years ago."

"But you used it to know for certain that my mother loved my father."

Donyon nodded. "Yes. I admit that's true. One of many things I'm not proud of. I should have pretended to see nothing. I should have let her go when she first willed it. She might yet be alive."

"No, she likely would've met the same fate." Gailea felt the tightness in her throat as she defended him, in whatever small way. What he had done to her and her family was inexcusable. Even still, she couldn't accuse him falsely where accusation wasn't due. "I can blame much of her unhappiness on you. But she would have died anyway, or at least risked death, in the name of seeking peace between Rosa and Adelar."

"And how I have dishonored that wish, ever since." Again, he sought answers in the flames, perhaps, Gailea thought, to avoid looking at her. "Hiding, locking myself away, growing stagnant...."

"Are you being sincere now? Or simply telling me what I want to hear?"

"You likely think I am ignorant of my faults. But I'm no stranger to them. They haunt me closely. I have trapped myself here, inside my own mind, with my guilt and regrets constantly poisoning me."

"And plagued with the guilt of trying to murder me and my children?"

Donyon's eyes narrowed. "That accusation I still do not understand. Whatever I may have done to cause your mother pain, I never sought to lay a single hand against you or your children."

"Then explain *this*." Gailea grasped the side of her chair and leaned forward, the grip necessary to keep herself from lashing out. "Explain a young mother fleeing with her children and friends through the woods. Imagine me, besieged by Sprites bearing *your* crest, attacking my friends, killing them. And then imagine me being forced to hand over my children to one of those friends so they could flee and be brought to safety!"

Disgust filled Donyon's face. "I swear to you I have no knowledge of these horrors of which you speak. I did hire those Sprites—hired many—to search for you. They were to bring you and your children safely to me. I intended to offer you refuge, for what you had done for my father and me. I had no knowledge that it turned out so hideously. Eventually, I guessed that perhaps you had already found somewhere to hide with your family where you didn't wish to be found. I stopped looking, hoping it was in peace that I left you."

He looked at her again, and Gailea hardly knew what to think or say. All these years, she had hated him, thinking that he had hated her and everything she loved. Now, her biggest reason for hating him was in question, and even if he spoke the truth, which she yet doubted, she wasn't certain she was ready to except this or the responsibility to stop hating him.

"I can't be sure yet if you speak truth, or if you feed me deceptions to make me pity you. But whether or not you intended to take my children's lives, the fact remains that you still managed to separate me from them."

"I assure you, knowing that I caused such pain will haunt me, just as your mother's pain haunts me every day. Especially seeing that pain so vividly, gazing it straight in the eye. I see her—I see her in you. You're so like her, Gailea, and not just in your appearance. In your strength, your speech."

"I saw the way you looked upon the Eagle earlier. You resent the creature. You blame it for taking my mother away from you."

Donyon shook his head. "No. No, that's not it. Seeing the Eagle...it too was like seeing a ghost of sorts. If anything, I was first shocked with horror and then filled with a sort of sad yearning. A bittersweet taste of a memory if you will. I loved your mother."

"*No.*" Gailea inhaled a trembling breath and fought her tears, determined to show no weakness to this man who was, in his own way, a monster just like other rulers she had known. "No, you didn't love her. Maybe you thought you did. But you wanted to possess her, to own her. You would stop at nothing to make that happen. That is not love!"

"My love for your mother was born of a desperate situation. I admit it was tainted. But it was sincere, as are my affections for you and your children."

He reached for her hand, but Gailea sprang up. The chair clattered back. The Guardians' music ended on an abrupt note. Gailea glared at Donyon, his face blurred by her tears. She wiped them roughly away and stood shivering with rage. "No. I don't care what excuses you give. It's *your* fault my children and I are divided. It was *you* who tormented my mother for years. Her own writing is clear proof of this!"

"Her writing?" Donyon's face turned gray. "You found some sort of—"

"Yes. Pages of her diary. My sister gave them to me— the same sister Rosa now holds captive, accusing her of being the one behind their plague!"

"Your sister?"

"My mother's very words declare your selfish and bitter heart. I wish I had known years ago what I know now, that I was a fool to hand the kingdom to you. I thought it would be safer in your hands. But you're just as corrupt as Moragon and Alistor and Crispin—"

Her voice broke at Crispin's name. She took a shuddering breath, near collapse, but she held firm and stared at Donyon, needing him to see her hate, along with every single hurt that he had caused her.

Chamblin was suddenly at her side, placing his hand on her shoulder. "Perhaps, with all due respect, Your Majesty, it is best you leave us to rest for a time."

"Yes." Donyon rose to his feet. "Yes, of course."

He stared at Gailea, mortified. His lips parted as if to say more, but then he turned, bid them good day, and left the room.

Once he was gone, Gailea spun and allowed herself to fall against Chamblin, her tears flowing freely.

"Gailea?"

Gailea couldn't answer Iolana. She couldn't answer any of them. All she could feel was the agony of this place pressing her from all sides.

"Chamblin, I don't want to stay here," she cried. "I don't want to be here...."

"I know, I know. Come, let's get some air."

Cradling her against him, he led her out into the hall and exchanged a few words with the guards. They led Chamblin and Gailea to a small alcove with a velvet windowseat. Gailea readily unlatched the windows, swinging them open wide. Crisp, cool air washed over her, filled her lungs, and helped dry some of the tears drawn from so much resentment and anguish.

She cried her last and then, still letting Chamblin hold her, her sobs turned to shaky laughter. "Well, that's it then. I'm sure you've always thought me a bit crazy. And now you've seen it."

"You're not," Chamblin said with surprising sternness. "I'll not let you talk or think that way. This place, it's one giant, awful memory for you. It makes you see and remember things you'd hoped never to face ever again."

"I can never forget. Now that I'm here, it's brought everything rushing back to me with the same force of the ocean rushing over us when the Eagle first dived beneath the waves." She fought back another rush of tears.

"I know you like to seem stalwart as an oak tree, and you are. But showing emotions doesn't weaken you or make you crazy. I'd be more concerned if you showed none at all."

"I hardly know what to think," Gailea whispered. "I've thought all this time that he wanted me and my children dead. Now he denies it. But I don't know whether to believe him. He could easily be lying to gain my sympathy."

"Even if what he says is true, there's no need to jump right into trusting him."

Gailea nodded, and her head brushed against Chamblin's chest. It was sturdy, and she could feel his warmth beneath the silk tunic that was soft against her cheek. He held Gailea a little tighter, and Gailea let him. For once in a long while, a man's touch made her feel more solid, cohesive. Instead of feeding upon her strength, he added his to hers.

"Gailea, if I may ask a delicate question, has there ever been anyone else? Have you ever loved anyone besides Ragnar, someone more worthy? I think you deserve to if you haven't."

Gailea released an exhausted sigh. "Not loved, no, but cared for…yes, there was someone else, but he is lost to me now. But in a happy way. As long as he's taking good care of my sister."

"I'm sure he is," Chamblin said, rocking Gailea gently. "Ashden is indeed a worthy man. I'm sure he's doing everything in his power to keep her safe and comfortable. I pray you someday find a man who can provide the same for you."

Gailea silently hoped the same. She didn't know how it could be so, for as long as Crispin lived, she was bound to him, unable to give herself fully to another. At least she could savor the comfort of such a dear friend as Chamblin. For now, such sweet, simple gifts were enough.

~*~*~

Gailea opened her eyes, stretched, and moaned. Darkness still enclosed her. She turned over, hugged the person lying next to her....

And sat up with a start. No, this wasn't right. She had fallen asleep by herself, in one of the bedchambers granted by Donyon. Chamblin had carried her and laid her in the bed. Who had snuck in here with her? Perhaps Iolana or Nerine?

The person woke and forced her down on the bed. Now the moon shone pale through the window, and she saw Crispin's face looming over hers, his purple eyes violent with madness and sheer abhorrence. When she screamed, his fingertips clawed deep into her arms as he hissed, "What's the matter, love? Ashamed to lie next to your husband? Still dreaming of whoring around with the glorified stable boy? His days are numbered as are the days of that little bastard you continue to parade around as my own. It embarrasses me, sickens me."

Gailea cried for help and tried to wrench away. She sang out defensive spells but could summon none of her magic.

"Shut up, you insolent wench!"

He slapped her hard across the face, and a bright white light stunned her.

When it faded, she stood in a familiar hall, shrouded in shadows, and another man stood before her. A man with pale skin, flowing ivory robes, and a long braid of green hair plated intricately down his back. Chevalier, the sorcerer. As he spoke, Gailea wondered if she had traveled back in time.

"The Dusk's source is hidden between the eyes that gaze across the sea."

She didn't want to speak to him but found herself asking, "What does that mean?"

"It's a riddle," Chevalier said. "It's ancient history, ancient lore. But it's more than that. I assure you it's all based in truth. And should we ever escape our bonds, we must make certain that Moragon never lays so much as a finger on it."

"Then be done with your riddles and tell me where it's hidden."

Chevalier scoffed. "Unfortunately, your mind is not as well guarded as you think it is. If I tell you outright, then the secret may be exposed to Moragon, and then what value would my plan have? I can, however, tell you of another treasure—"

Gailea woke with a sharp gasp. For a while, she lay breathing hard, struggling to fill her lungs.

When she did, she realized that she wasn't lying down. She stood in a hallway, the same in which Chevalier had shared his revelation of the Prism, where he had hidden it and how he'd hoped it would someday lead to Crispin's downfall. But what of their exchange regarding the Dusk? That was just a dream; it had never happened. Did it hold any significance, or had her mind conjured it because of this place?

At any rate, she had been sleepwalking—just as Darice had.

Frightened, Gailea fled back to her room and bolted the door shut.

She didn't know what any of it meant. She didn't know if her fears alone had invoked such realistic dreams, or if they'd been triggered by some darker force. She could only pray that Donyon would make up his mind soon so they could flee this cursed land.

CHAPTER 35

BETWEEN THE WAVES

Gailea stood by the window of her antechamber, holding the baby, and laughing at something Tytonn, her friend, the royal horse master, had just said. Darice stood nearby, smiling at the scene. Tytonn grinned at Gailea and reached out to cradle the baby's head.

Crispin flew at them. Rings of fire burst from his fingertips, slinging around Tytonn's wrists and ankles, and binding them with blazing fetters. Tytonn cried out as his skin reddened, blistered and charred.

Helpless, Gailea clutched her son closer. "Crispin, stop! What are you doing?"

"Quiet, wife, or I will throw your little bastard right out that window."

Gathering what mental strength she could, Gailea released a high-pitched trill that sent Crispin spiraling across the room and landing hard against the far wall.

Gailea bolted out the door and burst down the hall.

But someone grabbed her arm. She flung a stunning spell at them, but they easily deflected and held on fast. It was Chevalier. She cast a frantic glance at the door, fearing what Crispin *would do if he saw this. Would he think she'd betrayed him by lying with the sorcerer too?*

Then she realized her arms were empty.

"Release me!" she screamed. "Crispin has gone mad. I must find my son!"

"The king has been mad a long time. You only blinded yourself from seeing it! If you want to stop him, stop Moragon, then find my creation!"

Gailea strained against his grip. "Your crea—I don't understand—"

"Where is my Dusk? I sent you to find it ages ago!" Gailea still tried to wrench away, sobbing, but he drew her nearer, his green eyes lit with desperation, giving them a ghostly glow. "No! You will answer me. Didn't I give you a gift to protect your children? You owe me this favor. You must do this for me!"

"To think I once pitied you. But you were always Moragon's monster, a beast always on Moragon's leash. I don't know why you are here! You can't be real. Why can't I escape you?"

"Sing the right tune, and you shall."

Silence fell. Then she heard it: a thin whisper of a melody floating toward her, distant and indistinguishable—

Gailea woke with a sharp inhale, a drowning woman finally breaking the surface. A few shafts of moonlight revealed that she stood in an old study. Thick dust and cobwebs shrouded the room's few furnishings. A long, narrow table with torn scraps of parchment. An overturned wooden stool, its velvet seat torn and weeping its feathers. A huge bookcase, empty and now without purpose. The air was heavy and smelled musty. Above it all was a mixture of scents Gailea couldn't quite identify. Herbs, dried leaves, long-dead flowers, and something bitter and medicinal that made her wince. But it was familiar.

Her gaze strayed to the room's stained-glass windows, and she understood at once. This was Chevalier's old study chamber. That colorful window over there was where he'd kept the Prism for her.

Between the dream and the comingled scents, the past was pulling, urging Gailea ever closer. She crept from the room and hurried back to her chambers, all the while wondering: why did Chevalier keep plaguing her dreams? Did he still live and send these visions to help her? Why would he be so keen on her finding the Dusk, the most horrific magic he had invented, that held the power to consume one's mind and poison one's body with just a few drops? Did he know something about Moragon she did not? Was he helping her...or was he now doing yet another evil master's bidding?

She had seen what devastation the Dusk could do. The tiniest bit had killed Queen Marlis, and in the most horrendous way. She had no desire to find it, but the possibility of Moragon regaining control over this deadly poison was unthinkable.

Still, she could not fathom how to find out if it even still existed.

When Gailea reentered her bedchamber, she hoped the quiet might ease her mind back into a dreamless sleep, but through the remainder of the night, she found little rest. She spent most of it thinking too much and praying.

As dawn began to fill the sky with its hopeful golds and oranges, she strayed to her window and gazed down into the courtyard below where someone on horseback rode up to one of the guards, passing what was likely a message to them. The sight of the horse tugged nostalgic strings inside Gailea's heart. She dressed in the clothes provided her, a long, blue-green velvet sleeveless tunic over a long-sleeved, white linen tunic, a gold satin corset embroidered with flowers and leaves, and fresh hose and boots. Throwing the warm, blue-green cloak over her shoulders, she stole quietly from the room.

Approaching two guards patrolling the adjoining hall, she caught their curious gazes and announced, "I'd like to take a walk outside, down to the stables. Would His Majesty have any opposition to that?"

"No, Lady Gailea," one guard replied, while they both gave a respectful bow of the head. "He has permitted you to traverse the castle and grounds at will."

"Thank you." Gailea curtsied at them before hurrying down the hall. She made her way toward the path they had taken last night, down the stairs and past several quarters toward the kitchen, by no means wishing to stray anywhere near the king's chambers. The sad and frightening memories from that wing of the castle outweighed the joyous, enough that she had no desire to reenter their shadow or grant her mind more fodder for its strange dreams.

Delving down into the servants' quarters, she passed several women and girls hurrying to the kitchens, or away from them to deliver firewood. Some ignored her in passing, while a few dared to glance upon her in surprise, and even moreso when she granted them gentle smiles or polite nods. Being so near the kitchen invoked a different sort of pain, but one that was more manageable. Growing up a scullery maid had been harsh in many ways, but at least she'd always had the comfort of her sister nearby. And that was before anyone knew about her magic, when her music was her own and she could find true enjoyment in it, ignorant to how much heartache its gift would cause her a few years hence.

At last, she emerged from one of the ordinary, wooden doors into the outer courtyard. Staying near the the gray stone wall ringing the courtyard, she made the long trek to the stables. Out of everything she had witnessed of the castle thus far, they were the one thing she was glad to find had not changed.

Slowing her pace, she entered the stables, running her hands along the weathered wood. Horses ate hay or watched her from their stalls while a young man shoveled straw into an empty stall. As Gailea approached, he glanced up and paused in his work, brows raising in curiosity.

"Good morning, milady. Is there something I can help you with?"

"No..." Gailea smiled at him, softly. While he didn't otherwise resemble Tytonn, there was a gentleness in his face that reminded her of him. "I just came to take some fresh air and visit the horses. I used to come here frequently, many years ago. They comforted me, and I would do my best to return the favor."

She stopped before one of the stalls, gazing at a gray mare who reminded her of her horse, Silver, who had well served her in her escape from Adelar. Singing a soothing melody, Gailea carefully approached the horse and ever so gently stroked her velvety nose.

"She seems to like your song, milady, as do I. You've a gift with horses."

Gailea nodded, unable to reply otherwise. The familiar sensation of petting a horse and singing to it to gain its trust, coupled with the boy's words, toppled the protective walls that had been fighting to shield her heart since before they'd arrived. A deep, yearning sorrow overtook her, and she wept silently, all the while singing to the horse and stroking it.

The boy returned to his work, sometimes humming along to Gailea's melody. A few other workers popped in and out, delivering fresh straw or hay, checking on the horses, chatting to them.

"Lady Gailea, are you all right?"

Gailea jumped from her reverie, wiping tears away

and withdrawing as much of her calm composure as she could before turning to look up at Donyon.

"How did you find me?"

"The servants. I went to your chambers to ask if we might take a walk and talk together, but the servants alerted me that you'd already beat me to the walk. Forgive me if I've intruded upon some private moment. I was only hoping to have a moment to talk in private before we depart today, if I may."

Gailea studied him warily. "Depart?"

Donyon motioned beyond the stables with a questioning look, and Gailea nodded.

As they circled the courtyard, Donyon continued, "I have told my Council I will be accompanying the Guardians back to Rosa. Many of them were not keen on the idea, but I reminded them of history. The brother and sister who built our two kingdoms once stood hand in hand, fighting enemies together, even once they'd moved across the waves to their own dominions. Perhaps it is time to consider some sort of resolution, a peace treaty perhaps. But more than that, above all, I would not deprive you of your family yet again. I *will* help you save your sister."

Gailea inhaled a shuddering breath. It had been a long night. She was still weary and shaken from her nightmares and their confusion. But this news was enough to restore some of her drive to press onward. Because of him, her sister would be spared. He was, in essence, risking his life for hers.

"Thank you," Gailea said quietly.

"You're welcome." A melancholy smile filled his face, and Gailea noticed the envelope he clutched, its edges brown and frayed with age. "It is possible that going to Rosa is one of the few noble things I've ever done. But if today should be a trap and I should die, and if Amiel should be generous enough to grant me entrance into the Forever Havens, I do not fear. Rather, I'm comforted by the idea. For the chance to see Gillian again, if I am allowed. To ask her forgiveness. And then, to be reunited with my family."

Gailea gasped. "Your family?" It had never occurred to her that Donyon might have a family. Monsters didn't deserve families. Much as she wanted to deny it, the bittersweet longing that filled his face now, along with his coming to Rosa for Darice, made him feel more human.

"Yes," he said. "During my exile from Adelar, before you helped me take the throne, I had a family. A wife, a child, happiness, though perhaps I didn't deserve any of those. But we were set upon by thieves, and while I used every spell I could think of, my magic then was young and untamed. The thieves overpowered me, and I was left for dead on the side of the road. When next I opened my eyes, I discovered my wife and boy lying dead at my side."

"I'm sorry," Gailea whispered. "Very sorry for your loss." The words rang cold in her ears, as stilted as if rehearsed. She hardly knew what to feel toward this man. An urge for compassion warred with her lingering grief, the roots of which stretched deep.

"I will leave you to get ready," Donyon said, his sad tone turning solemn. "We'll depart as soon as possible. But there is something I wanted you to have, especially if I should not return to Adelar."

Pausing their walk, he extended the envelope toward her.

"What is it?" she asked, taking it into her hands. Carefully opening the fragile parchment sealed with wax reflecting the Adelaran signet, she removed the folded parchment and opened it just enough to glimpse the handwriting.

Her mouth parted slightly, and she took a deep inward breath before she found her voice. "This is my mother's."

"Yes. These are some of her last words. I have kept them all these years. But when you mentioned the diary pages, I thought it more fitting that you keep them now with the rest."

Gailea folded the envelope back around the pages. "Thank you. These mean the world to me."

"I am glad. Glad I can give you this small offering of peace between us. I know you will not like me or trust me, now or possibly ever. But if we must travel together, let us do our best to be allies. For the sake of Rosa and Adelar. For the sake of your sister."

Gailea nodded slowly. His words rang true. Even such a gracious gift did not wash away her distrust or the years of anger she'd cultivated toward him. But it made her more able to accept him as the final member of their Guardianship.

Donyon gave a small smile. "Well then. I take my leave. I shall see you later, as soon as everyone is ready." He departed across the courtyard toward the castle.

For a time, Gailea stood holding the envelope. She stared down at it, gripping it as Donyon had done. This was likely the last piece of Gillian he'd possessed. What a great sacrifice for him to hand it over. She yearned to read it, to glimpse just a little more of her mother's past. But her mother deserved her full attention, and she could not grant that now.

Instead, clutching it to her breast, she hurried back toward the castle to rouse the others, eager to leave the nightmare of Adelar behind once and for all.

~*~*~

Along with everyone they had transported to Adelar, Donyon and six of his personal guard joined them on the trip back to Rosa. As before, Dei managed to accommodate these extra bodies with ease, and the flight seemed to flash by like lightning. Soon the Rosa Isle crept along the horizon, grew into a thick green line, and then took shape into an island covered in coniferous forests, with Rosa's great wall peeking over the trees.

Donyon stared at Rosa with a solemn frown. He had boldly refused his Council's pleas to bring even more guards, hoping that the Rosans took this as a sign that they could trust his innocence and desire for friendship. Now he looked as though he doubted his decision.

"Are you afraid?" Gailea asked.

"Yes. I'd be a fool not to be. It's been an age since I set foot here, and then not on the friendliest of terms."

"I felt the same, returning to Adelar."

Donyon gave her a curious look. "I appreciate your empathy. Though I'm certain the fear for you was far greater."

They glided over the city walls. Guards shouted to one another from the walls and watchtowers, and horns announced their presence. As Dei winged them toward the castle and landed in the outer courtyard, Rosan guards marched toward them, surrounding the familiar figure of Delia's head advisor, Lord Rhys.

"Donyon, King of Rosa!" Rhys declared. "The queen orders you to come down at once, unaccompanied. You will be escorted into the castle separately."

Anxiety flared inside Gailea, along with an indignant anger. Donyon may not be a trusted ally yet, if ever, but he was a Guardian.

"Donyon is one of us now. As Guardians, we are sworn to protect one another. With all respect, Queen Delia already holds one of our own captive, my sister, whom she has threatened harm should we return without both cure and king—threats she made without any mention of a fair trial at that."

"I take my orders from the queen, milady." Rhys spoke the words quietly, looking remorseful as he felt forced to deliver them. "She has made herself abundantly clear on this matter."

"I will go." Donyon moved to the side as if to dismount, but Gailea's sharp words stopped him.

"No, you will not." She fixed her fierce stare on Lord Rhys. "Allow me to likewise make myself abundantly clear. We have brought the cure, as promised. We will deliver it together, or not at all. You can threaten my sister, but we both know that without this cure, many more innocents will die, a fate Her Majesty abhors, or she would not have sent us to Adelar in the first place. We could easily command the Eagle and he would wing us away. If you attack us, we can defend ourselves with our music. I'll say it again: we stay together, or the cure stays with us." Gailea kept her stare locked on the guard as evenly as she could, hoping he would accept her logic.

She breathed relief as Rhys looked defeated and said, "Very well. Grant us the cure, and we will escort you safely, if heavily guarded, to your quarters while waiting to see if the cure works as intended. If not, then we will likely be forced to take Donyon prisoner, or else fight you for him."

"Only in exchange for a fair trial." Chamblin leaned forward to speak around Gailea. "For both His Majesty Donyon and the Lady Darice."

Rhys nodded. "Be it done."

Everyone dismounted Dei's back, helping one another slide down. As the Adelaran guards touched solid ground, more Rosan guards marched forward with swords drawn, separating them from the rest of the party. Gailea opened her mouth to protest, but Rhys held up his hand in a sign of warning.

"You said that the Guardians stand together as one. Adelaran soldiers do not fall under that title. Her Majesty expressly forbid the presence of any Adelaran soldiers in her court."

Gailea swept a glance across Donyon and then the rest of the Guardians and Echelon. All looked weary and frustrated, but Donyon, several Echelon, and even Lorelei and Mikanah nodded.

"Very well," Gailea said.

"We will escort them to quarters outside the castle walls where they may rest as long as you are guests in Rosa."

"And what of their safety?" Chamblin asked. "I'm sure the Rosans beyond these walls think no more favorably of the Adelarans than those on this side."

"They will be granted sufficient protection from the Rosan guard." Rhys spoke the promise sincerely, but he shifted on his feet, and his hands clenched and unclenched. He grew impatient, or perhaps worried that his queen did. "Now, before I escort you, I must be certain of the cure."

That much seemed fair. Gailea nodded at Donyon who met Rhys' gaze as he slowly reached inside one of the large leather pockets secured on his belt. He drew out a leather bag, untied the string, and delicately lifted a few of the bright magenta berries into his hand.

Rhys gave a single nod, looking satisfied. "Come, follow me."

Donyon slipped the berries back inside the satchel. Together, the Guardians, Echelon, and Rosan guards followed Rhys inside a pair of red cedar doors set into the side of Castle Rosa. Once again, they delved inside plainer corridors, winding up a stair until they emerged into the finer golden grandeur and tiled floors of the castle's inner chambers.

Rhys led them inside the familiar withdrawing room with the long table, lamps and hovering white flames providing both light and warmth. Some of the guards dispersed at intervals around the room's perimeter, while others stayed right behind Rhys who once more addressed Gailea.

"I will now take the berries to our healers. Amiel willing, they will prove to be what you say they are, and then the cure will be mixed and distributed to those in need with all efficiency."

Donyon removed the leather sack, and Rhys took it gently. "Thank you. One of the ill is a child, a distant cousin of the queen. If the child is healed in time, Her Majesty will be eternally grateful to you—and to you all."

"What about my sister?" Gailea's voice broke, and she sang a soothing melody inside her mind as she focused on keeping her composure. They were so near and yet so far from seeing her sister released safely. Another song drifted ever so subtly to her. Chamblin, singing his own calming melody right behind her, allowing her to steady her voice and ask again, "How is Darice?"

"In good health. And Ashden keeps her in good spirits."

"May I see her?"

Rhys' face fell. "I'm afraid that is not possible. But rest assured she is in safe hands. Ashden won't let any of other prisoner bother her with so much as an unkind word. He's also been a great help in the prison quarters. He's earned my respect, and I'm not the only one, to be sure."

"Thank you. If you can, at least send my greetings to my sister. Let her know we are here safely with the cure."

Rhys bowed his head in a respectful nod. "This I can do, my lady. Now then, I must be off."

While Rhys departed, the Guardians sat at the long table, the Echelon gathered around them. Gailea gazed anxiously at the Rosans ringing the room. Their presence, the lack of windows. Gailea breathed deeply as she felt the walls steadily closing in, almost wishing instead for Adelar's airy room with the horse décor.

"Perhaps we should practice our music until he returns."

Iolana spoke the words in a small voice. She sat tall, looking resolute, but her face showed a plain weariness mingled with worry. Though it was yet early afternoon, she looked like she could lay her head on the table and sleep many hours.

"That's a good idea," Lorelei said, presenting her lyre. "Why don't we teach Donyon one of our soothing melodies?"

The king sat stiff in his chair, face drawn into a solemn frown. "I would appreciate that highly, though I've no instrument of my own."

"Use your voice, Your Majesty," Chamblin said. "As most of us do."

"Which one shall we do?" Lorelei asked Iolana.

"*Raya Nocturna*," she replied.

Lorelei strummed on her lyre, and Gailea and Chamblin chimed in with the repeating refrain:

"*Raya Nocturna:*
Shine your light
Into our night
And fill us with peace."

Chamblin glanced curiously in Gailea's direction, nodding toward the case slung across her side. Her nerves felt too on edge for her to explain why she sang instead of playing. Instead, she merely sang on, hoping that using her voice would provide a more intimate experience for her, make her feel more one with the music and allow its soothing to reach her more deeply.

While Gailea couldn't say she felt peaceful over the next few hours, she at least felt distracted enough to have some small semblance of calm. In between singing and teaching Donyon simple charms of defense, she prayed that the cure's development went well, for the people of Rosa, for the queen's cousin, and thus ultimately for her sister.

Finally, Rhys returned to announce Queen Delia's summons.

"It seems I've good news to report. The healers were able to use the berries to craft a successful cure."

"My sister is free to go then?"

"Of that, I'm not sure. I was only told to bring the Guardians at once."

Hope had started to rush inside Gailea's heart, but now dread rode up in fresh waves. If the cure took effect, there seemed no reason to hold Darice captive any longer. What if Queen Delia changed her mind or demanded some greater, impossible task to prove her innocence?

Inside the throne room, Rhys took his place beside the rest of the queen's counselors who gathered around her throne, speaking with her in hushed tones. More guards than usual ringed the dais and the walls. On one side of the dais stood Darice, with her hands bound, but with considerably fewer guards at her side. Gailea mused at the irony. Had she wished it, Darice's light magic was powerful enough to stun half the throne room. Ashden stood right behind Darice, massaging her shoulders. Both watched the queen intently.

The Guardians stopped at the foot of the dais. Echelon and Rosan guards formed several arcs behind them.

Gailea locked eyes with her sister. Shadows beneath Darice's eyes revealed that she had slept little, but she granted Gailea a shaky, hopeful smile.

Queen Delia beamed down at them. Her appearance was slightly more unkempt than usual, but glee shimmered in her eyes. "Welcome, Guardians. Early this morning, as I was tending to my little cousin, his fever faded. The boils on his skin have already disappeared into faint scars. I have you to thank for that—and you, King Donyon." She turned to him. "I'm eager to dissolve the tensions between our kingdoms once and for all—especially as a much greater war approaches our shores. You have proven your desire to establish trust between our kingdoms, and I believe the discussion of a treaty may be forthcoming. However..." Her gaze strayed to Darice. "There remains the mystery of how the plague entered our midst. There seems to yet be no explanation other than it entering through Darice here."

"Your Majesty." Ashden stepped beside Darice and gave a short bow. "If I may. I think in the time Darice has been kept here, both you and those in charge of her care can testify to her character. Perhaps the disease did enter through her. I cannot deny this possibility. But perhaps she was merely a pawn. I think we both know she would not bring purposeful harm to anyone."

"If I may add," Lorelei said, "Your Majesty, something along those lines. My mother was a healer, and she taught me that there are those who can carry a certain disease, sometimes for years, and be invulnerable to its effects, while passing it onto others."

Darice cleared her throat. "It is true that, when I was younger, I never seemed to get the disease myself, though I was around many who did."

Chamblin took a step forward and gave a respectful bow. "I would add to this theory, Your Majesty. I have done my fair share of traveling. In the Western Realm, they say that a foot that never takes a step is soft but weak, while the foot that travels hardens and grows strong. Perhaps being isolated inside your great walls has made you more vulnerable. This could have just as easily happened in reverse. An immune Rosan could've just as easily borne some deadly illness to the Adelarans."

The queen watched each of them closely, seeming to consider all their words. "Though it does not please me to think of my kingdom as weak or ignorant, as of late, I have had to make certain admissions. If we do not step outside ourselves, the world will simply cave in on us. But even if Darice were an innocent carrier, as you say, then why was she found in the garden on two occasions? Near the water, and more than that, soaked head to toe?"

"Darice was sleepwalking," Gailea said. "In my stay at Adelar, I too had nightmares. Twice, and on both occasions, I woke up in a completely different part of the castle."

"As have I."

Everyone looked at Donyon in surprise.

"I've been too full of pride to admit it before, terrified I was going mad. But I think it's some sort of sign. As evil closes in, as Moragon grows more powerful, I think it affects us all differently. My healers say some are more sensitive to evil auras than others. I've woken up in some odd places. I can only imagine the same must have happened for Darice here as well."

Delia studied Donyon for what seemed a long time. No judgment reflected in her gaze, but rather a humble sort of respect.

Then, looking to the council members on both her right and left, she said, "What say you? I believe the evidence pointing to Darice's possible guilt to be more and more dwindling, insufficient to declare her a harm and threat to the crown. Do my advisors offer any further argument or insight on this matter?"

The Council turned to one another, whispering, muttering, and shaking their heads. Gailea's heart sped, and Darice seemed to hold her breath, leaning forward on her tiptoes as if ready to leap in the air the moment the hopeful verdict was uttered.

At last, Rhys, closest to Delia's right said, "No, Your Majesty. We can offer no argument."

"We give the same answer," said a woman on Delia's left.

Delia nodded and faced Darice with a smile. "Then, Lady Darice, I declare you innocent. Forgive my haste to judge you. The Adelarans and Rosans have been enemies for a long age. But today I'm reminded this was not how it was meant to be, and perhaps it is time that age passed for good. Guards, release her."

A guard stepped forward, and within no time, Darice's chains fell away.

"Your Majesty," she said, stepping toward the dais, "you are fully forgiven. You were only protecting your own, as we all strive to do during these dark times."

She bowed, and the queen bowed her head in return. "As I will continue to do. I welcome you all back as guests of my castle. However, as long as you're here, I feel it's only right and fair for my people if I make certain you are sufficiently guarded, to prevent further incidents from occurring. Feel free to explore the castle grounds but know my guards will be watching you. And do not be alarmed either by the extra guards placed outside your rooms at night."

"From one monarch to another, I would not expect otherwise."

Delia's eyes flashed surprise as Donyon spoke, but

then she watched him steadily as he bowed low. "Thank you for so graciously hosting us, even myself. I will be honored to discuss a treaty with you as soon as it would suit you."

"Thank you, King Donyon."

The queen dismissed them, and a host of Rosan guards led them back their chambers. Once in the withdrawing room, Darice hugged Ashden and the girls close, before sweeping Gailea into a tight embrace.

"I told you we would set things straight," Gailea whispered into her ear.

"I knew you would. Thank you, sister."

"Well, what say you?" Chamblin cast a playful grin around the room. "What better way for musicians to celebrate a moment's victory and reprieve than with a bit of music?"

He began singing a silly song, its rhyming words filled with nonsense, perhaps meant for children. Gailea didn't have the heart to playfully scold him for the choice of song. Rather, she found its youthful joy refreshing, especially as she joined him with her flute and everyone else joined hands and set to dancing, skipping, and laughing around the table.

As she played, Gailea watched her sister with grateful tears, granting a silent prayer of thanks to Amiel that she had not lost yet another person dear to her heart.

CHAPTER 36

NOCTURNE

Once again, Adelaran walls taunted Gailea, seeming to close in with each passing second.

They had not tarried long in Rosa. Donyon had promised Delia they would remain in correspondence regarding war plans, as well as a peace treaty, but in the meantime, he expressed his unease at leaving his kingdom any longer than necessary. There was still the matter of persuading him to accept his Guardianship, a point he seemed less than eager to embrace. He said he needed another night to sleep on it and that they would discuss the matter in the morning.

Gailea couldn't fathom why he insisted on being so stubborn about such important issues, especially when they had defended him as a Guardian to Lord Rhys, and furthermore when he spoke as if protecting his kingdom were the most crucial task. Didn't he understand that joining the Guardians was the only chance he had of truly ensuring Adelar's safety?

Gailea lay back on the bed and closed her eyes to escape the insufferable walls. She had requested one of the vastest guest chambers, with many windows permitting much sunlight by day and now, by night, moonlight and starlight. She had hoped the open setting would set her at ease, but it didn't.

Her body was suddenly floating. She watched it float along blue and white currents, like foam and waves. Soft music surrounded her, creating the colors and light.

Eventually, she stood upright, and the blue hues faded away to reveal the castle's large, familiar gallery. Moragon walked beside her, and the music lingered, however faintly, in the back of her mind. It sounded like a lullaby, and its soothing tones made her want to drift to sleep, but Moragon's sharp gaze demanded the opposite, as did his next words:

"I asked what you wished to study today? Mandolin? Flute? Harpsichord?"

Gailea suppressed a yawn as she considered. What would keep her the most awake, the most on task? By using herself as an instrument, of course. Then she was sure to stay awake.

"Voice," she said. "I wish to practice my voice."

Moragon tilted his head in amusement. "It's been a while since we tried that. No tricks up your sleeve like when you shattered the windows of my dining hall, I trust?"

"No, Your Majesty," Gailea said, though she couldn't be sure if this was true.

"Very well. Choose a song. There are hundreds ripe for the picking." He motioned wide to the bookcases and the desk filled with sheet music.

Gailea frowned. This wasn't right. Moragon had always picked the music for her.

As if guessing—or likely reading—her thoughts, he said, "I trust your judgment at this point in our relationship. Besides..." He slipped a hand around her shoulder and held it there firmly. "Even before your Guardianship, you were privy to songs I wanted you to teach me yourself."

Gailea shook her head. This wasn't right, the timing of this memory made no sense. He shouldn't know she was a Guardian.

"Ahh, but this is no memory," Moragon answered as if she'd spoken. "No, don't resist me. I've never seen your thoughts as vulnerably as I do now. I should have tried it this way ages ago."

Gailea tried to pull away, but he clutched her to him, hissing in her ear, "Where is it? The song Chevalier taught you?"

"I—I don't know. He didn't tell me any song."

"Then go—find it!"

He shoved her, and she fell against the desk. She caught herself, trembling all over but refusing to move or to look back at him.

"Your king commands you to find the song. It must be here, somewhere."

Gailea stared at the sheets of music scattered across the desk. Fear blurred her mind, blurred the notes on the page until they became an incoherent jumble, little more than splotches of ink smeared together.

Moragon was behind her again. Right behind her. Gripping her shoulders, leaning his face into her hair, inhaling, letting his lips brush against her neck. She shivered and then froze still as he whispered, "I know about your children. You think they are perfectly safe in Hyloria. But there are clues. Don't think I couldn't find them, should I will it so. And don't forget a night like this, the night when we stood so close, ready to consummate our marriage. Don't be fool enough to think that can't still happen. You will always be the one I created from a slave into a queen. The others after you were mere replacements, their potential pale in light of yours. But you are still only a queen, and I am your king, and your king commands you to find the song."

He released her again. She fought back tears. Why was her mind so suddenly vulnerable?

She began searching wildly while his sharp gaze watched her every move.

After what seemed an age, her gaze fell across a manuscript bearing the illustration of two islands, each with a giant stat-

ue. The caption read, "The Song Caught Between the Waves." Rosa. Adelar. Chevalier's clues. The song Moragon sought— was it linked to finding the Dusk?

Gailea quickly shielded this idea from her mind, but Moragon was already marching toward her, eyes ablaze with fury. "What did you learn, what did you see?"

Gailea sang at the top of her lungs, flinging Moragon against the fireplace.

In the dim, empty gallery, the sobbing woman bolted, as if hunted by her own nightmare.

She fled the room, screaming, "Where is he? Where has he gone?"

~*~*~

Iolana hurried down the corridor. After taking a walk to quell some of her wild nerves, she had decided to heed the note in her pocket. She drew it out for the millionth time, reading its summons over and over:

Meet me in my chambers come midnight.

Mikanah's desperation showed in the hasty, uneven scrawl, a stark contrast to his usual, rigidly neat penmanship. He had slipped the folded parchment into her hand right before she had retired to her room for bed. She had tried to ask if they could meet right away, but he had already vanished.

Iolana hastened her steps, praying that at last he would show her the affection she'd been craving. The past few days had been torture. Darice's capture. Being thrust back and forth between two kingdoms that hated one another, with possible death or imprisonment lurking around every corner. Gailea distracted with concern over Darice's capture and a palpable anxiousness at returning to the place that once imprisoned her. Iolana had wanted to be strong for Gailea but had found herself immoblized by the all-too-familiar terror of feeling helpless. She had turned to Mikanah, hoping they could comfort one another, but he'd been as strongly plagued by fear as her.

Now that a moment of peace descended, even if it was a mere calm before a much bigger storm, now was her chance. Mikanah had refused her advances up until this point, but he was as drained and overwhelmed as her, as much in need of comfort. Maybe he wouldn't admit it right away, but she would convince him.

"Where is he? Where is he?"

The question came shrieking with all the chilling force of a banshee, followed by a figure in flowing bed-clothes running down the hall. Iolana backed against the wall to prevent being trampled as Gailea rushed down the hall, eyes frozen open in wide-eyed, unblinking fear. Servants dashed aside or braced themselves against the walls as she passed, staring in alarm. Gailea barreled forward and Iolana nearly cried out, terrified she prepared to crash right into the wall, but then she wheeled around the corner, disappearing down the adjoining left corridor. Several Echelon and Adelaran guards rushed from the righthand corridor after her.

Even as Gailea raced out of sight, Mikanah rounded the corner. He staggered to a halt, panting hard, his ferocious gaze locked on Iolana.

"Which way? Which way did she go?"

"Toward our bed chambers," Iolana said. "Mikanah, what—?"

But he had left her behind, dashing down the hall in pursuit. Iolana hurried to match his long strides. A few of the Echelon rushed after them.

"Mika, what is it? What's happening?"

"I don't know." His voice was strained as he ran. "But I can guess. I should've guessed before. My dreams,

Gailea's, Donyon's, Darice's sleepwalking. I think they're all linked."

"You're still having dreams too?"

"They never stopped. But ever since arriving here again, they've intensified. I think they're tied most strongly to this place. I have an idea, but for once I damn well hope I'm wrong."

Iolana wanted to ask what he meant, but fear choked her words. They sped down the corridor, several Echelon soldiers on their heels. Gailea was already out of sight, but her pleading screams pulsed down the corridors, drawing them after her. Down the hall, doors were slamming open, with a shaken Darice first to rush from her room, then Lorelei, Ashden, and Chamblin.

"What was that?" Darice demanded. "Is that Gailea?"

Iolana paused to catch her breath while Mikanah continued his pursuit.

"Yes. I had thought she might be sleepwalking. Her eyes were wide open, but she didn't seem to see me."

"Follow me." Darice led them down an adjoining hall. "I think I can tell where she's going."

As they ran down corridors and stairwells, Gailea's voice diminished, and Iolana worried that Darice's memory of the castle had faded after so many years. Then, after a few moments, Gailea's shrieks met their ears once more. As they rounded a corner, they saw her racing down a vast hallway, its lofty ceiling supported by stone archways.

They turned another corner, and two grand double doors rose into view at the other end of a passageway. Several guards flanked the doors and drew their swords against what must have seemed like a crazed woman rushing toward them, and Iolana's heart sickened. Gailea wasn't going to stop, and the guards didn't understand. They would spear her straight through.

"Don't attack!" Darice cried. "Please!"

The guards slammed back against the wall, slumping down into a heap while Gailea ran straight between them. She didn't slow, not even as blood pooled beneath one of the guards who reached out to her. Something dark trembled in Gailea's heartsong, and Iolana knew that this was not her Gailea. Someone or something else was at work.

They all rushed inside the room, a massive structure flooded with moonlight and starlight from the tall windows and the candlelight glowing from the branching chandeliers overhead. The light shone across the checkered black-and-white marble floor. Several long dining tables with tall-backed chairs stood on one half of the room. On the other side of the room, two young ladies swept ashes from the cold fireplace. Several others scrubbed the floors or dusted the glass encasing several statues. All looked up in alarm as Gailea stood in their midst, trembling, and screaming, *"Where is he? What have you done with him?"*

Donyon raced through a pair of doors on the other side of the room, sword hanging in its sheath around his waist. Four knights raced on his heels, bearing Adelar's bear crowned with stars on their breastplates. Caution filled the king's face as he crept toward Gailea, hand outstretched. The knights trailed after, but he held a hand up behind him in a silent command for them to hold still.

"What's wrong, Gailea? What do you see?"

"Adel!" she shrieked, flinging a wild glance in Donyon's direction. In a single step, she had reached him and grabbed him, clawing at his robes. "Adel! The statue of King Adel that stood outside the castle—what have you done with him—?"

Gailea collapsed to the floor with a wail, her voice

gravelly from screaming. Tears wracked her body.

Donyon lowered himself to her level. He hesitated a long while, as if contemplating what to tell her.

"It was damaged," he said at last, in a quiet, even tone. "During a battle my father and I fought against Ragnar's troops. Only the head and shoulders remained untouched. It would have been sacrilege to abandon it, so we preserved it, brought it inside. It's now safely contained on a pedestal beneath Icean glass. It's right over there, in fact."

Gailea jumped to her feet and whirled. Her gaze found the bust statue inside the glass, and she flew toward it. She threw herself on the glass, weeping hysterically.

"Gailea, what is it?" Darice asked, rushing over to her. "Please, what's wrong? This isn't like you at all."

"My children," she sobbed. "He is here—he is everywhere—don't you hear him? I must do what he says. I must have Adel. He will kill my children. He will tell Crispin where to find them!" She sank to her knees and hunched over, pounding her head against the pedestal and whining, "Go away…go away, go away, go *away!*"

"Gailea, come out of it!" Darice fell beside her sister, gripped her by the arms, and shook her. "You're still sleeping. Wake up!" She slapped her across the face.

"What are you doing?" Iolana demanded, reaching for Darice. "Can't you see she's upset enough?" Someone caught her from behind and held her tightly—Mikanah. She fought against him, but he only said, "Let her be."

"Everyone, sing with me!" Darice flung the command over her shoulder. Together, they lifted their voices to mimic her mind-healing charm as fervently as they could. Gailea wailed, seemingly unaffected. Chamblin led them in another healing melody, then another, but none seemed to penetrate whatever vicious spell held

Gailea in its grasp.

While the others sang on, Darice leaned close to Gailea, still holding her arms as if attempting to ground her in some reality. "Something has taken hold of you, sister, just as it did me. It wants you more than it ever wanted me. But you *can* be released. Free yourself, Gailea. Command it to go. By Amiel's grace, you have that strength!

Darice sang the spell *Dumkana*, magnifiying both the volume and strength of the Guardians' voices. Gailea fought as her sister held her, screamed, kicked, tried to throw punches that Darice dodged. Ashden darted forward and helped restrain Gailea until at last, with a great gasp of breath, she fell limp in his arms. Everyone ceased singing.

As Ashden cradled Gailea, panic gripped Iolana. Nerine breathed heavily beside her, voicing aloud what Iolana dared not:

"Is she…she's not dead?"

"No," Darice said. "Only spent from the experience."

Gailea's eyes fluttered open, slowly at first. Then, they shot open wide and glanced frantically at Darice. "Where is he?" The words slurred together. "I know he's still here—where did he go?"

"Who?" Darice took her hand. "Who was here, sister? Who had such a control over your mind?"

"Moragon," Mikanah said. "He's here."

Iolana felt her heart nearly fly from her body at this declaration. Mikanah's gaze drew across the room, fixated with loathing on a singular point. The Guardians whirled, and as Iolana turned with them, terror ripped through her, especially as the dark melody she had heard quivering in Gailea's heart moments before floated to her again—faintly, for it was well guarded—confirming the nightmare standing before her and bringing it too vividly to life.

Moragon stood in the empty space in the middle of the room. He clasped his hands behind his back and raised his chin, a familiar proud smirk playing at the corners of his lips. He and Donyon, who had drawn his sword, slowly circled one another. Ashden gently passed Gailea into Darice's arms before approaching Moragon, singing a charm to shield his mind from mental attacks, while Lorelei's heartsong flowed with both fear and concentration as she prepared her magic. Many of the Echelon rushed over, swords drawn, hands raised and poised for magic attack.

"Help me up," Gailea muttered.

"*No*," Chamblin knelt at her side. "You're too weak. You're sitting this one out."

"*Help me up*," she insisted. "Or I'll do it on my own."

His frown was clearly disapproving, but he and Darice helped Gailea to her feet and the three of them joined Ashden and Donyon.

Iolana crept up to Mikanah, who stared at Moragon with a steadily burning disgust. That burn seemed to grow with each passing second, consuming Mikanah's heartsong with erratic chords.

The Guardians, the Echelon, Adelaran guards, and Nerine all surrounded Moragon in a wide arc. The few servants who yet lingered fled the room.

Leaving Gailea with Chamblin, Darice stepped aside and raised her palms which glowed with white light. She pushed her palms together and then stretched them out, so quickly that her hands were a blur. She repeated this pattern until strands of light stretched between her fingers like a game of cat's cradle. Darice flung the light strands at Moragon, and they expanded into a glowing net, but Moragon stepped aside so fast Iolana didn't see him move. Her heart plummeted into her gut. When had he learned such a skill? Never before had she known him to possess inhuman speed.

In the next breath, he stood before Darice, snatching at her head as if to grip it, but instead his hand seemed to pass right inside her skull.

Darice screamed in agony, flailing. "Please, stop—don't hurt her! Leave Gailea alone!" She wailed, seemingly overtaken by nightmares just as Gailea had been.

Donyon charged straight at Moragon. Lorelei shouted for him to stop, but he ignored her. One of his Adelaran guards rushed forward, flinging a beam of fire at the ceiling. A loud snap alerted Iolana as one of the chandeliers plummeted. The guard shoved Donyon and Darice from harm's way as the chandelier crashed down at Moragon. Iolana braced herself, prepared to either see Moragon crushed, which seemed too good to be true, or else to see him perform some mental trick that would send the chandelier flying.

Neither happened. Instead, the chandelier passed straight through Moragon's body. He casually stepped away from it, his body quivering like a vapor and turning translucent a few moments before solidifying once more. Darice collapsed, panting hard. She tried to stand, but her legs trembled beneath her. Gailea fell at her side, singing a soothing melody while she sobbed, her entire body shaking.

"Just as I thought," Donyon turned on Moragon and lowered his sword. "It's an illusion, not the true Moragon. A Desthai, it's called, a type of demonic spirit."

"A wise declaration from the otherwise unworthy king," the Desthai sneered. Its voice was certainly Moragon's but contained a hollow echo. "The Desthai is merely a servant, a conduit to speak through, albeit a powerful and revered one—just like the servant he replaced." His gaze strayed to Mikanah. "Indeed, this young instrument made a most excellent conduit for my Desthai to travel in, even if it did take me some time to locate and regain control over him from such a distance."

Mikanah stared in utter horror. The Guardians, the Echelon, even sweet Nerine all turned to him, eyes wide with utter disbelief. Some of the Echelon watched Mikanah with clear judgment. Iolana took Mikanah's hand, but he stood too stiffly to hold hers in return.

"I've heard of these creatures in my travels," Chamblin said, a rare contempt in his voice. "They have no soul or will of their own, but once attached to a master, they can be sent into the minds of others to control them. Moragon would have been able to control the Desthai from afar, like he said, once he figured our location, though doing so accurately from this far would be difficult. Desthai can pass between bodies. He may have controlled Darice when she was sleepwalking. And Gailea, what did he do to you? Just now, what did you see? Did you tell him anything?"

"I...I'm not sure. it's all such a blur."

Iolana took Mikanah's hand. "Mika, did you know? Did you know about this?"

Mikanah glared down at her, blatantly hurt by the suggestion. The shock on his face had transformed into self-revulsion.

"No, I didn't know. If I had, I'd have abandoned you a long time ago, to protect you...and to protect the Guardians." He drew his hand away. Iolana felt the separation with an almost tangible pain and wished she hadn't been so hasty with her words.

"Wait..." Gailea glanced at the statue of Adel, and recognition flooded her face. "The Dusk magic. Moragon has been trying to make me search for clues to find the Dusk."

"The Dusk?" Lorelei's voice tightened as her gaze followed the Desthai's every movement, as though she expected the real Moragon to spring out from the demon's core at any moment. Iolana shuddered with the same intimate fear; though he didn't stand physically before them, Moragon's presence was tangible. "You spoke of that before. The Obscuro, shadow magic, that he dabbled in before."

"The Dusk is the cleverest magic and the aptest weapon ever invented by me and that fool, Chevalier," the Desthai said. "A few drops hold the power to either kill or ensnare the minds of hundreds at once. Perhaps I don't yet know where the Dusk lies hidden. Thanks to Gailea's own cleverness, I was unable to penetrate her every thought. But thanks to Mikanah here, I know precisely where Gailea is. And Iolana, and Lorelei—and you, Donyon." The Desthai swirled around to Donyon, his grin mocking. "I don't know how it is you escaped me twice, but rest assured it will not happen again."

"What do you mean twice?" Donyon aimed his sword at the dark spirit, his eyes fierce.

"First, when I seized Adelar. Then, when you were in exile. Alas, my men were sloppy with their work, cutting down only your hedge-born whore and her brat."

Donyon's face burned red with rage. "Foul levereter, you own no right to speak of their murder so callously, nor of them with such disrespect!" He sang a charm at the top of his lungs. Its angry strains echoed in the vast hall, and a sharp wind cut through, surging toward the Desthai. Once more, while his form wavered, he stood firm, unaffected, and Donyon roared a frustrated cry.

"We need to leave," Iolana said, trembling. "You heard what it said. Moragon knows where we are now!"

"Too true," the Desthai crooned. "I know all about you. But surely some of you must miss me. Lorelei?"

The Desthai glided over and hovered right before her. She held her ground, returning his cruel stare with her own, fearful but resolute.

"Or you, dearest Iolana." The Desthai floated toward Iolana and slipped inside her. A coldness wrapped around her entire body and then filled it. Iolana squirmed and stepped back instinctively, but he lingered inside her, violating her body by turning it to ice, violating her mind by filling it with a whirlwind of frightened thoughts that zipped so quickly through her that she couldn't concentrate on any singular one. The only thing she could grasp concretely was an overwhelming terror at being trapped once more, with no means to escape.

A healing charm reached her—Mikanah singing in her direction—and her mind broke through just long enough for her to realize that it was her own. Her will was still hers. She sang along with Mikanah, and at last the Desthai passed out the other side of her body.

Iolana collapsed, reeling dizzily, but Mikanah caught her and held her close, his skin ashen, as it has been since the Desthai appeared. "You won't have her this time, Moragon. She has defied both you and death and triumphed. You won't lay another hand against her."

"Oh, I *will* have her," the Desthai said, glaring viciously at Mikanah. "Her, and Lorelei, and Gailea—and every other creature that ever dared to oppose me, to throw away the gifts I offered them."

The Desthai transformed into a silvery, semi-transparent figure and shot into the air, flying straight toward the window.

"We can't let him escape!" Chamblin shouted. "Once outside, he'll be able to use the wind to travel back to Moragon!"

Darice rose to her feet and threw a beam of light

that wrapped around the Desthai like a rope and sent him crashing to the floor. He leaped up, solidified once more, and whirled, pure venom filling his gaze.

"Very well. If you want the war now, then so be it!"

The Desthai drew his sword and swung at them. The sword divided into a six-pronged blade, and shadowy tendrils spiraled out in all directions. One of the shadows passed straight through Nerine, and she gasped as though punched in the stomach.

The Desthai swung the six-pronged sword again, and shadowy darts sprayed in every direction. A few of the Echelon stumbled, paling, and looking like they might be sick. Cenwin raised her hands and commanded the flames still glowing on the candles of the fallen chandelier. The flames expanded, and fiery darts flung out at the Desthai who staggered back, stunned for a moment.

"It's affected by fire!" Cenwin declared. "Fire mages, unite with me!" Several Echelon and Adelaran soldiers circled the room, throwing darts and pillars of flame in the Desthai's direction.

"Guardians, chant with me!" Chamblin cried, his voice trembling; Mikanah had stayed near his side, doing his best to explain the chaos surrounding them. "I know a chant from China, used to cast out dark spirits. It may help!"

Chamblin chanted in a language like none Iolana had ever heard, the notes ringing bold and clear. Unable to grasp the words in her panic, Iolana simply vocalized the notes. The other Guardians joined in. Rage brewed in the Desthai's face, and he swung his sword in wild arcs, throwing several rounds of shadowy darts. Several Echelon aimed fire or lightning. Lorelei sang one of their repelling spells, *Segmunda*, to help deflect the Desthai's attacks. Nerine joined her while Darice flung beams of light at the Desthai.

One of the light beams reflected on the glass cases sheathing the statues. It bounced into the Desthai, passing through him just as he had passed through their bodies. His shadowy form flickered like a candle threatening to extinguish. He solidified once more, but with a renewed fury in his gaze. Releasing an ear-splitting shriek, he jumped up, circling the room to pass through each of them, and one by one, they collapsed to their knees.

Iolana held her head, shuddering as she saw herself *back in Moragon's castle, watching a host of Carmennans cheer as several proclaimed traitors were dragged to the stake. The soldiers came for her, as she knew they would. She could do nothing. Couldn't fight back, couldn't even touch them. She was tied to the stake, Mikanah tied with her. The flames were lit. Iolana sang the song that had spared her before, praying it would save them both from the fire. This time, she did not burn at all but hung on the stake completely unscathed. But Mikanah burned. The stench of his boiling flesh assaulted her, as did his agonizing screams. The heat of his body burning next to hers intensified until it was too much to bear. She cried out—*

Her entire body jolted. When her eyes flashed open, Mikanah was there, whole, unscarred, unharmed, shaking her. She was back in the Adelaran Great Hall. All around the room, Guardians and soldiers alike looked just as terrified, many of them still collapsed on the ground, moaning, holding their heads, crawling to get away from the nightmares Moragon had crafted through the Desthai.

Iolana swept her gaze around the room until she saw the evil spirit dragging itself across the floor toward the window. The nightmares had been its last stand. It meant to escape while they were all distracted.

"He's getting away!" Iolana shouted, struggling to her feet. "The dreams aren't real. Wake up and get him!"

"*Rustiék!*" Cenwin shouted at the top of her lungs. As she staggered to her feet, an arc of flame shot from her sword. Fiery tendrils coiled around the Desthai. The demon lay at her feet, writhing in its bonds.

"Keep singing!" Lorelei commanded. She advanced toward the Desthai, hand outstretched as she vocalized a different spell, keeping the demon locked in its blazing bonds.

Iolana resumed Chamblin's chant. One by one, the other Guardians broke free from the demon's hold and chimed in, moving closer to it, helping one another as they stumbled from the attack. Darice directed a beam of light that flowed from her palms and reflected off one of the glass cases directly onto the Desthai's form. Echelon and Adelarans added their streams of fire until the Desthai's shadowy form could hardly be seen through the flames.

The demon wailed and gave a final pull against its bonds. Then, with a high-pierced screech, it exploded. Embers and ash spiraled. The Guardians maintained their chanting—Lorelei maintained her song to hold the demon in place—until the smoke and ash cleared to reveal, in the fire's midst...nothing.

"Did it flee back to its master?" Cenwin asked, glowering with disgust at the patch of blackened floor. "Or is it gone?"

Chamblin leaned against the table, perhaps the only thing keeping the weary man on his feet. "It's gone. Destruction by fire and song. That's how I saw it done in the West."

"It seemed almost too easy." Gailea stepped forward, staring at the ground where the Desthai had raged only moments ago. Her wide eyes looked haunted as she fixated upon that spot. "I almost expect Moragon himself to rise from these ashes and slay us all in some final twist of hate and vengeance."

Her knees buckled, and Darice rushed forward, catching and holding her up, all the while watching the burned patch with a haunted gaze.

"He won't." Ashden stood beside them. "My people and I, we've seen similar spirits. I think this one sealed his own fate of destruction by disobeying Moragon's wishes."

"Why do you imply the demon's disobedience?" Donyon stared at the place the demon had lain, grief etched vividly on his weary face. Already overwhelmed, Iolana tried to push his heartsong away, along with the others floating around her, but it pulsed so fervently that she couldn't help but sense its longing refrains. "It seems the demon was doing exactly as Moragon intended, to murder us all, make another end of the Guardians."

"I don't think he'd want us all dead." Mikanah's voice was flat, his face devoid of anything but a vehement loathing. "I think he would mean to keep some of us alive, to use us...." He choked on his last words, and his fists clenched. Iolana wanted to comfort him but knew she couldn't in that moment. He blamed himself for the Desthai's presence, and nothing she could say to him would convince him of his innocence.

"Strange..." Gailea's gaze locked fiercely on Mikanah. Despite her wobbling limbs, she stood a little taller, prouder. "That you would presume to know any of Moragon's plans, considering that it was you he used to carry the demon that siphoned nightmares and would have likely sought to control us all before the end." She swept a meaningful gaze across several Echelon who gave a single nod before moving to surround Mikanah.

Iolana stepped in front of him like an instinctive shield, glaring at Gailea between the guards as hurt and righteous anger raged inside her. "You can't blame him.

You can't think he did this on purpose."

"Whether on purpose or not, Moragan was able to use him."

"Moragon *would* know him intimately." Lorelei seemed to wince as she declared the words, watching Mikanah with remorse. "Even if Mikanah didn't consciously allow the Desthai inside him, Moragon knows enough of his fears to use them against him. Have you had any nightmares lately?"

"I have," Mikanah answered stiffly.

Lorelei seemed to narrow her eyes in disappointment. Iolana braced herself, expecting her to scold him, but instead, her expression softened, and she said, "I don't know how a Desthai's powers work. But I've seen Moragon use mental magic to feed upon fear in other ways. We don't know how long the Desthai may have been planted in his mind, with Moragon waiting for the right opportunity to reach out and use him."

Iolana gave Lorelei an appreciative glance for defending Mikanah. Lorelei was often so composed that Iolana sometimes forgot that she understood what it was like to be manipulated by Moragon just the same as she and Mikanah did.

"Whatever the case, I agree that we should keep a close watch on Mikanah, at least for the time being." Donyon took another step forward, peering curiously at the ashes on the floor, the only remnant of the Desthai's existence just moments past. "You know, it's perhaps the most hideous irony." He knelt down, touching the ashes, rubbing them between his fingertips. "It felt so real. It felt like I was fighting Moragon, destroying him, enacting vengeance for my family at last. In the moment, it felt so real. And yet, it means nothing. Such a victory was empty. We triumphed over a mere pawn, a weak reflection of Moragon's true evil."

"Do you believe now?" Gailea shared a sober look with Donyon. "Do you understand how dangerous Moragon is? How easy it is for him to infiltrate your castle, despite your walls of water and flame? He would have had us all writhing on the ground, begging for mercy just like that demon."

"Yes, I see," Donyon said. "Too clearly, and much later than I wish I had. Let us meet in my Council chambers at once. This war won't wait another moment to be fought."

CHAPTER 37

REQUIEM OF DREAMS

The Guardians, Nerine, and Echelon marched after Donyon down the long corridor leading to the Council chambers. Like the corridor they had just turned from, tapestries lined both walls, most embroidered in softer shades of blue, silver, white, gold, and green. All depicted bears of various colors, and most of the bears were crowned with halos made of stars. In between the tapestries, bust statues carved from light gray stone were situated within arched alcoves.

The designs of the statues' crowns largely matched those of the crowns ringing the bears' heads, so that Iolana wondered if each bear was meant to represent some past Adelaran monarch. Her education under Moragon's rule had been restricted mostly to music, but he had made certain to teach her—and Mikanah, and others no doubt—who their enemies were and how to recognize their standards.

The tapestries and corresponding statues were crafted beautifully, and Iolana would have enjoyed pondering their history, but it was merely a feeble attempt to distract herself from the tension pouring from Mikanah. Once more, she picked up her pace, squeezing between the six Echelon who ringed him. Once more, he tried to hurry ahead, but she slipped her hand in his. He stiffened before allowing the touch, though he did not return its tenderness.

"What is it?" Iolana whispered. "What's wrong? The demon is gone now. We're safe."

"Only for a moment," Mikanah said quietly. "You know that as well as I. As soon as Moragon has time to regain his next breath, he'll be back, in some way or other." His gaze strayed to Gailea, who had done nothing but study him with an even greater distrust than usual. "Besides, don't you understand yet that I'm a monster too?"

"You know I don't believe that."

"You as good as said it earlier. When you asked me if I knew about the Desthai."

"I was scared."

"Fear often brings out the worst truths."

"Mikanah."

She squeezed his hand, so hard that he stopped in the hall beside her; the half dozen Echelon stopped too. Staring him straight in the eye, she said calmly, "I know you didn't bring that demon here on purpose. You don't have to prove anything to me."

"Sometimes, I think *I'm* the demon, that I'm just fooling myself into believing I'm human."

"But you're *not*." She watched the others as they disappeared inside the council chamber before refocusing on him. "Come on. Before they find us missing and take that as suspicious as well."

They hurried inside to join the other Guardians before Donyon's council table. This time, chairs had been brought in for them and they sat facing the king and his advisors while the Echelon moved to stand against the chamber's walls, alongside Donyon's guard.

"I know it's late," Donyon began. "I know we have been to a proverbial torture chamber and back this evening. However, considering the night's events and everything leading up to them, I believe a swift decision is in order. I try not to be a man given over to haste, as I was in my youth. But the demon's attack changes everything." His gaze strayed with caution to Mikanah. "I see the necessity of fighting this war against Moragon, and yet I still hesitate to join with the Guardians when it seems they cannot even protect their own from being possessed by one of his foulest servants. It seems you once served under Moragon?"

"Yes, Your Majesty." Mikanah glanced at the floor, looking disgusted. Iolana knew his contempt was only toward himself and hoped the king wouldn't misinterpret it.

"And you as well?" Donyon's gaze drifted to Lorelei, who nodded.

"And myself," Iolana voiced firmly.

Donyon's brows rose, but Celegrave beat him to a reply.

"So, not one but three of you might provide the perfect means for another of Moragon's evil spirits to infiltrate." He huffed, sweeping his arms dramatically across the room. "Another such demon might be inside this room even now, listening to everything we say, every last bit of our plans."

"If I may..." Chamblin bowed his head toward first Celegrave and then the king. "Creatures like the Desthai are magnificently powerful. Moragon may be as well, but he is not, like the Desthai, from a spiritual realm. I don't think it likely that he would have been able to summon multiple such creatures. Even so, perhaps there are some songs that may help protect the Guardians from further such harm, or bring to light if there are other dark workings among us?"

"There is a song," Lorelei exchanged a meaning glance with Gailea, "but neither of us have fully learned it. It was a piece we had discovered with the first Guardians, a spiritually powerful song that can overcome all manner of evils. *'Ah Lum Amiel,'* it's called."

"That's lovely," Nerine breathed. "What does it mean?"

Lorelei smiled gently at her enthuisiasm. "It's translated to 'Amiel is Light.' We stored its knowledge in the Chamber of Music, though I'm afraid that won't help us now."

"No, it won't," Gailea said calmly, and Iolana felt grateful at her subdued tone, a stark contrast to her recent hysteria. "But what would help for now is if I were to teach you a song-shield, a type of song-spell that protects against mental intrusion. It wouldn't be a bad place to start for now, until we can all learn and master *'Ah Lum Amiel.'* If the Desthai can only house itself in one person at a time, then even if one was inside this room right now, the rest of us could shield our minds from its intrusion."

"I could help as well," Lorelei said. "I've my own song-shield that I've used to guard against Moragon for many years."

Donyon looked wary but nodded. "There can be no harm in learning a new protection spell. Go ahead, ladies. Teach us what you think best."

Lorelei shot a questioning glance at Gailea who said, "I know you have other means of protecting yourself that the rest of us do not. So, while I trust the effectiveness of your song, perhaps it's best to use mine just in case, seeing as how it's proved to guard completely against mental attacks, with no outside aid."

Lorelei nodded, looking appreciative that Gailea hadn't outright mentioned the pendant fused inside her skin.

Gailea turned her attention to Darice beside her. "Would you help me, sister?"

Darice's brows raised. "The *Song-Shield of Salmana*, I take it?"

Gailea nodded, and she and Darice sang in unison. The melodies flowing from the sisters' rich alto soon blended warmly, making Iolana ease back in her chair, releasing her body's tension. Like many song-spells, it contained only a single word, *Salmana*, making it efficient and easy to memorize. The notes themselves created a lilting, haunting tune.

They listened for a few moments before gradually joining in. As Iolana sang, she felt an unknown power enclosing her mind, like some sort of intangible sheath wrapping around her thoughts, locking them inside. A thrill rippled through her, and she sang out more adamantly, her passion intensified. She had experienced many spells that had probed her mind, invading its privacy, but this felt like the exact opposite. Instead of vulnerable terror, she felt incredible security.

After a few moments more, her mind grew weary, and her concentration on the spell wavered before severing altogether. Jolted back to the present, she listened as Gailea and Lorelei finished singing; the rest had already ceased. Most of the Guardians looked astounded by the song's power, just as Iolana had been. Even Mikanah's expression had softened, ever so slightly.

"Well." Donyon sat back in his chair with a long sigh before straightening again and meeting Gailea's gaze head-on. "I must admit that if such an overwhelming song is but one of many that the Guardians have to offer,

I would be a fool indeed not to join with you and take advantage of the great protection such knowledge could afford Adelar."

"So, you will join us then?" Gailea's gaze locked seriously on his. "You will finally join us as a Guardian in the fight against Moragon?"

Donyon bowed his head in a humble gesture. "I will." Some of his advisors murmured, and Celegrave began to protest, but Donyon held up a hand to stop him, keeping his gaze fixated upon Gailea. "But only with your leave."

Gailea's mouth parted wordlessly for a few seconds before she could respond. "Me? You're a Guardian. I've told you we are all equals. My permission is not needed."

"All the same, I ask it. I know I've yet to gain your trust, but perhaps this may be the first step." His sincerity was apparent and Gailea's usual hardness toward him melted.

She seemed to ponder a few moments before sitting up in her chair, withdrawing her cool demeanor. "As you see, we have taken others into our fold that we are yet learning to trust. What matters most is that we've come together for a single purpose, to protect those we love, and others, by destroying Moragon and his reign. Of course, you must come with us."

"Thank you. I am humbled to be welcomed so graciously into your fold. Perhaps you and the other Guardians could give any details, any plans you might've had against Moragon before your delay here?"

"The Council of Loz has been gathering allies," Lorelei said. "We hope to march against Carmenna and destroy Moragon before he has the chance to unleash full war upon us. But because he has found a way to garner and control so much music, even without being a musical magician, the Guardians will likely be needed to personally defeat him."

"How is it that he obtained such musical power?"

"He started by finding strong musical mages," Gailea said. "I was his first protégé, before I even realized what he was. Then Lorelei here, then Iolana...." She glanced over to Mikanah but didn't speak his name. Iolana didn't know whether to be more relieved or suspicious. "He tried to use our music, manipulate it through the power of his mental magic."

"I'm sorry." Donyon glanced solemnly at each of them. "No one should ever violate the mind of another in such a hideous manner." As he looked away, Iolana thought she caught a glimmer of guilt in his eyes.

"There is also the matter of the Vessel," Lorelei said.

"The Vessel?" Donyon arched a brow.

Briefly, Lorelei explained what she and Mikanah had overheard regarding Moragon's plot to use the Vessel to complete his plans.

"Mikanah and I had thought it to be a warship that could hold and transport some sort of tremendous power."

"The Dusk!" Gailea gasped, wide-eyed. "Perhaps he means to use the Vessel to house the Dusk. Perhaps it's a craft that's strong enough to contain the Dusk without being destroyed the moment the substance touches it. In my nightmares, Moragon was searching for the Dusk, siphoning memories into my mind that never happened. It was clear he knew something, but not enough to find it. But for some reason, he thought I did."

"Are you sure the dreams were entirely from Moragon?" Chamblin asked gently, leaning forward on the table to peer in her direction. "Perhaps someone tried to send you the dreams as a warning, to find the Dusk and hide it from Moragon, but Moragon's Desthai intervened."

"But the only person that could've done such a

thing..." Gailea paused, looking overwhelmed at her own realization. "Chevalier himself. He did appear in my dreams as well. He's the sorcerer who invented the Dusk under Moragon's command. Perhaps he placed some protective charm on the Dusk's whereabouts. He could have sensed Moragon's Desthai searching for the Dusk. He could have sent the dreams to warn me, but then the Desthai distorted them."

"Or, the Desthai may have been the first to send the dreams, and then Chevalier intervened. Whatever the case, if Moragon wasn't quite sure what he was looking for and if Chevalier was determined to protect it at all costs, the dreams could have melded together in a sort of twisted, confusing mess."

"This Vessel," Darice studied her sister with sympathy. "You don't think the nightmares were linked to it? Maybe the word 'Vessel' is more symbolic of a chalice or, perhaps in this case, a spirit, that houses nightmares to make people go mad. You don't think the Desthai could have been the Vessel?"

"No..." Gailea's frown deepened with growing pensiveness. "Moragon won't have sent his most valued weapon into our midst without any protection surrounding it. The Desthai was merely a tool to learn as much as he could from us. Donyon," her gaze flashed seriously to him, "before we go anywhere, the matter of the Dusk must be handled as soon as possible. From my dreams, I was able to piece some things together, and if I'm correct, we'll want to move as quickly as possible. The Desthai never made it back to Moragon, but if Moragon was controlling him, we have no idea if he was able to learn anything from my dreams. I think I was able to block him out but can't be entirely sure. I believe one half of the Dusk's source resides in the statue of King Adel, the other in the statue of Queen Rosa."

Donyon's eyes flared with passion. "Then let them be destroyed at once! I'll go myself, shatter them to shreds—"

"*No*," Gailea said firmly. "I'm still uncertain if some form of the Dusk is hidden directly inside the statues, or if it's some kind of song or spell or element that can breathe the Dusk into existence. Whatever the case, it's possible that in destroying the statues, we would *unleash* the Dusk. We don't know how it might spread. Countless numbers could die, by touching it, breathing it. The Dusk must be extracted and disposed of carefully."

A cold shiver waved over Iolana. She had seen so much wickedness at Moragon's hands that she couldn't imagine what depraved havoc he might wreak with such a formidable substance as the Dusk.

Donyon sank back into his seat, clearly anxious. "I can make certain the statue of Adel is dealt with before our departure, but Rosa, we don't have time to go back there and find out about their statue, do we? The Eagle has left, now its purpose is complete. And lingering in Rosa is as good as staying here. We'd be too easily targeted."

"You're right, Your Majesty," Chamblin said. "Which is why I propose, in your absence, that you appoint an Adelaran ambassador. Have them go to Rosa and explain the situation. Before we leave, you can also write a message with your seal to send on ahead. Faina here has light magic that can send messages quickly. Have both statues placed under close guard by your most trusted magicians until they can be reckoned with."

Donyon seemed to consider the matter. "The Adelaran court is home to magicians of many skills. They have surrounded the statue with many shielding charms, spells that would entrap any who seek to lay hands on it. If Rosa allowed and has need, we could also send some of those magicians to watch over their statue as well. Does my council make any opposition?"

"None, Your Majesty," Celegrave said, albeit gruffly. "Only that it may be difficult to find someone willing to play the part of ambassador. Peace between our kingdoms is delicate. Like an infant's flesh, newly formed and still easily wounded. Any Adelaran may be wary of setting foot on Rosan soil."

"If their king can do it safely, then surely I can find one brave man who is willing."

Mikanah scoffed beside Iolana. "I don't think this is a matter of willing or not. It needs to be done, and people will do what their king tells them to."

As Donyon turned his sharp gaze to Mikanah, Iolana shifted uneasily, humming the song-shield they had just learned in a vain attempt to calm her nerves, while wishing she had the power to extend its protection to Mikanah. This king had mental powers, just like Moragon. Would he break his word and use them to probe Mikanah's thoughts and intentions, now that Mikanah was under scrutiny for the Desthai?

Gratefully, the king only said, "Be that as it may, I do like to offer my counselors the opportunity to make choices of their own will, as a willing servant is far often a more impassioned and persuasive one. If none speaks up, then, yes, I will be forced to choose an ambassador for this matter of high importance."

"I will go, Your Majesty," said another of the counselors, a man who looked only a few years older than Mikanah.

"Conall. Are you certain you're up for the task?"

Conall pursed his lips, clearly worried at his decision, but he lifted his chin, looking moreso determined. "I am. I will represent my kingdom with full honor and courage. If the dawn of a new alliance is to be formed between our two kingdoms, then the Adelarans must show the Rosans we do not fear them."

Celegrave's expression wavered between skeptical and impressed as Conall spoke, but he held his tongue, unlike the two men beside him, who muttered to each other.

The king nodded graciously at Conall and said, "Thank you for your generous offer. Once I am finished speaking with the Guardians, I will speak further with the Privy Council on these matters. Fellow Guardians, what of our immediate plans once we depart from here?"

"Now that the Guardians are one unit," Gailea said, "we can begin to train as one. We must increase our repertoire and learn more of the pieces we've archived. Many of you already have a strong musical knowledge. But there is much more to learn. Especially *Ah Lum Amiel*."

"*Ah Lum Amiel*," Nerine spoke each word slowly, face filled with the reverence that Iolana felt such a song likely afforded. "Just the name makes me feel peace."

"As well it might," Lorelei said. "It's a song born of the purest forms of light and musical magic. An ancient spell, and a prayer to Amiel Himself, to implore His grace and power. No one is quite sure of its origins. It may have been created by the celestial beings who guard Amiel's throne. The Olwins, they are called."

"Its purpose and power is to dispel all manner of darkest magic." Gailea waved her hands in the air, in a symbolic gesture of driving evil away. "Had we known it, we could have used it against the Desthai. To achieve its full power, it requires the power of eight. But it is such a complex, potent song and requires such intense concentration that most of us would likely have faltered, our spirits were so weakened by the demon. We need ample time to learn, practice and perfect it. The other pieces we teach you before *Ah Lum Amiel* will prepare us. Like exercising a muscle, we'll start small and build our way up."

"And where do we go?" Donyon asked, "to learn these songs?"

"We return to Loz. To the Chamber of Music. Now that the Guardians are joined as one, you will each be officially appointed. You'll be gifted with your instruments, which will strengthen your spirits and your magic. From there, we will commence training, as well as plans with the Lozolian Council regarding war."

"Very well then." Donyon swept an affirming glance across them. "Tomorrow, we make for Loz as our first course of action."

"Your majesty." One of the advisors leaned forward, gazing with concern at his king. "I understand this mission is of the utmost value for Adelar's ultimate protection, but so is your presence here. Who will protect and rule in your stead?"

Donyon nodded at the man. "A wise question. One we will discuss further once the Guardians and Echelon are dismissed. Which, if there is nothing further?" He turned to them again, head tilted in question, weariness descending on his face once more.

"Actually..." Gailea's gaze drifted down the row of Guardians to land on Mikanah, and Iolana felt her chest tighten, like an invisible hand squeezed her heart. "There is one thing more. There's the matter of what to do with Mikanah, at least until we can reach Loz and learn *Ah Lum Amiel* to guard against any further mental intrusion on Moragon's part. Does everyone agree, at the least, that he should continue to remain under close guard by the Echelon and, perhaps, Your Majesty, any guards you might spare?"

An icy silence doused the room. Iolana watched Mikanah warily. Anger brewed inside his gaze, whether more for himself or for Gailea, she couldn't tell. The more she watched him, the more a fresh anger began to burn in her as well.

Iolana locked eyes with Gailea. "Why should Mikanah be placed under such strict inspection? Lorelei, myself, even you—the Desthai could have entered through any one of us. Moragon tried to control you too, through the dreams. Why point to Mikanah as the singular possible threat when we all served him?"

"I was never his servant," Gailea reminded harshly. "I fought that fate with every breath in me. Down to my last, if I'd had to."

Iolana started to retort, but Lorelei spoke first, impatience edging her voice, "We are not all so fortunate, Gailea. Not all of us who tried were able to completely resist him."

Some of the fierceness faded from Gailea's face. "I know. I didn't mean to speak so carelessly. I only find it difficult to believe that Mikanah has renounced all loyalty to Moragon."

"You don't have to defend me." Mikanah cast an apologetic glance in Lorelei's direction, and Iolana gripped the edge of her chair in frustration; lately, he didn't show her even that much affection. "Unlike the rest of you, I chose to serve Moragon of my own free will. I wanted the same power Moragon had, to feel some sense of control over my life, and to avenge my brother. I still want that. I'm still filled with hate. I don't deny it. But I choose now to fight fully against Moragon. I have come to care for the Guardians. I would not endanger any of you knowingly. If you don't believe that, you must know that I would not endanger Iolana."

He shifted his gaze to her, his dark, fathomless eyes pleading.

Iolana met him with a small, encouraging smile. At least, she meant it to be encouraging. His words had chilled her. He had *chosen* to serve Moragon. He had said this before, but it hadn't fully sunk in until now. The Desthai's insidious grin at Mikanah had been so knowing, so conspiratorial. Gailea's suspicions, the demon's implied partnership—could any of this be true?

The direction of her thoughts shocked her, *galled* her. But she refused to let it show. Beneath the table, her fingers dug into the soft material of her skirts, curling into tight, solid fists. Fists trembling with effort and ready to attack anyone who continued to accuse Mikanah. Even herself.

"I love Mikanah," she said, voice unwavering. "And I trust him. I will defend him. He is innocent. Just as much as Darice was innocent in poisoning the waters at Rosa."

Gailea scrutinized her, as if searching for a vulnerability in Iolana's armor. *No, you will not find one.*

Then the older woman looked once more to the king. "Donyon, all I'm saying is we don't know what Mikanah is capable of, whether on purpose or not."

"We don't know what any of us may be capable of," Lorelei said, sounding more frustrated. "Which is why I think we need to remember to treat one another with equal respect."

"And with equal caution," Donyon said firmly. "For now, I will have extra of my guard stand watch over your chambers. The castle grounds are yet yours to explore, but my guards will be ordered to follow you. This is for the protection of all." His gaze swept across them and landed lastly on Gailea, focusing on her with obvious inquiry. She gave a curt nod and sat back in her chair, seemingly satisfied.

"That is enough for now. The Guardians are dismissed. I ask my Council to stay behind so we may make preparations for my absence and for the protection of the Adel and Rosa statues."

As the Guardians, Echelon, and Nerine departed the Council chamber, Iolana cast a frustrated glance in Gailea's direction. She hated harboring even the smallest ounce of anger toward the woman who had served as a necessary mentor and friend. Chamblin came up beside Gailea, placing a hand on her shoulder, his face reflecting clear compassion as he spoke what were likely words of reason and comfort. Iolana wanted to be happy that Gailea had such a dear friend, but the sight drove her anger a little deeper, turning it to desperation as she realized: she needed Mikanah. *Now.*

Mikanah strode from the room as quickly as possible, staring straight ahead into a sightless void as several guards trailed after him. Iolana raced to catch up. This was her last chance before they left Adelar, possibly her last chance in a long while. She would not miss seizing this opportunity, not when the need for it pressed so imminently.

"Mika," she said, catching up to him and shoving the piece of folded parchment into his hand. "If this still stands, I'll see you in an hour's time."

~*~*~

Iolana knocked on the door to Mikanah's bedchamber.

"Come in," he answered from within.

Iolana glanced at one of the guards flanking his door. The guard nodded, and Iolana slipped inside.

Like her own chambers, Mikanah's was small but finely furnished with a four-poster bed, a desk and chair, a small wardrobe, and a rug sprawled before the fireplace. Once more, the pattern of bears and stars gazed up at her. The blue, gold, and silver threads shimmered in the starlight and moonlight pouring through the large, diamond-patterned windows thrust open. He knelt before the fireplace, throwing more kindling onto the blazng flames, and Iolana wondered if he'd had one of the servants start the fire or whether he'd done so of his own spontaneous will. Her heart sped as she imagined the latter. Just like old times, when they used to steal away in one of the unused rooms of Moragon's castle.

Mikanah rose slowly to his feet, staring at her. An anticipating silence wavered between them, with only the flames crackling softly.

Iolana took a few steps forward, and he did the same. For a few moments, they circled one another, watching each other all the while, as if sharing some ritualistic dance. The yellow-orange firelight gave his dark skin a copper sheen, like the celestial warriors from children's tales who lived in the stars. Unbridled yearning pulsated vividly inside his heartsong, opposing the fear gleaming in his eyes, a fear she hoped he would let her tame.

"What's wrong?" she asked. "What are you afraid of?"

"Aren't you afraid of me? After tonight, the demon, after everything they believe me responsible for? Everything you know that I've been?"

"No," she said firmly. "No, I'm not."

"You should be." His voice and expression turned to pure ice. He froze in place, and so did she. "What if I do something to you? What if I try to control you like I did all the others?"

"I don't know what you did to them. And I know you

won't tell me. But I'm not afraid of you. I don't care if you're different. I don't care what you are, what you've become. You're still my Mika, and I need you."

She circled closer, reached out to him. He slapped her hand aside. Still, she approached him, until his back pressed against the wall, allowing her to bridge the gap between them. "Fear is a choice. I will no longer choose to be ruled by fear. And I won't let you be ruled by it either."

She reached up again and touched his face. His body stiffened, and his face pulled into a disgusted frown. She didn't trust any of his resistance, didn't believe a single moment of it. She took his face in her hands, pressed her body close to his, and kissed him. His stony shield shattered as he pulled her even closer, devouring her lips in an ardent kiss.

His fears transformed into a wild energy, and his kisses consumed her again and again. Her need and his became one. The two of them were obsession, driven by their hunger to possess one another.

Iolana jumped up, wrapping her arms and legs around him. He carried her and laid her on the soft rug, tangling his body with hers. His hands trailed beneath her skirts and chemise, up her thighs. Their bodies danced, and he took the perfect lead. For once, as she submitted, as their bodies became a twisted web of kissing and touching, she was willingly, freely trapped.

Their lovemaking seemed to last a glorious age.

Then, at last, they lay still, and the surreal experience that had lasted an eternity now seemed cut off, over far too soon. A bittersweet parting, Iolana thought, as they lay next to one another. She watched him, admiring, still desiring, but satisfied enough, her nerves and body soothed.

Mikanah closed his eyes and breathed hard. His

skin shone bronze in the orange firelight, glistening with sweat. He opened his eyes, and the fire reflected in them. Iolana wanted to lean over and kiss him again but was too awestruck by his beauty. She didn't want to end the dream of him lying by her side, looking this way. She wanted to admire him for as long as she could.

Mikanah did not speak or look at her for a long time. The dreamy veil began to lift as she searched his face more closely. His brows and lips bent into a frown. She tried to listen to his heartsong, but it was silent, shielded by his own will, or perhaps by the spell they'd learned earlier. Propping her head up on one hand, she said, "That was beautiful. It was everything I've been longing for."

For a few moments more, he did not look at her.

Then, he turned toward her, his gaze sharp as a blade. "Was it?" He sounded more accusing than doubtful, as if he refused her compliment the permission to be true.

Iolana lay stunned, not knowing how to take his words. Her heart hurt, but she fought back tears. Maybe she just misunderstood him.

"Don't *you* think so?"

His eyes narrowed, as if trying to detect something within her. He looked prepared to say "no." Instead, he answered in a tone sincere yet abruptly sad, "Yes. Yes, it was beautiful."

He sat up and turned his attention to the stars outside the window, and again, Iolana didn't know how to respond. She didn't understand why he should feel any apprehension at the wonderful gift they'd just shared, let alone sorrow, and could only feel more hurt at his lingering distance. She hated how uncertain he made her feel. She wanted to ask what was wrong. But she couldn't read his heart and knew that he had veiled himself entirely from her. Asking him would provide no further answer.

In a weak attempt to feign ignorance at his changed mood, she said, "Will you...will you come to bed with me?"

He released a long sigh. The noise cut bitterly into her heart, and even moreso his next words:

"I'm sorry, but I have much to think about. Please just go."

"What is there to think about?"

She couldn't stop the question from spilling out. It was her last desperate attempt to tell him how he broke her heart. She had not anticipated him pushing her away yet again. She had tried to be patient with him, had tried to understand. But she couldn't. She had given her all to him, and still he rejected her.

Quietly, she rose and stole a final glance at his face. He was still beautiful, and she longed for him to look at her, apologize, beckon her for another kiss. But he didn't. He only watched the stars, his gaze hard-set and impossible to decipher.

Iolana turned and left his chamber without another glance back.

THE FOURTH MOVEMENT

"Arise, shine; for thy light is come,
and the glory of the Lord is risen upon thee.
The people that walked in darkness have seen
a great light:

they that dwell in the land of the shadow of death,
upon them hath the light shined."
~ Isaiah 60:1-2; Isaiah 9:26

CHAPTER 38

THE CHAMBER OF MUSIC

Mikanah felt the excitement flowing through the other Guardians in waves of nervous energy as they followed Gailea and Lorelei through the Lozolian Council's Headquarters.

They had slept through the morning before joining in the Adelaran Great Hall to share a midday meal of roasted pheasant and duck, fresh-baked bread with butter, baked fruits, salads, spiced wines, and an array of other culinary treats. While they feasted, it was revealed that Conall had been appointed as the steward who would travel to Rosa, along with one of the older advisiors, some of Donyon's most trusted knights, and magicians skilled in the arts of concealing and protecting who could guard the statues. In Adelar, the remainder of Donyon's counselors, led by Celegrave, would rule and make collective decisions for the realm in Donyon's stead.

After their meal, the Guardians, Nerine, Echelon, and eight Adelaran soldiers joined in the courtyard to sing *The Lozolian Summons*, the transportation melody that Gailea, Lorelei, and the old Guardians had created in case of emergencies. When all eight Guardians were joined together, the song could transport them instantly to the Lozolian Council Chambers. While none of the Echelon or Adelaran soldiers possessed musical magic, the song had the power to encompass and transport anyone within a certain radius of the musicians singing it.

Mikanah wished there were other songs of transportation that could take them other places besides the Council chamber. Why couldn't they just land in Moragon's courts in the blink of an eye? Slaughter him in his sleep before he had the chance to devise some new, wicked plan against them?

After a brief welcome from Lynn Lectim and the Lozlian Council, Gailea started leading them to the Chamber of Music. As they wound through the halls of Castle Iridescence, Mikanah posed his question.

"Creating transportation portals is an arduous and precise task," Nerine explained as they delved down a long, wide staircase. "On occasion, someone may be born with the gift of transportation. These individuals can learn to transport anywhere at any time, even across entire countries in a single moment. But most everyone else must rely on portals."

Gailea gave Nerine an impressed look and added, "Lynn and the first Octavial Eight, we were able to find a fairy gifted in transportation. However, crafting the portal and combining it with our musical magic took several months. So, you can see, even for someone born with the skill, crafting a portal is no easy feat."

As they continued along, Mikanah could feel Iolana breezing past him again. Every time she almost walked astride with him, she would rush ahead or fall back.

Their arms brushed this time, and Mikanah dared to glance up at her. She stared straight ahead, her expression cold as stone, except for a glimpse of lingering sadness that she could not hide.

As they descended deeper toward the castle's core, a draft made Mikanah shiver. The halls darkened, lit only with orbs of white light that floated along the ceiling as they delved beneath the earth. A dank, stale smell wafted to his nostrils, making him sneeze.

"Why is it so depressing down here?" Chamblin asked. "Even as a half-blind man, I can tell it's terribly drab. I've half a mind to take out my pipa and charm the place, brighten it up a bit."

"Don't—please," Gailea said, rolling her eyes in her usual manner. "The Chamber of Music is so deeply buried for its protection. The corridors we've passed through have all been laced with security charms. Lorelei and I have been undoing the charms so that we can pass through."

"At last!" Lorelei cried. "It's like being home again."

Mikanah saw nothing special about the plain wooden door with iron hinges set at the end of the corridor. More than anything, it looked like a gateway to a prison or even to the sewers. Being this far under ground, either was possible.

Through the door was another corridor lined with Echelon on either side, with what appeared to be a plain stone wall at its far end. A song flowed faintly toward Mikanah. Gailea and Lorelei must be using some charm, perhaps to prove they were not intruders.

As they all stopped at the blank stone wall, Gailea and Lorelei sang another song, this time in an ancient-sounding language that Mikanah did not recognize. The white outline of an arched door appeared in the wall and began to glow. Light poured forth all along the outline, brilliant enough that Mikanah had to shield his face. In the next breath, the light faded, and he glanced up in surprise at the stone door with an iron handle now built in the wall where the light had glowed just moments past.

Gailea reached out and turned the door's handle.

Together, they all passed through the door into the room beyond.

Gasps echoed among the Guardians, Nerine, and some of their guard. Mikanah stared along with them, his anxiety expelled for a few moments by the magnificence surrounding him.

They had entered a circular room, its cavernous ceiling indecipherable. Columns of light spilled down from above, and within them, tiny musical notes and symbols floated—quarter notes, eighth notes, treble clefs, bass clefs, sharp and flat symbols—all seemingly comprised of light themselves, representing every color in the rainbow and every shade in between. The colorful music notes twirled in the columns of light, constantly spinning, reflecting bright shimmers with every turn.

In the midst of the room, a great stone rose from the floor. Its smooth black facets shimmered in the pillars of light surrounding it. Magic pulsed tangibly from within, and Mikanah guessed it might be the stone that sent out waves of musical magic to detect new Guardians.

Along the wall that circled the entire chamber were unbroken lines of massive oak shelves, staggered much like the coliseum seats in Moragon's theatre. They were nearly packed with books and scrolls, along with bound sheets of parchment turned into music scores. Resting on one shelf directly across from the entrance were musical instruments, all made of pure Icean crystal, transparent and sparkling with an iridescent sheen, with an ageless beauty that conveyed both strength and serenity.

"So, this is it," Donyon breathed, breaking the silence. "The legendary Chamber of Music. I feel a fool for almost letting myself miss such a wonder."

"With all due respect," Gailea said, "I think it's not ancient enough yet as to be called 'legendary'."

"To me, it is," Donyon said. "When you isolate yourself from the world, talk of any such wonder seems legendary."

"The time to wonder and awe will come later. Let us begin the initiation. Guardians, join hands. Nerine, stand back with the others. You may sing with us if you like, though of course the song's magic will not affect you."

Nerine stepped back with the Echelon and Adelar soldiers while the Guardians joined hands.

"Donyon, the rest of the new members have been taught this initiation piece. Due to the limited time, you'll have to learn it by ear, I'm afraid. This song will strengthen our bond and that of our combined magic."

Donyon nodded. "I will do what I can. What instrument shall I choose? I have limited experience."

"The choice is not up to us. Apparently." Iolana's clipped words were clearly aimed at Mikanah.

Gailea seemed thrown by Iolana's mood, but she dismissed it. "The spell that grants you these instruments has taken inspiration from your spirits and your strengths and weaknesses, as well as any experience you may already have with certain musical instruments. Your instrument's magic will respond only to you. Many song-spells are just as powerful if not moreso when sung, but playing your instrument for the first time will strengthen you. You *will* be more powerful after this initiation, most of all when we are joined altogether in song, as we prepare to do now. At the end of the song, I will lift my hand like so." She raised her hand to demonstrate.

"Hold the last note until I swing my hand down. Then, at that moment, we must each sing the note corresponding to the note of our Guardian's mark, completing, and thus sealing the initiation spell."

"I'm afraid I don't know what my note is." Donyon pushed up his sleeve, glancing at his mark, *Ut*, with a confused frown. "That is, I am familiar with the Lozolian solfége. But I never did possess a knack for identifying notes on sight. By hearing though, if someone could sing my note for me, I could quickly memorize it."

"Of course." Lorelei smiled warmly at him before motioning to all of them. "In fact, I think it would be best if we all practiced our designated notes, to make certain we each understand how to find them before beginning the appointment ritual."

Gailea voiced her agreement, and the Guardians broke into small groups, singing their notes to one another, helping them adjust where needed. Mikanah easily found his note *Mi*, and together, he and Ashden sang Donyon's low *Ut*. Donyon mimicked and practiced several times to ascertain he'd memorized it.

Once everyone finished practicing, Gailea began the *Sonata of Appointment*. Lorelei chimed in with her soprano. Iolana was next to join, her high soprano harmonizing perfectly. Iolana's face tightened with concentration, her ire and anxiety clearly giving way as she shared the others' excitement.

Mikanah smiled to himself as he began singing. He felt excited too. Even if she wouldn't look at him, they were sharing this sacred moment.

Mikanah and Ashden's flexible baritone, Chamblin's bright tenor, and Darice's warm alto all joined in, weaving together to create a perfect harmony interspersed with moments of dissonance. Donyon's bass joined last, wavering at first, singing notes here and there as his face knit in deep concentration. As the other Guardians repeated the first several refrains, he sang more confidently, providing a rich, warm layer.

As the song intensified, so did Mikanah's exhilaration. The might of both the songs and the instruments pulsed toward him. So much power at his fingertips. So much potential for all manner of musical spells to use against Moragon and Reynard and force them to their knees.

Gailea lifted her hand then, and Mikanah held his note, as did the rest of the Guardians. As Gailea swung her arm downward, they belted their designated notes in unison: Donyon sung the lowest *Ut*, Ashden *Rey*, Mikanah *Mi*, Chamblin *Fa*, Darice *So*, Gailea *La*, Lorelei *Ti*, and Iolana *Ut*. The tones of their voices blended beautifully, even as the notes themselves overlapped with a strange yet compelling dissonance.

Their voices swelled like the finale of a symphony, and a brilliant light enveloped them. When it faded, a musical instrument hovered before each of them, except Gailea and Lorelei who drew their respective flute and lyre from their shaped leather cases. They now reached for their instruments, admiring. Music began to swell the room once more as they each played woodwinds, strings, a horn.

But Mikanah could only stare at the crystal violin hovering before him, twirling slowly mid-air. Light glistened off its smooth surfaces, and the point of its bow gleamed sharply like a sword. The thrill coursing through him crashed and turned to pure fear. This was how he'd seized power before, with *this* instrument, by torturing countless souls. Was this how he would redeem himself now? *Could* it be?

He glanced up when Iolana played her new, high-pitched fife. She showed it proudly to Nerine who blew a few screaming notes on it, making the two girls laugh with glee.

Their laughter could not reach Mikanah. He felt like the ruins of the old statue of Adel: lost, more broken than before, defeated and crumbling. What he and Iolana had shared last night was beautiful, his hands rippling over her soft skin, their bodies melting as one, his lips pressing against hers in long, fervent kisses. Since he had first seen her in Pakua, he had wanted nothing more than to be with her intimately, over, and over.

But he had resisted, especially when she had pursued. Under Moragon's guise, he had done more than torture minds with his music. He had tortured bodies. He had learned how to use his music to lure young ladies, lie with them, make them give up their virtue and thus shame them in the eyes of Carmennan society, and their faith, for those who practiced the latter more strictly. Sometimes, they gave their bodies in exchange for their lives, sometimes in exchange for information, and other times simply because it pleased Moragon.

How could he be certain he hadn't also seduced Iolana against her will? If he had, he had needed no violin to do so. How much more lethally persuasive would he be with this new weapon in his hands?

"Mikanah?"

Mikanah's head shot up. Lorelei stood beside him, strumming a gentle melody on her lyre.

"I don't know if I can do this," Mikanah muttered. He cast a quick glance about the room. The others were distracted, even Gailea as she played a duet on her flute with Darice, who'd likewise received a flute, and Ashden, who plucked away on his new lute.

"You're afraid," Lorelei said. "You're afraid because you've used this instrument before."

"It's no instrument," Mikanah snapped. "It's a weapon of torment and destruction."

"No. This is not the same. You used your violin in Moragon's courts to sway people for evil purposes. But you don't serve Moragon now. You serve the Guardians."

"That's what I'm afraid of. I do care for the Guardians. More than I thought I would. What if I use this—this thing, to lead them astray?" He glared at the violin. He wanted to snatch it up and smash it, but he knew it wouldn't likely shatter, being made of Icean crystal. Moreso, he didn't want to show disrespect in front of the Guardians who yet accepted him in their fold.

"Mikanah."

Lorelei's sharp voice drew his attention back to her, and she looked him straight in the eye.

"*You* are in control of yourself now."

"The Desthai—"

"Was not of your choice." Lorelei played a sharp chord on her lyre before lowering it and resting her hand on his arm. "Any of us might have been a victim of the demon without knowing. But *you* are no demon."

Mikanah scoffed. "You didn't disagree when Gailea advocated that I be closely watched as one."

"Because I don't trust Moragon not to misuse you again. But I believe that you yourself are no monster. Perhaps especially because I see this very struggle now. This instrument was given to you for a reason. It's an instrument of great emotional influence. You can use all of that *against* Moragon this time. You can use all of that for good."

Mikanah studied Lorelei, awed at her words, at the sincerity with which she spoke them. He didn't know why he was so surprised. From the first, Lorelei had always been the one Guardian, aside from Iolana, of course, whom he'd felt deep down that he could trust. Perhaps he had forgotten this, after the demon and the accusations that had followed.

"You're right," he said. "I am in control of myself. I've made some terrible decisions in the past. Selfish decisions. I don't know if I can be redeemed, but I will do my best to undo the damage I've done under Moragon. I will use this instrument, this time not for him, but to triumph over him."

He reached out, snatched the violin, and played several melodies riddled with passion—the passion of love, the passion of hate, combined into a single song. He only stopped playing when he realized all eyes were watching him, impressed, even Gailea.

"You have a compelling talent, Mikanah," Chamblin said, plucking a song on his new crystal mandolin. Nerine followed him, playing on his old pipa.

Donyon approached Mikanah. "You've a true gift. I don't think I've ever heard such ardor poured into music before. It's most inspiring."

"Any type of magic that is fueled by intense motivations is always the strongest," Lorelei announced to the Guardians. "It's what we need. Though I would caution against being led too firmly by hate." She turned to Mikanah. "Use your *love* for the Guardians, or for Iolana if that's stronger, to drive your music. Hate often breeds only more hate."

"Hate, in some cases, is a good thing," Donyon said. "A hatred for evil—that is righteous. The kind I think we all have against the false king." He clutched his trumpet with the same pride as someone receiving a new sword. "It feels unwaveringly strong. The instruments are made of Icean crystal, yes? They're unbreakable?"

Lorelei nodded as she rippled her fingers along her lyre strings. "I'd recommend bringing them with you everywhere, even into battle. Your voice may be your most powerful tool, but you never know when your instrument can come in handy."

"Indeed." Gailea walked up to them, flute in hand. Her gaze narrowed at Mikanah and his violin, ever so briefly, enough to make him shift a few steps away from the group. "Speaking of battle tactics, we can now go about the task of garnering and learning song-spells that may aid us most in fighting Moragon. There are many songs and other pieces of attack and defense. We have already taught you several, but there are others we may learn."

Gailea motioned to the glistening notes twirling in the white pillars of light. "These represent…" She paused, looking at Chamblin with concern, then started again, more descriptively. "These music notes hovering before us each represent a certain magical music work that the Guardians have collected since our formation. The light columns protect them, and only a Guardian can summon or awaken them."

Gailea lifted the flute to her lips and blew a short trill. Several music notes, all a deep crimson hue, zipped over to float before her. A cry of amusement alerted Mikanah as Iolana and Nerine both rushed over. Darice and Ashden hurried after them. Donyon strode over, face filled with concentration. Murmurs of wonder echoed from the surrounding Echelon and Adelaran soldiers. Gailea played a lower trill on her flute, and a larger number of notes and symbols zipped over. This new batch reflected sunny golden hues.

"Astonishing magic," Donyon breathed, gingerly reaching out to touch one of the hovering notes. It flashed a bright red and played a quick, frantic tune, all the while spinning midair.

"The red notes represent all of the songs of direct offense and attack we've collected, while the gold ones are song-spells of protection, of defense. At first, we had to search through them every time, to find the exact song-spell we wanted. However, the tunes used to summon each individual note have all since been transcribed in this book."

Gailea held out her hands and vocalized a short melody. A shape blurred past from one of the bookshelves, and suddenly a large book was in her hands, an illuminated manuscript, judging by the gold coating the pages' edges. Mikanah had witnessed several such tomes in Moragon's libraries.

Opening the book, Gailea carefully ran her hands across the elegant words, music notes, and elaborate illustrations surrounding them. She leafed through, seeming to admire the pictures of swords, fire, rain, sun and moon, knights, and ladies. Her expression softened with sadness, and the longer she stared at the pages, the deeper she seemed to delve into some memory or other intimate thought.

"The first Guardians and I...we recorded this book together."

She smiled faintly, and though she looked at them, her gaze seemed to peer straight through them, seeing instead into that distant past. A touch of compassion pricked at Mikanah. Six of this woman's closest friends had been murdered by Moragon. Mikanah couldn't fathom surviving such severe torment. Losing Iolana alone had made him lose all desire to live. And yet, live on Gailea had, and honorably. Perhaps she would never like or fully trust him, but he marveled now, seeing her pain, and knowing that she had accepted him perhaps as best she could.

Gailea seemed to force herself back into the present moment as she looked at each of them. "Many of the songs we discovered were passed down orally, so we captured their knowledge inside the floating music notes. As Donyon demonstrated, they will play their contained song when touched. We did transcribe many of them…" Gailea motioned to the shelves containing scrolls of parchment. "…but not all. I think the best order of business may be to start transcribing whichever ones we think may prove useful, to take with us. We can't memorize all of them while we're here. Iolana and Nerine, would you be prepared to utilize your skills from the academy?"

"Yes of course!" Nerine nodded eagerly. Eyes gleaming at the chance to help in whatever way. Iolana nodded too, though she clutched her fife tightly, face pulled into a hesitant frown. Mikanah couldn't resist a small smile. The practical side of music never had been Iolana's favorite lesson.

"Before you girls begin, best to find the songs that are already transcribed, so we aren't wasting time. If you tap one of the notes or symbols twice instead of just once, you'll find that it corresponds to one of the parchments on the shelves—if it's already been transcribed, that is." She touched a floating gold treble clef. It flashed and zipped across the room to one of the far shelves, where a golden gleam emanated. Gailea walked over and held up the parchment. It glowed for a few moments more before fading, and the music note returned to hover inside the column of light.

"See here? On this parchment is the song-spell *Hovaria* that allows you to hover in the air for a few moments after jumping. The melody is written out, along with the spell-word. *Hovaria* is useful if avoiding hot liquid or thorns or other dangerous substances underfoot." She paused to glance up at the observers around the chamber. "If any of you would care to help as well, we'd be so grateful! Collecting and transcribing so many songs will be a lot of work."

A few of the Echelon and Adelaran guards stepped forward, looking eager and somewhat humbled. Two Adelaran men claimed that they had experience transcribing music and would be happy to help in that regard.

One by one, everyone tapped the music notes twice to see if they would disperse to locate one of the parchements on the shelves. Songs of invisibility, stealth, various songs of attack and defense—the chamber swelled with the sound of Guardians playing a myriad of powerful tunes. Fire and electricity flew, wind gusted, people temporarily turned invisible or still as stone, shields of defense appeared and glistened. Musical spells filled the Chamber with sound and color. Some of the songs utilized magic words or even full verses, while others were formed only from specific melodies. Such a spectacle of so many varieties of magic, crafted from mere song, amazed Mikanah, distracting him from his worry over the instrument he now wielded.

Once all the floating notes and symbols had been tested, they sifted through each to determine which might be useful as they journeyed to Carmenna and ultimately to war. Then, Iolana, Nerine, and the two volunteer soldiers were granted quill and parchment to begin transcribing those songs. Gailea, Darice, and Ashden helped with this work. Donyon likewise volunteered his services, much to Mikanah's surprise. As a king, his education had likely afforded him the opportunity to learn how to write music, but Donyon astounded Mikanah in his acts of servitude. Such humility felt out of place for even the most generous of rulers.

After another two hours of rigorous work, the remaining songs they'd selected had been transcribed. Gailea and Lorelei said they should all rest their minds. They would have plenty of time to continue learning and practicing the collected songs during the remainder of their stay in Loz. Before departing, they would meet with Lynn and the Lozolian Council to discuss plans for the coming war. Meanwhile, they would practice and memorize as many spells as they could.

Emerging from the Chamber, they returned to their quarters in the castle, except for Mikanah, whose feet strayed along with his restless mind. Exhaustion clung to his body. Perhaps his mind should be equally weary, having trained on so many song-spells, but he had always absorbed new spells like a sponge, same as Iolana.

Mikanah wound through the castle, accompanied by two Echelon guards. At least they had decency to follow him at a distance this time. Then again, perhaps they simply felt more at ease in their own domain. Considering the number of Echelon and servants he passed in the halls, anyone would be a pure fool to try anything nefarious.

Mikanah wound through the halls, decorated with tapestries depicting various past kings and queens and other nobles, each wearing Loz's crest of a golden sword within a silver cross, until, scaling one of the towers, he came to a dovecote surrounded by small, open windows. Doves perched on the rafters and windowsills, tilting their heads as if wondering at the man who had invaded their private sanctum. Mikanah scowled. Even here, he was unwanted. Even here, too many eyes watched him.

As he inhaled the night air, he wished its chill would blanket his heart with the frost that had served him so well in the past. In his time with the Guardians, his protective, stone-cold walls had begun to melt. His emotions now blurred his clarity, especially about Iolana. She still hadn't spoken to him, still wouldn't look at him. He couldn't blame her.

And yet, a part of him wondered if he did. She had

pushed and pushed until his defenses had given way and he had accepted. Had *she* actually been the one to seduce *him*? Was that even possible?

A grunt reminded Mikanah of the Echelon's presence. They felt too close in this small space. He wanted to yell at them to go away, but even if they were stupid enough to obey, he'd likely bring more suspicion upon himself. With a sigh, he retreated back down the tower steps.

Mikanah wandered the castle halls, but there was no place of reprieve, no place he could feel alone, aside from his own chambers. Even they felt too constricting, but it was better than traipsing aimlessly, with so many eyes watching, waiting for him to mess up.

He neared the corridor containing his chambers when a voice called, "Mikanah? Are you alright? You seem troubled."

Mikanah froze and snapped his gaze toward Donyon, examining the man through wary eyes. While Donyon had portrayed himself as a sincere soul thus far, Mikanah was no stranger to the deceit of kings, and their means of manipulation to get what they wanted.

"Perhaps, if you would welcome a talk, you would feel more comfortable speaking in private, in your own chambers?"

Mikanah scrutinized the king, unable to discern whether he detected any deceit in the man. Like Moragon when he'd first met him, Donyon seemed to hide his motives cleverly.

Mikanah nodded and muttered, "Yes, your majesty."

Donyon followed him into the next corridor. As Mikanah entered his room, Donyon commanded the Echelon to remain outside the door. Again, Mikanah wondered if this man meant to earn his trust honestly or for some alternative motive. He supposed the Echelon could listen easily enough from outside the room if they chose to, but whatever the motive, Mikanah appreciated this small allowance of privacy.

He offered the small armchair to the king and drew over the chair from the desk for himself. They sat before the fireplace. The Lozolian crest of the cross and sword was carved into the mantle's center, flanked by knights riding their horses, swords drawn as they charged into battle. Mikanah glanced away as their bravery taunted him.

"It's been a long day," Donyon released a long sigh. He folded one leg across the other nonchalantly, and a slight smile touched his otherwise weary face. "Being appointed as a Guardian, learning a plethora of new musical pieces, it's impressive beyond words. Especially when one considers how quickly they developed the Chamber with its complicated protections. It feels like an ancient institution, but it's hardly a couple of years old."

Mikanah agreed with the king on this point. "Incredible sometimes, what necessity will drive people to do. Being in the Chamber was the most overwhelmed I've felt in some time."

"Overwhelmed…" Donyon touched his chin thoughtfully. "That is an apt word to describe what I experienced today. So much magic surrounding me, flowing through me as I was appointed. I almost wondered if I would lose control, or if it would control me. But I think that is the benefit of the Guardians learning and working together. None of us must bear the weight of so much power single-handedly."

Mikanah had wondered if Donyon directed such statements specifically toward him, but the king's gaze looked distant, as if he had unwittingly conjured some deeper memories inside himself.

"I feel it too," Mikanah admitted quietly. "All this new

power flowing through *me*. But the more I receive, the less I trust myself with it. I *think* I want to use it for good. But what if I'm still being used by Moragon? And if I'm not, what if I'm just using all this power for myself?"

"You doubt your ability to make a good Guardian—a good leader," Donyon suggested.

"I know I'm no leader," Mikanah muttered. "I spent much of my life a coward. I've hurt people, tortured people, done things that would make you despise me if you knew."

Mikanah hoped his words would drive the king away so that he could return to his solemn brooding. In fact, he expected as much.

Instead, the king said, "Would it surprise you to know that I lived my life in much the same way?"

Mikanah glared at him. Was he bluffing? Spinning some moral tale in an attempt to lift Mikanah's spirits?

Donyon watched him intensely. "Listen well as I tell you something. I too never saw myself as a leader. I saw myself as weak. I did what I was told, often to save myself from punishment, other times for the empty pleasure of gaining my superiors' approval. From as young as I can recall, I was declared 'destined' to be king, despite having no royal blood."

Mikanah's brows rose. and he leaned forward. "You aren't of royal descent?"

Donyon adjusted in his seat with a sigh. "I am not. You see, my father was a great Adelaran lord, close friend of King Weston, the late King of Adelar. He had no son but had always valued m*e* as one. He did have a daughter, but she died." He paused and glanced away. Again, his gaze looked far off, troubled. Mikanah wondered if he would finish speaking or if he'd become paralyzed by another unpleasant memory.

Finally, the king looked at him again, continuing

quietly. "There was a time when I wanted to become a priest. I desired a quiet life of spiritual servtitude in an Amielian shrine. I never expressed this desire, as neither my father nor King Weston would have entertained it. More likely, they'd have mocked it. Suffice to say, I didn't want to be king. But then, when King Weston died, the throne was left to my father and soon enough passed to me. I was forced to take responsibility. I've not always done the best job. Up until yesterday, my people were at war because of my own blind spite. But despite all our flaws and fears, we must keep on, learn, and grow. I see a hidden strength in you, Mikanah. You are angry, yes. But you may turn your fury into a raging force against Moragon."

Donyon rose to his feet, announcing that he should get back to his own chambers and rest for tomorrow's musical training and Council meetings. He advised Mikanah to do the same before bidding him goodnight and leaving him with his thoughts.

Mikanah stared into the flames, hoping some illuminating answers might leap at him. He was bewildered that someone as strong and sure as Donyon could have shared even a fraction of the same sort of past as him. Could Donyon be right? Could he someday become the Guardian and protector that Carmenna deserved? And what of Iolana? What would—or should—he do regarding her?

CHAPTER 39

HARMONY WAVERING

The next morning, the Guardians and Nerine joined with Lynn Lectim and the rest of the Lozolian Council inside their Council chamber. Extra chairs had been brought inside the room, allowing them space at the triangular table with three equal-length sides, crafted from a white marble flecked with silver. Banners hung between the long, narrow, stained-glass windows surrounding the room on two walls. Male and female soldiers were embroidered on the tapestries, golden swords within silver crosses stitched across their breastplates.

Gailea eased wearily into the seat beside Chamblin. Nightmares had impeded her sleep last night, devoid of controlling magic and evil spirits, but troubling enough to steal the full rest she had craved after yesterday's intense musical training. Her mind had plagued her with visions of being in Adelaran court, under Crispin's rule. Distorted memories of their marriage had assaulted her until at last, she saw the war, when she'd fled him with her children. Only this time, Crispin had woken from her lullaby to capture and chain her inside the castle's prison, shackled hopelessly to the wall right where her old mentor Aline had been.

Thus, Gailea felt devoid of the patience and wit needed to discuss war plans. Glancing at Chamblin, her irritation deepened into anxiety. As they were driven further toward danger, his eyesight diminished. He had survived thus far with their help, but could they protect him well enough from Moragon's wrath, within the confines of his own domain, surrounded by his mentally warped armies?

Her attention drifted to Nerine, sitting farther down the table between Iolana and Darice. Concern mixed with further dread as Gailea wondered if the girl should be here at all. Before she could voice this worry, one of the counselors spoke:

"Excuse my ignorance, if it is indeed at fault, but it would appear there are nine of you present. And yet, I had thought the Octavial Guardians limited to eight in number, as their name depicts?"

The man drummed his fingertips together, looking more curious than concerned, unlike some of his comrades. Redford, Gailea thought his name was. He had dark skin, auburn hair, and wore a dark green robe with a gold sword and silver cross stitched across his chest, the same as every other counselor present, aside from Lynn who dressed in her usual pink and green robes.

"Nerine here isn't a Guardian." Iolana touched her friend's arm. Nerine chewed her lip, pink flushed touched her cheeks, and Iolana quickly added, "But she's been a steadfast companion through all our travels. She's a very skilled water Nymph."

"That she is." Donyon nodded in Nerine's direction.

"She managed to swim beneath the magic barriers encompassing Adelar, a feat thought impossible for hundreds of years."

"Impressive as that is, I don't understand how that's linked to her presence here, at this Council meeting." Redford gave Nerine a kind, sympathetic look. "We're here to discuss war plans. This seems no place for a child."

"Perhaps not for most, but my point was that Nerine has proven herself both brave and capable, just as much as any Guardian. She may even be one of the best musicians among us."

Gailea leaned forward, hoping to catch Donyon's glance, but he didn't turn in her direction. She seethed inwardly. How could he speak so matter-of-factly about this matter?

"Redford makes a valid point," she said. "It's not as though Nerine intends to accompany us on this new mission."

"Why wouldn't I?" The innocence in Nerine's tone further made Gailea want to shake sense into her. "I've come with you this far, and as King Donyon says, I've done everything I can to prove myself useful."

"But this is a war, love." Darice's gentle tone drew Nerine's attention to her. "We've been through much danger already, but nothing like what's to come. I've seen war. So has Gailea." Darice nodded toward her, meeting her gaze. "War is no place for anyone, but least of all a child, and so needlessly."

"I'm no child." A rare indignation-tinged Nerine's voice. Gailea liked to see the girl stand up for herself but wished she would do so under any other circumstances.

"How old are you?" asked a female counselor with long, dark brown hair.

"Fifteen and a half."

Redford snorted. "Only a child cares for menial details like half-years."

"Or someone who's observant."

Gailea's eyes blazed at Chamblin beside her, but he either didn't see her or chose to ignore her.

"I'm not saying that I advocate for her to follow us to Carmenna, right into the very molten core of danger. But we must give credit where credit is deserved. And I think we must also let her choose for herself, as we have thus far."

"And I think sometimes there are choices we must let others make *for* us, for our own good!" Gailea nearly shouted the last words. She was already on edge at the idea of a war she would be much more directly involved in than when Donyon had taken Adelar from Crispin. Her patience spent, she found it difficult to contain both her worry at placing Nerine in any further danger and her frustration that others seemed to have no interest in discouraging her from such foolishness, especially others like Chamblin, who ought to know better.

"Gailea."

Nerine spoke Gailea's name gently but firmly. Gailea gazed down the table at the girl who watched her steadily, sitting straight, chin lifted in a resolute way that deepened Gailea's dread.

"I know you worry for me. I know you all do. But I've chosen to come with you all this way. And I think that Chamblin's right, that if I want to come with you further, even all the way, that is also my choice. And if you or anyone tries to force me to stay behind, then as Donyon points out, it's not as though I couldn't still find a way. How then would you stop me? Imprison me? Cast a magic spell on me?" Nerine fixed her gaze on Gailea, narrowing her eyes to reveal a glimmer of hurt before looking away.

"Such dramatic statements." The woman who'd already spoken rolled her eyes. "Again, signs that this girl is just that: a mere girl."

"Then by your definition, I too was a 'mere girl' when I was involved in my first war." Lynn's tone was kind, but she directed a pointed gaze at her fellow counselor. "I was hardly thirteen when I first came under the care of the Great Fairy, Gemina, and when her island came under attack by the Mass."

Gailea breathed deeply, vainly trying to quell her trembling nerves. "Lynn, surely you can't be suggesting that Nerine should come with us?"

Lynn returned Gailea's exasperated stare with a level one of her own. "Had I not been there to help Gemina, she and everyone on that island might have died. True, I could have died just as well, but that was my choice to make. I chose to risk my life to save another. And I say that Nerine should be free to choose the same."

"I second that, if only for her safety," Chamblin said. "Otherwise, what's to stop her from pursuing us? Better she stays in our sights than to be lost unknown in some senseless mission of following us in secret, where she could far more easily fall into the wrong hands."

Chamblin looked toward Gailea with a sympathy-filled gaze, and Gailea sat back in her chair, feeling defeated. Hating truth did not alter it, and she knew Chamblin spoke truth. Nerine had proved that she could not, *would* not be stopped. If she was stubborn enough to follow them, best that happen in their watchful care than out on her own, leaving her to the threat of Moragon's symbolic but all-too-real wolves.

"What do you choose, Nerine?" Lynn gazed right at the girl.

Nerine sat tall, chin still lifted. "I choose to stay with the Guardians."

"So let it be done," Lynn said. "Now that's settled, let's turn our attention to sharing the war plans the Council have been discussing lately."

As talk turned to war, Gailea's attention waved in and out. This was perhaps the last and thus most vital conversation they would have directly with the Lozolian Council before delving inside the war itself, but Gailea's mind drifted with exhaustion and dread. Iolana was still a child herself, and yet as a Guardian, it would be nearly impossible for Gailea to argue against her involvement. Wasn't it enough that she had come to care for Iolana like her own child, much as she had tried to resist doing so? Must she see another of her pupils plunged into senseless peril? If only Nerine could understand the risk of what Moragon could do to her.

Needing distraction, Gailea shifted in her chair and did her best to tune into the Council's plans. They were doing all they could to garner the support of the surrounding island kingdoms for the inevitable war. Adelar and Rosa were committed to joining their fight. The Council would send messages to the Guardians while they traveled, updating them on war plans.

The Guardians' purpose in Carmenna would be to resume Lorelei's search for the heir, while making their way toward the borders of Castle Alaula, to be ready for battle there. One of the Echelon soldiers questioned the decision to attack such a well-fortified castle, but Lynn declared that they couldn't wait for Moragon to come to them. He wouldn't be foolish enough to do so, and the longer they waited, the stronger whatever magical Vessel he was preparing would likely become. Lynn stated also that finding a true heir and giving the people hope for life beyond Moragon's rule might empassion the Carmennans and help them overcome enough of their fears to draw more of them to their side of the fight.

"An heir?" Donyon asked. "An heir to what?"

"To King Noheah's throne," Lorelei said. "When I was last in Carmenna, I researched rumors of a true, bloodline heir. I do believe one may still live. Once we're back there, I intend to continue my search. As we travel across the land, I hope to gather more clues, and hopefully, some real answers."

"Excellent. It would certainly aid us to have a leader the people feel they can rally around."

Gailea's focus waxed and waned again until at last, she heard Lynn announcing the Council meeting adjourned and the Guardians dismissed to rest and prepare for tomorrow's voyage.

Gailea jumped to her feet, eager to leave the Council room behind, to clear her mind with fresh air. Chamblin said her name and reached out to her, speaking gentle words that might have been an apology or some comfort regarding Nerine, but Gailea politely excused herself before hurrying from the room, directing herself toward the gardens.

Entering the inner courtyard surrounded by the castle's high, gray stone walls, she breathed deeply, relishing the clean breeze rippling over her. Castle Iridescence was too far inland for the salt air to reach, but it was situated on a smaller island in the midst of a lake that served as a great moat. The water of that lake was clear as crystal and cleansed the surrounding air. It cleansed her lungs now, seeming to disperse some of the anger, hurt, and fear flowing through her in what lately felt like endless waves.

Familiar laughter snared her attention. Across the lawn, between the rows of rosal and moon blossom bushes, Iolana and Nerine walked, arms linked. They laughed again, and the sound soothed Gailea, inasmuch as it broke her. They sounded exactly how they should be: simple schoolgirls, two close friends sharing some secret joke.

Gailea stepped instinctively toward them but then hesitated. She shouldn't interrupt such rare joy, should she? And yet, this was her last chance to try to persuade Nerine away from her reckless decision.

Picking up her pace, Gailea hurried past the trellises hanging with grapevines and the rows of neatly pruned bushes and stopped before the girls who now walked beside the grand fountain, its phoenix statue spreading its wings to the sky as arcs of water gushed from its beak. The girls admired the fountain, but as Gailea cleared her throat, they glanced up in surprise.

"Gailea! You came for a refreshing walk as well?" Iolana asked, as she and Nerine both smiled warmly.

"I did. And I don't wish to interrupt yours. But if I could only have a moment to speak with you, Nerine?"

Nerine's demeanor transformed. Her smile faded into a worried frown which then deepened as hurt gleamed unabashedly in her eyes. That look alone pained Gailea so that she almost wished she hadn't spoken, but a stronger part of her knew she must.

"Nerine?" she prompted again.

"If you're wanting to persuade me not to come, you won't." Nerine's tone held a fervent decisiveness.

"Nerine, I must say I admire this new streak of courage and confidence, but I must also say that there are times when it is best to know when to contain such traits. I believe that now is one of those times, that you'd be better off returning to the school, where you're safe."

"Return to the school. And do what? Study while I know my friends are out here, fighting, maybe dying? When maybe I could have done something to save them, if I was there?"

Gailea opened her mouth to reply, but Nerine pressed on, "Everyone has always underestimated me. But not anymore. I practice my water magic all of the time. I pick up on songs quickly. I can help. I will help. I'm coming."

Gailea stood, struck silent as Nerine's pain seemed to flow toward her in tangible waves. Though Nerine had directed her frustration at "everyone," Gailea noticed the intensity of her gaze and felt that Nerine spoke mostly, if not only, toward her. Before she could think of how to answer, Nerine bid her good afternoon and, squeezing Iolana's arm, turned them around to continue their walk through the garden.

Her strength waning at last, Gailea collapsed on the side of the fountain. She glanced down at her reflection, only for one of the small goldfish to pop up beneath the surface, altering it with ripples. After a few moments, the waters stilled and her reflection was whole once more, but it was too late. Gailea had seen the distortion. No matter how hard she tried, she couldn't see the girls through any other lens other than that of her own youth, yearning to spare them from every evil she had endured.

But she couldn't spare them. Lorelei and Iolana had suffered even more than her at Moragon's hands. She hadn't been there to save them then, and she couldn't save Nerine now from throwing herself at the same horrendous perils.

Gailea wept freely, releasing the tears her body had stored since the nightmares, since Adelar, since everything.

CHAPTER 40

AH LUM AMIEL

With new songs, instruments, and magic in tow, the Guardians and Nerine set sail the next afternoon for Carmenna. A unit of twenty new Echelon guards accompanied them. The Lozolian Council had agreed that fresh, well-rested soldiers would be of more use to the Guardians than those who had spent the past few weeks traveling far and wide with them.

Lorelei climbed up the stairs and stepped on deck of the large wooden ship, shielding her eyes from the bright sunlight overhead. Wind whipped past her, giving her an unexpected shove. She caught herself on a nearby crate. The Council had set them sailing on a merchant's ship that commonly made deliveries to Carmenna, to prevent any immediate suspicion upon their arrival, and all of them had been granted gray and blue linen tunics and cloaks to help them blend in more naturally. Even the Echelon wore common Carmennan garb over chain mail or leather tunics. They stood scattered across the deck from bow to stern, scanning the open waters for any signs of danger, keeping the Guardians in their sights at all times.

Lifting her head to inhale the salty air, Lorelei watched as the wind filled the ship's two great sails. Then, she set to searching for Mikanah. She had spent her morning trying to draw a map of Carmenna, as much as she could remember, and especially Castle Alaula. Chamblin had accompanied her for a while, granting her advice where he could, but he had only visited Carmenna twice before, and this coupled with his limited eyesight made it a challenge for him to help as fully as they needed. Mikanah would surely be able to recall any details her memory had overlooked.

Lorelei walked toward the stern, scanning the ship. Sailors shouted to one another, turning the rudder and adjusting the sail lines. Her glance fell upon Chamblin, who now taught Nerine various songs on his mandolin while she mimicked on his pipa. Nerine's face bent in full concentration as she mastered song after song with impressive swiftness. If Chamblin could help Nerine's confidence match the level of her skill as a musician, she might well prove one of the strongest magicians of them all.

Ashden and Darice sat not far away, practicing together on their respective lute and flute. Below deck, Gailea practiced with Iolana, while Donyon had barred himself in his room, ciphering through maps and old texts and penning letters containing further instructions to his people.

Everyone seemed hard at work. All except for the one individual she seemed unable to locate.

"Lorelei?"

She jumped a little and whirled to face Mikanah, who had just come up from below deck as well, joining her.

"Just the person I wanted to see," she said. "Are you busy?"

He frowned, even more sullen than usual. "No. I'd thought to see Iolana, help her with songs, but she's occupied with Gailea."

"All the better," Lorelei said brightly, hoping to distract him. "I need your help with a task."

"What task?"

"None of the armies coming to aid us in Carmenna have ever been inside the castle walls. It's well fortified, and it'll be moreso with Moragon's droves of mentally dominated soldiers. We can likely infiltrate the castle through the caves, but once inside, there are some things I don't remember. I'm trying to construct a map. I thought perhaps you could help me."

Mikanah's stormy gaze lightened with interest, and he followed her back down the stairs into the ship's hull. They walked through the single corridor lit by lanterns overhead before branching into one of the two cabins they'd been granted to share.

For the next few hours, they toiled, pouring over the large, half-drawn map spread across the floor, quills and ink at the ready. Mikanah delved fully into the task, clearly relieved to have something to focus on. By the time they had several detailed maps sketched, Nerine popped in to announce their evening meal had been delivered in the other cabin.

Lorelei and Mikanah joined the Guardians in the other room lined with small bunks. Some of them sat around the wooden table with chairs, while others perched on the ends of the bunks to eat their meal.

"How goes everyone's progress?" Lorelei asked as she tore off a piece of biscuit, popping it into her mouth with a bit of salted pork. "Mikanah was a great help to me today, making maps of the castle. I was also able to map out some of the cave networks that lead inside the castle. That may be our best chance of infiltrating."

"That's good work," Chamblin said, with a proud smile and nod at Mikanah. "I'd be glad to examine the maps with you later. Well done."

"Thank you," Mikanah said, "though I cannot take all the credit Lorelei would give. My memory may have been an important asset, but her attention to detail helped everything come together."

He exchanged a polite nod and smile with her before his gaze drifted to Iolana. She had been staring at him with interest, but now she focused on her stew, looking annoyed.

"Gailea and I have been equally busy," Iolana said, "mastering the songs we learned in the Chamber."

"I think that's been the goal of many." Chamblin grinned and patted Nerine on the arm. "Even Nerine has picked up several tunes rather quickly."

Gailea swept a glance across everyone. "I think now that we've had some practice, it's time we begin teaching you *Ah Lum Amiel*. I'd suggest a joint practice session once we've finished our meal?"

"To which I might suggest we play up on deck. Nerine and I were quite relishing it earlier, with the glory of the wind and waves to motivate us." Chamblin winked at Nerine, and she returned the gesture with a light-hearted laugh.

After lunch, they grabbed their instruments in their cases and headed back on deck. They gathered on the starboard side, around a couple of crates. Mikanah helped Chamblin perch on the edge of one of the crates. Nerine and Iolana joined them on the other crate, Nerine fiddling with the frayed end of a rope. She smiled at Gailea but then glanced away, and Lorelei wondered. The two women had hardly spoken that morning except to share brief niceties, and an odd tension seemed to hang between them.

Lorelei and the other Guardians stood facing those sitting on the crates. Gailea and Lorelei asked everyone to wield their musical instruments and led everyone in several of the protective and offensive song-spells they had been mastering, reminding them of the importance of the intent behind each song.

"For example," Lorelei said, "when practicing *Segmunda*, the song that can physically push your enemies away from you, be sure you're not picturing one of your companions in your mind. And remember that the songs themselves can be practiced without using magic. It all depends on your intent when playing them."

After running through several pieces, Gailea sheathed her flute in its case and let her serious but well-meaning gaze fall on each of them. Lorelei smiled, recognizing the expression as one she often wore while teaching at the academy. She wondered if teaching them now brought Gailea any comfort, or if it only reminded her of days past that she could never return to. After her father's death, Lorelei had felt the latter a long while any time she glimpsed one of his carvings.

"Now," Gailea revealed two sheets of folded parchment from a pocket in her dark blue tunic and unfolded it. "I was studying *Ah Lum Amiel* earlier, and its melody, while lengthy, is simple enough to memorize. But the intensity with which one must sing it, the amount of purpose one must pour into it, that is what makes learning and using it a most challenging feat."

"What do you mean by 'purpose'?" Nerine's eyes shone bright with curiosity at Gailea. Perhaps Lorelei had imagined the tension between them after all.

Gailea smiled at Nerine. "The purpose of the song is to cast out evil, dark spells, dark spirits. The greater the evil, the more one must focus on the *purpose* of casting out evil as one sings. When our armies go up against

Moragon, there's no telling how powerful he will be. In the moment we face him, we must want nothing more in the entire world than to destroy him and every evil thing he has ever done."

"I don't think that will be a problem," Mikanah muttered, while Chamblin nodded beside him.

"Agreed." Donyon grabbed one of the ropes stretching diagonally overhead, bracing his foot on the edge of a crate to steady himself. "But while we're on the subject of war, there is one question that perhaps I should have posed already. The Carmennans are already likely to be untrusting, having been usurped from a wicked outside ruler. Who's to say any of them will join with us? How do we convince them that our realms—mine, the Rosans, and others—are not simply coming to take their kingdom as Moragon did?"

"The heir," Gailea said, looking to Lorelei, seemingly just as confused she repeated what they already knew. "If we find the heir, that will help us."

"Yes, of course." Donyon waved a dismissive hand. "But I mean, what if we never find such an heir? Or even if we do, convincing this person to join us could be another difficult matter."

"I don't think it will be a challenge," Mikanah said. "Everyone in Carmenna who isn't under Moragon's control abhors him. If they can be convinced that they have a hope of succeeding, I think such a man will jump at the chance to fight him."

"Or woman," Gailea suggested.

Mikanah looked at her curiously, but she spoke to Lorelei. "You remember what we discussed some weeks ago, when you first came to Pakua?"

"I do." Lorelei's gazing at Iolana was enough to alert everyone as to her meaning—everyone but the center of their attention.

"What is it?" Iolana asked. "Why is everyone looking at me?"

"You can't be serious," Mikanah snapped, the bite in his voice indicating he had guessed very well the direction their conversation prepared to take. "I can't believe you'd be so eager to paint that target on her back, Gailea. I thought you cared more for her than that."

"'Eager' is the last word I'd use to define my feelings on the matter, I assure you."

"*What* target?" Iolana demanded. "What are you all talking about?"

"We had discussed the possibility…" Lorelei kept her voice gentle toward Iolana. "And *only* the possibility, of your being the heir."

Mikanah leaped to his feet, his glare livid. "Ridiculous!"

"Is it?" Lorelei challenged him. "Iolana was one of his favorite musicians, much like you, Mikanah. But then, all of a sudden, he wanted her dead. If she was one of his favorites, there are very few reasons he would have wanted to kill her. Even if she defied him, he might have kept her alive, unless there was some deeper reason for not doing so."

"You think *I* am descended from royalty?" Iolana's tone was as disbelieving as Mikanah's. She stared at Lorelei as if she were mad.

"You know nothing of your parents or family," Gailea said. "It's a possibility I am loath to consider, but one we must keep open."

"And you couldn't have mentioned this to any of us before now?" Mikanah said. "You didn't think this was important for us to know, for *her* to know—?"

"Stop, Mikanah." Lorelei held up a hand to silence him, ignoring as he muttered beneath his breath. "No one kept information from you or her on purpose.

There were other matters to contend with at the time. Only Amiel knows who the heir is, but for her safety, we can't rule her out as a possibility."

"Amiel," Mikanah said with a scoff. "If *this* is Amiel's will—"

"Amiel," Nerine interrupted, firmly and with reverence. All eyes turned to her. "Perhaps now would be the best time to learn the song. You'll all have to work together to sing it, right? What better way to unite the Guardians in harmony instead of all this bickering?"

"The girl might be wiser than the lot of us thrown together," Chamblin said, with an admiring glance in her direction. "When we confront Moragon, *that* will be an ultimate test of trust, of being able to work together. I say she's right. I say we try the song."

Everyone looked to Lorelei and Gailea expectantly. Lorelei studied Gailea, who nodded in agreement.

"This is one song which the Guardians must *sing*," Gailea began. "You can play it as well, but it is only with your voice that you can create the deepest purpose necessary for the song to work. It must come from your innermost hearts and souls. Its power can be strengthened at its conclusion, by each of us singing our notes that match our Guardians' marks, just as we did for the *Sonata of Appointment*. Darice, would you mind holding the parchment for me, so I can read it while leading everyone?"

"Of course, sister."

Darice held the first page of the folded parchment in front of Gailea who said, "Listen closely, and when you are ready, join in."

Lorelei raised her lyre, Gailea her flute. Gailea blew a long note on her flute and then, together, they began. Lorelei sang as she strummed. Once Gailea had led Lorelei through the entire piece, she lowered her flute and sang with her as they began the song over again. Her rich alto blended with Lorelei's soprano to create the majestic words, *Ah Lum Amiel: Amiel is Light*, over, and over.

Mikanah joined with both his voice and violin.

Iolana sang in her high, clear soprano, and Nerine joined her. As Nerine's soprano blended perfectly with Iolana's, Lorelei glanced at her with amusement. The younger girl's eyes reflected an unusual confidence, and her voice never wavered.

Chamblin chimed in next, then Ashden with Darice, and finally Donyon. Together, their voices swelled as they had inside the Chamber of Music, entwining like roots of a new flower plunging into the soil, creating a solid foundation. Then, like the leaves and petals of that flower blossoming for the first time, their song expanded. The harmonies became more balanced, as did the traces of dissonance. Their voices became one voice, as the petals of their newly planted union reached for the sunlight.

The song rushed to a crescendo. Gailea waved her hand in a sign for them to sing their individual Guardian notes. Then, at last, the song ended, leaving only the rush of the ocean waves in its wake. The Guardians looked exhausted but exhilarated at once, some of them panting for breath.

Lorelei's heart flew inside her. "Did you feel it? Did you feel how...how powerful we were?" She grappled for the right word. *Powerful* simply didn't feel vibrant or alive enough, but she wasn't sure any word would.

"It was like I wasn't even myself anymore," Mikanah eased down on the crate, eyes wide with blatant astonishment. "I couldn't have my own fears or desires. I couldn't be selfish. There was just the song and everything it was meant to do."

"We were truly one." Iolana swept a wondering glance across them all. Her gaze lingered longest on Mikanah before resting on Gailea. "Even our heartsongs. I couldn't distinguish them. All I could hear was *Ah Lum Amiel.*"

"*Ah Lum Amiel,*" Nerine beamed up at Lorelei and Gailea. "Amiel is Light."

Gailea smiled gently at Nerine. "Yes. And we have just experienced a glimpse of the magnitude of the light we can create, the inner light that will be necessary to expel the Moragon's darkness. Right now, we feel spiritually energized. We weren't fighting against any enemy just now, and so we feel only strengthened by the song's magic. However, once we're fighting against Moragon, it will take everything in our power to focus on the unity we just felt and will likely prove physically exhausting."

After chatting a bit more, they parted ways, except for Iolana who said something to Gailea that made her stay behind. Worry crept back into Iolana's face, tainting the peace that the song had granted her, and Lorelei wondered if she expressed more concerns about the heir theory.

As they headed down the stairs below deck, Lorelei touched Mikanah's shoulder, stopping him from entering his quarters after the others. He turned toward her, his eyes reflecting a now almost ghostly surprise.

"Did the song really effect you that poignantly?" Lorelei asked gently.

Mikanah nodded but looked past her, his gaze distant as if he reached to understand the words he spoke. "It really did. I don't know if I should only be impressed, humbled, or concerned by how much the song seemed to take hold of me. It didn't feel manipulative or controlling like any piece Moragon ever had me perform. Rather it filled me with this sense of peace and goodness that I couldn't stop from taking over me, but I also didn't want to." He let his gaze meet hers. "Is that what it's like, to have have faith, hope?"

Not wishng to alarm him with the sudden tears form-ing in her eyes, Lorelei only nodded, her heart swell-ing with unexpected emotion as he hinted at the hope nestled just beneath the surface of his own heart, if only he would allow it to grow and thrive.

"What a wonder it must be to possess that all the time," he said, "not just in a few fleeting moments of singing. I hope I could find that some day. That we all could."

His demeanor grew solemn once more as he bowed and entered the men's cabin.

Lorelei entered her own quarters and laid down in her bunk, letting her tears fall quietly as she thought, *I hope so too.*

~*~*~

After several more days of practicing songs, map-making, and discussing strategies of how to proceed once they landed, the shores of Carmenna loomed into view.

Among the music the Guardians had gleaned from the Chamber was a song-spell called *Supressario* that could make them elusive for a few minutes at a time, allowing them to blend in with their background. They would use this spell and other protective charms as they advanced toward Castle Alaula. They may not have the power to conceal whole armies, but they could be careful to keep themselves safe.

Supressario itself required much concentration and would wear them out if used too often, but they took advantage of it as they departed their ship in three row boats. Three Carmennan sailors rowed them to the rocky shore before returning with the small vessels to the ship.

The Guardians, Nerine, and Echelon slipped into the thick cover of the nearby woods. The soldiers found a clearing well-secluded by a thick wall of trees and brush, and there they set up camp.

"No one should wander far from the camp without Echelon escorts," Gailea said. "As we get further inland, we can start taking turns making trips to various towns, to try to learn more about the heir. If we go alone or in pairs, it'll look less suspicious than for all of us to go around asking questions."

By the time camp was set up, night had fallen. Instead of a fire, Darice and Iolana created orbs of floating light around the clearing. Iolana's orbs only emitted light, but Darice taught her a simple song-spell, *Flárlia*, to enhance the heat they emitted. Their glow was fainter than fire and gave off neither smoke nor smell and, if necessary, could be extinguished by singing a short series of notes.

Some of their party seated themselves in small groups scattered across the clearing, while the remaining Echelon patrolled the perimeter. They had all agreed it was best not to practice their music at night. An ensemble sounding from the middle of the woods was sure to draw attention. Gailea had taught them *Dumkana* to diminish or magnify sounds, but it worked best in enclosed spaces. Darice knew a spell that could further muffle the sound of their music, but it needed the power of sunlight, so they would wait until day when they were on the move again to practice.

Gailea sat with Chamblin on an old log. Drawing his mandolin over his shoulder, he played softly. His ballade soothed Gailea as she watched Mikanah, Lorelei, and Donyon. The three of them pored over a map together, though Mikanah kept shooting intense glances in Iolana's direction. Iolana sat beside Nerine while Darice plaited the Nymph's hair into an intricate braid. Nerine all the while tried to talk to Iolana, but she kept glancing over at Mikanah, clearly distracted. Nerine looked upset, until Ashden said something that made her laugh.

Chamblin shifted his focus to Gailea, though still picking out his tune. "You're having a hard time. You've had a hard time since Adelar."

"Do you think I'm too mistaken? In my fears? My distrust of the boy?"

Chamblin shook his head. "I want to trust Mikanah. I've always wanted to trust him. But until this war is past, and we see how he truly conducts himself, we don't really know. If confronted by Moragon, he could change loyalties again, whether purposely or not. Between the two of us, I think Nerine has a better head on her shoulders than him, or than any of us at times, despite her being the youngest of us."

Gailea twisted the hem of her tunic, pained as Chamblin brought up Nerine's name. They had spoken little since their encounter in the gardens, nor did Gailea truly know how to approach her. She never meant to imply that Nerine possessed inferior potential or skills.

"Nerine is intelligent. Suited for war? No. I stand behind my previous defense, that she would be best off returning to the school. She's still a child."

"Yes," Chamblin agreed with a thoughtful head tilt, "but she's grown more than I think you've had time to notice. She misses you, you know. You should pay her more heed."

Gailea frowned as his words stung more sharply than the last. "I haven't ignored her if that's what you're implying. I've just been rather busy, as we all have, dealing with demons, Council matters, planning a war."

"Others have still found time to encourage her. She needs that more from *you*. She feels even more directionless now that everyone else is an official Guardian, especially with you spending more and more time with

Iolana. She doesn't say it, but I can tell. It's her own kind of jealousy. She feels left out—"

Everyone glanced up as two Echelon men led another young man into the clearing. He bore the Lozolian standard on his tunic, but a small metal pin shaped like a blue rosal framed with flames showed that he was likely Rosan-born. A leather bag was strapped around his shoulder. From within, he presented two envelopes and said, "I am Brodach, a messenger of the Lozolian Council. I have a message from the Council and another message from Adelar."

"Thank you, sir." Donyon strode forward and took the letter extended to him.

Gailea took the letter addressed to the Council. "Thank you. May Amiel grant you a safe journey back."

"Thank you, my lady, and Your Majesty. May Amiel be with you as well—*all* of you."

The messenger dipped his head and folded his hands before him, prayer-like, muttering indecipherable words. A soft blue light glowed along his skin. It brightened, the rays expanding to encompass him like a shimmering, transparent jewel for just a moment before he and the light vanished.

"Who was that?" Iolana's voice was edged with an abrupt sharpness as she glared at the spot where the young man had stood.

"A messenger from the Council."

"Oh." Iolana returned her attention to Nerine as Darice finished braiding her hair.

"What is it?" Darice asked her. "You look shaken."

"Reynard had the same power," Iolana said quietly. "Of instant transportation. I guess my mind was playing tricks on me, made me feel like that messenger might be an enemy."

"Reynard *has* the same power, not *had*." Mikanah glanced up from the maps in Iolana's direction. "I'm sure Reynard's powers haven't diminished, any more than his favor with Moragon."

"Yes," Iolana shot him a sharp look, "but it can be nice to speak of things as if they're mere ghosts of the past. They *are* the past, for us anyway."

"For now."

Iolana narrowed her gaze at him before tearing away and helping Darice add small wildflowers to Nerine's braid. Mikanah sucked in his breath, looking angry, but said nothing more.

"What news from Adelar?"

Ashden's question drew Gailea's attention back to the letters. She sat on the log beside Chamblin while everyone watched Donyon with anticipation.

Donyon opened his note and scanned its contents. "The alliance between Adelar and Rosa still holds. Conall has been most successful in joining the two kingdoms peacefully for our cause. They will send a fleet of soldiers to Carmenna in a few days' time."

Donyon gave a firm nod, seemingly satisfied, as Gailea unfolded the second parchment. "The Lozolian Council has been able to gather a few more allies. The Elves of Sallusay will join our cause, as will Abalino. Bedlington remains neutral…"

"As ever," Chamblin muttered with a roll of his eyes.

"…but Moragon has gained a new ally as well. Spaniño has joined him. Our one grace is that Prismatic has refused to send him aid. Ellion prefers to keep his armies to himself, what with all the unrest and civil war there."

"Praise Amiel, indeed," Chamblin said. "An army of Prismatic soldiers gifted in light and illusion magic might have meant our undoing. The Spaniños can send large numbers, but as a race, they've no inherent magic. Any further news?"

"The Council promises to keep in contact with us as frequently as they can. We'll meet up with the armies once they arrive in Carmenna, along the northern forests bordering the castle." Gailea handed the parchment to Donyon. He scanned its contents before passing it along to Lorelei. "We'll write the Council back, tell them our latest plans, ask them to send whatever Echelon they can spare and our other new allies."

Donyon nodded. "I can help write such a letter, first thing in the morning."

They relaxed for a while then, with Chamblin strumming a soothing serenade on his mandolin. Ashden joined in with his lute, while Nerine harmonized with her voice.

Eventually, the girls lay down to sleep, while Donyon and Mikanah moved to sit by one of the larger light orbs, studying their maps once more. Darice and Ashden walked over to join Gailea and Chamblin on the log. As Gailea shifted, she felt something press softly against her thigh. Curious, she felt along the side of her tunic, then slipped her hand inside her pocket to reveal another small envelope, sealed with a wax seal depicting a rosal.

"What's that, sister?" Darice leaned in, running her hands through her long dark hair as she rebraided it.

"I don't know. I just found it in my pocket. I wonder if the messenger could have left it, though why and how?" She opened it, unfolded the parchment within, and read it.

"Well?" Chamblin asked after a few moments.

Gailea reread the letter, first raising her brows in amusement before furrowing them with worry. "It's from Lord Celegrave. Saying how glad he and the Council of Adelar are to have a daughter of both Rosa and

Adelar leading in battle, and that they would have been prouder still to see someone like me lead their lands, if such were possible."

Chamblin's face twisted with deep thought. "That's a mightily gracious compliment. Too gracious. If I may lend my thoughts?"

"You may."

"It sounds like, well…as if they truly would want you for their queen."

"I thought the same," Darice said.

"Yes, it rather does sound that way, doesn't it?" Gailea's gaze drifted over Celegrave's words yet again. As much as she didn't want to, she couldn't deny their possible disloyal implications. A shiver waved through her as she imagined being queen again.

She folded the letter, shoving it back into her pocket. "A ridiculous notion. I've no desire to rule again, over Adelar or anyplace else. I have no desire to live in Adelar, or even set foot there again if I can help it. Adelar may help us win this war, but that's as far as my ties to them extend."

A sigh drew Gailea's attention to Ashden. Darice had formed more of her small light orbs. She held one, soothed by its warmth, while Ashden passed another back and forth in his hands, studying it with a weary expression. "I hope, when this is all said and done, that our world can be as it was when we joined together singing *Ah Lum Amiel*. Wouldn't it be wonderful, if all kingdoms could be united under the protection and solidarity we felt while singing that song? What a shame that such peace must be a struggle."

"Yes," Gailea said quietly. She let her gaze drift between Iolana, who slept peacefully, and Mikanah who now sat beside her, staring emptily at one of the light orbs, face pulled into a taut frown. "What a shame indeed."

CHAPTER 41

REYNARD'S KEEP

Over the next few days, the Guardians traveled to various towns. They scoured the southern cities, taking turns seeking clues regarding the heir. Gailea, Ashden, Darice, or Chamblin would pose as outsiders passing through Carmenna, sometimes visiting kin or friends. Having heard war rumors or stories of the jovial King Noheah who had come before Moragon, they would pose questions that seemed innocent enough yet could easily prove helpful, if answered honestly. Chamblin's charisma often won him willing conversationalists, though none had yet divulged anything of use.

Lorelei had scoured many of the southern cities in her previous quest with no success, but she was hopeful that as they traveled further north, their luck might change. Now and then, she would take turns seeking information as well, sometimes taking Mikanah with her. They would slip into whatever role they had agreed to pretend, such as being travelers long estranged from Carmenna who had heard of the late King Noheah's downfall and wanted to know what had happened to his family, and why was this Moragon king instead?

No matter whose turn it was to spy and question, Echelon always accompanied them, from a safe distance, browsing the marketplace or having an ale at whatever tavern the Guardians stopped in, wearing Carmennan garb and making themselves blend as naturally as possible.

Those who camped in the woods outside of town would spend much of their time practicing song-spells and sword skills. They focused on songs new and old, but always, their greatest concentration was on *Ah Lum Amiel*.

Meanwhile, reports from the Lozolian Council arrived steadily. Their allies continued to increase, but so did Moragon's. The smaller island kingdom of Nadia agreed to defend Carmenna, while its larger and more ruthless cousin, Rozul, sided with Moragon. Time was quickly unraveling. Like a wilting rose, soon their last moments would be stripped away, leaving only the core—the war itself.

As they traveled, they purposely used a wandering route that sometimes brought them nearer to Castle Alaula, sometimes reversed their progress. But they were now two-thirds of the way closer to the enemy's lair, and several days' journey from the next village, Dismas, which housed Reynard's Keep. A castle had once existed there too but had been destroyed in battle. With a scowl, Mikanah said the keep had been renamed when Moragon gifted it to Reynard.

In the previous town they had searched, they had heard tales of a mistress that King Noheah had frequented in Dismas, a girl named Komeah, with powers of shapeshifting. Her family was slaughtered when Moragon rose to power, but the girl's body was never found. Many believe she had changed form and escaped, along with her child.

"Reynard's Keep rests not far from the village," Lorelei said as they wound through the wooded path leading into Dismas. "We'll have to be extra careful, but it's imperative we search this town. If we can find some birth records or other information, we may be able to prove at last who our heir is."

Iolana grasped her stomach, feeling it tighten. She had grown used to talk of the heir. After all, finding him or her was an essential part of their mission to persuade Carmenna to join the fight to liberate its people. But until now, she had been able to keep her worries on that topic at bay, worries stemming from Gailea's suspicions that she herself could be the heir, that the nature of her blood was why Moragon had been so eager to spill it.

Now, those worries overflowed, carrying the promise that she would never rule. She would never trade her newfound freedom for a larger prison disguised by elaborate silks, jewels. She had taken that freedom for herself, and she would not give it up again. She would die again first.

She wished she'd never discovered the suspicions of her being the heir. The only benefit had been watching Mikanah make his protective speech about her, proving he still held some affection for her. They hadn't spoken since Adelar, and she was trying her best not to infringe on his heartsong. Long ago, she had promised not to invade the thoughts and feelings of others the way Moragon had. Survival had driven her to break that promise with many, but with him, she wanted to remember it.

"Iolana?" Nerine walked up beside her. "Are you okay? Are you ever going to tell me what happened between you and Mikanah?"

"No," Iolana sighed. "It's none of your business." She picked up her pace, but Nerine pursued her.

"No, I suppose it's only my business when you need someone to share your feelings with, to make *you* feel better."

"It's not like that. I'm sorry if I'm not there for you the way you want. But right now, that's not the most important thing on my mind."

"It never is," Nerine muttered. "I've risked my life for you and would do so over and over again. But I'm beginning to wonder if you would even care if I dropped dead right in front of you."

Guilt tugged inside Iolana. Nerine must be upset to speak so harshly, but Iolana didn't have the energy to care for her. She clutched at the sides of her tunic, twisting the fabric anxiously.

"You sound like a little child. Why don't you go talk to Darice or practice with Chamblin for a bit?"

Nerine glared at Iolana before storming off to walk alongside Ashden and Darice. Remorse pressed deeper inside Iolana's heart, but she pushed it aside. Now was a time for survival. And to survive, for her, was to sort out things with Mikanah. But when and how?

As they snaked through their thick woodland path over the next few days, practicing music as often as they could, any chance to confront Mikanah eluded Iolana. She noted Gailea's distrusting eyes upon him. She watched Nerine stare at him in jealousy. Iolana wanted to comfort him, assure him that she still trusted him. But he clearly wasn't ready to talk.

At least, that was the excuse she made herself believe. Deep down, she knew she couldn't risk further rejection from him. To keep from falling apart as they drew closer to Moragon's domain, she needed to cling to her belief, whether real or fabricated, that he still cared for her, still wanted her.

As they neared Dismas, a mist began to cloak the land.

The watchtowers of Reynard's Keep loomed between the treetops. Iolana felt her stomach churn as the keep reminded her of Moragon's towering abode.

The mist thickened, obscuring their view, and slowing their journey.

"Well," Chamblin quipped as Nerine described their predicament, "at last, this is the first time on our adventure that the blind man is not the main person at a disadvantage."

Gailea huffed. "This is not the time for your *always* ill-timed humor."

"If my humor is always ill-timed, then I would say this is precisely the time."

"Darice," Ashden interrupted loudly. "Perhaps you and Iolana could produce some of those handy light orbs to guide our way."

"I'm trying." Darice lifted her hand. Her fingertips illuminated, and a flare of light flickered inside her palm before extinguishing. "This mist—it feels like it's blocking my magic somehow."

Iolana cupped her hands, humming the *Luma* spell inside her mind. Her hands glowed faintly before fading altogether. Fear swelled inside her. She couldn't lose her magic, especially not here, so close to enemies. "I—I can't feel mine either."

"Mine as well," Donyon said. "I've had the most terrible headaches since the mist descended, and my healing charm hasn't helped."

Several low notes snapped Iolana's attention to Gailea who blew on her flute before lowering it, eyes wide in alarm. "For the first time, I can barely feel my music. My magic is still there. I can feel it in my core. But it's as though my ability to access it is fading."

"It's likely some kind of protective spell," one the Echelon men said. "To guard Reynard's Keep. The Echelon will protect you though. We've plenty a sword and bow to keep you safe."

"It does make me wonder what Reynard's hiding," Mikanah said with contempt.

Iolana agreed with him in silent reluctance. Reynard was as much a monster as Moragon, even moreso in how he chose to blindly obey him. Why would Moragon have granted Reynard the keep at all, if not to conceal some dark purpose they schemed together?

"I say we investigate," Donyon said. "Let's set up camp. We'll decide who will enter Dismas to search for clues about Komeah and the heir. The rest of us can try to learn about the fortress and the goings-on there."

~*~*~

The Echelon had located a small clearing several miles outside of Dismas, surrounded by thick bushes and trees, and it was there they set up several tents clustered close together. An Echelon man had purchased various elemental powders at the last town, including one that, when sprinkled around the area housing their tents, could muffle the sounds within. The mists did not seem to affect its magical properties. While this wasn't as effective as the spells they had used to muffle sound before, Nerine was grateful they had some form of shielding.

Nerine stepped outside one of the several tents. She had been practicing songs with Iolana. Despite the mist restricting their magic, she still wished to be diligent about learning the songs. Mikanah had entered, asking to speak with Iolana, and it had taken every ounce of Nerine's will not to snap at him to leave them in peace. Iolana had been clearly distressed at his silence the past few days. Nerine would be happy for her friend if the two of them made amends, but she doubted this, and

Iolana hadn't been herself since Mikanah had showed up. Rather, he seemed to intensify her impulsive nature while doing little to soothe her frantic soul.

As usual, Mikanah had ignored Nerine's presence as he'd entered the tent, focused solely on Iolana. She had looked first shocked as Mikanah entered and then worried as they disappeared into the woods together. Lorelei had set off for town to investigate about the heir, while Darice, Ashden, and Chamblin had left to visit one of the taverns in town, to see what gossip might surface about the fortress. Gailea and Donyon met inside a tent with one of the Lozolian messengers, discussing news and war plans.

Through the mist, Nerine could glimpse only a few stars, but she knew the sky was blanketed with many more. How many thousands of millions shone above? How did Amiel ever distinguish an individual star from among so many? Or perhaps He didn't, and like those stars, she was just another soul after all, her dim light outshone by the brilliance of those burning more brightly than she ever could.

Except tonight. The mist had neutralized everyone else's magic, but her water magic remained fully intact.

Tonight was the night. Tonight was her chance to prove her worth, both to the others and to herself. To show Iolana she could be more than just a blindly faithful companion, to show Mikanah she had a purpose here at all, and to show Gailea that she was not some helpless little girl in constant need of protection. She could *do* things. She had overheard one of the Echelon saying that Reynard's Keep was located along the borders of a lake. She would start there, to see what she could learn.

Nerine concentrated hard until she transformed herself, flesh and bone morphing to water, and then—the most difficult shift of all—from liquid to vapor. Her new form quivered with excitement as she floated through the forest, past the tents, past the Echelon, blending almost perfectly with the mist.

She remained as vapor until she began to gasp for air from the strain of the spell. Changing back to her solid Nymph form, she slipped silently through the trees, letting the cool night air refresh her lungs. The clouds shifted overhead, darkening her path even further. It was almost impossible to see, and even harder to know which way she should go. She stood still for a moment, hands raised, feeling the air, absorbing moisture into her skin. Any new source of water would be difficult to detect since she was already surrounded by so much moisture from the mist, but she thought she sensed fresh water to her left.

She continued in that direction for a while with no results. She tried a different way, then another. Or at least, she *assumed* she was changing paths. Perhaps she simply revisited the same one over and over. Whatever the case, the water she had sensed never drew any nearer. The wise thing might be to admit defeat, but she didn't want to. She wanted to do something useful for once.

A distant yell broke through Nerine's thoughts, making her jump. The yell culminated into a scream, followed by a roar of incoherent words. A few yelps followed, and then another series of screams, ear-splitting.

Nerine stood in place and shivered. The noises haunted her to the depths of her soul. She considered shapeshifting into vapor again to hide, but the screams didn't seem to come any closer. Did the wretched sounds come from their camp? Had some sort of monster or other danger besieged her friends?

Heart pounding, she fled toward the discordant symphony of shouts, howls, yells, screams, and indecipherable jumbles of what might have been spells, but if so, their words were too distorted to make out, or perhaps in another language. The cries fluctuated between anger and fear and eventually pain.

Nerine tumbled into a space in the woods where the mist had thinned out some. The stars shone faintly above, guiding her path just enough for her to see that a massive stone fortress rose before her. Lights shone dimly from a few of its windows. In one of the towers, shadows moved, rising, and falling along with the creature's shrieks, which were magnified by the lake nestled beside the fortress.

Nerine had found Reynard's Keep. She could still prove her worth after all.

~*~*~

Iolana followed Mikanah through the woods, led by his hand in a sort of daze. Many days had passed without his uttering a word to her, and now he acted like a desperate lover ready to run away with her.

Finally, he stopped and released her hand. She watched him pace back and forth between two trees. He sighed loudly, an almost growling noise. His frustrations seemed to rest on the tip of his tongue and yet refused to make it past his lips.

"Mikanah, what is it? Why won't you talk to me? You've been so distant since the night we spent together, in Adelar. Are you angry with me?"

"Angry?" Mikanah froze in place and stared at her, looking incredulous. "If anyone should be angry, why should it be me?"

"If you're not angry, then what? Why do you draw away at my every attempt to touch you?"

She walked up to him and drew his face toward hers. His eyes widened, wild like those of some beast she tried to tame. Mikanah closed his eyes and inhaled deeply, inching closer until their bodies touched. Ecstasy flooded Iolana as she felt the heat flushing him. Twining her hand in his, she moved it to her waist. She stretched up and teased his lips with hers, and he began to respond.

With a cry, he tore away from her.

"Why are you doing this?" Iolana demanded.

"I don't want to be like that anymore. I don't want to treat you like I did them."

"Who?"

"Everybody!" he roared. He didn't look at her, but desperation shone clearly in his eyes. "Everybody that Moragon ever ordered me to manipulate!"

"I'm not being manipulated. I want to be with you of my own free will, because I love you."

She stepped forward, but he held out a hand to stop her. "No. I can't be sure I'm not using you, and neither can you. We're all we've ever known."

"Which is why we've always been perfect for each other. Mikanah." She stepped toward him again. "You've always been that one safe place where I could just breathe and let go. You've always been the one person who can make me believe things will be okay. I want you to still be that. If you won't, it breaks my heart. I have Nerine's friendship, and I've found great strength from Gailea, but I want to find strength in *us* again."

"*Gailea?*" Mikanah scoffed. "I appreciate that she cares for you. But you know she hates me. She would be your new idol?"

Iolana savored the sudden fight in his voice. At least she had struck some chord, triggered some reaction. "She's just trying to protect me."

"From monsters like me?"

"*You're* the one trying to make me see you that way."

"Because you need to see it, the truth. I may not be

the same monster that Moragon is. But I've done many horrible things. I—"

"What things?" Iolana cried. "I know about the women before me. I know what you were then, what he made you do."

"He *made* me do nothing!" Mikanah threw his hands in the air, shaking in frustration. "I chose to! I chose to obey his every whim!"

"Did you really though?" Iolana's voice broke in exasperation. She felt desperate to make him see himself as she did. "I don't excuse any of your actions, but I can easily forgive them. We were all prisoners. We all responded differently to Moragon's threats and torture."

"Yes, you responded by choosing to serve him as little as you could. Whatever you may have known about me before, I can promise you my actions were a hundred times more horrible once I thought you were dead." He winced at these last words.

"You might let me judge how horrible they are for myself, if only you'd share them with me."

"No. They are not your burdens to bear."

"You know, maybe you're right." Iolana tried to put all the force of her emotions into her next words. "Maybe they're not mine to bear because there's really nothing between us after all. Maybe I was wrong to trust you when everyone else didn't. Maybe Amiel was trying to warn me, and I ignored Him."

Mikanah glared daggers at her.

"If that is what you believe," he said quietly, "then I don't understand why you're fighting so hard to reignite whatever we once shared. Perhaps there *is* nothing between us and never was. If fairy tales are what still give you comfort, you're fooling yourself. It's all the same. Faith in any god is manipulation, only under a different master, a different name. But if that is what you choose, then so be it."

He stormed away, but Iolana ran after him and grabbed him by the arm. His muscles beneath her hand were stiff as stone.

"Mikanah, I'm sorry. I'm only repeating what you seem to keep believing yourself. It's frustrating because I don't understand at all. You say that you've manipulated me. You say you're no good for me. Then, when I try to agree, you get defensive and say the opposite. Which is it?"

Mikanah said nothing as he stared vacantly into the trees.

"You don't know, do you?" Iolana pressed. "You don't know what to think. About yourself, about any of it. You don't even know how in control of yourself you are, or how much you're in control of me. You definitely don't know how in control I am of myself. I love you, I choose you. That holds, no matter what." She moved to stand in front of him and took his hands in hers. "Be with me. Tell me your secrets…" She stepped closer still, took his face in her hands, and stretched up on her toes to whisper in his ear, "Love me. Love me as you once did. Enchant me if you must, only love me, please—"

Mikanah shoved her away. With a cry, Iolana staggered back. Catching herself on a tree, she stared up at him. The fierce rejection in his eyes could not be real. Surely, he would offer his hand at any moment, help her up, pull her to him and make everything right.

"There is your answer," he said coldly. "See how dangerous I am to you, just with physical force? Imagine if I exerted that force over your mind. Maybe that's all I ever did with you. You're right. I don't know what to think anymore. And I'm not going to hurt you even more by trying to find out."

Mikanah turned and fled the clearing.

Iolana scrambled to her feet, calling his name. She ran through the trees searching for him, but he had vanished like a puff of smoke. Angry tears rolled down her cheeks as she wandered the woods, lost but not caring to be found, except by him.

~*~*~

Nerine crouched in the reeds at the fringe of the lake and stared across its glassy stillness toward Reynard's Keep. The screeching and yelling had ebbed, as had the mist. Nerine wondered what kind of thing could make such hideous, earsplitting noises. A great monster? A wild beast? Perhaps even another demon like the Desthai?

Wading out into the water, Nerine prepared to morph into her liquid form. From there, she could easily glide across the lake, approach the tower, and search for some underwater passage inside.

An arm grabbed Nerine, and she spun about, chanting a spell to create a small wave that pushed the person into the lake with a splash. Several figures stood before her—Darice, Ashden, an Echelon woman Nerine recognized as Marla, and two Echelon men. With a gasp, she realized who she sent flying into the waters just as Chamblin surfaced, sputtering. He clambered onto shore, and Nerine rushed over, kneeling beside him.

"I'm so sorry! I—"

"You needn't apologize..." Chamblin waved the matter aside before frowning sternly in her direction. "Your little spell only shows what I've always admired in you, your studiousness, greater than anyone else's here, I'll warrant. What you *should* apologize for is sneaking off in the middle of the night and coming all the way out to Reynard's Keep. Are you mad, girl?"

"I wanted to be helpful." Nerine took a deep breath and tried to sit tall before Chamblin. She hated the disappointment on his face. He, above all people, usually defended her, even when Gailea and others disapproved. "I'm sorry I worried you. But I heard these terrible screams."

"We heard them too," Darice said, holding Ashden's arm. "It's what drew us in this direction."

The screams started up again but with less intensity, as though the creature grew tired.

"Whatever it is," Ashden said solemnly, "it's angry and has known much suffering. I once lived with certain Fury clans who took delight in tormenting beasts for sport. The beasts wailed much like this creature is."

"So, it's some kind of animal then?" Chamblin asked.

"Or else it has been taught to behave like one. Maybe the townsfolks' rumors were based in truth after all. What if Reynard is performing some experiment on people who've gone missing in recent years?"

"You could be right," Nerine said. "Moragon uses his magic to control people, make them his slaves. What if Reynard is doing the same sort of thing? The mist seems to be connected to the creature's screams. When the screams get louder, the mist grows thicker. The quieter it is, the mist lessens."

Chamblin's brows rose. "That's impossible. No beast or human would be able to harness such power. Not enough to cover the entire forest with a substance that renders all magic useless."

"Maybe no ordinary creature," Darice said. "But maybe it's another demon."

"Maybe indeed. Which makes me furthermore glad we found you before it did. That fortress is likely to be overrun with guards and traps of all sorts. It's no place for you."

"Why *shouldn't* I be the one to go?" Nerine sighed, growing frustrated, something she was accustomed to lately but hated for it to be caused by Chamblin. "I could easily change into my water form, find a way inside."

Chamblin placed a hand on her shoulder, gazing with solemn concern at her. "I know you're right. I know also that I cannot stop you. But I would beg you to stay here. Ashden and I and the Echelon here plan to get closer, see what we can find out. You could stay with Darice, keep a lookout."

"You can hardly even *see*," Nerine reminded him gently. "How is it safer for you to go?"

"It may not be," Chamblin admitted. "But I do have more years, more experience, and Ashden as a worthy guide."

"And Darice?"

"Frozen by fear, I'm ashamed to admit. Every time I get near the screams, all I can imagine is the Desthai, creeping back inside my mind."

Darice shivered, and Ashden placed his hands on her shoulders, meeting her gaze. "There is no shame in this fear. Choosing not to risk a similar danger isn't cowardice. It's wisdom."

Nerine took her hand. "If I must stay here, I'll keep a close watch on her."

Darice smiled at her. "We'll watch over each other."

"I'll stay as well," Marla declared, moving to stand beside them.

Chamblin looked relieved. "Well, come on then. Ladies, I would lie low in the bushes, wait here for us to return."

Marla led Nerine and Darice over to a thick cluster of bushes, and they crouched down. Nerine peered through the branches, watching as Chamblin, Ashden, and their two Echelon escorts disappeared inside the veil of mist which thickened as the screams began once again, culminating with greater force.

A bright white light flashed past. Nerine jumped and then sighed relief, laughing a little.

"Scared me too," Darice said, taking her hand. "Must've been just a firefly, or perhaps a sprite?"

More lights darted past, zipping between the bushes. Nerine reached out with cupped palms to try to catch one, when Marla abruptly grabbed her wrist.

"These aren't fireflies," Marla whispered. "They're hunting lights. We can't let them notice us. We need a safer place to hide!" Marla bent low to the ground, motioning them to follow. Darice dragged Nerine toward the woods after them, but Nerine resisted.

"I'll hide down in the water. I can change to my liquid form. It'll be safer for me. You two hide in the trees. Come and get me when you know it's safe."

Marla's eyes pleaded fiercely for them to move, while Darice seemed to hesitate. But as more lights sped past and the creature's distant screams intensified, she nodded, and the two women darted for the trees.

And none too soon. Moments later, soldiers rushed past, their footfalls muffled by whatever boots they wore or perhaps some spell. Nerine crept from the bushes into the nearby reeds and sank down into the water, transforming her body into its liquid form. The guards seemed to hurry past without detecting any signs of Marla and Darice, but Nerine's heart lurched all the same. What if they were after Chamblin and Ashden? What if they had already been caught?

Drifting forward a little, Nerine parted the reeds and peered through at the fortress. It wasn't all that far away. If Chamblin and Ashden had been taken, perhaps she could find out. Even if they were safe, their plans had likely been thwarted, so perhaps she still had a chance at discovering some information on her own. She could easily glide to the fortress and back again within a few minutes.

Blending perfectly with the water, she swam close and hugged the fortress's side, gazing all around for any sign of guards or other dangers. The creature's screams mounted, more pleading than before. A twinge of pity vibrated in Nerine's heart. However evil or powerful the creature might be, however Moragon sought to use it against them, she still hated to hear it suffer.

Diving beneath the water's surface, Nerine scaled down the wall, searching for an opening. In the stories her parents had read to her, old towers always held secret passages and sewers and other hidden entrances. Sure enough, part of the wall had crumbled away at its very base.

Nerine squeezed inside and let the water carry her up until she broke the surface. The creature's screams were closer. A few thin shafts of light filtered through the wooden floor above. There were no other signs of life or danger.

Nerine pulled herself up out of the water onto a cold stone floor. She sat shivering, fumbling in the dark. Her hands met with several small objects, which sent some of them clattering, others rolling noisily away. She held her breath, but the monster's cries soon drowned all else.

Creeping forward a little more, Nerine's hands met with something else. Cold, hard, circular, then another and another, each heavy in her hands. Links from a chain, she realized, running her hand along its length. At once, she shivered and scuffled back. She'd read about enchanted chains, the kind that trapped unwanted visitors and made them meet with an early grave. She left them alone but pocketed a couple of the curious little items she'd knocked into earlier. Perhaps they would give some indication of just what was living here. She would examine them properly when there was more light.

Nerine hugged the wall and stretched up, listening as the monster's yells subdued at last into quieter moans. It sounded as though she might be right below it.

A mournful noise rose from the creature then, an eerie yet musical noise, as if it tried to comfort itself by mimicking some song.

Footsteps thundered overhead. Nerine held still.

A man's voice demanded, "What's the plan? Where are we taking it?"

"To His Majesty as soon as possible," said another man. "I don't think we should let it grow any stronger, or even the king won't be able to control it."

"Help me move it, then. We'll need to be careful."

Roars erupted from the creature with renewed strength and increased passion, shaking the whole room and making debris rain down. Terrified that the monster might crash through the ceiling at any moment, Nerine dove back into the water and fled the tower.

Nerine flew through the waters, not daring to take a breath until she had pulled herself back onto shore.

No sooner did she climb from the reeds, flinging a wild look over her shoulder at the fortress, than hands grabbed her. She screamed and fought against them, but they whirled her around—

Chamblin grabbed her face and forced her to stare up at him, dazed but silenced.

"I'm sorry," he said, drawing her close and hugging her. "But Reynard's guards were just on our tail. Some-one's alerted them that spies are in the area. Nerine." He held her by the shoulders. "Why, my child? Why did you go after you promised not to? Darice was terrified for you. We found her and Marla both distraught."

"I'm sorry," Nerine whispered, trembling. She began to cry, overwhelmed. "I just wanted to help."

"Oh, my dear girl..." Chamblin held her again. His kind, tender embrace only made her cry more. "When will you learn, you don't need to prove yourself to us? We all know you're wonderful and smart and helpful. We just want you to be safe."

"I'm sorry," she repeated. "But I *did* learn things. I got close to the monster making all that noise. Someone said it was nearly powerful enough. They were getting ready to move it to Moragon's castle."

"We're *all* going to be taken there if we don't go," Ashden said, crouched low and feeling along the earth. "Footsteps. I think more guards approach."

"Let's hurry back to camp." Chamblin led Nerine after Ashden and the two Echelon men. "We can talk about what you found later. For now, we must make sure that the others are safe."

CHAPTER 42

ALLIEGIANCES

Mikanah wandered through the woods, plowing through thick brush, not knowing or caring where he went as Iolana's accusation pounded inside his head:

"You don't know, do you?"

"You don't know at all," he muttered, dragging himself on.

He was meant to be a Guardian, sworn to protect and keep the innocent safe from evil. But he couldn't stop questioning his purpose, his motives. He sang *Ah Lum Amiel* to himself as often as he could, but what if it wasn't enough to drive away other demons Moragon might send his way? Maybe evil was too deeply imbedded inside his nature for him to avoid.

"Mikanah!"

His name shot through the mist like a bolt of lightning. Mikanah hurried his pace, flying blindly through the veiled woods.

"Mikanah, *stop!*"

The voice—Lorelei's—seemed to come from everywhere at once. Mikanah drew his blade. He didn't want to fight her, but he would if he had to, to get away.

"*Stop this instant!*"

Fury flooded her words, and before Mikanah knew it, something collided with his sword and sent it spiraling through the air. Something else knocked into Mikanah, making him sprawl on his stomach. He rolled over onto his back, only to find the tip of a sword pointed straight at his heart. Lorelei stood on the other end of the sword, staring at him with a fierce frustration.

"You will not draw your sword against me or any other fellow Guardian again, nor will you seek to abandon us. Is this made clear?"

"Lorelei—"

"I will stand here all day if need be. I may not be able to cause you direct harm, but you will not rise without making yourself pass through my sword. Are we clear?"

Mikanah nodded slowly. She drew back her sword and offered her hand. He took it, but as he stood to his feet, he snapped, "If the Guardians are meant to be equals, then how do you get the right to order me around?"

"You were putting us all in danger. Flying recklessly through these woods without an escort. The same as your girl here when I found her. Racing through the trees, screaming your name like a banshee. We're lucky we didn't have a whole string of Reynard's men on our heels."

Mikanah glanced up past Lorelei. A few yards away, Iolana stood flanked by two Echelon guards, her face pulled into a taut frown, eyes blazing with obvious anger and embarrassment.

Lorelei lowered her tone to a near-whisper. "Truly, Mikanah, you of all people should understand the danger. What could've possessed you to parade around with her in the middle of the woods?"

"We were only talking," Mikanah said, reaching for a good excuse but finding none. "We didn't mean to go far."

"It doesn't matter how far you go! You know the possibility of what Iolana might be. You're always acting like you have such a desire to protect her. Why then remove her from our guards?"

Mikanah stared at Lorelei. There was nothing he could say. She was right.

"I don't know what's going on with the two of you." Lorelei took a step nearer, her voice still low. "But at this most pivotal point in our journey, there is no room for a lover's spat. Save that for when, or *if*, we survive the war. For now, you've wasted enough of my time, precious time I could've already been in town, asking about the heir. This mist may be a nuisance, but while it persists, I wish to use its cover to my advantage. So, you two may either head back to camp, or accompany me to town and be of some use."

Mikanah glanced at Iolana, questioning, but Lorelei blocked his view of her. "She does not make your decisions for you. Are you coming or not, Mikanah?"

"I will come," he said, praying Iolana would choose the opposite. "I will do what I can to help you."

Iolana's answer proved to him yet again that prayers were futile. "I will come as well."

"Then let's go. I will allow no further delays."

Lorelei started forward.

Mikanah hesitated before following. Then, he picked up pace, hoping to apologize.

"Mikanah."

Iolana had caught up and now walked by his side, a quiet yearning in her gaze. She longed to touch him but would not, fearing the agony of rejection. He knew this because he knew her. He knew he had caused such pain.

"Iolana," he said quietly. "Lorelei is right. I shouldn't have abandoned you. And you...you were right as well. I don't know who I am, *what* I am. What our future holds, if it holds anything. But right now, in this moment, maybe we should just try to work together. As we once did."

"I could do that. If you could just promise that you still love me."

"I do," Mikanah said fervently. "I do love you. I'm just not sure I love you as I should."

"I know. But Mikanah, I need to feel *some* connection with you to get through this. I need you to understand that. So, let's work together, as you say. Let's help Lorelei. We'll pretend it's one of my old rebellion missions. I mean, it sort of is, isn't it? And after all, you always wanted to be part of those."

She smiled up at him. Sadness shone visibly in her eyes. Uncertainty of the future was so difficult for her. It always had been.

"Look at you," he said, hoping to encourage her. "As wise a leader as ever. Perfect for a queen."

Iolana's smile faltered. "I don't want to be queen. If I really was the heir...which I can't even fathom...."

"You would make a good leader. Righteous, just, fair. You were always 'queen' at heading the rebellion meetings."

"Being queen would only be a more elaborate prison. I want to be free. I want to go back to the school and learn things with Gailea and Nerine."

She didn't mention a future with him. This stung, but he understood. He'd just asked her not to count on the promise of their being together, and so she couldn't afford to imagine it.

In silence, they walked side by side, following Lorelei and the Echelon from the woods and down a hill heading toward town, led by the moonlight shimmering dimly through the mist.

~*~*~

Gailea and Donyon pored over the large maps spread on the ground while two Abalino messengers stood with their wings tucked behind them, explaining the latest Council news. The force of Donyon's concentration was aimed at the map as he marked in detail, and Gailea watched his every move, double-checking that he marked correctly.

"Bad tidings from Prismatic," declared Gethin, the shorter and more senior of the two messengers. "Their king has agreed to send aid to Moragon from the north. But the numbers they're meant to send are small, and Carmenna's northern border is mostly surrounded by cliffs, so it's doubtful the Prismatics would be able to land or attack from that direction anyway. They would have to sail around to the northeast or northwest shores. This means that Abalino may be able to use our airships to hold off the Prismatics from reaching Moragon's shores. Our light magic rivals theirs and may also hold them at bay."

"Yes," Donyon muttered, deep in thought. "Also, as we try to open the southern gates and take the wall, your air attacks may be a key distraction. Thankfully, our allies are greater in number. Though I know numbers are not everything."

"No. They are not," Gailea said firmly. "And especially because we don't know the nature of Moragon's Vessel, the most important part of this war will be breaking through Moragon's forces to find it, and Moragon, as soon as possible. We must destroy the hub of a wheel to stop it from turning. Lorelei has mentioned underground caves we could use to infiltrate."

"Indeed. We'll ask her more about them." Donyon turned back to the messengers. "What news of our other allies?"

"Rosa and Adelar are sailing from the northwest even as we speak," Gethin said. "Sallusay will also depart shortly. Loz sends some aid, though they're still trying to quell the uprising in Prismatic—which also works against us. Some of the Lozolian soldiers sent to aid Prismatic are being captured and forced to join Moragon's side. Loz is trying to withdraw its soldiers, but it's a messy affair. Spaniño will also come from the west to aid Moragon, but they should pose little threat to Sallusay. The Sallie Elves have the power to travel underwater, undetected. Our greatest threat lies in that of the Meleeóns from the south."

"The pirate kingdom," Donyon muttered. "Is it the pirates who have joined Moragon's side, or King Irian?"

"Both. But their involvement is spearheaded by the king. It seems he has joined with the pirates."

"Hypocrite," Gailea snapped. "He would execute pirates left and right for petty crimes yet use them for his advancement in this war."

"He has huge numbers of them too," said Rian, the younger messenger. "Fleets filled with fierce, unabashed warriors. Many of the pirates have been promised both gold and pardons. False promises, no doubt, but Irian will use them to fuel his cause. He doesn't have any magic. But he has an obsession for collecting magical artifacts, much as Moragon has for musical artifacts. We think he might have heard of the Vessel."

"So, Irian wants to join with Moragon and obtain access to it?" Gailea said. "That's a stretch of a goal to achieve. The man must be a fool."

"He is," Gethin said with an annoyed curl of his lip,

"but a ruthless one. His people know how to fight on the seas. The hope is that our allies will beat the Meleeóns here. Once on shore, the playing field will become more even."

Gailea traced the islands on the map until her fingertips rested on a particular kingdom. "What of Hyloria? They could also be a powerful ally."

Especially to Moragon, she admitted with a shiver, *if he and Crispin somehow made amends.*

"Neutral," Rian said. "And likely to stay that way. They're busy enough containing Ragnar. Apparently, he tried to rise up against the royal family. Besides that, the Hylorians have seen enough of civil war in recent years. They don't wish to involve themselves in the wars of others."

Gailea breathed a huge sigh of relief to hear that Marlis' family had been able to subdue Crispin after all.

Donyon, scowling at the northern edge of the map, nodded toward it. "Our armies will meet together right along the northern borders of the woods facing the castle, correct? And the Guardians will also continue marching in that direction."

Gethin nodded. "Rosa and Adelar should be the first to reach Carmenna and make camp. By the time you reach the castle, their camp will provide a safehold for you to rest."

"What of the Ethual?" Rian blurted with an impatient glance at his companion. "Shouldn't we speak of them too? They may be the most important bit of news we can offer."

"Which is why I meant to turn my focus to them once other plans were thoroughly discussed." Gethin granted Rian a gentle smile, even as the younger man flushed red at his own overenthusiasm.

"The Ethual?" Gailea questioned as fresh hope shot

through her. "Are they meant to be our allies too?"

The Ethual were a well-renowned academy of elves, fairies, and other scholars who dedicated their entire lives to mastering the arts of healing. Their reclusive home was said to be a giant structure that floated somewhere in the clouds, just like the Abalinos' kingdom.

"The Abalino royal family is acquainted with several of the most prominent Ethual," Gethin explained. "The Ethual largely keep to themselves, training healers to send out into the world. They choose to abstain from all aspects of warfare. However, there was one occasion in our Realm's history during which they banded together to risk their lives during war, to save many a fallen soldier."

"During the Age of Dragons," Donyon said, sharing a wondrous look with Gailea that reflected her same hope.

Gethin nodded. "Yes, the very same. The Ethual came then because that war served a good and righteous purpose. Abalino ambassadors were sent to the Ethual, to implore them to help us. The Ethual despised learning what Moragon has done, torturing the minds of so many Carmennans. They are eager to help with healing, but they won't come until the fighting has ceased. On the day of battle, messengers will be dispatched to the Ethual. Amiel-willing, they will be ready and willing to come as soon as the last battle is laid to rest."

"Amiel-willing, indeed," Gailea breathed, praying it would be so. After all, aside from the Carmennans' mental brokenness, there would no doubt be many others in need of both physical and emotional healing by the war's end.

After a few more tactical plans were discussed, the messengers took their leave with the responses Gailea and Donyon were sending to the Council.

Donyon made a few final notes on one of the maps.

After waiting for the ink to dry, he rolled it up and scooped up the rest before heading toward his tent.

"You know," Gailea said, trailing after him, "despite your inability to take back your own realm, you have quite the knack for planning the conquering of other lands."

"Planning a war and executing one are two different skills. And they are both made easier with willing armies and wise counselors. Neither of which I've ever had in abundance."

"Still, I can't help but wonder if you're like the pirates the messenger spoke of." When Donyon turned to her in surprise, Gailea met him with a hard, penetrative stare. "You could be quite the powerful king if you obtained the Vessel or whatever other source Moragon gains his power from."

Though his chin was held high with pride, hurt shone in his eyes. "Gailea. I understand if I can never be more to you than the monster that tormented your mother. But I do not aid Carmenna from false friendship. I wish you would read those last accounts I gave you. Perhaps then you would not cling so tightly to this need to fear and distrust me—"

"My lady! King Donyon!"

One of the Echelon men rushed up to them, breathless. "Spies. Reynard's men, scoping about in the woods. The other Guardians may be in danger."

Gailea and Donyon looked at each other in alarm.

"Mikanah and Iolana were out there," Gailea said. "I thought they'd be with Lorelei, but—"

"We'll search for them at once." Donyon gestured to the guard. "Come. All available Echelon will help us."

CHAPTER 43

THE SETTING SUN

Iolana and Mikanah wound through the streets of Dismas after Lorelei. Stone houses and shops lined the streets. Many of the buildings boasted straw-thatched roofs and second or third floors that jutted out on all sides. When Iolana asked why, Lorelei explained that the larger size of the higher floors allowed for more space within. The lower levels were built smaller all around to make more room for the cobblestone paths snaking through town. The omnipresent mist was less vexing here, but overhead, clouds had since veiled the night sky. Everything was lit only by a thin film of grayish starlight, along with lanterns suspended mid-air here or there.

As they turned onto a winding road, Lorelei slowed her pace. The road's disheveled stones had been mostly buried beneath the mud, and their boots made a strange squelching noise. With each step, the mud tried to suck Iolana's feet under. She jerked her feet up, shuddering as she recalled how it felt to slosh through the mass grave, struggling to pull herself from the muck and the tangle of so many corpses. The longer they spent in Carmenna, such memories seemed to revive themselves more and more, both during her sleeping and waking thoughts.

"I believe this is it."

Lorelei's announcement drew Iolana's thoughts back to the present. Iolana followed her gaze to the weathered wooden sign painted with a faded red-and-yellow sun that hung above the building, reading *The Setting Sun*—the inn that the tavern keeper at their previous stop had suggested they visit. Its silver hinges suggested that the building, perhaps the whole town, had once been very fine. Now, shutters hung limply, filth clung to everything, and cracks raced up and down one of the windows.

"This is our destination?" Iolana questioned. "This will lead us to what we're looking for?"

"Come," Lorelei said, stepping inside.

As they followed her, Iolana took deep breaths. Was Mikanah as afraid as her of what they might find within? All the recent talk of her being the heir had been unsettling enough, but now, the idea of finding concrete proof made the idea feel far too real.

Inside, *The Setting Sun* had a far warmer appeal than expected. Cobwebs and dust lined the bar and dining area, but a fireplace blazed, and lanterns reflected a friendly glow. A few Carmennans ate, drank, or talked to one another at one of several wooden tables.

Lorelei led them over to the bar, where each took a seat on a tall, wooden stool.

Iolana saw Lorelei's eyes shifting to examine her surroundings. What was she watching for? Lorelei always looked so collected and confident. Iolana envied her, much as she envied her evident bond of trust with Mikanah. Sometimes, he seemed to trust Lorelei more than he trusted her.

At the fluttering of anxious heartsongs, Iolana's interest was piqued. She glanced around and spotted a group of men sitting not far to their left. Swiftly, she dropped her gaze, but her ears were still at work:

"Did you hear the beast not long ago? Always shouting, screaming, roaring—but I swear I never heard it bellow like *that* before. What do you think it means?"

"The nobles are brewing some kind of madness up in that fortress. Probably for *'his* madness'."

"Do not speak treason so openly. I'll gladly cut off your head to spare my own."

"What can I get for you, my pretties?" The innkeeper stood at the counter before them, a middle-aged man with a worn knit tunic and a leather waistcoat that had seen much better days. But they were clean and patched carefully, and his manner was impish, not intimidating.

"We've been away from Carmenna for some time," Lorelei said. "Is this still an inn?"

"Yes, lass." He leaned across the bar, smiled at her. "We have some lodgings available tonight—for the right price." His gaze drifted to Iolana, and he grinned. It wasn't predatory, but Iolana tensed and could feel Mikanah do the same beside her.

"We don't seek lodgings," Lorelei said. "We seek information." She leaned forward and gazed past the innkeeper, toward an older man pushing a broom across the dusty floor. "That man there. He may be old enough to know what we seek."

The innkeeper glanced over his shoulder. When he looked back at Lorelei, his smile had faded into a disappointed frown.

"Helbrek," he called. "This young lady would like to speak to you."

The white-haired man Lorelei had indicated paused his sweeping and walked over. Iolana noted that the long, jagged scar stretching across his cheek perfectly matched the description that the keeper of the previous tavern had given them.

"What can I do for you this evening?" he asked with a grin.

"I'm looking for family of mine," Lorelei casually explained. "I was told some might yet exist in this town. I know the name of only one, a distant cousin. I'm told she's long since dead. But I thought perhaps if I could find someone who knew of her, I could find the rest of my family. Apparently, she stopped here once, about seven or eight years ago."

Helbrek chuckled. "Well, I can't promise to remember every single face that's come through those doors the past eight years. But go ahead. Test me. If the face or form was particularly striking, I may recall."

"I think her face would indeed be memorable. And if not, the name. And if not the name, the story. Or maybe all three together will ignite your memory. Her name was Komeah. She would've had a small child with her. And she might have once worked in the castle."

Helbrek's smile vanished, and his mutter was barely audible. "I'm sorry. But we know nothing of that name here."

He turned to leave, but Lorelei reached out to touch his sleeve. "Please, fate may lie in your hands." She'd lowered her voice further, not easy for Iolana to follow. "If I don't find my family, their lives may be forfeit. But if I could find them, especially Komeah's child, it could mean hope for many beyond myself."

Panic thrummed inside Iolana at Lorelei's boldness. She listened more keenly still as Lorelei leaned across the bar and continued, "You know of the rebellions that have been cropping up. A war is brewing. Armies on both sides are ready. But wouldn't the people be greatly heartened with someone of hope to lead them?"

"How can I know you're not a spy—on either side?" Helbrek glanced nervously about the bar before looking back to Lorelei, pleading. It seemed he could hardly dare to believe her sincerity but wanted to desperately. "If I breathe a single word to you, truth *or* falsehood, it could be my head."

Before either of them could speak another word, the innkeeper had rejoined them, wiping down a mug with a tattered cloth.

"You know, I might be able to help you as well, if you might first do me a favor." He arched a brow, and a corner of his mouth pulled up in a smirk.

"What sort of favor?" Lorelei kept her voice even.

Iolana grabbed the sides of her tunic, clenching it in her fists as she prayed the man wasn't about to name some devious act. He disappeared through a door, only to reappear with a large basket of laundry in tow. He set it on the counter beside Lorelei, and Iolana barely repressed the urge to gag at the sour-smelling cloths and garments. As the innkeeper leaned one elbow on the edge of the basket, Iolana wondered how he didn't pass out.

"My laundress has taken ill. It's been a terrible burden, trying to keep things running smoothly, what with extra duties to take on. You can imagine that keeping customers happy is a mite challenging when I'm hard pressed to provide them with fresh linens and the like. What do you say? A good deed for a good deed."

Lorelei's body tensed ever so slightly, and she took a deep, slow breath. It seemed her composure at last wavered, or perhaps she tried to contain herself from reacting to the stench.

"Very well then," she said at last.

Iolana released the breath she had been holding.

Seeming overly impatient to obtain information could have made them look even more suspicious and lose their chance. At least in making this trade, they might stand to accomplish what they'd set out to do here.

"That's the spirit." The innkeeper beamed and stood up straight, pushing the laundry basket toward Lorelei. "The laundress is just down the lane. Make a right at the first corner, then you'll go to the end of the next lane where you'll find a pool enclosed by a wall. The laundresses should still be working this time of night. Find a woman named Wana and tell 'em old Pelekah sent you. Oh, and be sure to give her this, for her trouble." He presented a copper coin from his pocket and handed it to Lorelei.

"Yes, of course. Thank you, Pelekah." Lorelei pursed her lips into a curt smile before hefting the laundry off the counter. Mikanah hopped down from his seat to take it from her, and she gave him a grateful nod before leading them from the inn.

As soon as they stepped outside, Iolana gulped the fresh air. Unpleasant smells of sewage wafted to her on the breeze, but they didn't overwhelm as much as the sour laundry had in the inn's warm, cramped air.

Pelekah's instructions led them to a small space enclosed by a weathered stone wall, just as he'd promised. A shallow pool of water covered roughly three-fourths of the area, with a small tunnel on the far side that Iolana guessed served as a conduit. Three Carmennan women had stationed themselves at large wooden basins around the pool. One of them scooped water into a bucket and poured it into her basin, while the others scrubbed clothes and linens on rough wooden boards angled inside the basins. Clean laundry had been slung over ropes strung between the walls to air out. The scent of fresh herbs drifted to Iolana, washing away some of their laundry's pungent stink.

As they took a few steps forward, the woman nearest them glanced up with a curious frown. "You're new here. If you want your turn at one o' the tubs, you'll have to wait. We've all got enough work still to last us another two good hours or so."

"We're just making a delivery," Lorelei said. "We were told to find Wana. Pelekah at the *The Setting Sun* sent us."

The woman's brows rose, showing amusement for a brief second before she nodded toward one of the other two women across the grass. "Right over there." She turned and called over her shoulder, "Wana, you've got company. Pelekah sent 'em."

"He sent more work along with them, by the looks of things."

They approached, and Wana glanced up at them with a frown before glaring with disdain at the pile of laundry. As Mikanah set the basket down, her face wrinkled with a deeper disgust.

Lorelei held out the coin in her hands.

"Pelekah sent this for your trouble."

Wana's brows rose, and excitement gleamed in her eyes as she snatched the coin. Holding it so that it shone in the moonlight, she muttered, "Coming from Pelekah, it's often not worth my trouble at all. But I see tonight he's gifted me with a rare and valuable beauty. See this handsome face here?" She took Lorelei's hand and held it palm up, placing the coin in its center. Iolana leaned in, curiously studying the face etched on the coin, a king by the fact that he wore a crown.

"This type of coin hasn't been seen since before the days of King Moragon."

"You mean during King Noheah's time?" Lorelei glanced up at the woman.

"Yes, and far before that. The man on this coin represents King Noheah's great-great-great-grandfather, King Nolanah. A gracious ruler if ever there was one, or so they say. Could just be a myth. Gracious kings are hard to come by in any kingdom, so says I."

Lorelei nodded, keeping her steady gaze on Wana, while Iolana wondered at Wana's audacity. While she didn't speak outright treason, her words were no compliment toward Moragon.

Wana folded Lorelei's hand over the coin before withdrawing hers with a tired smile. "Return this to Pelekah. Tell him his money isn't needed today. The rascal's done me a good turn often enough that I'll do this bundle for nothing, and gladly. Though, he'd best not expect to make a habit of it either."

Lorelei's eyes flashed the same surprise that Iolana felt. What a generous gesture for a laundress. They were known to do some of the hardest work for the most menial pay.

"Thank you very much. We'll return this to Pelekah at once."

They departed the laundry pool, and Iolana hoped their completed task would be enough to prove their friendliness and trust to Pelekah. How, she didn't know. The task had certainly seemed too easy, and she hoped they weren't wandering into some trap.

As they entered the inn and approached the counter, Pelekah walked over to greet them with raised brows.

"Back so soon?" he asked.

"Yes. Wana said to return this to you." Lorelei handed him the coin. "Said you'd done her enough favors that she was glad to do you one. But she made certain to warn that you don't make a habit of it," she added with a playful smirk.

Pelekah chuckled. "Come. You've proven yourselves

friends indeed. Follow me. I'll show you to more private quarters. Then I'll see about fetching Helbrek, see if he's up to finishing your chat."

Pelekah stepped through a swinging half-door that led from behind the counter. They wound around the corner after him, through another door and down a short, plain hallway. Iolana prayed fervently that they weren't being led into a trap. Thanks to the mist, their magic was still all but useless. They carried swords, but Iolana wasn't overly confident yet in her ability to wield a blade, while Lorelei's pendant forbade her from using her sword to its full extent, unless the mists had stolen that magic too, which would be equally unsettling.

They followed Pelekah through another door at the end of the hall, into a small room. At least, it appeared small at first glance, but Iolana quickly realized this was because it was so stuffed with things. Several crates and a wooden chest. Shelves on one wall lined with packages wrapped in cloth, mugs, and barrels. A small wooden table with chairs centered the room, and lanterns floated at intervals along the walls, granting a friendly, orange light.

"Wait here. I'll find Helbrek."

Pelekah departed and shut the door, dousing them in quiet.

Iolana shivered, aching at the anticipation of what would happen next.

"Seems an awful lot of trouble they've put us through," Mikanah muttered. "Wouldn't it have been more expedient to tell them we're Guardians, show our marks to them?"

Lorelei scoffed, and Iolana cast him an annoyed stare.

"Expedient, yes," Lorelei said, "to prison or worse if these people are Moragon sympathizers. Such rash actions are what get people killed the fastest. Especially those on the wrong side of a rebellion. On the wrong side of anything."

The door opened then, and Helbrek walked in wearing a smile, his previous fear seemingly erased, which made Iolana's intensify. Why would a simple favor like delivering laundry make Helbrek or Pelekah suddenly open to trusting them?

Helbrek pulled up one of the wooden chairs, joining them at the table. "Pardon my earlier hesitation. You understand these are troubling times. One never knows the form one's enemies may take, even the form of lovely ladies and a handsome young man like yourself." He nodded at each of them. "So, you side with the Defiance?"

Lorelei tensed nervously, but she spoke with confidence. "We haven't directly met with anyone in Carmenna from the Defiance, though I've met many in Pakua and support their cause."

Helbrek laughed softly. "I can assure you that you've met with several such people this very night—myself included, but also Pelekah and the laundress."

The dread gripping Iolana's heart eased just a little. Did this man speak truth? Had they found allies after all? She glanced at Mikanah, who kept his solemn gaze steady, indecipherable.

"What do you mean?" Lorelei's voice was purely curious, and her shoulders seemed to relax a little.

"The coin you you exchanged is used as a sort of code. If Wana keeps it, then we know the person sent to her isn't to be trusted. If she returns the coin, then we know they're an ally. Did Wana touch you at any point?"

"Yes, she took my hand." Lorelei turned it over, glancing at it wonderingly before looking back to Helbrek. "But what has that to do with anything?"

"Wana possesses a sixth sense. A unique type of magic, if you will. She cannot intrude upon the mind. But in touching someone, she can search out their emotions, sense whether they are sincere. If the three of you have been traveling closely, she likely would have picked up on the auras of all three of you, just by taking your hands. It would seem you've proven yourselves sincere indeed."

"You can help us then?" Lorelei retained a sense of calm, but Iolana could hear the eagerness in her voice.

Helbrek nodded. "Yes. It seems you take interest in the rumors of King Noheah's bastard children. Why so? Even if the rumors proved true, how could three young folk like yourself use them to help Carmenna?"

Lorelei leaned forward, gaze fixated on Helbrek. "My companions and I here stand with the Lozolian Council. Loz and others are prepared to wage war on Moragon. I know that most of King Noheah's bastards were slaughtered. But one may have survived. Born to a woman named Komeah. Tell me: Did she exist? Komeah? Did she have a child?"

Helbrek leaned even closer across the table so that his forehead nearly touched Lorelei's. Iolana leaned in to catch all his words.

"Yes. Yes, someone of that name came by all those years ago, just as you said. With a child. Boy or girl, it was hard to tell. It was a pretty child, I'll tell ya that. Komeah had been a favorite of King Noheah before the royal family was murdered. He had gotten her a house and everything. They were lovers for many years. Then His Majesty, Moragon—or Samil as he was then—came into power. While on the run, Komeah stopped here. I gave her a night's shelter, but I didn't let her stay long. Those were frightening times for us all. They still are, though I expect we've gotten more used to them...."

Iolana's chest heaved as she contained a sudden urge to cry. As much as she loathed the idea of being Carmenna's heir, she couldn't help wondering: what if this man spoke about her mother? What if she learned some small piece of her family's history, right here and now?

"Can you confirm her death?" Lorelei asked.

Helbrek shook his head. "No one ever seemed certain what happened to her or the child. But if she was born here, you might check the old sanctuary down the westward road. They keep records of births and deaths and the like."

"Thank you so much," Lorelei said, rising to her feet. Iolana and Mikanah did the same. "May Amiel crown you with many blessings."

Helbrek recommended they stay for just a little while longer, to share a drink to not raise suspicions of their sudden coming and going. Lorelei agreed, much to Iolana's chagrin. While a wise choice, she couldn't stop the whirlwind of emotions forming inside her mind. Was it really that crazy to hope she had just learned something about her own mother?

After their reprieve, Lorelei breezed from the inn, Iolana and Mikanah on her heels. As they walked, the mist began to thin out, and Iolana felt a tingling of magic returning to her body. They trekked the winding trail a little ways further until the streets opened to a wide patch of grass turned gray and withered from the stark cold. A solitary stone building rose against the forest at the town's outskirts. By the white lion painted over the double wooden doors, its six feathered wings shimmering with mother-of-pearl, Iolana knew it was an Amielian sanctuary. As they approached, she stared up at the emblem of the flying beast in awe.

"You've never seen a sanctuary," Mikanah said, so softly Iolana could barely hear. The stillness of the place demanded silence as much as its reverence demanded respect.

"No," she whispered. "I never have."

"I did once...but it was with Moragon. He was punishing some holy man or other he claimed had betrayed him. The building we saw was more beautiful. Candles in the windows. Colorful glass. People praying inside. It was serene and majestic. You would've liked to see it."

"But this will do just as well," she whispered as Lorelei pushed open the wooden doors and they slipped inside.

The clouds must have parted, for moonlight shone through what remained of the shattered windows. Their remains surrounded the room, their jagged edges shimmering with splendid reds and blues and greens. Rows of benches flanked the rectangular room, and a dais stood at the far end.

"There were probably musical instruments there once," Mikanah explained softly. "Music is important in formal Amielian worship. The sanctuary I went to, there were all sorts of instruments."

Lorelei led them alongside one of the walls, running her hands across the stones searchingly. "Moragon silenced the music of all sanctuaries and shrines. We're searching for a way downstairs. That's where these places often keep their records."

She led them past the benches, up the dais, and behind a small curtain. There, a door waited, and within, stairs led beneath the ground.

"My father," Lorelei said quietly as she stared down the winding steps. "Before things went bad, we used to attend sanctuary." She hesitated, looking as though she had wandered into a far memory. "I can feel my magic starting to return, with the mist thinning out. Iolana, are you able yet to create some light?"

Iolana sang *Luma*, and a small but steady orb of light appeared in her hands. She passed it to Lorelei and created two more orbs of light for herself and Mikanah. Without another word, Lorelei wound her way down the stairs. Iolana and Mikanah followed.

When they reached the bottom of the stairs, the space opened into a vast chamber. Books and scrolls lined the massive shelves. Many desks showed where scribes might have translated or studied. Papers scattered across the floor. Ink had spilt and dried in hardened patterns.

"Well, I suppose we start here," Lorelei said. "Start looking for anything that might have a connection to the name 'Komeah.' Or anything else remotely related to the royal family."

Lorelei wandered over to a table and began sifting through papers.

Mikanah lifted a tattered parchment and glanced at it before throwing it back down. "What a monumental task."

"There's a lot of history here," Iolana said. "But maybe we can divide the tasks. Play to our strengths. You're a fast reader. You always were. And you're tall. Maybe you can check the shelves, and I'll start looking through the desks, on the floor."

Mikanah studied her curiously. "Yes…yes, perhaps. I'll start looking at the shelves up top. We'll let one another know if we find anything."

He wandered off to climb the ladder beside one of the shelves, and Iolana scurried off down the rows of books.

She took several deep breaths, fighting back sudden tears. She should be elated that they were no longer quarreling, that they could work so well together. But perhaps that was all they had ever done, work well together in hard times. Maybe they couldn't do that in a normal life.

Iolana sank down and set her orb of light on a shelf, focusing on the old texts and records. The first pile she came across was collections of maps. Then religious rituals, histories, legends. Every part of Carmenna seemed housed inside this sanctuary, except for the birth records they sought.

After a while of searching through the various papers on the floor, Iolana stood and began wandering the shelves, observing row after row of history and religious texts.

At last, she came to a long shelf stuffed with tiny scrolls. They were each tied with a string, and secured to each string was a small piece of paper with a bit of writing. Iolana leaned close and whispered the words out loud, "Jara, Jasmina, Jemina...."

Heart racing, she ran her fingertips along the names. For the most part, they still seemed to be in order. Her heart skipped as she drew near the "K" names. She searched through them, and at last her hand halted over two scrolls with the identical name of "Komeah."

Trembling, Iolana grabbed both and plopped back down in her sea of parchment. She snapped the strings with her hand and then hesitated. What if she truly prepared to uncover the truth behind her past, her family? How would she feel if the scroll revealed Komeah as her birth mother? Would she be disappointed if it didn't?

Inhaling deeply, she unrolled both scrolls. Her glance skipped across the words. Her heart sped to the point of wanting to erupt inside her. One scroll gave the account of Komeah's birth, the other of her death. The death account spoke of Komeah's child who had survived her.

The description of that child was undeniable. Iolana

swooned and snatched out her hand, catching herself on the bookshelf to keep from falling over. She stared at the parchment's revelation, too overwhelmed with shock to understand how else to feel.

"Mikanah!" Iolana cried, scrambling to her feet, steadying herself on the shelf as she trembled all over. "Mikanah, Lorelei! I've found something!"

Rounding a corner, she skidded on a piece of parchment and ran right into Mikanah, who helped her catch her balance.

"You found the records?" he asked. For a moment, his eyes seemed devoid of all fear, filled only with pride toward her.

"Yes. Everything Lorelei discovered at the inn is true."

"Well done!" Mikanah said, catching her up in an embrace.

Iolana laughed shakily and allowed herself to sink inside his comfort.

"Oh, Mikanah," she whispered into his chest. "Do you think we can ever be more than what we've always been? After the war is in the past, do you really think there might not be anything for us? Even after all we've been through together?"

"I think there might be hope. After the war, we'll start over. At least..." He drew back from the embrace just enough to grin down at her. "I assume you'll want me as your king consort. And if not that, your bodyguard at least."

"Both of you, hush!" Lorelei commanded, reaching them and taking hold of Iolana's arm.

"We found the scrolls," Mikanah said. "Iolana found them."

"They prove what you said, about the heir."

"All the more reason to draw silent and still," Lorelei

whispered sharply. "Guards are milling outside. Their armor shows a symbol of two swords crossed before a tree."

"Reynard's crest," Mikanah almost growled the words, and Iolana shared the anger starkly painted across his face.

"We need to get out of here before we're trapped," Lorelei continued. "My magic is starting to return, but it's not strong yet. Keep your swords ready. Fighting may be a necessary evil."

The joy that had transformed Mikanah into a new soul entirely vanished from his face. Iolana kept near to him, one hand pressed over his heart, the other drawing his face to hers.

"It will be all right," she said. "Everything will be all right now. We're so close."

"Yes," Mikanah muttered, before making a miserable attempt to smile at her again. Taking her hand, he led her after Lorelei, who skirted along one of the bookshelves, peering out as if expecting their enemy to burst through the stacks of parchment at any moment. She motioned them after her, and they trailed close behind.

Each step crunching across the ancient papers sounded like thundering footsteps inside Iolana's anxious mind. She held her breath and released it only when they had cleared the papers and scurried up the steps.

Mikanah released Iolana's hand and pushed past Lorelei.

"Let me go ahead, scout for danger—"

"No!" Lorelei snapped, shoving him back. "I can go. I have my pendant to protect me—"

The sound of glass breaking shattered their conversation, and they froze. Lorelei crept up the stairs, peered through the doorway, and then ducked back.

"They're inside now."

Iolana's heart sank all the way to the floor.

"My magic is a little stronger," Lorelei whispered. "I might be able to conceal us long enough to get us out of the sanctuary. But if we are to have a chance, we must make no noise, and we must run as soon as we reach the woods. Are you ready?"

Mikanah nodded and tightly grasped Iolana's hand. Iolana's belly churned with nausea. Could she cheat death yet again?

Lorelei sang the spell *Foláchia Seche* under her breath. A film descended over Iolana as the spell took hold, muffling the sounds beyond the stairs, though not enough to block them entirely. When she turned toward Mikanah, she gasped to discover he'd disappeared entirely. Iolana's pulse drummed as panic nearly conquered her, until she felt the touch of his hand. Of course: the songspell's gossamer cloak hid him, even from her.

Footsteps approached, seeming to match the wild drumming of Iolana's heart. Heartsongs besieged her on all sides, melodies of cunning and purpose, harmonies of discontent, rhythms of fear.

"Come on!" Mikanah whispered, dragging her up the stairs.

They flew after Lorelei with all the swiftness and silence of deer fleeing their hunters. Iolana didn't look at the guards swarming the sanctuary on either side, searching the benches, and throwing them over. She just kept running, praying she was still invisible.

They burst outside, helped one another over the crumbling stone fence enclosing this part of the town, and delved into the woods.

They ran until Iolana's lungs burned.

At last, Lorelei allowed them to stop. She held her side, panting. "I think we made it."

"Let's get our bearings," Mikanah said, holding Iolana close. "Make our way back to camp—"

The word ended with a roar of pain, and he shoved Iolana to the ground. She glanced up, horrified at the arrow now protruding from his arm. Blood trickled down between his fingers as he touched the fresh wound.

"Come on!" Lorelei shouted as more arrows arched overhead.

As they dashed after Lorelei through the woods, Iolana heard Mikanah uttering a song that she recognized as a spell meant to dull pain. He snapped off the end of the arrow and cast it aside. Then they picked up pace and Iolana prayed that, by some happy miracle, they would stumble across their camp and that the others would come to their aid.

CHAPTER 44

FROM DUST TO ASHES

Mikanah whipped his head to look over his shoulder as he, Lorelei, and Iolana ran for their lives.

The arrows had ceased, but Reynard's men pursued in plain sight now. Their armor glinted in the moonlight like the cold steel of their swords, becoming increasingly more visible between the trees' black silhouettes.

Then, they poured from the woods on all sides.

Everyone drew their swords. Mikanah's gleamed in the slivers of moonlight spared by the clouds above, and he realized this was the first true fight that he had ever faced wielding Jerah's Justice. He and the spirit of his brother would conquer Reynard's men together. He promised himself this, even as more soldiers poured from the woods all around them.

Reynard's men met them with full impact. Mikanah stayed near Iolana, striving to shield her even as she stepped in front of him, swinging her sword protectively. Mikanah struggled to brace himself against the soldiers' strength. Three could not stand against so many.

"The mist's receding even more!" Lorelei shouted above the fury. "Our magic should return now!"

Songs flew as the three Guardians tried desperately to push back the waves of soldiers threatening to drown them. They sang *Segmunda* to throw several back, but more swarmed in on all sides. Their magic seeped back inside them too slowly, and Mikanah cried out in frustration as he failed to summon its full force. Cutting down a soldier with his sword, he silently cursed the mist. It needed to lift faster.

"*Mikanah!*"

Mikanah wheeled around.

Everything seemed to happen in surreal, slow motion.

Arrows bombarded him at top speed, and so did Iolana, knocking him to the ground. He thanked her and began to help her to her feet, but she fell against him and then slumped to the ground.

Blood pooled beneath them.

Her blood.

The sight of so much of it, of Iolana gasping for breath, ignited an insatiable rage inside Mikanah. All other sight and sound faded away. He swung his sword with a ferocity he had never known existed inside him. He sang one of Darice's elemental ballades, *Elén-elén*, pushing the song's force through the sword, and arcs of light burst from its tip, stunning dozens of Reynard's men. He had locked up his hurt so many years, and this—*this* was the last straw, seeing her suffering, with him helpless to protect her, except to keep the soldiers at bay to prevent them causing her further harm.

The enemy raged on all sides as he stood over her, dealing blow after blow. Yet for all his efforts, the more he felled, the more surrounded them. Was there no end to the bastards?

A blinding light flashed. When it receded, Darice stood in their midst, her skin, hair, and clothes merging into a single, white glow. A song rose from her to flood the air, along with a light that branched out and knocked many of their enemies to the ground.

As Lorelei and Darice fought on, Mikanah fell to his knees.

In that moment, all he knew was Iolana.

He took her in his arms, cradling her head. Arrows protruded from her side and back in a brutal, blasphemous invasion of her vulnerable flesh. He wanted to rip them out but couldn't bear to bring her more harm. Pain glinted in her eyes, as their spark of life faded.

"Why?" His voice and body trembled violently. "Why, Iolana?"

"Because," Iolana whispered, her voice staggering, along with her breaths, "you're too precious." A small smile wavered on her lips.

"No." Mikanah held her closer still. She winced at the touch, and he winced at her pain. He wanted to touch her, to comfort her, to give her what she had begged him for, but now his touch could only hurt. "No, I am nothing. I have always been nothing. A coward. You've done far more good than me. You've always sought to save other people while I chose to save myself."

"You're wrong," Iolana drew a long, rasping breath. "You saved me...all those years, I would not have survived without you." She gripped his arm with her fleeting strength, commanding his full attention. "We did it, Mikanah. Everything I ever fought for, all those rebellion meetings, we did it."

Mikanah wept, Iolana's face blurring in his tears. "I don't understand. All of it means nothing now if you're gone. You're supposed to be Carmenna's queen, and mine." He brushed a stray curl from her damp face. Shivers pulsed through her body, which burned with a violent fever. Reynard's poison, tipped on the arrows. A loud sob escaped him as he realized that even if he could seal her wounds, there was no cure for the poison. "How can I protect you if you leave me this way?"

"Maybe I can't be your queen," Iolana whispered. "But you will always be my king...and as your queen, I give you a last command to kiss me."

He leaned over and kissed her ever so tenderly. He felt her exhale and drew back to see the last light leaving her eyes. With a shuddering breath, he gently closed them.

Then he sobbed and crushed her to him, crying freely. His tears came in an uncontrollable rush, but no matter how long and hard he wept, they could not soothe his torment. Nothing could. Nothing except for her sweet eyes to awaken, her lips to laugh and say it was all just a trick or a bad dream. He would forgive her, if only she would wake up, wake up, *wake up*....

All around him, madness raged as the other Guardians and Echelon arrived. The sounds of battle gradually faded, replaced with Ashden saying, "Gailea, it's too late. Please, stay here!" Gailea's frantic cries, "No! It can't be true! Let me go!" Chamblin and Ashden holding her back. Nerine screaming. Darice weeping as she held Nerine. Donyon praying to the heavens in anguish.

All of them seemed so distant and insignificant. All that existed, all that mattered, was her.

Then Gailea was beside Mikanah, taking Iolana from his arms into hers. And he let her. Perhaps Gailea hated him, but she had loved Iolana just as fiercely.

Mikanah's gaze wandered over the sea of fallen soldiers. Some groaned in agony, while others lay frozen still. Blood poured visibly from some, but not others, likely stunned by Darice's light spell or immobilized by some other song. An urge to drive his sword through each of their hearts, whether alive or already dead, filled him, but he could not leave Iolana's side. His attention snapped back to her as Nerine fell beside Gailea, sobbing so violently she began to retch. She reached a trembling hand toward Iolana and cried, "Let me hold her, please. Just for a moment."

Gailea clung to Iolana's limp body, ignoring Nerine. She rocked back and forth, her gaze distant, and hummed in erratic tunes, as if she could create some melody to bring Iolana back to life.

"Gailea, *please*," Nerine pleaded.

Chamblin knelt behind Gailea and placed his hands on her shoulders. "Gailea. Let her have a moment."

"What do you know?" Gailea choked out. "What do you know of losing children? Let me have my time with her!"

"Nerine suffers too. I know Iolana is dear to you. But she is not yours!"

"She *is* mine! I found her, I saved her, I alone know what she went through—"

"She is not Ashlai or Merritt!"

Gailea stared up at Chamblin as if he'd stabbed her straight through her heart.

Fighting tears, he said more gently, "She is yours. But not yours alone. You do not get to own all this pain. Let us bear it with you. Or if you will not, at least let others release their grief. Let Nerine hold her."

Gailea's head bowed. She let Chamblin draw Iolana away, and Nerine tenderly held her in her lap. In cradling Iolana, she wept such great tears that she began to transform into her liquid form. Her hair turned into rippling waves that closed around Iolana in a sort of cocoon, as if to soothe her wounds. Much of the blood washed away. As Mikanah watched her, a tender pain shot through him.

Suddenly, Nerine gasped, and her hand flew to her cheek. Something glinted there. A shape. A familiar word. Iolana's Guardian mark, *Ut*, etched in golden light.

"What is that?" Mikanah demanded, feeling the growl as it rose low in his throat. "What *is* it? Don't tell me—it's impossible—"

"The Council would have sensed a death," Lorelei said, her voice numb as stone. "These are pivotal times. To go without a Guardian for too long could be lethal to our cause. They likely made an emergency appointment."

"This girl holds none of Iolana's strengths," Mikanah snarled, his momentary affection for Nerine vanished as he released the venom pent up inside him. "She is weak. She will bring shame to the Guardians and to Iolana's memory."

"Place one further word of hurt against the girl," Chamblin seethed, glaring up at him, "and I will see to it that another Guardian must be chosen this day."

"But he's right," Nerine cried. "I don't want to be a Guardian. I don't know anything. I didn't ask for this—"

"You lying little witch!" Mikanah growled. Nerine stared up at him, wide-eyed and trembling like cornered prey. With every shiver that passed through her body, every tear that welled in her wide eyes, Mikanah's resentment mounted. "You wanted what she had, her power, her magic. You were jealous even of *me*. It was written plainly on your face every time you looked at her. Now you would seek to steal her place as a Guardian—"

"Enough, Mikanah!" Lorelei thundered. "Leave the girl in peace. You know it is not our choice to be Guardians. I think you would remember that full well, of all people. I'm sure Nerine doesn't wish for this fate right now any more than you did then."

"She doesn't deserve it either way. What did she ever do for Iolana, for any of us?"

"How dare you!" Nerine shouted. "I loved her. I did whatever I could to protect her!"

"You followed along like a faithful dog who has no other master to cling to. When she became queen, no doubt you would've licked her boots just to keep her favor!"

"She's not the heir," Lorelei said, her voice stiff as stone.

Mikanah glanced up wildly. "What did you say?"

"Iolana. She couldn't have been queen. At least not by blood."

Mikanah's mind spun so hard that his head ached. If her death was all for nothing, he would go insane. He would jump up and throttle the nearest person to him, Nerine perhaps.

"Mikanah," Lorelei said, turning to face him and holding up a small scroll. He recognized it as one of the two Iolana had found in the shrine. Upon opening it, she read, "'A boy named *Mikanah*, after his grandfather, born with a dark blemish shaped like three musical notes near his left eye.' It's you. The heir to Carmenna is *you*."

CHAPTER 45

THE PHOENIX RISING

S ilence engulfed the Guardians, drowned them to choke what little had remained of their goodwill toward one another.

Gailea was the first to recover from the shock, lunging at Mikanah. Chamblin and Ashden grabbed her again, barely holding her.

"He did this! He knew all along! You accuse Nerine of jealousy, and yet we know you've always wanted power. You'd stop at nothing to overthrow Moragon!"

She wrenched free and flew at Mikanah. Before he knew what hit him, she had slammed him back against a tree. He lay stunned and almost wished she would finish him off, but then the urge to fight swelled inside him and he jumped to his feet, dodging her sword's blow. He dove down, grabbed his blade, and blocked another blow.

Blow after blow they wielded at one another. Melodies soared, countered only just in time by other melodies. On they battled, until Mikanah's feet abruptly froze, rigid and solid. The ice-cold sensation flowed upward through his body. As it passed through his arm, his sword dropped to the ground. His chest froze next. This was it. He would not be able to breathe, and death would at last release him from the tormenting cycle of life. Dimly he watched Gailea surge forward.

A warm light blinded him, melting away the icy spell's hold on him. When it cleared, Gailea cowered on the ground, shielding her gaze. She glared up at Darice, who held up glowing palms and said, "Enough, sister."

"No. No, he killed Iolana. I won't let him murder an entire kingdom. I won't let another tyrant rise to power!"

She scrambled to her feet, but Chamblin held her in check. Without hesitation, she flung her arm back to wrest free, her fist striking his lip. His hand flew to his mouth, and Gailea finally fell still. With a choked sob, she turned toward him, trembling. "I'm sorry. I'm sorry." She buried her face in her hands, weeping afresh. Chamblin muttered something reassuring and gently rubbed her shoulder.

In the pause that followed, Lorelei's voice sounded louder than it probably was. "Did you really know nothing of this?"

She held up the scroll. Her gaze narrowed at Mikanah, accusing him. Of all people, he had expected her to remain on his side. But it didn't matter anymore. None of them mattered.

"No. I knew nothing. You can all stop your worrying. I don't want to be king. I want only to mourn for Iolana and give her a proper burial. And then I'm going to march on Moragon's gates to do what I should have done years ago." He moved toward Nerine. "You. Get away from her."

When she didn't move, he shoved her aside with a snarl, lifted Iolana's corpse into his arms, and stormed with her into the woods.

~*~*~

Mikanah knelt on the hard ground, with Iolana resting in his arms.

After collecting leaves from the surrounding peepal trees, he had pulled the rest of the arrow from his arm and pressed the leaves to his skin while singing a healing charm. The wound still throbbed but was now sealed, and the herbs would ward away infection.

Not that it mattered. Nothing mattered. The feel of her lifeless body shot the deepest chill into the core of his soul. Everything else, the trees surrounding him with their heart-shapes leaves, the grass beneath him, seemed to mock death with their enduring life.

"Mikanah?"

Lorelei knelt beside him. Normally, her closeness would warm him, but death was a coldness that no one could melt. In Iolana's death, he had died too.

"Mikanah, you know we can't linger here. We have to take her back."

"I know. I just wanted some time with her." He glanced up at Lorelei. "But I'm not staying here once she's buried. I can't. There's nothing left for me. Only my hatred for Reynard and Moragon. Their deaths can't undo anything, but the desire to bring them about is the only thing fueling me now."

Lorelei watched him closely. Her eyes didn't judge this time.

"You can't go alone. Moragon's guards would kill you before you got remotely close to his castle."

Her voice trailed, wavered even. Tears shone in her eyes.

"Do you know why it's been easier for me to trust you than for some of the others?" she whispered. "Not *easy*, just easier?"

Mikanah shrugged. "No. I always assumed it was your nature. To trust people, give them chances."

"I suppose that's part of it. But the main reason is because I *know*. I was once a prisoner of Moragon's. Just like you, just like Iolana."

"I know," Mikanah exhaled wearily. If she came to grant comfort through their shared torment, she knew she was wasting her time. Her story was far and away different from his.

"No," Lorelei said firmly. "No, you don't. Not even Gailea really knows. For years, my father and I were able to hide my musical powers from him. But once he knew, he desired to use me in any way he could. Because of my pendant, he couldn't physically harm me. The pendant also helped me protect my mind, made it easier for me to learn spells to keep him out. I don't know if he ever knew my secret. If he did, he was unable to remove the pendant or else never tried. He started using other means to manipulate me instead. But even then, I refused to become his queen and submit fully to him. Rather, I made an attempt on his life. Perhaps the most foolish, reckless thing I've ever done. That's how I ended up on the pyre."

"The pyre," Mikanah whispered. His heart raced, springing to life again with her words. He stared at her, bewildered. He glanced down at Iolana's face, her closed eyes, her closed lips. All pain was erased. She might have been sleeping if not for how empty and cold she felt.

Looking up at her, he asked, "How? That's the same way he tried to kill Iolana, with fire. But how did you survive? And why didn't the pendant protect you?"

"The pendant's magic is made of earth and herbs and healing charms. Fire is its main weakness, and it's the one reason I wonder if Moragon might have known about it. Perhaps, because he could not remove it and use me as he wished, he found the one way I could be destroyed. By refusing him, I made myself his enemy. A woman not only opposing him but then attempting to take his life? I would make him a mockery. He could not abide that.

"So, before I knew it, I was being sentenced to death. I would burn as a traitor to Carmenna. While I was sitting in my prison cell, I tried desperately to think of a way to escape. I knew many spells, but none that might help. But I had an ability, the same Gailea has, to create song-spells of her own. I composed a song and called it *The Phoenix Rising*, praying it would work. No one had ever created a song-spell to cheat death and survived, as far as I knew. But it was my one hope. I scribbled the song on a piece of paper and wedged it between the stones of my cell's wall, hoping that if it saved my life, it might someday save another's.

"It saved mine that day. As the flames were lit, I sang the song, focusing its every intent on keeping me alive. I woke up buried, surrounded by the stench of bodies and the feel of cold flesh. I could hardly breathe, but I managed to climb free of the grave. Then I ran from that place. I had never been more frightened or felt more alone. But my prayers kept me strong, and Amiel kept me safe. I fled to Loz. People had to know what Moragon was doing, the depth of his depravity. People had to know why he must be stopped—"

"Lorelei," Mikanah interrupted softly, staring down into Iolana's face once more. A breeze ruffled her hair, concealing her face. Ever so gently, he shifted her growing weight in his arms before brushing the curls from her face once more. "Lorelei, you saved her."

"What? Saved who?"

"Iolana. The song you created and left in your cell, *The Phoenix Rising*, she used it to escape Moragon too. Lorelei." He looked up at her, meeting her gaze which stared wide and ghost-like at him. "I'm so sorry for everything I've been. I've been a fool to her, to everyone. I ask your forgiveness, though I don't expect it."

A sob escaped Lorelei's throat. She closed her eyes, taking a few, shuddering breaths. Then, opening them again, she gave him a wan smile. "I give it to you, willingly. And I ask now that you return to the Guardians. This is *our* fight. We have *all* been hurt by Moragon now. And the people need a leader to give them hope."

Panic flared inside Mikanah, along with a burning anger. Iolana would have made a vastly more fitting leader. She had always cared for people, had dared to help them at risk to her own life, as proven in her ultimate sacrifice to save him. How could he live up to everything she had stood for when he had done the exact opposite?

"I will not promise to take the throne," Mikanah said. "I see how it corrupts, and I have no desire to become what Moragon was."

"No one can force you to take the throne. If you wish to name another as king, the Council can help with that. But for now, you are the blood-born heir of Carmenna. And the Carmennans need you. Your people need you, to help them know they can win this war."

"They're not my people."

"They are. And I know you care about them."

"If they are my people, then I have only ever done them wrong. I'm no better than a man who beats his wife and children."

"Perhaps such a man may be redeemed. That road to redemption will be long and arduous, perhaps the hardest you've ever taken, but I believe you can take it all the way, if you so choose. Choose to take all that wrong and put it to right."

Mikanah stared at her, at the hope in her eyes. She believed in him. He had long since ceased believing in himself. But if she would follow him into battle, then he would lead. She had saved Iolana, had bought him a few more precious moments with her. For that, he owed her his life, his allegiance. After the war, his life could be forfeit, but until then, he would not disappoint her.

Most of all, he must not disappoint Iolana. He had failed her in life, but now he must honor her death by striving to become what she had always imagined him to be. She had believed in him too. She had been his first and strongest supporter. He would redeem himself for her or die trying if that's what it came to.

"I will heed your counsel. I will return to the Guardians. No matter how much they may hate or despise me, I will stay by their side. And I will help them fight until every last shred of Moragon's evil is utterly destroyed."

Nerine stared at the wisps of thin smoke curling up from the smothered campfire. She watched their patterns, all the while fiddling with one of the small, wooden objects she had found in the fortress just hours ago. They were intricately carved figurines of horses and soldiers, toys that might have once belonged to a prisoner's child and, in this moment, mindless distractions from her sorrow at Iolana's death.

As the gray light of dawn tinged the sky, exhaustion pressed heavily on her, and a growing hunger gnawed at her stomach, but she had found it impossible to either sleep or eat.

They had set up camp deeper into the woods. The mist had not returned, allowing the Echelon and Guardians—Nerine scoffed as she reminded herself that she was now saddled with such an undeserving title—to once more surround their camp with spells that muffled any noise. Several Echelon had also retraced their steps, using elemental spells to shift the earth and grass enough to hide their footsteps.

Ashden and Darice sat on the ground across from Nerine, picking at a small pheasant that Ashden had roasted inside the white light glowing in their midst. Donyon paced, hands clenched, jaw set. Chamblin sat beside Nerine, looking utterly weary. They had all offered their comfort to Nerine, and at first, she had embraced it.

Now, she shunned it. There was too much to feel. Too much she couldn't afford to feel. Not at this crucial time. Not now that she would be forced to fight as a Guardian. She had trained alongside the Guardians thus far, hoping she might do some good. She had believed in that possibility. Now that she was one of them, she didn't know if she could ever live up to their expectations. What difference could a naïve girl make in such a great war?

The sound of someone clearing their throat made Nerine glance up. The sight of Iolana in Mikanah's arms induced fresh sobs. She sat weeping quietly, staring at her dead friend.

Lorelei had entered the camp with them and said, "We will wait for Gailea, and then we will give her a proper burial."

The crunch of someone treading on leaves and grass alerted them as Gailea entered the camp, followed by four Echelon guards carrying shovels. She stopped and stared at Iolana. Her eyes were glassy, her face wet with fresh tears.

"The time will come," Lorelei continued quietly, "for us all to mourn over what happened here. But for now, there is still much to do and plan. We must bury Iolana and move on. We cannot linger here. Reynard's men will report to him, who will report to Moragon."

"Yes," Donyon muttered. "I'm sure Moragon wouldn't mind sparing the expense of war to see us all slaughtered here in the woods."

"Must we bury her here?" Gailea asked. "Won't they desecrate her body, Reynard's men?"

"Not if we do things quickly, while the mist is still gone and we have our magic."

"I wonder if the monster in Reynard's Keep is gone too." Nerine's voice was hollow, but she forced the words out. If true, they could be important for everyone to know. "If Reynard and his men already moved it, perhaps it was linked to the mist after all."

Lorelei fixed her curious gaze on Nerine.

"What monster are you talking about?"

"While you were gone, some of us were exploring around Reynard's Keep. Something was screaming inside like it was being tortured. Maybe a monster, a demon...Reynard said they were going to move it to Castle Alaula soon."

"We scouted that way while removing traces of our footsteps," an older Echelon man said. "We heard no screaming or other such noise."

"Perhaps we may be lucky enough then that the mist doesn't return," Lorelei said. "But we must not rely on that. We have our magic for the moment and should bury Iolana as fast as possible, while we can protect both the body and graveyard with secrecy charms."

"That means we won't be able to find her again," Mikanah said, his tone devoid of any emotion. His gaze looked as vacant as Nerine wished she could feel in that moment. "This is goodbye."

"Yes..." Lorelei's gaze locked on Mikanah, his pain seeming to become hers. "This is goodbye."

"Then let us each pay our respects, together and in peace." Ashden gazed tenderly at Iolana, while Darice hugged his arm and rested her head on his shoulder, her tears softly falling. "Even though my clan questions the existence of an afterlife, we believe the body is just as sacred in death as in life. Iolana's spirit, if it endures, would wish for us to come together now as one."

Mikanah's stony expression softened with tenderness as he gazed upon Iolana's face. "In peace, she strived to live. In peace, let us lay her to rest."

The Echelon prepared a grave, using the shovels they had brought with them. One by one, the Guardians sang various songs to wrap Iolana in protective charms.

They each took a few moments to bid her farewell. Mikanah held her the longest and kissed her forehead before allowing Chamblin to gently pull her away. Nerine laid Iolana's crystal fife across her breast. There had been a short debate on whether Nerine should be allowed to keep and use it, but Chamblin had reminded them that the instruments responded magically only to their appointed Guardian. Nerine felt relieved. Using Iolana's fife would feel too intimate, remind her too starkly of her loss.

Mikanah and Lorelei sang to lower Iolana into the earth. The first bit of dirt cast into the grave made Nerine's heart lurch. She remembered Iolana's tale of escape, and for a moment, she almost feared they were making a mistake. What if Iolana woke as she did last time, with no one and nothing to greet her except darkness?

"Say your final goodbyes," Lorelei said. "Once we turn away from the grave, we won't be able to see it again. We won't find it or know where it is. No one will."

Deep in her heart, Nerine knew her friend would not wake this time. She watched solemnly as the grave was filled, and as the last of the protective charms were sealed. She glanced a moment more upon the grave and then turned to walk away. She hadn't gotten to tell Iolana goodbye, not really. She hadn't gotten to tell her many things, nor would she. Lingering here was futile, except to drive her pain deeper.

"Nerine."

Nerine paused and turned back. Mikanah watched her, his expression empty again. All signs of the grave had vanished. Fresh green grass grew all around, blended perfectly as though the burial had never taken place.

"You did well," Mikanah said quietly, "using your magic to see that she was clean, that all the blood was gone. She looked peaceful. She could have been sleeping."

"Thank you," Nerine whispered.

"What's that?" he asked. "In your hands?"

"Oh..." She cupped the wooden figure in her palm. It was a tiny knight riding a tiny horse.

Mikanah nodded at the figure. "May I?"

Nerine nodded and passed it to him. He held it up close to his face, a hint of curiosity breaking through his numbness.

"Its craftmanship is exquistite, like the ones your father used to carve...."

He nodded at Lorelei as she walked over. He held the figurine toward her, and she took it, examining it curiously before handing it back to Nerine. "Where did you get it?"

"I found it when I swam out to Reynard's Keep."

Lorelei's gaze met hers in astonishment. "*You* swam out there yourself?"

"Yes. The monster there, it sounded like some kind of creature or beast, or maybe even human. Whatever it is, it's certainly alive. I got close enough to hear its cries. Then I heard it sing to itself once they were done with it. The guards said it was getting too powerful, that it had to be moved to Castle Alaula as soon as possible."

Asking to hold the wooden figurine once more, Lorelei absently traced the miniature knight's edges and contours with her fingers.

"I know this is mad," Mikanah said, "but from that description, it sounds like that thing could be the Vessel. Maybe it's not a ship after all and we've been wrong all this time."

Lorelei glanced between him and Nerine in astonishment. "You really think the Vessel could be human?"

Nerine shrugged. "Maybe not quite *human*. But I don't think it's entirely malicious either. The way it sang to itself after they tortured it…I think maybe it's being forced against its will. Maybe there could be a way to even save it."

"Don't be ridiculous," Mikanah snapped. "When will you leave your fantasy worlds behind? Iolana is dead. Nothing good killed her. Some evil creation of Moragon's caused that mist."

Nerine's body tensed, and her fists curled as she fought back a fresh wave of anger and grief. Staring straight at him, she said, "Not everything that came from Moragon was evil. Iolana was practically raised under him. But you can't deny the goodness in *her*, her eagerness to *fight* evil."

Mikanah made no reply.

Without another glance back, Nerine turned and headed toward camp. The further she walked from the grave, her last memory of Iolana, the deeper her anguish rooted. So much had happened that night that it seemed like many nights wrapped into one, excruciating eternity. She wanted nothing more than to fall into her tent and sleep until every last ounce of heartache had disappeared for good.

CHAPTER 46

PREPARATIONS

The next day saw their departure from Dismas. Mikanah couldn't decide whether he felt relieved to leave behind a place filled with such wretched memories, or whether he grieved leaving the place where he had spent his last moments with Iolana. Perhaps he felt a strange confliction of both. In leaving Dismas, he left her final resting place. He left her behind entirely. And yet he knew she would follow him forever, like a bittersweet ghost.

Before leaving Dismas altogether, Lorelei and Mikanah returned to the inn to speak once more with Helbrek and Pelekah in private, gathered around the small wooden table in the back room.

"Where's your other pretty friend?" Helbrek asked.

"Dead," Mikanah said.

The faces of both men fell, and Helbrek muttered, "Sorry I am to hear that."

"She died saving my life."

"And while helping gather information vital to our cause," Lorelei added. "We found proof of who the heir is." She paused, watching as Helbrek leaned in and Pele-kah sat up straight. "He sits beside me now. Mikanah, the son of Komeah and the late King Noheah."

Shock flashed in Pelekah's eyes, while Helbrek dead-panned.

Pelekah was the first to break their bewildered si-lence. "I'd like to believe there's some hope of a better, possibly even worthy, king to rally around once Mor-agon falls. Better that than watching our kingdom fall into even greater shambles than it has already. But I don't understand how this can be. Where is the proof?"

Lorelei explained quickly and showed them Kome-ah's scrolls. Only after she had told her tale in full did Helbrek find his voice. "I can't confirm whether I entire-ly believe your story. But the details fit and could be used to convince other members of our Defiance. Whether or not he is the true blood-heir, if we could convince others that he is, that may grant the Defiance a more united cause. Currently, we are quite scattered. Young man," Helbrek gazed at Mikanah squarely, "are you prepared to see this great task through? Do you accept the burden of being Carmenna's future king?"

The word "king" rang in Mikanah's ears with the weight of a hammer striking an anvil. His past few days had been spent grieving Iolana and making himself numb to all else. Now and then, thoughts of his apparent lineage and the vow he'd made to follow through would crop up, but he would shove them aside, reminding him-self they were far in the future. All that mattered right now was destroying Reynard and Moragon. He could worry about being king and all that meant afterward.

Now, he realized that such a fate might loom fright-eningly closer than he wanted to admit. Keeping his voice level, he did his best to answer diplomatically. "I don't feel ready right now, no. I don't know the first thing about being a good king. But I've seen enough of Moragon's torment to know I want to see him destroyed. And if Carmenna sees fit to make me its king in his stead, I'll spend my entire life learning how to be a king who is in every way Moragon's opposite."

For Iolana, he thought. Not for this old man questioning him, or the innkeeper, or the rest of Carmenna which perhaps ought to be his motivation. But for Iolana, so that her memory and every ounce of faith she had placed in him might someday not be in vain.

"The Defiance members are spread far and wide," Pelekah said. He sat with arms crossed, disbelief still plain on his face. "We can hardly even be called a Defiance anymore if I'm being honest. Moragon's soldiers occupy most towns and villages. Many of our blacksmiths are forced to make weapons and armor for them. It's been difficult to make plans when we are so few and they're so numerous. There are a few hundred of us scattered about. But if you could persuade current members of the Defiance, they may be able to rally others. And we would gladly meet you in battle and help in any way we could."

"How would we do that?" Lorelei asked. "Convince other Defiance members, even find them?"

"The largest gathering is in the town of Omah, several days north of here. If you can convince them to join with you, they will send out messengers to other towns, gather their support. If they won't join with you, I myself will be pleased to meet you on the field of battle." Pelekah beat his fist across his heart.

"And I," Helbrek said fervently. "I don't lnow what good an old man like myself might do, but I would do whatever it is."

"Here..." Pelekah jumped up and wandered over to one of the old chests. Kneeling down, he unlatched it and raised its lid. His hand slipped inside a pocket hidden inside the velvet lining of the lid, then emerged to reveal a small, leather bag tied with a drawstring. As he handed it to Lorelei, Mikanah heard the coins jingle inside.

Lorelei pulled one out, and Mikanah stared wonderingly.

"These are the same as the coins we gave the laundress," he said.

"They are. Head for Omah. Find the locksmith, Bane. Show him one of these coins. Keep the rest. They may come in handy in other towns."

"Thank you." Lorelei slipped the pouch into her tunic pocket and rose to her feet. Mikanah and the two men did the same. "Thank you so much for everything. May Amiel watch over you until we, hopefully, see you again."

~*~*~

Their journey to Omah after that had proved a solemn procession.

Mikanah wandered mostly in a state of numbness. He dreamed of Iolana by night, sometimes holding or kissing her, other times watching as she was burned or or struck through with arrows. He saw her so vividly at night that thinking on her during the day became too overwhelming, and so he did his best to numb his thoughts.

The same could not be said for other members of their party. Gailea wept often. He could especially hear her crying at night. Darice or Chamblin often mourned with her, holding her, or playing soothing serenades and other melodies in an attempt to console her. Nerine clung to Ashden and Darice even more than usual, though other times she would walk alone, looking as distant and detached from her grief as Mikanah tried to feel.

Every now and then, Mikanah felt the urge to walk over, say some kind or encouraging word to any of them, but that would mean acknowledging his torment afresh. It was better to keep those feelings at bay as much as possible. Lorelei would likewise try to comfort him by distracting him with a new song or some random topic of conversation, though he all but ignored her. Letting her kindness in would also force him to acknowledge his pain, too great for anyone to face.

As they traveled, they discussed what to do regarding Nerine. There was no time for her to travel to Loz and then all the way back to Carmenna. None of the Echelon messengers skilled in transportation magic had means to transport another person along with them. They would have to make do without Nerine being officially appointed. She would rely solely on using her voice for spells, and they would have to hope their unified magic would still be strong enough to overpower Moragon. Lorelei and Gailea thought they had hope, as long as they had harnessed *Ah Lum Amiel* to its full potential when the time came.

At last, they came to Omah and found Bane, the locksmith. Mikanah went with Lorelei, letting her do most of the talking for him. After showing Bane the coins, explaining that they were friends of Pelekah and Helbrek, and expressing their desire to meet with the town's hidden Defiance, Bane had agreed to arrange a secret meeting. Apparently, there was an underground cave not far from the town where they continued to meet from time to time. Hidden by protective charms, it was one of few places that Moragon's soldiers had not yet infiltrated and corrupted.

Mikanah stood in that cave now, alongside Lorelei, Gailea, and Bane. Eight of the Echelon guard stood behind them. Despite Bane's promise that the cave was well-fortified, they had placed their own charms inside the cavern as well, to prevent any sounds from traveling outward. Four Echelon patrolled outside, while the remaining eight had stayed with the Guardians back at their camp in the woods.

They all faced the one hundred fifty or so Carmennans, men and women alike, many younger but a few with graying hair. Watching the sea of faces—solemn, curious, skeptical—made it harder for Mikanah to barricade the emotions wanting to overflow from inside him. Shoving back another wave of grief, he let his anger rise more fully to the surface. He must be careful not to come across as another mad tyrant. But if he could direct all his anger at Moragon, perhaps he could persuade others to their side.

"Welcome, my friends," Bane said, his voice full in the cavern's open space. "I have gathered you here tonight to speak with these possible new friends and allies of our cause. They are sent by Pelekah from Dismas. I will allow them now to speak for themselves."

He nodded at Mikanah, Lorelei, and Gailea, who nodded in turn. Lorelei turned then to address the crowd:

"Greetings, my dear fellow Carmennans. I thank you for being brave enough to let us share in one of your meetings. I assure you that we share a single purpose, to destroy Moragon and all his cruelties. My name is Lorelei. These here are Mikanah and Gailea. We are all part of the Guardians, musical magicians chosen by the Council of Loz to safeguard the knowledge of song-spells. That includes protecting them from people who would misuse them, like Moragon."

"Gailea," a woman shouted from the crowd. "Isn't she the one they say destroyed Moragon's rule in Adelar with a single song?"

A rush of exhilarated whispers swept through the onlookers.

"It was not as thrilling or heroic a tale as that," Gailea said, her smile strained. "I did manage to help take Moragon's throne from him, as I did with Ragnar, his nephew gone mad. But I did so through risk of my own life. And through war, as will we have to do now. Only on the other side of war can peace return to Carmenna."

"We're ready to fight," a bearded man said, shaking his fist in the air. "We've been ready to fight for years. If death scared us, we wouldn't keep meeting this way."

"But why should we fight for *you*?" said another woman. "A handful of magical musicians? Even if you're the most skilled in all the land, you can't stand against His Majesty."

"All valid points," Lorelei said. "To attempt to breach Moragon's forces on our own would be nothing less than a suicidal mission of martyrs, and it would do nothing to further our cause. We have the aid of the Lozolian Council, who have been gathering allies from other kingdoms. At least two thousand Adelaran and one thousand Rosan soldiers sail for Carmenna as we speak. Not to mention the Sallie Elves and Abalinos."

"All that's good and well, but how do you intend to reach *him*?" The bearded man crossed his arms, skeptical, though his interest seemed piqued. "The castle is surrounded by thick walls, with cliffs on three sides. An endless chasm spans before it. His archers are skilled."

"We must indeed cross many obstacles," Gailea said. "The Abalinos will help us breach Castle Alaula from the air. We also know secret passages through the caves inside the surrounding cliffs. We will use these to infiltrate the castle and let our armies inside."

"And we will do all of this under one banner, one name." Lorelei curled her hand into a tight fist before motioning at Mikanah. "The man standing beside me, Mikanah, is the rightful heir to the throne, by blood. The last surviving heir of the royal family. Would it not be good to see a Carmennan on the throne again?"

Ripples of mingled joy and suspicion waved through the crowd. Mikanah listened solemnly. How could they trust him? How could they look up to him as king, as any kind of leader? He stared at them, drawn like a magnet by the feel of so many eyes watching him, and summoned a song-shield, humming it continuously in his mind. Perhaps he wasn't meant to worry, being surrounded by Echelon and some of his fellow Guardians, but neither had spared Iolana from death, and he knew they couldn't protect him either.

"What of our supposed king?" a man shouted from the crowd. "Will he say nothing? How can we stand united with a man who has no encouragement for his people? Many rulers are filled with words but are empty of actions. A man with no words must be even less so."

"A man with no words may be fuller of thoughts and ideas," said another. "Silence can be the wisest virtue. Besides, he is a friend of the Council. Lynn Lectim is well-known for her wisdom and intuition. She helped decipher many a friend from foe during the Mass Wars. I say we trust her judgment."

"How will he lead us?" a woman challenged. "What *kind* of king will he be?"

"I've heard all about this young man," said an elderly woman. "He was once the instrument of Moragon. He enslaved hundreds with his music!"

Gasps and murmurs erupted and soon culminated into full-fledged yelling and arguments. The Echelon stepped forward, surrounding the Guardians. Lorelei nodded at Mikanah, the command in her eyes fierce. Mikanah had guessed that one way or another, the truth would rear its ugly head, but their journey to Omah had granted them more than enough time to plan how they might respond to different scenarios.

Mikanah stepped forward and mentally prepared his rehearsed speech. By now, it was a well-ingrained memory, words that he could repeat while sleeping and sometimes had in his dreams.

"My good people!" he shouted, his voice filled with command. The crowd's noise diminished. Whispers still raced, but most turned their attention to Mikanah, some with loathing, others with hope, but all expectant. He swallowed hard. So many faces, wanting, hoping for something he didn't know he could ever give them. But he must try, for Iolana. If only for Iolana.

Glancing across the crowd, he found a young man about his age, whose face was flooded not only with an admiration for him, but with a fiery desire for change. He was ready to fight. He was ready to listen. He was ready to do whatever needed to be done to annihilate their common enemy. Perhaps this young man could grant Mikanah the motivation he needed to make his words, however rote, sound real and fresh and meaningful:

"My dear people. You are wise to distrust me. But I hope I can prove to you that you are not *right* to distrust me. I did serve Moragon. I did enslave and torture our people. I don't deny it. Moragon murdered my brother, as well as the girl I loved most in all the world. At least, I thought she was dead. She escaped his wrath, only to fall recently to the bloodthirst of Reynard, Moragon's closest servant.

"I had no one and nothing to love but myself...and in truth, I don't even love myself. All I had was the hope to achieve power and wealth and prestige and use that to gain vengeance for my family. I knew nothing but hate. It kept me alive, kept me motivated.

"Then Lorelei risked death to find me. I was made one of the Guardians and shown a better way. Hate still fuels me against Moragon, but so does love for others. As Guardians, none of us lord over the other. We share power, and a strong will to protect. In becoming your king, I would wish to rule in the same manner, fairly and justly toward all. The girl I loved, she used to lead rebel groups just like this one. I'm trying now to do what I should have done long ago, to follow in her footsteps, to face death in order to save our kingdom, restore it to its former freedom and peace."

"The girl," said the elderly woman who had spoken before. "What was her name?"

A tenderness shone in her eyes and sad smile. Mikanah could tell she knew, even before he released the name in a breathless tone,

"Iolana. Her name was Iolana."

Murmurs rose again. Excitement replaced fear on a few faces.

"I knew her," the old woman said. "I once worked in his majesty's castle. I was a simple maid, with no musical talents to speak of, or any other magic, so His Majesty paid me little heed. I managed to escape one day on a cart delivering meat. Before that, I attended her meetings on several occasions. She was brave, determined—fearless. I will follow you, young man, to honor her memory. I will trust you because *she* trusted you, and she had a way for seeing people, seeing their hearts."

"Thank you," Mikanah said, standing truly humbled at this woman's love for Iolana and her willingness to so assuredly pledge loyalty to him because of her. He addressed the entire crowd again. "The first armies should arrive in a couple days' time. Anyone else who would aid us is welcome. We will have armor and weapons, should you need them. Every one of you is important to this cause. By standing together as one unit, as the Guardians do, we can overcome Moragon. The more who stand with us, the harder we can make him fall. Who will stand with us then?"

Cheers erupted from the crowd. A few skeptical faces slipped away, but many came forward, eager to declare their loyalty and ask what they could do to help the cause. Lorelei gave them instructions to travel north, to meet with the armies who would soon camp along the northern fringes of the woods outside Moragon's gates.

Bane and another man promised to send messengers to other towns, to grant similar instructions to other Defiance members. Many came up to speak with her and Gailea. One man had known Lorelei's father, and two women praised Gailea for her bravery during the war in Adelar. Perhaps Mikanah's speech had helped sway them, but it seemed that Lorelei or Gailea would be the ones to gain them many more followers.

Mikanah turned and hurried toward the cave's entrance, eager to get back to camp. He didn't have the energy necessary to face the people, to pretend to feel their hope as he answered their questions. He was exhausted. Speaking of Iolana had been the final straw in a long, taxing day.

"I suppose you *do* make a rather convincing king after all."

Mikanah's entire body grew rigid at Gailea's words. They had spoken little since Iolana's death, but they didn't need to. As he turned to face her, he could once more feel her distrust.

"I am doing this," she said quietly, "helping you, for the sake of the Guardians, for the sake of Carmenna and all the other kingdoms in danger of Moragon's wrath if we do not win this war. But if you do, after all, take the throne—"

"I will not."

"But if you do, as you likely will, for I have not yet seen a man who could resist the temptation of its power, then I pray that you do not take your example of how to be a king from those you have known. Amiel knows I have not yet seen one worthy of the title."

"What of Donyon? Is he not worthy? Or..." Mikanah crossed his arms and lifted his chin. "Would *you* wish to be queen in his stead? I saw the way the people looked at you in Adelar. They would have worshipped you as their queen."

Gailea's gaze seethed. "I have *no* desire to rule."

"Neither do I. Whether you trust it or not, it's the one thing we have in common."

Gailea stared at Mikanah a long time. He couldn't tell whether she believed him.

"Come," she said at last. "The other Guardians will be expecting us to report to them."

~*~*~

"How did it go?" Chamblin asked as Mikanah and Gailea entered the giant tent. By night, it served as the female Guardians' sleeping quarters. By day, as the largest of their tents, it served as a place to make plans.

"It went well," Gailea admitted stiffly as they sat with the Guardians and Echelon already gathered. "Mikanah charmed them right into his grasp." Her unfriendly gaze shifted in Mikanah's direction, and he glanced away, too exhausted to put up a fight.

"Indeed, he did." Lorelei hurried into the tent after them. "We were most successful. The Carmennans we met with today are eager to join us."

Donyon cleared his throat, drawing their attention. "Very good indeed. I apologize for keeping Chamblin to myself, but he was key in finishing preparations. His memory of the sea, of the lay of the land, is phenomenal."

"Not as phenomenal as my diplomatic skills," Chamblin said with a playful smirk, "or so I like to think. Though clearly, you managed without me."

"What remains to be done?" Ashden asked. He sat beside Darice, absently moving his hands in swirling patterns over the earth, and Mikanah noted the small plants sprouting up from the ground around him. "Before the armies arrive?"

"If at all possible," Gailea said, "we need some way to get word to the Carmennans on the *inside* of the castle, those who are Moragon's slaves but not yet turned to his side. They may help our armies get inside. Once we're in, we'll use *Ah Lum Amiel* to free the minds of those he has controlled."

"Is there a song we might use?" Darice asked, hugged close to Ashden's side. "We've used songs of speed and light to get messages more quickly to our armies. Are there any songs we might use that could penetrate Moragon's walls and get messages inside?"

"We have *Foláchia Seche* for invisibility, or my camouflaging charm, but I'm not sure we could control either from a distance. Reluctant as I am to suggest this, it may be more feasible to use such a charm to sneak someone in. Perhaps one of us could go inside, free his servants, and convince them to our side, while others go in to open the gates."

Mikanah cringed at the notion of any of the Guardians inside Moragon's walls. "I may have escaped those walls once, but that's a miracle I feel certain Moragon won't allow again. If any of us goes in, we need to be ready and certain in our plan. And we need to be prepared for the worst possibility of not coming back out alive."

"I think we're all prepared for that possibility already," Gailea agreed with him, her gaze less harsh as it met his.

"I could do it," Nerine said. "I'm good at slipping in and out unnoticed."

Mikanah sent her a sharp glance, but she ignored him. Hadn't she heard a word he'd just said? He had once thought her overly timid, but now she would straddle the line between bravery and madness.

Chamblin placed a gentle hand on her knee. "We know you are, but it would be too dangerous. This isn't another way you in which need to prove yourself to us."

"What about the Echelon?" Donyon asked. "Surely some of them have magic that they could use to sneak inside. I mean no ill will toward them in saying this, but they are more dispensable than the Guardians, since we are necessary to kill Moragon and, Amiel-willing, to find and destroy his Vessel. Besides, imagine if one of us fell, and a new Guardian was appointed miles and miles away? They would never reach us in time—"

"Your Majesty, forgive me for interrupting."

They all turned toward the Echelon woman, Marla, who had just entered their tent. She breathed hard, her eyes wide.

"The armies have just sent word. Rosa and Adelar, some of their ships dock at this very moment on the northwestern beaches. The Abalinos' airships are above us. Pakua will begin to arrive soon as well. Nadia and Rozul were both on their way, but it seems a skirmish with each other has delayed them."

"What a wonder." Chamblin's tone dripped with sarcasm as he shook his head. "But at least the rest of the armies are early."

"Yes," Donyon said. "They are early, and they are ready. Let us prepare to set out to meet them and share in their readiness."

CHAPTER 47

THE CALM BEFORE THE STORM

The armies of Rosa, Adelar, and Pakua spanned the breadth of the shore that stretched beneath the sweeping, tree-lined hills.

Their numbers weren't immense, being four thousand, all told, but the sight of them was an abundant feast compared to what Gailea had expected she might see. Moragon's numbers were likely to outmatch theirs, with Prismatic, Spaniño, and Meleeón being larger kingdoms, not to mention Carmenna itself, largely under Moragon's control. The Lozolian Council's spies had surmised that Moragon's troops would be at least seven thousand strong, and it was surmised that nearly half those numbers were comprised of Moragon's mind controlled Carmennan slaves. The numbers may even out more once Sallusay and Abalino arrived, but that didn't change the well-fortified nature of Castle Alaula itself. Even so, Gailea allowed herself to feel a moment of gratitude and hope at the fact that not everyone had chosen to stand with Moragon, lured by his cunning promises or cowered by the threat of his mental strength and growing military reach.

"It's a beautiful sight, isn't it?" Lorelei said.

She and the other Guardians stood with Gailea at the forest's border, fairly beaming as they looked down at the sea of tents, fires, and soldiers. Lorelei was more openly enthusiastic than Gailea herself. Gratitude aside, she dared not gloat over their meager chances, but she mustered as much confidence as she could.

"It's more than I hoped for."

"Where are Moragon's armies?" Darice asked. "The Prismatics and all the others who claimed to rally to his side? You don't think they've abandoned him, that we could be so fortunate?"

"Likely not," Donyon said. "Some may be holed up in his castle, others perhaps hiding in the surrounding cliffs and caves. Come. We must meet with our captains, welcome them, and share our plans."

Together, the Guardians and Echelon entered the camp. Soldiers wearing all manner of colors and crests nodded, took off their caps, or bowed in their direction. Standards waved on flags: the flaming blue rosal on gold from Rosa, the golden bear crowned with silver stars on light blue from Adelar, and the two silver swords and purple lyre on black from Pakua, the latter representing Carmenna's true colors.

Donyon inquired about the location of the captains' lodgings, and they came to two larger tents. A soldier indicated which tent the captains had gathered in, and Donyon led the way inside.

"Your Majesty!" cried one of two red headed Rosan captains. "And the Guardians. Welcome."

"Good too to see comrades from Loz," said a dark-haired man wearing an Adelaran crest on his breastplate. He nodded at the Echelon.

Donyon introduced everyone to each other. The two Rosan captains were Maddok and Iagan, and the two Adelaran captains were Nilson and Brentley. At the invitation of Iagan, a short, wiry Rosan man, they sat around the tent's perimeter.

"Welcome," Donyon said. "And thank you again, my faithful people and allies. It is good to see a taste of home again, safe, and whole."

"I'm afraid not entirely safe and whole," said Maddok, the taller of the Rosan captains who sported a great red beard. "One of our ships was attacked and overrun by the Meleeón pirates on our way here. Our men fought them off bravely, and the Rosans came swiftly to our aid. But the attack was unexpected, and the ship lost. Fifty of our best men, slaughtered or captured."

Donyon's expression turned solemn, his momentary joy erased. "I'm deeply saddened to hear this. They will be honored as soon as possible, and I will help send word to their families."

"This leaves the people in fear," said Brentley, the Adelaran captain who had first welcomed them, his face drawn into a weary frown. "In the time it took you to arrive, unrest has cropped up within the camp. Some are afraid. They want to go home. They view the war as futile—"

"Announcing Pono, Captain of the Pakuan armies."

The tent flap parted, and a Carmennan man wearing the royal family's crest ducked inside. He swept a solemn look across all gathered before nodding in Lorelei's direction.

"My lady. It's good to see you once more. And you, Lady Gailea."

He bowed his head at her in turn, and Gailea returned the gesture, relieved to see his familiar, friendly, and reasonable presence.

"It's refreshing to see you again, Pono." Lorelei smiled at him. "Everyone, Captain Pono and my father were good friends."

"And what an honor that friendship was." He met her gaze with a slight, somber smile of his own before seating himself beside the other captains.

"I do appreciate," Gailea said, "having someone among us who is hopefully neutral in the camp's petty quarrels."

"We should lay the petty quarrels aside altogether." It was the first Nilson had spoken, his voice comparatively quiet in the shadow of his fellow Adelaran's boldness. "There are more important matters at hand to discuss."

"Indeed." Maddok crossed his arms, thoughtfully stroking his beard. "We should be joining together to stand against our enemy, not each other."

Donyon nodded toward them. "As Pono has joined us, perhaps we should bring everyone up to date on our plans."

"What of the Abalino captain?" Mikanah asked. "Shouldn't he be present too?"

Iagan tossed his head as if ridding himself of a fly. "He refuses. Ever since the Meleeóns' attack on the Adelarans' ship. Meleeóns are generally good shots with the arrow and cannon and have warred with the Abalinos times past. Captain Harbin is quite cautious about risking any Abalino's life unnecessarily, including his own. But he sends word promising that they have their airships ready. The moment we're ready to attack, Moragon's walls will be bombarded with magic and arrows from above."

"The Abalinos are normally a reclusive people." Chamblin's tone was thoughtful as he mentioned the winged people, and Gailea recalled one of his recent tales from when he'd visited their floating city, during which he'd admired not only the craftmanship of their architecture, but their vast respect for protecting all living things, most fiercely that of their own people. "We're fortunate to have their aid at all. And I'd say the same for the Sallie Elves. As such a small kingdom, they've got true guts and heart alike to take part in this war alongside us."

"The Sallies!" Donyon's brows raised as his eyes flashed sudden remembrance. "What of them?"

"I was getting to them next," Brentley said. "It seemed fair to start with the bad news and work our way toward the good. The Elves have used their underwater ships to wage a surprise attack on the Prismatics. They've cut them off. There's very little chance the Prismatics will reach Carmennan shores anytime soon now. The Sallie Elves themselves should arrive here shortly."

Gailea breathed a huge inner sigh, as though she'd been holding her breath unawares, and mingled shock and gratitude flashed across the faces of everyone gathered.

Donyon spoke for them all. "That is wondrous news indeed."

"As for our armies," Nilson's soft voice was eager in a way that demanded attention, "both Adelarans and Rosans, we'll surround his castle as much as we can, though most of its northern border is encompassed by the cliffs and therefore cannot be reached."

"Which is where the Abalinos come in handy," Chamblin said.

Donyon exhaled deeply, face pulled into a frown that showed the gears inside his mind were turning, along with the worry he tried to hide by lifting his chin and making his voice robust. "If the Prismatics remain at bay, this will make our numbers more even. But there is still the matter of breaching the castle. We must opt for the element of surprise as much as we can. Moragon sees us gathered at his gates. We cannot surprise him that way. But the underground caverns...."

"They lead inside the castle," Pono said. "Someone could sneak in, open the gates. The Abalinos could distract Moragon's guard from the air if need be. The only problem is that the passages inside Castle Alaula are nigh impenetrable, our scouts tell us, and that the caves hide them well."

"I know the way."

Everyone looked at Lorelei. Gailea sucked in her breath while Donyon looked ready to protest, but Lorelei stopped him:

"I know how opposed we've been to sending any Guardians inside straight away. But I have coalescence magic that would allow me to fuse with the walls, if necessary, to avoid being seen. I could sneak about easily enough."

"I could join her," Mikanah said. "I know the castle like the back of my hand. I will stand by Lorelei, to protect her."

Donyon studied Mikanah skeptically, and Chamblin muttered beside Gailea. Staring at Mikanah like he had gone fully mad, Gailea said, "Do you truly have a death wish for yourself, or for us all, in fact?" He scoffed— ever so slightly, but she caught it—and this further fueled her frustration. "Any Guardian delving into blatant danger is risky, but it's also a risk we've foreseen. We've known all this time that Lorelei knows the castle and caves better than any of us. We've also known that we, as Guardians, would be forced to face other dangers before confronting Moragon himself. But to place yourself in that kind of danger not only as a Guardian, but as Carmenna's heir?"

"Isn't that what you've all been wanting?" Mikanah's words were almost as tense as his body as he crossed his arms, gesturing with one hand as he continued, "A leader who actually acts like one? Who takes control, who actually does something? Or would you have me be Moragon, sitting back and watching while I send all of my minions to die fighting for me?"

His gaze practically seethed, but as her irritation mounted, Gailea sensed the hurt hidden behind his anger. The desperation. Maybe he really did have a death wish. He had spoken very little of his grief at Iolana's passing. In fact, beyond a cutting remark here and there, he had expressed very little emotion at all. She tried to choose her next words carefully, but Chamblin beat her to it:

"A king dying for his people prematurely, before the war's even begun, may not be the best way to encourage them. More likely, it may cause them to lose heart, to see their future king fall so easily."

"Or it could rouse them to righteous anger and make them fight all the more." Donyon glanced in Chamblin's direction before looking at Mikanah. "I am not advocating that you throw yourself into this. But if it's for the right reasons, if this is how you wish to fight for your people, then at least ask yourself how and why? Yes, you know the castle well, but do you think you could make it without having Lorelei's coalescence powers?"

"I could use the song-spell Gailea taught us to camouflage myself. Or the one granting temporary invisibility." He nodded stiffly in her direction, not meeting her gaze. "And I have my mental skills. I can command Moragon's forces with my music if necessary—only, if necessary," he added quickly, with an uncomfortable glance at Lorelei who stared with the same obvious disapproval as Gailea.

Donyon turned to Lorelei. "Would you have Mikanah accompany you?"

"If he insists." Lorelei's stare lingered on him. "We

got out together once. I suppose we could get back in. His skills could prove most useful."

"I suppose that's settled then. We'll discuss these plans more at length once the other captains arrive."

The Guardians and captains agreed and, making plans to speak later, departed the tent for their own.

Nerine trailed after Chamblin, Darice, and Ashden, asking if they could practice their music together, while Gailea wandered toward the tents that Brentley and Nilson had indicated they might use for their own. Choosing one and hoping that it hadn't yet been claimed, she peeked her head inside—

And quickly withdrew it. Several Adelaran and Rosan soldiers had gathered within. Gailea prepared to walk away from what had surely been a private meeting, but then she hesitated upon hearing her name from the muffled the voices within. Her heart lurched. Who were these strangers, and what could they possibly be talking about? They were days, perhaps hours away from war. There should be no secrets among their allies at this point.

Gailea crept along the tent and knelt beneath a large tree. She clutched the fabric firmly in one hand and sang *Gizemia's Revelation* inside her mind, concentrating on that specific area of the tent until she had torn a gap in the sound-dampening spell enclosing the tent. Then, she sang *Dumkana* to magnify the voices just enough until she recognized Nilson, still quiet but far less meek. Leaning in, she focused hard on what was being said:

"For all his previous folly, Donyon seems to have grown bolder, more confident. He *has* been a faithful king to us. Perhaps we should reconsider."

"Confident or no, he still cannot be trusted," said another man. "He has proven time and time again his inability to lead. Ever since his wife and child died, he's lost his fire. A sad fate, but sad though it is, we cannot allow sympathy to weaken us. Adelar cannot go on as it has all these years."

"But see how he has taken up the mantle at last? Found his courage with the Guardians? I was surprised he dared leave his borders at all."

"He hopes for the glory of battle, an alliance with Carmenna, the power and security that would bring him. But don't fool yourself. Once he has obtained this victory, he will slink right back into his hole. He has no thoughts to expand Adelar, only to shield what little remains. Once Moragon's threat is removed, he will return to his old ways. We'll be trapped once more like rats."

"I fear the same," said yet another man, his voice strangely familiar. "We are a weakening breed. A dying breed. If we remain isolated, we will vanish, and our proud magic will mean nothing. I don't trust Donyon. He has always been a man of fear and isolation. But there is one bolder than him. A most powerful ally, a fearless ally. The one eavesdropping on us right now, through a crack like a little mouse. I know you're listening, Lady Gailea."

Gailea froze in place. Her first instinct was to run, but the man who had seen through her trick had also just praised her. He seemed a possible friend, though by the near treason he'd spoken against his own king, she would do best to exhibit caution.

"Please, my lady. Come in. Speak with us."

Gailea crept around to the front of the tent and ducked inside. She glanced across the small crowd gathered. Three Adelarans, four Rosans. She made up the eighth member.

Included were Nilson and Iagan, the Adelaran and Rosan captains who had just helped plan their war strategy alongside the king they now sought to turn against.

Her glance lingered on another familiar face, Brodach, the Rosan messenger who had slipped her the secret message.

Iagan extended his hand. "Worry not, my lady. You have no enemies here."

"I'm not so sure I would agree." She swept a fierce look across them all, letting Iagan's hand linger awkwardly midair. "Men threatening Donyon, and thus my fellow Guardian, sound like enemies to me."

"Quite on the contrary. We are rather most loyal subjects willing to die for you."

"But you are not so eager to die for your king?" She looked to the Adelarans, striving to keep an even tone.

"Donyon is not *my* king," Iagan said. "But yes. All of us here would sacrifice the king's life for yours."

"Is that your intention?"

"That is our intention," Nilson said. "Though I begin to doubt." His brows furrowed, matching the frown that seemed to reflect some inner conflict.

"It's too late to turn back now," another of the Adelarans snapped. "Your magic is needed, Nilson."

"Wait," Gailea said, clenching her fists beside her and calling several defensive spells to her mind. As their motives grew more clearly apparent, she fast grew uncomfortable. "Do you truly mean harm against Donyon? He is a Guardian. His magic is necessary to help defeat Moragon."

"We know, my lady," Iagan said. "Which is where Nilson holds the key. He is a rare gift amongst us. His is the power to transport, not just himself, but another at the same time. He could bring the replacement Guardian here in the blink of an eye."

"But why *kill* Donyon?" Gailea asked, trembling inside.

"You needn't pretend to claim loyalty." Brodach met

her gaze head on. "Everyone here knows your own distrust against him, a distrust which we share. If such displeased you, Donyon would not necessarily need to die. Even if we could devise a way simply to corner him into a position of surrendering the throne, we would gain a new, deserving queen."

"You would really think to place me on the throne in his stead," Gailea said, her voice flat as she fought to strike down every ounce of panic flitting inside her at the mention of returning to Adelar's throne. "You would have me rule in Adelar once more?"

"Yes, my lady." Iagan took a step toward her, gesturing as his speech grew more emphatic. "You've been victorious twice in battles, whereas he has only once, and then only by your aid. You are strong and bold and wise, and the blood of both Rosan and Adelaran nobility flows through your veins. You could unite our kingdoms, and together, we could be unconquerable. Getting rid of Donyon would clear your path to the throne. What say you? Should he fall or else be persuaded into surrendering his crown, would you rule in his stead?"

Gailea stared at Iagan, bewitched by the entire situation. She felt utterly stunned, as if she watched the scene from outside herself. Surely, this must be some bizarre dream she would soon waken from.

"I will consider it," Gailea lied, lifting her chin and sweeping as confident a look as she could across them. "And I will vow to keep this conversation between us. But only if you promise me that no harm will befall Donyon until I have had time to think things through and come to you with my answer."

Iagan nodded firmly. "You have my word."

"And that of your companions?"

Words of agreement echoed about the tent.

"I will now take my leave. You've given me much to

think upon. Thank you, gentlemen."

The men bowed their heads, thanking her as she exited the tent.

Gailea hurried through the camp, her head spinning so fast she thought it might fly off. All this time, she had thought the Rosans were encouraging her in her fight against Moragon, but the enemy they sought to tear down was one of her allies.

Of course, it was still difficult to entirely consider Donyon an ally. For a moment, she allowed her thoughts to wander, to consider what it would mean if the man who had tormented her mother was dead. Another cowardly ruler cast from his throne for good. He deserved this. He had never been worthy of being king.

That didn't mean he deserved to be murdered by his own people—by her. Nor would it serve the Guardians any purpose to kill one of their own, especially someone who had been training with them long enough to have a decent number of song-spells in his arsenal. But perhaps things could work out well enough in the end. She need not become queen herself, but she could help in both dethroning Donyon and choosing someone in his stead that she and the Adelarans found equally worthy to rule.

Gailea needed to breathe. Air. Clarity. She made her way through the crowd of soldiers and tents on the stretch of green grass bordering the northern forest facing Castle Alaula. She headed up a slope into the woods for some peace. Years of anger and loathing begged her to be all right with everything she had just learned. Only a single word from her, and the traitors inside that tent would do all they could to bring whatever fate she wished for Donyon to fruition.

"Gailea?"

Gailea breathed a sigh of relief at the familiar voice. "Chamblin." She turned to grant him as much of a smile as she could muster. "What are you doing here?"

"Well, it's fine to have your company as well." He placed his hands on his hips, tilting his chin away from her in mock insult, making her laugh a little. Grinning at her in a satisfied way, he motioned at the trees. "Honestly, it seems we both fancied the same sort of reprieve. A few moments' peace and quiet in the serenity of the woods. My eyesight is better some days than others, but my other senses remain keen as a young child's. It grants me comfort, to hear the breeze in the trees, feel it on my skin, inhale the earth's rich scent. It can be rather jarring, surrounded by all the sounds of soldiers practicing for battle without being able to fully see."

"I can't imagine." Gailea focused on keeping her voice gentle. Maybe comforting Chamblin as he so often did her was the distraction they both needed. "I've always liked the sounds of the forest myself. When I was a girl, I would often sneak from the castle into the King's Wood. There was a creek I was especially fond of. The feel of the water on my skin, its coolness, gentleness. The song it seemed to sing." Spreading her arms wide like the branches of the trees, she closed her eyes and inhaled deeply. "I can almost imagine it now. I would go there whenever I could, but especially when I was overwhelmed." Lowering her arms, she opened her eyes to share a smile with him.

Chamblin frowned in concern. "Is that what drove you into the woods now? Do you feel overwhelmed? Perhaps worried about the battle tomorrow?"

"It's me who should be asking you that, isn't it? You're the blind man, after all."

"*Nearly* blind, thank you so much. And that doesn't mean I can't, or won't, fight. I still have my trusty underhand skills." He brandished his sword, waved it with an artful flair, and then performed several quick moves.

"Any enemy who tries to touch you, I'll bring them right to their knees."

Gailea laughed again despite herself. "Endearing fool that you are, I'm sure I can protect myself. Besides, you don't actually plan on joining us in battle, do you?"

Chamblin cocked his head, clearly confused. "I've joined you so far, haven't I? Haven't gotten myself killed yet."

"No. But it's one thing to fight a single demon and another to stand against an entire army. You can't possibly fight with us."

"I appreciate this sudden concern for my well-being, but all the Guardians will be needed to destroy Moragon. It takes the power of eight to fully manifest *Ah Lum Amiel.* Isn't that what you said yourself? If you want to waste your energy worrying about anyone, I'd say it's best directed at Nerine."

"Nerine? Why?" The protest spilled from Gailea, and she took a step back as a bolt of distress shot through her.

As Chamblin stared in her direction, his frustration was almost tangible. "You've hardly spoken two words to her since Iolana's death. And even before then, your concern for Iolana consumed much of your time and resources."

Guilt stung Gailea at his blunt words, but she shoved it down and said, "Nerine has my sister and Ashden and Lorelei. They all adore her. She doesn't need me right now."

"You can't really make yourself believe that," Chamblin insisted. "I certainly don't. She adores you most of all. Always has."

"Nerine was my student before Iolana. You *know* she is important to me. But you must understand if I can't be there for her right now."

"I might, had you been there for her at all on this

journey. What about when she used her water magic to save us on the ship? Or when she swam beneath the barriers into Adelar? Not to mention her most recent feat, stealing inside Reynard's Keep to obtain information on that monster—"

"Yes, and why would you even let her go into that fortress? If you're so concerned for her, why allow such recklessness?"

"Not recklessness. Bravery. And a clear desperation to gain *your* approval."

Chamblin stepped toward her, and this time, he didn't merely look toward her. He looked straight at her, gazing right into her eyes. Perhaps because he stood close enough to view her face, or perhaps his waxing and waning vision had granted him a few moments of clarity. His eyes locked on hers, taking her aback before breaking the walls she had been scrambling to keep secured tight around her heart. She hadn't even realized she had built such a sturdy fortress but now, in one breath, Chamblin had both illuminated that fortress and brought it crashing down.

Gailea sank to her knees, sobbing.

After a few moments, Chamblin's arm wrapped around her. She tried to shrug him away, but he didn't let her. He kept holding her, until she let herself trust him, sinking against him as she cried.

"You're right," Gailea whispered, forcing herself to take as deep breaths as possible, quelling the overpowering tears. "I know you're right. I can tell I've hurt her. And I've wanted to talk to her. I've gotten the sense she doesn't want to talk to me. But I can't honestly say I've tried hard enough or tried much at all. It's just so hard right now. I don't know why it's hard."

"If I may shed some possible illumination?" Chamblin's gentle tone, devoid of any accusation, made her sink against him a little more. Her mind fought against her—she didn't deserve his grace—but she fought back, knowing that she needed it. She nodded against his shoulder.

Chamblin kept his arm braced around her, rubbing her shoulder in soothing circles. "I think, and of course you may correct me if I speak anything untrue, but it seems to me that, well, with Iolana, you saw much of yourself in her. That made you draw to her, want to have that connection. Help her, even though I think a part of you knew she wouldn't really want to be helped. Not deeply enough. You knew she wouldn't stop loving Mikanah, sabotaging her own heart. Then Nerine, who carries her own pain but has always been the more sensible, open to a more stable sort of connection with you, you shy away from her. On purpose? I don't think so for a moment. But I think because of all the loss you've endured in your own life, that it's difficult for you perhaps, to choose to love someone who is good and solid and steadfast. Whether because your heart fears suffering more loss or for some other reason, I think you struggle with seeing the love that's right before you, ready and available if only you'd reach out for it."

Chamblin gave her a gentle squeeze before continuing to rub her shoulder.

Gailea remained silent a few moments, allowing Chamblin's words to infiltrate her heart, struggling to comprehend them. There was some truth in his words. Exactly how much truth, she couldn't be sure. Perhaps part, perhaps all.

What was clear was that she had indeed resisted getting too close to Nerine, or to anyone in a long while, with whom she might develop such a lasting, deep relationship. Iolana had needed her, and Gailea had wanted to do everything in her power to save her. But she was never hers to save. Nerine needed her too, in a way that she could possibly fulfill, if she chose to open herself to it.

"I know you care for her," Chamblin added gently. "But she won't know it too if you don't show it. We're on the eve of an immense battle. Go to her. Hold her. Comfort her."

"You're right," she admitted again, practically collapsing against him, weary and defeated. "I should go to her. I'm just not sure I have the strength. I don't know if I have it in me to choose to do what I should. Perhaps I've neglected her, but not on purpose. I'm still wrecked from Iolana's death. The pain is bubbling so near the surface that it frightens me. If I were to try to talk to Nerine now, make amends with her, I might only end up hurting her more deeply, which neither of us can bear."

"I understand," Chamblin said, his voice gentler still. "Just promise that you'll do it soon, before it's too late. Death is not the only thing that's impossible to repair."

"I promise."

Gailea pulled away from Chamblin at last. Wiping away her tears, she stood to her feet, and Chamblin stood beside her. He watched her, and his compassionate gaze made her glance away, uncomfortable once more.

"Will you come back to camp now?"

"Soon. I just need some time alone, to collect myself."

Chamblin lingered a few moments. He clearly wanted to reach out and comfort her further, but Gailea stood her ground. Any further gestures of affection or comfort might make her collapse again.

When at last he turned to leave, she called out, "Chamblin."

He paused and faced her, quizzically.

She continued, "Promise me something too."

"Anything."

"In battle, promise me you'll stay close. I can't…I can't lose someone else that I…." *Admit it, say it: someone you love.* But her mind once more forbade her. "Someone I care about."

"I promise," he said with a tender smile before heading back toward camp.

As Gailea watched him go, she roughly brushed away a few tears. The further he walked from her, the more deeply she felt another sudden realization. Her heart screamed that she should make him come back, that she should tell him, but her mind continued to hold her in check, whether by reason or fear, she couldn't tell.

Maybe if they both pulled through the war, she would tell him. Or maybe it was better this way. After all, she remained lawfully married to a madman who would likely never find mercy enough to release her from their bond. Maybe it was better that she didn't allow her feelings for Chamblin to grow. Or, if she couldn't stop them from growing, that she at least did so in secret.

She didn't know what was best, and right now, she couldn't know. She could only focus on one war at a time, and the greatest one prepared to erupt tomorrow.

CHAPTER 48

THE STORM BREAKS

The sun had just begun to rise, painting shades of pale pink and gold across the horizon. Black clouds settled above, transforming the rest of the sky into a solemn ocean of gray.

Nerine stood on one of the grass hills overlooking the beach and bordering the western edge of the forest. The spot reminded her of when she, Gailea, Drewit, Valarie, and the rest of the first Guardians had once played music together on the slopes of Willardton that overlooked the ocean. She couldn't have imagined then that almost all of them would be murdered. Or that she and Iolana would be so close by while those murders took place. Or that Iolana, whom she had loved with all her heart, would be murdered too just a few short months later. She could never have envisioned that instead of standing on a hilltop admiring the ocean with friends, she would instead stand and survey the armies expanding before Moragon's threatening castle.

Reaching into her pocket, she touched the familiar, soft bit of cloth. She had ripped it from the hem of

Iolana's tunic before they had laid her to rest. It was the only bit of Iolana that Nerine had, and she had wrapped it around one of the small wooden figurines from Reynard's Keep, to help prevent her losing it. Nerine clutched the figure wrapped in cloth now. She must be bold like Iolana had taught her, like her parents had shown themselves to be all her life, like she had been that night she swam out to the keep. She trembled at the thought of joining the fight that could break out any moment. Even moreso, she trembled at the idea of what she prepared to do. But she was entirely resolute. She would serve the Guardians well, and if she perished doing so, then so be it.

With a deep breath and a continuous prayer for Amiel to help her push through the anxiety squeezing her heart, Nerine made her way back down the hill. Leaving the beach behind, she wound through the sea of tents situated just outside the northern edge of the woods and spanning before Moragon's castle. Further north, the castle plainly loomed. Castle Alaula was enclosed on three sides by cliffs rising high above it. The cliffs pressed close to the outer wall protecting the castle. In front of the castle, instead of cliffs, was a huge gaping abyss, deterring any outsiders that dared to get inside.

The Guardians had agreed to meet at sunrise, to see Lorelei and Mikanah off on their mission to infiltrate the castle, to free what servants they could of Moragon's mental shackles and open the gates.

Entering the large tent, Nerine found that the rest of her fellow Guardians had already gathered. Gailea glanced up as she entered, watching her with a noticeabe eagerness. Gailea had tried to speak with her last night, but Nerine had excused herself early to bed. With a curt nod, Nerine drew away from Gailea now, refusing to meet her gaze. Gailea was the one person who might sway her from doing what she prepared to do, and she could not allow that.

"Are you sure we're ready?" Lorelei asked Mikanah.

"Yes," Mikanah said. "We have everything we need."

Nerine cleared her throat. "I'd like to come along."

Bewildered glances turned in her direction. Gailea and Chamblin both looked horrified and opened their mouths to retort, but she cut them off.

"I won't hear any excuses this time. I am a Guardian. I'm just as important as any of you and just as capable of taking risks. I *want* to go. I've sensed underwater rivers flowing through the caves. I can be of help."

"There are no rivers as far as I've ever seen," Lorelei said. "Are you certain—?"

"Lorelei," Gailea interrupted, her voice breaking with clear exasperration. "The girl suggests risking her life to join you, and your only thought is to ask about the lay of a land you already know perfectly well?"

Gailea's gaze shifted to Nerine, sharply imploring. Uncertainty pricked at Nerine, along with guilt, forcing her to look away from her teacher once more. She must be free to make her own decisions, to prove she was worthy to stand with the Guardians. "With all due respect, Lorelei may not know as much as she thinks. The rivers, I think they may be hidden between layers of stone. But they *are* there. They flow deep and powerful. I can command them, if it becomes necessary to do so. Use them to tear open the rocks, make a way of escape."

Gailea gave Lorelei a pleading look, and Nerine breathed deep, struggling to hold back the flood of emotions she couldn't quite comprehend. Did Gailea show pure concern for her safety, or was this just more of the same, Gailea doubting her as ever? Gailea tried to meet her gaze again, but Nerine refused.

Lorelei gave Gailea a sympathetic glance before turning to Nerine. "We don't have time to argue. We've got to go, now. Whether you come along is up to you. Only know that my coalescence spell will work only for me. I cannot conceal all three of us inside the walls, except perhaps for a few seconds."

"I can make myself a puddle of water," Nerine said. "That could allow me to slip beneath doorways, scout the way ahead. And in my full water form, I'm immune to swords and other physical attacks. I can only hold that form for a few minutes at best, but it may come in handy."

Lorelei nodded. "Let us go then without delay. If Moragon discovers we've gotten inside, he will likely choose to attack. We'll do our best to open the gates before this happens." She looked to the other Guardians. "May Amiel be with you in our fight."

"Amiel be with you as well," Darice said, hugging Nerine while Ashden placed a hand on her shoulder.

Securing their maps, several vials of different-colored elemental dusts, and weapons, Lorelei, Mikanah, and Nerine started away from the camp and into the woods. From her place at the rear of the group, Nerine shot a final glance at Gailea. Gailea met Nerine's gaze, and now Nerine was certain that her pleading radiated pure concern, the first sign of affection she'd shown Nerine since Iolana's death. A bittersweetness flitted through Nerine, and she tore away with a shuddering breath. Gailea's gaze was filled with questions and an earnest yearning that seemed to mirror what Nerine had felt these past weeks. Why now, when there was no time to say even a small fraction of the plethora of things that she wished could be said between them?

Nerine's longing intensified into a pain that made her wipe away a few sudden, angry tears. She couldn't be overwhelmed by this rush of emotions. She couldn't allow herself to feel anything that might tempt her to turn back.

They descended deeper into the woods, heading for the cliffs rising on the castle's east side until the sounds of the camp faded away, replaced by a hushed stillness. Even the wind lay dormant. Nerine wondered if Moragon had bewitched the forest itself to obey and reverence him.

They continued toward the cliffs, passing just close enough to the castle that they could glimpse its mighty towers leering between the trees. Nerine's entire body shuddered. So, this was where Iolana had practically been raised a slave. The sight alone of Castle Alaula intimidated her, as though it was a villain all on its own to be conquered. She couldn't imagine how much more intimidating Moragon himself must be, the true villain she had heard so many terrible stories about, and yet that's all they had been: stories. Now, as they plodded steadily through the woods, she felt like she hurtled toward a danger that was too startingly real.

They emerged from the woods to skirt along the cliffs, with the ocean crashing against the rocky shore beside them. After an hour or so, the cliffs that rose above the castle on its northernmost side towered before them. Lorelei felt along their massive frame and then seemed to disappear inside them. Her hand peeked from the rock, waving them forward, and Mikanah disappeared after her inside the stone walls. Nerine hurried over and realized there was a narrow passage through the cliffs, nearly impossible to see, and slipped inside.

Darkness enclosed them.

"We can't summon light or fire here," Lorelei said. "This part of the cave forbids such magic. But I know the way. I'll sing a song, to keep us from getting separated."

Nerine's hands touched the walls as they went, guided both by the tune Lorelei hummed and the water's rhythm surging inside the cliffs. Her fingertips pulsed, aching to draw strength from the rushing waves.

After what might have been an hour, maybe two, Lorelei commanded them to halt. When she spoke again, her voice was so close to Nerine that she could feel her breath on her cheek.

"We're close to the part of the cavern that connects to the castle's outer wall, which means we're close to where guards will be posted. When we get closer still, I will use my coalescence to lead the way. Nerine, I trust you to use your magic to transform, if necessary, to avoid being seen. Mikanah, you'll have to follow my lead. Our sole mission right now is to reach the gates and open them as soon as possible. Are you two ready?"

Nerine and Mikanah agreed quietly. Although Lorelei said nothing more, Nerine sensed the vibrations of her footfalls and followed after her. As they delved deeper inside the cliff, the tunnel branched out into three different directions, forcing Nerine to listen extra hard to Lorelei's footsteps. Sometimes, they seemed to fill the passages and surround her. Nerine moved as slow as she dared, pausing to ascertain she could still sense Lorelei's footsteps while also making certain that Mikanah still moved behind her. The last thing she needed was to dive down the wrong passage and get hopelessly separated in the dark.

As water began to drip from the ceiling, running down the walls and trickling cold between her fingers, Nerine was reminded of when she and Iolana escaped the water tunnels leading from the school. If only Iolana could be beside her now, rushing to defeat the man who had ultimately stolen everything but her spirit from her.

After traversing the cavern awhile longer, a dim, distant light shone at last. Lorelei slowed, and Nerine gratefully matched her pace. They paused before a narrow fissure rent in the stone. A black, shimmering film covered the fissure, almost like a mist. Nerine guessed it might be a glamour spell of some sort that concealed the cave's entrance and wondered also if it was strange that she could see it. A visible concealment charm wasn't much of a concealment charm at all.

Lorelei braced herself against the wall of the cave and peeked out from the fissure. Then, she drew her head back and whispered, "This leads into a stone corridor, right inside the wall. At the end of this corridor is a door with two guards. The door will likely take us inside one of the guard towers posted around the perimeter. I'll try traveling through the wall and seeing if I can render them unconscious."

Lorelei leaned back against the wall. Her lips parted as she chanted too quietly for Nerine to hear. Sweat glistened on her body, and tremors quivered through her. Nerine watched, fascinated but scared in the same breath. Was the spell working?

All at once, Lorelei fell inside the wall and vanished. Nerine stifled a cry of surprise. Mikanah looked equally bewildered.

Seconds ticked past. Anxious, Nerine closed her eyes, quietly chanting the spell to change into her liquid form. Mikanah whispered beside her, demanding to know what she was doing, but she ignored him, focusing all her attention on transforming every fiber of her being first to water, and then to mist. She shifted from side to side in the passage, making certain her magic was stable enough to hold her form. Then, she drifted out of the fissure to see if she could glimpse what was going on.

No sign of Lorelei in sight. Nerine glanced back at Mikanah, only to find herself staring at a solid stone wall. So that was the purpose of the black mist spell, to make the cliffs look solid from this side while alerting someone on the other side that things weren't as they appeared. How clever Lorelei had been indeed to discover such a trick from the inside of the castle. Perhaps she'd used her coalescence spell to sense that this part of the wall wasn't solid.

Nerine turned back to the corridor, quivering as she struggled to hold her mist form. When no signs of Lorelei surfaced, Nerine began to panic. She had read tales of fairies and elves who used coalescence magic, only to get stuck inside walls, trees, or rocks, suffocating or starving to death.

A hand darted out beside the leftmost guard and threw a glittering dust over his head. The guard slouched down, eyes closing.

His companion drew his sword and struck at the hand protruding from the wall. Lorelei drew it back inside, and the steel struck stone instead. Instantly, her hand darted out again, rendering the guard unconscious as she had the first.

Nerine solidified once more and rushed over, Mikanah on her heels. No sooner had they reached the door than Lorelei tumbled from the wall, right into their arms.

"Thank you," she gasped, looking dazed. "There are some sort of invisible barriers here, preventing use of musical magic. There's no way I can put all the guards in the castle to sleep with powder, even if I had enough. Nerine, can you turn into a puddle and slip beneath the door, long enough to see what we're up against?"

"Of course," Nerine said, both thrilled and relieved. Becoming vapor again might have spent most of her strength, but she could hold her water form for a longer period.

"Then go quickly and come right back."

Nerine chanted the transformation charm inside her mind. She focused hard, repeating it until she felt the liquid coursing through her body and then becoming her body. For a few moments, she stood in her perfect liquid form. Then, releasing her shape, she collapsed to the floor in a formless puddle.

From there, it was easy to spread herself thin and slip beneath the door. Instantly, she detected the warmth of bodies and glanced up through the thin watery film. A guard stood on either side of the door. Guards patrolled the hall, as well as the adjoining hallway a few yards ahead.

Slowly, she slid across the floor, hugging close to the stone wall, and keeping herself spread as thinly as possible. Though the torchlight did not illuminate the corridor well, a puddle moving of its own will would be suspicious, to say the least.

Nerine paused at the end of the hall and looked both ways. The connecting hall stretched long, and dozens of men were on guard for as far as her eyes could see. Getting past them without being noticed would be impossible.

Nerine shifted back to the two guards by the door. She shaped herself just enough so that she formed a hand and placed it to the outer wall that was built right against the cliff. She felt for the pulsations she had sensed earlier and soon located them. The river flowed strongly inside the caves that were just beyond the wall. She could focus on its rhythm and draw on its power. But she would have to act quickly before the guards had time to sound an alert.

Concentrating hard, Nerine drew herself up into her full-body water form and slammed both hands against the wall, sensing for the river's currents. Bewilderment flooded the faces of the two guards. One of them raised his sword and slashed at Nerine. She closed her eyes, braced herself, held her form, and sure enough, the blade did little more than splash right through her.

Nerine continued pulling the power of the river inside her. Then, singing an elemental ballade, she began converting the water's waves into sound waves, commanding them to flow faster and faster until their short, choppy undulations screeched high and shrill.

The guards threw their hands over their ears, wailing in pain, and staggered to their knees. Blood ran between the fingers of some. Their comrades rushed down the hall to aid them, but as soon as the sound met their ears, they too collapsed.

When every guard in sight lay in a moaning, miserable heap, Nerine returned to her puddle form and slipped back beneath the door.

Mikanah and Lorelei stood covering their ears but thankfully showed no signs of blood or other injury.

"What did you do?" Lorelei demanded. "We heard the most terrible sound."

"I didn't want to harm them," Nerine said, "but it was all I could think to do. There are too many of them. So, I used the water inside the underground caves and converted it into sound."

Lorelei stared at her, incredulous. "Where did you learn such a trick?"

"In Rosa, there was a library. One of the guards took me there. I learned quite a few water tricks. I couldn't test all of them there, of course. But when I swam beneath the water barriers surrounding Adelar, I ran into a host of vicious sea creatures. The only way I could get past them was to try the sound wave theory. Thankfully, it worked."

Lorelei shook her head. "You truly are a marvel."

Nerine shrugged. "I'm only doing what Water Nymphs do."

"But to learn it from a book and apply it so readily is no small feat," Mikanah agreed, unable to hide his surprise.

Nerine was surprised at any interaction from him that wasn't a show of disdain or arrogance, but she only looked at Lorelei and added, "I can unlock the door now. From there, I'll do my best to stun any guards we encounter."

Nerine touched the keyhole. Transforming only her hand into its liquid form, she reshaped her fingers until the water shifted perfectly into the key's shape. Then, twisting her arm, she felt around until the lock clicked open.

"Another new trick?" Mikanah asked.

Nerine nodded, unable to feel anything but annoyance at his compliments. Perhaps he merely hoped to encourage her now that his life was directly on the line, reliant on her magic, since his was null and void. Whatever the reason, she didn't trust this rare show of friendliness.

"Yes, actually," she said. "Come on. Let's go."

They stole inside the hall where the guards lay moaning in agony. A few tried to snatch out as they hurried past, but the trio easily dodged them and made their way to the adjoining corridor.

"The gate can be reached eventually from either direction," Mikanah said, "but if I recall, this way's the fastest." He nodded to the left.

They stole down the hall, encountering a few guards here and there. Nerine knocked them down with waves of water while Lorelei and Mikanah uncapped one of the vials hanging from their wrists, throwing various dusts and uttering spells that made some of the guards drop to the ground, unconscious. Others froze still as stone, immobilized, and yet others fell with mouths open in what looked like silent screams of pain.

When the dusts were nearly depleted, Mikanah and Lorelei turned to using their swords. Lorelei defended Mikanah while he injured the guards. Nerine helped by transforming into a puddle, slipping beneath the guards' feet to make them fall.

"The gate," Mikanah said after a while. "It should be around the next corner. Slow down and be quiet. We'll have to scout it out."

Nearing the corner, they drew as still as the stone walls. Nerine whispered to ask Lorelei if she wanted her to go ahead, but Lorelei was already fusing with the wall and had soon disappeared.

Seconds ticked past. Minutes dragged by. Nerine looked at Mikanah, at the panic steadily mounting on his face. His panic soon turned to pleading, and with a single nod, Nerine dissolved into a puddle again and slipped around the corner.

Dozens upon dozens of soldiers filled the hall, but Nerine noted that they weren't dressed in the same full plate armor as the guards they had just felled. Rather, these seemed to be an equal mix of men and women clad in thick leather breastplates over long leather tunics, with leather armbands, boots, and round leather helmets, all a dark brown color. Moragon's crest of the phoenix and harp was painted across their chests, same as the previous guards, but Nerine wondered at this inferior protection. Perhaps even Moragon couldn't gather the proper resources to properly outfit all his soldiers.

Then again, the closer she looked at them, the less she felt like "soldiers" was a proper way to define them. Some stood like still sentinels while others patrolled, but any movements were stiff and strangely mechanical, while their eyes seemed to stare vacantly, as though entranced. Perhaps they were some lesser rank in Moragon's army, their minds succumbed to his mental magic to the point of ceasing to have their own thoughts.

Pity waved through Nerine, but she did her best to ignore it. Helping to open the gates must be her primary focus. She slid down the hall toward the gate, but no signs of Lorelei lay in sight.

Suddenly, fingers crept from the wall and moved ever so cautiously toward the lever surely meant to raise the gate. Nerine's glance found another lever; there were two. Twins that likely had to both be pulled in order for the gate to open.

With a loud gasp, Lorelei fell from the wall. She stumbled and barely caught herself on the nearest guard, struggling for breath. The soldier shoved Lorelei to the floor and swung his sword, but Nerine stretched up into her liquid body form, throwing him back with a wave of water. Lorelei scrambled to her feet with a grateful glance at Nerine before drawing her blade.

More soldiers swarmed them. Nerine blasted them back with jets of water. Lorelei struggled to block their attacks with her sword, looking out of breath and disoriented from being trapped inside the wall for so long. Nerine tried to inch closer to the levers that would open the gate, but a wall of guards forbade her each time.

Mikanah rushed in, wildly swinging his sword. The next few minutes became a whirlwind of swords and spells. Some of the guards threw fire, lightning, wind, and stunning charms. Nerine managed to neutralize some of the spells with her water.

"Lorelei, Mikanah!" she shouted as an idea leaped inside her. "Focus on the gate! Don't worry about me!"

She blasted back more guards with waves of water, forcing her way through their hordes and focusing on her new goal—the outer wall, on the other side of which flowed their one chance for freedom.

CHAPTER 49

CRESCENDO

Gailea sat on her horse atop the long, gently sloping hill and peered out at their armies. The horses
were gracious gifts brought by the men and women of
Carmenna's Defiance who had joined their ranks early
that morning. Ashden, Darice, and Chamblin flanked
Gailea, while Donyon was somewhere near the front of
the ranks. He had insisted on standing by his people and
leading them personally into battle, promising to join
the Guardians as soon after as he could.

Carmennans, Rosans, Adelarans, Sallie Elves, and
Echelon—the latter were two hundred strong, all the
Lozolian Council could spare as the conflict in Prismatic
continued to rage—stood behind and before them, covering the stretch of green field between the northern
forests and the the great chasm before the castle. Somewhere above, hidden amongst the clouds, Gailea prayed
that the Abalinos floated in their airships.

Gailea stared beyond, past the wide chasm and up at
the massive outer wall surrounding Castle Alaula. The
wall seemed deserted, but Gailea knew better, as did

Pono and the other captains. They had gathered that morning with the Guardians to make final plans. They waited either for the gates to open and the drawbridge to be lowered, or else for Moragon's forces to send the first attack.

"This seems a waste of time," Ashden said, drawing his horse a little closer to Gailea's. "I know we're giving the others a chance to open the gates and let us inside. But perhaps it would've been better to attack and grant them a diversion?"

"I've wondered the same," Gailea said. "But the castle is sturdily shielded by both the wall and cliffs. The longer we can hold off an attack, the more lives we may spare."

A loud, tortured yell snapped them from their conversation. Further down the hill, several horses whinnied and stepped away from something. One of the Rosans leaped off his horse to rush over to it, only to be struck down with a gut-wrenching cry.

"Chamblin, raise your shield, and stay near me!" Gailea cried, glancing up just in time to block the rain of arrows. She sang *Segmunda*, and several arrows deflected, scattered into the nearby woods. She flung a terrified glance in Chamblin's direction, but he had lifted his shield, and Ashden drew his horse up beside him, chanting spells.

As more arrows poured from the wall, Gailea glanced up, but no one stood in sight.

"They're invisible!" Pono shouted. "Protect yourselves!"

"We can't just sit here and let invisible warriors slaughter us!" Maddok yelled. "We need either to retreat or find another way in!"

A gleaming white light swooped from the skies, parting the thick clouds. Then another, and another. At first, the shimmering masses were a blur, but then they slowed their pace, and someone cried, "The Abalinos' airships!"

Abalino men clad in silver armor dove from their flying ships, which were crafted to look just like ships that sailed the ocean. The Abalinos zoomed down on white wings like bolts of lightning and spiraled right along the wall, knocking into their invisible foes who screamed as they plummeted into the chasm. Beams of light blasted from the silvery blue airships soaring on huge white sails overhead, and the winged warriors shot arrows seemingly made of pure light. Pono, Maddok, and the other captains on land gave orders, and the front-most archers released volleys of arrows at the wall.

"Quick!" Gailea shouted. "Sing *Gizemia's Revelation* with me!" Gailea began singing the same revelation spell that she had used to push through the enchantments surrounding the tent where the traitors had plotted against Donyon. If more of them sang it now, they may be able to push beyond their enemies' shield of invisibility and possibly dispel it. As Gailea sang, she focused every ounce of her attention on the castle wall. Darice, Chamblin, and Ashden joined in. The warriors on the wall flickered, like a lamp struggling to be illuminated. Then, the Guardians triumphed as hundreds of Carmennan soldiers stared down at them, fully visible.

For a moment, they stopped shooting. In the next, fire blazed on the tips of their arrows. The arrows arched across the sky in an array of shimmering colors. Ashden sang deflection spells and Darice crafted a large shield of light. Several Abalino warriors darted about, forming their own shields of light to protect as many of the soldiers on the ground as they could. The armies below shot their own volleys of arrows, some illuminated with fire or crackling with electric energy, sending many foes tumbling from the wall. Gailea and Chamblin continued the revelation song-spell. Gailea exerted extra effort, as she felt a force pressing back mentally, struggling to resurrect the invisibility barrier.

Someone shouted a command from the wall. The archers released their arrows again, but this time, the arrows multiplied mid-air. Each arrow split into five, ten, twenty. Abalinos rushed through the air to throw up more light shields. The soldiers on the ground raised their physical shields, some too late. Horses, men, and women fell with a shriek. Flames leaped from the dry ground where the arrows landed, spreading fiercely. Fire fell in the woods just behind them, setting the trees ablaze. A band of Sallie Elves raised their hands and sent waves of water after the flames, but the fire did not diminish. It merely flickered with black shadow before devouring the forest, creeping steadily toward them. The fire spread in the fields on either side, blocking any route to the ocean.

"What is this madness?" Nilson demanded as he and Iagan rode up beside Gailea, eyes wide with terror.

"Black flame," Gailea said. "It's what Moragon used to kill hundreds of sorcerers. Water cannot put it out." She paused to cough as a great gust of smoke choked her.

"We can't stay here," Ashden declared, sweeping an alarmed glance across the armies. "We'll be trapped between the fire and the chasm."

The horses nearest the flaming trees began to panic, rearing and kicking. More arrows rained from the wall, knocking down both horses and soldiers. Dozens fell. Abalinos spiraled from the heavens, fire waving from their wings.

"We're surrounded," Maddok said. "The only escape from the fire is forward." He nodded grimly at the chasm.

"There are Forest-footer Elves amongst the Echelon," Gailea said. "Ashden, ride out and find them. Use your earth songs to uproot the trees. Then, have the Elves construct ladders or bridges that will reach across."

Ashden nodded and commanded his horse into the sea of panicked soldiers.

"Follow him," Gailea said to Nilson and Iagan. "Listen to what he says."

They galloped after Ashden.

"What shall we do, sister?" Darice asked.

"What you're doing already, defending where you can. Chamblin, stay close to Darice. I need to concentrate."

Gailea closed her eyes. Breathing deeply, she focused on the image of the great castle wall, letting all else fade away. She hadn't tried the song she prepared to try now in several years, and even then, it had been an experiment. Attempting to localize it to a single area now could put their armies at risk, not just Moragon's. What's more, she needed to reserve enough strength to use *Ah Lum Amiel* afterward. Praying her crazy idea would work, she sang her lullaby, altering the notes to transform it into something else new so that she could, hopefully, direct it at Moragon's armies alone.

Commands, shouts, the clash of swords, the hiss of arrows, the whoosh of light and fire spells, the crackling of black flames, the creaking and crashing of trees as they broke and fell—one by one, Gailea eliminated these and all other distractions from her mind, letting her lullaby fill it to the brim. The song flowed from her mind down into her heart, and from her heart into her whole being, until it flowed out of her in wave after fierce wave. She saw nothing but the warriors on the wall with their flaming arrows. She heard nothing but the song. She *was* the song.

Only when her body trembled with exertion and she almost blacked out, did she open her eyes and inhale a great gasp of air.

"Gailea?"

Someone's hand rested on her arm. Chamblin had turned in her direction, both his and Darice's faces flooded with concern.

"I'm all right. I just need to recover."

Looking ahead, she held her breath. Had she been consumed in her song that long, or had the Forest-footers simply made swift work?

Their armies cramped closer together now, packed tight as the fire chased them toward the chasm, but the Forest-footers had constructed a great ladder. A tree flew past overhead and began reshaping itself mid-air. Vines joined the tree, until another giant ladder hovered above them. The Abalinos held the massive structure and carefully guided it in place. The two ladders spanned across the chasm to the great wall where Moragon's armies lay fast asleep from Gailea's song. Commands rose from the Rosan, Adelaran, and other captains, and their armies began scaling the ladders across the giant chasm.

Steadily, their armies poured onto the wall. Abalinos dove low and carried more men and women across the gap. Gailea and others shouted commands not to slay Moragon's soldiers that had fallen from the lullaby. Such an act would be an injustice, especially considering that many might be mindless puppets and not true servants.

One by one, and then almost at once, Moragon's soldiers woke from their slumber, while more poured onto the wall. Spells, swords, and arrows flew once more. Soldiers were flung from the ladders, shrieking as the great chasm swallowed them. Those still on the ground beyond the chasm cast magic spells and arrows up at Moragon's reanimated armies, trying to help their brethren

717

on the walls.

Flames roared as fire arrows again met their mark, consuming more of the woods. Soldiers pushed against each other in a panic, accidentally shoving some of their comrades into the chasm. Horses reared, maiming their own soldiers. Smoke cloaked the armies.

Gailea sang a wind charm to part the smoke. Chamblin and Darice joined her, and the smoke began to dissipate. It had nearly cleared when, in a rush, it returned in full force.

Gailea focused intently on her song, but the smoke only intensified. She tried another song to shrink the smoke. Nothing. As it curled up over the wall, across the chasm, and covered the armies, and as her music grew abruptly void, she realized it wasn't smoke at all.

"The mist!" Gailea shouted. "It's rendering our songs useless, just like before. Start using *Ah Lum Amiel*! It's the one song that may have power to repel the mist, or, at the least, it may sway any enslaved servants of Moragon back to our side!"

Gailea closed her eyes and flooded her mind with *Ah Lum Amiel*. As Darice and Chamblin's harmonies reached her, she adjusted her volume and pitch to blend with theirs as perfectly as possible. Then, singing on, she opened her eyes.

All magic attacks had ceased on their side. The mist had stolen their armies' abilities to use anything but sword, knife, halbard, and bow. More of their comrades continued to fall from the giant ladder. Others were struck down by the flaming arrows. The fire prison closed tighter and tighter around them, forcing them ever nearer the chasm.

Gailea and the Guardians pushed their song as hard as they could, and some of Moragon's soldiers began pulling Echelon, Rosans, Adelarans, Sallie Elves, and fellow Carmennans up onto the wall. Others stood looking dazed before turning against those who still fought for Moragon.

While Gailea sang on, she scanned the walls, searching for any other trapped souls who might need the song's call to liberate them. Her gaze locked on one of the archers standing atop a tower. He had nocked an arrow on his bowstring and aimed at the armies beyond the chasm as they poured toward the wall. He lowered the bow and arrow, only to raise it again. Uncertainty wavered on his face. His eyes widened in a panic, as though he couldn't decide what he was meant to be doing, whose side he stood on.

Gailea concentrated on him, sending the full force of *Ah Lum Amiel* in his direction. Gradually, the man's distress changed to wide-eyed awe. Lowering his bow, he pressed a hand to his heart. He gazed in wonder at his hands before feeling his face, looking bewildered as the song dispelled every lie that Moragon's mental instrusion had wrapped him in. Now, *Ah Lum Amiel* wrapped his heart in a pure peace, illuminating the truth of who he was. Taking his bow again, he aimed instead at those of Moragon's soldiers who yet fought on his side.

"It's working!" Darice shouted. "The song is freeing them!"

Gailea glanced back at the shrinking space between their armies and the forest as the black flames crept along faster and faster.

"Sing on!" she commanded. "Keep singing 'til we all make it inside!"

~*~*~

Nerine blasted another soldier with a wave of water before collapsing back against the wall, taking a breath-

719

less moment to savor her small victory.

As another soldier swung a knife at her, she transformed back into her liquid form and his blade splashed right through her without harm. She pressed herself against the wall, applying pressure where her hands touched the cool stone. Swords speared her rippling body, creating tiny waves in what had been her flesh. The soldiers staggered back, bewildered.

Mikanah kept as many of their foes at bay as he could with his sword, though his movements grew clumsy as more soldiers rushed at him with fresh strength. Blood flowed in thin rivulets from a thankfully shallow slash he had received in his side. Lorelei hovered near Mikanah, striving to shield him. Every now and then, a sword strike or a blow with a shield would knock her breath away, but she would recover a few moments later, uninjured, determined to block Mikanah from as much harm as she could. While quick on her feet, her own clumsy steps proved that her energy fast faded.

Nerine pushed her hands toward the great currents rushing in the caves beyond the wall, searching for any cracks, until at last she found one. It was narrow but long, and after all, water could fit through any crack. Shaping her hands to reach through it, she plunged her hands inside. She shivered at the impact as she and the mighty underground river became one entity. The water's power threatened to overthrow hers and blast her away, but she braced her feet, doing her best to keep herself rooted while focusing on keeping her connection with the water. She chanted a summoning spell to lure the currents in her direction, commanding them to flow toward her.

A scream snared Nerine's attention, and she stared in wonder as Moragon's guards turned on each other. Lorelei and Mikanah looked equally bewildered, but then they darted toward the levers to open the gates and lower the bridge.

Two guards blocked their path. One sliced a gash in Lorelei's arm, and she stumbled forward with a cry. She caught herself on the wall, even as the wound sealed itself.

Nerine closed her eyes, concentrating fully on the feel of the river's current cycling through her...no, wait. That was the wrong sensation. She needed to bring the water *toward* her, not *through* her. Chanting her summoning charm, she kept her arms in their liquid form but solidified the rest of her body, praying she could complete her task before being struck down. She gave the waves a final pull.

A deafening explosion shuddered through the entire cavern as the rocks ruptured and waves of water gushed through. The length of the outer wall crumbled in a domino affect. The river surged inside. Some of the guards scattered, while others were swept away by the mighty currents. Nerine changed back into her water form, letting the currents carry her. Upon surfacing, she glanced around desperately for Lorelei and Mikanah but saw no signs of them.

As the cavern continued to collapse, Nerine surged along the waves between the crumbling walls. The ground quaked, and the wall fell away to reveal great armies fighting beyond the chasm. As Nerine rushed past, she prayed that Lorelei and Mikanah had made it safely from the cave. The waters carried her away too swiftly for her to go back and look for them. Everything lay now in Amiel's hands.

~*~*~

Gailea, Darice, and Chamblin sang *Ah Lum Amiel* with full force. Donyon soon joined them, adding his magic to theirs.

Arrows and magic rained from the outer wall. Light arrows and beams of light soared from the Abalinos' airships as they dove a little lower. More Carmennans were loosed from Moragon's mind-enslavement spell to engage the fight against their brethren who still served him.

"*No! Please!*"

Gailea flung her attention to the wall where a woman cried a blood-curdling scream as her male companion stabbed her through. A light of recognition filled her face, the last sign of life before she slumped over.

Sickness clawed at the pit of Gailea's stomach. In singing *Ah Lum Amiel*, they had freed many from Moragon's hold already. But it was impossible to know whose side all the rest were truly on. They could still be slaughtering hundreds of innocents. Gailea sang more forcefully.

Suddenly, an even thicker mist than before descended, blurring her concentration, and choking her lungs. Her mind reeled, and she nearly blacked out. When she was able to look up again, she saw others falling around her. Abalinos rained from the skies, shot through with flaming arrows. Their white wings shimmered as they plummeted like falling stars, a grotesquely beautiful scene.

The mist rested thickest at the wall, and those whose minds had just been freed turned to fighting for Moragon's side once more. Everyone scaling the walls dropped like flies as more arrows flew. The wall of fire closed in, packing the armies closer and closer until some of the horses and soldiers spilled over the edge into the chasm. Others jumped in willingly. Gailea parted her lips to sing, but the mist had rendered her voice hoarse and dry. Try as she might, her magic could not breach the mist's potency. Even *Ah Lum Amiel* was now dead in its shadow.

A nearby cry alerted her to the sight of Moragon's forces descending the ladders. Several Adelaran and Rosans soldiers met them head on with sword and shield, but in the absence of their magic, they soon lay injured, while others were plunged into the abyss. Moragon's soldiers blazed through, throwing fire, lightning, and other attacks, stunning many, killing others.

Gailea's heart fell inside her, but she cried out, "Come on! We must aid our fellow soldiers!" Drawing her blade, she urged her horse forward, Chamblin, Darice, Ashden, and Donyon close on her heels.

Everywhere, both friend and foe fell, but the ground was more heavily stained with the blood of their own than that of their enemies. Gailea's attention darted up to the sky, but it had grown still. As arrows rained more freely from the walls, she prayed the Abalinos had not retreated altogether.

The ground rumbled beneath her feet.

A massive explosion boomed.

Chunks of rock flew from the cliffs surrounding the castle. Water spurted forth like geysers. The outer wall circling the castle caved in. Moragon's soldiers began retreating from the wall and toward the castle, but many were blasted forward into the chasm. Gailea, the Guardians, and their armies retreated as far and fast from the chasm as they could while rock, dust, and debris shot toward them in an unearthly fireworks display.

As Darice screamed her name, Gailea looked up to see her raising a great shield of light, blocking a chunk of rock that surged straight for them both.

"The mist!" Gailea said. "It's lifted!"

Chunks of rock slammed into the ladders made from trees, splintering them, and destroying their path to the castle. Several Adelarans and Echelon rushed forward, lifting and waving their hands, commanding the falling stones to form bridges across the chasm instead.

Gailea galloped forward. "Help them! If the bridge is destroyed, those rocks will be our only way in!" She sang a summoning spell, drawing the rocks and stones toward her to form a steadier bridge across. Chamblin, Donyon, and Ashden joined in her song, while Darice deflected bits of falling rock with her light shield. Gradually, a makeshift bridge of sorts paved their way over the chasm to Moragon's fortress.

Echelon and Adelarans directed the stones and chunks of rock to craft a second bridge. Several bright forms darted from the skies, creating shields of light—the Abalinos had not abandoned them after all. They raised their light shields to create a singular, protective dome, preventing as many rocks as possible from striking the land-bound armies.

Several bridges of criss-crossed rock, timber, stone, and other debris were formed. Soldiers scrambled across, and moments later, the drawbridge came crashing down.

"Armies, march forward!" Captain Pono shouted. "We take the castle!"

With a deafening cry, the armies surged across the drawbridge. Others climbed across the makeshift bridges. Abalinos swooped after them.

Together, Gailea and the other Guardians rushed over the drawbridge into Moragon's domain.

CHAPTER 50

BURNING CRESCENDO

As soon as Gailea's steed thundered across the bridge and passed through the gates into the outer courtyard, Moragon's armies met them, ready and waiting, hordes of Carmennans, along with hundreds of Spaniño and purple-haired Meleeón soldiers.

The mist descended once more, but clear patches formed here and there as *Ah Lum Amiel* persisted.

Darice and Chamblin flanked Gailea on their horses. Darice had constructed a light shield around Chamblin who sang on, despite looking terrified. Gailea couldn't imagine how he felt, enclosed inside an onslaught of yells, screams, spells, and clashing weapons. Then again, perhaps it was a blessing that he couldn't fully see the madness. The sight of so much blood and agony sickened Gailea.

"Where did Ashden and Donyon go?" Gailea shouted. "We need to find them and make it inside the castle. Keep singing *Ah Lum Amiel*, and let's go!" Finding Moragon was of the utmost priority, as was locating his Vessel, whatever that may be, and especially if it created the immobilizing mists. Best they didn't waste any time, to allow Moragon to show them the extent of its powers.

"Darice! Gailea!"

Ashden limped toward them. Blood stained his leg through a gash torn in his trousers. Darice spurred her horse to his side and jumped down beside him. She pressed her hands to the wound, singing a charm to seal it.

"Thank you," Ashden said, wincing.

"It's not a perfect fix," Darice said. "But it'll stop the bleeding."

"Take cover!"

Gailea whipped her head toward the fiery horror plummeting straight toward them from the surrounding cliffs, great blazes of flame, enclosed by formless masses of black, transparent shadows. Leaping from her horse, she yanked Chamblin from his. He yelled in alarm as she threw them both to the ground, shielding him.

"What's going on?" he shouted. "I can see blurs of red, like the sky's raining blood."

"It may as well be," Gailea said. "It's some kind of shadow flame."

The streamers of fire and shadows cascaded all around them, as though a volcano had exploded nearby, spewing both fire and the blackest magic. The flaming masses blasted onto the courtyard with a thunderous roar, sending soldiers flying by the dozens.

As a blazing rock fell straight for them, Gailea rolled with Chamblin to the side, only to knock her head against a sharp rock. Her head throbbed and her vision swam. Blinking, she managed to see clearly enough to glance up. Through the new light shield Darice had raised, Gailea glimpsed one of the Abalinos' airships weaving back and forth over the courtyard in erratic patterns. A blazing hole in one of the sails showed where the raining fire had struck, and it swooped dangerously near the ground, knocking into several soldiers. Some of the Carmennan and Meleeón soldiers leaped onto the rope ladders dangling down, mounting the ship. One of the Abalinos toppled overboard. Feathers had been torn from his wings, and he fell like a stone into the chaos below.

"I can lead us to Donyon!" Ashden shouted above the fury. "I saw him just moments ago!"

"Let's go then!" Gailea said. "We all need to reach Moragon as soon as possible—*ah!*"

The burn inside her head magnified, digging deeper, like a thin piece of glass through her skull. What was happening? She hadn't hit her head with that much force.

Everything turned black, and in the next breath, *flames flickered before Gailea. She muttered a spell to banish them, but their heat only strengthened. Screams echoed shrilly, and through the flames, faces implored her. Ashlai and Merritt, calling her name. Tytonn shrieking as the executioner split his skin open with the whip's fiery tendrils. Iolana, bound to a stake and pleading with her to make the fire stop. The four of them disappeared in a cloud of ash and smoke, only to rise from the dead and repeat the torment anew. Gailea ran toward them, snatched at them, only to miss them every time and watch on, forced to relive their deaths over and over—*

With a gasp, Gailea snapped from the vision. She whirled around, searching wildly for her children—and found herself caught in the throes of a huge battle. The Carmennan castle, Alaula. Moragon. The Guardians. Yes, she was still here. The vision had been so vivid, she could've sworn she had fallen right inside it, into a real place, but here she was, with Chamblin holding her while frantically singing *Ah Lum Amiel*.

She spotted Donyon through the wild waves of fighting warriors. He swung his broadsword in wide arcs, cutting down foe after foe. Nilson, Iagan, and Brodach fought the enemy in a defensive shield around the king. Donyon prepared to wield a final blow on one of his targets when, seemingly without reason, he collapsed to his knees. The sword slipped from his hands, and he held his head, shaking and muttering. His mutterings soon rose into desperate pleas:

"Stop, bring them back! Bring back my wife!"

Gailea rushed for him, heart pounding, and realized the mist clung more thickly than before. Donyon was losing his family and suffering, helpless, just as she had been moments ago. She must use *Ah Lum Amiel* to free him, as Chamblin had done for her.

As she reached the king, Brodach held up a hand, and she froze in place.

"C'mon!" Iagan shouted, spearing the sky with his sword. "See the chance Amiel has granted us—swift and painless—do it now!"

Nilson glanced between Iagan and his king like a man trapped between two worlds, unable to choose one as his own.

"Then I'll do it!"

Iagan swung at Donyon. Nilson parried to defend the helpless king, only to be speared in the side by Brodach. Iagan again struck at Donyon, but Gailea rushed at them, screaming, *"No, not this way!"*

She blocked Iagan's blow. Iagan came at her, but the uncertainty on his face increased with each swing. Torn between completing his mission and not wanting to risk harm to the woman he desired to call queen, he turned and fled into the sea of warriors.

Gailea whirled then to find Brodach still before her. He panted hard, his eyes wild. Nilson's blood dripped from his sword, and for all the blood and filth surrounding Gailea, the sight of it made her stomach churn anew. Donyon had regained his mind and flew at the treacherous Rosan. Their swords clashed. Gailea prepared to aid Donyon when the sound of a name caught her attention.

"Lord Reynard!"

Gailea whirled around. Anger boiled inside her as she searched for the man whose soldiers were responsible for slaughtering Iolana. The girl's image flashed fresh in her mind, her death fresh and very real. As a Carmennan soldier surged across the courtyard toward another Carmennan man wearing a finer suit of armor than anyone else, with Moragon's crest painted proudly across his breastplate, Gailea vowed that the sight of Reynard's corpse would soon be just as real.

"Lord Reynard." The soldier motioned at him. "This way!"

Enraged, Gailea rushed at Reynard. Her blade met its mark on the back of Reynard's leg, one of few exposed places between the plates of his armor. He yelled as his knee buckled beneath him, but soon he regained his balance and swung his broadsword in a wide arc. Gailea dodged the blow successfully, but a sharp pain ripped through her skull, just as it had before, throwing off her concentration. On Reynard's next swing, the tip of his blade met with her shoulder and sent her sprawling on the ground. She inhaled sharply, fighting through the fresh pain. Rolling onto her back, she raised her sword to defend herself against Reynard's next blow, but it never came. Shaking, she pulled herself to her feet, watching as Reynard raced toward the castle, surrounded by a host of soldiers. Absolute coward.

"Gailea, watch out!"

Chamblin's frantic cry was followed by a shout, and she whipped around to find him sprawled on the ground, clutching at the wound pouring fresh blood from his side. A Carmennan solider stood over him, blood dripping from his sword. Her fury enflamed, Gailea blocked the second blow that the soldier aimed at Chamblin, making him whirl and focus on her instead. She was at once assaulted by the spectral sight of her dying children but refused to believe them, instead singing *Ah Lum Amiel* once more. The nightmarish visions continued to flash in and out of her mind, but she pushed through their fear, using anger to fuel the power of her every sword strike.

Just as she swung again, the warrior's face abruptly transformed into that of a girl's, for just a moment, and then back again. The sight caught Gailea off guard and she instinctively staggered back, confused as to whom she was fighting. Again, his image flickered, this time replaced by a girl's entire body before returning to his own form. The flash of fiery red hair for those few seconds sent Gailea's heart careening inside her.

Then the soldier's form changed a third time, remaining steady: now Gailea saw a young woman with long, golden hair and vivid violet eyes: Elda, Crispin's sister. But this couldn't be her. Hadn't she burned to death? Gailea found herself reluctant to strike, each swing more hesitant and faltering. What a great irony it would be, if poor, kindly Elda had somehow made it out alive, only to be snatched up by Moragon and used here now.

Something slammed against Gailea's skull with a sickening crack.

Everything was a gray haze before her eyes. All turned black, then gray again. She understood that she was opening and closing her eyes, now lying on the ground. When her senses returned, she mouthed Crispin's name and tasted the blood on her lips. The sounds of the war raged all around her, but they seemed muffled, distant. She reached up and touched the blood from the new wound on her head.

Slowly, she sat up, her vision waxing and waning as the pain pounded inside her skull. She looked down at the blood staining her hands and the surrounding earth.

Then, stumbling to her feet, she saw Elda once more, sword raised, poised for the kill.

"Elda!" Gailea cried.

"Yes? Gailea, is that you?"

Gailea gasped at the unfamiliar yet familiar voice, but before she could respond, she was interrupted.

"Gailea!" Chamblin shouted. "What's happening? What are you seeing?"

Gailea turned dizzily in the direction of his voice. He stood nearby, likely hoping to protect her. Despite the terror in his face, he continued to clutch his sword.

"I see a girl who's familiar to me," Gailea said. "She shouldn't be here!"

"Is she one of the enslaved?" he asked. "Can we free her with the song?"

Gailea turned again, head swimming until she was nauseous, and found Elda once more.

This cannot be her, Gailea thought, though every sense railed against this logic. *This is not her,* she repeated over and over. *Elda could never speak. But Moragon can make anyone his puppet. What if he's controlling her and has given her that ability?*

Gailea sang *Ah Lum Amiel,* even as she raised her sword and circled Elda. Chamblin sang too. Surprise flashed on Elda's face, followed by irritation that swiftly mounted into rage. She swung her sword. The soldier's image flickered upon hers this time.

"It's not really her!" Gailea shouted, to herself as much as to Chamblin. "It's just one of Moragon's tricks!"

She ceased singing and focused all her energy into countering the false Elda's sword strikes. Fighting the façade of Elda took every ounce of Gailea's strength. Even though the song had proved the truth behind this cruelly deceptive image of her dear, late friend, doubt made Gailea want to talk to her, reason with her, make absolutely certain.

Gailea and the false Elda circled one another until Chamblin stood directly behind the imposter.

"Chamblin!" Gailea cried. "Right in front of you!"

Chamblin ran forward clumsily and swung his sword low, managing to slice a gash behind the false Elda's knees. As she collapsed, she swung her sword around until the flat of its blade whacked Chamblin in the side, making him tumble backward. Gailea took her opportunity and speared the girl through the chest. She shrieked and reached toward Gailea, her eyes pleading. A final wave of doubt ripped through Gailea, but as the girl lunged, Gailea aimed and swung her sword again. When she opened her eyes, the soldier's dead body lay on the ground.

Trembling head to toe, Gailea found Chamblin, doubled over and gasping for breath, and rushed to his side.

"Chamblin, you brave idiot!"

"Are—are you all right?" he coughed.

Gailea stood mortified, desperately fighting tears. "I should be asking you that! But—but yes. Thank you. The woman that soldier appeared as, she was once dear to me. I worried she might be real, and I...."

Gailea's words trailed when she noticed the large, red patch of blood seeping through the torn cloth bound around his waist.

"Your wound?" she gasped.

"I've stemmed the bleeding as best I could. The only healing charms I know aren't helping it in the least, thanks to...." He motioned at the mist obscuring so much around them. The haze had thickened once more.

"We must reach the castle," Gailea said, fighting a rising hysteria. "We must find the others and reach the castle. Stay near my side, and don't fight unless absolutely necessary. We'll need all our strength to sing and bring down Moragon, and with your injuries, we don't need you passing out."

Gailea scanned the throngs of soldiers, and her gaze lighted upon Donyon. He fought nearby, against a Meleeón warrior with a long, curved sword. She wanted to rush to his aid, but what about Chamblin? He couldn't risk further harm, and he would be certain to follow her into any battle if he thought he had the slightest chance of keeping her safe.

A beam of light shot past, knocking several of the Meleeóns to the ground. A band of Abalinos flew down toward them, throwing spheres of light, except for one, a broad-built man, who led Darice and Ashden. Beams of light circled their feet as the Abalino's spell carried them safely through the air. The Abalino let the two Guardians down to the ground before rejoining his countrymen in the sky, where they darted back and forth, stunning as many foes with their light beams as they could.

Shrieking sliced the air as a new round of flames wreathed in shapeless black shadows plummeted from the cliffs. The overrun Abalino airship lingered in the heavens, but it now blazed like a giant sun as flames burned from its masts and flags. The ship slowed its pace, rocking uneasily mid-air.

"It's going to crash!" Ashden shouted. "Take cover!"

Gailea grabbed Chamblin's hand and hurtled with him toward the castle. Darice, Ashden, and Donyon bolted after them. Moragon's forces started to pursue but turned back as they realized the Guardians were racing right underneath the shadow of the teetering ship.

"Gailea, we can't!" Darice cried. "If it falls, we'll be killed!"

"This is our one chance to reach the castle!" Gailea shouted, while hordes of soldiers scattered. The fire spread across the hovering ship, consuming its entire length. Flaming bits of wood and cloth spiraled down through the mist, spearing soldiers who couldn't move fast enough.

"Keep running and sing!" Gailea cried. "The doors are in sight!"

She sang *Ah Lum Amiel* with full force inside her mind, striving to shove the mist aside in hopes to summon the rest of her music. The ship creaked overhead. Fiery pieces of timber tumbled downward, and sparks ignited the sky. Chamblin tripped and nearly fell, but Gailea caught him, helping him along. As the shadow above them grew larger, Gailea glanced up and saw how close the deteriorating ship was to crashing.

Finally, they rushed up the steps and stood before the castle's massive double doors. Gailea, Ashden, and the others pulled at them, but they were sealed tight.

"I'll have to sing a charm to open them!" Gailea said. "But I'll only be able to sing it if the rest of you keep singing *Ah Lum Amiel* to keep the mist at bay!"

Darice, Chamblin, Ashden, and Donyon sang *Ah Lum Amiel* while Gailea chanted *Abré, Abré, Abré* over and over, pushing against the doors and focusing her every intention on opening them. Above, the Abalino ship lurched and then split. Half of the ship hung down, swinging loosely on what feeble splinters remained to hinge it in place. Fire flew everywhere. Soldiers rushed toward them, surely hoping they would open the doors and let them into safety.

No, their swords were raised. They knew who the

Guardians were. They meant to slay them, sacrificing their own lives, if necessary, to prevent them making it inside the castle.

Gailea panicked. Her grip on the song faded. The soldiers were upon them. They all turned and raised their swords, the mission for the doors abandoned. Try as she might, Gailea couldn't concentrate long enough to attempt opening them again. The mist returned. Ashlai's wailing face flashed before her again, then Merritt's and Tytonn's and Iolana's. She saw their faces in the embers raining all around them. She saw them in the ship blazing above.

Ah Lum Amiel poured toward them from a girl's sweet, high voice, so intensely that it stunned even Gailea. In her full water form, Nerine glided up the castle steps toward them as warriors plunged their swords straight through her without harm. Gailea stared with full awe, especially when she saw the effect the song had on Moragon's enslaved soldiers.

Though the dismal rain of fire and ash continued to shower them, and the mist continued to shadow them, many of Moragon's soldiers stood blinking in wonder, eyes bright and awake for their first dawn after unfathomable years of darkness. Gailea watched their disbelieving faces as they studied their hands and turned them over again and again. She could well imagine their thoughts: These were *their* hands. They put their hands to their hearts—*their* hearts, pumping faithfully inside. Their minds were *their own*. Their souls were *their own*.

Gailea turned back to the battle at hand, only to find it had ceased. Almost every single one of the soldiers bearing Moragon's crest stared at each other in wonder, or blankly at their surroundings as if trying to remember how they had gotten there at all. A band of Meleeóns still fought to reach the Guardians, but the newly freed

Carmennans barcaded them.

Gailea lowered her bloodstained sword. She wiped it on her tunic and sheathed it. Then, placing both hands to the door, she commanded the others to sing with her. The mist had momentarily dispersed. Already, it began to encroach again, but there was just enough time, if they focused.

Their song-spell worked: the locks clicked, and the doors creaked open. The Guardians sang on, pushing with all their might.

"Hurry!" Ashden shouted.

Someone slammed against Gailea. She flung a glance over her shoulder. The blazing ship's magic had faltered at last, and now it fell from the sky.

Gailea and the Guardians squeezed through the panicked masses pushing inside the castle. The ship collided with the ground with a tumultuous crash as the crowd's screams pierced the air. The last of the soldiers scrambled within. Flames reached inside the castle, but everyone hurried to shut the doors, blocking out the raging inferno.

CHAPTER 51

A HARMONY STRANGLING

A fresh onslaught of soldiers met them inside the castle's sprawling entrance hall.

"Keep singing *Ah Lum Amiel*!" Gailea shouted.

The Guardians banded together, keeping the song alive while parrying magic and swords from the encroaching armies. The freed Carmennans, along with the few Echelon, Adelaran, and Rosan soldiers who had entered the castle with them joined the fray, ringing the Guardians so that they could focus solely on singing.

Fire, light, electricity, wind, intense speed and flight—a whirlwind of spells surrounded Gailea. She sang with every ounce of energy and determination she could muster, striving to catch a glimpse of the action beyond the soldiers veiling them in their protective ring. As far as she could tell, most of the soldiers attacking were Carmennans. This spurred her drive to sing. Most or perhaps all of them might be fighting for Moragon against their will. The more they could free, the less blood need be shed.

After what seemed an eternity of singing that made Gailea's voice start to crack—Darice's voice next to her wavered, and Chamblin's turned breathy as he grew paler from his wounds—the sounds of fighting died down and ultimately diminished. The remaining soldiers stood still, regaining their breath, wiping blood from their swords and halberds.

Gailea pushed forward to survey the scene. Many shocked faces were illuminated in the glow of the lamps lining the walls and the candelight dazzling from the branching iron chandeliers overhead. Several hundred Carmennans stood dazed, staring at their hands and arms, feeling their faces or hearts, just as those freed outside had done. Dozens of bodies lay dead as well, and Gailea said a silent prayer for them and their families. They could never know which of those slain had truly fought for Moragon, and which had died vainly, their minds free from his clutches now only in death.

"You're the Guardians," a Carmennan woman said. "We were taught to hate you and attack you at all costs. But...that was not *me* who was taught that. It was the me he created."

"Who are we?" asked another, her voice shaking. "How did we come to be here?"

"Moragon used his mental magic to ensnare your minds." Gailea tried to keep her explanation as brief as possible. Exhaustion crashed heavily on her, and their biggest fight was yet to come. She wanted to steal a few moments' reprieve if she could and knew the others must feel the same. "He also used musical mages against you, forced them to serve him, just like he forced you. He's used their magic to keep you trapped inside his spell of servitude, but no more. You're free."

Murmurs of confusion mingled with wonder. Gradually, as shock turned to awe, several people called out, recognizing a friend or loved one and reuniting with them.

A deep sigh behind Gailea made her turn to Donyon who stood staring at the crowd, his gaze solemn and distant. He watched as an older man swept a young woman into his arms, folding her in a tender embrace. Donyon stiffened and swallowed hard, blinking as his eyes gleamed with fresh tears.

Heart aching with guilt, Gailea reached out and lightly touched his arm. "I'm sorry you had to see whatever memories the mist made you relive, both now and then, when it first happened."

"They were so close, right there in my arms...." Donyon held out his hands which trembled. He drew them toward him, as if imagining the weight of clutching his dead wife and child's bodies. "Just like before, they escaped my grasp. I couldn't save them. I couldn't save them." As he dropped his arms, hopelessness seemed to crash down on him, replacing his lost gaze with sorrow as he allowed a few tears to fall.

"It's not your fault," Gailea said softly, wincing at the sting of her words. Had she ever believed them herself, when she had lost anyone she loved? Could he? Was there hope for either of them to heal from such loss?

She couldn't be sure. Instead, she added words which she knew they could both understand and hope in. "We'll avenge your family, and mine. We *will* defeat him."

Donyon gave a single nod in reply and seemed to dive into deep thought. Gailea let him be, turning her attention to the rest of her companions. Darice and Ashden had propped Chamblin against a wall. Gailea rushed to kneel at his side. The cloth wrapped around his waist had been removed, showing an even more ghastly blood stain on his tunic.

"How are you feeling?"

Wincing as he breathed deep, Chamblin mustered a wan smile. "Believe it or not, I have felt worse."

"I was able to stop the bleeding," Darice said to Gailea. "Either the mist's power doesn't reach here, or else *Ah Lum Amiel* dispersed enough of it for our magic to return. I was able to use one of my light songs to seal his wound. Unfortunately, he did lose much blood and strength, and I don't know if we can fully prevent infection or stop his pain."

"Not altogether, but we may be able to soothe it," Ashden said, holding out several herbs. Gingerly, Gailea touched them to Chamblin's wound. He sucked in a sharp breath, but she kept her hands in place, singing one of her healing charms. Gradually, his breathing returned to normal.

"How is that?" Gailea gazed hopefully at him as he leaned his head back against the wall, no longer knitting his brows or gritting his teeth.

"It's better. The pain is there still, but better. Manageable, at least." He smiled up at her a little more fully. "Thank you."

"Does anyone know where we might find Moragon?" Donyon asked, glancing about at the Carmennans. "To free the rest of your kin, we must destroy him."

"He may be in the throne room."

Gailea and the others glanced up at the woman who had spoken. Hunched slightly over, face mapped with wrinkles, her jet-black hair streaked with gray. A dark gray dress cloaked her petite frame.

"I saw Reynard headed in that direction. If I had to stake my life on a guess, the most likely place for him to go would be to Moragon's side, to lick his master's boots and defend his pathetic life as always. But beware." The woman's eyes narrowed, watching them fiercely. "There is something else. Moragon has brought some new evil inside the castle, just days past. Some creature that shrieks and wails. Could be a monster, could be a demon of some sort. No one has seen it, but we think he keeps it close by when he can."

Gailea shared a suspicious glance with her fellow Guardians.

"The Vessel?" Donyon muttered.

"Perhaps. Perhaps it truly is some beast meant to harness whatever new dark magic he's been learning."

Darice shared a worried gaze with her. "Or perhaps the Vessel is still a ship, as originally thought. Something large had to hold or carry all that mist. Maybe this new creature is simply an additional part of his plan."

"The Vessel could still be a monster or demon," Ashden said, "if instead of holding the magic that formed the mist, it is in fact creating it."

"The Vessel could be the mist's origin." Gailea shuddered as she considered such a terrible but real possibility.

Donyon met her glance, his expression grim but resolute. "The only way we can find out for certain is to find Moragon and confront him."

"Indeed." Gailea stepped forward to lead the way when she realized this was not Adelar. For a moment, she had thought it was. The visions she had been battling had fractured her mind, allowing old fears to seep inside and force her back to that dark place. She turned to the woman in gray. "What is your name, good woman?"

"Pua, milady."

"And can you lead us to the throne room, Pua?"

Pua nodded and grinned up at her. "Certainly. Such would grant me great pleasure."

"Thank you, Pua."

Donyon addressed the Carmennans once more. "We're sure to meet more foes along the way, as well as more of your brethren in need of freeing. Any who wish to join us, to fight alongside us, are welcome to. If any or all of you wish to stay behind and rest, that is also your right."

Talk passed swiftly through the crowd. Most chose to stay behind, but a couple dozen vowed to see the Guardians safely to the throne room.

As they prepared to set out, Chamblin took Gailea by the arm and said, "Finding Moragon will ultimately do little good without also finding Lorelei and Mikanah."

Gailea halted in her steps. "You're right. I was so swept up in everything else, but Nerine. Surely, she can tell us. In fact, I'm surprised she didn't mention them. Nerine? Where's Nerine?" She turned all about, anxiously searching the sea of faces. "She was right here. What if she—when the ship fell?"

"She was in her water form." Ashden granted Gailea a sympathetic look. "She's a smart girl. I'm sure she's fine. Perhaps she's gone to fetch Lorelei and Mikanah and bring them to us."

"Just as we need to find the throne room," Donyon said.

Gailea breathed deeply. She didn't want to press on without Nerine in her sights, but staying put here and waiting for Moragon to send some new horror to torment them would do no good. She prayed that Amiel would protect Nerine, Lorelei, and Mikanah and lead them back together. Then, with a permissive nod at Donyon, she started after Pua, the other Guardians and two dozen Carmennans following.

"If we encounter other Carmennans," Gailea said, "do your best to defend yourselves without killing them, if you can. It's impossible to tell which are your brethren and which truly serve Moragon. We Guardians will do our best to free their minds before things must come to more death."

In silence, they wound through the castle. Torches and lamps made orange halos and shadows bounce eerily about the walls and the tapestries woven in Moragon's blacks, whites, and reds, while gray light streamed through the high windows.

Here and there, they met small bands of soldiers. The Guardians stayed close together, singing *Ah Lum Amiel*, while the Carmennans surrounded them, doing their best to parry blows or injure their opponents without slaying them. Many soon stood bewildered, their minds freed. Some stayed behind to guard those who truly served Moragon and keep them from rejoining the fight.

Pua turned their trek upward. At the crest of a wide flight of stairs overlaid with a red cloth, their path curved around a circular wall. Doors were set at intervals, and a pair of tall, ornately carved doors rose into view, along with a host of guards flanking the door on either side.

"Halt!" One of the guards angled his halberd in their direction.

Pua paused, and the others stopped behind her.

"We seek an audience with His Majesty," Donyon said. "We hope to discuss terms of peace, to place this hateful war to a final rest."

While Donyon spun his story, Gailea sang *Ah Lum Amiel* beneath her breath, directing it at the guards. Chamblin, Darice, and Ashden sang along with her.

"His Majesty has expressly ordered that no one may approach him except for the Guardians."

"I am one of the Guardians." Donyon pushed up his sleeve, revealing his mark before motioning to Gailea and the others. "These four also."

The guard opened his mouth to speak, but then he let it hang open. His brows furrowed, and confusion seemed to fill his face. Murmurs rippled through the guards as the song's clarity descended upon them. Eyes widened, murmurs intensified, and one man threw down is halberd with a cry of alarm.

"Melbrook, what's wrong with you?" one of the guards demanded of his comrade.

"I—I'm me again." Melbrook touched his breast-plate, ran his hands along his face. "I hadn't known I'd been lost, but I know I'm suddenly found." He stared up at the guard who'd addressed him, wide-eyed. "We shouldn't be here, helping that tyrant. We need to help them—" He flung his hand in the Guardians' direction. "They're the only ones who can stop him—"

The man who'd questioned Melbrook speared him, and several Carmennans screamed as the halberd ran all the way through his side. Gailea clutched her head as it reeled, humming one of her soothing charms. The song did nothing to ease her anxiety, but at least it kept her from passing out.

As the freed guards and those true to Moragon turned against one another, the Guardians and the Carmennans who'd come with them rushed forward to help. Darice defended as many people as she could with small light shields, Gailea and Chamblin flung their enemies back with *Segmunda*, and Ashden and Donyon defended with their swords.

Outnumbering Moragon's true supporters, they soon made quick work of their enemies and rounded them against one wall. Some of the Carmennans held their treacherous countrymen, forcing their arms to their sides or behind their backs. Fire, shadow, and other spells rippled along the fingertips of some as they strained to break free.

"Guard these traitors," Donyon commanded. "Do with them as you see fit. If Moragon truly is beyond these doors, we will want no distractions in confronting him."

"Nor would it be safe for you to face him with us," Gailea added.

One of the young women marched up to Gailea boldly. "We would gladly stand and fight him with you, milady."

"Thank you." Gailea mustered a grateful smile. "But Moragon sees you only as pawns. He would just as soon torture or kill you, now you've broken free from his grasp. This is our fight to face."

"I was once a ward of the jail," a Carmennan man said. "We'll escort these traitors to the prison cells and have them wait further judgment there."

The Guardians thanked the Carmennans, and Pua for leading them to the throne room.

Gailea watched as the Carmennans led their enemies out of sight.

Then, alongside her fellow Guardians, she turned to face the red doors adorned with a golden phoenix spreading its wings over a golden harp. Her stomach plummeted, and she inhaled several shuddering breaths, trying vainly to calm her sudden whirlwind of distress. The last time Guardians had faced Moragon, almost all of them had died. Of course, they hadn't known then that they faced him, or what they were up against, but Gailea wasn't certain they knew what they were up against now either. None of them had ever stood in his presence. None of them knew just how deranged his methods could become if he wanted something badly enough. And he wanted the Guardians dead very badly indeed.

With a wave of his hand and the spell *Abré*, Donyon commanded the doors open.

Together, they stepped inside.

Curiously, the room beyond the doors was not round shaped as it appeared from the outside. Within was a long, rectangular room. Whatever this strange illusion, it was indeed the throne room.

"Welcome, Guardians," Moragon's voice echoed from across the chamber. "At last, you come to me, the perfect instruments to complete my collection."

Gailea stood, paralyzed by fear. All she could hear was the coldness of his voice, empty of anything but a lust for his own gain. The vast room seemed to shrink around her into a single point, Moragon, sitting on the throne perched on the dais far across the room. His eyes found her, as did his smile, and suddenly, she was back in Adelar after all, under his tutorage, forced to both teach and learn from him. Then, backed into a corner, forced to take his hand in marriage, to become his bride, his queen, the most valuable treasure he had ever stolen. Trapped, just like the musical instruments encased in glass, scattered throughout the room between the lofty stone pillars.

The feel of Darice tugging on her hand brought her back to reality. As they walked down the long red carpet and approached the throne, she tried to sing a charm to calm her mind, but magic barriers cloaked the room too thickly, and she knew Moragon had likely seen her thoughts. She suddenly wanted Chamblin, but he stood leaning against Ashden, looking paler. Blood dripped from his side again, as though his wound had reopened, or perhaps the magic sealing it was disabled in this room.

"Come forward—no, not all of you. Gailea. A personal reunion is in order, don't you think?"

Gailea almost reeled at this personal address, but then she stepped forward. Donyon snatched her hand, but she pulled gently away.

"Let me," she whispered. "Don't try to follow me. He has the power to stop you anyway. When the time comes, you know what to do."

Gailea walked toward the throne, her heart thundering with anxiety. As she neared Moragon, his face became more defined, his sharp jaw line, snowy skin, jet black hair, and his sneering, self-righteous gaze. Anger flared inside Gailea. His smirk revealed his certainty that he was already victorious. She picked up her pace.

She stopped before the dais. Keeping her gaze locked on Moragon, she lifted her chin high. Perhaps he could read the fear pulsing from her heart into every inch of her being. But he would also see her defiance, her willingness to break through that terror and stand against him now, just as in the past and to the bitter end.

"Gailea," Moragon said, false tenderness tingeing his voice. "After all these years, you remain to me the greatest mystery, and the greatest treasure that ever eluded my grasp. It's been a long time, hasn't it, since we spoke face to face? Save for my attempts to reach you with the Desthai. I commend you for escaping his grasp, just as you once escaped mine. Like a cat with nine lives. More capable of escaping death than that abomination, Chevalier."

Gailea scoffed. "Abomination? For a man who's fought so hard to rid his world of those he considers such, you certainly have done a fine job of turning yourself into the very same."

Moragon's eyes narrowed a little, but his voice remained falsely pleasant. "Fear ran rampant through that sorcerer's heart, making him weak. Even his attempts to interfere with the Desthai's visions were cowardly. Any man can act brave when miles away across the ocean, guarded by powerful new allies. But I can see that you've still not let fear control *you*, have you?

"Your spirit. It is that I have always worshipped most in you, besides your musical prowess. You were always my favorite, and so, despite everything that has happened between us, I will give you this final chance: I can cut you down and eliminate the rest of your nine lives in one fell swoop, along with your beloved Guardians. Or you can join with me. Become my queen after all. Rebuild the past on the foundations of my mental power and your musical strength. That is how it was meant to be. That's what Amiel made us for. His destiny brought us together."

"Do not stand there and insult my faith," Gailea snapped. "You don't care for Amiel. You would make yourself a god. You would twist my beliefs and use them against me. I would never take your hand in marriage. This is as true now as it was then. Amiel did not create you to enslave thousands to murder thousands more for you, and He did not create me to join you in this cause."

Moragon's smile vanished, shedding his mask of flattery. "I will not attempt to force your hand. That failed long ago, and I do learn from my mistakes. You can come to me willingly, or..." He leaned forward and lowered his voice. "...perhaps I will reveal the location of your children's whereabouts to my dear nephew, your husband."

Moragon eased back against his throne and sat tall, looking more than pleased with himself.

Panic flitted through Gailea, but she tried to control it. Was this a ruse? Was there any way he could know where her children were?

"I don't know *yet*, Gailea. But if your thoughts keep screaming so loudly, I'm sure you'll reveal that information to me soon enough."

She silently sang *Ah Lum Amiel*, lowering the anti-magic barriers around her just enough to sing the *Shield of Salmana* and craft a protective wall around her mind.

"I know things that would destroy you as well," she ventured. "Chevalier's secret. For all your trickery with the Desthai, you still don't know where it's located, do you? If Chevalier is dead, then the Dusk's secret dies with him. But by your words, he is alive, and were he to get his hands on it, you know he could overthrow you. Don't think him incapable. You saw what the Dusk could do."

Venom seethed from Moragon's gaze, and his hand darted out. Gailea gasped in pain and fell to her knees, feeling the fresh sting on her cheek as if he had physically slapped her. Moragon placed his hands together and then began drawing them apart, repeating this motion over and over as he sought to pry inside her mind. Gailea's head throbbed. She fought to keep her mental shield in check, but she could feel him forcing his way in.

The others raced toward her, but they too fell beside her with a cry, holding their heads. Donyon burst up the dais steps, but with a snap of Moragon's fingers, the mist descended, cloaking the floor around them. Donyon collapsed on the stairs and gasped for breath. Then he groaned out loud, holding his head and shaking it. The Guardians' anguish flooded Gailea's thoughts in a haunting symphony, providing the tool Moragon needed to tear a hole in her mind and siphon his nightmares inside:

She was with Moragon in his chambers in Castle Adel. They prepared to join intimately, to add her power to his.

She escaped.

Only to fall prey to Crispin.

She watched Tytonn being tortured to death. She begged Crispin to spare her children, but this time, he flung Merritt from the tower and forced her to watch her little boy land on the cold stones far below, becoming nothing but a spray of blood in the blink of an eye.

Ashlai grew up into a beautiful maiden, a proud warrior. Fighting alongside Moragon and leading a great army. Gailea sat on a horse on Moragon's other side. Her hands were bound, her lips enchanted so that no sound could come out. Moragon gave some command, and their armies charged toward Loz's Castle Iridescence. Moragon would rule the entire world as they knew it. Gailea fought feebly against him, but he easily channeled her music into himself, singing great chords that collapsed the Lozolian armies. Gailea remembered then that he had taken her power long ago. All that mattered had been destroyed or corrupted.

No, Gailea told herself as they thundered forward. This isn't happening. Ashlai isn't grown. He's blending fact and fiction. Merritt is alive. Merritt is alive, and your power is still your own. Sing Ah Lum Amiel. *Sing, sing, sing!*

With a gasp, Gailea opened her eyes. Her vision reeled. She caught herself on her hands and knees and sang, shakily but surely, battling against Moragon's attacks on her mind and heart.

Slowly, she struggled to stand. Moragon pushed her down, but she sang on, fighting through it.

At last, she staggered to her feet, glaring up at him.

"Bravo," he sneered. "But what do you think to do now, Gailea? Your fellow Guardians are trapped, and the rest are not even present. You never could unite amongst yourselves, could you? A pathetic excuse for those meant to safeguard the entire musical realm of Loz."

Ignoring him, Gailea turned to her friends and shouted, "Sing! Chamblin, Donyon, Darice, Ashden, all of you, sing!"

They continued to shout, wail, and claw at the ground. Donyon wept great tears, scratching at his face until he drew blood. Gailea feared he would tear his very eyes out and fell beside him, trying to pry his hands away.

"Donyon, stop this madness! It's not real!!"

"Oh, it's very real to him!" Moragon thundered. "The death of his wife and child, only one of many regrets now playing out before him. The destruction of his entire kingdom at the hands of his own people, shredding each other apart. Your sister watches her father die as a slave, alone and starving in a cell; she never shared that with you, did she? Ashden watches Darice die, slaughtered by his kin who refuse to accept her outside heritage...and Chamblin. Oh, dear Chamblin *is* a sentimental fool, isn't he? He's watching *you* die. He tried to save you, even right after you told him how much you hate him, great oaf of a man that he is. But it was all in vain. You couldn't stand against my magic, and neither can he."

Gailea's attention flew in Chamblin's direction. He sprawled on the ground, arm outstretched as if reaching for her.

"Gailea," he cried pitifully. "Gailea...Gailea, please, please come back to me...."

He called her name over and over, crawling and reaching everywhere. He pulled himself across the floor, and blood stained the stones where it oozed fresh from his wound.

Gailea knelt beside him. "I'm here, Chamblin. I'm alive, and I'm right here."

He only continued to chant her name, unable to hear her voice through the nightmares. Fighting back tears, Gailea sang *Ah Lum Amiel* to him. As the mist receded around them, she touched his wound, prepared to heal it, but a force flung her hand away.

"No," Moragon said. "They will fight through the darkness same as you. They will sink or swim, same as you."

Gailea flung a hateful glance at him. "The Guardians are one. We stand together as one. We help one another as one. The others will be here soon. And together we will end the torment you have caused."

"The others are indeed coming. In fact, they're very close, the rest of my instruments, the most powerful and beautiful I've collected. But you were the favorite,

Gailea. That grants you a special place in my mind. That makes you alone undeserving of death, no matter how you may wish for it time and again before this day is through."

He swung his hand through the air, and Gailea spiraled back, slamming into one of the stone pillars. Her mind blacked in and out. The visions crept inside once more. She fought them, but as the pain overtook her, so did the darkness, swallowing her whole.

CHAPTER 52

SMOKE AND MIRRORS

Nerine transformed into a puddle, just before the giant, blazing airship crashed down. Fire and wood splintered in all directions. The weight of the ship's impact momentarily suffocated her, causing her to nearly lose her shape, but she focused all her energy on remaining as a puddle until she could move to safety. She slid from underneath the ship, careful to avoid the patches of flame, for while water couldn't be pierced, it could boil. She could sense the heat radiating toward her and slipped away from it as fast as possible.

When at last she left the ship behind, she stretched up into her water-body form. The battle still raged all around her, but she'd wandered quite a distance from the castle's front doors. She ran around the side of the castle and ran its length until the sounds of battle faded. While she could still hear them well enough, they no longer screamed in her mind, ringing in her ears. Nerine collapsed back against the wall, turning into her solid Nymph form once more to catch her breath and a few moments' reprieve.

As she glanced down at her hands, she saw how they trembled. In fact, she was shivering head to toe. Not from cold or any injury, but from pure overwhelming emotion and exhaustion. Freeing so many of the Carmennans with *Ah Lum Amiel* had invigorated her spirit, but performing such strong magic, while also holding her water shape, had strained her body. All the same, she couldn't abandon her fellow Guardians. They were all needed to take down Moragon together. She needed to find them as fast as she could. She gave her body a couple more minutes and then, limbs shaking, she drew herself to her feet and started back toward the front of the castle.

A wailing made her hesitate. At first, she thought it must be the wind, but something familiar in its sad, pleading tones made her wait and listen. As the wailing peaked into a protesting scream, she recognized it as the beast or demon or whatever creature had been locked in Reynard's Keep. The creature that the guard there had declared was becoming too powerful. As its shrieking climaxed, Nerine felt an urge to help it as much as to figure out what it was. If it was some new weapon Moragon meant to use against the Guardians, maybe she could do something to stop it.

Nerine crept along the wall, heading toward the back of the castle once more and listening intently as the cries grew nearer. Rounding a tower to the castle's back wall, Nerine paused. The cries were clearer here than they'd been thus far. Crouching, she listened at the grate along the bottom of the castle. That might be her best chance of slipping inside and finding the monster. Taking a few deep breaths to compose herself, she transformed into a puddle and slid down inside the grate.

Nerine drifted across the cold, stone floor. Pausing at the next corner, she peered around to ascertain no guards or soldiers were in sight. She stretched up into her full-body water form and finally solidified once more, leaning against the wall catching her breath. Then, she glanced up at the narrow, dank corridor filled with stale air and dimly lit by torches set in iron sconces at intervals along the wall.

Letting the creature's wails and screams guide her, Nerine traversed the corridors lined with cold iron doors. Within, she could hear people stirring, moaning, or talking in low voices. She sped through the dungeons as fast as she dared. Part of her wanted to help each of these poor, imprisoned souls, knowing many were likely innocent of true crimes, just as Iolana had been. But she pressed onward. The only way she could help them was if she helped the Guardians.

At each corner, she would pause. Guards patrolled some of the corridors, and she used her puddle form to slink past them. While she couldn't be harmed in her full-body water form, she didn't wish to raise any suspicions and ruin her chances of finding the creature. Her body ached with the effort each time she solidified again, but thankfully, the guards she encountered were few and far between.

Approaching footsteps alerted Nerine, and she held still in the shadows, flattening herself against the wall. The creature's cries intensified in both strength and volume. It was coming closer, and fast. Nerine braced herself against the wall.

"This way, and hurry!" a man shouted. "Before you lose all control of the beast. I'm not sure how long my charm will contain him."

"Yes, Lord Reynard," several others replied.

Nerine's breath quickened, and she placed a hand over her mouth to muffle its sound. The footsteps and shrieks grew louder until at last, they came into view, walking past in the hall running perpendicular to the one she stood in. The first man she saw was dressed in fine plate armor, Moragon's crest proudly displayed on his breastplate. Nerine guessed he must be Reynard, as he led the four guards carrying a small, gangly creature by gripping its arms so tightly that she wondered they weren't torn right off, especially as it pulled and wrenched against them. Its cries pierced Nerine, sending shivers down her spine and through every inch of her body. While its shape seemed human, it was impossible to tell, as the hood of its cloak veiled its face.

Nerine lingered in the shadows until they had passed by. Even then, she waited until the creature's screams had started to fade. Then, she darted around the corner after the small entourage. While they had turned a corner out of sight, the creature's noise carried enough for her to follow at a safe distance.

~*~*~

After what seemed an age of being carried through the great wall along the river's swift currents, the water slowed, and Mikanah and Lorelei came to a standstill. They floated in the newly formed moat, gathering their bearings. They still floated inside the outer wall surrounding the castle. While the frontmost wall had been destroyed when Nerine blasted the river through it, parts of the back wall remained. Bodies of injured and dead soldiers floated on the water around them. Blood stained the water with threads of crimson.

"Let's try that door," Lorelei said, swimming toward a wooden door set in the wall.

They climbed from the water and passed through the door. The castle towered before them; they'd entered the inner courtyard. Sounds of battle reached them faintly from the front of the courtyard. The only life back here was the neighing and pawing of horses in the stables to their far left. Recognizing the area, Mikanah motioned Lorelei to a small door in the base of the castle's back wall, and they entered the castle.

"Let's find Moragon," Mikanah said, "and hope the others find us."

Mikanah led them up the set of stairs and down the adjoining hallway, headed for the front of the castle. He paused at one of the windows and frowned as he surveyed the bloodbath swathing the courtyard below. Fire and shadow magic spiraled from a flying ship. Soldiers fell by the dozens, to magic, to the sword, some by flaming arrows. Desire burned brightly inside Mikanah, fueled by anger and a yearning for justice. He needed to be down there, fighting alongside his people. No— he needed to be fighting Moragon, shoving his sword straight through the bastard's skull—

"*Mikanah?*"

Lorelei spoke his name with emphasis. Realizing that she had tried to get his attention several times already, he looked up at her.

"We must keep going. For their sake." She nodded at the window. "We must keep going."

Mikanah breathed deeply. "Yes. Yes, we must. But where would we find him? Sooner or later, we're going to run into trouble, some guards or other resistance. We can't just wander aimlessly, and we can't use up all our strength and magic before fighting him—"

"I know where he is."

Mikanah's head snapped up. A woman had just entered the hallway, seemingly appearing from thin air, but as he noted the woman's face and the tapestry hanging at its skewed angle beside him, he understood instantly.

"Pua," he spat, glaring at the wrinkled woman who

stared up at them, her smile unnervingly calm. Mikanah recalled several song-spells of attack, ready to stun or mame the crazed Moragon-worshipper at the first sign of trouble.

"You're the woman." Lorelei stepped forward to partially shield Mikanah; irritated, he stepped up beside her. "The one who helped me, before turning on me."

"I had to, my dear. 'Twas the only way to prevent my turning on the Defiance." Pua lifted her hand, and something gleamed a faded gold. A coin. Lorelei gasped beside Mikanah, even as he realized that Pua held one of the coins depicting King Noheah's face and emblem.

"Impossible!" Mikanah scoffed, shaking his head. "You're one of Moragon's most loyal spies. Time and again I've seen you bring countless harm to innocent people. You can't possibly expect us to believe you're on our side. On the Defiance's side, no less."

Pua arched a brow, and a smile curled on her lips. "Those are bold words from one who tortured so many innocents yourself. And yet, despite your faults, which are as egregious as they are numerous, you have swayed many into believing that you are capable of change, of doing good, of even being our true and just king."

Mikanah stood rendered silent. Much as he had always despised this woman for her cunning and cleverness, he had also admired her for her rare moments of clarity and truth.

"How could this be?" Lorelei asked. "If you're part of the Defiance, then why did you cause a disturbance that could've gotten me imprisoned again, or worse?"

Pua's chuckle was uncanny. "You forget how close I made myself to his majesty. I made myself useful enough for him to tell me things others would not know. Not the most important secrets; those he saved for a select few. But enough to be of help to the Defiance—and to you.

I knew he wouldn't seek to harm or imprison you, not that early in his game. I gave you just enough information to set you looking for the heir, which I see worked out well enough in the end. And then I resumed my usual role of the wench who'd gone mad over her love of Moragon."

Mikanah stood taken aback. Had this woman truly been a spy against Moragon all this time, without his ever guessing?

"Even if you were a spy for the Defiance, then how would we know? Anyone might have one of those old coins. How do we know you're speaking truth in saying you know where Moragon is, instead of leading us to some trap?"

Pua tilted her head, looking strangely thoughtful. Quietly, she said, "Just earlier, I ran into several of your Guardian friends. I led them to the throne room, to confront His Majesty. But one was missing. Your girl, Iolana, where is she?"

Mikanah flinched at the fresh stab of pain at the sound of Iolana's name. "She...she fell. Reynard's men killed her."

"I know. The bastards," Pua sneered. "If you make it out of that throne room alive, I do hope you're the one to spear that noxious skamelar straight through. But Iolana..." Her voice turned abruptly gentler as she spoke her name. "...did she ever speak of a servant woman who came to visit her in prison? Who would bring her an extra bit of food or water now and then?"

Once more, Mikanah stood dumbfounded. Pua could be making it up. There could have been another woman who served Iolana, and Pua had merely seen or overheard about this woman's kindness. But the strange serenity in Pua's face as she spoke of Iolana told him that, against all incredible odds, she must be telling the truth.

"You helped save her," Mikanah forced the words from his suddenly dry throat. "You threw the cup that showed her where Lorelei's spell was hidden."

Pua's head bowed in a small nod. "I did. Because of my role as a spy for both Moragon and the Defiance, I had to play my cards carefully. I wasn't able to attend many of Iolana's Defiance meetings. But I knew who she was, what she was, what she stood for. Just as I knew your father, way back in the day, Lady Lorelei."

Lorelei's breathing grew shallow beside Mikanah, and he glanced over at her. She stared wide-eyed at Pua, brushing away a few tears. Terrified she might pass out on the spot, Mikanah firmly took her hand.

"You knew my father?" Lorelei managed to say.

"I did. Master Lorens. What a good man. Kindly and brave, just like his daughter. But now, if your curiosities are satisfied, we have wasted enough time. I only just left your friends in the throne room, but a few minutes under Moragon's wrath is more than enough time for him to take whatever twisted vengeance his mind has formulated."

"Thank you," Mikanah said, pulling Lorelei after him. "We can find our way from here."

"Very well. Amiel grant you all speed and protection."

Mikanah and Lorelei sped through the castle. They passed several dozen guards along the way, freeing the minds of those they could with *Ah Lum Amiel* and fighting those who attacked them.

Suddenly, a wailing met their ears, rising with such ferocious torment that Mikanah froze in place and drew his sword, terrified that Moragon played some new, cruel trick to distract them. Lorelei began chanting songs beside him and drew her own sword. They stood back-to-back, waiting as the wails culminated into shrieks, stabbing Mikanah to his core.

Then, as a familiar face loomed around the corner, the screams faded to the back of Mikanah's mind. He stared as Reynard approached, suddenly incapable of doing or feeling anything apart from an overwhelming hatred, rage. Briefly, he noted the person—or monster, it was hard to tell—straining against the four guards who carried it, clearly at Reynard's command. Clutching his sword so hard that his hands burned, Mikanah shouted down the hall,

"Still relishing the sport of torturing helpless creatures, are we, Lord Reynard?"

Lorelei hissed some warning beside him, but he ignored her as Reynard's glare met his, first with shock, and then with recognition as his face twisted into a grin.

"Mikanah, old friend, welcome back!" Reynard flung his arms wide in an overly dramatic gesture. He halted, and the guards behind him did the same. The creature's maddening screams echoed between the walls.

"Why don't you let that poor soul go?" Mikanah took a step forward, sword clenched, poised to fight. "You've clearly already driven it to madness, just as you did my brother."

"I can assure you that this *thing*," Reynard flicked his hand at it, "is neither poor nor helpless." He waved his hand then, and the guards took this as a command to drag the creature back the way they had come.

Its screams started to diminish, but they rang just as clearly in Mikanah's mind, dredging up every ounce of loathing he'd ever felt for Reynard.

"Are you going to do it or not?" Reynard spread his arms wide again. His tone mocked him as he added, "Or will you just stand there, playing your moves safely like always? Even your brother, pathetic wretch that he was, at least had the guts to fight back—until he threw himself from that window, proving himself a coward—"

Mikanah lunged.

Reynard drew his broadsword, parrying Mikanah's first strike with the flat of his blade. Lorelei rushed up behind Mikanah, singing *Fraziolda* to freeze Reynard in place.

"No!" Mikanah shouted over his shoulder. "Reynard is mine!"

Lorelei looked uneasy but released Reynard from the spell.

For the next few minutes, Mikanah and Reynard circled each other, blocking each other's blows. Tension poured thickly between them, and Mikanah drank in its poison, letting it fuel his mounting hatred. Beneath his breath, he vocalized one of the songs he had once played on his violin, a song that had made hundreds if not thousands submit and bend to his will. Mikanah had always existed in Reynard's shadow, haunted by every cruel thing he'd enacted upon Jerah, but now Reynard would kneel in Mikanah's shadow.

Mikanah poured every ounce of his loathing, frustration, and years of unfathomable pain into his song. Reynard swung his sword, but the movement was slow and clumsy. He swung again, but his arm paused midway, bending not to his own will, but to Mikanah's. Reynard growled in frustration, but as he tried to jerk his arm free, Mikanah's song forbade him.

Mikanah sang forcefully, all the while imagining exactly what he wanted Reynard to do, and Reynard did it. He fell to his knees before Mikanah. He raised his sword above his own heart, arm trembling as he struggled vainly to resist. He twisted his other arm behind him, yelling out as the bones crunched. He twisted his feet, snapping the bones in his ankles. He should have fallen from the pain, but Mikanah forced him to remain kneeling, sweat pouring from his face.

"Mikanah, end this!" Lorelei shouted.

"Don't tell me how to take my vengeance!" Mikanah shouted back, singing in his head to hold Reynard in check. "Do you have any idea how this man tortured my brother? And you saw how his men mercilessly hunted down Iolana, killed her like some animal."

"I know, but torturing him like this won't right any of those horrible wrongs. You named your sword Jerah's Justice. So, take your justice and be done with it!"

Mikanah hesitated, staring with pleasure as he watched Reynard's face contort with pain. He could break every bone in Reynard's body. He could force him to spear himself through with his own sword. He could make him tear out his eyes with his hands. Mikanah admitted that he would enjoy watching Reynard's torment.

But none of that would bring his brother back, or Iolana. And they had a much bigger enemy yet to find and conquer.

Mikanah gripped Jerah's Justice and pierced Reynard straight through the heart. Reynard's eyes widened, and a grunt fell from his lips. Then, as Mikanah released him from his spell, he collapsed, dead.

Mikanah breathed heavily, staring down at him as Lorelei placed a hand on his shoulder.

"How do you feel?" she asked gently.

Mikanah studied Reynard as his blood spread beneath his corpse. His body was a limp, empty shell of flesh. The light of life in his eyes had been snuffed by a dull emptiness. He had died just like any other man would on the battlefield.

"I feel a strange peace and satisfaction," Mikanah said quietly. "Reynard's gone. He can't hurt anyone anymore. It's over."

Lorelei squeezed his shoulder, as if both to comfort him and to say, *But it's not over yet. We still need to find Moragon.*

"Come on." Mikanah wiped his sword on the edge of his tunic before picking up his pace to resume their pursuit toward the throne room.

CHAPTER 53

A MELODY UNRELENTING

As Mikanah and Lorelei neared the throne room, a pain began to jab at the back of his head. He touched it and drew back his hand, expecting to feel blood, but there was none.

"I feel it too," Lorelei said, digging her fingers into her temple.

"It's Moragon," Mikanah said. "He knows where we are. He's trying to infiltrate our minds. Use *Ah Lum Amiel* to resist him."

Mikanah silently repeated the song. Here and there, a flash of some horrible scene broke through, but Mikanah sang harder and fought them off, fueled by the power of the song, his determination, and his mounting rage.

The double doors of the throne room loomed into view. Mikanah and Lorelei stopped before them. Sounds of torment echoed from within. Cries, moans, screams. Lorelei squeezed his hand to draw his attention. "The honor is yours, my king. We may be equals as Guardians. But in this moment, I follow you."

Mikanah looked at Lorelei, incredulous. She watched him with a new respect, and her encouragement strengthened him.

He thrust the doors open and led Lorelei inside.

The other Guardians clustered near the foot of the dais, wailing, shrieking, clawing at their heads. Moragon sat tall on the throne, staring proudly at his handiwork. His gaze found Lorelei and Mikanah as they marched forward. Lorelei rushed to tend the others while Mikanah stopped before the dais, shielding himself by repeating *Ah Lum Amiel* in his mind.

Moragon rose to his feet.

"Mikanah, my most faithful friend. Aren't you going to bow to your king?"

His voice was edged with an icy warning. Good. Mikanah was ready for a fight. He had stood in this place of servitude too many times, but now he would rip Moragon from the throne that was never his. Mikanah stepped forward, but Lorelei jumped up and firmly grabbed his wrist, stopping him.

"We didn't come here to bow to you," Lorelei said. "Nor shall anyone bow to you ever again. Mikanah is the true king."

"Little Mikanah?" Moragon arched a brow and, after affording Mikanah only the briefest dismissive glance, laughed out loud.

"You've named my chief puppet as your king? Surely you could do better than *that*, Lorelei."

"I am your puppet no longer," Mikanah said, his loathing building inside him with each passing second. "You can't control me anymore."

"Perhaps." Moragon tilted his head. "But even if you're no longer my servant, that doesn't make you my liege."

"But his bloodline does." Lorelei glared fiercely at him. "Mikanah is King Noheah's blood and thus true heir to the Carmennan throne."

A rare moment of shock gleamed in Moragon's eyes. He glanced away, seemingly distracted by some private thought, and Mikanah wondered what he plotted next.

"We've come to finish you, Moragon," Mikanah said. "Submit now, or taste death swiftly."

"Submit?" Moragon's gaze snapped back to Lorelei, narrowed like a viper focused on its prey. "Look around you." He motioned to the Guardians; they had quieted, as though Lorelei had calmed their nightmares, but still lay on the ground. "I don't think it is *I* who shall submit this day. It would not be fitting, would it, Lorelei? A true king never submits. But a true lady always does."

Mikanah waited for Lorelei's retort, but it never came. She had closed her eyes. Her lips moved quickly as she sang *Ah Lum Amiel*. She trembled head to toe, and a harsh sob escaped her before she sank to her knees.

"Lorelei!" Mikanah fell to her side, terrified to see her on the verge of breaking. He glared at Moragon. "What are you doing to them?"

"Not I," Moragon said. "But another, my Vessel. Had she learned the value of submission, I might have granted the same honor to your whore, Iolana—"

"Don't call her that!" Mikanah snarled. He held Lorelei more tightly as she whimpered.

"Iolana was never anything to me," Moragon said. "She could have been. But her gift was too unstable, and she incapable of controlling or tempering it. She was merely a replacement for Lorelei, a toy to distract myself with until the Vessel was complete. As for you, Lorelei, Gailea has rejected my hand, but you can still join me as my queen. You came closer to it than she ever did... *intimately* so. Would it not be wrong, by your faith, to take another's hand after being so close?"

Lorelei trembled more violently but sang on, fighting against him.

"Lorelei," Mikanah said sharply. "It's not real. None of this—"

A frightful chord resonated in his mind, consuming it. Then another and another. Dreadful, exquisite music, flowing with ten times the force his violin had ever wielded. Suddenly *he was surrounded by a ring of flames. Iolana called to him from the fire, burned, died, turned to ash, and rose again only to suffer anew. His brother fell from a tower beyond the flames and landed in them. Dozens of other faces, then hundreds, leered from the fire, all accusing him.*

It isn't real, he told himself, furiously singing to drown out the horrific images. *He's putting this into your head!*

Just like that, the flames vanished. Mikanah had won.

But where was the throne room?

He was still in the castle—the bedroom with the lavish linens in which he now found himself was familiar—but why was he here?

One by one, the women were paraded inside. One by one, Mikanah seduced their minds with his violin before seducing their bodies.

"Mikanah!"

Lorelei? No. No, not Lorelei. He never did this to her. He wouldn't do this.

"Mikanah!"

Mikanah flailed, nearly slapping her as she whirled him around. He breathed hard, staring at her in a daze. They were still inside the throne room. Lorelei was standing before him, fully awake and aware and unharmed. She reached up and took his face in her hands.

"Mikanah. You're all right. He's showing us lies."

"Oh, am I?" Moragon sneered. "Go on then. Tell her, Mikanah. Tell her of these so-called lies. That you didn't seduce a single one of them. Steal their virtue, their secrets, in some cases, their very spirits. They were never the same after you. Some of them killed themselves for wanting you to love them. If I were you, Lorelei, I would sever this growing affection before he consumes you as well. Before he clings to you like a leech and sucks the very life from you, just as he did to Iolana."

"It wasn't like that," Mikanah pleaded. "Not with her. We were free—she was willing—"

"Sing," Lorelei commanded, holding his face more firmly in her hands. "Sing the song and free yourself. Free the others."

Mikanah gazed deeply into her eyes. Strong, stalwart, prepared to fight. If she judged him, she laid all that aside for what they must do. Moragon's visions began to float back to him, threatening to rip his mind apart once more, but as Lorelei sang, Mikanah sang with her.

Gailea sat up, blood trickling from a wound in her head. She crawled next to Chamblin, singing *Ah Lum Amiel* with passion. A true tenderness shone in her gaze as she held him, singing until at last, he broke from his nightmares with a gasp. Gailea continued to hold him, and he sang with her.

One by one, the Guardians joined in. Gailea and Chamblin sang until Darice was freed, and she freed Ashden. They sang to Donyon until clarity returned to the king's face and mind.

Together they rose, Gailea supporting Chamblin, and faced the usurper on his throne. *Ah Lum Amiel* rang out, even as waves of a dark song floated to them, the mist curled around them, and nightmares wavered at the fringes of Mikanah's mind. He struggled against them, knowing that somehow, Moragon used a song-spell, chanting *Nux, nux, nux*, repeatedly in various notes and pitches, and in a tone Mikanah had never heard before.

It was a voice so surpassingly, irresistibly lovely it was impossible to believe it came from this demonic tyrant.

The two songs warred with one another. Mikanah felt Moragon's song—could it really be Moragon singing so serenely?—trying to claw his mind open again. Despite an aching desire to give all his attention to this new melody, Mikanah clutched his head and fought until all but *Ah Lum Amiel* was shut out. The mist cleared away at once, and his musical magic returned to him full force.

Moragon's song held for but an instant until its childlike purity changed. It grew in volume and depth into a terrible, booming melody that resounded throughout the throne room. Sound took on physical form, with fire streaking and shadows surging in all directions. Moragon seemed to be in one place one second and another place the next, spewing spells like a madman.

Darice's hands glowed a bright white, and she raised them high. A grim shadow careening toward Lorelei's head stopped mid-air. One by one, Darice halted Moragon's spells so that they hovered above, frozen in place, unable to make impact.

Until one of his many spells spun off the wall and slammed into Darice. Her feet flew from underneath her, and her concentration severed. Instantly, her holding spell failed, and chaos erupted as fire and dark energy rebounded off the walls and pillars. Stone exploded. The ceiling began to crumble and cave in. Everyone screamed and leaped out of the way.

One of the pillars crashed toward Mikanah, who dove to the floor. Coughing and rubbing his aching side, he glanced up through the rising dust to see Moragon slipping behind the throne and out of sight.

Mikanah scrambled to his feet. Filled with white-hot determination, he ignored the pain covering his bruised body and sprinted after Moragon.

CHAPTER 54

THE INDOMITABLE VESSEL

While Mikanah had confronted Reynard, Nerine had chosen to pursue the creature.

The guards wound the beast through several corridors. Nerine encountered several groups of Carmennans and other soldiers along the way, but most paid her little heed, focused on fighting each other. For those who did attack, she would transform to liquid long enough to prevent harm to herself or else blast them back with a wave of water.

At last, the guards' path turned down a narrow, seemingly deserted corridor which connected to a long flight of spiraling steps. Nerine lingered on the bottom step, listening for the monster to reach the top before continuing her pursuit.

A clattering noise came toward her, and she panicked. Had she been discovered after all? Did the guards throw some weapon or other means of attack at her? Quickly, she shifted her body into its water form, groaning with the effort. After a few seconds, her weary body forced her to turn solid once again and she staggered back against the wall, breathless, her vision turning black for a moment.

The clattering ceased, and the slamming of a door echoed above. Carefully, Nerine began her ascent, scanning the steps for any sign of danger. About halfway up, a familiar sight caught her glance. She stooped to pick up two figurines of knights riding their horses, each exquisitively carved. Nerine wondered whether the guards or the creature had dropped it. It was very much like those she had found in Reynard's Keep, beneath the creature's prison. But what use would a monster have for what seemed to be simple children's toys, with no magical or other apparent value?

Pocketing the figurines, Nerine finished her ascent, coming at last to an iron door at the top of the steps. Nerine pulled on the door, only to find it sealed tight. Finding strength enough to transform her right hand to liquid, she reached inside the lock, molding her hand to fit inside the gears and turning them. Satisfied, she pulled on the door handle and then pushed, only to meet the same results.

She tried again to manipulate the lock's mechanisms. Nothing. Peering inside the keyhold, she sang *Gizemia* to see past the charms shrouding the door, but she saw nothing. The door was protected by magic beyond her abilities.

Nerine hurried back down the stairs, determined to take note of any tapestries or other decorations to help her find her way back. If she could find the other Guardians, one of them may be able to get inside the door and help her stop the beast after all, before Moragon could use it against them.

~*~*~

Mikanah chased Moragon through the shadowy halls.

Every time Mikanah thought he'd lost track of the mad king, he would catch a glimpse of him disappearing around the next corner. He knew Moragon purposely led him somewhere. As Mikanah pursued, his mind raced with a million questions. What memories had Moragon alluded to that had filled Lorelei with such obvious agony? And where was Nerine? Had Moragon already captured her?

Mikanah's tunnel vision locked onto Moragon as he disappeared through a wooden door at the end of the corridor. Moments later, Mikanah passed through the door inside a familiar tower with a long staircase winding steeply upward. His footsteps echoed as he rushed up the stone steps, and when he emerged through the door at the top, he found himself drinking in cool air. The mist seemed to have dispersed up here entirely, though dark clouds lingered overhead, and hints of ash, smoke, and possible rain bit his nostrils. From this vantage point, he could see the battle still raging in the courtyard far below, though the wind sang too sharply for him to hear more than what sounded like distant cries.

He suddenly realized where he stood. His special place, the wall walk where he and Iolana had enjoyed so many sunrises together. Or so few, it now seemed.

"Brings back memories, doesn't it, Mikanah?"

Mikanah whirled and drew his sword, regret turning to rage as he beheld his old master. Beside Moragon, another figure crouched low to the ground. Hunched over and clad head to toe in tattered gray cloths, the creature's stance conjured thoughts of gargoyles, like those that guarded the castle's rooftops.

The figure hung its head low, so that its hood covered its face. Spindly legs peeked from beneath its tunic, and arms poked from sleeves that were too short. Its brown skin stretched thin over its bones. Wisps of white hair blew from its hood. A low wheezing pulsed from the creature. It looked like it could collapse and die at any moment, but a song radiated faintly from it, a mighty song etched with power, pain, and passion. The song was controlled, contained somehow. The concentration on Moragon's face revealed some connection between the two of them.

"Do you admire him?" Moragon asked, stroking the creature's head. It winced but allowed the gesture. "Do you envy him, my Vessel? This could have been you, after all."

Mikanah stared, and for a few moments, bewilderment outweighed his anger. This frail pile of bones, this corpse cloaked in rags: *this* was the Vessel? More powerful than the Desthai?

"This could *still* be you," Moragon continued, his voice soft, almost gentle. "Or perhaps taking Reynard's place would be more desirable? I am told you were the one to fell him, after all. A great loss. But even he was not as powerful as you. Perhaps I made a mistake, in choosing him over you. And perhaps now is my time to rectify that mistake. After all, it seems you are heir to the throne. The true, blood-born heir. With my power and your prestige, who wouldn't bow to us? You should never have been one of the Guardians. You were both born and taught to rule over others. That future is now within your reach, if you will but grasp it. Everyone you love is gone. But everything you worked so hard for may yet be obtained."

Mikanah stared at Moragon, struck silent. It should be easy for him to defy Moragon, to throw his suggestions to the wind. But while the sight of the pitiful creature snarling beside Moragon disgusted him, it somehow also allured him. He could feel a strange energy emanating from the creature. Moragon's hand still rested on its head, and tendrils of thin black mist curled up from its body.

"What of that thing?" Mikanah asked. "What would you do with it?"

"Oh, powerful as he is, you'll find he's very submissive. Why, I would surely pass on before you, leaving you with a mighty kingdom and an unstoppable Vessel at your command. You could rule entire worlds."

Mikanah took a deep breath. The idea of all power in his hands. To never be below anyone or anything ever again. To never again lack control over his life. To use his power for good.

He looked once more to the Vessel. As compliant and cowed as this creature appeared, Moragon's fierce grip on its head was hard enough to turn Moragon's knuckles white. No, Moragon neither trusted nor gave freedom to anyone, no matter how much an ally, no matter how loyal.

As long as Moragon lived, he would never allow Mikanah to do what he willed. Bowing to Moragon to obtain the crown meant giving up at least half his right to rule. Moragon would never allow him to be the kind of leader he desired. Guilt and pain would repeat themselves until Moragon took his final breath.

"A king doesn't rule alongside another," Mikanah said. "I will take my kingdom or die trying. You took away everything I loved, but I won't let you do that anymore to anyone else."

"You blame only me?" Moragon tilted his head. "Are you certain you didn't kill them with your cowardice? Inaction, they say, is the worst evil. Your whore was reckless, but at least she *did* things. She fought for what she believed in. What do *you* believe in, Mikanah? Power, control, recognition, these are all you have left to fight for. They are the greatest desires of your heart and have been for some time. Why do you think I chose you as my chief musician? I would have made you my number one servant from the start, if we didn't share the same ambitions. But because of that, I knew I must never entirely trust you."

Mikanah's hands grew sweaty, and he readjusted his grip on the sword. He saw the great hatred in the king's eyes, and his heart trembled. "Yes, we are similar." Saying the words aloud, words he'd known to be true, seemed to heal some other, more ancient wound he could not define. "Our lust for power, our hatred. I still hate you. I will always hate you with every fiber of my being, to the bitter end. I did have choices back then, and I chose wrong. But I'm making what I hope is the right choice now. I choose to fight you, so that at least *your* hatred may be dispelled from this world."

"You're certain you want to do this?" Moragon slightly twisted the hand resting on the Vessel's head, and the creature uttered a faint whimper. "You don't understand the strength of my Vessel. His musical power feeds into me, even as my mental powers feed into him. We are like a parasite and its host, each playing both roles until, as one flesh, we become infinitely strong. With our combined strengths, you could take down the other Guardians in a single breath."

"Some of them may hate me," Mikanah said, "but for all the reasons I hate you. And I will not fault them that. Rather, I stand with them."

"Very well then. My offer dissolves with your words. Let us have less talk and more music. Let us see what you have learned, or perhaps forgotten, in my absence."

Ever so quietly, Moragon began to sing:

"Kakill t'ake gakur dakians, kakill thakem akall, kakill; cakonskaum kae thakem, cakonskaum kae thakem akall...."

It was more of a chant, in a language Mikanah couldn't recognize. Maybe it was the language of whatever horrific realm had spawned the Vessel. Or maybe it was some made-up tongue entirely, composed by Moragon and the creature for the sole purpose of destroying the Guardians. Moragon's fascination with languages wasn't as great as his obsession for musical magic, but it was enough that Mikanah wouldn't wonder at him completing such a feat.

Whatever the song's origins, Mikanah felt the weight of its energy pressing on him, seeking to bend him under its submission. Mikanah tried to step forward, but his feet dragged, and his sword pulled his arm down, as though made of the heaviest stone. Grounding himself, he sang *Ah Lum Amiel* quietly and slowly, striving to counter Moragon's song and its seeming intended purpose of crushing both his spirit and body.

The Vessel released a mingled cry and moan, a pleading, pitiful sound, and Mikanah realized that it, not Moragon, was the source of the song. Somehow, Moragon had found a way to latch onto the creature's mind and channel its music through himself. The Vessel snarled, and the black mist shimmered along his slight frame before rising from his skin and hair, sweeping in toward Mikanah. Focused purely on *Ah Lum Amiel*, Mikanah intensified both his volume and purpose.

Moragon's deep voice resonated with a force that Mikanah would not have thought possible, even for such a powerful man. The strength Moragon drew from the Vessel radiated toward Mikanah, stifling his own voice. His breathing labored, and his concentration began to falter. Darkness closed in. Memories of the past suffocated him. He saw Iolana, dying once more. He saw Lorelei and the other Guardians and all his fears of failing them, just as he had failed Iolana and his brother. He knew these fears were induced by Moragon and the Vessel's song, that Moragon was controlling him again. But the more vivid the horrors grew, the more difficult it became to fight through them. His lungs heaved, denying him his very breath, and his feet staggered against his will.

Of a sudden, Gailea's rich mezzo-alto voice thrummed in the air like a bath of warm golden sunlight on a wintry day, and with it, her power added to his. The shadows clouding his mind began to diminish, just enough to calm his heart, renew his focus, and help him stand tall. Darice's clear alto joined her sister's, along with Donyon's thundering bass. Chamblin and Ashden joined next, with Chamblin leaning on Ashden for support. The act of standing and singing riddled Chamblin's face with pain, but he pushed through, letting his tenor soar. Ashden summoned his lute from its case strapped to his belt, echoing *Ah Lum Amiel* on its strings while singing along.

Mikanah sheathed his sword then and drew his violin. A vicious smirk crossed Moragon's lips, and for a moment, Mikanah faltered. But then he remembered Lorelei's encouragement. He had used Moragon's violin for his evil. He would use the Guardians' violin to destroy that same evil. Placing the bow to the strings, he played while singing on.

Mikanah closed his eyes, letting *Ah Lum Amiel* fill him from the inside out until he felt nothing else, saw and heard nothing else except its rich purity reverberating through him and from him. Moragon's corrupt chant tried to claw its way inside Mikanah's mind, but even the visions Moragon tried to thrust on him appeared as little more than gray, flickering blurs.

A loud noise made Mikanah's eyes fly open. Moragon stumbled over his own feet and had to catch himself on the wall with both hands. Abruptly released from his master's touch, the Vessel fell over with a cry.

Setting his violin aside, Mikanah drew his sword and rushed at the evil creature. Now was his moment.

"No!" Gailea shouted. "Lorelei warned us not to harm the Vessel—only Moragon!"

Mikanah threw a glance over his shoulder, staring at Gailea as if she were mad.

"Where is she?" he demanded. "Where is Lorelei?"

"On our way here, we ran into Nerine. Nerine had something important to show Lorelei. They both warned us not to harm the Vessel!"

"Well, they're not here now, and he'll get up any second! Now might be our only chance!"

Ignoring Gailea's shouts, Mikanah swung his sword, but the Vessel leaped up and glided to the side. Mikanah stared, caught off guard. How was this fragile wisp of a demon, monster, creature—whatever it was—capable of moving so fluidly? Mikanah attempted another blow, only for it to swerve to the side yet again. This time, it released a sad, high melody that rose and fell. With each crescendo, the creature seemed to plea, but every time his voice dipped into a lower pitch, an overwhelming sense of despair emanated tangibly from him. The song nearly broke Mikanah's heart in two. He couldn't determine why, but he wouldn't be fooled by its trickery. He took another swing.

Only to be blocked by Moragon's sword. Moragon sang again, drawing ragged breaths and power from his Vessel, which bore its master's weight again from his merciless grip on its shoulder. Clumsily, Moragon wielded blow after blow at Mikanah who easily blocked.

One of Mikanah's blows met their mark, and with a sharp hiss, Moragon fell to his knees, grabbing at his side. The other Guardians sang on, clustering behind Mikanah, except Chamblin, who leaned against the wall, looking pale as death. Their song had broken Moragon's, but the Vessel's strength endured. Who knew what damage it was capable of on its own? Mikanah turned toward it and thrust his sword at the small figure.

"*Mikanah, no!*"

At Lorelei's shriek, Mikanah barely managed to control his momentum but did so before his blade hit home. Lorelei and Nerine hurried across the wall toward him.

"Lorelei, we need to finish this," Mikanah said. "We must end this while Moragon's down. The Guardians can't keep singing forever!"

"I know, but it's not what it seems. Mikanah, he's your brother, Jerah!"

Mikanah staggered as the shock of Lorelei's words slammed into him. Then, his anger flared, and he clutched his sword tighter, prepared to deliver a lethal blow to this creature that obviously gripped her in its deceptive claws.

"Lorelei, whatever this thing is, it's just distorting your mind, saying whatever it can in a desperate attempt to save its pathetic life."

Mikanah swung his sword again, but Lorelei practically screamed the spell that rendered his body immobile from the neck down, perfectly frozen.

"Lorelei, we don't have time for this. I'm serious!"

"And so am I!" Lorelei shouted, releasing him from the spell. She gripped his arm, staring up fervently into his eyes. "Please just listen—and look, just *look* at these! Do you remember these? Nerine!"

Lorelei ripped the small items from Nerine's hands and thrust them before Mikanah who stared and lowered his sword a little in surprise. Tiny wooden figurines of two soldiers on a horse, each detail exquisitely carved.

"They're the ones my father used to carve!"

"I don't know what that has to do with anything, but it needs to be destroyed, Lorelei! We don't have time—"

He swung his blade again, but Lorelei sang *Segmunda*, flinging him back just enough for him to fall backward, dropping his sword. He scrambled for the blade, screaming at her to stop as she reached for the creature's hood and pulled it back.

A boy's brown, starveling face stared up at them beyond the lank white hair. He cried out and shielded his face, as if even the morning's gray light seemed unbearable to him. But the longer Mikanah stared, the more he realized that what the child feared was scrutiny. He was in terror of being seen. Despite his ghostly appearance, something familiar registered in the boy's face. Mikanah glanced from the boy's sharply watchful expression, fixated directly on him, to the wooden toys Lorelei had dropped and now rolled at the boy's feet.

Distracted for a moment, the boy picked one up. He turned it over, examined it closely. He tapped it, licked it, sniffed at it. For a moment, his wild gaze lightened, perhaps with remembrance, perhaps with some semblance of what might have been joy, had he ever been capable of such a pure feeling.

Mikanah stared at the boy, hardly able to feel anything but an overwhelming sense of bewilderment. Years ago, it would've been a dream come true, but this boy, this nightmare, couldn't be what he was.

And yet, as the boy looked up at Mikanah, the same glimmer of life sparked in his eyes. He stared straight into Mikanah's eyes, and Mikanah stared at their light brown color, their shape so like his, and he knew by whatever miracle or devilry, he gazed into his brother's eyes.

"Jerah."

The moment Mikanah uttered his brother's name, Jerah's expression transformed. The light of flickering joy extinguished in his eyes, replaced by a mask of loathing. Gripping the toy hard, he glared up at Mikanah and seethed,

"You did this. You left me here. You abandoned me. You promised to protect me, but you let them destroy me. You didn't even look. You just believed their lies. And now you would try to kill me."

"No," Mikanah said, his voice breaking as sorrow broke through his surprise. "I didn't know. I couldn't have known."

"You never looked for me. Not once. You were glad to be rid of me, so you could take your place as Moragon's favorite."

"Don't listen," Nerine cried. "Don't listen to him. It's Moragon. He doesn't really know what he's saying."

"...I was in the background, all the time, watching and waiting. Training for our king in ways you never could have handled. I am his favorite, and always will be. And you won't take that away from me."

The boy's accusations rambled on. Moragon still crouched on his hands and knees. He tried to push himself up but trembled, seemingly stuck in that position. His lips moved, fueling the boy's words. Or maybe it was too late and Moragon and the boy had become one flesh. Maybe there was no redemption for his brother.

No. Mikanah wouldn't believe it.

Crouching down, he said, "Jerah, are you in there? Please, Jerah, if there's anything left of you, please, show me somehow—"

Jerah lunged, snarling at Mikanah, and grappling for his neck. Mikanah jumped back, even as some invisible force seemed to yank Jerah back. Moragon had managed to stand, leaning heavily against the wall, shaking violently. Jerah writhed on the ground and whimpered, his voice quiet and broken, "It hurts...make it stop...it hurts...*Mika!*"

Mikanah spun to face Moragon, aiming his sword straight at his heart. "Tell me! Tell me how to free him!"

Moragon gave a mockery of a laugh, a sound like rattling bones. "Truly, I've tuned the perfect matching set in raising you and your brother. Your entire life's training was always this, to prepare the way for his grand debut. Alas, that this grand performance may be his last. For the only freedom either of us will find now, from each other or this world, lies in death. Jerah's fate is now bound to mine, and mine to his. Kill one of us, and the other falls."

Mikanah stared in wild panic at the Guardians. Sympathy shone from Gailea's face, and from Lorelei's, but none seemed able to tell him what to do. Should he end his brother's misery? Was death the only way? He gripped his sword, wanting nothing more than to spear Moragon's heart. But what if the man held some secret key to freeing his brother?

"Jerah?"

At the sound of this gentle call, Mikanah turned back to his brother. Nerine, in her pure water form, knelt before the ghostly boy. Her hair flowed in long blue tendrils, extending toward Jerah who looked up at her. Pain was etched deeply into the premature lines across his face. Weariness stretched deeper still within his eyes. But Mikanah could see the tiniest hint of light flickering in those eyes, however briefly, as he stared at the water maiden kneeling before him. Mikanah remembered how the mist had held no sway over Nerine's magic. Could she also, by some miracle, break through Moragon's hold over his brother?

"Jerah," she whispered. "Listen to me. Please, try as hard as you can. Your brother never forgot you. He still loves you. Do you remember this?" Solidifying one hand, she picked up one of the wooden figurines and held it up to him. "You don't want to hurt people with your music. Don't you want to just play again?"

As Jerah reached for the toy, Moragon yelled a spell that sent Nerine flying back against the wall before crashing to the ground, returned to her solid form, and unconscious. Gailea screamed and rushed to Nerine's side, and Lorelei joined her while Jerah lunged at Moragon in fury.

Moragon flicked his hand at Jerah, but the boy sang what Mikanah recognized as a song-shield; Moragon had tried to attack his brother. Mikanah braced himself, barely containing his urge to spear Moragon through.

A sudden anxiety pierced through his anger as a horrific vision flashed through his mind—*Jerah attacking him while screaming profanities and words of hatred*—but Mikanah quickly sang *Salmana* to erect a song-shield around his mind. Moragon's hold on Jerah and his music may be severed, but he would still seek to destroy him with his mental magic.

"The healing charms aren't working!"

At Lorelei's cry, Mikanah whipped his head in her direction. She knelt with Gailea beside Nerine, both of them with their hands pressed to Nerine's temple.

"It's one of Moragon's mental tricks," Gailea snarled, standing, and stepping toward him. "Let us finish him, once and for all! Push back his magic with *Ah Lum Amiel*, together now!"

A high, keening wail interrupted her, and they all stared at Jerah. He hunched over Nerine, reached forth a thin, trembling hand, grasped the wooden figurine, and held it tight. Then he crawled over to where Gailea, Darice, and Donyon stood. Huddling next to Darice, he turned toward Moragon, whose face flashed with alarm.

Jerah's lips parted, and he sang:
"Ah Lum Amiel."

One by one, the Guardians rejoined the song. Even Chamblin, still leaning on Ashden, face filled with anguish, bravely rejoined the song. With a yell of rage, Moragon picked up his sword and swung at Mikanah who blocked him. Moragon pulled himself to his feet, and he and Mikanah battled as Moragon poured every last ounce of strength he had into his sword strikes. He chanted dark spells, trying to force his way into their minds, but the Guardians fervently held their notes, while Jerah's voice pierced high with the call of *Ah Lum Amiel*.

At the song's finish, Gailea raised her hand and brought it swiftly down, the signal for the Guardians to each sing their respective notes. Over and over, they sang the notes that blended in waves that shook the castle's very stones.

Mikanah's blade met its mark, spearing Moragon's other side. As Mikanah pulled his sword back, Moragon staggered against the wall, doubled, and gasping for breath. He tried to lunge, but Gailea rushed over, raising her hands, and singing *Fraziolda* to freeze him in place.

"Do it," she said, staring Mikanah solemnly in the eye. "Grant the final blow."

"I would, but my brother…" He gazed in torment at the boy who watched him, singing on. "I don't know if he'll survive. I don't know how connected he and Moragon still are. I don't know if I have the strength."

"Mika."

He turned to his brother and saw a calm new determination in Jerah's eyes. The boy nodded, and Mikanah recognized it as his blessing. Jerah was ready to die if it meant the destruction of the man who had annihilated any chance he might have had at a normal life.

With an anguished cry, Mikanah thrust his sword through Moragon's heart.

Moragon remained upright only by the strength of

Mikanah's grip on the sword hilt. When Mikanah withdrew his weapon, the false king crumpled at his feet, still and, at long last, silent.

Just as Moragon fell, Jerah's tiny form collapsed and lay motionless. Lorelei took him into her arms, listening for his breath, murmuring healing charms. No signs of life stirred.

"Mikanah," Lorelei whispered, weeping softly as she looked to him. "I'm so—"

"Mikanah, watch out!"

Chamblin's cry rang out just a second before a burning pain sliced through the middle of Mikanah's back. Instinct made him whip his hand behind him and yank the source of pain. His vision blurred, and he felt himself turn cold as he stared at the dagger in his hand, covered in his own blood.

Flinging the weapon aside and taking a breath to clear his mind, he whirled to find Moragon propped on one elbow, clawing his way across the stones toward him, his eyes pure venom. As he reached at his belt for another knife, Chamblin flew at him, bashing his pipa over Moragon's skull. Chamblin slammed the pipa over Moragon's head again, and the instrument splintered apart. Blood trickled from Moragon's fresh head wound, but he managed to mutter a curse that knocked Chamblin off his feet with a groan.

Mikanah started dizzily toward Moragon, only to watch in amazement as Gailea flew forward, spearing her sword straight through Moragon's neck. Moragon collapsed, and Gailea finished what she'd started, severing his head from his body.

Then, with a gasp, Gailea flew to Nerine and held her, begging her to awaken. Chamblin leaned against the wall beside her, struggling to push himself up. Ashden hurried over and touched a cluster of herbs to his wound, chanting a healing spell. Gailea looked at him hopefully, but Ashden said, "The wound may be too deep for our skill."

"Mikanah...."

He looked back to Lorelei who held Jerah toward him. Gently, Mikanah knelt and took his brother from her. His slight frame rested as light as air in his arms, and Mikanah hugged him gently and wept. This was likely the only embrace his brother had known in years, and yet in death it meant nothing.

"Only the Ethual may be able to save us all," Lorelei said.

The Ethual. The healers that the Abalinos were meant to have traveled to, imploring their aid.

Endless moments slipped past. Mikanah didn't believe that his prayers would be heard, but he prayed, nonetheless. It's what Iolana would have done, and he felt powerless to do more.

A ray of light parted the heavens.

Then another, and another, and....

A great tiredness abruptly weighed on Mikanah's body. His vision began to fade in and out.

"Mikanah!"

He collapsed. He could feel Lorelei grasping his hand, could hear her voice crying out and then fading.

His senses numbed. He felt panicked but couldn't move, couldn't scream for help. He was dying, he was leaving Lorelei, and he had no way to tell her.

"The Ethual—they are coming!" he heard her cry, even as he thought he saw a golden chariot descending from the clouds, pulled by white horses. Or perhaps it was just a dream. Or perhaps he was dying and by some luck, his soul had found eternal rest and peace after all. Perhaps he would meet Iolana and his brother. Perhaps death would be less terrible than this life after all, and they would be together at last.

CHAPTER 55

THE HOUSE OF ETHUAL

Darkness had surrounded Mikanah for the longest time, but now he opened his mind to various shades of green. A soft light danced all around him, as did the gentlest breeze, cool and healing. What a sweet dream. Memories of a battle, of fire and evil songs and someone he loved dying beside him wafted faintly with the breeze, but he easily shut them out, focusing only on the greens and the fresh, sweet air.

Then, after a time, he realized it was not his mind that had conjured such a lovely scene. Rather, his senses had returned. He blinked and stared at a stretch of light green cloth above him. His body was stiff, almost numb. He concentrated hard, until his fingers closed around the softness. At last, he shifted his legs and moved his head. Though he groaned from the effort, there was no pain. With some determination, he pushed himself until he had propped up on his elbow, just enough to look around and gather his surroundings.

He lay in a huge canopy bed with green linens, inside a vast room. Dozens of similar beds lay scattered throughout, hosting men and women clad in green robes just as he was. Bandaged wounds were visible on some, scars on others. Some walked about, while others nestled in the same safe slumber he had just stirred from. Other men and women in white, gold-trimmed tunics breezed about, carrying various herbs, potions, and trays of food.

In the beds, Mikanah saw Adelarans, Rosans, and many of his fellow Carmennans. He felt his spirits lift a little as he realized so many Carmennans had been spared and hoped their minds could heal from the years of torture he and Moragon had caused.

Across the room, Gailea sat on the edge of a bed, talking to Chamblin who leaned up against a pillow. His face was less pale than when Mikanah had last seen him, crumpled against the castle wall. That suddenly seemed an age ago, and Mikanah shook his head, trying to clear it. Either much time had passed, or else this sacred haven distorted time.

"Don't worry, you're not losing your mind."

Mikanah's gaze snapped toward the familiar voice. Lorelei sat up in the bed next to his, smiling at him.

"It's about time you woke up." Her grin was playful, a rare but refreshing sight.

"What do you mean? How long have I been asleep?"

Lorelei shrugged. "Time is a blur here. Several days, perhaps a week? I don't know. The Ethual aren't focused solely on physical healing, but on emotional and spiritual healing as well. Everyone wakes up in their own time, and not before the Ethual consider you healed enough, ready enough. The Ethual don't want us to remember what happened all at once. They say the pain of this would be too overwhelming. It will all come to you in time. But not quite yet."

Mikanah forced himself to sit up the rest of the way so that their eyes met on the same level. "Trust you to be philosophical first thing when I wake up."

Lorelei grinned. Then, at the sound of laughter, she leaned forward to gaze across Mikanah's bed, smiling at something. Mikanah turned toward the bed on his other side. Shock darted through him as he recognized his brother, Jerah. He felt a confused sort of thrill. Was this a mere dream, and if so, should he feel as elated as he did? Hadn't his brother been dead many years? And yet, there he sat, different than Mikanah remembered with his white hair and light brown skin, but his face was most certainly Jerah's. He propped up against a mountain of pillows, smiling at a blue-skinned girl who sat cross-legged on his bed, facing him. Nerine, Mikanah thought her name was. Ah, yes, the Water Nymph who had saved Jerah, but from what or who?

From you, the words echoed from deep inside his mind, as the hazy memories reshaped to form a clearer picture. An arrow of mingled joy and pain pierced Mikanah's heart as he watched the tender scene and, slowly, began to remember.

Nerine cupped her hands, turning them to liquid. They began to ripple, until bubbles formed. Jerah made no sound, but the pure wonder shining in his face spoke volumes. He slowly reached out to take one of the bubbles into his hands. It popped, and he glanced over, terrified, at Nerine. She smiled gently and returned her gaze to the bubbles, and he did the same.

His white hair had been trimmed neatly, and there was a bit more meat on his bones. This, coupled with the happiness Nerine seemed to bring him, made him look almost like an ordinary boy. Almost. He had never been that. He would never be that. But if Nerine could give him even a fraction of that, Mikanah owed her his life.

Mikanah's heart rejoiced at seeing his brother alive, safe, his body made whole, cheered by Nerine's presence, and then it sank as he wondered whether his brother would be truly happy to see him. Being rejected by Jerah after discovering he was alive and after nearly losing him again might break him altogether, but he knew he had to try. Displaying love and affection had never been his strongest gift, but Jerah deserved a lifetime of him trying, if that's what he wanted. Mikanah would never force his brother into a relationship, no matter how the loss of that chance might shatter him.

"Jerah?" he called, ever so gently.

Jerah and Nerine both looked up. A light of recognition sparked in Jerah's eyes, and he smiled warmly at Mikanah. Mikanah sat astonished. Perhaps he was dreaming after all. Or perhaps his brother's full memories hadn't returned yet and he didn't know to be hurt and angry at the brother who had abandoned him, however unknowingly.

With a hopeful smile, Nerine prompted, "It's good to see you awake. He keeps asking for you."

Mikanah hesitated. Then, returning her smile, he looked at his brother and said, "Would you mind if I come over there to see you?"

Jerah nodded and waved Mikanah over before pulling a large book into his lap. As Mikanah pushed his legs over the edge of the bed, his limbs stiffened in protest. He stretched his legs in front of him and lifted his arms, twisting about to erase some of his stiffness. A dull pain pulsed in his back, and as he found the white bandages wrapped around his torso, another memory returned to him, of Moragon throwing the dagger and Gailea being the one to ultimately end his wicked reign.

After stretching a few moments more, Mikanah stood

to his feet, holding the bed for support as his body quivered weakly. Carefully, he bridged the few steps from his bed to Jerah's and stood admiring his brother's every movement. Even the smallest things, from exhaling to shifting on the bed, meant that Jerah was alive.

Jerah sat looking at the book sprawled open on his lap. He turned the pages, closely examining the brightly colored illustrations, running his fingertips along their lines, shapes, and colors, paying close attention to each detail. As Nerine crawled over to sit beside him, he looked up, smiled at her, and pointed to a picture. He raised his hands and wiggled his fingers, before pointing to the picture once more. Nerine nodded, smiled, and imitated him.

Then, glancing up at Mikanah, she said, "It means rain. Gailea has been teaching us words that Jerah can use to talk with his hands. She once had an old friend who communicated that way. He told me that for so long, he only ever used his voice for music, and that was such a terrible thing for him. I don't know if he'll ever *want* to talk. But he's very smart. He understands perfectly well and picks up new words quickly. Come. We'll show you."

Jerah looked up at Mikanah. A bright smile sparked in his eyes. He patted the bed beside him and then placed a hand to his heart.

"That means 'please'," Nerine said.

"Thank you," Mikanah said, humbled by his brother's acceptance. He sat on Jerah's other side and watched in amazement as Jerah and Nerine created word after word with their hands. At times, they told whole stories while Nerine narrated aloud, stories of princesses and fairies and knights and other happy things. Mikanah tried to follow along, soaking up as much of the hand language as he could.

At some point, Jerah drew a small object from beneath his pillow and cradled it. The object appeared to be a little clay jar that had been painted a serene sky blue, with a few tiny cracks etched in its surface. Mikanah wondered if he should ask what it was when his brother caught his glance and held it toward him.

"Do you want me to show him?" Nerine asked.

Jerah nodded and handed the jar to her instead.

"This is his favorite story right now. Darice taught me a light charm to help tell it."

She pulled a small leather pouch from her pocket, grabbed a pinch of a yellow powder, and dropped it inside the jar. "Once there was a little jar who felt lonely. All the other jars in the potter's shop were beautiful with their bright colors, their intricate designs. Many people came to the shop each day to buy the other jars. But not this little jar. The potter had dropped him once, and now he was full of cracks, no good to anyone, or so he thought."

Jerah reached out and ever so delicately traced his fingers along the jar's cracks. He didn't need to say anything for Mikanah to comprehend the sad hauntedness in his eyes, the grief etched along his furrowed brow. Jerah was that small, unwanted, cracked jar. Mikanah's heart broke with his brother's pain as Nerine continued,

"But what the jar didn't know was that he was the potter's favorite. The potter loved him very much, especially for his bright blue color, like the sky on a sunny day. One day, the potter brought a gift. A candle, which he lit and set inside the jar. Suddenly..."

Nerine paused to utter a spell. A bright light flared inside the tiny clay jar, and Mikanah jumped in surprise. The light softened but did not extinguish. Instead, it glowed steadily from within the jar. Its rays sifted through the cracks, shining whimsical shapes and patterns across the walls and the canopy bed's curtains.

"...the jar shone the loveliest designs across the walls of the shop. From then on, people would come into the shop and stare at the cracked jar in wonder, and many asked to buy him from the potter. But the potter would let no one take him away. For he had known all along what a gift the jar was. He had not seen a cracked vessel, but a vessel that could be filled with light and joy and become something greater and more beautiful than anything he could've ever imagined."

A soft grin dispelled some of Jerah's sadness as he watched the jar in his hands, turning it slowly to let the light shine through the cracks and dance across his face. Mikanah wiped away a few tears and smiled at Nerine in grateful humility.

"I would've never thought to see such hope on his face. Thank you."

"You're welcome. Getting to know him, help him, has been the greatest honor."

Nerine told more stories then, and Jerah joined sometimes with his hand language. They did not speak of the war. They did not speak of Reynard or Moragon, or Jerah's time as the Vessel, or his time before that when he was imprisoned. They did not look back, nor did they look forward. They enjoyed the moment for what it was, getting lost in the fanciful tales Nerine told—favorites she had learned from Chamblin—and the healing found within them. Even Mikanah felt the burdens of his heart lift a little.

After a time, Jerah yawned wide and began to look weary. He glanced up at Mikanah, patted the pillow, and then turned his head sideways and placed a hand to his ear.

"You're tired?" Mikanah said. "Of course. I'll let you sleep—"

Jerah snatched Mikanah's wrist and shook his head.

Stay, his eyes pleaded.

"I will," Mikanah said. "I'll stay with you 'til you fall asleep."

A tenderness filled Jerah's face. He made his next gestures slowly, watching Mikanah with the most serious, intent look. He pressed his palm over his heart. Then he crossed his arms over his chest, and finally, he touched his hand to Mikanah's heart.

"He says he loves you," Nerine whispered.

Mikanah stared at his brother, incredulous. Even though they had sat talking for a few good hours, even though Mikanah had tried to immerse himself in his brother's world, he hadn't known how much any of it meant to Jerah.

For the first time since Iolana's death, Mikanah wept freely. Smiling at his brother through his tears, he said, "I love *you*, Jerah. More than anything or anyone in the world. I'm going to take my place as king. I'm going to be a good king. I'm going to fight to correct all the wrongs I caused. And that means I'm going to take care of you. You will never have to be afraid of anyone ever again."

Jerah glanced away, his face falling into an uncertain frown. Surely, he found it difficult, perhaps impossible, to believe that anyone could keep him from harm, but Mikanah would spend the rest of his life striving to fulfill that promise.

Jerah sat looking contemplative a few moments before looking up with a slight smile. He patted the bed again. Together, they lay back on the soft mountain of pillows. Jerah snuggled close, and Mikanah held him. Nerine lay on Jerah's other side, conjuring bubbles once more. Jerah's breathing soon steadied as he drifted to sleep.

"Nerine?" Mikanah said softly.

"Hmm?" She glanced over at him before refocusing on her bubbles.

"I owe you an apology. What I said at Iolana's death—I was blinded by my own pain. I was wrong. We needed a Guardian to replace her and finish the fight she began. That's what she would have wanted. And no one better could have been chosen than you, as Iolana's closest friend."

"Thank you," Nerine said, her smile turning sad. "But I think I must apologize too. There were times when I blamed you for stealing Iolana from me. I almost resented you. But I realize now how selfish that was, and that I was just as obsessed with Iolana as she was with you. I'm not mad anymore, or resentful. Because I understand her better now. Anything she loved, she needed. Her needs consumed her. There was no room for anything else. I don't even know why she let me come with her." She breathed deeply but couldn't stop her tears.

"Because you were a good friend," Mikanah insisted. "I promise you. I know she was consumed by our problems, in her love for me, for Gailea. But she did care for you. And you were good to her. You must learn to stop denigrating yourself, just as you have to stop worshipping her."

As Nerine seemed to ponder this, Mikanah considered his own words, letting their truth strike his heart with a fresh but needed pain of understanding. In the same sense that Iolana had allowed Nerine to worship her, so he had allowed Iolana to worship him, to a great fault. In his pathetic attempts to spare her the cruelties he'd exacted on other women, he had treated her with no greater dignity than he had treated them. He could never make that up to her, a truth that would haunt him forever. His only hope of redemption was to help others like her, and his brother, and the countless others wronged at his and Moragon's hands.

Mikanah continued, "You're stronger than you think. Look at how you saved my brother. You saw a beauty in his beastliness that few others would have. I see the joy and happiness you bring him. I did promise to care for him, and I will. But I also wonder if he can be happy with me."

"He's your brother. He loves you. He wants to be close to you. It's nearly all he's talked about."

Her words touched Mikanah deeply. "But I can also see how he cherishes you. I can't take him away from you. Why don't you come with us? When we finally go to live at the castle, come stay with us. If not to live with us, perhaps to visit at least?"

"I would love to. But do you think it will be wise? To have him go back to that castle where he endured so much pain?"

Mikanah's heart lurched. He hadn't thought of that, neither for his brother or himself. The thought of living in the place where he had both met and dealt so much torment, of being imprisoned there with its cold memories, churned his stomach. What greater damage might it do to his brother to step foot there again?

"I guess there's still a lot to figure out," Mikanah admitted. "Only promise me that, no matter what, you'll remain a part of his life, one way or another."

"That I can gladly promise," Nerine said with a grin.

Her attention drifted back to Jerah, and she hummed a sweet melody. As Mikanah absorbed her peaceful song and watched the bubbles dance their comforting patterns across the bed's canopy, he too drifted to sleep beside his brother.

~*~*~

When Mikanah next awoke, it took him a moment to remember all that had happened, and then to believe it. But sure enough, as he sat up and stretched, he saw them. Jerah and Nerine, soundly asleep. They had cuddled close to one another, Jerah with his head on her chest, Nerine with her arms wrapped around him. Mikanah placed a hand tenderly on Jerah's head—his hair was as soft as it was snow-white—and bent down to kiss him.

Then he swung his legs over the side of the bed and looked around him. Night had fallen. Most people slept, except for a few healers milling about, administering herbs or changing bandages. Lamps illuminated the room with a soft orange glow, and moonlight shone through the tall, paned windows, full and milky white.

Mikanah slid from the bed and almost wandered to his own, but he was suddenly wide awake. He instead turned his sights to a pair of glass doors thrust open, emitting a soothing, cool breeze. Beyond the doors stretched a balcony, and upon glimpsing Lorelei's familiar figure, he wandered over.

She stood leaning against the railing arched across the front of the balcony, facing the heavens, and for a moment, Mikanah turned his interest to the same, finding nothing but stretches of star-scattered sky and clouds all around. Way up here, hundreds of thousands of stars dazzled, more than anyone could ever count in a lifetime. He recalled the legends of the Ethual, how their healing houses floated high above the earth, separated from the rest of the world and all its troubles.

An unexpected sound drew his attention back to Lorelei. Her arms folded against her chest which rose and fell with quiet sobs. Tears streamed down her cheeks, and she looked unusually vulnerable. Mikanah hesitated at first, but when she neither looked at him nor made any sign of rejection, he let his hand touch her shoulder and then slip around so that he held her. She fell into his touch, resting her head on his chest and weeping.

After a long while, Mikanah said, "Lorelei, what's wrong? When we faced Moragon, he said things that… that troubled you." He paused, considering his words. Offering comfort to another person was still somewhat foreign to him, and he didn't wish to intensify whatever pain she was experiencing by saying too much. Gently, he added, "I know you never told me all your story."

"I couldn't at the time," she whispered. "I had been trying to forget for so long. But this place, it makes you remember things. It makes you confront them, so that you can heal from them. The past few days, the memories have been returning. I've been fighting through them, and I hope I'm almost on the other side."

"Tell me," Mikanah said, holding her a little closer. "You know what I am, what I was. Your tale can be no more terrible or shameful than mine."

She nestled closer to him. "When we stood before his throne, seeing him look at me that way again, like he was in perfect power and control and always would be, and then speaking those words, the words he spoke to me so many nights…." Her voice faded to a whisper, and her breath shuddered as fresh tears found her again.

"If you don't want to tell me, you don't have to," Mikanah said, terrified at how she clung to him.

"No," Lorelei said. "It's necessary. Only by going through the pain can we be healed. This is what the Ethual believe.

"Mikanah, I told you that the reason it was easier for me to trust you than it was for the others was because we had both been Moragon's prisoners. That was only part of the truth. The other part was because we were both also his willing servants. I had to believe that you could break free and be healed because I had to know I had a chance of being healed too, from my own past."

She choked these last few words, struggling through tears. Her body tensed in his, but he held her a little closer. Surprised as he felt by this revelation, he needed her to know that he didn't judge her for it.

"Go on," he said, "if you want to. You can tell me anything you feel ready to. Whatever it is, whatever you feel, I promise to listen without judgment. I could never judge you for your past. Not after what I've done. And not after what you saved me from."

"Thank you," she whispered against him, before clearing her throat to speak a bit louder. "Though, I realize it isn't you or others I've been worried about. I've been worried about judging myself, that I'd be unable to forgive myself. This place has shown me just how many memories I had buried.

"Moragon could never take my magic by force, because of my mother's pendant. But then, as I grew older, he manipulated me in other ways. Moragon was the first man to ever make love to me, and at first, I told myself that it *was* love. He was very passionate, and I told myself that perhaps he *could* love me, despite all I had heard of him. I came to love him, and he knew this. He knew it as intimately as he knew how fiercely I loved my father, who remained his prisoner for many years. I've told myself that I served Moragon to spare my father punishment and torture, and that's true. But the other side of that truth is that I did love Moragon. Or at least, I loved whatever my naïve mind imagined him to be."

Lorelei shuddered against Mikanah, who barely resisted the same reaction. The idea of Moragon not only seducing a strong, compassionate woman like Lorelei, but tricking her into something as sacred as loving him, revolted him to the core.

Taking a deep, slow breath, Lorelei continued, "At first, he was almost like a father figure. I craved that desperately, with my own father ripped away from me. As I grew older, he became more a romantic figure. I think I needed love so desperately that I was willing to have it in whatever way from Moragon. He never let me spend time alone with any other person. So, I suppose it was natural that instead of hating him and making myself feel even more isolated, that my mind and body convinced me to love him instead.

"Sometimes, I would accompany him as he questioned spies and other suspects. He trained me to decipher truth-tellers from liars. I became rather skilled in detecting deceit in others. I never directly tortured anyone. But I often helped in making decisions that led others to a torturous fate. This went on several years before Moragon started having other mistresses. This broke my heart, enough to shatter the distorted view of him I'd created. I saw that he had only used me, and I had let him. I didn't want to hurt others anymore, like he had hurt me. I stopped obeying him. He tried to force me to marry him, but I would not. As retaliation, he killed my father." Her voice trembled again. "Can you imagine what it's like, to love someone for years, to make yourself believe they could love you too, only to realize they have so little regard for you that they make you watch as they murder the one person who matters to you?"

Lorelei sobbed afresh. Mikanah didn't know what to say. He only continued to hold her, hating how intimately he and Lorelei truly understood one another. Moragon had made them each watch as the one person they'd loved most was murdered. Mikanah had always held Lorelei in high regard, but he wished he could connect with her for any other reason but this.

Eventually, Lorelei calmed enough to resume speaking. "After that, Moragon and I, we both stopped pretending. I refused all service to him. And he, in turn, became more brutal with me...especially in his bed chamber. I could no longer pretend that anything resembling love existed between us. He tortured me with cruel mind games that filled me with fears and guilt and made me wish for death many times over. That was before I had mastered how to block him out of my mind altogether. I was forced to keep on with him. 'A true lady does her duty and always submits.'"

Anger flared inside Mikanah as he recognized Moragon's words from when they'd faced him in the throne room.

"And then one night," Lorelei said, "I snapped. I'd had enough. I had been practicing my music. I thought I was strong enough. We dueled, and I tried to kill him. We fought for a long while, but he eventually overpowered me. I paid that night for fighting him, and then he threw me in prison. He'd finally seen how powerful I was and thought I was better off dead."

Her voice trailed again. She'd ceased crying but now rested, almost dead weight in his arms. Her spirit had threatened to break as she'd faced Moragon and now, in telling her darkest secrets, it seemed to have fled her altogether. The idea terrified Mikanah. He had only ever seen her strength and needed to help her remember it.

"It's not your fault," he said, gently but firmly. "You were used by Moragon. You did what you thought you had to. You survived, and more than that, you rose to become everything your father would've wanted. A Guardian, a protector of Carmenna."

Lorelei pulled from Mikanah so that she could look up at him. The moon rose behind her, illuminating the crest of her long dark hair like a crown. Her gaze was sad, weary, almost empty as she searched his. "I know it's not my fault. Deep in my heart, I know that. But sometimes, my mind speaks louder and bolder than my heart, screaming the opposite. I loved Moragon. And for a long while, I even enjoyed my time with him. With that madman, who slaughtered hundreds, if not thousands. I served him. *Willingly*." She touched her heart. "My pendant has protected me from physical harm, immediately healing me from any wounds. But even its powers can't erase the pain I endured at Moragon's hands, or the pain I helped him bring to others."

"*It's not your fault*," Mikanah repeated. He lifted her chin, so that her gaze met his. "We both served him, in order to survive, but also because we believed that at some point, it would bring us happiness. Moragon manipulated us both by pretending to be exactly what we needed. He played the role of a fatherly figure after stealing yours, and later a romantic figure. For me, he played the role of the father I never had. The things Moragon did to you? I was no better than him. Just as bad, if not worse. I seduced so many women. I was never violent with them, but I still used them. Over and over again. I'm awed now that you were willing to place so much trust in me, knowing how Moragon did the same disgusting things to you as I did to others. Thank you for believing in me, that I could become something and someone else. I don't deserve your faith in me any more than I deserve my brother's forgiveness, but I value it just the same. And if Jerah can find it in his heart to love and forgive me, surely you also deserve to open your heart to forgiveness for yourself and love from others."

She smiled slightly as some of the hopelessness dissipated from her gaze. "Perhaps...perhaps here, in the House of Ethual, we may learn how to heal even from those deepest wounds and move forward."

Mikanah's heart raced as she looked up at him. He

stared at her, though not with the same consuming intensity as he'd so often studied Iolana. Maybe he'd clung to Iolana so tightly because of the constant fear of losing her. Instead, as he looked at Lorelei, he felt something fresh in his heart, something he feared because he couldn't quite define it. And yet, it was something he wished to embrace, like a newly planted seed. He continued to watch her, filled with soothing and admiration.

"I think," he said, trying to choose each word carefully as the thoughts came to him, "that I am not ready, *yet*, to be king. Standing here, in this moment, I feel peace. But I've only just woken up in this new world. I may feel reborn, but...I know there is much doubt and resentment and fear inside me, things that I probably can't control yet, things that might still control me. I want to be a strong king for Carmenna, the king they deserve. I don't wish to become another self-centered tyrant like Moragon. I hope my waiting doesn't make you too disappointed."

Smiling a little fuller at him, she said, "It makes me very happy. A wise king recognizes his faults and weaknesses. He recognizes when he needs counsel. And you shall have it if you wish. It's already been arranged. You may stay here longer than the others to receive all the healing you need. The Lozolian Council has also agreed to send teachers to begin instructing you how to be a good king."

Mikanah stood humbled. "That is all greatly appreciated. But who will watch over Carmenna while I'm here? Would you act in my stead, as my steward? You likely know the inner workings of court life and Carmenna more than anyone."

Surprise lit Lorelei's eyes. "If you so wish. Though I can't claim to have the experience necessary. I do have a heart for Carmenna, but I would require many counselors to lead with me. Captain Pono, perhaps? And other leaders who managed to keep from being subjected to Moragon's rule."

Mikanah had always been one to handle matters on his own, often to his downfall. Knowing the Guardians had provided him a positive glimpse into how much more secure it felt to have experienced allies teaching and aiding you.

"I think that's a wise idea," he said. "If Pono and others will help you, truly, I would be humbled to have you rule in my stead." He hesitated before adding, "I'm sure that Carmenna would flourish from the counsel of so wise and clever a queen such as yourself."

Lorelei stood thrown off guard. It was only for a moment, but he caught her short intake of breath, the excited gleam in her eyes.

Then, lifting her head, she returned to her calm, proud stance and said, "Steward, Mikanah. Steward— not queen. Your offer is tempting, I admit. But I would not seek to take your place. You *will* make a true and righteous king someday."

He did not mean for her to replace him, but he kept his true meaning hidden inside his heart. He had plenty of time to reveal it, should the right moment ever come along.

Instead, he asked, "Lorelei...do you really think I will ever find peace? Iolana wanted me to, but I don't know if I can."

Lorelei looked reflective as she spoke seemingly to herself, as much as to him, "I think that, with the worst over, you can focus on what is necessary. Healing, leading a normal life. I think you can find the peace Iolana spoke of, if you just keep searching, always keeping your heart open. Whether that peace comes initially from a renewed faith, or from helping others, or from a change you choose to make within yourself, strive to find it and, by Amiel's will, you shall."

Mikanah let Lorelei's encouraging words wash over him and melt just a little more of the doubt from his heart.

"Thank you, Lorelei."

Lorelei smiled again, letting her defenses slip away. Her gaze admired and encouraged him. It even hinted at the same affection blossoming in his heart toward her. She slipped gently from his arms and back into the House, leaving him to his thoughts.

Mikanah silently breathed a word of thanks to whatever had led him to this place. Whether it was Amiel, fate, or his own newly acknowledged inner strength, he wasn't yet certain.

He then looked to the stars and whispered a goodbye to Iolana, promising her that she would always be with him. As the stars shone at him, he could feel her music playing inside his heart. He lifted his hand in a final farewell, leaving their struggles behind while heading toward a new future brimming with possibilities.

DAWN OF THE FUTURE

Gailea rose carefully from the chair by Chamblin's bedside, massaging her neck muscles. She had visited with him nearly the entire afternoon, and after he fell asleep, she too had dozed in the setting sun's warm embrace.

Moonlight gleamed on everything as she moved through the airy room toward the corridor that would lead to her private room. She had been deemed well enough to have her own chamber. On her way, a song drifted to her, a high soft melody. Glancing about the room, her gaze fell on Jerah's bed. Nerine sat by his side, stroking his snowy wisps of hair, and smiling down at him with all the tenderness of a sister for her brother.

"Nerine," Gailea said softly, walking over to stand beside her.

Nerine glanced up in surprise and ceased singing. A concerned frown filled her face. Not for herself, but for Gailea, who wiped away a few tears.

"Gailea? Are you all right?"

"Yes. Seeing how far Jerah has come already under your care is astounding. I don't think anyone else could have done it."

"It isn't me," Nerine said quietly. "The Ethual are responsible for healing him."

"All the same, you've done a wonderful job in caring for him, just as you did for Iolana, and for all of us. I ask your forgiveness, for failing to acknowledge what a bright and gifted girl you are, with so much to offer. Truly, I am humbled by the strong woman you've grown into."

A gentle smile brightened Nerine's face. "It's all right. I was wrong too. When you spent so much time with Iolana, I was jealous at first...for a while, honestly. When you tried to protect me, I didn't understand. I thought you felt like I was incapable of being useful like Iolana, like others. But that wasn't your fault. I've always felt small, inferior." She paused and tilted her head, looking as though she realized some of her thoughts for the first time even as she expressed them. "My parents are so intelligent and accomplished. They sent me to Lynn Lectim so I could discover my own gifts, but I felt lost there. With you and all the Guardians, I felt at home. And I wanted to find a way to prove to you, but especially to myself, what I was capable of."

"And so, you did. Stay as you are, Nerine. Stay strong in your kindness and your ability to see the good in others when everyone else has given up hope in them. Those gifts will see you farther in life than many others are ever able to go."

A deep tenderness filled Nerine's face. "Thank you, Gailea."

Gailea reached out laid her hand on Nerine's, squeezing gently.

Then, she left her to rest alongside Jerah once more and stole from the healing wing toward her private quarters.

As she wandered down the long hall, passing several Ethual women and men in their white-and-gold robes, she wondered how big the House really was, how many rooms it held. In all the books and stories and legends, no one had ever claimed to have seen it from the outside. Its location remained a secret to all but the Ethual themselves.

Gailea entered her room with a grateful sigh. The room was small but cozy, with a soft bed, a fireplace, two wooden chairs with a table, and several books to keep her company. Softly singing the spell *Luma*, she formed several orbs of light to hover and about the room, their soft white glow mingling with the firelight. Then she changed into her nightdress and brushed her hair, thinking with mild relief that she wouldn't need to go to the trouble of turning it auburn anymore. Her name would spread across the Lozolian Realm, as would the names of the other Guardians. She would simply have to lay as low as possible and trust that Amiel would continue to keep her children safe and hidden from her husband.

She prepared to climb into bed when a knock sounded on her door. With a weary sigh, she pulled on her robe and walked over to answer it.

"Donyon," she gasped. How strange, to see him dressed just as simply and plainly in green robes as anyone else in the House.

"May I come in and talk for a moment?" he asked, smiling gently at her.

"I suppose," Gailea said, standing aside. She motioned to the two chairs, and they pulled them near the fireplace, sitting together.

Donyon drew something onto his lap, a large, frayed

envelope. "I had this sent for, from our camp. I was hoping that here, of all places, might be the perfect spot to resolve things that need resolving." He leaned forward and handed the envelope to her. "I know what you did for me, out on the battlefield." The hurt gleaming in his eyes was plain. "For that, I am eternally grateful. Still, I don't expect forgiveness from you, for what occurred between your mother and me. Only an understanding, so that you can know the full truth."

Firelight danced soft, orange circles across his face. He looked older, in both a weary and wise way.

Guilt tugged at Gailea. She curled her hands, debating within herself. The words were right on the tip of her tongue, but necessary though they were, she didn't wish to feel the shame associated with breathing them to life. But Donyon had proven himself a loyal Guardian and deserved that much:

"I must ask your forgiveness as well. The plot against your life, I knew about it, but I stayed silent. I didn't know they would attack then and there. But I had overheard a conversation and said nothing about it. For that, I was wrong, and I deeply apologize."

Donyon forced a strained smile. "Your betrayal is hurtful, but understandable. I forgive you, even as I thank you for sparing my life." He glanced down then, motioning at her lap. "Please…"

Turning her attention back to the envelope, Gailea took out the parchment within, unfolded it, and began to read.

The letter was Gillian's final correspondence to Donyon before her death. A wave of emotions rushed over Gailea, just as they had upon first reading her mother's diary accounts, but the emotions seemed to happen in reverse this time. The deeper she read, the more she felt her defensive self-righteousness stripping away:

"That day, as you and my father chased me down the halls and I escaped to the Veil, you tried to stop him. You risked your life by defying my father to buy me the time I needed to escape. For that, I thank and forgive you and hope you can find peace as I have...."

Gailea sank down in her chair, overcome as compassion pushed away her hatred and pride. She read the letter through several times before remembering Donyon sat in the same room with her.

"So, you helped save her, after all," Gailea said at last.

Donyon nodded and smiled sadly. "It was perhaps the one good thing I had done for her in many years. A part of me was afraid that in loving Callum and running off with him, your mother would lose her magic to him. I didn't like the idea of her being in a country filled with such hostile civil war with no way to defend herself. But in truth, my greater opposition to her leaving stemmed from my selfishness. I loved her, but my ideas of love were distorted back then. I was told what to do, what to feel, whom to follow. I had not yet mastered the art of having my own mind and making my own decisions.

"But I did that day. I realized how unhappy she would be if she remained trapped with me in Adelar. So, I released her to find her joy, wherever it led her. In the short time she was alive after that, I hope she found it."

"She did. I'm sure she did. The way she loved Callum..."

Donyon's countenance fell a little more. "I *did* love her, Gailea. If you believe nothing else, please try to believe that."

"I do," Gailea promised. "I refused to see it before. But I see it now, in your sacrifice."

"My father and the king were both furious. They threatened to take the rights to the throne from me. False threats perhaps, as neither of them had any other heirs."

"I'm glad they didn't." Gailea leaned forward and placed a hand on his. "We were each prisoner in our own homes. We each clung to that one person we thought could save us. And we were each wrong. But we have both fought through and are now stronger for it."

Donyon glanced down at her hand on his. His sadness turned to a wistful tenderness. With a small twinkle in his eye, he said, "Does this mean you can stop hating my being one of the Guardians?"

Gailea looked down, her smile rueful. "I think it means I can stop hating you altogether." She lifted her softened gaze to his. "If my mother granted you forgiveness, Donyon, so I should follow her example."

His smile grew a little fuller. "Thank you, for your forgiveness, your generosity. You truly would have made Gillian proud." His expression sobered again. "There is one other thing. Messengers arrived earlier. Rosa and Adelar have successfully found the sources of the Dusk magic."

Gailea sat back a little in her chair, uncertain whether to feel more glad or wary at this news. "What exactly did they find?"

"Texts detailing exactly how to recreate the Dusk, find the necessary ingredients. Glass vials filled with a shimmering red substance that moves not unlike the mist that Moragon had Jerah use to incapacitate our magic."

Gailea shifted in her seat. "Yes, I believe Moragon had a hand in helping Chevalier invent the Dusk. He likely tried to emulate that magic as closely as he could when creating the mist. Thank Amiel he did not succeed. What is being done with what you found?"

Donyon motioned toward her. "What would *you* recommend?"

Gailea glanced away, contemplating as carefully as her tired mind would allow her. She didn't like the idea of the Dusk's fate resting with her advice. And yet, short of Chevalier himself, she didn't know anyone more experienced with the Dusk than her, and who knew where to find the sorcerer, or if they would even want to?.

Moragon had sent her the dreams through the Desthai to make her find the Dusk. Chevalier had intercepted parts of those dreams and may have even sent some of his own. The question was, why? Would Chevalier acknowledge the danger of his creation and seek to destroy it? Or would he use it to lord over the world as they knew it, becoming the kind of terrible master who had once enslaved him?

Gailea looked up at Donyon. "The Dusk inside the glass vials, we can't destroy. We don't know how, and trying could unleash the Dusk and kill innocent people. We don't know how capable it is of spreading. I propose we find someplace to hide it, far away from Adelar or Rosa. Somewhere deeply secret and secure and closely guarded at all times."

"And the texts?"

Burn them all, was what she wanted to say.

"Hide them as well, but separately from the Dusk. There may come a time they are needed, if ever we find someone who can use them to figure out how to destroy the Dusk for good."

"Thank you for your counsel. I will reach out to the Lozolian Council. Surely Lynn or one of the other counselors may have some knowledge of a suitable hiding place for the abomination."

Gailea doubted if the Dusk could ever be buried deeply enough but didn't voice this. It would be hidden away at last, and she must take what comfort she could in hoping this would be enough.

Donyon rose to his feet then, and Gailea did the same.

"I must away to my chambers, to make ready to depart. I'm heading back to Adelar tonight with my messengers. Take care, Gailea, and may Amiel continue to bless you on your healing journey. My only regret is that I shall miss tomorrow's send-off. Give everyone my love if you would."

"I will," Gailea promised.

With a bow of his head, Donyon bid her goodnight and left.

~*~*~

Early that next morning, the Guardians gathered on the shores of Carmenna to bid Darice and Ashden farewell. The sun had just begun to rise, and Ashden had just finished readying his provisions to bring on board the trading galleon that would take them home. Darice had agreed to accompany him, and they were to marry as soon as possible. He had asked Gailea's blessing, which Gailea had gladly granted.

Gailea smiled tenderly at him and said, "We both knew it would come to this, in the end."

She turned then to her sister and played with a lock of her hair.

"It's turned almost as golden as my natural color." A few strands of dark brown remained in Darice's hair, but soon it would completely match Ashden's sandy hue, reflecting her heart's choice to love him forever.

"Indeed," Darice said with a twinkle in her eye. "And I'm surprised yours hasn't begun to change either."

"Into what?" Gailea quipped as her cheeks flushed hotly.

Darice laughed playfully. "I suppose you didn't inherit that part of your mother's magic anyway."

That was true enough. Gailea wasn't fully Adelaran, as Gillian had been. If Gailea was meant to transfer her looks and powers to someone she loved, her hair would have turned red on its own long ago when she loved Crispin. Thank Amiel she hadn't passed any of her musical power along to that madman.

Darice caught her in a tight embrace then and whispered in her ear, "You're sure this is all right with you? I feel like we haven't had the chance to talk as deeply on the matter as we should have."

"What else would there be to say?" Gailea asked, taking her sister's face in her hands, and leaning in so that their foreheads touched. "I stand by what I said weeks ago in Pakua, and days ago in the House. My blessing is yours. You deserve this happiness. I will miss your shining light and Ashden's calming spirit. But I can think of no one more worthy for you to share your heart and magic with."

"Besides," Chamblin said, joining them with a mischievous grin and leaning on his temporary cane, "I'm sure the Guardians will find someone to replace you in no time."

Gailea lightly tapped his arm with the back of her hand. "They're merely moving away, not abandoning their place as Guardians."

Darice laughed lightly. "Glad to know we'll be missed."

"You will be," Lorelei assured her, taking Darice's hands.

A figure rushed past in a blue blur and threw her arms around Darice's neck. Darice stumbled back, looking like the air had been knocked out of her. Then, she wrapped her arms around Nerine, warmly embracing her, as did Ashden.

"I love you both so much," Nerine said. "I'll miss

you." She gave them a final squeeze before releasing them and rejoining Jerah and Mikanah. They sat a few feet back from the others, and Jerah dug in the sand for shells, humming to himself.

Once the sailors and cargo were ready to depart, Ashden and Darice boarded the small boat that would take them to where the ship was anchored. As the sun rose on the ocean behind them, Darice raised her hand in a final farewell. Gailea raised her hand too, smiling through her bittersweet tears.

Ashden's warm tenor and Darice's alto filled the air. Soon the sailor rowing the boat took them against the tide, and those on the beach listened as the wind and waves carried Ashden and Darice's song away with them.

Lorelei wandered down the shoreline, and Mikanah rose to follow her. Nerine trailed after them, and the three splashed in the shallows, laughing and talking. Every now and then, Nerine would pause to wave at Jerah who would wave back with a smile before returning to his seashell search.

Gailea turned toward the group of Echelon who would escort her back to the House of Ethual once she was ready. She smiled to see Chamblin among them, though she quickly turned it into a mock frown. "You're not convincing me with that silly grin of yours. I can tell you're still in some pain. Why you came all this way, I don't know. You shouldn't have left the healing wing yet. Darice would have said goodbye to you up there."

Chamblin shrugged, leaning on his cane. "I wanted to see them off."

Gailea sighed and shook her head, feigning exasperation. "Stubborn a fool as ever. Then again, when *have* you been one for following the rules of what's acceptable? Playing that contraption of yours all hours of the night...."

"If you're referencing the pipa," Chamblin said, his smile turning into a pout, "I fear it was a war casualty. I don't intend to see the likes of it ever again, unless I'm so lucky to come by another."

"Well, then, consider yourself lucky indeed."

Chamblin stared in confusion as Gailea motioned to one of the Echelon guards who stepped forward. She nodded at him, and he pulled the instrument strapped behind his back over his neck.

Gailea took the pipa and passed it to Chamblin who received it with all the shock and tenderness that she imagined a father should have when holding his first-born. His brows rose as he ran his hands along its smooth surface. Then, as he plucked a few notes, he laughed out loud.

"Gailea, it's magnificent! How did you ever come by it?"

"I was speaking with Lyra, one of the Echelon. Her brother makes instruments. I asked if I could commission him to design a new pipa for you. It's his first, so I hope he was able to get it right."

Chamblin strummed a few chords and danced a few steps. "It feels right enough to me. What a wonderful gift, to have found someone who could replicate such a divine instrument."

He hugged the instrument to him, and Gailea playfully rolled her eyes before smiling, letting his joy fill her with warmth.

"I'm almost afraid to tell you, for fear you'll react with such enthusiasm that you'll float right off the ground and fly away but...there is one thing still that you're missing. One more surprise to be discovered."

Taking one of his hands, she guided it to the pipa's handle, carefully leading his fingers over the shapes carved there.

Chamblin slowly sucked in his breath. "My name, the Chinese characters—*unbelievable*! What sorcery could you have used to replicate them?"

Gailea beamed, finding his radiant joy impossible to resist. "Right after we killed Moragon, as we were waiting for the Ethual to arrive, I noticed your pipa. Smashed and splintered beyond repair, but the handle was still intact. I kept it, knowing that if we made it out alive, you would want it back. I hope it's all right, having it added to a completely different instrument. I hope that doesn't taint how special the original was to you."

"Of course not. If anything, it makes this one more extraordinary than any gift could be. Crafted by not one, but two dearest friends." He smiled tenderly at her before adding, "It seems as though other things were found too. I hear you and Donyon were able to reconcile."

"Yes," Gailea admitted. "We have made our peace."

"I'm glad. And proud of you."

"It's not just him. Amiel saw fit to put many in my path last night. I spoke with Nerine too and even made peace with Mikanah."

Chamblin's brows rose. He looked surprised at first, and then an amused smile crossed his lips. "And now he sends *me* your way."

"Yes, in that He does have a sense of humor, in the way He constantly throws you in my path." Gailea sighed, still pretending annoyance. "Is that the real reason you tagged along this morning, so I can make peace with you as well?"

"I wasn't aware we were embattled."

"We're always arguing about *some*thing."

Chamblin tapped a finger on his chin and twisted his face into a deep, comical frown. Then, his expression brightened with a broad grin. "Nope. Can't think of a single thing."

Gailea returned his smile, but only briefly. A lingering guilt tugged at her heart, singular in nature and yet no less potent than any other wound she had started to heal from. In fact, in that moment, it felt greater than all the rest.

"What is it?" Chamblin asked tenderly. "I may not be able to see your face clearly anymore, but I can feel your silence. What else troubles you?"

"Chamblin..." For a moment, she fought back the fresh tears that hit her with surprising force. Being so long in the House made it nearly impossible to hold onto any emotion, to bottle it and show what she once thought was strength but now recognized as mere pride and fear. "Chamblin, I went to the Ethual healers. I begged them to fix your blindness, to restore your sight. But they said it was impossible. That the impact of Moragon's attack, the darkness and depth of it...they said maybe if you'd found the right healer immediately, but now...I'm so sorry."

"Gailea..." The deeper tenderness in his voice tore at her heart, as did the compassion filling his face as he stepped closer. "I have already accepted your apology many times, even though an apology was never warranted. I would sacrifice myself again and again to save you, even if it meant my life. And if I was blessed by some miracle with many lives, I would give them all to save you. Don't you understand that? How dear you are to me? Why do you continue to let this guilt imprison you and throw a wall between our friendship?"

Gailea's tears fell freely as she answered, "I don't know. I think because...because I feel as though every good thing I've ever had, everyone I've ever loved, I've somehow managed to be a danger to them. I feel horrible for what happened to you, but I think it stretches deeper than that."

"I think the House reveals many pains. Revelation is simply the start of healing, and these wounds may take longer to heal than others. But I promise you again, you did nothing wrong. Moragon's evil had nothing to do with you. Nor does your husband's."

Gailea gazed up at him through her tears. At first, her heart resisted him, as it always had. But then she allowed herself to smile and take his hand. "Thank you, Chamblin. You're a true friend. I will be honored to continue having you at my side."

"Good." Chamblin smirked and lifted his chin. "I assure you there's no getting rid of me anyway, so it's easier for us both if you comply."

"Don't push it."

"Wouldn't dream of it." Lifting one hand, he ever so gently touched a lock of her hair. "My eyes can still see enough to tell your hair has been changing. Have you fallen in love with some golden-haired prince that I'm not aware of?"

Gailea chuckled. "No, my true color is blonde. I changed it when I was first on the run, trying to hide my identity."

"Mmm...you know, I talked to the healers as well. They said it could be a mere matter of months—weeks, even—before I lose my sight entirely now. If I may...if it isn't being too bold...might I have a lock of your hair? I can still see your face, dimly. I can tell when you smile if I'm close enough. And I can still see the color of your hair. That's how I'd like to remember you when my sight fades altogether. As my strong-willed friend with the red hair that matches her fiery spirit."

Gailea gazed up at him, incredulous. How could she ever deserve such a sincere friend?

"You sentimental fool," she teased. "I suppose it's not asking *too* much."

Chamblin reached inside the pocket of his green tunic and presented a small knife. Handing it to her, he said, "Best you do the honors. It wouldn't do for me to spoil the moment by accidentally cutting off your ear or the like."

Unsheathing the knife, Gailea knelt in the sand beside the gentle tide. Studying her reflection in the ocean's clear shallows, she searched her hair. Much of it had lightened to a soft strawberry blonde or faded to gold altogether, much more than she had realized. But just underneath, at the base of her neck, she found a curl that was still streaked with auburn. Carefully, she cut it, took a bit of ribbon from her pocket, and tied it about the lock of hair. Then, she placed it and the knife in Chamblin's hands.

"Thank you," he said, pocketing the knife while gently holding the lock. "This is all I could have wanted, a token of our friendship, which I hope will extend long past this moment. But what about you? Where does Gailea Fleming hope life will take her, now that all this evil is put behind her?"

Gailea glanced at Jerah nearby, her heart aching, then stared out toward the ocean. "To my children. I want to be with my children."

After a moment of listening to the waves crashing nearby, she turned her gaze to Chamblin's face, still so familiar and endearing and someday, perhaps...more.

"We may have lost a great deal in this war," Gailea said, wearing a soft smile despite herself. "But there is much yet to be found."

THE END

Dear Reader,

Thanks so much for taking the time to read *Symphony of Crowns*!

The Gailean Quartet was inspired by the choir class I took in college and especially my choir teacher, who provided a refuge for me during a very difficult time in my life.

If you'd like to help me out, please leave a review for me wherever my books are sold. I absolutely love hearing from my readers. Discovering a new review and reading what others have to say about my work truly makes my day. It also helps other awesome readers like yourself discover my book so they can enjoy it too.

On that note, God bless, happy reading, and may you be inspired!

I look forward to seeing you in my next book.

~ Christine E. Schulze

THE AMIELIAN LEGACY

More Books
by Christine E. Schulze

T he *Amielian Legacy* is a vast fantasy comprised of both stand-alone books and series for children and young adults. *The Amielian Legacy* creates a fantastical mythology for North America in much the same way that Tolkien's Middle Earth created a mythology for Europe. While it's not necessary to read any particular book or series to read the others, they do ultimately weave together to create a single overarching fantasy.

~*~*~ Young Adult Books ~*~*~

The Amielian Legends:
A Young Adult Fantasy Collection
(Can be read in any order)

Larimar: Gem of the Sea
The Chronicles of the Mira
The Crystal Rings
Bloodmaiden

Lily in the Snow
One Starry Knight
Pirates of the Dawn
Narwhals in the Stars

The Gailean Quartet
Prelude of Fire
Serenade of Kings
Symphony of Crowns
Requiem of Dragons

Beyond the Veil: A Gailean Quartet Prequel

The Stregoni Sequence
Golden Healer, Dark Enchantress
Memory Charmer
Wish Granter and Other Enchanted Tales

~*~*~ **Children's Books** ~*~*~

The Adventures of William the Brownie

The Special Needs Heroes Collection
In the Land of Giants
The Puzzle of the Two-Headed Dragon
The Amazing Captain K
Puca: A Children's Story About Death

Lozolian Timeline

B.Z.S. = Before Zephyr Split

A.Z.S. = After Zephyr Split

This method of naming refers to the sacrifice that the great fairy Zephyr made in order to split the original Loz apart into multiple islands, thus saving it from being destroyed in flame during the first Age of Dragons. Queen Grishilde the Silver later declared that the new islands be named in Zephyr's honor, hence the name "Zephyr's Islands."

This became a sacred turning point in Lozolian history. Thus, all important historical events in the Lozolian Realm and surrounding area are referred to as happening either **B.Z.S.** (Before Zephyr Split) or **A.Z.S.** (After Zephyr Split).

I. First Age of Dragons, 1325 B.Z.S.

Wars led by Grishilde the Silver against the Great Dragon, 1325-1327 B.Z.S.

II. *Zephyr Split*, March 9, 1327 A.Z.S.

The wars led by Grishilde the Silver culminated when

the fairies of Loz (at this time there was no official Council) joined together to split Loz into separate islands, thereby stopping the massive fire that the Great Dragon would have used to decimate the entire land. To complete the spell, the fairies had to disperse at the last moment, barely escaping destruction by fire themselves.

One fairy, Zephyr, was unique in that she was born without the ability to fly; because she could not fly, she could not flee the small piece of island that was consumed by flames and thus died, sacrificing herself to help the other fairies complete the spell.

Zephyr's Islands include Hyloria, Aquanitess, Spaniño, and Carmenna, amongst others. The largest island, which yet housed the capitol of Iridescence, took the name of "Loz" in place of the much larger predecessor from which it had been formed.

III. First Age of Peace, 1327 A.Z.S.

IV. Surpriser Curse, 1330-1430 B.Z.S.

Books: *The Legends of Surprisers* (or *The Legends of the Seven Kingdoms*)

On the massive mainland east of Zephyr's Islands lay the Seven Kingdoms. One of the kingdoms, Labrini, sought to make itself lord over the other six kingdoms. The kingdoms were soon divided. War broke out. The seven peoples who had once loved each other as brothers and sisters slaughtered one another.

The three great fairy sisters who guarded the Seven Kingdoms, Keziah, Gemimah, and Kerennah, intervened, placing a curse upon the peoples which gave them animal-like features. Until they stopped quarreling like beasts, they would look like beasts. But more than that, if all seven kingdoms did not reunite peacefully within one hundred years, the curse would complete itself, the people would turn completely into beasts, and their humanness, their kingdoms, their history—everything they held dear—would be lost forever.

V. Age of the Mass, 1410-1443 A.Z.S.

Mass War, 1440-1443 A.Z.S.

During this time, a sect of fairies known as "the Mass" came to power through use of a dark shadow magic that would later be known as "the Dusk." Their primary focus was on using the Dusk to usurp Loz and "purge" it from all those born without magical blood.

To protect against this growing threat, the first official Lozolian Council was formed. The Council consisted of various magical leaders from all across Zephyr's Islands and the Seven Kingdoms. The renowned Lynn Lectim herself was one of the core founders of the Council.

A year later, Lynn Lectim's Academy was established at the behest of Lynn Lectim. She believed that, in order to properly defend themselves and their homes from dark magic, magical peoples should have the chance to be educated by those with expertise in various magical fields.

During this time, it was also revealed that Zephyr was still alive. She had been disguising herself as the phoenix Brandi. This was how she escaped the flames during the Zephyr split, by shapeshifting into a phoenix at the last possible moment; while she could not fly in fairy form, she could fly in phoenix form. She remained in phoenix form for some time, letting many believe she was dead, in order to elude certain enemies and carry out certain tasks. She was quite useful to various quests leading up to the breaking of the Surpriser Curse, as well as in the Mass War.

* Formation of First Lozolian Council, 1440 A.Z.S.
* Founding of Lynn Lectim Academy, 1441 A.Z.S.

* Mass Defeat by Queen Grishilde the Red and Sir Willard, 1443 A.Z.S.

The Mass was originally founded and led by Sir Willard of Loz. Toward the end of the Mass War, he was entrusted with the care of his niece, Aribella, a brave youth with a keen desire for both mercy and justice. Through Aribella, Willard came to see the error of his ways, left the Mass, and joined the Lozolian Council to fight against the evil entity he had originally created. In the last battle which occurred on the grounds of his mansion, he sacrificed his life to complete a magic ritual that would ultimately allow Queen Grishilde the Red's armies to triumph over the Mass.

Willard left everything, including his estate, to Aribella. Aribella in turn gave the house to Lynn to use as the Lynn Lectim Academy's first actual building; before then, the students had lived in tents and tree houses and conducted their studies in the woods. To this day, Willard's Mansion still stands and serves as Lynn Lectim's middle school. An elementary school, high school, university, and chapel have been built on the grounds as well, offering all magical students a full education.

VI. Age of Music, 1450-1487 A.Z.S.
Books: *The Gailean Quartet*

VII. Second Age of Peace, 1487 A.Z.S.

VIII. Second Age of Dragons, 1491-1493 A.Z.S.
Books: *The Gailean Quartet*

IX. Third Age of Peace, 1493 A.Z.S.

X. Age of Shadow, 2325 A.Z.S.
Books: *A Shadow Beyond Time* (*The Hero Chronicles* reboot)

About the Author

Christine E. Schulze has been living in castles, exploring magical worlds, and creating fantastical romances and adventures since she was too young to even write of such stories. Her collection of YA, MG, and children's fantasy books, *The Amielian Legacy*, is comprised of series and stand-alone books that can all be read separately but also weave together to create a single, amazing fantasy.

One of her main aspirations for *The Amielian Legacy* is to create fantasy adventures with characters that connect with readers from many different backgrounds. Her current focus is to include racially diverse characters and also those with disabilities. The latter is inspired by Schulze working with adults with autism and other developmental disabilities at Trinity Services in Southern Illinois.

Schulze draws much of her inspiration from favorite authors like Tolkien and Diana Wynne Jones, favorite games like *The Legend of Zelda*, and especially from the people in her life. Some of her exciting ventures include the publication of her award-winning *Bloodmaiden*, as well as *The Stregoni Sequence* and *The Chronicles of the Mira* with Writers-Exchange. Her books for younger readers include *In the Land of Giants* and *The Amazing Captain K.*

Christine currently lives in Belleville, IL, but you can visit her on Facebook, Youtube, or her website: http://christineschulze.com

CPSIA information can be obtained
at www.ICGtesting.com
Printed in the USA
JSHW022245270623
43721JS00006B/95